T3-AME-189

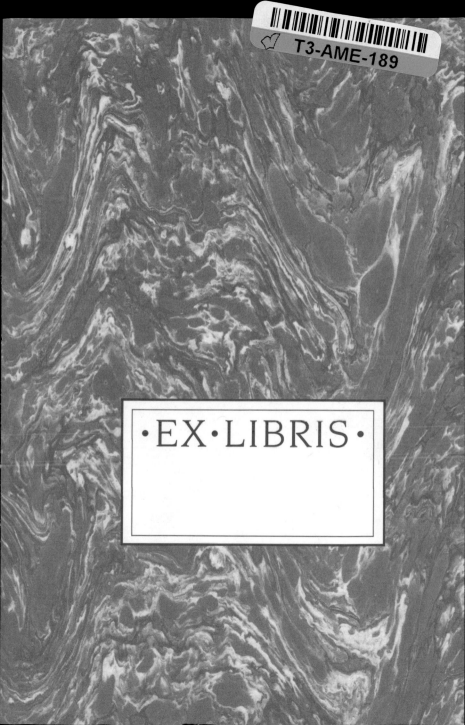

· EX · LIBRIS ·

READER'S DIGEST

CONDENSED BOOKS

JEFFERSON'S MONTICELLO
by Bradley Clark

READER'S DIGEST CONDENSED BOOKS

VOLUME 3 1995

THE READER'S DIGEST ASSOCIATION, INC.
Pleasantville, New York

READER'S DIGEST CONDENSED BOOKS

Editor-in-Chief: Barbara J. Morgan
Executive Editor: Tanis H. Erdmann
Senior Managing Editor: Marjorie Palmer
Managing Editors: Thomas Froncek, Herbert H. Lieberman, Joseph P. McGrath,
James J. Menick
Senior Staff Editors: Dana Adkins, Anne H. Atwater, M. Tracy Brigden,
Catherine T. Brown, Thomas S. Clemmons, Maureen A. Mackey,
Angela H. Plowden-Wardlaw, John R. Roberson, Ray Sipherd
Senior Editors: Linn Carl, Christopher W. Davis
Senior Associate Editors: Catharine L. Edmonds, Barbara M. Harrington,
Paula Marchese
Associate Editor: Ayesha Pande
Managing Editor, Copy Desk: Jeane Garment
Assistant Managing Editor, Copy Desk: Jane F. Neighbors
Senior Staff Copy Editors: Maxine Bartow, Tatiana Ivanow, Marilyn J. Knowlton
Senior Copy Editors: Claire A. Bedolis, Jeanette Gingold, Daphne Hougham,
Charles Pendergast, Miriam Schneir
Senior Associate Copy Editor: Alexandra C. Koppen
Associate Copy Editors: Fay Ahuja, Barbara Booth, Arlene Petzal
Editorial Administrator: Donna R. Gataletto
Art Director: Angelo Perrone
Executive Art Editor: Soren Noring
Art Editor: Clair Moritz
Senior Associate Art Editor: Katherine Kelleher
Director, Book Rights: Virginia Rice

International Editions

Executive Editor: Gary Q. Arpin
Senior Editors: Bonnie Grande, Eva C. Jaunzems, Antonius L. Koster

Reader's Digest Condensed Books are published every two to three months at Pleasantville, N.Y.

The condensations in this volume have been created by The Reader's Digest Association, Inc., by special arrangement with the publishers, authors, or holders of copyrights.

With the exception of actual personages identified as such, the characters and incidents in the fictional selections in this volume are entirely the products of the authors' imaginations and have no relation to any person or event in real life.

The credits that appear on page 576 are hereby made part of this copyright page.

© 1995 by The Reader's Digest Association, Inc.
Copyright © 1995 by The Reader's Digest Association (Canada) Ltd.

FIRST EDITION: Volume 219

All rights reserved. Unauthorized reproduction, in any manner, is prohibited.
Library of Congress Catalog Card Number: 50-12721
Printed in the United States of America
Reader's Digest and the Pegasus logo are registered trademarks of The Reader's Digest Association, Inc.

CONTENTS

PRIZES

ERICH SEGAL

Adam Coopersmith

Sandy Raven

Isabel da Costa

All three are brilliant scientists.
All three are driven by a
great desire: to win the Nobel
Prize. All three are shadowed
by private dilemmas—of love,
betrayal, and personal tragedy.
One day each will become
famous. But only one will travel
to Stockholm to hold the gold.

Prologue

Diseases desperate grown
By desperate appliances are relieved,
Or not at all.
                              —*Hamlet,* Act IV

THE Boss was dying.

He was losing weight, growing paler and thinner. And feeling an exhaustion no amount of sleep could relieve.

"Skipper," he confided to his closest friend, "Boyd Penrose is a lousy liar."

"Come on. He's not the White House physician for nothing."

"Listen, I'm dying and I know it. There's a cold black wind tearing down the corridor of my chest. I can even hear the wings of the angel of death flapping in my bedroom when I'm left alone."

"I'll call Penrose."

"No. If I can't wring it out of him, nobody can."

"We'll double-team him. He can't outface both of us."

Forty-five minutes later a bedraggled Boyd Penrose, looking not at all like the admiral of the navy that he was, stood straight-backed and tight-lipped in the regal bedroom.

"Come clean, Boyd," Skipper demanded. "You're hiding something. Has he got some fatal condition you're too chicken-livered to divulge?"

Penrose lowered his head and sighed. "Skip, I wish to heaven you didn't have to hear this. He's got lymphosarcoma—it's a cancer of the blood and tissues."

There was a shocked silence.

"All right, hold the sackcloth and ashes a minute," said the powerful patient at last. "Let me hear the wretched details." Turning

9

to the physician, he asked, "What are my chances of recovery?"

"That's just it, Boss," Penrose answered. "This isn't one of those numbers you get out of alive."

Another silence.

"How long have I got?"

"About five, maybe six months."

"Great. If I'm lucky, at least I'll get my Christmas presents."

Skipper's face was gray. "I don't get it. There must be some way of fighting this monster."

They looked toward the doctor again. "As a matter of fact," he confessed, "there are three different labs—Harvard, Stanford, and Rockefeller—developing drugs to combat this disease. But they're still a long way from getting FDA approval."

"Forget the formalities, Boyd," the Boss growled. "The White House can get me anything we ask for. How do you decide which is the best gamble?"

"Well, I can call up a couple of heavyweights and, keeping total anonymity, find out what they think of the relative merits of the three medications."

"Good idea. Why don't you start right away," Skipper suggested. "Use the Boss's office. The phone's secure."

The admiral was back in less than an hour. "I don't believe it," he mumbled, shaking his head. "The first choice of all the guys I called was the same character—Max Rudolph. He's the immunologist at Harvard who's developed those special mice."

"*Mice?*" the sick man asked with exasperation. "What in hell's name do mice have to do with my life?"

Penrose looked his patient straight in the eye and said softly, "They could save it."

1 **ADAM** Max Rudolph sat in his darkened penthouse lab at Harvard Medical School waiting for signs of daybreak over the Charles River. Having been informed that the blood and other tissue samples would be delivered at precisely six a.m., he had arrived early to be sure that none of the night owls on his staff would be working at their benches when the courier arrived.

There was a single exception: He had summoned his protégé, Adam Coopersmith, to meet him at five a.m.

Physically, they made an odd couple: Max, mid-sixties, short, bespectacled, and almost bald; Adam, tall, wiry, with a shock of dark brown hair, younger-looking than his twenty-eight years.

"Max, you pulled me out of the operating room—this better be important."

"It is," his mentor announced.

"You sounded so mysterious on the phone. What the heck is going on?" Adam demanded.

"My boy," Max answered gravely, "for the first time in our professional lives we're going to do something unethical. A life is at stake. Certain corners will have to be cut."

"You've never done that."

"Yes, but I've never had the President of the United States as a patient before. Admiral Penrose called me from the White House about a patient he described only as a senior Washington personage. He insisted that I not ask any more."

Max conveyed to Adam verbatim the medical information given on the phone by the Washington physician. And their awesome assignment.

"Max, that's an enormous responsibility."

"I know. That's why I had to share it with somebody."

They were interrupted by a loud grating sound at the end of the hall. They watched as the elevator doors opened and a black-leather-jacketed courier appeared. He was carrying a carton about the size of a cigar box. "Dr. Rudolph?" he asked.

"Yes."

"Do you have some sort of ID?"

Max pulled out his wallet and showed his driver's license.

The courier handed over the package and receded into the shadows. The two scientists then walked down the corridor to a room stacked floor to ceiling with cages of mice, all scampering to and fro, blissfully unaware of their unique qualities.

When transfused with human blood and other tissue, the systems of these special mice became carbon copies of the donor's. This meant that reactions to whatever they were subsequently given were miniature but precise reflections of their human model. The humanoid mouse was just one of Max's many scientific achievements.

11

"All right, Adam. We have three possibilities. They could cure, kill, or even do nothing. What do you suggest?"

"Four sets of six mice each. We inject them all with the patient's blood and then treat each group with varying strengths of the medications. The fourth crew obviously gets placebos."

By seven thirty, when the day staff began to straggle in, they had already infected a third of the mice.

Adam called the obstetrics ward. He listened and then announced with evident pleasure, "All's well—eight pounds, eight ounces."

"Lucky people," the professor murmured.

As they descended in the elevator, Max permitted himself to yawn. "Shall we visit the House of Pancakes before we turn in?"

"I promised Lisl I'd watch your cholesterol," Adam protested. "I don't want to lose my best friend to a lipid-soaked pancake."

"Okay," Max sighed histrionically. "To salve your conscience, I'll eat them with margarine."

2 ISABEL ISABEL'S DIARY, NOVEMBER 16: *My name is Isabel da Costa. I am four years old and live with my parents and big brother, Peter, in Clairemont Mesa, California. About a year ago Mom and Dad found out that I could read on my own. They got very excited and took me to see a lot of people who gave me all sorts of different things to read.*

I really wish this hadn't happened, because Peter doesn't want to play with me anymore. Maybe if I keep this diary a secret, he might like me again.

NOTHING in Isabel's parents' backgrounds suggested that their child would someday be called a female Einstein. Indeed, her father, Raymond, twice failed the qualifying exam for a doctorate in physics at U.C. San Diego.

Yet the department admired his enthusiasm and offered him the nonfaculty position of junior development engineer—which involved the preparation of apparatus for lectures and experiments. It was not what he had dreamed of, but at least he had a legitimate connection with a university lab. He was so dedicated that he soon became indispensable. His reward was Muriel Haverstock.

One day this plump, vivacious brunette music major, suffering from a phobia for science, pleaded for Raymond's assistance. "Oh, please, Mr. D.," she begged the stocky, red-haired supervisor. "I need this course to graduate, and if you don't help me, I'll never get this oscilloscope to work."

By the time Ray had shown her how to measure the resonance of RLC circuits, he was smitten. He gathered his courage, then invited her to dinner.

"Sure," she answered. "If you don't mind waiting till after my orchestra rehearsal."

His heart leaped. "That'd be great."

"Okay, why not drop by the auditorium around seven thirty."

Raymond arrived early and sat in the back row watching Edmundo Zimmer conduct Bach's Double Concerto in D Minor. To his surprise Muriel had been chosen to join the concert mistress in playing the exquisite duet in the largo movement.

"Actually, I came here to study English," she explained over dinner. "But when I got into the orchestra, Edmundo completely converted me to music. He's so charismatic—and not even bitter about his accident."

"What happened?" Raymond inquired. "All I could see was that his arms were kind of stiff."

"He was a rising young cellist in Argentina when he was in a car crash. Both arms were paralyzed. Now the closest he can come to being a musician is conducting our bunch of amateurs. I really admire his courage."

As they got to know one another, Raymond confessed that he was already mired in scientific failure, that he would never rise above his current station. Paradoxically, this made Muriel admire him more. For Raymond seemed to accept professional disappointment with a strength of character similar to Edmundo's.

They married. And lived unhappily ever after.

AFTER graduation Muriel found a job teaching music at the Hanover Day School and continued playing with the orchestra until late in her first pregnancy.

On July 10, 1967, Raymond da Costa became the proud father of a son, already sprouting red hair like his own. He vowed that Peter would have the advantages he himself had been denied when growing up, and he pillaged the library for books on enhancing a child's brainpower.

Muriel was pleased that he was taking such an interest in Peter's development, until she noticed the darker side.

"Muriel, I'm going to have the kid evaluated. I don't think he's living up to his potential."

"But he's barely two years old," she reprimanded him. "What on earth do you expect him to be doing—nuclear physics?"

"No. But I'm afraid Peter's no genius."

"So what? He's still a sweet, adorable child. Do you think I'd love you more if you were professor of physics at Princeton?"

He looked her straight in the eye and answered, "Yes."

Muriel felt Raymond would be less preoccupied with little Peter's mind if they had another child. On the ides of March, 1972, Muriel went into labor and shortly afterward brought forth a bouncing baby girl. A *girl*—Raymond had been unprepared for this possibility. His own idiosyncratic, unscientific expectation was that he would have only sons. But Muriel was overjoyed. She was sure that Ray would quickly be captivated by their new baby's charm and not cherish any absurd fantasies of sending her to Yale while she was still in Pampers.

At first her instinct seemed correct. Raymond was attentive and affectionate to his bright-eyed little girl, whom they named Isabel. Muriel spent many happy hours reading to her lively daughter, who seemed fascinated by words and rather adept with them. As a toddler, Isabel was already speaking in complete sentences.

But the most astounding discovery was yet to come. As Muriel was cleaning up after Isabel's third birthday, scraping ice cream off the rug and scrubbing jellied fingerprints from the wall, she overheard a tiny bell-like voice: " 'Babar is trying to read, but finds it difficult to concentrate; his thoughts are elsewhere. He tries to write, but again his thoughts wander. He is thinking of . . .' "

Muriel had never read this story to Isabel. Clearly, her daughter had simply unwrapped a present and decided to peruse it herself. Muriel was stunned. She quietly slipped from the room and summoned Raymond from his study. Now both parents stood in the doorway dumbstruck, watching their pretty little girl recite flawlessly from the book.

14

"How could she learn all this without us noticing?" Muriel asked.
Raymond did not answer. He did not know how bright his daughter was. But he resolved to spare no effort to find out.

3 SANDY The *Time* cover story about Sandy Raven, Ph.D., was entitled, "The Man Who Discovered Immortality":

> "When I was a kid in the Bronx, I was a classic example of the guy who got sand kicked in his face."
> Nobody kicks sand in this man's face anymore.
> The acknowledged leader in the brave new science of genetic engineering, Professor Sandy Raven has already made history by receiving the first federal approval for clinical trials on reversing the aging process.
> Still in his early forties, Raven has paved the way not only for increased human life-span but for the potential arrest of fatal illnesses and the regeneration of tissue in wasting diseases such as muscular dystrophy and, ultimately, Alzheimer's. He has received numerous awards and is widely regarded as a likely Nobel winner.
> "Sandy's achievement was probably the most important breakthrough of the decade in the battle against cancer," says Gregory Morgenstern of M.I.T. "It dwarfs anything I've ever done. He deserves all the honor and glory—and money—that I'm sure he's going to get."

"GOOD Lord. Did you see how they quoted Morgenstern, Dad?" Sandy fumed.
"Yes, sonny boy," the older man muttered uncomfortably. "But it's only natural for a cover story that they would trace your career and go back and speak to the people who knew you along the way. After all, Morgenstern did win the big one. How the hell are they supposed to know the skeletons in his closet? Listen, it could have been worse, kiddo. They could have mentioned Rochelle."
"Yeah," Sandy acknowledged. "Thank heavens for that."

CURIOUSLY enough, Sandy Raven did not look back on his formative years with any anger. He was only marginally aware of his parents' mutual hostility, and he always recalled his childhood as a time of purest love. Not anyone's for him, but his own secret passion for his classmate Rochelle Taubman—the belle of P.S. 161. She was slender and strikingly beautiful, with high cheekbones, shiny auburn hair, and deliquescent eyes, while he was pudgy and bespectacled, with a complexion reminiscent of oatmeal.

She barely knew he existed, except when finals approached and she cajoled him into helping her prepare for their math and science exams. He did not feel the slightest bit exploited. The mere fact that she sweetened each tutorial session with phrases like "You're wonderful, Sandy" or "I'll love you forever" was recompense enough. And yet when the testing period ended, she ignored him until the end of the next semester.

And in the interim Sandy would merely pine.

THE only child of Pauline and Sidney Raven, manager of Loew's Grand theater, Sandy had just been accepted at The Bronx High School of Science when his parents divorced. Shortly thereafter his mother married a wealthy jeweler and relinquished custody of her young son.

Sandy could have gone to live in Los Angeles with his father, who had moved there to be a movie producer, but he was determined to study at Bronx Science. He spent the rest of his high school years shuttling from one grudging relative to another.

JUST before the end of school at P.S. 161—their last school year together—Sandy made certain to mention to Rochelle that his dad was now a junior executive at Twentieth Century-Fox. Once again she remembered Sandy's existence. She rushed to him and declared, "I don't know how I'll bear being without you. I mean, next year you'll be at Bronx Science and I'll be at the High School of Music and Art. When will we ever see each other?"

"There's always the telephone," he replied with a touch of sarcasm. But then he chivalrously volunteered, "Any night you need help with your homework, just call me up."

"I will, I will," she chirped. "I guess I never had a chance to tell you, but I was sorry to hear about your mom and dad splitting."

"Thanks," he replied. "I suppose it's better for all of us."

"But will you ever get to see your father?"

16

"Actually, he's just sent me a bus ticket so I can spend the summer with him in Hollywood."

"Gosh, that sounds so exciting. I wish I could go too."

Oh, Rochelle, he thought, his heart drumming. If only I *could* take you with me.

SANDY would never forget his first visit to California.

It was nearly lunchtime when Sid's Chevy arrived at the gate of the Twentieth Century-Fox studios. The guard immediately recognized him, gave a salute, and smiled. "Good morning, Mr. Raven. This is pretty late for you."

"Yeah. I had to pick up my boy at the station."

The guard waved them through with a cordial "Hi there, young fellow. Welcome to Tinseltown."

Sid drove slowly to his parking place so that his son could drink in the sights of the studio. Stagehands were busy putting up an elevated railway track, while others were nailing up what looked like a row of old-fashioned brownstones—the set for *Hello, Dolly.*

In the commissary, a cavernous dining hall whose façade served as one of the buildings in *Peyton Place*, there was an elevated platform reserved for major moguls—a category for which his father did not yet qualify. The bigwigs would be joined by whichever stars were filming on the lot at that time. Today it was Charlton Heston, wearing an astronaut's gear.

Yet the most startling view was of the plebeians' eating area, which seemed to have been attacked by a legion of gorillas casually munching sandwiches and swilling coffee. Sid explained that they were extras from an epic called *Planet of the Apes.*

Everyone seemed to know and love Sandy's father. As they ate their tuna on rye with pickle, Sidney was greeted by innumerable simians as well as other Hollywood animals. Sandy was awestruck.

"Musicals are in," Sidney declared to his son over that evening's chili. "And I've got a notion for a blockbuster. It's called *Frankie*—a song-and-dance version of *Frankenstein.* It's a guaranteed hit. And do you know why, sonny boy? Because it's one of the surefire stories of all time. For centuries men have dreamed of actually growing life in the laboratory. So all we need is a new twist." He then inquired of his son, "Any ideas for a gimmick?"

17

"Well," Sandy said, proud of the opportunity to parade his learning, "you could have Dr. Frankenstein be a genetic researcher building his monster with DNA."

"What's DNA?" his father asked.

"It's really the latest thing," Sandy said, waxing enthusiastic. "Back in '53 two guys in England named Watson and Crick deciphered the code of life—the genetic material we're all made of. DNA stands for deoxyribonucleic acid. I mean, Dad, it's right where science is at. I bet every guy in my school will see this movie twenty times."

"But kiddo, not everybody goes to Bronx Science. I'm afraid your concept won't fly with Mr. Z."

Sandy felt embarrassed, thinking he had gone down in his father's estimation for having made so foolish a suggestion. He vowed to keep his big ideas to himself from now on.

THE visit provided many opportunities for heart-to-heart conversations, during which Sandy had revealed his unflagging passion for Rochelle. His father tried to be sympathetic, though platonic love was an emotion beyond his ken.

On several occasions they took long walks by the ocean in Santa Monica, sharing their aspirations for the future. The older man dreamed of making big pictures with big stars for big money. And most of all, to have his work designated as "A Sidney Raven Production." Biochemistry was the realm in which Sandy wanted to dominate—especially the genetic side. And then, ever prone to rhapsodize, Sidney conceived of a time not too distant when—in a single year—he would win an Oscar and his son a Nobel Prize.

Father and son had grown closer that summer than they ever were when they were living together 365 days a year.

4 **ADAM** Suddenly, at the beginning of the third week, the blood count in the second set of mice began to improve dramatically. Forty-eight hours later it was certain: The animals' systems were clear. The human cancer had been cured in its mouse surrogate.

Max and Adam were now confident that their drug would work on the patient himself. Of course, there was an element of uncer-

18

tainty, since they had not completed the normal cycle of FDA trials. But then, they had a White House concession.

With the generosity that characterized his relationship with Adam, Max Rudolph deputized him to deliver the serum personally to Washington and monitor the results.

THE admiral was puzzled when he met Adam that night at National Airport. In addition to his overnight case, the lanky Harvard doctor was carrying what looked like a square lampshade with a handle.

"What's that?"

"It's a surprise for the patient," Adam answered with a tiny smile.

Penrose nodded and led his Boston colleague to a limousine waiting on the tarmac. The two men rode in silence for several minutes before Adam realized that the lights of Washington had receded and they were now in the countryside.

"Hey," he said, confused, "what's going on? Are we going to Camp David or something?"

"No," the admiral answered, "the patient's in Virginia." He paused and then confided, "And it's not the President."

"What? Who else has got the clout to get hold of three unapproved drugs?"

"Our patient is Thomas Deely Hartnell."

Adam's jaw dropped. "Otherwise known as the Boss? Former ambassador to the Court of St. James's? Adviser to every President, right and left?"

Penrose nodded. "And a man to whom you say no at your peril. I hope you'll forgive the subterfuge, but I sensed that Dr. Rudolph would not have extended his patriotism beyond the Oval Office."

Neither would I, Adam thought with annoyance.

Perhaps the admiral read his thoughts, because he said earnestly, "Let me assure you, Dr. Coopersmith, Thomas Hartnell is a very worthy human being—and a valuable asset to this country. You should have no qualms about what you're doing."

"Ow!"

Adam stood silently in the elegant bedroom as Penrose injected the serum into Hartnell's buttock. Then the two men turned the

19

dignitary onto his back and gave him a sedative. When Hartnell was comfortable, Adam, with the panache of a magician, whisked away the cloth from the object he had carried into the room and announced, "Voilà, Mr. Hartnell, a gift from Immunology Lab 808, and specifically its director, Max Rudolph."

"A mouse?"

"Well yes, zoologically speaking, I suppose so. But this little fella's rather unusual—he has the same blood chemistry as you do, and we thought if you saw him frisking around, it might give you an idea of what you'll be like in a couple of weeks."

After waiting for the sedative to take effect, Penrose led the visiting scientist to a majestic drawing room, where members of the patient's inner circle were tensely waiting to hear what had transpired. The admiral quickly made the introductions.

"All we can say at this point is that he's resting comfortably," he declared. "And now I'll leave it to my learned colleague to spell out the procedure we've put into effect."

Despite the lateness of the hour, Adam felt an unexpected surge of energy. He was a born teacher, and his manner charmed the audience as he discoursed on the development of a retrovirus that could be transported directly to the cancer cells that had gone amok. Its "disguise" would allow it to penetrate the nucleus of the malignant cell, where the alchemy of DNA transformed foe back into friend. Pausing, he smiled. "In other words, it makes a bunch of Hell's Angels suddenly turn into the Vienna Boys Choir."

Surveying his high-powered audience, Adam was puzzled by the presence of a tall, striking blonde. Her horn-rimmed glasses and conservative suit seemed to him deliberate attempts to camouflage her beauty.

Yet Antonia Nielson was far too young—a fairly recent graduate of Georgetown Law School, it later emerged—to hold important government office. And she was even too youthful to be a politically acceptable wife for a sixty-year-old man.

But she was the ideal vintage for a Cabinet-level mistress.

The only question was: Whose?

As Adam spoke, she smiled several times at his witticisms, and he began to think that he had seen her somewhere before. And then it struck him. To set the mouse cage down on the patient's night

20

table, he'd had to displace a leather-framed photograph of Hartnell and a ravishing young woman. He now realized it was Antonia, without spectacles. His question was answered.

As the various guests departed, none of them neglected to kiss Antonia. It all appeared perfectly friendly, except the way the Attorney General held her. Indeed, if she had not been so clearly the Boss's girl, Adam would have suspected a liaison with the country's chief legal officer.

Unexpectedly, she took the initiative as she and Adam emerged from the mansion to a blue sky marbled with the first pink streaks of morning. Adam's driver was waiting patiently, but before Adam could climb inside the car, Antonia materialized next to him and asked in soft, confident tones, "Doctor, I know you're staying at the Watergate. May I offer you a ride?"

Adam smiled. This was an unexpected gift. "Only if you'll agree to have a very early breakfast with me."

"Fine," she answered. "I'll even make it for you myself. But you'll have to let me cross-examine you while we drive."

"With pleasure," Adam responded. "Just let me retrieve my impedimenta and liberate the driver."

As they sped toward the capital, Adam quickly realized that her gesture was not romantically inspired. To be sure, she was anxious to talk to him, but as a doctor. "He's *got* to live, Adam," she said. "Honestly, what do you think his chances really are?"

"Miss Nielson—"

"Please call me Toni."

"Toni, I can only say that what Max has done gives Mr. Hartnell a better shot at licking this killer than any other man on the planet."

"Oh, that's wonderful. Thank God!" she exclaimed with relief. "I mean, he's such a good person. No one knows him better than I. Beneath that gruff exterior he's loving and sensitive."

Forty minutes later they were in Toni's small, expensively decorated flat. While she stirred the batter for oatmeal pancakes, the phone rang. "Take it, Adam. My hands are full."

He picked up the receiver, listened for an instant, and covered the phone. "Sounds like a mistake. Some secretary's asking for Skipper."

"Oh," she said casually, taking the phone from him. "That's

21

me. It's my old tomboy nickname." Then, speaking to the caller, "Morning, Cecily. Put him right on, please." She paused for a moment and then exclaimed warmly, "Hi, sweetheart! Feeling better yet? . . . Yes, I'm here with Dr. Coopersmith." She listened for a minute and then asserted, "Yes, yes, I *did* notice he's attractive. What should matter to you is that he really knows his stuff, and I honestly think this drug is going to work." In another minute they were exchanging kisses down the line, and she hung up in a buoyant mood. "I guess you know who that was."

"Yeah," Adam responded, trying to mask his disappointment. "Everybody's boss."

"Except mine." Toni grinned.

"What makes you so special?" Adam asked.

"I'm his daughter," she replied.

Well, well—Hartnell was her father. That changed things somewhat. Except where did "Nielson" come from?

"Mr. Jack Nielson was a childhood folly," Toni explained later. "We were at law school together at Georgetown, and quite frankly, I think he was more in love with my father's influence than he was with me. He turned out to be a louse."

"I'm sorry," Adam commiserated.

"Well," she said breezily, "it was what they call a learning experience. And now I'm immunized."

"Against what?"

"Against emotional involvements," she said quietly.

THAT evening Toni drove Adam to a dinner party at her father's Virginia mansion. Though on doctor's orders the Boss did not attend in person, it was a high-level evening befitting the nature of the house: two Senators, a senior columnist from *The New York Times*, the Secretary of State, and the Attorney General. All except the last had brought a companion. Before the evening ended, Admiral Penrose turned up in time to join Adam in a thorough examination of the patient, and then immediately departed.

Toni stayed a bit longer, but she beckoned Adam into a corner for a confidential chat. Pressing something metallic into his hand, she murmured, "Take my car and just leave it in the garage. I've got a spare set of keys. Will you be able to find your way back?"

He nodded, understanding all too well what was happening and unable to keep from feeling hurt. "Yeah," he muttered. "I suppose so. How will you—" He stopped himself. "I guess that's none of my business, huh?"

"I guess," she whispered.

Okay, he consoled himself. It was all a meaningless tease. Toni was not available after all. She had unblushingly gone off hand in hand with the Attorney General.

Yet the next night she insisted upon taking Adam to dinner at La Renaissance. He was puzzled by her interest but had already seen enough of her lifestyle to permit himself a few cynical observations. "Does your father approve of you going out with a married man?"

"He's no one to talk," she replied casually. "He stopped supervising my social life when I broke up with Jack. Anyway, he and . . . my friend were college classmates. So how can he object?"

She was not the least self-conscious in discussing these details. And since this relationship was clearly dependent on her "friend's" domestic obligations, there were even several nights in a row when Toni was unfettered and could invite Adam to one or another Washington festivity.

One evening as they were walking home from a performance of *Swan Lake* at the Kennedy Center, he was in a carefree mood and actually danced for a few seconds in imitation of the prince. She surprised him by executing several steps in response.

The whole incident was out of character for them both. Their defenses were suddenly down, and they confessed to one another that, as children, they had each studied ballet.

"What made you quit?" he asked. "I mean, you have a perfect dancer's body."

She smiled. "Thanks for the compliment. The stupid truth is that I was always so tall that none of the boys could lift me. What stopped you from becoming the American Baryshnikov?"

"Two reasons. My mother was the pianist for the class, and I only joined as an act of loyalty. Also it was a way to hurt my father for the shabby way he treated her. Imagine an Indiana steelworker having to tell his buddies that his son was prancing around in tights."

"What happened to your mom?"

"She died when I was twelve. He killed her."

23

"What? You can't be serious."

"She was trying to bear him another kid, and she got toxemia in the late stages of pregnancy." His anger was emerging now. "It was a heartless thing—when she got into trouble, my father bullied the doctor to hold off delivery to make sure the baby she was carrying would live. In the end they lost both of them."

"Who took care of you?"

"I took care of myself. Unlikely as it sounds, I took up a sport— platform diving. It meant that for at least a couple of seconds—in my head—I could be completely alone, thirty-three feet above the rest of the world. Soon all I wanted to do was get away from home. And my only chance was getting an academic scholarship. My grades were better than my diving. Ever hear of Shimer College?"

"Frankly, no."

"Nobody has. It's a small, progressive offshoot of the University of Chicago, a kind of incubator for premeds anxious to save a few years. I channeled my anger into studying, and by some miracle I got into Harvard Med."

"No doubt with the goal of keeping women from dying of toxemia," Toni suggested gently.

"And saving babies," Adam added. "I was a grand old man of nineteen. I may have been academically prepared, but I was a social misfit among all those smooth Ivy League graduates. I suppose that's why I only felt at home with the other lab rats."

"Is that how you met Max?"

Adam nodded. "I finally found a father I respected. While I was finishing my residency in ob-gyn, Max wangled me a research fellowship. He didn't just teach me immunology, he taught me life. I mean, the first time I was invited to his house for dinner, I knew that Max and Lisl had the kind of relationship that gave marriage a good name. She's a Kleinian analyst—does wonders with children. They took me under their wing."

"Do they have any kids?" Toni asked.

"Me, I guess. Now it's your turn to be up close and personal," he responded, hoping his candor had eased her own inhibitions.

But she suddenly pleaded the lateness of the hour, explaining that she had to be at work early the next morning at the Department of Justice.

BOYD PENROSE PHONED AT three a.m. "Coopersmith, I've just read the Boss's numbers, and those lymphocytes are making a comeback. I think we've turned the corner, old buddy."

Overflowing with euphoria, Adam called Boston and conveyed the good news to Max. As he hung up, there was another ring.

"Hi. I got Boyd's message too," Toni said ecstatically. "Your line was busy. Were you on with Max?"

"Yes. I just reported to him."

"Would you like to report to *me* for an impromptu party?"

"Why not?" Adam agreed.

When he arrived at her apartment, Toni was intoxicated with joy. "Oh, Adam," she wept, hurling her arms around him. "You've done it—you've saved my father!"

Suddenly she was kissing him on the lips. It was unexpected but far from undesirable, and he welcomed it wholeheartedly.

NATURALLY, Adam did not leave Washington until the third blood tests came through. They were—in Penrose's words—squeaky clean. Boyd and Adam agreed that it was safe to tell the patient that his recovery was certain.

Hartnell was overwhelmed. He summoned Adam for a private conversation. "Now you listen, Coopersmith. I've got a hell of a lot of influence, and thanks to your chief, I'm going to be around to wield it for a long time. I owe him. Now tell me, what would Max Rudolph want most in the world?"

Adam moved closer to the bed and said almost in a whisper, "I don't think anyone alive deserves the Nobel Prize more."

"No problem," the Boss murmured.

5 ISABEL Once more the demons had been awakened in Raymond da Costa. After his son had gone off to school and his wife to work, he was free to nurture his daughter's genius.

One of the advantages of his nonacademic appointment in the physics department was that he was not obliged to punch a time clock. Therefore he was constantly testing Isabel, desperate to see how far the horizon of her intelligence stretched.

Having been blessed with a truly gifted child, Raymond was passionately curious to learn when she would be capable of making

25

the connection to abstract thought. He devised a simple test. "Isabel, I'm picking a number, but I'm not going to tell you what it is. I'll call it x." He took a piece of paper and scribbled:

$$x + 5 = 12 \qquad x = 12 - 5 \qquad x = 7$$

"Do you understand, darling?"

"Sure."

"Now I'll write a secret formula: $x + 7 = 4 + 11$. So, what does x stand for?"

The little girl pondered for a moment and then blithely announced, "X is eight."

Raymond gaped. She had not merely crossed the threshold of abstract thought but had pirouetted through it like a ballerina.

Of course, Muriel concurred that their daughter was a prodigy, but she was determined that Isabel would not become a freak. This intensified her confrontations with Ray. They were at loggerheads on the question of sending Isabel to elementary school.

"Elementary school will just hold her back," he argued. "Don't you think that would be unfair to her?"

"She needs playmates her own age. That is, if you expect her to grow up to be normal."

He did not, as she had feared, lose his temper. "Look, honey," he reasoned. "Normal is simply not an adjective that applies to Isabel. Believe me, she enjoys the time we spend together. In fact, she can't seem to learn enough."

After some painful soul-searching, Muriel stayed firm and, despite Ray's grumbling, enrolled Isabel in grammar school with her peers. With the proviso—and with Ray there was always a proviso—that the moment Isabel came home from school, she would be under his exclusive tutelage. With no distractions.

Two afternoons a week Muriel would see violin pupils at home, sometimes lending them Peter's long-discarded quarter-size fiddle. One day she left the violin on the coffee table, and Isabel picked it up. Copying the others, she placed the instrument under her neck, grasped the bow, and scraped it across the strings. The result was a raucous screech that brought Muriel from the kitchen to the living-room door. There she stopped to observe.

After a few more attempts Isabel was able to bow an A string, which grew clearer with every stroke. She then began to explore the string with her first finger until she found a B. It was not long before her experiments yielded a C-sharp.

Muriel was too ecstatic to keep this discovery from Ray. Although he too was excited, he was worried that she might now try to seduce the girl into the realm of music. "Gosh, that's fantastic, honey," he murmured. "She's not much older than Mozart was when he began to play. But did you know that Mozart was also a mathematical genius? His father made the crucial decision that someone of his son's age could never have made."

"Which you are now making for Isabel?" she asked.

"Precisely. The girl's a scientist, and maybe even—yes, I'll say it—another Einstein."

Muriel was incensed. "Did *you* know that Einstein was also a fine violinist?"

"Yes," he answered. "But it was a hobby, a kind of recreation."

"Are you implying," she asked, barely able to control herself, "that the Almighty has decreed that Isabel will become a scientist?"

"I'm not implying anything," Raymond shot back. "I'm simply saying that I won't let anything stand in the way of my daughter's development. That's it, Muriel—the discussion is closed."

AUGUST 10: *There are two invisible people haunting our house, and the way my parents talk about them, you'd think they were members of the family.*

One is Albert Einstein. I looked him up in the encyclopedia and read that his ideas were so extraordinary that at first people refused to believe them. I feel very uncomfortable when Dad predicts that someday I'll make these kinds of discoveries. Frankly—and I'm ashamed to admit this—I'd rather be compared to Brooke Shields.

The other ghost is Wolfgang Amadeus Mozart. He lived in the eighteenth century and was—as people like to call me and make me cringe—a "prodigy."

Dad goes crazy whenever Mom mentions Mozart. Fortunately, they came to an agreement that I could do an hour of music a day.

Peter watched them fight without saying a word. Later he came to my room and said, "Boy, am I glad I'm not smart."

6 **ADAM** After his return from Washington, Adam had wondered whether to tell Max about that final conversation with Hartnell. But his mentor had already been upset to learn that the man for whom he had compromised his principles was not, after all, the President of the United States. And the fact that someone like the Boss had offered to help obtain him a Nobel might stigmatize the prize forever in Max's scrupulous estimation.

In any case, whenever someone suggested that Max should have long ago earned the Nobel, he always commented dismissively, "Well, if it must come, let's hope it's not for a while. T. S. Eliot was right when he said, 'The Nobel is a ticket to your own funeral. No one's ever done anything after he got it.' "

"COME into my office," Max told Adam. "I want to talk to you about an important project."

"Something new? How long have you been hiding it from me?"

"Oh, about ten years." And there was something about Max's tone of voice that sounded as if he was not exaggerating.

Moments later they were locked within the glass-walled partitions of his office. "This is very difficult for me to discuss," the older man began uneasily. "Tell me truthfully, have you come across any rumors about why Lisl and I didn't have children?"

"That's none of my business."

"Have you never heard it whispered that I didn't have a family because it would distract me from my research?"

Adam looked his boss in the eye. "First of all, I've never heard it, and most of all, I don't believe it for a minute."

"I'm glad," Max responded. "The truth is, we both desperately wanted a baby. In fact, Lisl was pregnant at least fourteen times."

"Fourteen?"

"Well, a great number of them ended so early that only a doctor could have determined that she'd been pregnant at all. There didn't seem to be anybody in our ob-gyn department who could shed light on the matter. So I took the investigation into my own hands. I soon discovered that a sizable number of women go through this agony many times before giving up completely. It's a catastrophe and a mystery, which to this day remains unsolved."

"How come you never once mentioned this to me?"

"I didn't want to burden you with something that neither of us could do anything about. But I've been gathering data over nearly ten years."

"All that time behind my back?"

Max nodded. "I've been moonlighting in the Marblehead Gynecological Clinic, specializing in patients with repeated miscarriages." He patted his computer and said, "Everything's in here. All I need is the benefit of your brain."

"Okay, boss. But I still sense that if Batman's calling Robin, it means he's already on the trail of a solution."

"As a matter of fact, I am, Boy Wonder. I think you'll agree with my basic hypothesis: that these miscarriages might result from the woman rejecting the fetus as a foreign body. My experiments with mice have shown that certain females carry their own antigens, which are toxic to the baby." He lowered his head sadly and murmured, "I am afraid my little Lisl is that kind of mouse."

"You must have suffered a great deal," Adam whispered.

"No. She suffered—I just endured." And then, regaining his gruff tone, he ordered, "Now let's get to work, shall we?"

WITH the data, the technicians, and the mice already in place, it was relatively easy for Adam to move his investigation from the confines of Max's obsession to the open benches of Immunology Lab 808. The information already gathered had given them leads with which to begin. Moreover, there had been progress in other areas of the field. As Max explained, "Researchers at Sandoz are well along the way with an immunosuppressant that will transform organ transplants into everyday occurrences."

"Great," Adam said. "Now all *we* have to do is discover an analogy that would suppress the autoimmune reaction in pregnant females."

Adam worked demonically. Whenever he was not seeing patients or delivering babies, he was in the lab. Late one afternoon Max found his protégé hard at work. Eyeing him with disapproval, he demanded, "How many hours of sleep did you get last night?"

"A few."

" 'A few' is not a scientific answer," he admonished. "Even your great brain has to recharge. So finish what you're doing and we'll go out to Newton and get some decent food into you."

Twenty minutes later they were in Max's vintage Beetle, sputtering along Commonwealth Avenue in the growing winter darkness.

As the older man failed to stop for the second red light in a row, Adam scolded, "Pay attention. Your mind's a million miles away. You shouldn't be driving at the best of times."

"At least *I* got some sleep last night," Max replied. "Now sit back and listen to this Schubert." He turned up the volume.

Adam relented. At that instant he took his attention off the road—a lapse for which he would castigate himself the rest of his life. As they reached the crest of Heartbreak Hill on Commonwealth Avenue and began to hurtle downward, two teenagers on bikes suddenly appeared directly in the path of the car.

Max swerved to avoid them and, skidding on a patch of ice, lost control and crashed violently into a tree.

The silence after the accident belied its gravity. For a moment Adam sat there motionless, in shock. He listened intently but could not hear any sound of breathing. Reaching over to feel the old man's pulse, he knew this was merely a pretext to touch his mentor for the last time.

Slowly he was gripped by an agonizing awareness. He's dead. My friend, my teacher—my father—he's dead. And it's all my fault.

He was still sobbing when the squad cars came.

LISL took the news bravely. "He was so headstrong, my Max," she murmured. "I should never have let him drive." She then realized how shaken Adam was and touched his hand. "Stop blaming yourself. You have to accept that terrible things like this happen."

But why to Max? Adam grieved. Why to such a saintly man?

Lisl called one of her close friends, who was more than willing to sit with her while Adam went through the grim procedure of making the funeral arrangements.

At six p.m. Eli Cass, the press officer from Harvard, telephoned for details of the accident to add to the release he was rushing to complete for the next morning's Boston *Globe* and the wire services. "Dean Holmes said it was only a question of time before Max got the Nobel," Cass remarked.

"Yes," Adam replied numbly. "He was probably the leading immunologist in the world."

In the living room, Lisl had been joined by Maurice Oates, the Rudolphs' lawyer. "I wouldn't be discussing Max's will so soon," he apologized. "Except that it's emphatic about there being no service at his interment. Otherwise the testament is straightforward." He paused and then looked at the tall young doctor standing ashen-faced in the corner. "He wanted you to have his gold pocket watch."

"I'll get it," Lisl offered.

"No, no," Adam said. "There's plenty of time for that."

"Please," she overruled him. "If I don't give it to you tonight, you'll have nothing of Max's to go home with."

Suddenly, heedless of the others in the room, she fell into Adam's arms. And they both began to sob for the terrible loss of the noblest human being they would ever know.

ALTHOUGH it was nearly midnight when Adam left, Lisl was still surrounded by several friends and neighbors.

Adam's phone was ringing when he reached home. It was Toni.

"It was on the eleven-o'clock news," she explained. "Are you okay?"

"Not really," he replied bitterly. "I should have been driving."

There was a silence. Toni did not know what to say. Finally she asked, "When's the funeral?"

"Tuesday morning. There's not going to be any ceremony."

"Would it be all right if I came?"

"But you didn't even know him."

"Funerals are for the living, not the dead."

"I realize that. But I have to look after Lisl."

"I know," she answered gently. "But somebody has to take care of you."

There was a momentary pause.

"Thanks, Toni," he whispered. "I'd appreciate that."

THERE were two dozen or so gathered around Max Rudolph's freshly dug grave: the dean, colleagues, their wives, his lab teams and students. And standing discreetly among them was Antonia Nielson from Washington.

The undertakers, experienced with "silent" funerals, had pre-

31

pared cut flowers for the mourners to drop onto the lowered coffin as they passed by to pay their last respects.

Finally only Adam and Lisl were left. And as he held his flower, the lines from Hamlet emerged from his throat unbidden:

> *"He was a man, take him for all in all,*
> *I shall not look upon his like again."*

Then, unwillingly, he let fall his flower.
And Lisl did the same.

7 SANDY Sandy Raven returned from his first visit to the Coast tanned and confident—at least self-assured enough to phone the lovely Miss Taubman "just to say hello."

She seemed less than overjoyed to hear from him until he reminded her where he had spent his summer vacation. Her tone warmed, and she suggested they meet for coffee.

When he first arrived at the café, he looked around for her in vain. Then, with a jolt, he realized that she had been waiting for him all the time, and he hurried to her table. "Sorry, Rochelle, sorry," he apologized abjectly. "But I really didn't recognize you. I mean, you didn't tell me that you were a blonde now. And that you . . ." He glanced at her face and was embarrassed to say it.

But she finished his thought. "Didn't the doctor do a great job? You'd never believe it wasn't my real nose."

Sandy felt genuinely saddened, for in truth, she had been far prettier with her original physiognomy. The operation had changed her from soulful Madonna to Barbie doll.

"Yeah, yeah. It looks great," he responded dutifully.

"I was against it at first, but my agent insisted I wouldn't have a chance in the movies without a more classic profile."

As he signaled to the waiter, she launched into a narrative that would have made Narcissus blush. "Summer stock was unbelievable. I mean, not only did I get to do *Streetcar* and *Our Town*, but our final production was *Romeo and Juliet*. Joe Papp actually came backstage and spoke to me. But I'm waiting for your news. What's your father got on tap?"

He told her all about the studio, the apes, and about *Frankie*.

"That sounds brilliant. Have they cast the female lead?"

"I could ask my father," Sandy offered generously.

"Oh, you really are a beautiful person," she said joyously. "Call me after you speak to him. I'll be sitting by the phone."

THE news Sidney Raven conveyed was bittersweet. Bitter for himself, but sweet for her. It seemed the studio was retrenching, and Mr. Z. had qualms about putting money into yet another big musical, even though he loved the concept of *Frankie*. And yet Sid was confident that he could arrange for Rochelle to audition for the Fox Players' School. This was less an academy than a collection of potential heartthrobs being groomed for stardom by the studio. The next time they interviewed in New York, he would see to it that his son's inamorata would be auditioned.

"Oh, Sandy," she gushed on the telephone, "I wish you were here. I'd throw my arms around you and give you a big kiss."

I can always come over, he thought. But he didn't say it.

Sid was true to his word. That winter the scouts from Fox gave Rochelle a screen test. They decided that, if not a convincing actress, she was certainly worth accepting for her looks alone.

In her haste to depart for California, Rochelle somehow could not find time to contact Sandy.

8 ADAM When Harvard lured Ian Cavanagh from Oxford to take over Max Rudolph's chair and the directorship of the lab, the staff transferred its allegiance and proceeded with research as usual. But Adam kept a cool distance. He had great difficulty bringing himself into the glass-walled office where the Englishman lorded it over the domain that had once been Max's.

This was less deference than Cavanagh had expected from someone he regarded as junior. And whereas he called other staff members by their first names, he always referred to his predecessor's favorite merely as Coopersmith.

Lisl urged Adam to be conciliatory. "Have lunch with the man. Play the game. It won't take him long to recognize your abilities. But help him get to know you."

"I'm afraid it's too late for that," Adam replied dejectedly. "Apparently because of 'financial restraints,' he's had to slash my next year's budget—and my salary—in half."

33

Lisl reacted angrily. "Excuse me while I revise my opinion of him. By cutting Max's most cherished project, he's just proved how petty he is. He's probably intimidated by you, Adam. But you mustn't let him make you resign."

"No, Lisl," he said with fervor. "I won't."

To make up the shortfall in his salary, Adam signed on as a supervisor in obstetrics at the Lying-In Hospital. Since the terms of his new employment required him merely to be in the medical school area, he could actually work in the lab, able to sprint to the delivery room in less than five minutes.

His spirits were always buoyed by the sight of the newborns— wriggling, wailing, red-faced creatures. And yet he found it hard to discuss this aspect of his work with Lisl. He felt that, if anything, Max's death had exacerbated the pain of her childlessness. But as the months passed, she had begun to come to terms with her loss. At least enough to realize that he had not.

"You're a young man, Adam. You should be thinking about your own babies, not just other people's. Incidentally, how do things stand between you and that nice girl from Washington?"

Adam shrugged. "What can I say? I'm here, she's there. Geography just about sums it up."

"Why don't you see if you can dislodge her?"

Adam didn't wish to go into details about Toni's complicated social life. But when he got home that night, he telephoned Washington and invited himself for the weekend. Toni did not hide her delight.

SHE met his flight, and they sped off back across the Potomac in her car. Though they had kissed perfunctorily at the airport, there was an uneasy silence. In the apartment, Adam took off his jacket, donned an apron, and helped her prepare the salad. They worked like lab partners.

"Why are you so incredibly talkative?" she joked.

Adam turned and gave vent to the feeling of frustration that had seized him since he had entered her apartment. "I'm confused, Toni," he said candidly. "I mean, on the one hand you make me feel like I'm the only man in the world. And yet we both know you have this commitment."

"To my job, Adam. To the Department of Justice."

"You mean your employer, don't you?"

Toni did not disguise her irritation. But she paused for a moment and then put her hand gently on the back of his neck and whispered, "It's all over with him, Adam. It's been over since the minute I got back from being with you in Boston. I was going to tell you, but when Max died, it hardly seemed the moment. I'd discovered the difference between a man wanting you and *needing* you. I hope it doesn't sound presumptuous, but I honestly felt I made a difference in your life."

"You did. You do. I only wish you'd told me sooner."

The rest of that weekend was a kind of prologue to commitment. Toni finally felt secure enough to open her heart.

Her childhood had been antithetical to his at almost every point. While he had climbed above his father by mounting the diving platform, she had viewed the world from the height of the pedestal on which Tom Hartnell had placed her.

Adam realized that her predilection for mature men was an inevitable continuation of her deep attachment to the Boss.

He understood what he was up against, but he was man enough to confess his qualms. "Look, Toni. Nobody knows better than I how close you are to your father. Do you think your relationship with him would allow you to forge another?"

"I don't know." She shrugged. "Why don't we try taking things one day at a time?"

"Well," he answered with a smile, "I was working within the parameters of 'forever after.' Does that seem too onerous? In fact, why don't we go on a honeymoon this summer? Take a house on Cape Cod maybe. Then if we like it, we can get married."

"That's a novel idea," she said, her face radiant.

9 ISABEL Just after turning eleven, Isabel passed the final high school equivalency exams, theoretically making her eligible to go directly to college, depending, of course, on how well she scored on the Scholastic Aptitude Tests.

One rainy Saturday morning in October, 1983, Ray and Muriel drove Isabel to the local high school, where she took the SATs. On the first page of the questionnaire she requested that her results be

35

sent to the University of California at Berkeley and at San Diego, her hometown.

The Berkeley application, Ray explained, was just an exercise to see how she would be judged by the state's finest university. There was no question of her being sent away at so early an age.

Isabel scored a perfect 1600 on the two aptitude tests and had done so well in her achievement tests that both schools offered her advanced standing, while suggesting that she wait a year or two— perhaps to pick up a foreign language.

Undaunted, Ray proposed driving to Berkeley for an interview.

Muriel objected. "There's no point in going all that way when Isabel's not going to accept the place." She looked into her husband's eyes and immediately understood his plan. "No, Ray. This is where I draw the line. We're not moving to Berkeley."

"I've never said *we* were."

"You're out of your mind," she exploded. "Do you imagine any court would grant you custody of an eleven-year-old girl?"

Ray maintained a serene calm. "Who said a word about custody? We're not divorcing, Muriel. We're just doing what's best for our daughter. And if you really want her to be happy, you know damn well that taking her away from *me* will have the opposite effect. Think about it. Meanwhile, I'll take Isabel to Berkeley."

THE Berkeley dean of admissions had in his portfolio two somewhat disturbing communications. The first was from a high school examiner who had questioned Isabel orally. The second came from the girl's mother. Both warned that there was "an unnaturally close relationship between the girl and her father."

These unhappy predictions were borne out the minute Dean Kendall opened his door and beckoned Isabel inside. He pulled up short when he noticed that Raymond was tagging along after her. "Mr. da Costa," he said in an unmistakably chilly tone, "if you don't mind, I'd like to speak to your daughter by herself."

"Uh, yes," Raymond mumbled, ill at ease. And then to his daughter, "I'll be waiting right outside, darling."

Alone with the girl, Dean Kendall exercised supreme delicacy. "Isabel, do you think you could live in dormitories with other girls, some of them twice your age?"

"No," she replied happily. "I'd be living with my father."

"That would seem to make sense," the dean murmured. "But don't you think that would inhibit your social life?"

"Oh, no. Besides, I'm not old enough to have a social life."

When they were gone, the dean had an inner argument with himself. She's far too young. She should really go to a prep school. But if *we* don't take her, Harvard will. He composed a letter of acceptance to Ms. Isabel da Costa, offering her a place as a freshman in the class of '88 for a bachelor's degree in physics.

MURIEL was barely able to control her anger. "Ray, I hate your guts for what you've done to Isabel—*and* me. The only reason I won't take you to court is because, unlike you, I genuinely care about what happens to her as a person. I won't allow her to be the mutilated prize in a parental tug-of-war. Take her if you must, but at least don't shut me out of her life."

Suppressing his feelings of triumph, Ray responded softly, "Muriel, I swear it's what Isabel wants. You can ask her. Berkeley's got one of the greatest physics departments in the world. And we'll be home for every vacation, I promise you." He paused and asked, "Do we have a deal?"

"Yes," she answered acidly. "What we don't have is a marriage."

AUGUST 24: *For the first part of our journey I was excited, but the closer we got to Berkeley, the more I began to feel afraid. I mean, it's one thing to do college work with your father as the teacher. But it's a whole other thing when—as I imagined—I'd be sitting in a classroom with kids twice my age and maybe twice as smart.*

Anyway, by the time we reached Berkeley, I was on the verge of panic. And when we got to this dinky little place Dad had rented, I was almost hysterical at the thought of having to move all the millions of books to the second floor. And Dad had forgotten to pack my violin. Luckily, there were three Berkeley jock types living on the ground floor, and they helped us carry stuff up the stairs.

I lay in bed a long time, tossing and turning. Finally I realized what was keeping me awake. I crept out of bed, went over to my duffel bag, and pulled out my best friend in the whole world. And the moment I was back in bed with Teddy in my arms, I fell fast asleep.

10 **ADAM** Toni and Adam's solitude was highly populated, for the summer people who flock to the Cape are almost evenly divided between the who's who of Boston and the who's what of Washington. Still, they found plenty of time to be alone. Whether it was an early morning jog on the beach or a late evening clambake, they enjoyed being together. And the lovemaking got better and better.

On the final weekend of the vacation they reached a crucial moment. After an early morning walk they found themselves placing their suitcases on opposite sides of the four-poster bed in the saltbox cottage that had sheltered such happiness for the past weeks.

Suddenly Adam murmured, "I don't want this to end."

She gazed at him and echoed, "Me either."

After an awkward pause Adam said, "It doesn't have to, Toni."

"We'll only be an hour's flight away," she offered.

"No," he insisted, "that's not good enough. We belong together."

"Do you think you could live in Washington?" Toni asked. "The research facilities at NIH are as good as Harvard's."

"How about you? There are some very distinguished law offices in Boston."

"Adam, for me Washington's a very special place. My career's just taken off—and not only in government. Starting January, I'll be giving a seminar in con. law at Georgetown."

"Come on, Toni," he urged her gently. "There are plenty of good law schools up here—not least, the fairly famous one at Harvard."

She lowered her head and, in a whisper, said, "I knew it would boil down to this. But I didn't know how much it'd hurt."

He was at her side now, wrapping her in his arms. "Please, Toni," he implored, "I love you and I need you. Will you at least think about it? Let's take our time."

"I can't." Toni looked at him, her eyes shining. "I love you. I want to marry you. And if that means having to move to Boston, then I will."

"No WAY, Coopersmith. Not unless hell freezes over!" Thomas Hartnell bellowed, pounding his desk. "You're not dragging my daughter to that provincial mackerel-snapping excuse for a city."

"Dad, calm down, for heaven's sake."

"Skipper, you get lost so I can deal with this alone."

"No, dammit. It's my future you're discussing." Toni stood her ground as the two men in her life battled.

"Will you listen to reason, Mr. Hartnell?" Adam demanded.

"Nothing you say is of interest to me, Dr. Coopersmith. And before you bring it up—yes, I do owe you my life. But I *don't* owe you my daughter—she's even more precious. I mean, what's so damn special about staying at Harvard?"

Adam hesitated for a moment and then confessed, "Max Rudolph. I know this sounds crazy, but when I walk into that lab, he's still there. And when I ask him a question, he sometimes answers."

Adam, brave as he was in standing up to Hartnell's steamroller tactics, still could not bring himself to reveal his deepest motive: that he wanted to tear Toni away from her father's smothering influence.

"You're some kind of nut," Hartnell sneered. "Now I'm giving you exactly thirty seconds to about-face and march out of this house."

"No, Dad," Toni overruled him. "We'd need at least an hour."

"Wh-what?" her father stammered furiously.

"I'd have to pack. Because if he goes, I go with him."

Two months later Toni and Adam were married in St. John's, Lafayette Square, the so-called church of the Presidents, directly across the park from the White House. The incumbent in the Oval Office was among the guests, no doubt a gesture of respect for the man who had done so much to help put him there.

And Thomas Hartnell managed to smile while giving away his only daughter.

DR. AND MRS. Adam Coopersmith rented an apartment on the top floor of a Beacon Hill brownstone. Toni then dug in to cram for the Massachusetts bar exam. Both were passionate about their careers as well as each other. They would look back on this time as the happiest of their married life.

When Toni began to hunt for jobs, there was no lack of Boston law firms eager to add a thirty-year-old former assistant attorney general to their roster. Osterreicher and DeVane outbid them all.

Meanwhile, Adam was making progress. His new director had finally taken the time to examine Adam's study on idiopathic multiple miscarriages, and he now realized the potential of Adam's investigations. In the months that followed, Adam repeated Max's final experiments, using corticosteroids to suppress the embryotoxic reaction in pregnant white mice.

After much soul-searching—weighing the possible side effects of the steroids versus the good they might do—he reluctantly began to treat women whose tests revealed that they could not possibly have a child unless the killer toxins were somehow subdued.

Meanwhile, Toni executed what she lightheartedly referred to as a double play. In the same week, she received positive results from the Massachusetts bar and her beta subunit pregnancy test.

Her drive to excel at everything extended to pregnancy as well, and by sheer force of will she did not let morning sickness curtail her activities. In her thirty-ninth week she went into labor and expertly breathed her way through the birth of six-pound eight-ounce Heather Elizabeth Coopersmith.

Though not the first woman, Toni was the first lawyer to avail herself of the firm's excellent day-care facilities so she could return to work immediately.

AT THE weekly brown-bag staff luncheon Adam was beaming with joy. He read from a computer printout and then crowed, "We've smashed our own record. Thanks to the steroids, seventy percent of our worst repeaters have finally made it through their first trimester. It's either a miracle, or we're geniuses. But I'll render my absolute judgment when I see real babies."

And he did. They then witnessed a surprising development: Once these previously unsuccessful women had reached this point, almost all proceeded to deliver healthy children on schedule.

But the procedure was far from satisfactory. The pregnant mothers began to resent the side effects of taking steroids: the extra weight, swollen limbs, and bloated faces. Not to mention the risk—in rare cases, to be sure—of glaucoma, diabetes, and functional dependency on the drug. Max would never have approved.

Meanwhile, Adam encountered his own unexpected fertility problem. As Heather neared her third birthday, he began to rhapsodize about the possibilities of a second child.

"Heather's a handful already," Toni countered. "I don't honestly see how I can manage another little one and my legal practice."

"They're not little for long," he commented.

"I know," she said, on the verge of losing her temper. "But the baby still wouldn't sleep through the night for at least two years, and I'm not prepared to go through that again." She was crushing his dreams with the recklessness of someone deliberately stamping on delicate glass.

Adam sat silent for a moment, inwardly bruised, then almost involuntarily murmured, "I never expected this."

"You mean you regret marrying me?" she asked bluntly.

"Of course not," he protested. "It's just a dream I'll have to file under impossible."

Toni saw the growing rift between them and, to counteract it, put her arms around him affectionately and stroked his ego. "You forget something, darling. You need a lot of mothering yourself. I hitched my wagon to a star. I want to take good care of my boy genius so he can win the Nobel Prize. I promise you, we're doing the right thing."

As HEATHER grew older, her mother worked longer and longer hours, leaving Adam to make sure his daughter wasn't abandoned to the care of Toni's vast network of baby-sitters. There were times when he simply could not bear to leave the house even when Heather was asleep, lest she wake up with a nightmare and be comforted—or worse, neglected—by a paid surrogate. To his daughter's delight he would put warm winter clothing over her pajamas and take her along to the lab, where she would nestle up on the couch with her Kermit the frog, covered in a blanket, and sleep peacefully until he had to wake her up and bring her home.

There were, however, occasions when he was called out to emergencies and had to phone Toni and insist that she hurry home to take charge. One evening she was in the midst of a crucial partners' meeting and was extremely reluctant to leave. "Adam," she complained when he phoned her. "When will you realize that you're not

the only doctor in the world? You could hand the job over to somebody else."

To which he retorted in a flash of anger, "And when will you realize that a *mother* can't?"

MEANWHILE, there was an explosion in the lab that attracted world attention. Ian Cavanagh had earned his reputation—and his fortune—primarily in the service of Hematics, a biotech company that had engaged him to test their new artificial blood substitute developed for use by hemophiliacs.

His landmark paper demonstrating the efficacy of the drug elevated his standing in the scientific community—as well as the price of Hematics stock. Yet subsequent attempts by other laboratories to repeat Cavanagh's experiment could not replicate his success. There were increasing demands to see his initial data. The Englishman's lame excuse that the original spreadsheets had "gone missing" convinced no one.

When the science editor of the Boston *Globe* caught wind of the

brewing scandal, he blew the whistle, claiming that Cavanagh had falsified his evidence. Every major wire service picked up the story, and Harvard's terrible swift sword fell, instantly severing the scientist's connection with the university.

That morning, when Adam, still unaware, was approaching the lab's parking lot, a policeman waved him away.

"But I'm on the staff," Adam insisted.

"Look, Doctor, I have my orders. And besides, from what I hear, a lot of heads have rolled, and your parking permit might have been revoked."

Finally, in an act of total frustration, Adam abandoned his car on Kirkland Street and raced back toward the lab. Approaching the building, he was startled by a swarm of journalists, television crews—and the law. As he pushed his way through the crowd, Adam could see a Brooks Brothered university administrator politely but very firmly informing a disheveled Englishman that he was no longer a member of the faculty. He could, therefore, remove nothing from his former office except personal effects.

"And may I remind you, Dr. Cavanagh, that you've only got till noon before we change the locks."

Adam reached the tenth floor and went to his cubbyhole of an office to phone Toni to tell her that he had arrived safely through the tumult.

"You mean they didn't tell you? The dean called a minute after you left, but it was impossible to reach you."

"What's up?" Adam asked.

"You, my dear husband," she replied. "You are extremely up. Officially, as of twelve oh one today, you are the acting director of the whole shooting match. And their first three choices to succeed Cavanagh are you, you, and *you*."

Adam let out a whoop. He hung up and, heart still racing, immediately dialed another number. "Hello, Lisl. I've got some wonderful news," he said. "I'm going to be in Max's chair after all."

AT HIS first brown-bag lunch as director, Adam told his team, "I have this gut feeling that we're ignoring something obvious. Why don't we all demote ourselves to freshman med students and carefully analyze the physiological changes of a normal pregnancy. Maybe we can pinpoint the moment our problem women no longer need steroids to sustain their pregnancies."

They all nodded, continuing the exercise with pencils in their right hands and sandwiches in their left. Soon the answer was staring them right in the face.

"Why didn't anybody think of this before?" Len Kutnik, a junior research fellow, asked.

"Because we were working alone," Carlo Pisani suggested.

"Right, Carlo," Adam answered, and then articulated their new insight. "In the second trimester the placenta starts to work overtime producing estrogen and . . . progesterone. Maybe in early pregnancy these multiple miscarriages needed more of the hormone to fight the mystery toxin that was keeping the fertilized egg from implanting."

"It makes sense," offered Maria Suleiman.

"Then why don't we set up some trials?" Adam suggested. "To see if large doses of progesterone would protect the embryo till the placenta kicks in with its abundant supply. Any volunteers?"

All hands shot up. Everyone wanted to be on what looked more and more like a winning team.

It took several months to set up the protocol and find the subjects. By the middle of the second year Adam had tangible results. The progesterone worked.

DESPITE Adam's professional success, the most important thing in his life was his family. Toni, by contrast, seemed to derive most of her satisfaction from her career. Adam tried to convince himself that it was merely a phase from which they would both emerge, becoming closer and more loving than ever. He refused to see what was really happening.

They were simply running out of things to say to each other.

11 **ISABEL** Ironically, it was Raymond who had been unable to sleep the night before registration day. As Isabel slumbered in the adjacent bedroom, he paced the living room of their cramped apartment. What am I so worried about? he asked himself. And then he admitted to himself, It's inevitable. Tonight she's all mine. Tomorrow she'll belong to the world.

Dean Kendall was aware that a minor commotion was inevitable, and thus he permitted the reporters a quarter of an hour—"and not a second more, ladies and gentlemen"—to interview the prodigy.

Just a few minutes before noon Isabel stepped into Sproul Plaza, the forecourt to the university, as—uncharacteristically—Raymond hovered in the background.

"Can you tell us why you've chosen to major in physics, Isabel?" asked Natalie Rose of United Press International.

"I've always been drawn to figuring out how things work," the young girl responded amid the click of cameras. "That's how I broke my cuckoo clock when I was three."

Appreciative laughter.

The New York Times: "What about your music? Will you be playing with the university orchestra?"

Isabel shot a quick glance at her father and then answered, "Only if *they* give me advanced standing, too, and let me just play 'Spring' and 'Summer' of *The Four Seasons.*"

More laughter. She had captivated all of them.

Prizes

RAYMOND HAD OBTAINED AN indefinite leave of absence from his post in the San Diego physics lab. This left him without any visible means of support. He now chose to put his tutorial skills to work. With all the publicity, he had become a kind of celebrity. The printed index cards he posted on bulletin boards in the physics department brought more responses than he could accommodate.

Prudently, he had scheduled his tutorials for Saturday mornings or weekday evenings between seven and ten p.m., hours when he knew that Isabel would be in the next room, hard at work.

Sundays were the exclusive property of father and daughter. Weather permitting, they would go on an excursion, or a picnic across the bay in Golden Gate Park. It was at moments like these that Isabel, who was beginning to experience the physiological transformation to womanhood, could not suppress pangs of longing for the little things in life that she was missing. As her thirteenth birthday approached, she was struck not merely by the couples young and old walking hand in hand through the park, but even by the joggers breathing fresh air and chatting to each other as they passed down the treelined paths.

A young girl could naturally have discussed these subjects with her mother, but Isabel's thrice-weekly calls to Muriel were uneasy and awkward. Even had Raymond not been in the room, she would have felt somehow disloyal by confiding private thoughts to her mother.

Though it seemed that Isabel led a cloistered life, she was aware of the outside world through San Francisco's popular all-talk station. At night, as soon as she heard her father snoring, she would plug a pair of earphones into her clock radio and listen to callers discussing the latest controversies.

Understandably, Isabel was a frequent topic of campus gossip, most of it focusing on the fact that her father went with her to every class. In an early press interview he had explained that this was merely to be sure that Isabel understood the material.

Consciously, at least, Ray did not want to suppress his daughter's emotional development. And so he attempted the impossible, trying to provide her with a social life while still remaining in firm paternal control.

Once, as a treat, he took her for pizza at Nino's Brazilian, order-

46

ing a Coke for her and a pint of beer for himself. As Raymond and Isabel found a table, a group of shaggy types were grooving to jukebox music. If nothing else, their squeals of laughter indicated that they were high—and not on Miller Lite. Their apparent leader, motorcycle-jacketed and stubble-chinned, noticed father and daughter and pointed his finger. "Look! There's Humbert Humbert and Lolita."

Raymond's face reddened. He had, of course, read Vladimir Nabokov's famous novel about an older man with a sexual penchant for nymphets, and the intimation was a thousand-volt shock. He lost his temper completely, bellowing, "You shut your dirty mouth."

This merely intensified their mocking laughter.

To Isabel's alarm her father pulled himself to his feet. He lunged at the young man, swung, missed, then let out a strangled groan and fell to the floor.

The boy gasped in horror. "Somebody better call an ambulance. I think the old guy's cooled."

12 SANDY One day Rochelle Taubman vanished forever. Sandy Raven learned of this disappearance during a weekly phone conversation with his father. According to him, the studio did not believe that her original name had the ring of stardom. So Taubman became Tower, which not only rhymed with power but also suggested the height for which she was destined. And since there was no pizzazz to the name Rochelle, the object of Sandy's affections had been metamorphosed into Kim.

Sandy had also moved up in the world. In his senior year at Bronx Science, Sandy's project on the transmission of genes in fruit flies won him a Westinghouse Scholarship to M.I.T.

Those who believe that science is a religion regard the Massachusetts Institute of Technology as its Vatican. Situated in Cambridge, the university is a short jog away from Harvard. But while Harvard takes pride in selecting the whole man or woman—athletic, musical, artistic—M.I.T. cares only about the candidate's brain.

In this academy the fun aspects of college life were conspicuously absent. While in theory Tech students could go on dates, none of them would dare take time off from their slavery in the scientific salt mines. Their only brief glimpses of the outside world were through its electronic periscope—television.

It was here that Sandy was able to follow the progress of Rochelle's career. Though it had been a while since they had seen each other, he could still adore her on the tube. Thanks to the influence of the studio, she received regular invitations to guest star on series being shot under their aegis.

Sidney alerted his son to the fact that Rochelle would assay her most challenging role yet, as a deaf prostitute in a *Movie of the Week*. In the student union there was no wrangling among the guys about which channel they would watch: the title *Women of the Night* was too tantalizing to miss.

But while Sandy had come to venerate, his classmates had gathered to undress his beloved with their eyes.

"Man, wouldn't you like to be her bra?" grunted one of them.

"Shut up, you creep. She's a serious actress." Sandy's outburst shocked even him.

All eyes turned to the slight, pimple-faced figure, and someone said, "Who are you, Raven—her brother?"

"No. She's just sort of an old girlfriend of mine."

"Yeah, right," his antagonist countered. "Why on earth would a piece like that go out with a wonk like you?"

Sandy's eyes returned to the screen. It was displaying a commercial for Kraft cheese. "What's happened to Rochelle?" he exploded.

"You're a little slow on the draw, aren't you, Raven? The girl's name was Maisie and she's dead."

"Dead? But she just got on." Sandy was crestfallen. And could not keep from crying on Sidney's shoulder when they spoke on the telephone later that night.

"But Dad, you said she had a big part."

"Kiddo, you gotta understand how the business works," his father reasoned. "This wasn't some afternoon soap. It was prime time. You have no idea how many households she died in."

"Dad, where does she go from here?"

"Well, it's obvious, sonny boy—up."

"Do you really think so?" Sandy asked eagerly.

"Or down," his father added philosophically. "I mean, you never know in this business."

13 **ADAM** In the four years since he had been made director of the lab, Adam had become, metaphorically, the father of nearly two hundred children. By treating multiple-miscarrying women with large dosages of natural progesterone, he had enabled 174 of them to carry their pregnancies to term.

And yet, sadly, there were those whom even his vast knowledge and untiring effort could not help. Such a couple was Professor and Mrs. Dmitri Avilov, recent arrivals from the U.S.S.R.

Formerly a geneticist at the Soviet Academy of Sciences, Avilov was so much in the avant-garde of the field that several Western countries had urged him to emigrate. Finally, at a congress in London, the couple had sought sanctuary in the American embassy.

Avilov had already selected Harvard, not merely because of the generosity of their offer, which included a lab of his own, but also because of the med school's reputation for treating infertility. In more than five years of marriage he and his wife had not been able to achieve a pregnancy.

Now Adam sat across the desk from the tall, broad-shouldered Russian and his petite, full-breasted wife.

Anya Avilov was beautiful. She had large, deep-set brown eyes, short dark hair, and a cherubic heart-shaped face. Adam's patients did not normally radiate optimism. All of them were battered survivors of unsuccessful consultations with other specialists. But Anya's irrepressible cheerfulness seized his heart.

By contrast, her husband was dour and pompous. "What do you think are the prospects, Professor?" he demanded.

Uneasy, Adam shuffled some of the documents and began carefully. "From what I see here, Mrs. Avilov—"

"Actually," the husband interjected pedantically, "my wife is also *Doctor* Avilov."

"Really? What's your specialty?"

Somewhat embarrassed, Anya answered in broken English. "Is cruel joke of nature. But in Russia I was trained in *ginekolog*."

"Oh, I didn't know I had so charming a colleague. Do you practice here?"

She shook her head. "Not yet. Dmitri does not see patients, so he did not have to take boards. But I have to pass exams for foreign medical graduates, and my English is still very . . ."

Adam tried to steer the conversation back on course. "Dr. Avilov, as you know, amenorrhea can be caused by several factors, some of which are reversible. I suggest you see my colleague Dr. Rosenthal. Hopefully, the trials he'll run will help us pinpoint the problem."

Two weeks later the couple sat once again across from Adam. In the interim they had duly been tested by Dr. Rosenthal's lab.

Knowing that the very name of her condition would be like a dagger in Anya's heart, Adam began as gently as possible. "The hormone tests suggest that you're not ovulating. I'm afraid we're dealing with a case of premature ovarian failure."

"But she is so young," Dmitri protested.

Anya covered her face and began to weep. She then looked at her husband, her glance clearly begging for a sign of reassurance. But he remained silent.

It took the Russian several more seconds to realize that Adam was staring angrily at him. Nothing could possibly have been lost in translation: either you put your arms around her—or *I* will.

Anxious not to lose face with a colleague, Dmitri slowly turned and placed his hands on Anya's shoulders. After a moment the barrel-chested Russian rose, and his wife slowly followed him.

"I am sorry not to bring you good business," she said to Adam with a wan smile. "I shall have no babies for you to deliver."

Dmitri began to lead his wife toward the door.

"Wait," Adam protested. "You two should have some counseling. I'd like to—"

"With great respect, Professor," Dmitri cut him off. "I do not think such measures are indicated. We are scientists—all of us. We deal with facts, and we accept them as they are."

After they had left, Adam found himself whispering half aloud, "You arrogant bastard, you don't deserve a woman like that."

14 **ISABEL** Raymond da Costa was still on the floor of the restaurant when the paramedics arrived. The now remorseful hippie had placed his own leather jacket under the victim's head, while the restaurant owner had covered him with tablecloths to keep him warm.

Trembling with fright, Isabel watched as the paramedics lifted Raymond onto a stretcher and began to carry him out.

"Listen," the young man pleaded. "I was only joking, I swear."

"What difference does it make?" Isabel yelled at him, quickly following the paramedics out the door.

As the ambulance sped across the city, Isabel tried hard to hold back her sobs, but the sight of her father, disabled, and now disfigured by an oxygen mask, brought her to the verge of panic.

The ambulance shrieked to a halt in front of the battered doors of the emergency room of Alta Bates Hospital on Ashley. The ailing man was transferred onto a gurney and wheeled off.

Inside, the chief resident of the "pit" rapidly fired orders to his staff. It was only when they were about to speed Raymond to intensive care that the doctor noticed Isabel standing frozen and mute. "Who's she?" he asked gruffly.

"The guy's daughter," the paramedic explained.

"Send her to pediatrics and let her sit in the outpatient clinic," the resident commanded.

"No, no," Isabel protested. "I want to stay with my father."

Trying to restrain his own frayed emotions, the young doctor spoke as gently as possible. "Listen, kid, I've got my hands full, and I wanna be able to concentrate on your old man. So please let someone take you to pediatrics, and I'll phone them when it's okay for you to come down."

"I can find my own way," Isabel asserted.

Though she did not realize it, this was the first time in her life she had expressed this conviction.

For nearly three hours she sat motionless in a whirlwind of coughing, squealing, and crying youngsters. At last the chief resident appeared. He said, "Your dad's okay. He's had a mild heart attack, but there doesn't appear to be serious damage. The cardiologist will tell you everything you need to know."

THOUGH her father was heavily sedated, Isabel remained by Ray's bedside and tried to comfort him with words he could not hear.

Four hours later he half woke and called out, "Isabel?"

"I'm here, Dad," she whispered, taking his hand.

"Darling, I can't tell you how bad I feel about doing this to you."

"But Dad, you were trying to protect me."

"They say they want to keep me in for observation. Who's gonna

51

look after you? Maybe I can talk them into letting you sleep here."

"That won't be necessary, Raymond," a female voice interposed. Instantly, both turned their gaze toward the door.

Ray frowned but said nothing as Isabel leaped excitedly to her feet and rushed to embrace her mother. "Gosh, it's great to see you, Mom."

From Muriel's expression, the joy was clearly reciprocated. She then addressed her husband. "I've sent Peter to Aunt Edna and rearranged my schedule so I can stay here as long as necessary."

"*I* called her, Dad," Isabel asserted, and then, anticipating a hostile response, continued. "Whatever you two feel about each other, it was the right thing to do. I mean, for *me*."

MOTHER and daughter had so much to catch up on that they chatted endlessly.

"Are you enjoying your studies, sweetheart? I suppose you're too young to make friends with the undergraduates."

"Frankly, I'm really bugged by this age thing. I mean, everyone on campus can drive, and I've still got to wait three years."

"Don't worry, darling, nature has a way of making time catch up to you." At which point Muriel's gaze was inexorably drawn to her daughter's budding breasts.

"Yes, Mom," Isabel confessed with relief, "and I've started having periods too. I wanted to tell you on the phone, but Dad was in the room, and I was embarrassed."

Her mother's expression grew somber. "I wish I could rewrite history. Then I'd still be driving you to junior high school instead of visiting you at college. Anyway, your dad and I had an understanding that we would spend all the vacations together as a family. But somehow, the two of you always seem to find reasons why you—"

"It's not me, Mom."

"Well, don't you miss me?" her mother persevered, beginning to reveal her hurt. "Lord knows my heart aches for you."

"Me too. Maybe we could try speaking to Dad together."

Sick at heart, Muriel said sadly, "I don't really think that would help." She buried her face in her hands and began to sob quietly. "I'm sorry. It's just that I miss you so much."

They hugged each other tightly.

Finally, knowing she had to regain control, Muriel said cheerily, "I've got a surprise for you." She hurried into Raymond's room, which she had temporarily appropriated, and came back with—

"My fiddle!" Isabel cried with delight. "Thanks, Mom. I've really missed it."

"And I've brought you lots of music." Her mother smiled. "Actually, you'll discover, as I did, that being good at an instrument can improve your social life."

"Meaning?"

"Well, besides going to orchestra practice, I've been taking advanced classes with Edmundo. And when the Physics Quartet needed a second violin, they stretched a point and asked me to join. It's been wonderful—traveling, meeting new people." Muriel shifted gears. "Now, can I make us something to eat?"

"Great." Isabel's face brightened. "Dad's a terrible cook."

Thank heavens for that, Muriel thought.

THE next day Isabel took her mother to classes with her. As they were leaving the physics lecture hall, one of her classmates called out, "Hey, da Costa, your new bodyguard's a lot cuter than your old one."

After an alfresco lunch, followed by a cheerful shopping expedition, they returned to the apartment to find Raymond leafing through a copy of *Science*.

"My, I was beginning to wonder if something had happened to you," he remarked with a perceptible edge of disapproval.

There was an uneasy silence. "I'm glad you're feeling better, Ray," Muriel remarked.

"Yeah. I checked myself out. Actually, I'm fit as a fiddle."

Muriel suddenly had an awkward realization. "I guess I'd better call and see about flights this evening," she volunteered.

"Can't you stay, Mom?" Isabel asked. "We could all have dinner." A further thought tumbled out. "Like the good old days."

"By all means," Raymond added. "Isabel would really enjoy that."

"But then I'd have to stay over," Muriel explained as delicately as possible. "And you don't seem to have a guest room."

"There's always the couch," Raymond suggested.

Was he aware, she wondered, of how cruel he sounded? "No, I'm afraid I've never been a very good camper," she said with a smile. "It'll only take me a few seconds to pack."

WHILE rummaging through the medical reference library on his computer database, Raymond had come across an article asserting the theory that regular physical activity could raise a child's IQ between five and ten percent. Imagine how high that would put his Isabel! Thereafter he would set his alarm for five thirty a.m. and wake Isabel so the two of them could jog inconspicuously on the track at nearby Edwards Field. After all, his cardiologist had said that with a healthier lifestyle he could live to be a hundred. And he was damned if he'd let himself die without seeing his cherished daughter mount the podium in Stockholm.

Early one morning several weeks after their exercise routine had begun, Raymond emerged in his tracksuit to find Isabel seated at the dining table, still in the jeans and sweater she had been wearing the night before.

"Hey," he said with mock severity, "how come you're not ready for our pre-Olympic workout?"

She glanced with surprise at her watch and exclaimed, "Oh, my gosh, is it morning already?"

"You mean you haven't been to bed?"

"No. I got addicted to the fiendish problems in this book. They're like Cracker Jacks—once you start, you can't stop." She showed him the cover of J. D. Jackson's *Classical Electrodynamics*.

"But you're not taking electricity and magnetism this term."

"It's just for fun," she explained. "Karl told me that most of his Ph.D. candidates couldn't do half the questions, and I was so intrigued that I begged him to lend me his copy."

"Who's Karl?" her father asked suspiciously.

"Professor Pracht, my new adviser."

"Since when? What happened to Elliott Tanner?"

"Well, Elliott's going on his last sabbatical next year, and as he put it, he wanted to leave me with a good baby-sitter."

The department chairman's phraseology did not reassure Raymond. But he forced himself to smile and then prudently changed the subject. "Coming to work out?"

"I don't think I could go one lap." She yawned. "I'll have breakfast ready when you come back."

Raymond nodded and left for his workout.

Jogging seemed especially difficult for him today. Perhaps, he thought, because he was still in a state of shock. Electromagnetic theory was one of the fields he had flunked in his own Ph.D. qualifying exam. The moment Ray had been dreading had finally arrived. His daughter had transcended the limits of his own intellectual capacity. How could he now justify his role as her mentor?

IN MID-JUNE 1986 father and daughter drove back to San Diego for Peter's high school graduation. Ray urged his daughter not to reveal their plans for the summer. "We don't want your mother to talk you out of it," he said as lightly as he could.

Isabel was more concerned with how Peter would react to her, especially since she was so far ahead of him academically. Yet all anxiety dissipated as they drove up to the house and her brother ran out to embrace her, carrying a WELCOME HOME balloon.

The graduation exercises took place the next morning. Although there was hearty applause as he came up to the podium, Peter's brief moment of glory was dimmed when the spectators suddenly realized that if he was on the rostrum, his celebrity sister would surely be somewhere nearby. Dozens of eyes scanned the audience for the famous prodigy.

Peter did not seem resentful. That night, elegantly dressed, he set off in Muriel's car to pick up the girl he referred to as "my woman" and drive her to the graduation dance at the gym. When he returned in the early hours of the morning, he headed to the kitchen and was surprised to find his young sister still awake, leafing through a copy of *Cosmopolitan,* of all things.

"I never imagined you'd read stuff like that, Isabel," he joked.

"Come on, Peter. I'm not a complete freak," she answered amiably. "Don't you think I have any fun at Berkeley?"

He sat down and replied, "No. From what I see about you in the papers, you devote every minute to the pursuit of knowledge."

Isabel could not tell if he was mocking her or—as she hoped—offering her a chance to open up. "Look, Peter, I'm taking graduate seminars. I love the work, but there's a heck of a lot of it."

He asked point-blank, "Does Dad have a social life?"

The question stunned Isabel—and embarrassed her. "Of course not. He's married to Mom."

"Are you serious? It's more like a long-term cease-fire. Actually, I'm happy *she* doesn't sit home and mope."

"You mean Mom goes out with other men?" Isabel asked.

"Well, she goes to a lot of the musical evenings with Edmundo. Mom likes him, and they have a lot in common."

"Do you think Dad and Mom are going to, you know, break up?" she asked apprehensively.

"Well, they're hardly together now, are they?"

She was silent for a moment. Peter stood up and put his arm around her. "Listen, Isabel, I'm not saying any of this to freak you out. But what are brothers and sisters for? Besides, you're the only person in the world I can talk to about this."

Isabel looked at him with affection and whispered, "You know, I didn't realize how much I missed you until tonight."

"I'm glad," he responded with a quick hug. "I'm really looking forward to this summer, when we'll be together." He suddenly realized that Isabel had stopped smiling.

"So was I, Peter," she said plaintively. "But the department granted my request to get an early B.S. if I remain at Berkeley for the summer sessions."

"You mean *his* request, don't you?"

"Peter, we both agreed that it was the right thing to do."

Her brother's face reddened with anger and disappointment. "Sis, he's only using you, to compensate for—"

"I'd prefer not to discuss this anymore," she said firmly.

She had begun to march off when Peter called gently, "Isabel, let me say one more thing."

She stopped and turned to him. "What?"

"Someday you're gonna open your eyes and realize how unhappy you are. I just want you to know that whenever that happens—at any time of the day or night—I'll be at the other end of the phone."

Two days later, as her daughter was packing to leave, Muriel came in. "Listen, darling," she began softly. "Your father's told me of the new supersonic academic plans. I've given up trying to reason with him. He knows that even though I'm dead set against it, I'd never try to take you away from your studies."

Isabel looked at her mother's anguished expression and was at a loss for words. The best she could manage was a simple but sincere, "Thanks, Mom."

"On the other hand," Muriel continued, "your father and I have our own business to settle, and we've come to the conclusion that we might as well bring down the curtain on what isn't really a marriage anymore. We're going to file for divorce."

Isabel was rocked. For though she had observed the outward dissolution of her parents' marital bonds, she had nevertheless taken comfort from the illusion they maintained for her benefit. Yet now that it had brutally shattered, she felt compelled to confess, "Oh, Mom, I'm so sorry. I mean, I know it's all my fault."

"I somehow suspected you'd want to take the blame, darling. That's the crazy thing about divorce. Even the most aggrieved party feels guilty. But as strange as this may sound, one of the most important reasons I wanted to put an end to the unspoken tension is because—at least for the time being—you're the only thing keeping Ray alive."

15 **SANDY** During his first three undergraduate years at M.I.T., Sandy Raven's social pleasures were, to be precise, nonexistent. During summer vacations, encouraged by Sidney, he redressed this imbalance by dating young women on the West Coast. In Cambridge, however, it was painfully clear that being the son of a Hollywood producer was no big deal. He was neither tall nor dark nor handsome. But he resolved to change as much of that as he could. He bought a set of weights and embarked on a program that he supplemented with protein powder to speed muscle growth.

"I tell you, Raven," his friend Barry Winnick commented, "if this works for you, I'll try it too. I can see where you're getting stronger. But how exactly do you intend to achieve the triple goal you outlined to me? Especially the tall part. Why do you want to be so tall anyway? You're average height."

Sandy simply pointed to the many pictures of Rochelle pasted around the room.

"Man, are you *still* hung up on her? I'd have thought you'd gotten over her by now."

"I don't wanna get *over* her," Sandy replied. "I wanna *get* her. And I've read that she goes for hunk Hollywood types."

"Gosh, Raven," Barry muttered, "you're really off your tree."

Unfortunately, Sandy was not able to become hunk enough for Rochelle—at least this time. In the checkout line at the supermarket the following week he flicked through one of the tabloids and found the announcement of her forthcoming marriage to Lex Federicks, one of her classmates at the Fox Players' School.

The news broke the day Sandy received word that he had been accepted into the M.I.T. doctoral program in biochemistry. Otherwise he might have contemplated hurling himself into the Charles River.

During the weekly telephone call with his son, Sidney made a herculean effort to cheer the boy up. "Hey, kiddo," he commented. "I know how much you liked her. But believe me, marrying an actress is like jumping out of a plane without a parachute. It's exhilarating for the first few minutes, but pretty quick you're gonna hit the ground with an awful thud."

"I know how stupid it sounds," Sandy confessed openly for the first time. "And she's used me for a doormat since we were kids, but I love her. It's—how can I put it, Dad?—like some sort of disease."

SANDY may have been a step or two behind in the Hollywood social rat race, but he was a front-runner in his choice of specialty, for arguably the most important achievement in the late-twentieth-century study of the body was the discovery of the genes that composed it. As James Watson, the DNA pioneer, stated, "If you're young, there's really no option but to be a molecular biologist."

On the far but visible horizon was the possibility of discovering which chromosome carried which diseases—the different cancers, brain tumors, even Alzheimer's. If the specific gene were found, its defects could be studied and, with time, scientists could build the equivalent of a better mousetrap—a new, improved gene, which, like an unmanned spaceship, would automatically do its repair work inside the body. And in this real-life drama Sandy Raven was determined to become a hero.

THE M.I.T. GRADUATION DAY WAS doubly festive for Sidney Raven. Not only was his son receiving a bachelor of science degree with honors, but his latest release—the soon-to-be-legendary *Godzilla Meets David and Goliath*—was in its sixth week among the top twenty grossers around the world.

At Sandy's celebratory lunch it took only a few moments before the conversation got around to Rochelle. "She's going to be huge, Dad, isn't she?"

Sidney replied with evasion, "Mmmm . . . ," feigning a full mouth. But Sandy waited. "Listen, kiddo, let's not spoil the day."

"What do you mean? Is something wrong with Rochelle?"

"No—she's fine." He paused and then added, "It's just that her career's dead. The studio didn't pick up her contract."

"But why? I don't get it. She had so much going for her."

"Yeah, maybe. But she did lack one small thing—talent."

"Isn't there any way you can help her, Dad?"

"Listen, I've already gone out on a limb for her lots of times. You gotta realize Hollywood isn't a charitable institution. But if it'll make you happy, I'll see if I can get her some kind of job."

"Oh, thanks, Dad. Thanks," Sandy whispered affectionately.

A week later Sidney telephoned his son in Cambridge. "Okay, sonny boy," he announced. "I made all kinds of promises I shouldn't have, but your secret love won't be booted off the lot after all. Starting Monday, she's an assistant editor in the story department."

"You're really terrific, Dad. How did Rochelle take the news?"

"Well, she took the job like a shot. She's got a lot of spunk, that girl. As we were walking out of the interview, she swore to me that in a year she'd be *running* the whole department."

"Gosh," Sandy rhapsodized. "That's wonderful. Uh, did she, um, mention me at all?"

"Sure, sure," Sidney replied as convincingly as he could. "She sends her . . . love."

16 ADAM

Adam still hoped to reawaken Toni's maternal instincts. He persuaded her to move to a rambling three-story house in Wellesley Hills. Toni converted one of the smaller bedrooms upstairs into an office for herself, hooking up a computer not only to the firm but to her father as well.

Adam concentrated on making the garden a child's paradise. To the old oak in the back he attached a swing, and in a rare display of craftsmanship, he actually succeeded in building a climbing frame.

And to be sure that Heather's world was circumscribed with love, he would make a point of coming home for dinner every night, then reading a good-night story. When she was comfortably asleep, he would return to the lab.

His research was soon earning not only professional recognition but also the coveted prizes that would normally accrue to his gray-haired seniors. And all that glittered very often *was* gold. Even relatively minor prizes carried with them rewards in the twenty-five-thousand- to fifty-thousand-dollar category. And these honors created a momentum of their own.

One evening at dinner Lisl predicted that it would not be more than three years before he received the Lasker Award.

"Isn't that pretty much the stepping-stone to Stockholm?" Toni asked with uncharacteristic interest.

"Yes," Lisl answered. "The prize after the Lasker comes with a handshake from the King of Sweden."

"And a cool million dollars," Toni added.

"Not so fast, honey," Adam admonished her jocularly. "That's only if I don't have to share it."

"That's okay," Toni said. "It would still give us enough to buy the house we rented on the Cape this summer. But listen, I have to disappear upstairs to bone up for a deposition tomorrow morning. Would you excuse me, Lisl?"

"Of course, dear."

Adam looked apologetically at the guest Toni had abandoned.

Lisl patted his hand. "I'm afraid nothing in Boston can match what Toni had in Washington. She's probably feeling professionally nostalgic."

"I'd say resentful is more like it," Adam asserted.

"Does she still speak to her father so often?"

"Not really," Adam answered dryly. "I mean, rarely more than two or three times a day."

"Oh, that doesn't sound ideal. But in any case, she should never let her . . . attachment . . . affect her parenting."

Adam put his head in his hands. "How could I have known that she had an allergy to motherhood?" It hurt him to say it.

"Darling, you were madly in love. Would anything have dissuaded you?" Lisl said lovingly, trying to soothe his conscience.

He pondered for a moment and answered, "Frankly, yes." Then added, "Meanwhile, I'm trying to work fewer hours at the lab just so I can compensate for some of her parental shortcomings."

"That's good for Heather, but it's unfair to you," Lisl said. "After all, as I well know, research can't be a nine-to-five job."

"That's exactly what Toni tells me about her law practice."

IT WAS nearly nine o'clock in the evening. Adam had left the lab and was walking toward his car when he spied what he thought was a familiar figure. A young woman was standing by the curb, right hand covering her face, her body shaking. As he drew nearer, he recognized Anya Avilov, the unfortunate Russian to whom he had given such bad news several months earlier.

"Anya, is something the matter?" he asked.

She looked up, startled, her face wet with tears. "Oh, Dr. Coopersmith. Is nothing," she replied unconvincingly.

"Please tell me what's wrong. Come on. I'll buy you a coffee and we can chat." Before she could object, he took her by the arm and swept her to the coffee shop next to Children's Hospital.

His attempts at small talk were in vain. He could elicit only monosyllables to banal questions like how was she adjusting to life in Boston. "And how is Dmitri?" he asked.

"He has left me," she said abruptly. "He has found, so to say, a better deal. He has moved in with a woman."

I knew it, Adam thought. He had sensed that day in the office that Dmitri was on his way out of her life. "And you're all on your own? How do you pay the bills and that sort of thing?"

"He gives me money. Besides, I still work in his laboratory." She paused and then continued. "The woman is pregnant."

Adam was stunned. "Are you sure?"

"Yes. That was one of the first things he told me. I think he wanted to punish me. I am sure he would be more comfortable if I found another job"—she gestured hopelessly—"but I have not yet qualified."

"I have a lab," Adam replied impulsively. "I wouldn't ask you for a diploma."

"That is very kind," she answered. "You are such a good man, Dr. Coopersmith. So I will tell you what a nasty person I really am. I want desperately to hurt him for what he did. And I do. Now he comes in every morning and has to look me straight in the face. And begin the day with an upset stomach."

"Frankly, if I saw you first thing in the morning, it would make my day."

She blushed. "You flatter me, Doctor."

"Call me Adam. And I want you to take my offer seriously. I mean, promise me you will at least think about it."

She smiled. "I promise."

"Good. I'm flying to a conference in San Francisco for a couple of days, but I'll call you when I get back."

17 ISABEL Isabel napped as her father drove demonically through the night. They reached San Francisco as the first rays of the morning sun illuminated the Golden Gate Bridge.

"Ah," Ray remarked. "Home sweet home."

Isabel pretended to be asleep. But in her heart she still thought of the house they had left behind in San Diego as her home.

When they reached their apartment, Raymond had to push open the door, since the floor inside was piled high with mail.

"Anything for me?" she asked hopefully.

He was busy tearing open envelopes, grumbling to himself, "I can't believe this electric bill . . ." And then he noticed it. "This is your lucky day, Isabel. There's actually something for you." The letter was from the physics department.

She opened the envelope, stared at the card inside for a moment, and then smiled broadly. "Hey, this is really neat. Karl's invited me—I mean us—to a party."

"Who'll be there?" her father inquired suspiciously.

"Oh, just physics types," Isabel replied. "Karl sweeps them out of the lab one day a year to get some fresh air."

"That sounds very hospitable," Raymond averred, and thought that at least it would give him a chance to size up this Pracht fellow.

THE PROFESSOR'S HOME WAS ON Panoramic Way in the Berkeley Hills, straight above the university. It was definitely an up-market neighborhood. Ray looked around him with satisfaction. It was common knowledge that M.I.T. had been wooing Karl Pracht with a lucrative offer that Berkeley, a state university, could not possibly match. Judging from his house, the professor liked to live well; maybe he would, in fact, be lured to Boston.

Karl Pracht himself answered the door. He was lean and stoop-shouldered, with a receding hairline, and was undeniably attractive, especially when he smiled. Raymond disliked him instantly.

Pracht welcomed Isabel warmly and introduced himself to her father. "Glad you could come, Mr. da Costa. Come out into the back garden," he continued. "Isabel can introduce you to just about everybody. But I warn you, they're not all as bubbly as your daughter."

The young scientists were indeed, as Ray whispered to her, "all cut from the same cloth." Isabel smiled and quipped, "Yes—wet blankets." It was no wonder she shone like a Roman candle in their midst. They greeted Raymond with a respect he had not antici-pated. His confidence returned until a sudden thought struck him. He whispered to his daughter, "Isn't there a Mrs. Pracht?"

"There is, yes, but they're in the process of splitting."

"Oh." Even though Raymond himself was divorcing, he counted Pracht's dubious marital status as a point against him.

Two young boys, roughly sixteen and thirteen, were grilling vege-tarian hot dogs and burgers when father and daughter reached them with their empty plates. The elder chef, sinewy and bronzed, greeted Isabel jauntily. "Hey, you must be Ms. Einstein."

Ray frowned. "Come on, Isabel. We're holding up the line."

"On the contrary," the boy dissented. "*I'm* holding it up so I can get acquainted with God's gift to physics and—regardless of age and mental capacity—the cutest thing to happen in science since the apple that hit Newton on the head. May I introduce myself?" the boy continued.

"That isn't strictly necessary," Ray replied acerbically.

"Yeah," he agreed. "I'm just the backward boy with the fore-hand, sometimes known as the forward boy with the backhand."

"What?" Isabel exclaimed.

63

"Did that get you?" he asked, his eyes twinkling. "I rehearsed it on my kid brother all afternoon, didn't I, Dink?"

The younger chef nodded obediently.

"Is your brother's name really Dink?" Isabel asked.

"Not officially. He got saddled with George, but I gave him something more colorful. Which reminds me—I'm Jerry Pracht." Then, turning to his assistant, he commanded, "Dinko, take over the food while I show these VIPs to a table."

"There's no need for that," Ray began to protest. But the young man had scooped up their paper plates and led them across the lawn to a table. Then he elegantly placed the food down.

"Thank you," Ray said in dismissal.

"Mind if I join you?" Jerry sat down before either of them could answer.

Though fuming inwardly, Ray had to keep tight control of his temper. After all, this was the son of his daughter's adviser.

"I've seen your picture on Karl's desk," Isabel remarked.

"For use as a dartboard, no doubt," Jerry retorted. "I suppose he told you I'm not exactly a microchip off the old block."

"Actually, he told me you were rebelling at the moment," Isabel responded. "But that you're very brilliant."

"No, I used to be—cursed with an IQ around the Fahrenheit boiling point of water. But I gave it up when I quit school to take up tennis full time."

Isabel instantly knew she had met someone who would understand why she sometimes felt like a freak. And what's more, he'd been brave enough to escape from the monkey house of genius.

"But think of how much you could learn about the world," Raymond offered.

"I'm not exactly knocked out by the world. It's a polluted, overpopulated suburb of the universe. I'm more into space. In fact, the first question I ever asked was, Why do stars shine?"

"Really?" Isabel remarked, thinking of her own childhood curiosity. "Well, you had the right parents to ask."

"So did you," Jerry said, his instinct telling him that flattery in this area would get him very far indeed.

"Did your mother and father tutor you?" Ray inquired.

"Endlessly. I had to beg them to send me to school to get away

64

from the academic pressure." He grinned. "Of course, it was a school for 'special' children. That's where I met my pal Darius, who, like me, was crazy about the stars. We built a telescope, even ground a perfect twelve-inch F6.0 mirror. It's mounted on the other side of the garden. I'd be happy to show you."

"I would—" Isabel responded instantly.

"Some other time," Ray interdicted.

"Great," Jerry enthused. "I regard that as a firm commitment. Anyway, could I hear more about you, Isa?"

Raymond cringed at the mutilation of his daughter's name.

"I'm afraid I live a very dull life compared to you."

"I wouldn't say that," her father said, pouting.

"Well, it's true, Dad. You're too nice to rebel against—even for a game of tennis."

"What!" Jerry exclaimed histrionically. "You mean you don't play? Would you like some lessons, Isa? I'm not much at physics, but I'm one heck of a tennis teacher."

"Gee, that would be nice. I mean—" She glanced at her father.

"Isabel's got a punishing schedule, Jerry. I really don't know how she could manage it."

"No one appreciates that more than I, Mr. da Costa, but you'd be surprised how much I could accomplish on a Saturday morning." He turned to Isabel. "Why don't I come by this Saturday around ten? I'll bring an extra racket."

Before she could answer, Jerry glanced over his shoulder and quickly excused himself. "My poorly coordinated brother's causing havoc back at the grill. I'd better shoot over there and bail him out. See you Saturday morning, Isa," he called as he dashed off.

18   **ADAM**   It was the first evening at the medical convention in San Francisco. Adam had been enjoying a drink at the Top of the Mark with several West Coast colleagues. Now, as he fumbled with the key to his room, he could hear the telephone ringing persistently from within. It was Toni.

"Where the devil have you been? I've been trying to get you for the past three hours."

"Is something wrong?"

"Your daughter's in hot water at school," she replied. "It seems she and two friends were caught smoking in the girls' room. The headmistress claims that Heather provided the cigarettes."

Adam was angry. "Listen, honey, these meetings go on for another day. Can you hold the fort till then?"

"Yes. I just don't know if I can hold my temper."

Adam sat wearily on the bed. It couldn't be coincidence that Heather picked the one day he was out of town to cry out for attention. And then he saw the positive side to this event. It would be the ideal pretext to get some family counseling for all of them.

THOUGH Toni had vehemently objected when Adam first suggested consulting a therapist, he ultimately convinced her that they owed it to Heather.

After the initial interview the psychiatrist, Dr. Malcolm Schonberg, deemed a weekly meeting essential, "to reestablish the lines of communication among all the parties."

Ever the lawyer, Toni came to these sessions with a case already prepared in her own defense. "I can't help it, Doctor. I can't fight the Oedipus complex. I'm up against a perfect father."

"He's not perfect," Heather acknowledged. "But at least he tries. I mean, he actually listens to what I say. I hate it when you ask me things like what all my 'little friends' think about the Republicans' chances. I don't give a darn about politics. Maybe things'll be better if you take that Georgetown offer—"

"What Georgetown offer?" Adam interrupted, glaring at Toni.

Caught by surprise, she answered defensively, "It's just come up. Heather happened to walk into the room while they were sounding me out on the phone—"

"Hey, you guys," Heather exploded, "why don't you fight this out later? Right now you're supposed to be concentrating on *me.*"

As she began to sob, Adam embraced her and stared at Toni.

They drove home in glacial silence. Adam was furious that Toni had been making important plans behind his back.

When Heather had gone up to her room, Adam walked into the kitchen and confronted Toni. "What is this Georgetown business?"

"It's pretty flattering, really," she replied. "A visiting lecturer in con. law just finked out on them until the end of next term. I *was* going to talk it over with you tonight."

"What do you mean, 'talk it over'? You've obviously decided."

"As a matter of fact, I have. I could do the whole thing and be back the same night. I think I deserve a chance to spread my wings a little bit. And I could revive some Washington contacts."

"But what about Heather?" he asked, furious.

"I've got a lead on a fabulous nanny who's willing to come in on her day off," Toni replied.

"Nanny? I thought we agreed not to be parents by proxy."

"Okay," she said. "Then you can stay home every Wednesday."

"Come on. You know that's impossible," he protested. Then, smoldering, he backed down. "Maybe we should see if this nanny's any good."

TONI's weekly absence afforded Adam the opportunity to have regular phone conversations with Anya. He was able to monitor her mood—and lift it when necessary. He was sometimes tempted to propose a meeting. But then, he did not trust his feelings.

One Wednesday evening in mid-October when Mrs. Mallory, the nanny, was still tidying the kitchen, Toni phoned to say that she had missed the last flight back to Boston.

Adam frowned. "Don't tell me you gave a six-hour seminar."

"Not a chance," she replied good-humoredly. "But I dropped in on a cocktail party and sort of lost track of time. I'll stay at the Marriott and take the first plane tomorrow."

After he hung up, a thought suddenly struck him. Wasn't Toni's one-time patron, the former Attorney General, now a professor at Georgetown? At first he blamed himself for even entertaining such untrusting fantasies. Nonetheless, a half hour later he found himself dialing the Marriott Hotel at National Airport.

"Hello." Toni's voice sounded surprised.

Adam was relieved. "I'm just calling to say I miss you," he said in what he hoped was a convincing tone.

"Thanks, Adam," she replied. "I'm really glad you did."

After they bade each other good night, Adam could not help thinking that someone might have been with her. And in a curious way the notion suited him. For now he dialed Anya to propose a change in their plans.

"Hello," she said. "I'm so happy it's Wednesday night."

"Me too. I was just wondering—if I can get Mrs. Mallory to stay, I might be able to come over and pay a personal visit. Does that sound all right to you?"

"Do you even have to ask?" she replied.

AT LAST he found her house in Watertown. If the peeling paint on the wooden porch was any indication, it was indeed a dump, as Avilov had once described it.

Adam rang the bell to the upstairs flat. Anya buzzed him in, and he entered to find a cold and narrow stairway. To his astonishment, when she opened the door, she was wearing a parka. "Are you planning to go out at this hour?"

"On the contrary," she answered. "I am intending to stay in, and as you will soon see, it is much colder in here than outside. You had better keep your coat on as well."

The apartment was spare. The only source of real warmth seemed to be an electric heater—and Anya's personality. What furniture there was looked old and tired. As Adam flopped into an armchair, the springs twanged, making them both laugh.

"Well," she asked, "to what do I owe the honor of this visit?"

"I just wanted to look straight into your eyes. It's the only way I can tell if you're really happy."

"I am really happy." She beamed. And both of them understood that she meant it was because he was there.

"I know this is a stupid question," he said. "But how did a nice girl like you ever get mixed up with an oaf like Avilov?"

"Do you insist on all the gory details?"

"I'm fascinated by gory details," Adam replied.

"Then I had better open a bottle of wine—or two. It's a long story." As she filled the glasses, she recounted, "It all started in Siberia, where I was born. My father was a doctor who was guilty of being Jewish. He was assigned to one of the most famous labor camps in the whole of the gulag system, Second River.

"At school I wanted to go into pure science. And I wanted to go to the top of the mountain—Moscow. But in spite of getting the top grades, I was barely accepted by the local university at Vladivostok. They offered me a place not in pure science, but at the Institute of Medicine. Anyway, I accepted the place, and the moment I began

68

clinical work, everything changed. I loved the contact with other human beings, even if it was simply taking a pulse or blood pressure. When I got to deliver the babies, it made me think of obstetrics as a specialty. So once again I applied to Moscow. But this time I was accepted. And at the university clinic, no less.

"I was happy to be getting out of Second River. But I was also sad to be leaving my parents." Suddenly her voice grew soft. "My father was allowed to take me to the airport," she continued, her eyes filling with tears, "and I shall never forget his parting words. 'Annoushka, do everything you can never to come back here.'"

And now she was crying, racked with painful memories. Adam longed to take her in his arms and comfort her.

And finally he did. Her lips were so warm, her hands so loving. Anya had so much to give, and she held nothing back.

19 ISABEL

Jerry Pracht was the cause of Ray and Isabel's first serious argument. "I'm completely baffled by your interest in that unbalanced dropout," he told her.

"He's lively," she stated. "And independent. And besides, he's the first person I've ever met with an IQ higher than mine."

Ray was wide-eyed. "What makes you believe a thing like that?"

"Well," Isabel confessed, "I asked Karl straight out."

The doorbell rang, and Ray glanced at his watch. It was precisely ten a.m. The boy was nothing if not punctual. A moment later he was standing there in a blue tracksuit, dangling a pair of tennis shoes that had obviously known better days.

"I think these'll fit," he said cheerfully. "And what's more, they're golden. My brother wore them when I coached him to the Bay Area twelve-and-under singles title. Anyway, we'd better make it snappy. I only booked the court for an hour and a half."

"That long?" Raymond asked disapprovingly. "I want you to be sure to be back by noon. She's got a load of work to do."

"Oh, that's a shame," Jerry commented, and then addressed Isabel. "I thought we'd be able to have lunch at the club."

"Well, I'm sorry," Raymond overruled him.

The buzzer sounded again, heralding the arrival of Raymond's student. Sensing the moment propitious, Jerry signaled Isabel with a nod, and they both headed for the door.

Isabel was far from a genius at tennis. As she missed shot after shot, she grew increasingly embarrassed and could not seem to benefit from Jerry's tutelage.

"Don't let it worry you," he said. "In a few more weeks you'll probably make mincemeat out of me."

At five minutes to twelve he checked his watch and proposed, "Listen, champ, why don't we use our last precious moments to have some iced tea?"

Isabel smiled wearily. "I was hoping you'd ask."

As they sat down at a table on the terrace, she remarked, "I know you enjoy the shock effect of masquerading as an idiot, but just what exactly do you plan to do when you grow up?"

"That's the whole point, Isa," he insisted. "I *am* grown up. Sancho Rodriguez, my coach, thinks if I work hard, in another couple of months I should be ready for the pro tour."

"What about your astronomy?" Isabel asked.

"Hey, just because I'm not in school doesn't mean I don't devour every issue of *Sky & Telescope*. Or visit the Morrison Planetarium. Sometimes I sit up all night at my scope, watching the fireworks of the universe."

Suddenly they were interrupted.

"Isabel, do you know what time it is?"

Both youngsters were shocked by Ray's unexpected appearance. They had lost all track of time, and it was now well past her curfew.

"I'm terribly sorry, Mr. da Costa," Jerry said contritely, rising to his feet. "It's all my fault."

"Isabel's got a full schedule of homework," Ray declared sternly, "including a very important seminar paper."

Jerry was nothing if not resilient. "If you're thinking of her report for my dad, she delivered it last week."

"Oh," Raymond remarked icily, "does your father always discuss the details of his courses with you?"

"No," the young man conceded. "But he admired Isa's paper so much he mentioned the possibility of getting it published."

"Published?" Ray murmured half to himself. He turned to his daughter. "How come you didn't tell me?"

"This is the first I've heard of it. Isn't it exciting?"

"I'm sure there'll be many others," Jerry interposed. A glance at

70

Raymond stopped him from saying more. "Well, I don't want to stand in the way of scientific progress," he announced, beginning to retreat. And then, looking at Isabel, he added nervously, "Maybe you can stay for lunch next week, huh?"

"Thanks, Jerry," she said. "I had a really good time."

Raymond turned and led the way toward the parking lot.

JUNE 28: *Today I had what I guess was my first real date. I mean, it wasn't like Romeo and Juliet. But it was a few hours in the company of a boy who's a high school dropout—and light-years smarter than I.*

And we didn't even have a chaperon. At least not till the end.

Anyway, it's not likely to happen again in this century. Because I knew from Dad's cranky behavior that there was no point whatever in even asking whether I can play tennis with Jerry again.

JULY 7: *Jerry hasn't called yet.*

JULY 12: *Jerry still hasn't called.*

JULY 19: *Jerry's never going to call.*

JULY 26: *Dad let slip that Jerry had, in fact, called two days after our first date. But he made him promise not to ask me out till I finished my exams. I wish he had at least told me.*

20 SANDY

Sandy Raven was in the right scientific specialty. At the right time. At the right place.

Neighbors in the M.I.T. lab where he was toiling for his Ph.D. included both once and future winners of the Nobel Prize for Physiology or Medicine. They had been drawn, through various detours, from the four corners of the earth. There were also a few local prodigies.

Sandy was so dedicated that he did not mind associating himself with a figure generally respected as a "good loser" in the scientific community. Gregory Morgenstern's lifelong project had been a search for a genetic means of defeating cancer of the liver, a disease that is more extensive in Southeast Asia and tropical Africa than in the industrial world. These were not potential markets that aroused much enthusiasm among the large pharmaceutical companies. Morgenstern was therefore obliged to be a constant commuter from Boston to Washington, hat in hand, to seek federal funding.

Meanwhile, Sandy's horizons were broadening both intellectually and socially. Instead of remaining in the dormitory at M.I.T., he
accepted his lab partner Vic Newman's invitation to join him and
two others in sharing an apartment near Central Square. What
startled Sandy at first was Vic's casual description of their roommates as "a couple of girl grad students from Penn."

Girls? Females? The very idea of living in close proximity to a
nubile woman made Sandy weak at the knees.

"How do you manage it, Vic?" he asked. "I mean, suppose they
walk around in their underwear or something?"

Newman laughed. "I guess you're not a man of the world, Raven.
There's nothing like living twenty-four hours a day with girls to turn
off your hormones. I mean, after the first few minutes they seem
just like guys—except that Stella and Louise are incredibly bright."

"Okay, I'm game," Sandy responded, not without some inner
qualms.

Naturally, there were house rules. If, for whatever reason, the
door to any of their rooms was closed, this was to be respected in
every instance except a three-alarm fire. But since these were all
serious graduate students, they never had to bar their gates when
they were studying. Indeed, one of the nicest aspects of this think
tank—as Vic referred to it flatteringly—was that any of them could
seek another's advice on matters scientific.

21 **ADAM** As Christmas neared, the level of excitement
in the Coopersmith household intensified. Adam had
suggested they all go skiing at a terrific place in Canada, near Lake
Huron. Since it would be a long drive, he proposed that they invite
Charlie Rosenthal, his colleague from the fertility clinic, to join
them. Toni liked Charlie's wife, Joyce, and Heather was midway in
age between their two sons—which gave her two playmates.

Late in the afternoon of Christmas Eve, tired but exhilarated,
they reached the resort hotel at the tip of Georgian Bay. The
families separated, each to its own bungalow. At seven they all
donned boots and hiked off in high spirits to the main dining room.

The noise level was high and the alcohol level even higher. Sitting between the two Rosenthal boys, Heather was radiating hints
of grown-up beauty that tugged at Adam's heartstrings.

After the feast, as they were waiting for the baked Alaska, the concierge suddenly arrived and whispered to Adam that he had a phone call. Nodding, he excused himself and headed for the phone booths, wondering what could be the matter.

"This is Dr. Coopersmith."

"Doctor, this is Marvin Bergman. I'm the senior resident at Mass Mental. Sorry to bother you, but it's about Mrs. Avilov."

Adam suddenly went cold. "What about her?"

"She attempted suicide—ingested about thirty diazepam fives. Then she had second thoughts and called your service, which contacted us."

"Good Lord," Adam said. "Is she all right?"

"No problem," Bergman replied. "We got there in plenty of time." He paused and then continued. "Well, sir, obviously you're her ob-gyn. Do you know her psychiatrist?"

"She doesn't have one. Did she, uh, ask for me?"

"She did mention you by first name a couple of times," Bergman reported in a nonjudgmental tone. "But she's completely out of danger, so there's no real need to disturb your vacation."

"That's okay. I'll call Toronto and see if I can still get a plane. If by some chance she should wake, tell her I'm on my way."

Adam hurried to the front desk. There was one flight to Boston that evening he could catch. He asked them to book it and went back to the dining room. He bent over and whispered to Toni, "Could we talk outside for a moment?"

A worried look crossed her face as she followed him to the lobby.

"There's a problem. I've got to go back. Remember Mrs. Avilov?"

"The Russian?"

"Yes. She tried to commit suicide."

"That's awful." Toni's response was instinctive; then she abruptly realized there was something wrong with all this. "Isn't that a little out of your area? I mean, you're not a shrink."

"I know, I know. But I'm her only friend."

"Darling, you are on vacation. Why don't you let the psych department handle this?"

"Toni, I haven't got time to explain."

She scowled. "Adam, I've got all the sympathy in the world for this Avilov person. But practically every patient you see is a walking tragedy. What makes her so different? Is there something going on between you two?"

"For heaven's sake," Adam replied with exasperation, "I just want to be certain that she's properly taken care of."

They stared at each other, suddenly aware of how fragile their relationship had become.

"All right," Toni said with a sigh, stoically suppressing her own outrage. "How long will you be gone?"

"A day—two at the most."

"What about your daughter?" she demanded angrily. "This was supposed to be our big rapprochement."

"Can't we just say that I've had an emergency?"

"*We* aren't going to tell her anything. *You're* the one who has to face not only Heather but the other members of the jury. And Adam," she said tartly, "try to be a little more convincing with them than you've been with me."

22 ISABEL After ascertaining that Isabel was more than ready for the next day's world lit exam, Raymond suggested that they loosen up by going to the Holiday Bowl.

The cavernous bowladrome echoed with the clatter of tumbling pins and the shouts of spectators. As father and daughter sat on a bench lacing up their shoes, Ray looked off into the distance and a flash of anger crossed his face. "What is he doing here?"

"Who, Dad?"

"Your swain, Mr. Won't-take-no-for-an-answer Pracht."

Isabel's eyes widened. "Is Jerry here?" she asked excitedly.

Isabel had spent most of the lonely summer trying to come to terms with the fact that she would never see Jerry again. And yet now, unexpectedly, he was scarcely a hundred feet away.

He was standing in the approach area, holding the ball next to his cheek. His eyes were fixed intently on the headpin at the far end. Then he strode forward, firing the ball at the foul line. All the pins were scattered. It was a strike. His comrades cheered.

Isabel, who had been captivated by his agility and skill, involuntarily cried out, "Great going, number one nine four."

Jerry looked up, spotted Isabel, and called, "Hey, long time no see." He started toward her. "How come you know my number?"

"I bought *California Tennis* magazine. Sancho must be very pleased. You're over a hundred places higher."

Isabel could feel her father smoldering as he demanded, "What's all this nonsense?"

"Jerry's taken a leap in the tennis rankings," she explained.

"Hi, Mr. da Costa," Jerry said breezily. "I didn't know you guys were into bowling."

Just then a fresh-faced Japanese American girl in a red-and-white-striped blouse called out, "Lane twelve ready for da Costa."

Nudging his daughter slightly, Raymond tossed off a "Nice seeing you" to Jerry and began to move away.

"Me too. In fact, we've just wrapped up ourselves. Would you mind if I watched?"

"That would be great," Isabel interposed before her father could think of a politic refusal.

Suddenly they were interrupted by the appearance of an attractive blonde about Jerry's age. "Come on, Pracht," she called seductively. "Some of us have eleven-o'clock curfews, you know." Jerry nodded and then turned to the da Costas.

"Sorry, but I've got the only car. Maybe some other time?"

"Sure," Isabel responded, masking her disappointment.

Later on the way home Raymond commented, "Well, Isabel, I guess now you see why I don't want you hanging around with young people of that ilk."

"I don't know what you mean, Dad," she said, genuinely baffled.

"Since it's only twenty past nine, we can imagine what sort of mischief they'll get into before eleven o'clock."

Isabel understood only too well that Ray's remark was another attempt to discredit Jerry Pracht. Yet all she could think of was how much she would like to have been that other girl.

23 **ANYA** As she lay semiconscious in her hospital bed, Anya's thoughts took refuge in the past. It was lifetimes ago and a million miles away. . . .

To young Anya Litvinova, Moscow was the destination of a dream. By a stroke of good fortune—or in the opinion of some, bad luck—she had managed to secure a place in the overcrowded dormitory at the city's university clinic. She soon found out why the bed was available. It was the upper half of a bunk in a cubicle occupied by a bad-tempered future eye surgeon. Olga Petrovna Dashkevich had frightened off no fewer than six previous roommates in her first year of residency.

If Anya had learned nothing else, it was that good humor could erode even wills of steel. The gift of seeing the best in everyone was ingrained in her nature.

A month into the term Olga came down with a terrible flu and was forced to remain in bed. Not only did Anya bring her soup from the refectory but she even volunteered to take notes at a lecture Olga would be missing.

"I don't understand you," Olga commented bluntly. "I think you actually want to be my friend."

"I do."

"But why?"

"Frankly," Anya laughed, "I already have enough enemies."

ALTHOUGH the Soviet Revolution successfully abolished Christmas, on New Year's Eve the people awaited the arrival of Grandfather Frost, who came laden with presents for the children.

This year, for the first time, Olga was bringing a friend home for the holiday celebration. As their subway train passed through a succession of gleaming marble stations, she casually remarked, "I think you'll enjoy meeting my uncle Dmitri. He works in genetics. In fact, he's an academician."

Anya was amazed. "You mean you're related to a member of the Soviet Academy of Sciences and never mentioned it?"

"How else do you think I got into the surgery program?" Olga answered with a touch of self-mockery. "I'm not as clever as you."

In proudly disclosing the existence of her illustrious uncle, Olga neglected to mention that he was a bachelor. Anya respectfully shook his hand. "It's an honor to meet you, Professor Avilov."

"Please, please," the tall, wide-shouldered man insisted. "You must call me Dmitri Petrovich. Also, I don't think it's such an honor." He paused for a moment and then added with a grin, "But I do hope you'll consider it a pleasure."

They sat down to dinner—Olga, her younger sister, her parents, her maternal grandmother, Anya, and Dmitri. The meal was sumptuous, with no fewer than twelve cold appetizers. As they were eating the main dish, Olga's mother announced, "For this marvelous salmon we have Dmitri Petrovich to thank."

The grateful diners raised a toast to their benefactor: *"Na zdorovie."*

As if to the spotlight born, the professor held forth on the relative beauties of various cities of the world—with particular attention to Paris, where he had just delivered a paper. Had she been more cosmopolitan, Anya might have found him arrogant. But as a student from the provinces, she was totally captivated.

After they had welcomed the new year with champagne, Anya was helping Olga and her mother clear the table when she suddenly found her way blocked by the large frame of academician Avilov.

He gazed down at her and whispered, "And you, my little dove, why have you said nothing of yourself?"

Anya felt awkward and sputtered, "What could I possibly say that would interest a personage like you?"

"I am not a personage," he responded. "I'm just a person who finds you irresistible." He smiled broadly.

The next day Avilov invited Anya to hear him lecture at the academy on the genetic aspects of Huntington's disease. He was a brilliant speaker, able to make himself intelligible even to nonexperts in his field.

After the lecture Anya was fetching her coat when Avilov glided up to her and whispered, "We will meet in Seventh Heaven."

"What?" For a moment she was totally baffled.

"That's the restaurant on top of the television tower. I've booked a table for ten o'clock."

Seventh Heaven rotated slowly, giving the distinguished diners the opportunity to see the entire city between cocktails and dessert. Anya had never in her life seen anything like it. The guests were elegant, and there was a glint of real silver on the tables. She could not hide her uneasiness when Avilov ordered. "What is the matter, little one? Do you not like cutlets à la Kiev?"

"No," she stumbled. "It's just that—"

Avilov nodded. "I understand, Annoushka. It cannot have been frequently on the bill of fare at a place like Second River."

"You know about my family?" She felt more nervous than ever.

He nodded and replied gently, "What I can't understand is why your father never got recalled."

"I guess he didn't have any friends in the academy."

"He has now," Avilov replied, putting his large hand on hers. He looked into her eyes. "I'm the most selfish person I know," he conceded. "But perhaps I can make you like me."

"I already like you," she whispered.

"Enough to marry me?"

For a moment Anya could not believe what she had heard. Then she shook her head in dismay. "I just don't understand it. You could have any girl you wanted—"

"But Anya, you're not any girl. You're someone very special. You have a gift of happiness that's almost magical."

OCTOBER 21, 1982, was the happiest day of Anya's life. Now she was not only a diplomate in obstetrics, but at the matrimonial department of city hall she became the bride of academician Professor Dmitri Avilov. Her new husband had arranged a sumptuous reception at what would be their apartment on a high floor of one of the giant blocks bordering the Moskva River.

Anya felt like a princess in a fairy tale. For among the many well-wishers were the two dearest people in her life.

Her mother and father.

But that was lifetimes ago and a million miles away.

24 **ISABEL** Isabel da Costa achieved her goal—or more accurately, Raymond's—and in the late summer of 1986, at the age of fourteen, became the youngest graduate in the history of Berkeley. Summa cum laude in physics, Phi Beta Kappa.

Once again the press was out in force, and once again Muriel and Peter reenacted their familiar roles of loving mother and admiring brother. Though the TV cameras concentrated on close-ups of Isabel, when she graciously thanked her family for their support, they intercut to close-ups of Ray, the man she singled out as "still the best teacher I ever had."

During her brief visit home in June for Peter's graduation, she and her brother had forged a relationship that continued to strengthen.

Now, over dinner, they talked about their futures. Peter, himself entering college that fall, told her that he was thinking of majoring in physical education. "What's next for you, sis?" he asked.

"Do you have any suggestions?" she asked playfully.

"Actually, I do," he replied. "My advice would be to take a trip around the world. A couple of buddies and I are using the money we earned washing cars to go backpacking in France. I'd invite you to come along, but I already know what Dad would say."

"Gosh, I'd love to go, but it's urgent that I start on my master's thesis with Pracht right away."

"Isn't that a little bit premature, even for you?" Peter asked. "I mean, you haven't even done the coursework—or did you finish it all last night while I was sleeping?"

"I know it sounds strange," she said. "This is strictly between us—do you know anything about the theory of forces?"

"Only what I remember from *Star Wars*," he joked.

"Okay," she began. "Conventional physics recognizes four different forces in nature. Most everybody is familiar with gravity and electrodynamics—they operate over large distances. But then there is a strong force, which works over a short distance and holds atomic nuclei together, and a weak force—which is associated with the decay of neutrons outside the nucleus. Are you with me so far?"

"Let's just say I believe you—but go on."

"Well, ever since Newton, physicists have made about a zillion attempts to develop things called GUTs, or grand unification theories—some way of encompassing all four forces. Einstein tried, but even he couldn't find an answer. Lately, Karl's been collaborating with a team in Cambridge and one in Germany. They're all gathering data to prove the existence of a *fifth* force. That might be the key to the whole picture. If they're right, it's a megabreakthrough, and since nobody is closer to the material than Karl, I want to start this while he's still in our backyard."

Peter nodded and said with affection, "Isabel, for once I agree with you. Go for it. And may the fifth force be with you."

MURIEL'S final conversation with Ray was strangely poignant. They sat at the round, dark wood table of a college pub, its surface etched with initials of lovers and vandals.

79

"So this is it?" he sighed. "I'm sorry it had to happen this way."

"So am I," she answered quietly.

"I mean, we've lived this sham so long, I can't understand why it couldn't have gone on until the kids were a bit older."

"They're both strong enough to find their way in this world. On the other hand, at my age a second chance for happiness doesn't come along that often." She looked at him and murmured almost apologetically, "I want to get married again."

He hesitated for a moment. "Anyone I know?" he asked.

"I thought it was obvious," she responded. "Edmundo and I have grown very close."

"Isn't there already a Mrs. Zimmer?"

"Up till a few months ago," Muriel replied. "Then *she* found love with—of all people—the church organist. And actually badgered Edmundo for a divorce."

"Well," Raymond remarked, trying to mask his feelings of jealousy, "I guess you've been in love with him for years."

Muriel lowered her head. "I suppose so," she conceded. "But never the way I loved you."

Two weeks later Isabel, in a frilly pink dress, stood with Peter as a magistrate formally decreed that henceforth their mother would be Mrs. Edmundo Zimmer.

Another pair of siblings stood on the groom's side, a sister in her early thirties and a brother older still. Both Dorotea and Francisco had flown up from Argentina to honor their father, as well as to serve as legal witnesses. After the brief ceremony all six of them repaired to a private room at the faculty club for drinks and a small but elegant nuptial meal.

Both Muriel and Edmundo were in buoyant spirits, but they seemed especially touched that Isabel had come. She was so completely won over by the conductor's charm that she resolved to duke it out with Raymond if he tried to object to her visiting again at Christmas.

Her plane landed at Oakland just after nine p.m. And as she walked toward her father's outstretched arms, Isabel felt an inexplicable sadness.

He was everything to her. Or almost everthing.

But there was no music in Raymond da Costa's life.

25 **ADAM** Twenty minutes before midnight on Christmas Eve, Adam pushed open the door of room 608 at the Massachusetts Mental Health Hospital. A nurse was gently trying to lull Anya into slumber. Yet even though he was silent, Anya sensed his presence and turned her head slowly to face him. "You should not have come," she murmured.

"I had to," he countered. Uneasily he said to the nurse, "It's all right. I'm one of her physicians."

"Very well, Doctor." The woman made a discreet exit.

Adam sat beside Anya's bed. "Why did you do such a thing? I thought we were so happy together."

"That was why, Adam. It was Christmas—I was all alone. I missed you so terribly, and I realized we could never be together."

"Why not?" he inquired softly.

"You are married," she responded slowly. And then added even more emphatically, "You have a child. In fact, your entire life would have been happier if we had never met."

"No," he objected. "You're the most wonderful thing that has ever happened to me, Anya. All I want is to be with you." He wanted to sweep her into his arms, but she was tired, and ill. With soothing words he tried to loosen her grip on wakefulness. Remarkably, she resisted.

"Listen," he said, clasping Anya's hand tightly, "I've really got to go now. I promise I'll call every morning if you promise to start believing that I'm going to work things out."

"I will try." She smiled.

"That's my girl," he said encouragingly, and kissed her on the forehead. "And Anya, the next time you need to see me, try the telephone—it's less expensive."

Toni zoomed down the ski slope as if aiming straight at Adam, standing at the bottom. She braked to a halt in a flurry of snow scarcely ten feet away. For an instant neither spoke.

Finally Adam managed, "Well, the crisis is over."

She looked at him with eyebrows raised. "Is it?"

"Toni, for heaven's sake, I was making what I thought was a humanitarian gesture."

"All night? I called home every half hour. So unless you booked

81

into the Hilton, I can only conclude you were holding her hand."

"Come on," he said, raising his voice in exasperation. "Are you crazy enough to imply what I think you're implying?"

She stopped and faced him, and her words came out in tiny puffs of air. "Adam, you don't have to physically sleep with another woman to qualify as being unfaithful."

Adam's heart began to beat faster.

She pointed a ski pole at him and pronounced, "Let's just say you're on probation."

In the following days they kept up appearances for the sake of Heather and the Rosenthals. But the tension was palpable.

On the morning of their departure they clambered aboard Charlie's station wagon, the Rosenthals radiating health and good spirits, the Coopersmiths knowing that somehow their lives would never be the same.

26 **SANDY** The social high point of the year for those who worked in Gregory Morgenstern's lab was the chief's Fourth of July barbecue, where the scientists would disregard their own warnings against the cholesterol content of marbled steaks cooked over a carcinogenic charcoal fire.

On this occasion, after the evening fireworks, Sandy found himself drawn to a circle of young people seated under an oak tree, listening to a pretty freckle-faced guitarist with a reddish brown ponytail. She was wearing denim cutoffs and a Beethoven T-shirt.

Gosh, Sandy thought. If Rochelle was a goddess, this creature certainly qualifies as a nymph. Too bad I don't have the guts to talk to her.

At that point the singer coughed histrionically and uttered, "Will somebody please have pity and get this poor girl a beer?"

The normally reticent Sandy heard a cue and pounced on it. "I'll get it," he called out. He jogged over to the refreshment area, withdrew a bottle of Miller Lite from a metal garbage can serving as an ice bucket, and hurried back to the parched performer.

"Thanks," she murmured, taking a sip. "Where's yours?"

"Oh, I forgot," he confessed with embarrassment.

"Why don't you finish mine and get us both another."

After his third trip he had swallowed enough courage to sit next to her and introduce himself. He even emulated his father's style. "Hi, there. Raven's the name."

"Well, Raven," she responded gaily, "do you have any requests?"

"To begin with, it would be nice to know *your* name."

"I'm Judy Morgenstern," she replied. "Greg's my dad—and even though I'm not into science, I'm still his best pal."

"I don't blame him," Sandy remarked. "As Bogart said to Claude Rains, 'I think this is the beginning of a beautiful friendship.' "

"Oh," she said, brightening, "are you a *Casablanca* freak too?"

"I'm a movie loony. My dad's in the business. He's a producer."

"I guess lots of girls play up to you to get an introduction to your father."

"I wouldn't mind if *you* did," he responded.

"Not a chance." Judy strummed an angry chord. "The only thing I want to be less than a scientist is a movie star."

Sandy was thrilled. All time dissolved after that. They chatted endlessly about movies until it became clear that guests were finally starting to leave. Sandy made his way toward Professor and Mrs. Morgenstern to bid them good night.

Judy took his hand and whispered, "By the way, who's driving you home?"

"I am—that is, if I can find my car."

"Not in that state, you're not," Greg Morgenstern reprimanded as they approached him.

"Yeah, I suppose you're right, Prof," Sandy slurred.

"I'll drive him, Dad," Judy volunteered. "I switched to coffee about two hours ago."

When they reached the house in Central Square, she turned to Sandy. "You're really cute. Stop being shy and tell me if we're going to see each other again."

"Hey, lady, this is only the first reel," Sandy answered. "We'll kiss gently and look forward to the ultimate clinch."

And that was precisely what they did.

"Good to hear from you, sonny boy," Sidney Raven chimed from Hollywood. "How's life in the lab?"

"Fine, Dad. I've just watched the CBS *Movie of the Week*. Did you know that Rochelle was one of the guest stars?"

"Of course—I read *Variety* every day. That was the last picture she made before her contract ended. But I wouldn't worry about that young lady. Not only is she taking over the story department, just as she predicted, but she's also dating Elliot Victor, the head of Paragon. It looks like her next career move will be a quickie Mexican divorce from Lex—and another trip to the altar. Now tell me about you. Have you got a girlfriend yet?"

Sandy blushed inwardly. "I think I'm in love."

"Great," his father cheered. "Now maybe you'll get your mind off Ms. Tower and have a normal relationship. Tell me about her."

"Dad," his son replied, "she's so nice. I can't understand why she would settle for a guy like me."

"Hey," his father chastened, "where's your confidence? Is it someone you're serious about?"

"Could be. It's fairly possible."

"Then marry her before she gets away," Sidney counseled. "Reach for the brass ring. Otherwise," he finished wistfully, "you'll end up like me."

27   **ADAM**   From the second of January, Adam had visited Anya every day during his lunch break. Soon, however, the doctors were anxious to discharge her. Though Adam agreed that she was strong enough to cope with the outside world, he had misgivings about letting her go back alone to the dingy apartment in Watertown. But the psychiatrists had overruled him.

By now the compulsion to see Anya was so great that Adam sped to her place just to be with her for a few minutes, his behavior bordering on recklessness.

In the time since he had last seen her, Anya looked as if she had begun to grasp the tiller of her life. Wearing jeans and a maroon turtleneck, she was busily cleaning the apartment when he arrived. To his amazement there were even half a dozen books on a shelf that had been totally empty.

"Where did you get these?" Adam asked.

"I was up at dawn," she answered with a smile. "I walked to Harvard Square. Is a wonderful place—nothing ever closes, and the bookstores were full of people."

"Good for you," Adam said with admiration.

"On the way home I bought croissants . . . in case you came. Would you like one now with a cup of coffee?"

"Yeah, that'd be nice."

He sat down in the armchair and she on the far side of the sofa after placing the food on the low table. Adam could not help noticing the color in her cheeks. "Have you thought of going back to work—when you're ready, I mean?"

"Oh, I'm a little tired, but I feel I'm psychologically ready now."

"Well, I'd like you to come and work in our lab."

"But I know nothing about immunology," she protested.

"You're a medical doctor. You already know the basics. It'd take guts, but we both know you've got plenty of that."

Her eyes were now sparkling. She broke into a smile. "It sounds lovely."

"Good. When do you think you'll feel strong enough to begin?"

"I know you would want me to say tomorrow. But if you could possibly give me a week—and some proper textbooks . . ."

"Done," Adam agreed, and then fought the urge to put his arms around her. "I'm afraid it's getting late," he murmured lamely. "I mean, I have a family."

"Yes," she agreed. "It is good that we both remember that."

28 ISABEL
Isabel was making such splendid progress on her master's thesis that Raymond paroled her for a brief Christmas return to San Diego.

She had brought her violin, and on Christmas Eve the Zimmers had a real *soirée musicale*. Francisco Zimmer was a fairly accomplished pianist. And Dorotea bravely took up the cello, having for a time played in the Buenos Aires Symphony.

Despite his handicap, Edmundo could, as he put it, "at least make a tolerable noise" on all of the stringed instruments. Now that Isabel had joined them, the happy family gathered around the piano as a quintet—with one spectator.

As Peter joked, "Mom taught me that *somebody* has to be in the audience. I've developed my claps to a virtuoso standard."

Indeed, the evening was so joyful that it made Isabel feel pangs of sadness that Raymond had been left to celebrate Christmas on his own.

WHEN THE PRACHTS DECIDED TO throw a big New Year's open house, the corridors buzzed with rumors that M.I.T. had finally signed him up. Ray had misgivings about their attending the celebration. It would be difficult, if not impossible, to keep young Jerry from at least a minimal social contact with his daughter. Indeed, the moment Jerry caught sight of her, he moved through the crowd like a broken-field runner as the elder Pracht locked Raymond in conversation. "Hey, Isa, you can't imagine how desperate I am to see you. D'you know what number I am now?"

"As a matter of fact, I do." She smiled. "You're in the top fifty."

"And if I make the quarterfinals tomorrow, I'll jump thirty places. Say, do you think your dad would go ballistic if we took a walk in the garden? The view is absolutely breathtaking."

Isabel glanced over her shoulder and saw Raymond deep in conversation with Karl Pracht. She surprised even herself by answering, "Why don't we go before he can stop us?"

Suddenly Jerry's fingers were enlaced with hers, which caused a little tingle at the back of her neck. She walked quickly with him to the edge of the garden, and they stood there, gazing down over San Francisco.

"Isn't it terrific!" Jerry exclaimed. "I think my dad is crazy to give all this up for M.I.T., don't you?"

"You mean it's definite?" Isabel asked, unable to conceal her feeling of disappointment.

Ignoring her question, Jerry turned to face her and murmured, "Isa, I can't wait any longer. I'm going to kiss you."

She remained silent and motionless.

Thus, at twenty-five minutes before midnight on the last day of the year, Isabel da Costa let Jerry Pracht take her into his arms and press his lips to hers.

She so enjoyed it that she lost all sense of time. For all she knew, it might have been several minutes. And a little tingle became a full-fledged shiver down her spine.

"What's wrong?" Jerry asked, letting go of her.

Isabel wanted to say nothing was wrong. But she was suddenly afraid. She was not sure whether it was fear of being discovered by her father or her own growing ambivalence about her cloistered life. She broke away and hurried toward the house.

He addressed her from a few paces behind. "May I call you?"

"No," she said without turning.

"Will you call me?" he persisted.

For a moment she did not reply, and then, for an instant, she stopped, looked over her shoulder, and answered, "Yes."

29 **SANDY** Though he had not revealed it, Sandy had been deeply affected by his father's inability to establish a suitable new relationship. A professional success, Sidney had been a personal failure. He would love to have a woman of his own, but unfortunately it was never the same one. And Sandy was convinced that he'd confused his priorities.

True, Greg Morgenstern was not a giant in his profession, at least not yet. But he had a devoted family who worshipped him. Wasn't this the most important aspect of life?

Thus Sandy fell in love not merely with the Morgensterns' daughter but with their values. It was a heady new experience for him to join a happy, cohesive family for occasions like Thanksgiving, Christmas, and New Year's Eve. All of them—Greg, his wife Ruth, as well as Judy—opened their home and their hearts to him.

It took Sandy much longer to realize that Judy's feelings were greatly influenced by her father's admiration for him. It was never mentioned specifically, but it was clear that the greatest gift she could give her father was Sandy Raven as a son-in-law.

Independence Day became a double celebration on their calendar: not only the declaration of American autonomy but the anniversary of the first meeting of Sandy and Judy, who by this time were living together in Cambridge.

IF GREGORY Morgenstern possessed a flaw, it seemed to be an almost fanatic sense of honesty. When a biotech company lured away his second-in-command, he insisted upon going through an elaborate selection process before he finally chose Sandy. Furthermore, Greg was so maddeningly egalitarian that every paper coming out of their lab listed its authors alphabetically. It was almost as if Morgenstern had an aversion to eminence. Sandy theorized that this was what drew Greg to the urgent yet scientifically unpopular scourge of liver cancer: he would be left alone.

There were many theoretical cures for hepatic cancer, the most obvious being transplants. But this was obviously impossible on a large scale. Now Greg was leading a biological quest into uncharted territory. Since cancers occur when the usual checks and balances of cell growth cease to function, Greg hoped to produce an artificial protein that would restore the damaged gene to normal functioning.

"Is it a state secret, or are you guys near anything resembling pay dirt?" Judy asked Sandy over dinner.

"It's funny. I'm so close to the stuff, I find that impossible to answer. But if it's any indication, a film crew from *Nova* is visiting the lab tomorrow. Maybe they're getting some vibes."

"I'm really happy Dad's finally getting some recognition for all his unsung labor."

"Yeah," Sandy agreed. "And if this thing pays off, I'm afraid Greg will be inflicted with honors, probably even a Nobel. Do you think he'd like that?"

She looked at him with a gleam in her eye. "Not as much as the other project you've helped develop."

"What are you talking about?"

"I'm talking about being pregnant." She smiled. "By the way, does that make you happy?"

"Yes and no," Sandy answered, his cheeks flushed. "I mean, I love babies—but I don't believe in unwed mothers. Are you willing to do something about it?"

"Oh," she replied blithely, "I'll bow to convention and go legal. What about high noon tomorrow at city hall?"

30 **ADAM** In the past Adam had always succeeded in discharging his duties as a parent by tearing himself away from the lab to be at home for dinner. There he showed a genuine interest in his daughter's homework and waited until she was planted at her computer before returning to work.

Knowing Toni would herself be buried in her upstairs office at least until the eleven-o'clock news, it had long been Adam's practice to call about ten thirty to give her some indication of whether he was running out of strength or had been sufficiently inspired to spend an all-nighter. Lately his inspiration seemed to be in high gear. Not only did Adam stay out till dawn, he was sometimes too carried away to phone and forewarn his wife.

Charlie Rosenthal, the innocent if concerned bystander, thought Adam was "living like an ostrich." He advised his friend, "Do you honestly believe Toni doesn't suspect? Besides, Adam, adultery just isn't your scene. *Let Avilov go.* And let her go somewhere where she really has a shot at starting over."

"Dammit, you're implying that I'm being selfish."

"You are," Charlie stated curtly. "And you're on the slippery slope to disaster."

ADAM had been jolted by Charlie Rosenthal's blunt admonitions. During the weeks that followed, though he resumed their Wednesday night telephone conversations, he did not visit Anya. And yet he sensed his resistance was eroding.

Anya herself, consumed with guilt, accepted that though her moments with Adam had been the happiest of her life, they were now definitely at an end.

It had been nearly two months since Anya had begun working in Adam's immunology lab. She had started with menial tasks, but she was a quick study and assimilated scientific material at an astonishing pace. In less than a month she was promoted to the data section, collating the results of various experiments on computer.

It was nearly seven on a winter Wednesday evening when Adam noticed her closing up for the day. "How are you getting home, Anya?" he asked as casually as he could.

"The usual way. Number sixty-six to Harvard Square, and then the seventy-one, which takes me practically to my doorstep."

"It's dark and cold and the streets are icy," Adam remarked. "Why don't you let me give you a lift?"

She pondered for a moment, then smiled. "I'd be very grateful."

He was silent during the first part of the ride, stealing glances at his passenger. She seemed more desirable than ever. He knew he could not simply drop her off. As they were nearing Watertown Square, he inquired, "Have you got time for a quick bite?"

She hesitated and then asked deliberately, "Have you?"

"Uh, yes. My wife's in Washington today."

"That means your daughter must eat—"

"I can just give the housekeeper a call. She's used to my coming home at all hours." He tried not to think of Heather, for whom Wednesday dinner was special, since she had him to herself.

Anya smiled. "In that case, why don't we go by the market and I will buy a few things and make something simple."

THE apartment seemed to have undergone a metamorphosis, with new living-room wallpaper and a large, cheery Miró poster.

At first, conversation was awkward.

"How's your work going?" Adam asked.

"I love it." She smiled. "Your main project is very exciting. And you, Adam, are the most brilliant person I've ever met."

He smiled. "Well, while we're dishing out compliments, I can tell you have wonderful scientific intuition."

She blushed. "You flatter me."

"And another thing," he continued, moving closer to her, locking her eyes with his own gaze. "I love you, Anya."

"And I love you," she responded. "But what can we do about it?"

"We can give in to our feelings. We've been apart too long. I can't bear it anymore."

She did not try to move away as he took her in his arms.

ADAM had now crossed the Rubicon. Late one Sunday afternoon he reluctantly left Anya's embrace and, as he dressed himself, murmured, "I can't go on like this."

"Adam, I understand. If you told me this was the last time we would see each other, I would grieve. But I would accept it."

He turned and said passionately, "No, Anya, it's just the opposite. My life has boiled down to a single desire—to spend the rest of it with you."

But as he walked slowly down the porch steps, he realized that he was a coward. Counterbalancing the resolve he had so bravely displayed to Anya was the fear of hurting his family.

As he was putting his key in the lock of his car door, Adam heard the persistent ringing of the car telephone. He clambered in and grabbed it. "This is Dr. Coopersmith."

It was Toni, in a fury. "Where are you? Heather waited in the cold for nearly an hour."

"Heather?"

"Yes, Adam. You were supposed to meet her outside the skating rink at four. My watch says nearly six o'clock. You claimed you were going to the lab," Toni went on. "I called, but nobody had even seen you. So I got into the car and picked her up myself. Tell me the truth. What have you been doing?"

"Toni," he mumbled hoarsely, "we've got to talk."

"Okay, talk."

"No. Not like this. Face to face."

"Adam, I know there's someone else in your life," she stormed. "And since she seems to have such a hold on you that you'd let your own daughter freeze to death, you'd better stay away."

Her sudden silence puzzled him, until he could discern her weeping softly. At last she managed to say, "Just tell me where to send it."

"Send wh-what?" he asked with a slight stammer.

"The subpoena," she raged. "I'm calling the best divorce lawyer in our firm to have him nail you to the wall."

"Don't I even get a chance to speak in my own defense?"

"Of course, Adam. As soon as the court fixes a date."

31 ISABEL JANUARY 1: *Jerry kissed me. I confess it's something I had often dreamed about but never thought would really happen. For a second I was so scared, I was kind of dumb. And yet after another moment I realized that if your feelings about the person are strong, the rest comes naturally. I suddenly ceased worrying about my father and kissed Jerry back. It was the loveliest moment of my life. I only wonder when I'll ever get a chance to repeat it.*

IT DID not take Isabel long to ferret out the most secluded public phone in Le Conte Hall, her seminar building. As soon as Ray dropped her off, she would call Jerry, and they would chat until it was time for him to leave for the club.

Isabel's afternoon sessions in her carrel, exploring the theoretical possibilities for her master's dissertation, began to stretch out later and later into the evening. By mid-February she was putting in so many hours in the library after dinner that she looked haggard.

Uncharacteristically, even Raymond began to plead with her to ease up, but her only reply was, "I can't yet, Dad. I'm into something really important."

One evening just after nine the phone rang.

"Dad, come to the back of Le Conte Hall and pick me up right away. I can't talk on the phone. Please hurry."

Her tone was urgent. There was even a touch of fear in her voice.

Terrified, Ray rushed for the car. During the short drive to the campus he tried to imagine what might be wrong. He could only conclude that his daughter was truly ill. All the way to the physics building he berated himself for not heeding the signs of her fatigue.

The moment she saw the car, she rushed out laden with a pile of lab notebooks. Far from being pale, her face was flushed. "Quick, Dad. Open the trunk and put this stuff inside."

He obeyed wordlessly as Isabel climbed into the car.

"Let's get out of here," she urged like an escaping prisoner.

"Relax, honey," Ray said gently. "We'll be home in a minute—"

"No. Let's go someplace where we can speak really privately."

"Well, for heaven's sake, we're not being bugged or anything," he countered. And then, looking at her frightened expression, he relented. "Okay, I'll think of something."

Ray finally decided on Oscar's Den in Oakland, which was usually not student turf. They sat down at one of the booths, separated from its neighbors by tall wooden partitions. Raymond quickly ordered two coffees. The moment the waitress bustled off, he leaned toward Isabel and whispered, "Now, what is all this about?"

She replied with a single enigmatic syllable. "Karl."

"I don't get it," he said. "Has Pracht done anything improper?"

"No, no. It's nothing like that. Isabel's face revealed the gravity of what she was divulging and the pain it was causing her. "Karl's wrong," she said quietly. "His theory doesn't wash. I've gone over all his calculations again and again, and they don't jibe with his conclusions."

"But he's a world-class figure in the field," Raymond protested.

Isabel slapped the table. "Dad, I don't deny that. But this time he's wrong—dead wrong. I've come up with some ideas of my own, and I think my data argues conclusively against the existence of *any* fifth force."

Raymond was silent for a moment. "Do you realize what you're doing?" he finally asked. "You're throwing a firebomb into a roomful of some of the most important scientists in the world."

She nodded. "I know, Dad. I know. But I've never in my life been more sure of what I'm saying. I mean, the refutation isn't complex—its greatest strength is its simplicity."

"Who else knows about this?"

"No one. That's why I wanted to speak to you so desperately."

"Where's your proof?"

"In my notebooks in the trunk of your car. But if you want to see it boiled down into the basic formula, take a look at this."

She reached into the pocket of her flannel shirt and handed him a piece of paper. As he quickly scanned the data, Raymond found his anxiety rapidly transmuting into intense euphoria. "This is unbelievable," he murmured half to himself.

"Trust me, Dad, I'm right."

"I know, Isabel. That's why I'm so knocked out. Just imagine what an impact this will have. What a debut."

Isabel shook her head. "This is so painful. I don't think I can do it to him."

"Isabel, scientific truth is no respecter of rank or eminence. Its only criterion is integrity. You've got to publish your findings."

"I know, but it doesn't have to be right away. If I let the deadline for this year's conference go by, then there's no way of endangering Karl's appointment at M.I.T. I mean, what's my rush?"

"Come on," he remonstrated. "If Pracht were in your place, would he withhold publication?"

Isabel reflected for a split second and then answered quietly, "I think he would. I honestly think he would."

Ray shifted gears. "It's getting late, and you're incredibly tired. Why don't we discuss it again when our minds are fresh?"

"Okay, Dad," she replied, grateful to postpone the decision.

32 **ADAM** Three days after their telephone conversation, Toni had gathered her emotional resources sufficiently to invite Adam back to the house so they could both tell Heather.

Heather's reaction shook both her parents. Upon learning that Adam was leaving, she burst into tears. Her anger, curiously, was aimed at Toni. "You did this, Mom. You're so caught up in your career, you never pay any attention to him." She then implored her father, "You'll let me live with you, Dad, won't you?"

Adam melted with remorse.

During this entire conversation he was unable to look Toni in the eye. Yet she herself uttered not a syllable in rancor. That is, not in front of their daughter.

Finally the wounded girl went upstairs to telephone her best friend, who had gone through the very same ordeal.

Adam was now alone with Toni, who did not raise her voice but spoke barbed words. "Just don't let her farewell speech give you any ideas. She's got as much chance of living with you and Mata Hari as a snowball in hell."

"Wait a minute—" Adam protested.

"The court always finds in the child's best interests," Toni continued. "And whatever you think of me, I'm still the primary parent. That woman's not going to get near my child."

Adam was baffled. "Heather's never been at the center of your life. Why are you so insistent on custody?"

"I'm her mother. Do I have to say anything more?"

"Yes. You could say you love her."

"That goes without saying. Is it in Heather's best interest to live with some Russian babushka she doesn't even know?"

"Anya's a caring person. She'd be good to Heather."

"Does she have any experience with children?" Toni asked with an edge of cruelty in her voice.

"Do you?" he lashed back in anger.

His unexpected hostility hardened Toni's resolve. "You can't win, Adam. When you see what you're left with after this litigation, you'll be sorry we ever met."

ADAM slowly climbed the stairs carrying two old suitcases he had dusted off and brought up from the cellar. He shuddered as he passed Heather's closed door, through which he could hear muffled sobs, and hated himself for what he was doing to her.

He knocked and called, "May I come in?"

"No."

Adam spoke quietly but firmly. "Listen, Heather, I'll be leaving

95

soon, and I want to talk to you before I go. I'll be back in fifteen minutes, and I expect you to open this door."

While he was gone, she washed her face, combed her hair, and heroically pulled herself together. Her door was open.

Adam sat down next to her on the bed. "I know it may sound terrible, but this is going to turn out to be the right thing. Your mother and I were making each other very unhappy."

"That was no secret," his daughter muttered. "I wasn't exactly overjoyed either."

"Well, I guess we'll all have to start to rebuild our lives."

"Are you already involved with someone?" Heather asked. It was clear she dreaded the answer.

He said softly, "She's a very good person. I think you'll like her. Trust me, Heather. She's a lovely, gentle, caring woman."

There was a pause. Finally Heather found the courage to ask, "Tell me, Dad. Why did you marry Mom in the first place?"

He hesitated for a moment and then answered, "To have you."

Suddenly they were embracing, Heather in tears, he crying inwardly. "Please, Daddy, don't leave me," she begged. "I'll be good, I swear. I won't make any trouble for anybody."

Adam felt as though he had been kicked in the stomach. For a moment he even thought of capitulating. Anything that would not hurt his daughter more. But then he thought of Anya and the words exchanged with Toni, which could never be taken back. He closed his eyes and hugged Heather. He could feel her heart pounding.

Toni kept her word. In the negotiations with her lawyers—no doubt quarterbacked by the Boss—Adam was almost skinned alive. Naïvely he had chosen an old friend, Peter Chandler, to represent him, unaware that compassion and sentiment are not positive traits in divorce lawyers.

Not only did Toni petition for complete custody of their daughter, ownership of the house, and child support, she even sued for loss of earnings. Two senior partners from the law firm in Washington that represented the Boss testified that had she stayed in the nation's capital, her income would have been twice what it was in Boston. Peter argued himself dizzy. But the court upheld the relevance of the testimony and ultimately its validity.

The most egregious injustice was when the magistrate openly asked Heather which parent she would prefer to live with, and after she responded, "Dad and Anya," granted full custody to Toni on the grounds, however antiquated, that an adolescent girl was far better off with her mother. Battered and bruised, Adam was granted merely one weekend a month with Heather and only four weeks during the summer. No Christmas. No Thanksgiving.

Heather was devastated. "I don't understand it, Dad," she sobbed. "You're a much better parent."

"Yeah," Adam replied, smoldering. "But your mother's a much better lawyer."

That night Adam received a savage phone call from Thomas Hartnell. The Boss spoke with an icy calm. "Dr. Coopersmith, you have caused irreparable harm to the two things I love best in the world—my daughter and granddaughter. I intend to make absolutely sure that you regret your actions. I assure you that from this time forward I will be concentrating my life on finding a suitable vengeance. Now you go back to that Russian gal, and I hope she gives you all you deserve."

33 **SANDY** Most "civilians" balk at working more than forty hours a week. Yet serious scientific investigators think nothing of working night and day, including weekends. This is wonderful for the progress of mankind, but not for marriage and the raising of children. Sandy Raven, who had exchanged the vows of matrimony with the deepest of passion and the loftiest of intentions, became increasingly involved in the race against time, and against other laboratories, to find a cure for hepatic carcinoma.

Being a scientist's daughter, Judy fell easily into the pattern of being a scientist's wife. She knew from her own childhood that if she wanted her daughter, Olivia, to see anything of Sandy, she would have to bring her to the lab. Which she did, at all hours of the day and night.

Every Sunday night the family came up for air. They chose some ethnic eatery and tried to talk about something other than science.

One weekend they were joined by Sidney Raven, who had come east for the major city premières of his latest blockbuster, a seasonal offering called *Godzilla Meets Santa*.

97

"What's the news from Hollywood, Dad?" Sandy inquired.

"I think you can cover that by asking what's new with Kim Tower," Judy said, revealing to Sidney that she knew of her husband's obsession.

"Well," Sidney obliged, "the news is that Elliot Victor is on his way out of Paragon. And rightly, too, I might add. But guess who's succeeding him?"

Sandy looked at his father wide-eyed. "No, Dad. You don't mean it? Rochelle is going to be the head of the studio?"

"Yep. And she deserves it. The three pictures she produced made more money than the ninety-nine losers Victor supervised."

"Fantastic! But won't it be a strain on the Victors' marriage?"

"Not at all. Rochelle and Elliot are getting a divorce. I mean, it's a hell of a lot easier to get a husband than a studio."

Early the next evening Sandy was alone in the lab. Taking an unprecedented liberty, he breathlessly dialed Paragon Studios. After talking his way past three assistants, he was granted the honor of hearing her voice. "Raven, you old geezer. I thought you'd croaked with the dinosaurs."

Sandy was thrown completely.

"Rochelle," he managed to reply. "It's me, Sandy."

She burst into gales of laughter and remarked, "Oh, Sandy, it's *you*. My assistants thought it was your dad. How are you?"

In the instant before he replied, Sandy wondered if Rochelle had been joking. Would she have really addressed his father in so condescending—not to say cruel—a manner?

"I'm fine," he replied, suddenly tongue-tied. "I'm a professor at M.I.T., actually."

"That's great," she remarked.

"Rochelle, I've just heard about your promotion. I was so happy for you, I just had to call and say congratulations."

"Sandy," she said with fervor, "you're a truly beautiful person. Would you believe me if I told you that I miss you more than ever? I mean, there's nobody like you out here. Are you married?"

This can't be possible, he thought. The woman is about to be single again, and she asks me point-blank about my eligibility. Why did she wait so long? "Yes," he replied. "And I've got the most wonderful daughter."

"Oh, how I envy you." She sighed theatrically. "I'd give up the keys to the kingdom—even the keys to the studio—to have a darling little girl."

"Well," Sandy responded as he reveled in the attention she was paying him, "you're bound to find somebody worthy of you."

There was an abrupt silence. Then Sandy heard some voices in the background.

She returned apologetically to their conversation. "Sandy, listen, I've got to cut this marvelous conversation short. Why don't we talk again?"

"Sure, sure, anytime," Sandy said.

"Thanks again for calling—and loads of love to your wife and lovely daughter."

Though Sandy had no illusions that their relationship was anything more than platonic, it was not something he could discuss with Judy. For then he would have to admit that just hearing Rochelle's voice could still evoke in him pangs of regret.

34 ISABEL "Excuse me, Professor."

Karl Pracht peeked over a copy of *Science*, removed his feet from the desk, and acknowledged his unexpected visitor. "Ah, the good Mr. da Costa. Nice to see you." He motioned Ray toward a chair.

"Actually, I'd prefer to stand if you don't mind."

Ray's veiled hostility somewhat baffled Karl. "To what do I owe the honor of this visit?" he inquired.

Ray stared at the professor, unblinking. "Just tell me one thing," he said. "Has Isabel kept you up to date on her research?"

"Of course. I'm her adviser. Why—"

"Then you know," Raymond interrupted.

Karl Pracht leaned across his desk with a look of bemusement. "What are you driving at?"

"According to your reputation," Ray said, "you're of the school that believes in the existence of a fifth force."

"I've published a few papers on the subject," Pracht conceded.

"But never a full-blown exposition, never a complete soup-to-nuts discussion of the whole question."

It wasn't what Raymond was saying, but the bizarrely intense manner in which he was saying it, that caused Pracht—a normally placid individual—to lose his temper. "You know, Ray," he said, fast reaching the boiling point, "I've done my best to try to like you—and it hasn't been easy. Because frankly I find you untrusting, unpleasant, and uptight."

Good, Ray thought, we're getting to the nitty-gritty. "You're entitled to your exalted opinion. I've never been very fond of you either. Even less so of that hoodlum you call a son."

"You leave Jerry out of this," Pracht snapped angrily. "Just what is it you want of me?"

"I want you to publish my daughter's paper," Ray demanded. "Still, we both know you'd do everything in your power to suppress the masterful demolition job she's done on your cockeyed theory."

"Are you sure?" Pracht asked with a slight grin.

"You don't seem like a hara-kiri type to me. And what university would want you after Isabel's essay blows you out of the water?"

"I think I'll survive, Ray," Pracht allowed quietly, with a look of disdain. "My appointment at M.I.T. begins July first, 1988—no strings attached. That means if I forget how much two and two are between now and then, I'll still be the Winthrop Professor of Physics."

"A pretty empty title when Isabel's paper comes out." Ray played his trump card. "Listen, I'm willing to make a deal."

"A deal?" Pracht's tone was more curious than offended.

"You get six months' grace . . . and you take your cub to Boston."

Pracht studied Ray's expression like an ornithologist looking at an odd bird. "Mister, you belong in a loony bin. I only hope someday Isabel discovers what a creep you are."

"You're ducking the question," Raymond continued aggressively. "Do we have a deal or not?"

Pracht's gaze burned into Raymond's brain. "No, sir, we do not. For your information Isabel showed me her calculations, and the minute I saw them, I called up Dudley Evans, the editor of *The Physical Review.* He accepted her paper on my word alone."

Raymond was speechless.

"You see, the first concern of a real physicist is to learn more about the universe. It's great if he can be a pioneer in discovering

100

new knowledge, but that's secondary. The point is, we're all richer for what Isabel has done," Pracht stated passionately, "even *you*— you selfish, bungling bastard."

35 **ADAM** Thanks to Anya's modest salary as a lab employee and Dmitri's perverse "generosity," Adam and Anya had a roof over their heads. Leaky, but a roof nonetheless.

Heather was their houseguest the next weekend. For some inexplicable reason she adored their rickety apartment. And she had liked Anya instantly. Among other things, Anya had an unerring instinct for talking to younger people and soon had Heather feeling like a friend and equal.

"I was just thinking," Heather offered. "If I could move in with you guys, can you imagine how I'd do in my science homework?"

Adam smiled warmly. "Well, honey, you know how Anya feels. And how hard I've tried."

"Yeah," Heather acknowledged, clearly disappointed. "Do you think the court would reconsider if you were married?"

Anya turned to Adam, her eyes sparkling. "Did you put her up to saying that?"

"Not at all, darling. Nobody puts words into Heather's mouth."

"Absolutely not," his daughter concurred. "And speaking as a Boston bluestocking, I want to express my official disapproval of your unofficial shacking up."

Adam addressed Anya melodramatically. "Darling, for the sake of my daughter's sensitive psyche, would you marry me?"

She smiled happily. "Yes, my love, I will."

BUT the honeymoon would have to wait, for professionally they were making progress at a feverish pace. Other medical centers throughout the world had been helping them by running identical trials on women who had had five or more unexplained miscarriages in the first trimester. Results were now beginning to come in from the studies in Minnesota, Bonn, and at the University of Nice. These statistics were so astonishingly alike that Adam would never have dared to imagine them. It meant that if he could convince the medical community, doctors would be able to replace steroid treatment with natural progesterone and risk far fewer side effects.

Now the pharmaceutical companies caught wind of the profit potential in Adam's work. Clarke-Albertson, the most enthusiastic of them, was anxious to buy into his research.

After wining and dining the two Coopersmiths at the Colonnade, their vice president for public relations, Prescott Mason, turned to Adam and remarked, "My company has always seen to it that the jockeys get their share of the purse. A little extra pocket money never hurt anybody, did it, Dr. Coopersmith? And of course, if your research succeeds, you will inevitably attract the attention of the Swedish Academy."

Anya's face was glowing as she turned to her husband. "Haven't I always told you that, darling?"

"Come on. It's a real rat race," Adam protested.

"I agree," the executive said, "but Clarke-Albertson not only has resources to subsidize and ultimately market your work, we've also got plenty of influence in the Nobel situation."

"I'm surprised," Anya commented. "I'd have thought that was the last morally unspoiled domain."

"Oh, let me assure you," Mason responded. "They don't give the award to undeserving people. They'll pick you sooner or later. But wouldn't it be nice if the recognition came sooner?"

"Let me be absolutely candid with you, Mr. Mason," Adam responded. "There's only one appeal to me in any of this—time. This is one instance in which money can buy time, and that's the one thing I can't give my patients. They need answers as soon as possible, and if what you're proposing brings them even a day closer, then I'm morally bound to accept the best offer possible."

ADAM and Anya Coopersmith now became relentless hunters in the dark jungle of the immune system, and slowly but surely they were nearing their prey. Somewhere among the benign and benevolent cells that whirled through the body lurked a secret predator whose sole savage purpose was the destruction of the human fetus. The evidence pointed to the interferons, three clusters of proteins—code-named alpha, beta, and gamma—that guarded the body against viruses. A series of elaborate tests left no doubt: gamma interferon was a double agent—immensely useful against many diseases but lethal for healthy pregnancies.

The question now was how to destroy the would-be enemy while preserving the victim it tenaciously stalked.

The breakthrough occurred on their anniversary. They were hard at work in the lab, testing Anya's hypothesis that there might be a subtle structural rearrangement of the atoms comprising the gamma molecule in the reproductive area.

With the help of crystallographer Simon Hillman, they visualized the conventional molecule on a 3-D video screen and superimposed it on fetal tissue. Wearily pressing the ENTER key on her computer, Anya glanced perfunctorily at the screen, which she expected to show her bleary eyes yet another near-miss.

What she saw, however, made her blink into focus and finally let out a squeal. Adam ran over, thinking she had hurt herself. "Look, Adam. Look."

He just stared at the screen. His jaw dropped. "You were right," he murmured. "I never thought I'd live to see this moment. The receptor molecules are different—subtly different—but enough to cause all the damage we've been trying to prevent." He was dizzy. "After all this time, I'm suddenly at a loss for something to do."

Anya beamed. "We just sit back and wait for the ultimate scientific reaction—the telegram from Stockholm."

By LATE fall they had created a drug—dubbed MR-alpha to commemorate Max Rudolph, the man who had started Adam on this quest so long ago. Clarke-Albertson put the drug on their fastest track for commercial development and FDA sanction.

It took six months for the drug company to achieve Washington's blessing, and by then Anya had passed her qualifying exam. Thus when the good news was phoned through, the toasts could be raised to "Dr. Coopersmith and Dr. Coopersmith."

ADAM and Anya decided to spend their first advance from Clarke-Albertson on a house. They purchased one of the stateliest homes on Brattle Street. Anya, with irrepressible optimism, insisted upon designating a room for Heather, and had Adam invite her over to choose the color scheme. "I want you to feel that this is your home too," Anya commented affectionately. "And you needn't wait for your allotted time to come over." She reached into

103

her apron pocket and offered Heather a newly made front-door key. "You don't even have to call to say you're coming."

The young girl was deeply touched. "I'd like very much to give you a big hug," she said shyly.

"Darling," the older woman answered, "the feeling is mutual."

BUT not long after the Coopersmiths had bought their mansion, Adam shocked his wife and himself by proposing that they take a sabbatical. "How would you like a trip around the world?"

"That would be wonderful."

"We could stop in California and see some of our colleagues. Then Hawaii. After that we'll play it by ear. I've got some long-standing invitations to lecture down under, and we'll definitely visit your parents in Russia on the way home."

Anya was thrilled, and they embraced warmly.

Unselfishly, Heather encouraged them. "You guys deserve this. I mean, even old people go on honeymoons, don't they?"

Adam and Anya laughed at what they hoped was a joke. Then Adam asked, "But what'll happen to you on our weekends?"

"Well, something tells me Mom'll let you make up the time when you get back. And if she has to go to Washington while you're gone, I can always stay with Auntie Lisl."

"From what I understand," Anya remarked, "I don't think Toni likes her very much."

"Yeah, most of the time," Heather conceded. "But when it comes to a place to dump me, I'm sure she'll make an exception."

36

SANDY Late one night when he was alone in the lab, Sandy discovered the Golden Fleece—the molecular structure of the anticancer virus that he, Greg Morgenstern, and their staff had spent years seeking to replicate. And it was there in glorious Technicolor on his monitor.

Sandy was ecstatic. But before broadcasting the news to the world, he wanted to savor the delicious taste of being the only man on earth to know one of God's secrets. He walked into the deserted coffee lounge, opened the Frigidaire, and poured a glass of Perrier.

Giddy with excitement, he toasted himself out loud: "To Sandy Raven, the first in his Bronx Science class to win a Nobel Prize."

"Amen," said a voice.

Startled, Sandy whirled around. It was his father-in-law. "Greg. I thought you'd be asleep at this hour."

"No," his mentor answered. "I had this feeling that we were getting close. I woke up and was drawn back here like a magnet."

"We've done it!" Sandy suddenly exploded.

They raced to Sandy's lab station, where the computer still glimmered with its victorious construct and his lab book lay open at the page where the writing had come to a triumphal end.

"I can't believe it," Greg murmured. Tears welled up in his eyes. "Oh, Sandy, you can't imagine how I've dreamed of this moment."

"I can, Greg. This is like being on top of Mount Everest."

THE long evening of festivities began at five p.m. as champagne corks popped in Gregory Morgenstern's lab.

Greg was forced to make a speech. But with characteristic modesty, he downplayed his own role. "This is a team effort," he began. "And a team victory. And if it means the beginning of the end of one of the cruelest diseases ever to afflict man, then all of you should feel as gratified as I. And now I'm gonna share with you the cherry on the sundae." They all leaned forward as he murmured confidentially, "Guess when the news is being published."

"Oh, that's an easy one," Sandy volunteered. "It'll take us about two hours to write it up—"

"An excellent hypothesis, Dr. Raven," Greg pontificated tipsily. "But my special surprise is—the paper's already in the press."

Something about Greg's tone made Sandy uneasy. "What do you mean?" he asked.

"Well," Greg responded, "you'd all agree that *Nature* is the most prestigious journal in our profession. When I called the editor this morning, he was so happy for me—for all of us—that he held everything while I scribbled out a few pages and faxed them. It'll be in every lab in America by Wednesday."

"Wrong," Sandy interrupted. "In every lab in the *world*."

IN THE days that followed, Sandy walked on air.

On Wednesday morning he fell to earth with a thud.

Arriving at the lab, he found a cluster of staffers crowded around

105

a copy of *Nature*. Rudi Reinhardt, one of their star biochemists from Munich, noticed him and called out, "Hey, Sandy, can you believe this?" He held out the publication to him. "It turns out that our humble prof is a closet egomaniac."

Sandy grabbed the magazine, which was already turned to "An Antibody for Some Hepatic Oncogenes."

The listed author was Gregory Morgenstern, department of microbiology, Massachusetts Institute of Technology. He was the *only* author. All the collaborators' names were relegated to the first footnote and prefaced by the demeaning platitude, "I owe my deepest thanks to . . ."

In a move without precedent, the self-effacing Gregory had taken sole credit for what was not even a team effort, but really the fruits of Sandy's own sweat and brains. Sandy suddenly felt dizzy and then desperately sick. He barely made it to the men's room in time. Fifteen minutes later he appeared, chalk-faced, in front of Greg's secretary. "Where is he?" Sandy demanded.

Frightened, she stammered, "He and Ruth have gone to Florida for a few days. That's all he told me."

"When? What airline?" Sandy asked, browbeating her. "I know you must have made the reservations. You always do."

"Delta at noon. He's probably on his way there," she answered.

Sandy checked his watch—just after eleven. He raced to the parking lot and drove off like a demon.

As GREG Morgenstern and his wife were waiting to board with the other first-class passengers, he spied a figure hurtling toward them down the corridor. He tried to hurry Ruth into the passageway. Suddenly a hand grabbed his shoulder and spun him around. "Greg, you thieving bastard," Sandy shouted, shaking the older man. "You stole it. You stole my work."

As airline personnel and a police officer rushed toward them, Sandy continued to demand, "Why, Gregory? Why?"

"Please try and understand," Morgenstern pleaded. "It was like a stroke of madness. I've been playing second fiddle my whole life. And Sandy, whatever you may think, this project *was* my life. You're young, Sandy. Your time will come—"

This facile consolation cut the last thread of Sandy's self-control.

106

"My time is *now*," he insisted. "You should have given me credit." He shocked even himself by unleashing a blow aimed at Greg's head. Fortunately, it was deflected by a large policeman.

"Now what seems to be the trouble here?" the cop demanded.

Sandy and Greg glared at one another. It was Ruth who rescued them. "It's just a family argument, Officer," she said. "My husband and I are on our way to Florida. This other gentleman is our son-in-law and . . ." Her verbal powers failed her. She grasped her husband by the arm and led him off down the gangway.

Sandy took a deep breath, scanned the faces of the officials, and capitulated. "Like the lady said, it was just a family argument."

Though he would not have believed it, the worst part of Sandy's day was yet to come. Judy's reaction was the *coup de grâce*. She was furious with him. "You struck my father," she repeated in a hysterical litany. "How could you dare even touch him?"

"He stole what was rightfully mine," Sandy insisted, though a small part of him was ashamed of his behavior.

"You presumptuous fool!" Judy shrieked. "Whatever you did was nothing compared to the years my father put in."

"Judy, this has nothing to do with time. It has to do with brainwork. I *owned* the ideas that led to the solution. But even so, I would never have dreamed of not sharing the credit with him. He's a common thief."

"Stop it!" she screamed. "I won't let you talk about him that way!"

The fires of Sandy's own temper were stoked by indignation. "I don't believe this. You are actually defending his dishonesty—his theft of my solution? I mean, the courts recognize intellectual property, and your father's just robbed me of mine."

They fumed in silence for a moment, each waiting for the other to lash out. Sandy suddenly did not recognize the woman he had married. "I'll tell you one more thing," he said quietly. "You can't have it both ways. You can't be *his* daughter and *my* wife."

"Good. I agree," she hurled back. "After what you did today, I don't want to be married to you, Sandy."

37 ISABEL
As Raymond had expected, the publication of Isabel's article on the fifth force created a storm. But however magisterial her argument, it did not convince those scien-

tists who had spent their lives trying to prove precisely what she had demolished.

Pracht kept a respectful silence, but colleagues in universities all over the world did not feel any such noblesse oblige. If the girl was old enough to attack, she was old enough to *be* attacked. The articles published in the *International Journal of Physics* as well as in other distinguished periodicals were tantamount to hate mail.

Naturally she would be accorded space by these various publications to defend herself. But who could assist her? Raymond could not really be of any help. In fact, unwittingly, he increased her tension by voicing his worries. And Karl Pracht, who had magnanimously allowed her to dig his scientific grave, could not be expected to help pour earth on it as well. Isabel felt isolated, except for what moral support Jerry—who was away at a tournament—could give her by telephone. She was so busy formulating her counterattacks that she decided not to attend the ceremony to receive her master's degree and risk exposure to the media.

Just prior to his departure for Boston, Karl Pracht invited Isabel to lunch at the faculty club. He could not mask his displeasure when he saw that Raymond had come along. The conversation was friendly, though delicately avoiding any mention of the fifth force debate. Over coffee, Karl revealed the purpose of his invitation.

"Isabel, I have a feeling that you're going to find Berkeley a little less congenial from now on. I really think you should let me arrange a fellowship for you at M.I.T. I promise you'll find somebody world-class to direct your thesis, or failing that—humble has-been that I am—I'll do the job myself."

Raymond could see an unmistakable reluctance on his daughter's face when she told Pracht, "We'll think about it." And something made him suspect that she was somehow tied to Berkeley by the presence of Jerry Pracht.

"I think he made a lot of sense, Isabel," her father commented when they walked out into the bright summer sunlight. "I'd say we should take his offer and go to greener pastures."

JUNE 28: *I was desperate to talk to Jerry about Karl's invitation, especially since Dad was putting unbelievable pressure on me. At first I was disappointed when Jerry gave me a pep talk about doing "the right thing for myself." I guess I was hoping he would beg me to stay.*

"Look at it this way, Isa," he explained. "Starting this spring, Berkeley is going to be just a mailing address for me. So the only difference in our currently unsatisfactory relationship will be in the size of the phone bill. Right?"

After we hung up, I realized that if he was, in fact, going to be on the road so much, I might as well go and do my doctorate at the school Dad refers to as the top of the mountain.

SEPTEMBER 11: *Jerry was right. Moving to M.I.T. turned out to be a good idea in more ways than Dad and I had ever imagined. First of all, since I'm grown up now, nobody on the campus whispers or points fingers as I walk past. A lot of freshmen look my age.*

Also, I'm here incognito. This I owe to Karl, who arranged with the M.I.T. press office not to make any noises about my arrival.

In a sense Isabel was living a double life. First, her assault on the fifth force theory had given her a worldwide reputation. There were scientists both pro and con, and she was variously regarded as illustrious or notorious. Yet on the M.I.T. campus she was just another grad student sweating out the requirements for her doctorate.

Perhaps her most significant accolade was a follow-up article by Karl Pracht in *The Physical Review* reporting that he had repeated her various experiments and that her refutation of his argument had been correct. As usual, she was breezing through her course-work and keeping her profs on their toes. But they seemed to enjoy the challenge as much as she. In fact, Isabel could not recall ever being happier. At least intellectually.

Ray on the other hand had a great deal of time on his hands. In Cambridge there were not as many undergraduates anxious to be tutored by Isabel da Costa's father. True enough, he occupied himself with the domestic chores and reading through the mass of publications Isabel subscribed to, abstracting those he thought of importance. Yet it was hardly a fulfilling life, and he knew it. Isabel knew it as well.

In contrast to the unchanging routine of Isabel and Raymond's life, Jerry's schedule was highly erratic: different cities, different time zones, different motels. But he never failed to phone Isabel at a time when she would be able to talk privately. Though they had not met since midsummer, an astonishing intimacy was growing between them.

Jerry was young to be making the tour, especially on his own. He was getting beaten fairly regularly, and began to count it a victory when he was not totally shut out by the big boys.

He was nonetheless gaining a following. A great many of the female sports fans were more interested in the good looks of the players than in the quality of their play. And here Jerry Pracht gave even the flamboyant Andre Agassi a run for his money.

38 **SANDY** The greatest day in Gregory Morgenstern's life was the blackest in Sandy's. Scarcely three years after the publication of his discovery of the antibodies for liver cancer, Morgenstern was awarded the Nobel Prize for Medicine.

At the height of the emotional conflagration, Sandy, now divorced from Judy, had resigned his post at M.I.T., confident that he could easily find another. He was correct, for universities like Columbia and Johns Hopkins, informed of his role in the Morgenstern research, took the initiative and sought him out. After he wrote letters to several other major institutions, he was swamped with offers.

Yet the injustice so embittered him, he determined that from now on all his research would be motivated by advancement and material gain. The big money was in combating the aging process. Everybody was afraid of dying. A scientist who might stop the clock would have the world at his feet and millions in the bank. Hence, to all the establishments that interviewed him, Sandy pitched the idea of an institute to study cell degeneration.

In the end he accepted a professorship in microbiology, with a lab of his own, at Cal Tech. He had a variety of reasons. There was, of course, the prestige, the high salary, the state-of-the-art facilities. Not least was the promise of funding for an institute of gerontology. There was also the fact that his father was living in Beverly Hills.

And by moving to the West Coast he would be as far away as possible from Gregory Morgenstern.

Unlike diseases such as cystic fibrosis, which have been pinpointed to one particular chromosome, aging is controlled from perhaps as many as a hundred.

Some aspects of aging are visible. Though only thirty-two, Sandy himself was experiencing a trivial but painful example as he combed his hair each morning and strands of it came off in his hand. This is but a benign indication that other systems are gradually failing. Sandy and his colleagues discovered that an enzyme called telomerase could be used to prevent time's once inevitable erosion of DNA. In other words, as he joked, they could now "grow hair on a gene."

THERE had been an additional element in Sandy's choice of university—one he had not mentioned to his father—for his move to Cal Tech would place him in the same time zone and virtually the same city as the former Rochelle Taubman.

"Have you heard the news, sonny boy?" Sidney trumpeted down the phone. "Kim Tower—a.k.a. Rochelle Taubman—is succeeding Sherry Lansing as head of Fox. It's the highest executive position ever held by a woman in Hollywood."

"That's sensational!" Sandy exclaimed.

"Why not call her up? She'd probably be glad to hear from you. Remember, you knew her when she was a minnow. Anyway, I'm just going down to watch the dailies. Why don't you drive in and meet me at Chasen's at eight so I can buy you the best bowl of chili this side of heaven? We can raise a glass to Rochelle."

"Great idea."

WHEN Sandy gave his name, the maître d' reacted with a slight bow of the head and led him through the restaurant to a rich red leather booth.

Sandy ordered a glass of mineral water and scanned the restaurant in hopes of glimpsing a famous face. So engrossed was he in stargazing that he lost all sense of time. Suddenly he realized that it was nearly nine and his dad still had not arrived. He was about to flag the waiter for a phone when his father suddenly appeared. Normally dapper and fastidious, Sidney was disheveled.

"Dad, what's the matter?"

111

"I'm dead, sonny boy. You're looking at a walking corpse."

Sandy rose quickly, put his arm around the older man, and helped him to sit down. "Please, Dad. What happened?"

"When I went to see the rushes, she was there, waiting. At first I was flattered. Wow, I thought, the head of the studio's barely moved in and she comes down to see my stuff. So we ran the film. It wasn't terrific, but it wasn't terrible either. Then the lights go up, and she turns to me and says, 'This is crap, Sidney. And what's more, it's '60s crap.' " He shook his head in agony. "She told me I was out of touch. And then she said something worse. She called me a dinosaur. Said I was extinct and didn't even know it."

Sandy felt outraged and helpless. "What about the fact that it was you who started her off in the first place?"

"Come on. This town has the highest amnesia rate in the world."

"Listen, you've got every right to be upset," Sandy said soothingly. "But don't let her break your spirit. I'll buy you that chili dinner, and we can go for a drive." He beckoned to the waiter.

Watching his father eat mechanically, simply moving the spoon back and forth between the bowl and his mouth, Sandy realized he was a broken man. And now he had an overwhelming reason for contacting Rochelle Taubman.

39 **ISABEL** The fax arrived late one autumn evening at the beginning of Isabel's second year at M.I.T. It had first been sent to the department of physics at Berkeley, the affiliation Isabel had listed in her controversial article. The chairman then called the da Costa home in Cambridge. Isabel gave out a squeal of delight. "Yes, that'd be great. Fax it to the department. I'm sprinting there so fast, it'll still be coming out of the machine. Thanks. Thanks a million."

She hung up and turned to Ray. "You'll never believe this, but the Italian Academy of Science has chosen *me* for this year's Enrico Fermi Award."

"The Fermi?" Raymond gasped. "That's just about as close to the Nobel as you can get in physics. When's the ceremony?"

"To be honest, I was so knocked out by the news that I can barely remember anything else he said. Oh, Daddy . . ." She dissolved into tears of joy and threw her arms around him.

WHEN THEIR 747 LANDED IN Rome at dawn, the da Costas were met by the president of the academy, Raffaele De Rosa, and two members of the executive committee. On the long journey into the still sleeping city, one of the scientists read off the timetable of events. It included press conferences, luncheons, television interviews, and two dinners in Isabel's honor—one of them the night before the big event, which was the presentation of the awards in the Aula Magna of the University of Rome.

The da Costa's luxurious quarters in the Hotel Excelsior were graced by at least a dozen arrangements of flowers. Instinct drew Isabel to the most lavish of the bouquets. As she suspected, it was from Jerry: "Break a leg. Love, J."

She quickly hid the card in her purse.

AT LAST the gala evening arrived. The Aula Magna was packed with dignitaries, all bemedaled and bejeweled. Isabel, wearing a light blue taffeta dress, sat onstage at the center of a crescent of chairs reserved for the high officials of the academy. Raymond, who had donned a tuxedo, sat in the front row radiating pleasure.

Many of the distinguished guests could not help remarking how much tonight's honoree looked like a pretty Italian schoolgirl. They adored her before she even opened her mouth.

The actual presentation was made by Professor De Rosa. To enthusiastic applause, the radiant, dark-eyed seventeen-year-old gracefully approached the podium. Cameras flashed as Professor De Rosa shook her hand, gave her the plaque and an envelope, and returned to his seat, leaving her alone in the limelight. A sudden hush fell as she began, *"Carissimi colleghi, gentili ospiti . . .* [Esteemed colleagues, distinguished guests . . .]"

At first the audience assumed that she had memorized a few flattering words of Italian. But it quickly became apparent that Isabel would be speaking entirely in Italian. She began with some words of praise for Italian researchers, past and present, then modulated skillfully into a history of the Fermi Award itself. She concluded by offering her views as to the moral obligation of the modern scientist "not merely to seek truth but to *share* it."

The standing ovation lasted five minutes. If they could have given her another prize, they would have done so on the spot.

40 **ADAM** The Coopersmiths' grand tour began auspiciously enough. They charmed distinguished medical scientists from San Francisco to San Diego, even the legendary Jonas Salk, conqueror of polio.

Hawaii was intended to be a vacation, but Adam's medical colleagues there all pressured him for lectures—or at the very least a state visit. He ended up working harder than ever.

They broke their journey to Australia in Fiji, where only a third of the three hundred tropical islands were inhabited. At Suva, Adam called Heather to touch base. Then a small two-propeller shuttle took Adam and Anya to an islet that had more coconuts than people. They arrived exhausted and spent their first day sleeping and strolling on the beach. It was to fatigue that Anya ascribed the first incident.

The setting sun gave the sand a roseate glow as they walked back toward their palm-thatched *bure*. Adam suddenly glanced at his watch and said, "Uh-oh, what time's my lecture?"

Anya laughed. "We'll order one of those delicious cocktails, and you can address me on any topic that suits your fancy."

"No, seriously, I've forgotten what time I'm speaking. I'd better hurry and get my slides."

There was something in his tone that gave Anya a frisson. "Darling, you gave your last lecture two days ago in Maui."

His answer chilled her. For he gazed at Anya with the look of a little boy lost and asked, "Isn't this Maui?"

"No, my poor tired husband, this is one of the Fiji Islands."

Adam looked about him with an expression of mistrust. Then he retrieved the reins of his mental processes and joked, "I was just checking you for jet lag, Annoushka. I'm happy to say you passed."

Anya confidently dismissed her husband's harmless lapse.

FIVE days later, tanned and relaxed, they boarded a Qantas jet to begin what would be a triumphal tour of Australia.

It was hard to tell who enjoyed his lectures more—Adam or the medical faculties he addressed in Perth, Adelaide, Melbourne, Sydney, and Brisbane. They then returned to Sydney for a few days of idleness and opera.

A good night's sleep had restored Adam's effervescent spirit. He enjoyed Anya's excitement at the prospect of seeing *Eugene Onegin* in Russian at the Opera House that evening. In the afternoon he went out jogging while she had her hair done.

Yet when she returned to the room two hours later, she was puzzled to find it empty, with no note from Adam. There was plenty of time, so she did not begin to worry—that is, until she was dressed and ready and there was still no sign of him.

At six o'clock the police called her.

"Mrs. Coopersmith," the constable explained, "we picked up your husband wandering around the opera lobby in his running gear. He was in a bit of a state. But when he calmed down, he asked us to contact you as soon as possible. It took us a bit of time because, uh, he couldn't remember where you were staying."

41 **ISABEL** Buoyed by her Italian coronation, Isabel returned to Boston and immediately went to see Pracht.

"Welcome home, champ. *The New York Times* picked up some nice quotations from your acceptance speech. I'd say you had a promising future in science."

"Speaking of the future . . ." She hesitated and then began to fidget. "Uh . . . I'm not so sure you're gonna believe this, Karl. I've been thinking about the unified field theory. I mean, for my doctoral thesis I would like to see if I can formulate a hypothesis that interrelates the various energy forces."

"I don't believe it," Pracht said. "No one respects your talents better than I, but is there something perverse in you that wants to unravel the mystery that Albert Einstein left unsolved?"

"Karl," she countered, "I only said I'd give it a shot. Tackling the grand unified theory is a real challenge. Besides, if I fail, won't it be at least character building?"

Pracht reflected a minute and then pronounced, "I suggest you go out and buy a lot of aspirin."

"How come?" she asked.

"Because you're going to be hitting your head against a wall."

AT FIRST Muriel was speechless. And then she exclaimed, "Darling, you shouldn't have! I'm overwhelmed."

As Isabel watched ecstatically, her mother gingerly picked up the

115

Prizes

antique violin, a Giovanni Grancino of about 1710, which Isabel had insisted on buying for her before leaving Rome. Then, lest she profane such an instrument, Muriel merely played some scales.

"Oh, my Lord," she whispered. "This must have been made for the angels' symphony." She threw her arms around her daughter and hugged her tightly. "You're such a naughty girl. You must've paid a small fortune for it."

"That's okay," Isabel replied lightheartedly. "The Fermi Award *was* a small fortune."

"THAT was a wonderful thing you did for Mom, Isabel," Peter remarked that night when he and Terri, his pretty blond girlfriend, took his sister out for dinner. "She's dancing on air."

"I'll bet Edmundo flips when he hears her play," Terri offered.

"How come Edmundo's in Argentina again?" Isabel asked. "Has he got some kind of visiting-conductor post?"

"I don't know," Peter answered. "But there's illness in his family. Lately he's been going back there almost once a month."

"I know what you're thinking." Terri smiled. "But there's no other woman. He and Muriel are very devoted to one another. Actually, when he heard you were coming, he tried to postpone his trip, but you didn't give us enough warning."

"Well," Isabel said, "I'm giving everyone fair warning now. I'm going into hibernation until I crack my thesis—or just crack. As I told you earlier, I've picked the toughest nut imaginable."

"Sis," Peter said lovingly, "from you I'd expect nothing less. Which reminds me—is your adviser still that guy Pracht?"

"Yes, sure."

"Wow," Peter enthused. "Terri, that's Jerry Pracht's father."

His girlfriend could only echo, "Wow," and then, turning to Isabel, ask, "Have you ever met him? Is he as cute in person?"

"He's absolutely gorgeous," Isabel answered. "And you know something else? He's as smart as hell."

"I could tell that," Peter said. "I mean, the way he talked in his interview the other night."

"What interview?" Isabel demanded. "What did he do?"

"He just knocked off Boris Becker in straight sets."

Momentarily allowing her guard to drop, she murmured euphor-

116

ically, "Gosh, I wonder where I can call him. Do you know what this will do to his ranking?"

"Ranking?" Peter inquired with eyebrow raised. "Have you become a tennis nut too, sis?"

"For gosh sakes, I was just asking a simple question," she protested with embarrassment.

"To be perfectly honest, it was such an exciting match that I didn't pay attention to Pracht's new computer ranking." Peter grinned. "But let's put it this way, sis. All you have to do is spell t-o-p. Because right now that's exactly where your boyfriend is."

42 **ADAM** That night Anya could not sleep. Too restless to remain in bed, she got up and sat staring out the window with unfocused eyes. Her husband, sensing her absence, awakened.

"What's the matter, Annoushka?" He got up, sat beside her, and took her in his arms.

"Adam, I don't know how to say this," she murmured, "but I think you're having some . . . memory problems."

"No," he answered quickly. Perhaps too quickly. "You're talking to the guy they call the walking medical database."

This gave Anya an acceptable way of breaking it to him. "I know, Adam," she began. "Then maybe you'll understand the history of this case I know." As delicately as she could, she described the signs and symptoms of a hypothetical patient who demonstrated behavior similar to his own.

"Well, what you've described sounds like a mild stroke that's caused short-term forgetfulness. Your patient probably needs to see a neurologist. Now what is this all about?"

Hesitantly Anya told him of his various lapses, from that first incident in Fiji until today. There had been minor episodes in the intervening days. Adam listened mutely, then sat deep in thought. Finally he said in a toneless voice, "I remember . . . I mean, I have a vague sense of not being able to remember." He paused and then finally confessed, "Anya, I'm scared. Terribly scared."

She put her arms around him and hugged him tightly. "Don't worry, darling. We'll take the first plane home, and whatever it is, there will be somebody at Harvard who will make it right."

Adam, at this point completely lucid, said, "I don't think we should go home because of this. For one thing, whatever I may have will be grist for the cocktail mill. There are some terrific people here in Oz. Why don't we go to the university hospital and check the *International Medical Directory?*"

She nodded.

THE librarian at the university hospital had herself attended Adam's lecture the previous week and was delighted to let the Coopersmiths use the computer database. Anya seated herself at the keyboard and came up with a specialist, not merely in Sydney but one just a few floors away from where they were sitting.

"Why don't I go down and make an appointment?" Anya offered.

"No, no. They *know* me here." He thought for a moment. "See what you can come up with in New Zealand."

Anya knew it would appeal to Adam the minute she called up the information: Otago University Medical School, Dunedin, on the South Island of New Zealand, boasted one of the finest medical faculties in the world. The chairman of neurology, James Moody, owned an international reputation, and his hospital possessed a state-of-the-art positron-emission tomography brain scanner. They phoned, and an appointment was set for two days hence.

FROM Sydney they flew to Auckland, then changed for a connecting flight to Dunedin, where they spent a sleepless night. Next morning they appeared punctually at nine a.m. at the offices of the professor. He was in his mid-fifties, with a full head of white hair. After taking the shortest of histories, he suggested affably, "I know how worried both of you must be, so why don't we skip all speculation and go right to the machines?"

Moody had been especially accommodating to the Coopersmiths' request for discretion. Only a radiology technician was present. Moreover, the professor generously invited Anya to look over his shoulder at the screen in the control room. There she studied his face, hoping to discern a telltale expression. At one point he seemed to squint. Or was it a frown?

"What did you see, Doctor?" Adam asked anxiously as the professor and Anya helped him off the table.

"Well . . ." Moody began.

"Tumor—right?"

"No tumor, Adam," the professor replied. "At least none that I can see."

"Did you find anything out of the ordinary?" Adam asked.

"I'm afraid it could be A.D."

"No," Adam erupted, "not Alzheimer's. That's way off-base, Moody. I'm only forty-four years old. Couldn't a tumor produce the same . . . erratic behavior?"

The professor did not reply immediately.

Although petrified, Anya somehow found the strength to ask, "Is it possible you could be mistaken, Doctor?"

"Of course he is," Adam shouted. "Whatever lapses I may have had are the result of fatigue. My memory's perfect."

Moody did not take offense. He took a textbook from the shelf, found the appropriate page, and handed it to Adam. "With respect, Dr. Coopersmith," he said, "I ask you to look at those pictures." The book had two color images taken by a PET scan. "The one on the left side is an image of a healthy adult brain. Looks like a cheese-and-tomato pizza, doesn't it?"

Adam did not reply, for he was staring at the contrasting photo, that of a patient with Alzheimer's. It looked merely like tiny leftovers on a blue plate.

Moody then handed over four Polaroid color photographs. "These are the ones we took this morning."

Adam snatched the photos and stared at them. Anya peeked over his shoulder, trying not to give voice to her horror. For the dominant color was turquoise, with what looked like stains of blue ink.

"What— What do you suggest I do?" Adam asked helplessly, his fists clenching the arms of his chair.

"You will, of course, want to have a second opinion, further tests," the neurologist answered as softly as possible. "You're aware this thing isn't static. It goes in only one direction, and the younger you are, the faster. I can only suggest that you consider going home and putting yourself in the care of a Boston physician."

Anya agreed. "I think that's very wise."

Moody shook his head sympathetically. "This is going to be very difficult for you—for both of you. I'm terribly sorry."

119

43 SANDY Sandy Raven drove up to the inner gate of Twentieth Century-Fox. The officer in aviator sunglasses was a familiar figure who had been there as long as Sandy could remember. "Good morning, Mitch."

"Good morning, Professor Raven. Nice to see you." But this time he did not automatically lift the barrier. Instead, he came out and inquired, "Who're you gonna see today?"

Struggling to keep his composure, Sandy asked, "Would you call Miss Tower's office and ask if she could give me a few seconds?"

The guard did his best to camouflage his surprise. He returned to his booth and closed the glass window so that Sandy could not hear the conversation. Then the sentry emerged. "A-okay, Prof. She'll do her best to fit you in."

Sandy nodded to the officer, drove to the visitors lot, and parked his car. Marching back toward the main building, he passed through familiar sets that were now ghost towns.

He stormed up the stairs to the first floor, stopped to recomb his hair, then proceeded to the double doors that bore a gold plaque: KIM TOWER, HEAD OF PRODUCTION.

As he turned the knob, he realized that his palms were sweaty.

"Well, hello, Professor Raven," the secretary greeted him with an expert smile. "Miss Tower is tied up in a phone call, but you're next on her schedule. Can I offer you a cup of coffee?"

"No, thank you," Sandy replied tersely.

Moments later the intercom buzzed, and he heard Rochelle's voice asking whether he had arrived.

"Yes, Miss Tower. Shall I show him in?"

"No, no," said the voice. "He's an old friend. I'll come out."

One deep breath later, the inner door opened and there, in all her power and glory, stood Rochelle Taubman. She smiled. "Sandy, what a marvelous surprise. I'm so happy to see you. Do come in."

Thankfully, she did not offer her hand, nor—as he had worried during the night—did she offer her cheek to kiss. "Sit down," she said, motioning to one of the Barcelona chairs that formed a semicircle in front of her enormous marble desk. She returned to her own leather throne. "What brings you to Tinseltown?" she asked.

"Actually, I'm based out here," he replied. "I mean, I'm at Cal Tech. I'm part of their new genetic engineering program."

"Genetic engineering? That must be thrilling work."

There was a sudden silence, during which Sandy stared at her, wondering if she would give the minutest sign of *any* emotion.

Even Rochelle could sense that the magic of her beauty and the opulence of her office were ceasing to mesmerize Sandy. Wisely, she took the initiative. "I'm sorry about your father."

Unbelievable! he shouted inwardly. She's acting as if he were in a car accident, when she was the one who had run him down. "I'm sorry too." Sandy frowned. "But neither of us feels as bad as the man who gave twenty years of his life to this studio."

"And lost almost that many millions," she added.

"I don't believe that, Rochelle. I mean, those pictures he made during the first years were real gushers—and on a tight budget."

"I'll give you that," she said. "Sidney *was* an asset to the studio—in a different era. But our statistics tell us that the vast majority of our audience are teenagers. Now how can you expect a man in his sixties to understand today's youth culture?"

Sandy was outraged by her sophistry—and yet amazed by her resilience. "By that reasoning, Rochelle," he rejoined, "all pediatricians should be little kids."

She was stymied for a moment, then chose humor as the medium of response. "That's very clever, Sandy. I mean that." Then she glanced at her Rolex and stood up. "Oh, my gosh, I'm late for a screening. Give me a ring sometime and we'll do lunch."

Then Sandy exploded. "Rochelle!"

There was a barely perceptible flash of triumph in her eyes: she had finally cracked him. And dealing with hostility was not only her forte but one of the prime secrets of her success in Hollywood.

"Yes?" she answered primly.

"Forget his loyalty and all the years he broke his back for this studio. Think about just one thing—your own career. If it hadn't been for my father, you wouldn't be in this office right now."

Perhaps she was unaccustomed to being told the truth. But suddenly her temper flared. "That's your opinion," she said with a hostile smile. "Personally, I think it's a considerable overstatement. Anyway, it was nice seeing you, Sandy."

With that, she disappeared, leaving him still consumed with rage. How could he have ever loved this monster?

44 **ISABEL** Some of the greatest scientific discoveries are not made, but stumbled upon. Rising early one morning in her third summer at M.I.T, Isabel sat down at her desk, pencil in hand, and began to think. With her mental faculties still half slumbering, she started to doodle, just to bring thoughts into focus. Then suddenly she began to write figures, which gradually became equations. Working furiously, she felt a sudden craving for carbohydrates. Padding barefoot into the kitchen, she took out two frozen waffles, toasted them, saturated them with maple syrup, and carried them back to the desk for a high-calorie breakfast.

Gobbling the rich food, she glanced at the paper again. She could scarcely believe that the entire formulation had come to her complete, in a single burst of inspiration, like a great melody coming whole to a composer's imagination. As flawless as a snowflake. She thought, This could be it. But how could it be so simple?

Forty-five minutes later she poked her head into Pracht's office. "Karl, can you spare me a few minutes?"

"Sure, of course. What brings you here so early?"

"An idea has just popped into my head." She hastened to the whiteboard, picked up a colored marker, and began setting out the principles from which she developed the theory. Finally she concluded. "Well, what do you think, Karl?"

"Frankly, I'm having trouble making it sink in. Your theory is magnificent. And yet . . ." Pracht's brow was furrowed.

"What's bothering you, Karl?" she asked.

"Well, actually, Isabel, my mind's already rushed to phase two. I mean, there's no question this will cause a stir because of its sheer beauty. But there'll always be doubters. If only we could come up with a way of demonstrating that you're right."

"Well," she replied, "we're neither of us on the experimental side. But if you've got time, we could kick around some ideas."

Just then Pracht's intercom buzzed. "What is it, Alma?"

An unexpected voice preempted his secretary. "Dad, Isa's not in her office."

She fairly bounded from her seat. "Jerry! But isn't he supposed to be flying to England?"

Smiling, Jerry walked through the doorway.

Isabel unabashedly threw her arms around him, and they kissed.

Jerry smiled mischievously. "Hi, Dad. Am I interrupting?"

"On the contrary. I think *I* am," his father joked. "Aren't you supposed to be in Wimbledon?"

"I routed myself through Boston so I could see my special friends here. I've got till the day after tomorrow."

"Great. By the way, nice going with Becker."

"Thanks, but don't expect an encore. I was just lucky. Anyway, were you guys working?"

"We certainly were," Karl pronounced. "You arrived at a historic moment—Isabel has come up with a new unified field theory."

Jerry was staggered. "Fantastic, Isa. Congratulations. I want to hear this for myself. I probably won't understand it, but can I at least listen?"

"Fine," the elder Pracht agreed, and Jerry smiled broadly.

Isabel returned to the whiteboard and repeated her earlier performance, with a few more refinements that came to her on the fly. At the end of her exposition Jerry clapped.

"Brava!" he exclaimed. "That's a guaranteed Nobel winner."

"Your dad's pressing me for even more," Isabel complained with mock frustration.

"What else do you want, for heaven's sake?" Jerry demanded.

"Well," the elder Pracht replied amiably, "a demonstration would be kind of nice—experimental proof."

Jerry turned to Isabel. "What sort of conditions do you need?"

"A monster source of energy—and not even the five-hundred-GeV accelerator at CERN in Geneva could rev up enough."

Jerry thought for a moment, and then his face lit up. "How about a supernova?" he asked excitedly. "When a star collapses, there's a tremendous gravity field and a massive amount of energy."

Isabel brightened. "I think you're onto something, my stargazing friend."

"Wait a minute," Pracht interposed, waving his hands like a basketball referee. "The ion temperature in a supernova is high, but it's only a hundred keV or so. You need a million times that."

"Hold it, Dad," Jerry shouted. "What about the shock wave?"

Isabel pondered briefly and then exploded with joy. "Jerry, you're unbelievable. Now both you guys follow me." In an instant she was at the whiteboard once more. "The star shrinks down incredibly fast until it reaches a point where it hits bottom and rebounds, sending this really fast shock wave," she began.

Pracht, who was reveling in these youngsters' animated dialogue, played the troublemaker. "This is all very well, but I don't think I'll live long enough till the next supernova."

"You don't have to," Jerry replied. "There *was* one in 1987—"

"When the blue star Sanduleak detonated," Isabel added.

"Bingo!" the elder Pracht cheered.

"Astronomers in Chile caught on to it really early," Jerry explained, "but the most sophisticated data would have been at CSIRO in Australia. Their hemisphere got the best view of it. One of my old buddies from the astronomy club is working there. I can call and persuade him to send us the tapes." There was always someone awake at the observatory, so Jerry called and determined that the team at CSIRO did indeed have computer tapes covering the history of Sanduleak and would be happy to make copies.

"That's absolutely brilliant." Isabel beamed. "Do you want to write this up with me, Jerry?"

"No way," he answered. "*This* part is fun. That would be work."

45 **ADAM** Charlie Rosenthal cried. "I'm sorry, Adam. I'm so sorry," he sobbed. "You're my best friend. And there's not a damn thing I can do to help you."

Adam put his hand on his colleague's shoulder. "Hey, take it easy," he said gently. "The worst is yet to come. Save your tears for then. Meanwhile, tell me what specialist is going to get the pleasure of my case."

"I've asked around, and there's no question about it—the guy you should see is Walter Hewlett at Mass General. He's going to make history and pay a house call."

Charlie put his arm around his suffering friend as they walked from his study into the living room, where Joyce was talking to Anya. As the two women rose and started toward Adam, he suddenly exploded into ferocious rage.

"What do you people think you're doing?" he bellowed. "Coming into my house like this, invading my privacy—"

Charlie tried to calm him. "Take it easy, Adam. You've known Joyce for years. You were best man at our wedding."

Adam's reply electrified Charlie like a lightning bolt. "Who do you think you are? You are probably here to poison me."

Charlie addressed Anya, his eyes broadcasting shock and sorrow. "I think we'll go now. Make sure he takes those pills. Hewlett will be here before nine. Call me if you need anything."

Anya left the room to show them out. Less than a minute later she was back with Adam. He was bent over, holding his head.

WHAT most surprised Anya was that, for a senior scientist, Walter Hewlett was so young. "Thank you for coming over, Doctor."

"It was the least I could do, Mrs. Coopersmith. Your husband won't remember, but I was his student when he had to take over Max Rudolph's course in midyear. He was a great lecturer."

They entered the living room and found Adam staring at the fire. "Adam, this is Walter Hewlett. He was a student of yours."

"Really?" he remarked in a normal tone. "Since I only gave an actual course when I filled in for Max, that must have been in 1979. Am I right?"

Hewlett smiled. "That's exactly when it was. You've got quite a memory, Dr. Coopersmith." He opened his attaché case and pulled out a large manila envelope. "I've looked over the reports and the photographs you brought along from New Zealand."

"New Zealand?" Adam asked quizzically. "Why would I go to New Zealand?"

"Well," Hewlett answered, "I know you're tired, and it may have slipped your mind. But as I hope you know, I'm a neurologist and I believe you have a problem."

"Really?" Adam reacted glassy-eyed.

Walter nodded. "I mean, naturally we'll want to take our own scan. But to my mind, the pictures you brought along substantiate Moody's diagnosis." The young doctor paused and then said tentatively, "I think you've got Alzheimer's."

Adam's reply was quite unexpected. Still staring into the fire, he answered in a monotone, "So do I."

CERTAIN people had to be informed. First and foremost there was Heather. Since Adam was declining swiftly, she was doomed to lose him well before his actual death. Anya called Lisl, who proved a welcome source of strength. She insisted on being the one to tell Heather and Toni.

Unexpectedly, Toni wept openly. "May I see him?" she begged.

"That's something I think Anya has to decide," Lisl answered. "But he wants to see Heather very badly." She looked at Heather and said gently, "Shall I pick you up tomorrow after school?"

Heather nodded mutely. She was too stunned to cry.

46 ISABEL

Raymond da Costa was outraged. "How could you do such a thing? Don't you think I deserved to know before anybody?" He had never gotten angry with her like this.

"I'm sorry, Dad," Isabel said softly, "but there was no point in showing it to you until I knew I was on the right track."

"You mean you thought it would be too far above my head."

Isabel was trapped. In truth, she could have explained it to Ray in terms he would have understood but had balked at the prospect.

Suddenly her father was crying, his head in his hands, at the kitchen table.

"Dad, I apologize. I realize now I should have told you first." Isabel stood motionless, painfully aware that their relationship had been torn in a way that could never be healed.

Just then the telephone rang. She picked up the receiver. "Yes?" She listened for a moment and then said, "I told him." She paused and added, "Of course he was happy. Anyway, eight o'clock's fine."

As she hung up, Ray snarled, "Jerry Pracht?"

Isabel nodded. "En route to Wimbledon. He's invited me for dinner."

"He's a kid. He hasn't got a chance. He'll get knocked out in the first round."

Isabel lost her temper and shouted, "Even if he doesn't get the ball over the net once, it won't make me care for him any less!" She looked at her father. "Please," she said, "I don't want to hurt you. Let's go out for a nice relaxing jog, and I'll tell you about my thesis idea."

Raymond's feelings were almost instantly assuaged. "I'd like that, Isabel," he said warmly, "but lately I prefer to discuss my science sitting down. Can we do it over a glass of iced tea when you get back?"

"Sure, Dad, sure. That'd be lovely," she answered quickly.

She spent most of her run castigating herself for being so harsh with Ray. He had given her so many years. Couldn't she have taken a few more days to let him down more gently?

She entered the apartment and was relieved to see that his mood—at least superficially—had radically changed. She quickly showered, put on jeans and a shirt, and prepared to deliver her second presentation of the day.

Ray sat there enthralled by his daughter's genius. It not only sounded right but—like many great discoveries—seemed as if it had always been waiting there in full view. At the end of her exposition he rose enthusiastically and said, "I knew this was going to be brilliant, so while you were out, I shopped for all your favorite things. I'm preparing the most fantastic dinner you've ever seen."

"But Dad," she protested gently, "Jerry's picking me up."

"This is a great occasion for you," Ray muttered frantically, still on his own wavelength.

She spoke to him with emphatic calm. "I'm going to change now, Dad. And then when Jerry comes, we'll be going out."

Twenty minutes later she reappeared dressed in her best silk blouse and blue skirt. To her dismay Raymond was still fussing with the dinner arrangements, and significantly, a third place had been set. "You can both eat here," he said, bordering on hysteria. "I mean, Jerry's a nice boy. There's more than enough for—"

The front-door intercom buzzed then, and Isabel picked up the entry-phone receiver, listened for a moment, and then said quietly, "I'll be out in a moment."

She turned back to her father just in time to hear him gasp, "P-please . . . Don't leave me now." Ray clutched his chest and sank to his knees. His face reddened, and he began to sweat.

Managing to keep a cool head, Isabel pressed the entry-phone button and implored Jerry to hurry inside.

Jerry took charge immediately. "I'll handle this, Isa. Just call 911."

"Don't—" Ray lost consciousness and fell back onto the floor.

For Isabel it was a horrible feeling of déjà vu. She remembered the trauma of Ray's Berkeley attack and her fear while waiting for the doctors to pronounce their verdict. But this time the diagnosis was less ominous. "There was no cardiac implication," the senior resident at Cambridge City Hospital explained. "He must have had some sort of shock that drove his blood pressure sky-high. We've sedated him, and we'll monitor him for two or three days."

Since her father would sleep till morning, Isabel acceded to Jerry's suggestion that they have a bite. But, unable to exorcise her feelings of guilt, the highest gastronomic level she would allow herself was Dunkin' Donuts.

While they were on their third helping of French crullers, Jerry affectionately broached another subject. "Hey, remember a million years ago, when we were originally going out to have something fancier than this? I was going to make a big deal about it because I had something important to tell you."

"Tell me now."

"I've come to the conclusion that our relationship has no future if we're only united by a telephone wire."

For a moment Isabel thought he might be about to leave her. "Anything else?" she asked uneasily.

"Yeah. We should live in the same city."

Her heart melted. "I'd like that," she whispered.

"You better. I'm giving up eccentricity for you. And I'll cease to be known as Pracht the dropout."

"They're not going to call you that anyway," she responded. "Soon they'll be calling you Pracht the Wimbledon champion."

He looked at her with surprise. "Do you for one minute believe I'm going to leave you with a father in intensive care?"

"Jerry, don't be stupid. I've got lots of friends—"

He shook his head. "No, Isa. I'm going to stick by you."

"But what about—"

"Bouncing a ball on a grass court? Eating strawberries? I don't think that outweighs leaving you on your own. Besides, my beating Boris was sheer luck. Cinderella only happens once."

When he took her to her apartment, he saw the look of helplessness on her face as she opened the door. "Isa, please don't mistake what I'm about to say. But I think we'd both feel better if I didn't leave you alone tonight."

For a moment she did not know how to react. Then she whispered, "Thank you."

47 **SANDY** As he approached his forties, Sandy found himself leading two separate lives. His public persona was the distinguished scientist at Cal Tech, running his institute, organizing seminars, and directing dissertations. He was a star, and many of the young female scientists in his field were anxious to know him better. But he was still so numbed by his downfall at the hands of Gregory Morgenstern that he was unable to perceive his own loneliness.

On the weekends, however, the hermit became a hunter, stalking the explorations of others. The all-pervasive technosphere of northern California had engendered a spate of cottage industries. Dozens of young geniuses were working in their parents' garages, all trying to develop newer biotech wonders. Sandy would hear about their work on the student grapevine and seek them out.

Their predecessors were men like the legendary Dr. Herb Boyer, who made history with a little company called Genentech. Once upon a time—in 1978, to be exact—Boyer and his staff were working out of a modest lab on the San Francisco docks. Their breakthrough was the synthesizing of insulin—a protein vital to sufferers of diabetes. Two years later Genentech was floating on the stock market, and Boyer's share of the enterprise had risen to a value of eighty-two million dollars.

On the surface, Sandy was looking for a new Herb Boyer. In another, deeper sense he was also trying to find himself. By the late 1980s the university was paying him a basic six-figure salary plus a share of royalties in anything they might jointly patent. So the outlay of a few thousand dollars to buy half the shares of some fledgling's scientific dream seemed like a fantastic deal for both parties. Yet Sandy was scrupulous in all his dealings with these young Columbuses. Though he could easily have demanded a share of the credit as well, he had no desire to usurp their glory. He could never hurt another human being as he had been hurt.

Sandy had always been enthusiastic about neobiotics. In this tandem operation Francis, nineteen years old, and his "senior" partner, James, twenty-one, were devising an AIDS test so simple that it could be administered in the privacy of any doctor's office and yield accurate results in less than five minutes.

When it appeared that they would be the first to get FDA approval, Sandy put them in the hands of a good lawyer, who proceeded to negotiate for the initial public offering for the company. Their stock came out at five dollars. By the time the green light came from Washington, it had increased tenfold.

SANDY did his best to derive some enjoyment from his newfound wealth. He voluntarily increased the child support he paid to Judy and established a very substantial trust fund for their daughter, Olivia. And since he needed more space—if only to display the many awards he was receiving—he bought a seventeen-acre estate just south of Santa Barbara, with a twenty-room Spanish-style house. It needed a lot of renovation—which explained its "bargain" price of two and a half million.

Sandy urged Sidney to move into what his father grandiosely referred to as "the Raven compound," luring him with an entire wing of his own, with a separate pool and patio. Not to mention a twenty-seat screening room.

"Holy moly!" Sidney exclaimed. "Now all I need is something to screen."

HIS daughter's visits each summer were the high point of Sandy's year. And yet, in a way, they also saddened him. For Olivia had grown up so swiftly that he wished he could make time stand still. In the corner of the lab he'd installed at the compound, he put a special bench for her, for she had become a deep thinker at a remarkably early age.

She also showed an interest in her father's private life, and one day she came up to him in the lab with a tattered movie script under her arm. "Hey, Dad, you should really read this. It's one of Grandpa's old screenplays. He's thinking of shopping it around again. Remember *Frankie?*"

"Oh, yeah," Sandy remarked. "Musical chromosomes. That project was before its time."

"Right." Olivia's eyes twinkled. "Frankie's way of finding a wife should appeal to you. He concocts her in a test tube."

"What makes you think *I* would do it that way?"

She smiled wistfully. "Because honestly, Dad, you don't seem to want to try any other."

EVEN PROSTRATE ON THE Hollywood scrap heap, Sidney remained ever hopeful, still held captive by the Hollywood myth that just one picture could reverse the tide of his fortunes. Sandy offered to bankroll one of his father's cinematic projects, but the older man was a proud patriarch. "No, sonny boy," he insisted. "Like Sinatra, I gotta do things my way."

Sidney was a veteran with a track record. Admittedly, it was for what the trade regarded as schlock, but that was precisely what the television industry demanded. He also had a reputation as a dependable producer who got pages filmed. And with the passing of time the stigma of Kim Tower's banishment began to fade. One of the network chiefs, whose first job in the business had been as Sidney's office boy, sensed what a potential treasure the old man still was and signed him on.

Sidney was like a man reborn. He drove straight to Sandy's lab and hurried in without even knocking. "Hey, kiddo. Great news— I'm in business again!"

Sandy was elated. "Oh, Dad, that's wonderful." As he embraced his father, they both broke down and began to sob.

48 ISABEL

It scarcely made a column of newspaper space, but it wrote headlines in their lives. When Jerry Pracht, citing cartilage problems, withdrew from the 1991 Wimbledon tournament, there were modest expressions of disappointment but hardly an uproar or a dirge.

So much had changed in just a single night. Raymond, alone in Cambridge City Hospital, was not eager to go home. He realized how irrational—and foolish—his behavior had been. Part of him was terrified that he had already lost Isabel for good. But it was clear to him that if henceforth he was to play any part in her life, it would be a minor one.

When Ray did return from the hospital, he was chastened and docile. His behavior made it very clear that he was simply grateful to be welcomed.

Isabel too had begun to question Ray's role in her life. She knew that the charade of parent and child had to end, but she couldn't ask him to move out, and besides, she worried about him living alone.

Isabel officially became Dr. da Costa in late June. She also received an offer to be an assistant professor of physics at M.I.T. when her degree was awarded. The starting salary would be forty-five thousand dollars per annum.

Two days after Jerry had called his friend at CSIRO in Australia, a couriered package arrived for Isabel containing five reels of computer tape. With the help of a physics department computer consultant, they transferred the data into Isabel's computer. As he'd sat in Isabel's office finishing the setup, Jerry murmured, "See how easy this is, honey? Electronics will do all the work for us. Say, I hope you don't mind my bivouacking in your cell?"

"No." She smiled. "It's nice to have you in such close quarters."

"Just to keep us both sane," he suggested, "why don't I work the night shift, and you can have your own office during the day?"

"That's very generous of you."

"Isa, I'm a generous kind of guy."

BY EARLY July, Karl Pracht deemed the 985-word abstract of Isabel's thesis suitable enough to qualify as a letter. "That way, no reviewer can get his claws into it, and you can go public without being mugged," Karl had said. He immediately faxed it off to the editor of *The Physical Review,* who accepted it within the hour. Its appearance a month later caused a stir that reechoed in every physics lab in the world. The daring young girl on the flying trapeze had done it again. This time at an even greater height, and with no net below.

In the first weeks after publication Isabel lived on automatic pilot. She jogged at daybreak and stopped at the department on her way home to await the morning mail and see if any of the journals had printed a response. She would then meet Jerry in the lab to continue their frustrating investigation of every centimeter of tape. And yet the tension mounted to such a degree that Isabel could not even concentrate on the search for evidence that could silence her critics with irrefutable proof.

When the bouquets finally came, they were all theoretical. In the ensuing months scientists throughout the world, whether grudgingly or admiringly, came out in print to acknowledge Isabel's brainstorm. But none was able to suggest an empirical manner in which to test its validity.

IT WAS NEARLY FOUR IN THE morning when the phone rang. Isabel picked it up drowsily.

"Isa!" Jerry was calling from the lab in a state of unbridled euphoria. "I've got good news and bad news. I've come to the absolute end of the Aussie tapes, and I can now tell you that they give us megazilch."

"That's a downer. What's the good news?"

"The good news was my sudden notion that they didn't catch the explosion early enough. Our last chance was to get the data right from the source. So I contacted Las Campanas in Chile, where the blowup was first spotted. And down there they've got tapes starting only an hour after the event began. I got them to send the data on Internet. I've looked it over, and guess what? There was a small peak that faded into the noise after a few hours. But it was there. The guy calculated that based on the decay rate, it must have had a pretty high amplitude at the beginning. What's more, none of the theorists he consulted could explain why the peak should have been where it was in the first place. But your theory takes care of all that, doesn't it?"

"Oh, Jerry. I'm so excited I don't know what to say. I owe you so much. Thank you. Thank you for everything."

Then—if such were possible—he endeared himself to her even further by saying softly, "Hey, listen, let me speak to Ray. He deserves a bit of congratulations too."

She glanced at her father's bedroom door. "He's zonked at the moment. But I will call my mom."

The moment he hung up, she dialed the West Coast. To her surprise the sleepy voice that answered was Peter's.

"Hi," Isabel said jauntily. "What're you doing home?"

"Terri and I are just house-sitting for Mom," he answered.

His tone seemed strangely subdued, and Isabel began to sense that something was wrong. "Where's Mom?" she asked anxiously.

"I wasn't supposed to tell you, but she's taken the red-eye to Boston. It's nothing to do with you. There's a . . . problem. I'm sure she'd want to talk to you herself." He reluctantly conveyed the details of Muriel's flight. She would be arriving within the hour.

"Peter, is this something very serious?"

Her brother hesitated and then said gravely, "Yeah, sort of."

49 SANDY
Sandy forged professional links with as much zeal as he avoided sentimental ones. A great deal of work on aging and longevity was being done in Japan, where he had ongoing collaborations on "immortality genes." And yet the most important discovery in his life was Kimiko Watanabe. To be precise, it was she who found him.

They had in common not merely a passion for science but a history of personal loss. Kimiko's husband, a geneticist, had died at an obscenely early age, leaving her with twin sons, a pension ample to raise them, but no means of *spiritual* support. Yet he had shared so many of his scientific ideas with her that she almost felt capable of carrying on his work, with the slight obstacle that she had only a high school degree. Kimiko applied to study genetics at half a dozen Japanese universities and was turned down flat.

One day while she was rummaging through her late husband's files, she came across an offprint from *Experimental Gerontology* entitled "Synthesizing Telomerase." It was inscribed to Akira Watanabe with warmest personal greetings from the author, Sandy Raven, Ph.D., California Institute of Technology, U.S.A. Kimiko thought it might be worthwhile writing to Sandy and asking his help.

Sandy read her letter and immediately arranged for Kimiko to spend a trial year at Cal Tech as a special student. She jumped at the chance and, with the boys, made the long journey to Pasadena. Aware that this was a once-in-a-lifetime opportunity, she worked like a demon and at the end of the year was offered a place in a formal degree program on a full scholarship.

In the months preceding her arrival she and Sandy had exchanged dozens of faxes. He had telephoned her to confirm the details of her travel and housing arrangements. And yet, curiously, from the moment she arrived, all personal contact ceased. Communication with Sandy's office was now through his redoubtable secretary, Maureen.

Kimiko began to worry that she had in some way offended her benefactor. If that were so, the good news that she would be staying on provided the perfect pretext for righting things with Sandy.

"Will it be possible for me to see the professor in person for a moment?" she appealed to Maureen.

Maureen knew her orders: "Don't clutter up my life." And yet she had grown to like Kimiko a lot. "I can't guarantee that you'll get to see him, but why not take a chance on coming by on Tuesday at say, four o'clock, and I'll do the best I can."

WHEN Maureen buzzed Sandy to announce Mrs. Watanabe's presence, he bristled. "No way. I've got a meeting with the dean."

"Come on, Sandy," the secretary responded. "That isn't till four thirty. Why don't you just pop out for a quick hello?"

Sandy acceded grudgingly. He had pictured Mrs. Watanabe as a tired woman, drained of humor. He did not expect her to be pretty. Certainly not young and vibrant.

Kimiko smiled as she held out her hand and politely uttered, "I had to come by and thank you so much for everything, Dr. Raven."

Sandy was momentarily tongue-tied. Her radiance had pierced his defensive armor. He recovered sufficiently to ask, "Do you have time for a cup of coffee?" He motioned the lissome visitor into his office, while Maureen grinned with satisfaction.

THE following week Kimiko invited Sandy to dinner. What he liked most was the fact that she made no attempt to camouflage her motherhood. The boys sat at the table with them in their modest apartment near the campus, making polite conversation when spoken to. At the stroke of eight they excused themselves and retired to their room to study.

"What time do they go to sleep?" Sandy asked.

"Never before midnight. They have two sets of homework, since I also send them to Japanese school in the afternoons."

"Just a guess, but I'd say *you* don't go to sleep before three."

"You got me this chance, and I don't want to disappoint you."

"You haven't. And yet we Americans have a saying: All work and no play . . . You're a very attractive woman. In fact, I only wish I were ten years younger."

"Why?" She looked at him with undisguised affection. "You are not exactly ancient. And you are a very attractive man."

They talked until midnight. When she excused herself to say good night to Hiroshi and Koji, Sandy realized that it was time to go. Yet when she returned, they continued talking for another hour.

135

Only then did he force himself to leave, but not without making another date.

"What do you normally do on weekends?" Kimiko asked.

"Well, as you probably gathered, I live a peculiar life. On weekends I go shopping—a few hundred miles away in San Francisco." He told her about the garages and their brainy proprietors. "Why don't you come with me?" He quickly added, "I mean, the boys too."

On Saturday they left at dawn and drove slowly on the Pacific Coast Highway, stopping for coffee on the pier at Monterey. A short while later he booked them into a luxurious three-bedroom suite near the top of the Four Seasons Clift Hotel in San Francisco. They immediately left again to explore Silicon Valley.

Here Kimiko saw another side of Sandy. Whereas he was timid with adults, he was a kind of benevolent godfather with the fledgling inventors. They adored him and treated her like a colleague.

That evening they went to the hotel's crystal-chandeliered French Room for dinner on their own, leaving the boys to eat in the room. Kimiko only pecked at her food, and Sandy realized at once what was wrong.

"Kimiko," he said earnestly, "we shouldn't have left them up there by themselves. You're having real qualms, aren't you?"

She nodded. A moment later he had settled the bill and they were back in the elevator to rejoin Hiroshi and Koji.

Two months later Sandy struck gold—literally and figuratively. He identified a group of genes that promoted aging in skin cells and, during various trials, succeeded in reversing the degeneration. It may not have been permanent, but it looked as if the process could be repeated indefinitely. Overnight Sandy Raven became a household name. The media touted him as the creator of the ultimate dream: the promise of eternal youth.

Sandy was so harassed by the three-ring circus that he fled with his father to Lake Tahoe, where they rented a bungalow under the name of Smith. There the two men watched as the auction for Sandy's discovery reached dizzying heights.

When Corvax beat out Yves Saint Laurent with an advance against royalties of fifty million dollars, Sandy was outraged. "You can't get these guys to give even a million bucks for a cancer lab."

"Listen, don't knock the dough," Sidney answered. "As Liz Taylor said in *Cat on a Hot Tin Roof*, 'You can be young without money, but you can't be old without it.' But then again, take it from your old man—all the money in the world ain't worth more than a hug and a kiss from a good woman. Am I making sense?"

"Yes." His son smiled.

Sidney smiled back. "Is Hong Kong on target?"

"Well, you've got the right hemisphere—she's Japanese." Sandy grinned. "Only how did you—"

"I just kinda guessed that the rental of this joint didn't include the picture in your bedroom of the Oriental gal and her two kids. Is she as nice as she looks?"

"Nicer," Sandy replied, his affection showing. "I mean, I feel very comfortable with Kimiko—with all of them."

"Kimiko Raven." He tried it out. "It sounds different."

"Well, she *is* different," Sandy asserted.

Sidney looked at his son's face and saw new life. "I love her already," he said with feeling, "for what she's done for you."

50 **ISABEL** Muriel, exhausted from lack of sleep, was scarcely able to believe her eyes when she saw her daughter at the airline gate.

"How did you find out?" she asked, her worried tone in contrast to the strength of her embrace.

"Never mind that. What is going on?"

Muriel held her daughter's hand in both of hers, forcing back the tears. "Edmundo's ill—very ill." She paused to gather courage. "Huntington's disease. It's a kind of neurological time bomb. Ultimately everything falls apart."

"Oh, Mom, I'm so sorry."

"There's a professor at Mass General who's developed a radical cure. But it's still in the final stage of FDA trials, and I've come to see if he'll try it on Edmundo anyway."

"I'll go with you," Isabel insisted.

"No. Believe me, this is something you want no part of."

"Mom, there's no way I'm going to leave you alone for a minute."

Muriel shook her head in defeat and then realized that for form's sake she had at least to murmur, "Thank you, Isabel."

137

HE WAS TALL AND broad-shouldered, his black eyebrows flecked with gray. "Good morning, Mrs. Zimmer," he said in a heavy Russian accent. "I am Professor Avilov. Would you come in, please?"

Isabel rose. "I'm her daughter. May I come too?"

"Her daughter?" Avilov reacted with startled interest. "Well, I should think—"

"*No,*" Muriel said emphatically. "I don't want her involved."

"But my dear Mrs. Zimmer," he protested. "By the very nature of the disease, is she not very much involved?"

"No, Edmundo's not— Her father's Raymond da Costa."

The Russian scrutinized Isabel's features with a sudden glow of recognition. "Ah, are you not the famous physicist?"

Isabel nodded wordlessly.

"Let me tell you what an honor it is to meet you," Avilov pronounced with deference. Then, turning again to her mother, he said, "I had no idea, Mrs. Zimmer. But the fact that you have such a world-respected person in your corner, so to say, might help with the wretched bureaucrats in Washington."

Muriel could sense that this pompous professor would not be satisfied unless Isabel joined them. "Very well," she sighed.

They followed him into his large office, which was decorated with diplomas in many languages. "Please, ladies, sit down." He gestured gallantly as he positioned himself behind his massive wooden desk. Then he launched into a kind of lecture.

"Huntington's has no cure, no remission. Up till a few years ago they did not even know where in the human genome it was to be found. Then, working in this very lab, my distinguished colleague Professor Gusella determined that the gene for Huntington's disease resided on a strip of chromosome four. I was fortunate enough to clone the offending gene and, by using recombinant DNA, produce a protein which seems—at least in the laboratory—to restore the structure of chromosome four to its normal healthy state. This, I take it, dear lady, is the reason for your visit."

"Yes, Professor," Muriel answered as deferentially as she could, aware that the way to this man's heart was through his ego.

"My heart goes out to the many sufferers whom I hope someday to help. Yet imagine the irony when I, as a former Soviet citizen, say I am strangled by what is here called red tape."

Muriel lowered her head.

"And yet," Avilov boomed, "I see here a potential advantage."

"What, Professor?" Isabel asked, breaking her long silence.

The Russian suddenly pointed his finger at her. "You."

"I don't understand," she responded.

"Surely, Dr. da Costa, you are aware of the genetic dimension? Affected individuals have a *one in two* chance of passing it on to their offspring. If the authorities in Washington were led to believe that you were, in fact, Edmundo Zimmer's child, that a scientist of your magnitude were in such jeopardy, I am sure we would get, so to say, the green flag to treat the patient."

"My God," Isabel whispered, and then asked Muriel, "Do Francisco and Dorotea know about this?"

Muriel nodded. "They both insisted on being tested. Francisco was lucky, but Dorotea knows she's living out a death sentence."

"Oh, that's horrible," Isabel gasped. She clutched Muriel by the shoulders. "I'll go along with it," she said passionately. "It's our one chance to save them."

At this moment Muriel, overcome with emotion, grasped Isabel's hands. "There's something you have to know," she said. "This affects you in a way you never realized."

"I don't understand."

"You're in danger, darling. I mean, it's my fault." She began to weep. "It's actually the truth, Isabel. Edmundo is your father."

Praying she had misunderstood, Isabel gaped at her mother.

"Darling, try to understand. Edmundo was so warm and caring. He genuinely loved me. We had an affair and"—her voice lowered to a barely audible whisper—"after Ray became so obsessed with you, there was no way I could ever tell him."

"Stop it! I don't want to hear any more of this." Isabel had let go of her mother, who by now was weeping uncontrollably. "I can't believe this. I simply can't believe this." She was staggered, stricken with self-doubt. She had always defined herself as Raymond da Costa's daughter. She had lived with him—and for him.

At this point she again grew aware of the Russian doctor's presence. "Professor Avilov," Isabel declared. "I've changed my mind. I won't be a party to this unethical travesty."

"But Isabel," her mother pleaded, "you're in danger."

"I don't care!" she snapped, and abruptly buried her head in her hands.

"You owe it to the world," the Russian argued unctuously. "You are perhaps the greatest mind in modern physics and have a fifty-fifty chance of carrying the gene for Huntington's disease."

"Thank you," Isabel retaliated furiously. "You've just cast a giant shadow over my entire life."

"Not necessarily," Avilov remarked. "I can draw your blood, and within a week you will know your fate. It could be good news."

Isabel did not reply.

"Perhaps I should leave you two alone to talk about this."

"You expect me to talk to the woman who screwed up my life—and my father's? What she did was unforgivable."

"But if there hadn't been Edmundo," Muriel said pleadingly, "you wouldn't be you!"

Isabel seared her mother with eyes of fire. "Do you expect me to thank you for that?" She stormed out of the doctor's office.

THOUGH it was sweltering, Isabel walked the entire distance home from Avilov's office. She didn't hurry. There was too much to think about. It was not her own uncertain destiny that was preoccupying her most. Her principal concern was the fate of the man who from her earliest memories had loved and protected her. She swore a fervent oath that he would never learn of Muriel's betrayal.

She arrived back at the flat drenched with sweat. Her father's bedroom door was closed. Perhaps he was taking a siesta. She looked around. Glancing at the table they used for work and meals, she noticed a sheet of yellow foolscap propped up between the salt and pepper. Knowing instinctively what it would say, she picked it up with dread.

Dearest Isabel,

You have been a wondrous, loving daughter, more than I could ever have deserved. I realize that I've overstayed my welcome in your life and that your rightful place is with people of your own age—like Jerry, who's a wonderful boy.

Among many offers Pracht passed on (perhaps to get rid of me?) there was a last-minute opening for a physics teacher in one of those fancy prep schools. I guess my claim to fame as your father is my best recommendation. When I called him this afternoon, the headmaster said he would take me sight unseen.

As soon as I get settled, I'll give you my new address. From now on I'll be acting like a parent with grown-up children. I leave behind the only gift I withheld from you—your freedom.

Be happy, my beloved daughter,

Your loving father

Isabel was stunned. She knew—the way a patient on a local anesthetic knows—that a part of her flesh was being torn away. But all she could sense was the anguish she would feel when the shock wore off. Sitting, she put her head in her hands and began to sob.

She was jolted by the piercing ring of the phone.

"Isa."

"Oh, Jerry." She was overwhelmed with relief to hear his voice. "It's been the worst day of my life. Can you come over for dinner?"

"Why don't you let me take you out? I mean, we could be alone."

"We'll be alone," she said softly. "Dad's gone."

"What happened, Isa?"

"He's taken a job in a prep school, and would you believe that's the least of the earthquakes? I'm still in such shock. But let me tell you in person. Will you settle for spaghetti and meatballs?"

"Fantastic. I'll come by at seven."

Still in a hypnotic daze, she went out to the supermarket and bought the ingredients for dinner.

The phone was ringing insistently as she opened the door. Quickly setting down her packages, she hurried to answer it.

"Isabel, we've got to talk." It was Muriel. "I've checked into the Hyatt Regency. Now that this terrible thing is out, it has to be dealt with."

"Look, I can't think about it now. I'll call you in the morning."

"Can't we set a date for breakfast? Say, eight o'clock?"

"All right," Isabel replied. "I'm sorry, I have to go now."

JERRY had a bottle of red wine as well as a bouquet of roses, but his most precious gift was irrepressible good humor. Impulsively Isabel threw her arms around him.

141

He smiled. "Hey, I think I'll go out and come in again for more of the same."

"Don't be silly," she coaxed him. "Sit down so that I can depress you." She handed him the note.

He was clearly moved. "It took a lot of guts to write this. He's a heck of a guy. You should be very proud of him."

Somehow the approval of the man she loved, his words of affection, had a paradoxical affect on Isabel. She began to cry.

"Isa, what's wrong?"

"I've just found out he's not my father." She gathered the courage to tell him about Edmundo. But she did not mention his illness—selfishly perhaps, since she did not want to run the risk of scaring Jerry away on this of all nights. "Does it sound crazy that I'm angry with my mother for giving birth to me?" she asked.

"That's a real tough one. Frankly, I can't help feeling a little grateful." He squeezed her hands affectionately.

Oh, if you only knew the worst part, she thought.

By the middle of dinner, with some credit perhaps to the wine, they managed to talk of things other than parents, heredity, and fidelity.

It was nearing the time when Jerry usually made his departure. He stood up, moved closer, and put his arms around her.

After they had kissed, Jerry asked gently, "Isa, last time, when your dad was ill, I spent the night here on the sofa."

"Yes, I remember."

"I'd like to stay again, but this time with you."

Their eyes met, and without hesitation Isabel answered softly, "Please, Jerry. I'd like that very much."

51 ADAM

Paradoxically, for the Alzheimer's sufferer the disease is more painful at the beginning, when his periods of lucidity are longer. In the end those around him become the victims. For they know that though he is not lost to the world, he is lost to *them*. But even before the light completely fades, there is an unending series of humiliations.

Since she had so much to do to protect him, Anya hired Terry Walters, a beefy black male nurse with considerable experience in dealing with this ruthless disease. This enabled her to go about the difficult business of living two lives: hers and Adam's. She visited the lab daily, collecting the data gathered from various experiments and bringing it home, explaining to the staff that the prof had picked up a nasty virus that he simply could not shake.

In lucid moments Adam wrote comments in the margins of the reports, and Anya made sure his modifications were adopted. If his mind was blurred, she tried to imagine what the old Adam would have done and conveyed the response to the staff.

She had no alternative but to tell Prescott Mason of Clarke-Albertson. He was genuinely shaken.

Up till now Mason had been low-key, operating on the assumption that he would make his big move in three or four years. But after what he had just learned, he had to go into high gear, for the Nobel Prize could only be given to a man alive at the time of the voting. On more than a dozen occasions, in the most important research centers in the country, he took previous Nobel laureates and respected nominators into his confidence and explained that Adam Coopersmith was dying.

By the spring he had made considerable headway, having obtained numerous suggestions and recommendations, sent by letter and fax to Stockholm.

52 ISABEL

Jerry Pracht awoke to the sound of quiet sobbing. He got out of bed and went into the living room, where he found Isabel seated by the window, staring out at the rising sun. He went over and tenderly touched her shoulder.

"Isa, what's wrong?" he asked. "Is it something about last night?"

She put her hand on his. "No, Jerry. That was beautiful. It's what I have to live with starting today." She turned and looked at him. "I told you a lot of terrible things last night. But I left out the worst." She then told him about the specter of her heredity. "So you see, instead of being supergirl, I turned out to be a leper."

He put his finger gently on her lips. "As far as I'm concerned, you're the same person I've always known and loved. And nothing you've said will make me walk out on you."

She threw her arms around him. "I won't hold you to that, but it'll be nice to have you around as long as you can bear it."

"I'm going to do more than that—I'm going to help. Now, let's deal with things in chronological order. First, there's your mother. She's waiting for you in the hotel dining room, and I think the best thing is to get her on a plane home as soon as possible."

"That's for sure. I don't know how I'm going to face her. What do I say to her?" Isabel pleaded, at her wits' end.

"As little as possible. I mean, there's no way you can undo what she's done. But there might be steps you want to take."

"You mean to save Edmundo?"

"The heck with him. I'm only thinking about you."

AT FIRST Muriel was annoyed that Isabel had not come alone. But it did not take long for her to realize that this young man was an important part of her daughter's life. She accepted his presence and motioned for him to sit down and join them. Correctly assuming that Isabel had told Jerry everything, she spoke freely.

"Professor Avilov is anxious to try his therapy on Edmundo. But I think the price is your letting him test you."

Isabel shook her head in confusion while Jerry answered firmly, "Mrs. Zimmer, if she tests positive, there's nothing she can do except live in fear of an early death."

"You're not a doctor," Muriel objected firmly.

"Mom, he's my best friend," Isabel rejoined emphatically.

"I appreciate what he means to you," Muriel said. "But he doesn't have anything to lose."

Jerry rose furiously. "On the contrary, Mrs. Zimmer, the most precious thing in my life is at stake," he said softly, putting his arm around Isabel. "The girl I'm going to marry."

Even in the depth of depression Isabel was thrilled by Jerry's declaration. She took his arm as he continued to address Muriel.

"Now, if you don't mind, I've taken the liberty of booking you on the noon flight to San Diego. I'll go downstairs and wait in the car so you two can have some time to talk." He kissed Isabel and left.

Muriel began, "You must be very angry with me."

"I don't think that word is adequate, Mom," Isabel said sharply. "You betrayed Dad's trust."

"All I ask for is a modicum of understanding. Lord knows I did something wrong, but I'm certainly being punished."

Just then an alien voice interrupted them. "Good morning, ladies. May I join you?" It was Avilov himself, jovial and expansive.

Muriel looked up and answered helplessly, "Of course."

The Russian professor sat at the place setting that had been Jerry's. "I've come to announce that I've made special arrangements to treat Maestro Zimmer with my new therapy."

"Oh, that's wonderful," Muriel replied.

"Of course, I can give no ironclad guarantees. But nowadays many advanced medical techniques are being practiced in highly modern clinics in the Caribbean. There you do not need FDA approval to administer experimental drugs. I suggest that we all make arrangements as soon as possible to fly to St. Lucia."

"Thank you, Doctor. Thank you." Muriel was close to tears.

"Fine," the Russian stated, standing as abruptly as he had seated himself. "I will liaise with all parties concerned."

JERRY Pracht knew there was only one absolute way of reassuring Isabel. "Isa, let's get married right away."

"What? There's no way. I'm a genetic time bomb."

"In that case, I've changed my mind about your taking the test. At least that would give me a chance of getting you to say yes."

"That's the only reason I'd go through with it. And even if the results are terrible, at least I'd know. But if we let Avilov do it, there's not much chance of keeping the results under wraps."

"I agree. But I've asked around and located the one person who's least likely to divulge our secret to him. His first wife. She's now married to Adam Coopersmith at Harvard, and even though she's in immunology, when they first came over, she actually helped Avilov develop the Huntington's test."

PREOCCUPIED though she was, Isabel could feel a kinship between herself and the still youthfully attractive Russian doctor. Anya's eyes seemed to emanate a sympathy that could only have been nurtured by a personal acquaintance with tragedy. She fully understood the need for discretion and even insisted on drawing the blood herself. After taking it, she promised Isabel, "The very minute I learn anything, I'll call you."

Earlier that week Isabel and Jerry had gotten their first letter from Ray, on the gold-embossed Coventry Prep School stationery. On the weekend they drove down to see him. Despite the fact that they were obliged to hide so much, it was an enjoyable outing. Ray even embraced Jerry warmly as they exchanged good-byes.

When they returned to Cambridge, there was a message on the answering machine to call Dr. Coopersmith at her home.

"I thought you would be nervous, so I rushed the test through," she explained. "Anyway, I'm overjoyed to tell you that your chromosomal makeup doesn't—repeat, does not—have a dominant Huntington's gene. That means you can look forward to a long, productive—and reproductive—life."

Not only was Isabel herself in no danger of developing Huntington's, there was no risk to any children she and Jerry might have.

Putting the phone down, she turned to him and said with deep emotion, "Thank you for being you. And for being willing to stay with me either way."

53 **SANDY** It was only in 1994 that the money radically changed Sandy Raven's life. That year *Forbes* magazine added his name to its golden honor roll of the four hundred richest people in America.

Elevated to the pantheon of plutocracy, Sandy was besieged by telephone calls from adoring well-wishers—many of whom he had forgotten he even knew. He told Maureen not to put any of the callers through so he could at least have a few hours of hands-on time in the lab.

She disobeyed him only once. "It's Kim Tower."

It opened a torrent of feelings. The object of his childhood longings, the princess who had turned out to be a dragon and nearly destroyed his father. Now she who had ignored him was suddenly telephoning him of her own accord.

"Okay," Sandy capitulated. "Put her through." He could feel his blood pressure mounting as he waited for the connection.

"Hi, sweetheart," she purred. "How does it feel to be the talk of the town?"

"I don't know. How should I feel?"

"Like a nuclear firecracker," she suggested. "Why don't we get together, break bread, and talk about old times?"

Old times? Sandy thought. What do we have to reminisce about? But then, for reasons conscious and unconscious, he thought, Why not? "That would be great, Rochelle."

"What about tonight at the Bel Air? It's Friday, and we can stay up extra late."

"Fine with me," he answered. "I only hope you recognize me after all these years."

"Dollface," she replied, "lately your picture's been in the paper more than mine. See you at eight. By the way, it's my treat. *Ciao.*"

HE ARRIVED early to find that she was already ensconced in a corner where she could survey the room. Her hair was light blond at the moment, and even at a distance she looked like the magnificent superstar she might have become had it not been for her consummate lack of talent. Still, she had the aura of success about her.

This time she offered him her glowing cheeks to kiss. Simultaneously the sommelier poured the champagne. Rochelle raised a glass and toasted his success. "You know, I always knew you'd make it, Sandy," she said. "I mean, even when we were classmates." She gazed at her grade school admirer as if seeing him with new eyes.

His feelings were stirred. He was so bedazzled that he temporarily suppressed his anger at her long-ago cruelty to his father. And despite everything, he still wanted her.

"I have an idea," she said after dinner, leaning closer to him. "Let's go to my place for coffee."

"Why not?" By now he was bursting with curiosity at the reason for her sudden rediscovery that he existed.

"You know, I've got a sensational record as head of production."

"Yeah, your instinct's phenomenal," Sandy commented, still wondering where all this was leading.

"But I'm just a salaried employee," she continued. "The big money goes to the studio bosses. For a long time now I've been looking for an opening to make my move, and I think the time is right. I happen to know that our chief stockholder, George Constantine, is financially overstretched and is trying to lay off big chunks of the company."

"Well then, go for it," Sandy said encouragingly.

147

"With what?" she inquired in an unconvincingly helpless tone. "Even with my track record, the banks are still fundamentally sexist. I can't get anybody to subsidize me for an LBO."

Ah, Sandy realized, it's my money. "I don't even know what an LBO is," he lied. "Isn't it a cable TV network?"

"No, silly," she answered with an indulgent smile. "Leveraged buyouts are how the rich get richer. And with your kind of collateral, you could easily raise enough cash to relieve Constantine of his holding." She paused, looking at him meaningfully. "Well?"

Sandy evaded her question. "It's something to sleep on."

"I agree. Do you have a driver waiting?" she asked.

"No. Actually, I drove myself."

"I've got a Lamborghini that can make it from here to my place in under five minutes. Are you interested?"

"Rochelle," he replied in the understatement of his life, "I've always been interested."

NOT that he would have expected it to be any other way, but her home was just like a lavish movie set, with a second swimming pool right in the middle of the living room.

"Come on, dollface," she murmured sweetly. "Let me show you what a great cup of coffee I can make."

He followed her into a room whose sophisticated machinery could well have surpassed the kitchen of the hotel at which they had just dined. Everything sparkled—glass, metal, hidden lights.

"You were married once," she remarked offhandedly.

"Yeah," Sandy nodded. "It didn't agree with me. Or to be more specific, it didn't agree with her. But I'm certainly not bitter. I've got the most wonderful daughter."

"Oh, really?" she gushed. "You must tell me all about her." Quickly adding, "Sometime. But for the moment, let's be selfish."

"In what way?" Sandy inquired.

"What about a little skinny-dip?" she asked with nonchalant eroticism. Before he could respond, she gracefully undid the zippers and stepped out of her dress. Her body was magnificent.

"Come on, honey," she coaxed. "What are you waiting for?"

"I don't know, Rochelle," he answered softly. "But I think I'd prefer to pass."

148

She stared at him in disbelief. "What's the matter, Sandy? Scared you're not man enough?"

Her taunt helped him at his moment of indecision. "No, Rochelle. I think it's the other way around. You're not woman enough."

"What?" she shrieked with outrage. "I always knew you didn't have any guts. You're nothing but a little eunuch. Go to hell."

At this point his soul had broken free.

"Thanks a lot for the dinner," he said.

"Did you hear me?" she shouted furiously. "I said go to hell."

He stared at her with genuine indifference and answered, "You know the funniest thing, Rochelle—I've been there all this time, and only just realized it."

THE following Monday, since Kim's first meeting was off the lot, she did not pull up to the studio gate until nearly eleven. Usually, the minute he caught sight of her red Lamborghini, Mitch would lift the barrier so she could zoom through.

Today, for some reason, the barrier remained in place.

"Have you lost your touch?" she called out in mock anger.

The sentry came to the side of her car. "Miss Tower, I don't know exactly how to say this, but . . . you're not on my docket. I guess you don't work here anymore."

Kim exploded. "Ridiculous!" she snapped, reaching for her car telephone. "I'm going to get George Constantine on the phone right now, and we'll see who leaves this spot first."

Kim reached him on the other coast. The tycoon remained impeccably calm as the wrath poured into his ear.

"Listen, sugar," he explained cordially, "you of all people should know the way the system works—one day you're in, the next you're out. I'm afraid this is your day to be out."

The phone went as dead as Kim Tower's status in the town.

Mitch was staring at her, his face fully showing his satisfaction now that his superior rank had been established.

"By the way," Kim said with artificial sweetness, "can you tell me who's head of production as of this morning?"

"Oh," said Mitch with a poker face. "Mr. Raven—Mr. Sidney Raven. Now you have a very nice day."

54 **ISABEL** Dmitri Avilov waited on the runway at St. Lucia, a lush paradise of volcanoes and valleys. Though only the second largest of the Windward Islands, it held two special attractions for the former Soviet scientist: the ultramodern facilities of its private Clinique Ste. Helene, and the compelling coincidence that this tiny country had already produced two Nobel prizewinners, though none as yet in medicine.

Uncharacteristically sporty in his open short-sleeved shirt, Avilov scanned the cloudless skies for signs of the Piper Comanche ferrying the Zimmer family. He was tense. For all his confidence before patients, he was deeply apprehensive about the new genetic therapy he was about to undertake.

A moment later the small plane became visible. It circled the field and gracefully touched down. A nurse opened the passenger door and a white minibus drove out onto the field. The orderlies entered the plane. Then they bore out Edmundo Zimmer, placed him onto a stretcher, and carried him back to their vehicle. The other passengers—Muriel, Francisco, and Dorotea—followed.

When they regrouped at the Clinique Ste. Helene, Avilov explained, "The actual 'operation' has already been performed on the samples I took from his bone marrow. We have merely to infuse the recombinant cells and set them to work transforming the murderous gene. I think we can get right on with that. I'll see that he's installed in a room and start the transfusion. Since there'll be no immediate results, may I propose that the rest of you go to the hotel and unwind from the journey."

As the professor had predicted, nothing dramatic happened for several days.

One night at dinner Dorotea confided, "I've spoken to several doctors, and all of them concur that Avilov is on the right track. I asked him if he'd try the therapy on me as well, and he agreed."

"Isn't that taking a big risk?" Muriel asked.

"No," the younger woman replied. "I can't live waiting to be sick. If he can't cure me, I'd rather die immediately."

IT TOOK merely five days to show that Dorotea's fate would be reversed. Whatever Avilov's motivation, he was a superb scientist. And with each passing day it became apparent that Edmundo had become a unique medical phenomenon: a victim of Huntington's in remission. It was a momentous achievement.

Perhaps even worthy of a Nobel Prize.

"ISABEL, you've gotta grow up. It's time to pick up that phone and call your mother. I can understand you feel this urge to punish her. But there's no question about her loving you. Think about how much she suffered when you and Ray walked out on her."

Isabel sighed. "Pracht, you're so maddeningly mature—at least when it comes to other people." She paused for a moment and said softly, "I'm scared."

Jerry took her by the shoulders. "I can see that. You wonder how you'll react if . . . Edmundo is dead. But you must call her, Isa."

Jerry kept his hand affectionately on the nape of her neck as her trembling fingers dialed the numbers.

"Mom, it's me."

"Oh, Isabel, how are you, darling?"

"Never mind me," she protested. "How's everybody at your end? I mean, especially . . . Edmundo."

"Would you believe we're all fine? So far the gene therapy's worked wonders, and there don't appear to be any side effects."

"That's wonderful."

"How's that young man of yours? You will invite me to the wedding, won't you?"

"Listen, Jerry and I agree we're both too young to get married. Anyway, if and when, I promise I'll invite you."

"And Edmundo?"

"Mom, Jerry's made me see that I'm foolish to be angry at . . . your husband. On the other hand, I've made Jerry see that I only want one father. Am I making any sense to you?"

"I'm afraid so, darling." Muriel paused and then said softly, "Anyway, I'm really glad you called."

"So am I."

The moment she hung up, a broad smile of joy and relief crossed Isabel's face. "I did it, Jerry. Thank you." Her next words caught him off balance. "Now it's your turn."

"What do you mean?"

"I mean now *you've* got to grow up. I'm perfectly willing to love you as a tennis pro, or even as a high school coach if you want. But I refuse to marry a scatterbrain who doesn't know what he'll be doing in two weeks. Deep down I'm a very conventional person."

"Want to hear a terrible confession?" he offered. "I've discovered that I am too. So I'm going to hang up my racket and join the family business."

"You mean you're going into physics?" she asked excitedly.

"Not the theoretical kind," he replied. "I like to go hands-on, like microwave radiometer tapes and telescopes. I mean, look at it this way: If I grow up and get a degree, I might actually get to work in a grown-up observatory." He smiled sheepishly. "But I have one nonnegotiable demand."

"I tremble—what is it?"

"To get my bachelor's, I actually have to go through intermediate physics. And I want you as my instructor."

She began to laugh. "All right, but I'm warning you right now— fool around in my class, I'll flunk you without mercy."

He took her in his arms. "That's the way I want it, Isa, without mercy."

"Yes, Jerry," she answered. "But with all my love."

THE most important event in the scientific calendar was about to take place. The various committees in Stockholm were meeting to choose laureates in medicine, chemistry, literature, and physics. Their official announcements would be made in October, and the awards themselves presented on December 10, the anniversary of Alfred Nobel's death.

Nomination forms had gone out to the usual constituencies— previous recipients, heads of departments in the outstanding universities of the world, and assorted other dignitaries. There were also self-propelled candidates like Dmitri Avilov, who openly solicited letters of recommendation from influential colleagues.

55 **ADAM** Isabel da Costa's achievement completed the final dimension of Einstein's theory of the universe, and there was no hesitation among the members of the Swedish Academy of Science about giving her the prize. The meeting lasted less than forty minutes. Isabel's victory was secure.

Everyone in the Stockholm Establishment knew that the big battle to be fought that year would be at the meeting to pick the winner of the Nobel Prize for Physiology or Medicine.

Dmitri Avilov had laid the groundwork with foresight and patience. As early as the days when he had been a Soviet academician, he had visited Sweden every year, giving generously of his time, both socially and scientifically. Not only did he have grassroots support, but the timing of his success with Huntington's disease could not have been better.

Adam Coopersmith was not personally known to any of the electors, but Clarke-Albertson, the drug company, had succeeded in disseminating the secret of his grave illness. Moreover, beyond the obvious sympathy for the brilliant scientist, there was the consideration that by giving the award to Adam, they would also be honoring the work of Max Rudolph.

Sandy Raven's name was mentioned. Yet it was the consensus that he had already enjoyed his share of recognition and reward.

Then Lars Fredricksen, a respected senior member of the panel, spoke. "Honored colleagues, with all the sympathy in the world, I don't believe that scientists should be swayed by pity. If Coopersmith's illness qualifies him, why should Raven's good fortune *dis*qualify him? After all, his—"

Suddenly Fredricksen's assistant was at his side and handed him a slip of paper, which he quickly examined. "Mr. Chairman, I have more to say on this matter, but, for good and proper reasons, I request a fifteen-minute recess."

"As a gesture of respect to the distinguished speaker, the request is granted. We will reconvene in a quarter of an hour."

The physician rushed to a telephone. "This is Fredricksen."

"Yes, Lars. Good to hear your voice. I hope I'm not too late?"

"Actually, if you had called in an hour or so, I would have been able to tell you that your candidate had won the prize."

"Thank goodness you haven't succeeded yet. It's a long story, Lars. But briefly, I've switched horses. What would you say about Coopersmith's chances if you were to back down?"

The scientist was confused. "But I understood that Coopersmith was the candidate you wanted me to block. Believe me, it is not easy. There is enormous compassion for the man."

154

"Good, good. That means you can go back in there and harness that sympathy."

Fredricksen sighed wearily. "I know I'm in your employ—"

"Don't make it sound so crass, Lars. Let's just say I like to give tangible demonstrations of gratitude."

"However you wish to phrase it. To be honest, I would have voted for Coopersmith from the beginning."

"I'm very glad, Fredricksen. So long." Tom Hartnell hung up and sat for a moment, staring pensively out at the pond on his Virginia estate. He turned to his daughter and said, "And that's really what you wanted, honey?"

Toni lowered her head and answered softly, "Yes, Dad."

"After everything he did to you?"

"Adam's suffered enough," she answered. "Besides, he deserves it."

Her father could not suppress a grin. "If people always got what they deserved, I'd have been out of business long ago."

It was a little after four a.m. in the Coopersmith house on Brattle Street. Anya sat talking quietly to Adam's friend and colleague Charlie Rosenthal. She had long since given up hope of getting a full night's sleep.

"He seemed pretty stable to me," Charlie remarked with more hope than conviction. "I'm almost positive he knew me just then."

"He did, he did," Anya insisted, anxious to assuage Charlie's fears. "Do you know the most amazing thing? Up until a week ago we still had the remnants of a . . . sexual relationship."

"Yeah. That's one of the paradoxical aspects of the disease. While it's insidiously closing down all the systems, it keeps the sex drive intact for a long time."

The phone rang. "Who could it be at this crazy hour?" Anya wondered aloud.

"It might be my service," Charlie explained apologetically.

"Mrs. Coopersmith—I should say Dr. Coopersmith—this is Professor Nils Bergstrom of the Karolinska Medical Institute in Sweden. Forgive me if I've awakened you."

"That's all right. I wasn't sleeping."

"It gives me deep satisfaction to inform you that at noon today in Stockholm, two hours from now, we will announce this year's No-

155

bel Prize in medicine. And the academy will honor the invention of MR-alpha as first put forth in the *New England Journal of Medicine* by you and your husband and his team." Professor Bergstrom continued to speak, but his words were merely a meaningless flow of syllables. Anya found the strength to thank him and hung up. Now, with tears streaming down her face, she stared at her husband's friend. "He's won. Adam's won the Nobel Prize."

A moment later they were in Adam's bedroom looking down at him. His face—still unlined and still handsome—wore an expression of tranquillity. Anya touched him and said softly, "Adam."

Her husband's eyes slowly opened. He gazed at her and for a moment said nothing. His glance then fell on Charlie. Then back to his wife. "An-Anya," he murmured. "How are you, darling?"

She took his hand. "Adam, we've got something wonderful to tell you," she began. "You've won the Nobel Prize."

He looked at her incredulously and shook his head. "No, *we* won," he corrected her. "Without you . . ." And then, abruptly, his eyes glazed and he became silent, no longer present.

"He knew," Charlie insisted. "He was all there when you told him. Don't you agree?"

She nodded. Then the two of them helped make the disoriented patient comfortable, and Charlie left for the hospital.

When Terry Walters arrived to begin his day of nursing, Anya hadn't checked on Adam for nearly an hour.

Moments later she was startled to hear Terry roar, "Oh, Lord!" This was followed by the heavy tread of his footsteps as he raced into the kitchen. "He's gone—your husband's gone!"

"What do you mean?"

"He's not in bed. He's not in the john. He's not anywhere."

Then she and Terry thought as one. They opened the door to the garage. One of the cars was missing.

ALZHEIMER's had slowly but relentlessly deprived Adam Coopersmith of all his faculties. Now and then he had revisited his old life with enough awareness to make him despondent. The only thing he had not dared tell Anya was that he had resolved not to surrender to the disease its ultimate prey—his dignity.

The news from Stockholm had provided a neural stimulus, giving him a physical renewal he was unlikely to experience again. He knew this was the moment to act. He sat up in bed and, like an automaton, dressed and put on track shoes—an act he had not performed without assistance for several months. Car keys were strewn carelessly on the hall table. He picked up a set.

The garage door had been left open, so the only sound he created was the soft purr of Anya's Ford as he backed out into the street. As he drove toward the lab, he meticulously observed the rules of the road. He even parked in the correct space in the garage.

He took the elevator to the eighth floor in hopes of making a final visit to his lab. But spying several night owls still at their benches, he turned and walked to the fire door. Then, with dignity and grace, he mounted the steps and walked out onto the roof. Adam knew where he was and why he had gone there. He was not frightened.

He walked slowly to the edge and stood erect and proud as he surveyed the city bathed in the glow of the morning's early light. Then he sprang forward. And dived into the void.

Epilogue

LATE on the afternoon of December 10 the nobilities of blood and mind packed the Grand Auditorium of the Concert Hall in Stockholm for the ceremony at which the Nobel Prizes were presented. Seated in several semicircular rows onstage were some hundred and fifty members of the Swedish academies, in white ties and evening dress, for all to see.

At precisely four thirty, on a raised platform behind them, the Stockholm Philharmonic Orchestra began the royal anthem, and the audience rose as Their Majesties King Carl XVI Gustav and Queen Silvia entered from the right-hand side of the stage.

One minute later the new laureates entered in procession and took their seats in red velvet armchairs across from the royal party.

From a modest black podium bearing a large gilt copy of the Nobel medal, the chairman of the foundation delivered a brief introduction. The awards were then bestowed in the order listed in the benefactor's last will and testament. Physics was first.

In presenting Isabel da Costa, Professor Gunnar Nilsson placed her in a progression that began with Galileo, then reached—and

157

surpassed—Einstein. He also gratified the audience by noting the phenomenon of her youth; at the tender age of twenty-two, she was the youngest recipient ever of the prize. The royal party led the entire auditorium in a standing ovation for her.

Radiant in a blue satin gown complemented by a single strand of pearls, Isabel was a handsome young woman, whose dignity was ample demonstration that the circus aspect of her life was over.

They expected her to speak in Swedish, and she did. But only a single prefatory sentence: *"Ers Majestät, Ärade ledamöter av akademien, Jag tackar Er för denna stora ära* [Your Majesty, members of the academy, I thank you for this great honor]."

The rest of her strictly rationed words thanked, "My father, Raymond da Costa, without whose devotion and sacrifice I would not be here today, and my fiancé, Jerry Pracht, for his loving moral and emotional support."

The two men sat side by side in the audience, each in his own way profoundly moved. Ray was on the verge of shedding tears when Jerry affectionately whispered, "Congratulations, Dad."

Two months earlier, when Professor Bergstrom had called Anya on the morning of the fateful decision, he had not mentioned that this year the award for physiology or medicine was to be shared. The doctors had been persuaded to honor general advances in cellular transformation to combat disease—a rubric that covered not only Adam's achievement but also that of Dmitri Avilov.

When the organizing committee learned that Dr. Coopersmith's wife had once been married to the corecipient of the award, they nervously cooperated in "desynchronizing" the two scientists' schedules. Anya and Dmitri were not even seated together on the stage. But there would be no evading him when they were summoned by His Majesty King Carl XVI Gustav.

At last Anya Coopersmith and Dmitri Avilov were both invited to come forward to receive their honors. The king bestowed the prizes—first to her, as her late husband's representative, and then to him. Each of them now had an instant to express their thanks.

Even at so sublime a moment Avilov was still petty enough to want to punish Anya for being there. "I wish especially to thank my wonderful wife and beloved children. For it is for them, and their future, that we scientists do our work. And without them our life would have no meaning."

Anya had expected unpleasantness, yet she did not anticipate how much it would hurt. Her own speech balanced gratitude with regret. "This is for me a time of great joy and profound grief. Your recognition of the achievement of my husband and, before him, Max Rudolph, rewards not merely work of enormous scientific imagination but of great human compassion."

She caught a sudden glimpse of Lisl, seated beside Heather, gazing up at her with tear-filled eyes, moved beyond words. Instinctively Heather put her arms around Lisl.

The presentation was followed by a magnificent banquet for thirteen hundred guests in the Blue Hall of Stockholm's Statshus. For Isabel, the best moments were those that appealed to the child in her. She was transported by the almost make-believe moment when she stood before the eyes of the world, facing a real king, to receive a certificate and a gold medallion whose obverse showed a profile of Alfred Nobel. A check for one million dollars was at that moment being wired to her bank in Boston.

At the dinner Anya and Dmitri were once again diplomatically separated. After the dessert and toasts the guests repaired to the Gold Hall, where an orchestra was tuning up.

It was at this point that Dmitri made an attempt to force Anya to acknowledge his scientific apotheosis. As the musicians struck up a waltz, he strode over to her and with a deferential bow murmured, "May I have the honor of this dance, Anya Alexandrovna?"

She smiled beatifically. "I'm afraid I'm not allowed to," she answered. "Doctor's orders." Her glance indicated the physician in question, Charlie Rosenthal, who was seated at her left.

"Dr. Rosenthal," Avilov acknowledged grudgingly. "May I ask what brings you to Stockholm?"

"I'm here in a professional capacity," Charlie declared. "Dr. Coopersmith's my patient. May I tell him, Anya?" he asked.

She nodded her permission.

"It's this way," Charlie explained. "Anya's pregnant."

Avilov's jaw dropped. "What? That is impossible."

"No," Charlie explained. "It's completely possible. Idiopathic reversals of ovarian failure are well documented in the literature."

The Russian was flustered. "Oh, yes, of course," he babbled. He forced a smile in Anya's direction. "You must be very happy, Dr. Coopersmith," he said.

"I am, academician Avilov," she replied, deliberately recalling his former status.

"Well, Dr. Rosenthal," he proclaimed, "another triumph for medical science."

"No," Anya corrected him. "It is quite simply a miracle."

EARLY the next morning the victors, all lodged in the famous Grand Hotel, were awakened by singers heralding the advent of Saint Lucia, the Swedish Festival of Light.

To each of them, standing at their windows, this moment had its own special significance. Dmitri Avilov delighted in his own triumph. But then, even after the banquet, he was already hungry again. And he could not comprehend that the larder of honors was bare.

To Anya the gentle flutterings of new life within reminded her that Adam had not only been there in Stockholm but would remain with her forever.

Isabel and Jerry gazed out at the choristers, arms around each other. "Beautiful, isn't it?" she murmured.

"Isa, this whole thing has been beautiful. But the best part is that it's over. Now we can concentrate on something really important."

"Oh? And what is that, pray tell?"

"Each other."

They had won the ultimate prize.

ABOUT
THE AUTHOR

Erich Segal

Writing to us from London, where he lives with his wife and two daughters, Erich Segal explains why he was drawn to the Nobel Prize as a subject: "The Nobel has become synonymous with the *ultimate* accolade, and the appeal for me as a writer was that people would obviously sacrifice more to get this honor than any other."

Segal spoke to numerous scientists about who gets the prize, how, and why: "I know some people in Stockholm are upset at my suggestion that it is not merely scientific brilliance that gives you the prize, but let's face it, all of life is permeated by competition. How much more so must it be when we are dealing with the prize of prizes?"

Although Segal is best known as the author of such best sellers as *Love Story, Doctors,* and *Acts of Faith* (all three have been Condensed Books selections), he is also a respected classical scholar who has taught at Harvard, Yale, and Oxford. He has written screenplays, including the Beatles' *Yellow Submarine,* and done television sports commentary. In 1989 he shared an award with Mother Teresa and Sir Peter Ustinov—Italy's Premio San Valentino di Terni—for "furthering the cause of peace, love and understanding throughout the world." And if they ever start giving out prizes for versatility, he'd have to be near the top of anyone's list.

PHOTO: GREG GORMAN / GAMMA-LIAISON

Secret Missions

Michael Gannon

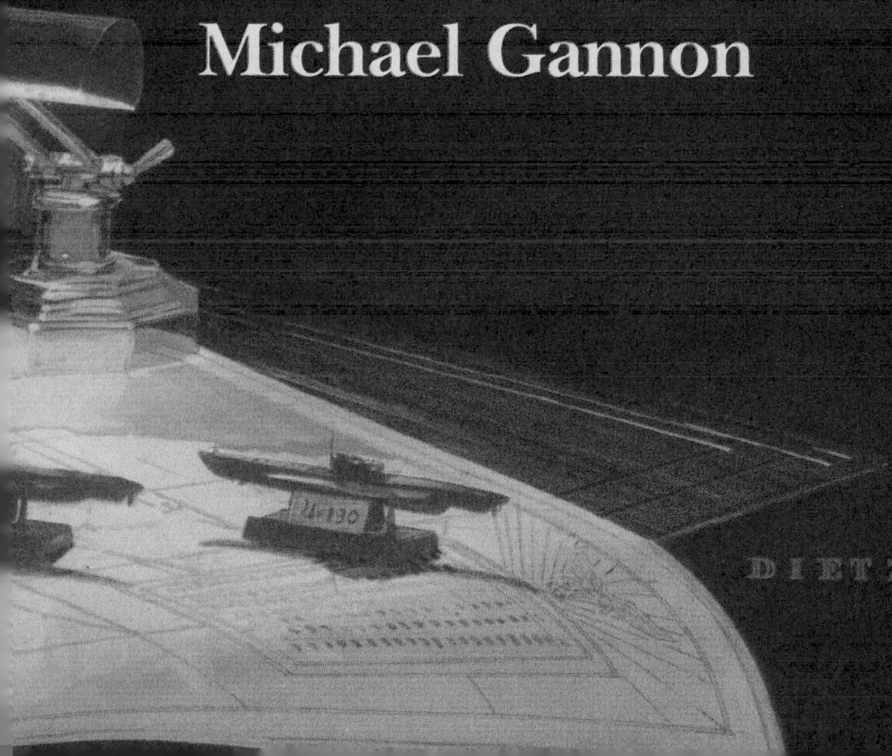

DIETZ

Secrets. In some lines of work they are vital.

For a Catholic priest, the secret of the confessional is sacred.

For a spy, secrets are the name of the game.

Now the game has begun, and both a Nazi spy and a Florida priest are about to discover that the price of keeping a secret can be very high indeed.

1

Thursday, January 15, 1942

To Peter Krug it seemed that his handlers could not have picked a less fitting site at which to test him for a mission to sand, sun, and aquamarine waters. The Pas-de-Calais coastline presented a scene of cold, compact ground under sullen clouds, the kind that came off the English Channel and hung forever in the winter. But, as Krug recognized, the atmosphere was irrelevant. The essentials were here: a military airfield, warplanes, and guards. On that basic stage his performance during the next twelve hours was all that mattered.

Worried that he might be challenged by forward sentries or by farmers who owned the land beneath his feet, though he saw no one in the dusk's last light, he hurried north over fields still furrowed where leeks and sugar beets had been extracted; and waded across the canals and irrigation ditches that, twenty months before, had barely slowed the 10th Panzer Division on its advance to Calais. Ahead he could smell the salt air of the Channel beaches. As twilight deepened, he began walking the final few kilometers through the woods that bordered the south perimeter of the old French airdrome at Le Touquet-Paris-Plage, now a key base of the famed Luftwaffe fighter wing Jagdgeschwader 26.

Nearing the edge of the woods, he saw the bright rotating airfield beacon and other lights of the airdrome. From his shoulder bag he withdrew a pen-size flashlight, a notepad and pencil, a towel, a pair of clean cotton gloves, and a can of aviation engine oil, which he emptied over his head, arms, and legs as a precaution against dogs. Then he buried the bag, which also contained bread, sausage, cheese, and water rations.

At the opposite end of the airfield Krug could see a long series of sandbagged blast pens. Day fighters. It had to be. He walked slowly and noiselessly, he hoped, out of the woods onto the airfield. He froze when he saw a guard to his left at some distance away—helmeted, rifle slung over his shoulder, pacing slowly, no dog, smoking a cigarette. A pinpoint of red light glowed on and off.

Krug was sure that he was too far away to be seen, but this was the first moment when he sensed—with a healthy twinge of fear—the vulnerability his civilian clothes imposed on him. There was no masquerade he could hide behind. In his black leather jacket and watch cap he was naked to the Wehrmacht sentries. At any moment, without challenge or warning, one of them could shoot him dead.

Well, if this was to be his line of work, he had best get at it. In a crouch he ran toward the blast pens. Better to go boldly than hesitantly, he thought, though he was on wide-open ground for much longer than he liked. Finally he reached the nearest sandbag revetment and threw himself inside it. Before him sat two of the older Messerschmitt Bf-109 day fighters, painted bright yellow.

Krug—whose background was in bombers—climbed onto the wing of the 109 nearest him, opened the hinged cockpit canopy, and with the aid of his penlight located the map pouch, from which he withdrew the pilot's handbook and logs. Next he reached for his notepad and began writing down the specifications for this type of Messerschmitt: horsepower, gross weight, maximum speed at various altitudes, rate of climb, turning radius, range, and armament. He quickly placed the documents back in the pouch, closed the canopy, and stepped down.

Emboldened by this success, and hearing no jackboots nearby, he proceeded to the next pen, and the next, and to the remainder of the day fighter pens, until he was satisfied that he had obtained all the information on day fighters—109s and Focke-Wulf 190s—that his handlers required. The data were now in his notebook. The pages were oily but legible. He sat behind a tail assembly in the last pen, leaned back against the sandbags, and rested.

BOOT STEPS. GUARDS. TWO MEN, very talkative. They came from the right and crossed the entrance of the pen. A dog on a leash preceded them. Krug placed a hand over his mouth and nose and closed his eyes, lest breath or tear give off a scent. The threesome passed by. Aviation oil had saved him. He breathed again and checked his watch. Then he crept slowly to the entrance and looked warily left and right. He saw the receding figures, but no one else.

It was time to take the second test. Across the grass airstrips, barely visible, stood the two-story white wood-frame fighter control center, with its railed observation deck. Three ground-level windows showed thin streaks of yellow light around the edges of their blackout curtains. No doubt these were the lights of the operations room. Krug began his run in the same low crouch he had used before, knees thrusting up close to his face. Halfway across the strips he fell to his elbows and surveilled the airdrome. No one. No guards visible. Security around here was certainly casual.

Up on his feet again and running fast this time, he soon found himself close enough to the control center to hear music from a radio. Then, quickly peering through a gap in the curtains, he could see an officer sitting at a long table, reading a book under a desk lamp and blowing thick clouds of Gauloise smoke. To the right a flight sergeant, no doubt a dispatcher, slept soundly in a camp chair. Behind him an open door led into a darkened room, perhaps a communications center. To the far right was the office Krug had set his sights on. A painted wood sign on the door identified it: GESCHWADERKOMMANDEUR.

He crept around to a darkened window and slowly pulled on it. Latched. He moved to the next window. Open! At age thirty-two he had the muscle strength, but not the agility, of his younger years; still, struggling, he managed to hoist himself up through the window. As he fell inside in the darkness, he barked his shin against a toilet bowl. He took out his penlight and surveilled the lavatory, found a door handle, and quickly entered the office, where he donned the clean cotton gloves.

Dead ahead was the commanding officer's desk, heavy with bric-a-brac and battle souvenirs. Krug stepped in front of the wood swivel chair and swept his narrow light beam over the papers on the desktop.

They were combat reports and correspondence—interesting, but noncritical. One by one he opened the drawers and examined their contents, which were mainly routine orders and forms—nothing worth stealing. The third drawer at bottom right was locked. Krug drew a steel pin from his pocket and had the drawer open in seconds.

He pulled from it twenty or so folders and one oversized envelope stamped GEHEIME KOMMANDOSACHE—Command Secret. The papers in the folders dealt with disciplinary matters. The envelope contained a lengthy landline cipher transmission and, attached, an Enigma-machine German-language decryption. Krug recognized its importance at once. After reading it through, he began copying the transmission. When finished, he placed the folders and envelope back in the drawer and turned the lock shut with his pin.

It was time to go. He was pressing his luck. From his jacket he withdrew his towel and wiped the CO's chair clean of any oil that might have come from his clothes. In the lavatory he also cleaned the door handle and, as he exited the window, the sill and siding.

Without incident he made the trees and found the spot where he had buried his bag. He slaked his thirst from the water canteen. The time was 0210. With his still gloved right hand he removed tan tropical-weight overalls from the bag and donned them to cover the engine oil on his clothes and body. And he waited.

After two hours Krug began to worry that he might not find the chance to pass the third test. But before long, to his relief, a lone guard, without a dog, came into view on his left, ambling in a lazy nonmilitary gait, a Mauser strapped over his right shoulder. He held a lit cigarette in his right hand. Krug checked the man's collar patches, his eyes straining in the darkness to make out the rank. When he was satisfied, Krug made his move.

Summoning up every vital power and mental edge, he crept out of concealment onto the airfield, behind his target. Then, with a rush, he went after him. The corporal turned when he heard Krug coming, lowered his rifle strap, and gripped the stock, at which instant Krug's right arm slammed against the sentry's side, turning him around. Krug knocked the gun away and pinned the sentry's arm behind his back at a painfully acute angle while, using the crook of his left arm, he pulled his victim's head back in a choke hold that he gradually increased in pressure, just enough to cause asphyxia without leaving a bruise. As the guard gagged, Krug whispered, "I'm sorry you didn't make sergeant. Be proud that you died for the fatherland."

Against his chest Krug felt the body's last warm tremors. He then picked it up and carried it to the edge of the woods, where he placed it in a seated position against a tree trunk. He straightened up the tunic and brushed the hair. Then he went back and picked up the Mauser and the corporal's helmet, examining the grass for signs of struggle. There seemed to be none. Next he placed the helmet on the corpse's head and strapped the Mauser back in place.

Krug had killed before, many times, but from twenty thousand feet, never at ground level. He was gratified that the kill had gone just as he had practiced it in training. At the same time, he was surprised how naturally—as though he were born to it—cold blood passed through his veins.

Back at his bag, he made a sandwich from the bread, sausage, and cheese. Newly fortified, and with all his test requirements met, he began retracing his path out of the woods, across the fields, and toward Highway 143 and the gully where he had hidden the Peugeot motorcycle. His copilot and crew were at the airdrome at Drucat, above Abbeville—standing by with the JU-88A-4 *Schnellbomber* that would take them back to Hamburg.

KRUG sat at a conference table in the Abwehr offices, a dreary three-story concrete building on Sophienterrasse in Hamburg. When his two handlers entered the room, he stood, but not at military attention, for all signs of military bearing had been drilled out of him during the last four weeks. The handlers motioned him to be seated, while they took chairs opposite.

Facing him on the left was Hans-Joachim Groskopf, director of the air intelligence technical section, a man of medium height with a ruddy, intense face and thick black hair. To the right sat Wolfgang Kettner of the SD—Sicherheitsdienst—the SS intelligence and security service headed by Reinhard Heydrich. Kettner was tall and dark blondish, with deep eyes and a mouth so thin and slanted it appeared to be a slash scar across his face.

From Abwehr gossip Krug had learned that Heydrich himself had insisted that one of his own men, Kettner, be involved in Krug's training, since so much depended on his mission's success. Four weeks were hardly enough to prepare an agent with thoroughness, but the surprise Japanese action at Pearl Harbor and the opening of full-scale German-U.S. hostilities had placed everyone on an accelerated schedule. Krug was the emergency point man.

"Glad to see you back, Krug," Groskopf said. "No scratches?"

"No scratches," Krug answered.

Groskopf smiled. "Let's get down to business. We gave you three test requirements. Which did you choose first?"

"The day fighters." Krug handed Groskopf the oil-stained pages from his notepad. "You'll find all the figures there."

Groskopf opened a folder containing typewritten sheets and began comparing Krug's data against his own for each day fighter type. It was not a cursory examination. Groskopf's motto was Victory through numbers. Under his exacting tutelage Krug had learned, if not mastered, the usual tools of espionage, most of which would be of little use in the mission at hand. Even radiotelegraphy would be no use, since he would be three thousand miles away from base, and since both Abwehr high-power stationary transmitters in the United States had been seized by the FBI in a massive agent roundup seven months before. Those raids had also netted a dozen producing agents, destroying the principal Abwehr ring in America. Only six senior agents remained in the country, although there were still scores of subagents and informants, including a lone radio operator and skilled forger in Florida.

Now that the Americans had entered the war, the air over Europe would soon be filling with fighter and bomber types of American design. The Luftwaffe desperately had to have—as soon as possible—data on U.S. aircraft performance. What the fatherland needed now, Groskopf and Kettner had told him, was a *Grossagent* of superior familiarity with military aircraft, a man of single-minded intensity, unbounded energy, and daring. They had decided that he was that man.

"Very well done, Krug," Groskopf said, lifting his eyes from the spread of papers. "You obviously got into the cockpit logs."

"Obviously," Krug answered.

"And you copied the data exactly, which is important," Groskopf emphasized. "We need to know performance envelopes in minute detail. Blue-sky figures do not help us. Do you suppose a Yankee agent could have gotten these same numbers at Le Touquet?"

"Absolutely," Krug said. "The security there is porous. I had no trouble at all. Neither would an enemy. I don't know how we're winning the war—if we are."

"That's enough," Groskopf cautioned. "The next requirement—"

"I'd like to get the third one out of the way," Krug said, looking at Kettner's hard face. "I killed a guard, as instructed, and I made sure he was not a sergeant. You can check."

Kettner spoke for the first time. "I already have. The base flight surgeon reported a sentry dead from apparent heart failure. He noted the faint odor of engine oil on the body and uniform, but explained it in terms of the environment. So you did well. But don't think you're going to get away with the kind of death certificate you want every time." Kettner leaned back in his chair and nodded for Groskopf to continue.

"The, uh, last requirement," Groskopf said, "was to penetrate the base commander's office. What have you got for us there?"

Krug tore three pages from his notepad and handed them to Groskopf. "What you have there," he explained, "is a command secret message from the general of the fighter arm, Adolf Galland, dated thirteen January and addressed to air wing and group commanders at Le Touquet, Caen, and Schiphol. It describes a fighter training program for a new operation called Thunderbolt. Notice that, on order from the Führer, absolute secrecy is to be observed."

Groskopf looked up, beaming. "Krug, you really got something here. I never thought you'd come out of Le Touquet with a document like this." Kettner, who never smiled, now smiled. Krug sat back and drank in the faces of the two men.

"You will be flying to Berlin this afternoon," Groskopf said. "Tonight you will be driven to the home of Admiral Canaris, the head of Abwehr. SS Obergruppenführer Heydrich will be a dinner guest. Tomorrow you will fly to Lorient, France, where you will report to Korvettenkapitän Viktor Schutze, commanding officer of

171

the Second U-boat Flotilla. After that you're in the navy's hands. Your orders are cut—pick them up at the desk as you leave. Henceforth you will be known by the cover name Homer."

"Why Homer?" Krug asked.

"Because you're going on a long odyssey."

"I think I'll accept it because of Winslow Homer, my favorite American watercolorist."

"Whatever," Groskopf said.

2

I T WAS what passed for winter in St. Augustine. Temperatures were in the high thirties after the passage of a dark cold front. The Florida sky was a bright transparent blue, with a dusting of cirrus. Men in jackets and mufflers played checkers in the heavily treed Plaza de la Constitución. Squadrons of gray-white gulls wheeled over the Matanzas River, waiting for shrimp boats, while, three thousand feet above, droning aircraft from Naval Air Station Jacksonville practiced flying in formation.

Adjoining the old Spanish cathedral, fronting the plaza, was the parish rectory, a Second Empire–style residence from the 1880s. Two sabal palms presented arms on either side of its front doors. Around the building and its narrow yard stood a three-foot-high molded-concrete wall.

Only the chilly temperatures made Father Anthony D'Angelo feel anything like at home in this rectory, nine hundred miles removed from his native Manhattan. From the window of his second-story room he could look out on a slice of the plaza and, closer by, the flanks of the cathedral and its campanile. He opened the window to take in the air, which both braced him and deepened his melancholy.

This was the kind of northern cold air in which he had spent all his previous Februaries. Pictures of those winter times rose before him, particularly those from his boyhood years on Forty-first Street when he and his pals played potsy and roller-skate hockey with pucks from the candy store, shot BBs at water rats along the East River, ducked into the museums—the Metropolitan and the Natural History—when it got too cold, traveled to the Bronx Zoo for a nickel, and rode their Flexible Flyers down the new snow in Central Park.

Odd that he could not summon many images from the period after he entered Cathedral College downtown, and then major seminary at Dunwoodie in Yonkers. Piety, he guessed, was less memorable than mischief. After that—well, life became more regimented and respectable but no less interesting, since in New York just looking about on days off was something to do.

It was not New York alone that he missed on this Sunday morning, however. It was having something to *do*, something other than Mass, baptisms, confessions, convert instructions, filling out marriage forms, teaching Latin at St. Joseph's, saying the breviary—and golf. He was surprised how little he liked golf, which, it appeared, was every other cleric's avocation. Too slow, he thought. And no real exercise to it. Why wasn't there a handball court in town?

St. Augustine just did not have that much to offer once you had seen the historic sites. There was a small art colony and an amateur theater company that was quite good. But over all, the venerable Spanish town was pretty darn boring—except, you could say, on weekends, when it filled with soldiers and sailors from nearby bases. Then it sometimes became the disorderly garrison town it had been in Colonial times. But Tony saw little of that. Rectory life and the collar insulated him from the multitude of sins he heard about only in the confessional.

Bishop Francis A. Garvey, chancellor of the diocese, had entreated the bishops of the priest-rich northern dioceses to lend him clergy to assist military chaplains in caring for the exploding numbers of Catholic soldiers, sailors, and airmen at Florida camps and bases. Archbishop Francis Spellman of New York, alone among them, had responded, and sent him Tony. It was not what Tony himself had wished for. He had begged Spellman's auxiliaries for permission to enter one of the military services as a chaplain. From his soul he detested the Fascism that had ruined his father's Italy and assumed wanton power in Germany, and he zealously willed its final destruction.

Instead, Spellman sent him on loan to Garvey to replace a Florida priest who *did* go into the chaplaincy. That hurt. Yet he could see that he was needed here in priest-poor Florida, especially now

173

that war had been declared and the state was filling up with tens of thousands of servicemen.

Bishop Garvey probably had a dose of saintliness. The legend on his episcopal coat of arms read VIRTUE IN HARD WORK—and the man worked all the time. Tom Murphy, the interim pastor, worked less hard, but if kindness and humor were virtues, Tom was making good grades, too. Tony liked Tom's way with his dog. "A Jack Russell terrier—he'll take a varmint to ground!" Tom would say proudly. Larry Byrne, the other assistant, with his pious, obliging, joyful nature, was heaven-bound, no question about it. As for himself, Tony was looking at a long stretch in purgatory.

He closed the window and looked at his watch: 11:05. Getting close to Mass time. He stepped into his Rogers Peet black worsted cassock and fastened a fresh linen collar around his neck. He checked the results in the dresser mirror, combed his black hair, wet his right index finger, and ran it across both bushy eyebrows, which, when he raised them up and down rapidly, caused the girls at St. Joseph's Academy to squeal.

Eleven ten—got to go. Tony opened the door of his room and walked down the stairway. He paused by the hallstand to read the lead story in that morning's *Sunday Times-Union* from Jacksonville:

SURVIVORS TELL OF TORPEDOING

EIGHTEEN IN TANKER CREW REPORTED MISSING

In one of the most dramatic sinkings reported in the war to date, the 8200-ton U.S. tanker *Pan Massachusetts*, holding 55,000 barrels of gasoline, was sunk in Florida territorial waters by a German submarine last night, U.S. Navy sources reported. Survivors say that the ship was hit by two torpedoes simultaneously, causing the gasoline to erupt in a blazing inferno, and that the U-boat then surfaced to shell the blazing hulk.

Tony laid the paper down and walked toward the sacristy. The damn Nazis, he thought. They've come to Florida!

THE rough weather front through which U-*Böhm* had just passed was only the latest among many miseries that Peter Krug had suffered aboard this bucking, twisting submarine. Its commander, Kapitänleutnant Günther Böhm, rode over the ocean's surface as

174

though he pined to be a rodeo rider in the decadent country toward which they were headed. A lookout just down from bridge watch told Krug there was a sky above as chaste as German crystal. Krug climbed to the conning tower to request permission of the first watch officer to go topside. To which his ear, pressed to the helmsman's voice pipe, heard back a laconic *"Nein."*

Arrogant Saxon, thought Krug of Oberleutnant zur See Wolf-Harald Franz, Number One, who unlike Böhm, never explained his orders. Thinks he's so professional, when in fact he's only an automaton, totally lacking in imagination, not to mention proper respect and courtesy toward those who are far more important to the Reich than he is.

As if sensing Krug's anger, the helmsman spoke up. "Herr Krug, we've entered the Gulf Stream. There's lots of American air bases ahead, and we might have to make an alarm dive."

Krug nodded. Don't tell *me* about American air bases, he said to himself. Grabbing hold of the ladder, he went below again into the dank, reeking dungeon that had been his home for five punishing weeks. Breathing the fresh, dry air on top would have been a delicious respite from the U-boat's foul enclosure, but unlike the rest of these poor dogs, he should be out of this stinking sewer pipe by tomorrow night.

From the edge of a bunk he watched idly as Second Watch Officer Klaus Baumann laid the heavy *Marine-Funkschlüssel-Maschine M* on the wardroom drop leaf and began deciphering a transmission handed him by the radio room. Laboriously Baumann punched the letters into the device, which resembled a typewriter except that its top had four turning rotors and its front presented a tangle of wires and plugs. He read the results from glow holes above the keyboard and wrote the German text letter by letter onto a pad. After completing the decryption, Baumann looked over at Krug.

"You might want to come with me while I hand this to the Old Man," he said. "It's got some stuff you would find interesting."

Krug followed Baumann into the control room, where Böhm was bent over the navigator's table examining the *Wegenkarte*—a meter-square chart of the Atlantic Ocean. Krug had spent a lot of time studying that chart on his own. Drafted to a 1:6,250,000 scale, it could hardly be expected to show much detail of coastal Florida, but to Krug's amusement, neither Jacksonville, the state's largest city, nor Miami, its most famous, was shown at all, while little Eden was prominently displayed, between Cape Canaveral and Jupiter. Emil Lorenz at Eden would get a kick out of that. A pineapple town of fifty people makes the *Wegenkarte!* But agent, radio operator, forger Lorenz had earned it.

"Herr Kaleu," Baumann said, using the accepted diminutive form of Böhm's rank, "here's a message I've just decrypted. I thought you might want Krug to know about it, too."

Böhm took the decryption from Baumann's hand, read it, then said, "It's from our refueling boat."

"Refueling?" Krug asked.

"Yes. U-*128*—that's Ulrich Heyse, our 'milk cow.' Part of his mission is to top off our diesel fuel."

Böhm's bright, round face was crinkled in a smile. "But the time U-*128* spends rendezvousing with us tonight," he continued, "will not be shown on her war diary, in order to guard the secrecy of your mission, whatever it is, from the bureaucrats in Berlin. I haven't the slightest idea why we're bringing you here or picking you up, but we do get our turn at the great American turkey shoot after we let you off."

"Turkey shoot," Krug repeated, relishing the allusion.

"Our orders are to proceed at slow cruise to Hatteras, sit on the bottom during the daytime, surface at night, and torpedo anything that passes by. Then, on the appointed day, we'll pick you up off Eden and go home."

"You better be there, Böhm," Krug said.

"*You* better be there," Böhm replied, handing Krug the decryption. "It looks like Heyse has had some successes."

Krug read:

ON 19 FEB. SANK TANKER 3000 TONS IN DB 9546. ON 22 FEB. SANK TANKER 12000 TONS IN DB 9439. PROCEEDING TO RENDEZVOUS AT 1700 TODAY IN DB 6848 WITH U-BÖHM FOR REFUELING. U-HEYSE.

Krug handed the message back. "Two ships in four days," he said. "Is that considered good?"

"Oh, yes—for someone who's pretty much standing still to save fuel," Böhm said. "*One twenty-eight* will meet us at 1700 hours, so it will still be daylight. The problem is finding each other." He pulled out a grid chart of Florida and adjacent waters. "DB 6848 is here." He pointed to a position about a hundred and twenty nautical miles due east of Matanzas Inlet.

Böhm went on to explain the difficulties that faced him and Heyse three hours hence. Although the two boats could take fixes on each other's transmissions, it was as much a matter of luck as of skill whether they would be able to see each other at or near the appointed hour. The problem was the U-boat's low silhouette and camouflage-haze-gray paint scheme. That was why the rendezvous was set at an hour and a half before sunset. American aircraft apparently did not fly that often or else did not know a U-boat when they saw one. Still, the lookouts would keep their eyes peeled. There were a lot of airfields nearby. You never knew.

"We should start receiving transmissions from *128* anytime now," Böhm concluded. "In the meantime, Krug, enjoy the last hours of your cruise. I don't suppose you have any complaints?" He smiled.

"Yes, I have, Böhm. I don't like that s.o.b. Franz. You have a real jerk for second-in-command."

Böhm was quick to answer. "An officer's value to a U-boat bears no relation to his likability. So long as Franz does his job, that's all that concerns me." He looked hard at Krug. "Since you brought up likes and dislikes, I may as well say you haven't exactly made yourself very likable. Your words and actions convey a certain nature and intent not in keeping with navy spirit. It's something about the chill in your eyes, the acid in your voice, the unnecessary salute you give each morning to the Führer's photograph, your unwillingness to engage in casual conversation. You're a dark mystery, Krug. The crewmen don't understand you, and they don't like you. If knowing that will help you conduct your mission, then I'm glad I said it."

Krug looked steadily ahead, expressionless. "You have something against the Führer?"

Böhm raised his eyes to the overhead. "Oh, don't be a fool. The photo is standard issue. We don't feel that we have to light candles before it every day. Any other complaints?"

"Yes," Krug said. "In all my years as a bomber pilot I have

177

never experienced such turbulence as you create by careening about on the surface over every storm-tossed wave you can find. I know these boats weren't made for my convenience, but yes, that's a complaint."

"It's a pretty silly one. This is your only means of getting to Florida, not to mention getting back, unless you would have preferred to take a blockade-runner to Argentina and then swim across the Rio Grande."

He was interrupted by the radio operator, Kurt Schneewind, whom everyone on board called Puster—"Blower."

"Message from U-*Heyse,* Herr Kaleu."

"Very well, Puster." Böhm read the decrypted message, after which he abruptly ducked through the hatch to draft a reply.

LEFT to his boredom, Krug climbed onto the still warm bunk he shared with one of the officers, lay back, and let his mind roam.

Böhm was right. Krug had exhibited too much of his brittle military-political side and not enough of the persona he had adopted for his mission. He should have used these weeks for projecting a certain warmth and friendliness—however feigned—for perfecting his conversational skills, and for establishing the look and eye of an artist, since those were the attributes he would have to display after landing.

A man could be hard in the conduct of his military and political responsibilities, yet soft in matters of art and the heart. On his other side, Krug persuaded himself, was the draftsman and painter of nature, the man of gentle habits, refined manners, and cultural high taste. Now the artist in him could serve the state, and the painter he once had been years ago would emerge again.

Watercolorist was to be his cover. He had proved to Abwehr officials that, like riding a bicycle, using a color wheel was a skill one never forgot. His demonstration paintings had been as good as what he used to turn out, exhibit, and sell in Chicago. In fact, his sense of color had matured.

SS Obergruppenführer Reinhard Heydrich, in fact, having seen the sample watercolors, had encouraged him to make pictorial art his leisure avocation during wartime. "An eye like yours should not be wasted," Heydrich had said to him during dinner that night at

Admiral Canaris' home in southwest Berlin. "Just as I try not to waste my ear."

Heydrich's meaning became clear when, following coffee, he opened a violin case on the piano bench and, after tuning his instrument, performed a Beethoven sonata with manifest virtuosity.

Krug found himself rendered breathless at the sight of this tall, hawk-nosed, blond, blue-eyed god of a man in field-gray SS service uniform—fencer, fighter pilot, chief of the SD and the Gestapo, who was also capable of tender grace and delicate emotion. Heydrich was the ideal mix, Krug exulted, of brutality and sentimentality—the perfect Nordic type, Siegfried incarnate.

When the concert was over, Heydrich stowed his violin and came around to where Krug sat. "We must talk, you and I," he said. Heydrich took Krug by the arm and walked him toward the far corner of an adjoining salon. "Did you know that in the war of '14–'18 our host, Admiral Canaris, was a military intelligence dynamo? He made a number of overland escapes, crossing borders dressed as a monk. He even once shot and killed a priest."

"A priest?"

"Yes. On one of his adventures he was arrested in Italy. He escaped by coaxing the prison chaplain into his cell, killing him, and walking out in the priest's cassock. The story has always amused me, since, like Reichsführer Himmler, I was raised a Catholic."

"I, too," said Krug.

"And that's the kind of thing you have to do in this business. We need active, aggressive men. We need totally ruthless men. That's why I insisted on our people having a role in your training."

Heydrich picked up a thin leather briefcase and took out a folder. "Let's see. Peter Krug, born in Hannover, 1909—son of Walter Krug and Barbara Dohler, pure Aryan bloodline, baptized Catholic, taken by family to Chicago at nine years of age, attended Lake View High School, took painting courses at the Art Institute, exhibited watercolors at Thurber Galleries, returned with parents to Hannover in '29, joined the Party in '33. You entered the glider program on the Borkenberge, received a commission in the Luftwaffe, flew bomber missions in Poland and France.

"Now, Krug," he continued, looking up, "you have to find out the performance characteristics of the American bombers, what their weak spots are. You will establish your center of operations in Florida?"

"Yes, Excellency. The bases there are full of bombers, I'm told."

"How's your English? Is it accent-free American English?"

"Better than that, Excellency. It's Chicago English—a very acceptable pronunciation that would give me entrée anywhere."

"Good. Now listen. A few things I want you to bear in mind: First, you must be absolutely cold-blooded. As a pilot, you've killed indiscriminately. Now kill selectively. You must be aggressive and totally ruthless. Second, be a bloodhound yourself, but never leave a trail."

KRUG was jarred out of the sleep into which he had drifted by Puster's hand against his shoulder.

"U-*128* is in sight, Herr Krug. The Old Man says you can go topside if you want to watch the refueling."

"Thanks, Puster." Krug grabbed for his jacket and mounted the control-room ladder. Climbing through the tower hatch onto the narrow steel bridge above, he took a position alongside Böhm, who, like the rest of the bridge detail, was wearing a double-breasted gray-green leather coat and pants. Oh, but the air smelled good.

He let his eyes follow the Old Man's binoculars to port. There was the U-boat! He could see it with his bare eyes—gray against an azure sea—headed almost directly toward them, hull down, its conning tower leaning back and forth with the waves. He looked at his watch. The rendezvous was running later than planned.

To either side of Böhm and aft, four lookouts surveyed the sea and sky, sweeping the sectors assigned to them with binoculars, searching for danger. Meanwhile, a ten-man deck force snaked a fuel hose out of its container and secured the nozzle at one end into a fuel bunker. U-*128* was pulling close, and Krug could see Heyse's deck force similarly engaged in laying out a hose. When the two boats lay to, Böhm used a megaphone to call across to Heyse, "Heil, *128*. Congratulations on your ships. We're ready."

"Thank you," Heyse shouted back. "Welcome to Florida. If you're ready, I'll send a dinghy with our line and bring back yours."

"Agreed," Böhm yelled.

While the two deck forces proceeded to their urgent and delicate business, Krug had leisure to lean against the periscope housing and take in the sunset. A vivid tangerine sun hung just above the horizon. Looking up, he saw the color change in luminous gradations to a mackerel sky. To paint this marine scene, he would lay down a wash of various hues for a misty, soft impression. . . .

"*Alarmmm!*" The dread scream suddenly came from starboard. "*Flugboot!*"

The lookout's hand chopped excitedly five points starboard off the stern. Böhm raised his glasses and confirmed the sighting, then took his megaphone. "Heyse! Flying boat!"

Diving was out of the question. And the connecting hoses meant that the boats could not even maneuver. There was only one defense. "Gun crew to antiaircraft," Böhm shouted. "Fire on my command."

With the fear that filled men who knew that death was approaching, the gun crew hurriedly manned the twin machine guns behind the bridge.

Krug turned to Böhm. "If you lend me your glasses, I should be able to tell you something about that aircraft." Böhm nodded and removed the strap from around his neck. Krug swung the binoculars around toward the aircraft.

"It's a PBY-5 Catalina," he said. "American navy patrol bomber flying boat. Carries four depth bombs on its wings." Krug paused, lowered the glasses, squinted, raised the lenses again, and gave them back with a smile. "I don't know what lucky star you were born under, Böhm, but that plane's got no bombs."

"No bombs?"

"The bomb racks are empty, and there's no interior bomb bay. The most he can do is spray your crew with gunfire. I think the combined antiaircraft of both boats can easily fight it out with him."

"Good." Böhm raised his megaphone to port. "Heyse! Enemy has no bombs. Repeat, no bombs. Guns only." He yelled fore and aft, "Deck force, take cover forward of the tower."

Krug watched, fascinated, as the PBY swooped down on them like a giant condor.

"Look alive now," Böhm directed the gun crew. "Here he comes. . . . He's in range. . . . Commence firing!"

The guns shook angrily: *Dacca-dacca-dacca-dacca* . . .

181

3

PATROL plane commander Lieutenant j.g. Beauregard Burke pulled the mike close to his lips and called for a new heading from the second pilot, who was taking his turn at the navigator's table below in the PBY-5 Catalina, designated P-10, out of Naval Air Station Jacksonville.

"Navigator, course home."

Burke barely heard the navigator's reply over the thunderous din of the engines overhead.

"Two nine zero, Bo."

"Two nine zero," he acknowledged as he reached for the throttle and fine-tuned the power. To first pilot Ensign Raymond A. Hope, seated at the controls on his right, Burke gave the first good news Hope or any of the six other men on board had heard after ten straight hours of flying. "We're headin' for the barn, old son."

Burke disconnected the autopilot, then muscled in the ailerons and rudder. After what seemed like five full seconds the flying boat responded. A slow turn completed and the high, long, flexing wing level again, Burke handed over the controls to Hope and eased his stiff frame out of the seat.

"Ray, maintain altitude and call me when you see the river."

"Aye, aye, Bo."

Burke removed his headset and ducked aft through the watertight bulkhead, passing through the navigator and radioman's compartment to the bunk compartment. He selected the lower port bunk, flopped down heavily, and withdrew a letter from his shirt pocket. The blue stationery was frayed from many openings and refoldings. Despite the pain it inflicted, he read the letter again:

> Dear Bo,
>
> You know that I'm a pretty direct person, so let me say right away that, as fond of you as I am, I've decided that the best thing is to break off our relationship. You have been the kindest, warmest, most considerate man a woman could desire. We had such good times together. But Bo, I am just not in a position to tie myself down right now the way so many women have done—

committing themselves to soldiers they rarely see, spending their days sitting around, immobilized, maybe for years.

Fortunately, I'm not the sort to need a man's company to do what I want to do. And an engagement would tie me down just when I'm thinking of breaking new ground. I'd like to go into military aviation myself and ferry airplanes. After the war I'd like a graduate degree in aeronautical engineering. Why should we tie ourselves down with promises that we know I can't keep?

It hurts you to read these words, of course, but I feel that you will understand. There will be many more people in your life. Who can resist your blue eyes, your dark brown hair, your Louisiana accent, your fine wit? You have so much going for you, Bo!

I know that you will have a wonderful life. Thanks with all my heart for being a short part of mine.

All the best,
Belle

Bo felt all alone. He missed his family in Plaquemines Parish. He missed his dog. He missed his former football teammates at L.S.U. He missed his fellow aviation cadets at Cuddihy Field and doing barrel rolls in N2Ss. He missed what he could have been, but was denied the chance to be—a fighter jock on a carrier. Bo daydreamed a lot about strapping on a F4F Wildcat, thundering off a carrier deck in the Pacific, and drawing beads on Japanese planes. But here he was, just a Catalina truck driver, and the biggest thrill allowed him in *this* craft was a thirty-degree bank.

Jeez, he felt down. And Belle's letter was the knife twister.

He remembered his first sight of her, at the tiny municipal airport north of St. Augustine—a tall slim figure in leather jacket and jodhpurs, long blond hair going on brown, rose cheeks. And what a vocabulary! She actually said what she thought. She was irresistible. She even flew airplanes. The only problem was, she preferred airplanes to kissing.

His misery was mercifully relieved by the first radioman, Pratt, who leaned low to report, "Lieutenant, a priority cipher from base."

Burke looked up. "Okay, Sparks, decrypt it. And please don't tell me it says the galley at base has run out of hot food."

"Aye, aye, sir."

Burke refolded Belle's letter, stood up to stretch, then worked his long legs through the hatch forward into the radio-nav compartment. He stood patiently behind Sparks' chair, waiting for the decryption. Finally the radioman swung around and handed Burke the message:

NET REPORTS U-BOAT APPROXIMATE POSITION 29 NORTH 79 WEST. INVESTI-GATE AND REPORT.

Burke turned around and laid the message before second pilot Ensign Samuel O. Singer, at the nav table. "How does this position square with our new course, Sam?" he asked.

It took Singer only a moment to check the coordinates. "With just degrees, no minutes, shown, that's a pretty big area. But our course home is taking us right through it."

"Thanks." Burke sprang for the pilots' compartment and took the controls from Hope. "I have it, Ray. Message received that a U-boat transmitted from somewhere ahead. Let's sweep the glasses."

With the binoculars Burke and Hope surveyed the ocean. The calm water was deep gray, except for the long, narrow hemorrhage of orangish red that poured from the dying sun.

"Bo!" Hope pointed. "Two objects three points off port bow."

Burke focused his lenses. "Two? Oh, yeah. I have 'em. Must be shrimpers. About eight miles off."

P-10 flew on. The report was that one U-boat stood somewhere near this position. Bo was reluctant to admit to himself the contrary evidence that gradually took shape within his glasses.

"Ray, if those are shrimpers, they're the first two I've seen with conning towers."

"Bo, those are subs! Maybe they're ours. How can we tell?"

"Only way is to dive on them," Burke said. "If they're ours, they'll wave, and if they're not, they'll shoot."

"Wonderful," Hope said. "Bo, we have no bombs, no guns."

"Get used to it, Ray," Burke said. "The rest of the world has gone to war, but the Florida coast navy is still training. The krauts may sink five hundred ships right under our noses, but we're not going to make a move until we're parade-ground perfect."

"Those subs are coming up fast. I see no flags or markings."

As P-10 descended to a hundred feet on glide attack mode,

keeping the two submarines slightly to port, Burke spoke into the mike. "Pilot to crew, we're descending on two suspected kraut subs. Prepare to receive ack-ack. Battle stations. Navigator, record exact coordinates, then break out your camera."

Now the two submarines were in full view, sufficiently detailed for Ray to see puffs of light gray smoke lift from the towers of both boats and curl toward their sterns.

"They're shooting at us!" he exclaimed.

Burke looked up to the port wing just in time to see it perforated diagonally across the fabric-covered airfoil. Tattered shreds of cotton and cellulose nitrate dope flapped in the wind.

"Turn away," Ray yelled.

"Hell, no," Burke answered. "Give him our whole broad underside? I'm going to bank against him."

As he stood on the rudder hard aport, Burke heard the metallic crack of rounds entering the fuselage. He hoped that none of his crew were in their paths. Fly, you lumbering wagon! Move it!

During the bank Burke could see the U-boats through his port window, the two black hoses connecting the boats, and, on each conning tower bridge, a man—an officer?—wearing a white hat. When P-10 was past the guns, he went to the mike again. "Crew muster. Normal sequence."

Burke carefully checked off the replies. "Hope, starboard pilot, unhurt; Singer, nav, okay; Bernard, flight engineer, okay; Pratt, first radio, okay; McClusky, second radio, okay; Martin, first mech, okay; Simmons, tunnel, okay." No injuries, thank God. "Bernard, damage report on wings and engines. Martin on hull."

Thirty-plus holes were counted in the wings, none in the engine nacelles. The port aileron was shredded but serviceable. The first mechanic reported eighteen perforations of the hull.

Singer handed up a slip of paper with the chart coordinates.

"Sparks," Burke called into the mike, "send the following message to Jacksonville: 'Sighted and engaged two U-boats at position twenty-nine point four two north, seventy-nine point four one west. Apparently exchanging fuel. Aircraft took incoming A.A. Minor damage. No personnel casualties. Recommend dispatch warships and armed aircraft.' "

Hope looked over. "What do you think they'll do at Jax, Bo?"

185

"They'll do nothing," Burke said. "Absolutely nothing. And our squadron has no depth bombs. I wouldn't be surprised if the war ended and we still had no bombs. Jax will sit on its hands."

Two hours later, squadron operations and training duty officer Lieutenant Frank Hudson motioned Burke to a chair in front of his desk at squadron headquarters and handed him a paper.

"This is a form that Fifth Naval District Norfolk has been using for operational reports. You had the first operational experience locally, so you get to be the first pilot to fill one out. It looks easy enough. Be sure to give as much detail as you can on the two subs—what they looked like, course and speed, armament, camouflage, that sort of thing."

"Actually, they weren't moving at all," Burke answered, "and I couldn't see any camouflage—they looked dirty gray and rusty."

"Whatever," Hudson said. "Just put it down on the form. And include your photos when they're developed. I'm anxious to see them. Now, what was it you meant in your message when you said that you engaged the two subs?" The tall, sandy-haired duty officer was well aware that Burke's plane was unarmed.

Burke explained that he had dived on the boats, since that was the only way to determine if they were friend or foe. He had been given no silhouettes or recognition books.

"And you sure found out, didn't you?" Hudson noted. "It's a good thing they didn't take out one of your engines. The Catalina's single-engine performance is marginal. At your low altitude, and no time to jettison anything . . ."

"I could be riding to Germany in a submarine," Burke agreed.

"You got it." Hudson sat upright and placed his forearms on the desk. "Yesterday evening we lost a ten-thousand-ton tanker off Jupiter. And early this morning an SOC-3 scout from Miami sighted and attacked a sub fifteen miles from Jupiter Light—"

"Well, how come Miami has depth bombs and we don't?" Burke protested.

"I don't know," Hudson said in a tone that revealed his own exasperation. "Fleet Air at Key West and Banana River also have DBs, and they're both training units."

"That ticks me off, sir. I'm the senior Cat pilot here. My crew has the top marks in the squadron. Can't you give us some bombs and ammo? Thinking about those subs sitting out there pretty as you please makes me mad. Getting shot at by them doesn't help, either. Meanwhile, sending me and my crew out on training flights with no weapons in the middle of a war is like sending a Boy Scout troop out into Bataan peninsula."

"Point taken," Hudson said. "I'll talk with the squadron skipper about it. Maybe we can detach you for a time to Norfolk, where you can load up with all the bombs you want."

"Thank you, sir."

"Meantime, finish the form."

"Aye, aye, sir."

THAT night Bo's call to Belle went about as well as could be expected. For security reasons he could not tell her what had happened to his plane earlier that day, though he was dying to.

"Don't you want to have a family someday?" he asked.

"Someday. Right now, like you, I want to fly. Jacqueline Cochran's organizing women pilots to ferry warplanes for the RAF air transport auxiliary. I'm trying to join up. In the meantime, I'm building hours. I have six hundred plus. I'm quitting my job next week so I can fly with the Civil Air Patrol, hunting submarines."

"What?"

"A CAP unit is starting up at Flagler Beach. The CAP is going to give us one-hundred-pound bombs—"

"What?"

"Bo, I've got to go. I won't change my mind about what's best for both of us. However, I'll be glad to receive your letters, but on two conditions. One, just news, no romance. If you break that rule, I'll have to have your mail returned to sender."

"Okay. And?"

"Two, buy some Ovaltine and send in the top for a Little Orphan Annie secret decoder pin. Then send your messages in Annie's secret code. I'll respond in kind. That'll keep our letters short."

"What?"

"Good-bye, Bo."

Bo went down to the riverbank and just sat for a while gazing at the impenetrable, glassy surface of the water.

Then he reached into his shirt pocket and retrieved the letter from Belle. Without reading it one last time, he tore it into small pieces and, kneeling, tossed the pieces gently into the water.

BELLE Hart ran after two boys across the fort green at St. Augustine, her Keds pounding the old Spanish path. Those kids, twelve or fourteen years old, were fast, but she bet they didn't have her conditioning. They could beat her in the short distance, but not the long. Besides, they were weighted down with the decorative brass pipes they had stolen from Orange Street Elementary. By chance, Belle had seen them on her walk home from her Work Projects Administration job as assistant playground director at Davenport Park. The boys were hauling the pipes out of a maintenance door, obviously to sell for scrap, probably so they could buy candy or go to the movies.

Darn those kids! Belle picked up the pace. Her lanky athletic frame bent to her will. As she made the turn onto Water Street, along the river, she saw the two boys halfway down the street. Flagging, they dropped the pipes with loud clangs, then doubled over, hands on their knees, gulping for air.

Belle caught up and grabbed both boys by their collars. "Now pick up those pipes. And come with me right away. Tommy Williams and Bubba Davis, I am surprised. Your parents will be ashamed of you."

"Where're you taking us?" Tommy asked.

"To the school superintendent's home," Belle told him sternly. "You can return his pipes and apologize."

"All we wanted to do was see *Captains of the Clouds*, with warplanes and James Cagney," Bubba said.

"If you ever do anything like this again, you will go before Judge Mathis, and he will send you straight to reform school. You won't like it there at all. No freedom, no friends—think about that!"

As they exited Water Street and reentered the fort green, Belle asked, "Both you boys go to St. Joseph's Academy?"

"Yes'm." "Yeah."

"Don't the sisters there teach you *Thou shalt not steal?*"

"Yes'm."

"You boys need some goals in life. Don't the sisters point out things

188

you can do when you grow up—provided you stay out of trouble?"

"What's there to do here?" Tommy said. "Shrimp boats, railroad, hotels, tourist stuff—that's the only goals in this town."

"You don't need to stay in this town if you don't want to. All you need is an education. Do well in school and you can do anything, go anywhere. When I was in college, I set myself a goal of learning how to fly, and I now have a pilot's license."

"Whaddaya fly?" Bubba said. "Bombers?" Both boys laughed.

"I'm going to whack you both over the head," Belle said, mock threatening them. After a moment she resumed, with a certain pride in her voice, "Piper Cubs, Aeroncas, Taylorcrafts."

"I'd love to go up in a plane sometime," Bubba said.

"Tell you what I'll do if wartime regulations permit," Belle said. "Stay out of trouble the rest of the school year, and come June, I'll give each of you a ride."

"Wow!" Bubba said. "Can we go out over the ocean?"

"A short distance maybe," she promised.

Suddenly Bubba pointed up in the air. "Look," he shouted. "There's a plane."

Belle looked up to see a blue balsa-wood-and-paper model airplane, its rubber-band engine spent, gliding in to a landing on the green, where two figures were running after it.

"Neat!" Bubba said. "That's Paul Ohlenburg from school. And Father D'Angelo's with him."

"Father D'Angelo's from the cathedral?" Belle asked.

"Yeah," Tommy said. "Everybody likes Father D'Angelo."

"Well, maybe I'd better talk with him about you two," Belle said.

"Oh, no!" they both protested.

Tony D'Angelo and Paul were examining some damaged landing gear when Belle approached with the two young miscreants.

"Hello," Tony acknowledged them.

"Father, I'm Belle Hart, a recreation director at Davenport Park. These students of yours stole brass pipes from the Orange Street school to sell so they could go to the movies."

"Is that right, boys?"

"Yes, Father," they answered softly in unison.

Belle explained that she was taking them to the school superintendent and that he could handle the situation.

"Well, if you don't mind, Miss Hart," Tony responded, "I'd like to go, too." He turned to the boys. "I really am disappointed in you."

The boys' heads hung in appropriate shame.

Then Tony said to Paul Ohlenburg, who was holding his wounded plane, "It's about time for your ride, anyway, Paul."

Tony explained to Belle, "Paul's father usually drives him home after school. They live at the beach. But his father called to say he was sick, and Joe Capona, the night watchman at Marine Studios, is giving Paul a lift on his way to work."

"That's nice of him," Belle said.

"Yes, it is. Tell me, Miss Hart, do you often spend your afternoons chasing down thieves?" He smiled.

"If you'll tell me, Father D'Angelo, if you often spend yours playing with model airplanes."

"Touché!" He laughed. "I deserved that. The answer is no. Paul just finished building his plane, and I asked if I could watch his test flights. I didn't build model planes when I was a kid. We didn't have much space for flying them where I lived in New York."

As Paul peeled off to await his ride, Belle continued, "I have to tell you, Father, I don't think you give much moral guidance to your Catholic people. Just look at these boys. Your church could do something more if it cared to."

"Well, what is your church, miss, and what have you done?"

"First Methodist," Belle answered, "and I think we have a pretty good record of showing our concern. Our young people visit the schools and churches of the poor in order to get to know them better as fellow human beings, fellow Christians, and fellow citizens. Do you do that?"

"No," Tony confessed, "we don't. We should. It sounds like a fine idea."

"But you won't," Belle said. "If you, the dominant religion in town, ever told me that your young people were doing the same thing, I'd feel a lot better."

During the pause that followed, Tony reflected on how unsettling it was to get dressed down by a young woman. He had never met anyone like Miss Hart. He shrugged his shoulders in discomfiture. What could he say? Probably humility was the best position to adopt.

"I'm learning a lot from you," he said.

Belle smiled. "I apologize if I've been too bold. Sometimes I'm a little direct. I like to go from point A to point B."

"Point A?" Tony asked. "I'm not familiar . . ."

"It's pilots' talk. I fly. A lot of pilots enjoy flying around the pea patch. I don't. I like going from point A to point B—direct."

"I see."

"If you'd ever like to go flying, give me a call. I can get you closer to heaven than you've probably been before—at least physically."

The invitation was a stunner. Not since he entered the seminary had any woman suggested that she and he be alone together in any confined space. Nor had he forgotten the clerical rule: *Numquam solus cum sola*—never be alone with a woman.

"I'd like that," he said, surprised at himself.

"Private flying's been curtailed for a couple of weeks because of the war," she said. "We're supposed to start up again in early March. Call me then. I think you'd enjoy it." She smiled.

Tony, totally undone, reached for his handkerchief and blew into it as hard as he could.

THERE had already been one nationwide FBI roundup of German aliens, in December 1941, and aliens had been ordered to reregister twice since then. Paul wondered how much longer he and his father, Hans, would be able to escape detection. They had reregistered as ordered. Their name, Ohlenburg, was too obviously German for them to do otherwise. But his father, an Abwehr contact, was skating on the edge of active espionage.

If the FBI caught on to his father, and he was arrested, Paul would likely go to prison with him. The thought was thoroughly depressing, not just because he feared what the Americans might do to them, but because the wonderful, familiar world Paul had grown up to love would disappear, perhaps forever.

That world was the ocean, the beaches, and the Intracoastal Waterway. Living on St. Augustine Beach, where his father operated the White Surf Cottages, Paul was addicted to his surroundings. Morning and night his nostrils savored the briny air. Daily his eyes feasted on the changing colors of the sea's expanse, his hearing resonated to the everlasting roll of swells becoming breakers.

That was his world, and the closer the hour came when he and his father were to pick up an agent named Homer from the same surf, the more apprehensive Paul became.

Two nights before, a transmission had come in. Subagent Lorenz in Eden relayed confirmation from the U-boat carrying Homer that the agent's landing was still on for just north of Marine Studios at 2300 tonight. That was four and a half hours off, and with his father bedridden with intestinal flu, Paul anticipated that he would have a much larger role in the landing than what was planned.

Paul's stomach was not doing so well, either, but the pain in his gut came from stress and fear. What would Father D'Angelo think if he knew? What would his classmates think?

At school he was a member of the civil defense team. He had helped tape the windows to prevent their shattering from the concussion in case of German bombs. No one ever mentioned the fact that he had a German name. None of the kids seemed to care. Every morning, standing at his desk, he pledged allegiance to the flag of the United States and gladly sang "America."

Paul honestly liked America. He liked the people, the casual life, the total freedom, the chocolate shakes, *Fibber McGee and Molly,* the cars—especially the convertibles. So why was he secretly trying to destroy America?

"Because of the higher principle," his father kept telling him, though Paul was never sure he understood what the higher principle was. Because of loyalty to his father, that was really why.

"In total war everyone is a combatant," his father had told him. "We are all in the trenches. No one is exempt from the great struggle." Paul prayed that something would happen to the U-boat, or to Homer, so that he would not have to be in the great struggle.

But that evening Paul's father, drained from his fever, told him, "Son, I think you're going to have to drive the pickup tonight."

4

TONY opened his breviary with every intention of getting in vespers before supper. *"Deus in adjutorium meum intende. . . ."* But his mind was not on his prayers. His concentration wandered. It had been happening to him a lot recently. He laid his head back on the linen antimacassar and listened idly to the hoofbeats as a horse-drawn tourist carriage made its rounds of the plaza.

He couldn't believe that he had said yes to Miss Hart's invitation. Bishop Garvey would kill him if he heard that he went up in a plane with a young woman. Tony could just see the stern-faced chancellor handing him a return ticket to New York.

But Belle—should he think of her by her first name?—Belle was more than a person of the opposite sex. She was an event—completely unlike any woman he had met before. Physically attractive, yes. But an independent mind. That was what had gotten to him. She thought her own thoughts, made her own rules. Deep down, did he wish he had the same independence?

Was he missing out on something here, something crucially connected to being human? Living with someone like Belle, Tony thought, would have to be a warm, exhilarating experience.

He laid his breviary aside and stood up. It was nearly time for the supper bell. Better slow down, he told himself. Your head is racing out of control, not to mention your heart. After supper better whip out a spiritual master, maybe Jacques Millet's *Jesus Living in the Priest*, so you can reinforce the theory that celibacy is a higher good.

Better shape up, Tony.

SNEAKERS off, feet propped on an ottoman, Belle Hart reached for that afternoon's St. Augustine *Record*.

The front page was all war: STATE OF FLORIDA ON WAR FOOTING; CITY TO HAVE AIR-RAID DRILL THURSDAY.

There was a knock on the door. "Come in, Mother," she said.

A trim, slightly graying woman came in with a cup of tea. "I thought you'd want this, dear. Did everything go well today?"

"Oh, yes. I survived the little rascals again."

"I also wanted to ask you about that air-raid warning in the paper. Do you really think we'll be bombed?"

"Oh, no, Mother. From where? Vichy-controlled Martinique is the closest place. No. This is all ignorant hysteria."

"Oh, I'm so relieved. I'd just hate to have to go through what the people did in London."

"No need to worry. St. Augustine is the last place they'd be interested in."

"Well, don't get a chill," her mother said as she left the room.

IN THE DINING ROOM TONY, LARRY, and Tom stood at their chairs as Bishop Garvey, in black cassock with purple buttons, sash, and piping, entered the room. Forty-eight years old, slight of build, with a square granite face and balding pate, Garvey walked in a slightly hunched-over position, the result of chronic arthritis of the spine. Standing behind his chair, he made the sign of the cross and gave the blessing, to which all at table, and Mattie Mae, the Negro housekeeper, standing in the kitchen doorway with a steaming bowl of chowder, responded, "Amen."

"Good evening, Your Excellency," Tom said.

Garvey nodded with a pleasant smile.

When Mattie Mae had ladled the soup into the bowls, Garvey laid his wire-rimmed spectacles on the table. Tony knew it as an unmistakable sign that the bishop was about to pontificate. Garvey had spent six years at the Vatican and had learned well how to do it. What was it to be tonight?

Garvey began with a recital of what the Nazis had done in Europe: the crushing of the Catholic peace movement in Germany; the pogrom against the Jews; the invasions; the air bombardments of civilians. "And now," he continued, "just in the last few days, the sinking of four American ships in the territorial waters of my diocese. The dragon is here, fathers. It has arrived, just as I've always said it would, but very few in the American church were listening."

Garvey expressed his dismay over the number of articles and editorials he had seen in the American Catholic press suggesting accommodation with the Nazis or, at the least, silence in the face of their global menace. There had been too much avoidance of the issue by the brighter heads in the hierarchy, while the dimmer bulbs had been allowed to establish the Catholic line that communism was America's number one enemy. But all along, Garvey insisted, the first enemy of humanity was the Nazi.

Heady stuff, Tony thought. You would not hear its like in too many rectories.

One thing you could say about Garvey—the man was a fighter.

PAUL Ohlenburg had the red Ford pickup gassed and packed with everything his father had said to take along: flashlight, socks, blankets, and a thermos of hot coffee.

"Don't leave here until one hour before the scheduled time," his father had told him. "You don't want to be hanging around down there any more than you have to. Remember, there's a watchman at Marine Studios. Keep well to the north. Park on the shoulder."

Paul was an emotional mess. He fidgeted, moved about his room, stared out the window. A half hour to go, just the half hour for *Fibber McGee and Molly*. He tuned in his radio and half listened, unable to smile as his mind kept switching to the world that was crashing all around him.

Finally, at ten o'clock, he grabbed his jacket, told his father that he was off, climbed into the Ford, and drove out the crushed coquina driveway onto the beach road.

KAPITÄNLEUTNANT Böhm came down from the bridge wearing red goggles, so as not to lose night-vision acuity, and leaned against the opening to his cubicle. He watched Peter Krug shave at the small washbasin underneath the lift-up writing table.

"I appreciate your lending me your cabin, Böhm," Krug said, catching Böhm's face in the small mirror.

"It's hardly a cabin," Böhm answered. "More like a cell. But you're welcome to it. That pitcher of fresh water is just for you, so you'll look presentable onshore." He watched Krug's long, bony face emerge as the whiskers fell away—a taut face suggesting tenacity of will, with a wide mouth and piercing blue eyes.

"I've been practicing my English by listening to Miami radio broadcasts," Krug said. "It all sounds very familiar."

"What about clothes?" Böhm wondered. "Is what you've got on there authentic American?"

"Yeah. The labels are all American, but they told me in Hamburg that the styles are a little out of date. My first task will be to stock up on clothes and shoes. I certainly have enough dollars."

"I hope their serial numbers are still in circulation." Böhm reached down to his bunk for a coastal handbook for the East Coast of the United States and opened it. "Headquarters told me your drop-off marker was Marine Studios, a saltwater aquarium just south of Matanzas Inlet," he told Krug. "But the bridge has not sighted it yet, and the place is not listed in the handbook.

195

I'd better get back on top. I'll let you know when we're ready."

On the bridge, Böhm lowered his goggles and raised his binoculars toward the shoreline. His lenses joined those of First Watch Officer Franz and the two starboard lookouts in sweeping the shore in search of a structure that Lorenz had told headquarters at Lorient no one could miss.

An attack on him now would be particularly dangerous, Böhm worried, since he had very little shoal water in which to dive. Just then, the forward starboard lookout stiffened.

"Herr Kaleu!" he shouted.

Böhm aligned his glasses with those of the lookout. "I see it." A narrow band of gray broke the black horizon. "That has to be it, a little to the south. Number One," he said to Franz, "have the deck force break out the dinghy."

"*Jawohl, Herr Kaleu.*"

"Number Two," Böhm called down the pipe, "bring Herr Krug to the bridge."

"*Jawohl, Herr Kaleu.*"

When Krug came up the hatch, Böhm led him down the exterior ladder to the deck, where oarsmen were lowering a black inflatable dinghy over the side.

"My instructions are to make certain you haven't left anything on the boat," he said. "Will you check one last time for the record?"

Krug shrugged and obliged him. He opened his bag and checked off its contents: birth certificate, lockpicks, penlight, batteries, Pyramidon headache tablets, and five thousand dollars in hundred-dollar bills. Then he pulled up his right sleeve and showed Böhm a narrow steel dirk in a leather wrist sheath.

"It's all here, Böhm."

"Then we'll see you off Eden on thirteen March," Böhm said, and shook his hand. "Good luck."

"Thanks. Same to you." Krug pointedly ignored Franz, who was standing nearby.

Stepping onto a rope ladder, Krug made his way down the side of the gently rocking hull into the pitching rubber dinghy. The oarsmen pushed off and began rowing smartly toward the shoreline. Krug looked back, fascinated to see, for the first time since

Lorient, the full broadside of the sea monster in which he had been riding. Truly sinister.

Krug peered ahead. The sea was inkwell black, with a moiré sheen from the reappearing moon. In the distance he heard the rumble of the rolling surf, and not long afterward he could see a long gray structure that must be Marine Studios.

The dinghy carried forward on the incoming tide. The crewmen used their oars to steer, and the rubber bottom bounced onto the American beach. One of the crewmen gestured for Krug to disembark. No sooner had he stood up in the swirling surf than the oarsmen rowed vigorously back against the breakers.

Well, here he was—back in America.

He turned to face the beach.

AFTER leaving his truck on the road shoulder and marching through the sand and cordgrass, Paul took a position in the dunes. He was stunned to see a lone fisherman heaving his line into the surf. There were *never* fishermen at this place at night. Darn!

It was Mr. Capona, the watchman for Marine Studios! What was he doing here fishing? Paul watched him walk back from the surf, set a long cane pole deep in a sand dune, and sit down. After about five minutes the pole flexed steeply. Mr. Capona ran into the surf, wrapped a yard or two of line around his open left hand and elbow, and ran back hauling what must have been a twenty-pound bass.

While his heart pounded, Paul saw a black, bulbous form emerge from the surf and a man step out of it. The boat from the submarine! The man had to be Homer! Paul could see him plainly. So, too, it appeared, could the fisherman, who ran heavily toward the boat, which was already receding from view. The two men faced each other on the beach, the fisherman gesticulating out to sea.

In the blink of an eye, the man from the surf grabbed the fisherman by a wrist, spun him around, and yanked his head back in a choke hold. For over a minute the two shadowy figures locked in a violent embrace. The struggle ended, finally, when the fisherman stopped thrashing and fell limp on the sand. Homer was on top of him in an instant. From his right wrist he drew a thin, bright object that he drove home with the ball of his right hand.

In the dunes Paul lurched to his left and vomited.

197

Disposing of a human body was not something that Paul thought he would ever do in his entire life. But here he was, with Mr. Capona's feet in his quaking hands, while Homer held the head and shoulders, hauling deadweight to the soft sand of the dunes, where Homer said they should bury him.

"Better to have a man disappear than to have him die of suspicious causes," Homer said. "Let's deposit this fellow where he won't be found until the next storm."

Was this really happening? Paul anguished as he dug furiously in the sand. He had done everything that he had prepared to do—flash his light, acknowledge the name Ohlenburg, and explain why his father was not there. But watching a man he knew being

killed and helping to bury his corpse—was this just a bad dream?

When they finally had the hole dug large enough, they lifted the body into it. Homer pushed the fishing pole in alongside and threw the bass on top of the body. Then he and Paul filled the hole. Paul knew that the questions that chilled his mind at this moment would never leave it as long as he lived: Was Mr. Capona really dead? Would he perhaps wake up in this sandy tomb? Did he really have to be killed in the first place?

It began to rain.

"That's good," Homer said. "It'll pack the sand so that this dune will look like every other. Let's get to your vehicle."

Paul led the way to the truck. "My father said you should ride in the back under these blankets until we pass the toll bridge."

Homer jumped into the back. "Okay, let's go."

Paul started up the engine and made a U-turn on the narrow coastal road. It was only a couple of miles until they reached the creaking wooden toll bridge across Matanzas Inlet, where Paul handed the tender a dime. A quarter mile past the bridge he stopped so that Homer could move into the cab.

IN THE main White Surf cottage Homer sat by Hans's sickbed.

"Your son said he knew that man."

"He gave Paul a ride home after school today," Hans said. "It's too bad the boy had to experience that."

"Can we depend on the boy's secrecy?" Homer asked warily.

"The boy is absolutely obedient and reliable, Homer."

"We can forget the code name now," Krug said. "I'll be going by my real name, Krug. Peter Krug."

"Yes. I know your real name. Lorenz sent me your documents." Hans reached for a general delivery envelope and opened it. "Here's your Illinois driver's license, an auto insurance policy, and the title to a car. It's parked out in back, a black 1940 Pontiac with Illinois plates—what I thought a Chicago man might be driving. Here's a Social Security card, three Army Air Corps IDs—one as captain, one major, one full colonel. Also a private pilot's certificate and the medical certificate that goes with it."

Krug examined the documents. "They certainly look authentic."

"Lorenz does good work," Hans said. "Now, private flying's been suspended for a few weeks. You'll have to watch the papers to see when it resumes. Any questions?"

"Yes," Krug said, "my watercolors."

"Oh, yes. In the trunk of your car you'll find a complete set, and a folding easel and stool—all used, as Lorenz instructed."

"Good. St. Augustine is supposed to have a winter art colony of some repute. I'll make myself known."

"Now, about your quarters. I've got you a room at the Alhambra Hotel, in the middle of town, starting tomorrow. The desk clerk there is Miles Zeigler. Everybody calls him Ziggy. He's a fund of information. But don't press him—he's a real American patriot type."

"Okay," Krug agreed.

200

Hans leaned up on one elbow and pointed down the hall. "We've got a room for you here tonight, second door on the left. Tomorrow Paul will drop you off at your hotel."

"Thanks." Krug stood up, tired and bored now. *"Gute Nacht."*

"Gute Nacht."

As Krug walked down the short hall, he caught a glimpse of Paul in his room. The light was out, the room silent. The youth was seated at the window, staring out to sea.

5

THE next day, after checking into the Alhambra Hotel, Krug walked the short distance to clothing stores on King Street. At one, he purchased a forty-dollar navy-blue gabardine suit with vest, a less expensive glen plaid double-breasted suit, a brown houndstooth sport coat, a tan sweater, several pairs of trousers, and an assortment of shirts. At a second, he bought a topcoat, two pairs of shoes, ties, and underwear. At a third, he found a money belt and a large suitcase. Back at the hotel, he changed into one of his new sets of clothes, then wandered about the small city center.

Certain of the narrow streets near the river were evocative of St. Augustine's Spanish origins, especially the houses with weathered arabesque balconies and sheltered gardens bright with red bougainvillea, green with hibiscus and oleander. No wonder, Krug thought, the quarter attracted artists.

The following morning, in his room, Krug broke out the watercolor box, easel, and stool. The varnished hardwood box had the look of long use, as did its contents, which was good. Ohlenburg had purchased wisely. The box had probably belonged to a professional, to judge from the quality and variety of sable and ox-hair brushes and the selection of watercolors. Krug made a short list of materials he would want to add, starting with paper. He needed blocks of twenty sheets lightly glued at the corners, large in size, cold-press, 140-pound weight.

Carrying his equipment to Aviles Street, he found the city's only advertised art supply store. The proprietor regretted that he had left in stock only three single sheets of the weight and size Krug required. Placing an order for three blocks of paper, Krug bought the available sheets and a cardboard case for finished paintings.

There was much to admire in the oils and watercolors that hung outside on the street's garden walls. But he could not linger today to study other people's work. Instead, he walked south and set up his easel on a corner of Aviles and Cadiz, where he could paint four different conjoining streetscapes on a single large sheet. The paintings were only exercises, but more rewarding than he expected, since they caught the attention of a passerby artist, Tod Lindenmuth by name, who introduced himself, stating that oils were his medium but he knew good watercolor work when he saw it.

Krug explained that he was just in from Chicago.

"I'm on my way to the Monson for coffee with Benoni Lockwood, head of the local art association. You should meet him," Lindenmuth said. "Why don't you join us?"

Over coffee at the Monson, a hotel on Bay Street, Krug took advantage of the chance to imprint his name and face on Benoni Lockwood, who seemed knowledgeable about every person who had raised a brush in St. Augustine. Lockwood named the artists who were active in the city that winter, which Krug made an effort to remember. After a while the conversation became boring, and excusing himself, he carried his equipment to the central Plaza de la Constitución, where he set up in front of the old Spanish cathedral. He concentrated for the next two hours, until he got hungry and headed back to the Alhambra.

IN HIS bedroom Krug took the sheet on which he had painted the streetscapes and turned it to its reverse side. Then, on the dresser top, he arranged several items that he had purchased at a drugstore that morning: an eyecup, a box of toothpicks, and three bottles of aspirin. He dumped the aspirin into the toilet and filled the bottles with the Pyramidon tablets he had brought from the U-boat. Then he filled the eyecup with water and dropped in a single Pyramidon tablet, stirring it with a toothpick until it was dissolved. Dipping the pick in the solution, he wrote carefully on the paper. The moist lines vanished as they dried.

After an hour Krug plugged in an iron that he had borrowed from the front desk, slipped a towel under the paper, and ran the hot iron over it. Brown-colored letters appeared: THIS PAPER WILL

SERVE JUST FINE. He stood up straight to admire the result, then tore the painting into small pieces.

He wondered what there was to do around this town while he waited for his paper to arrive on Saturday. He really needed to get to work. But there were no military airfields nearby. All he could do was practice his painting, eat seafood, and go to the movies.

He thought about the advisability of linking up with a woman for cover purposes. "Always travel with a woman" was Abwehr doctrine, since a woman companion deflected notice from a man's activities and rendered the couple innocent, feckless tourists.

Krug had no doubt that he could pick up a woman. From a decade of bedding Fräuleins, he knew that even without trying, he emitted an unconscious and automatic charisma.

He could afford to wait. The other sex would come to him.

He wondered if there was any gambling in town. That was the one side of decadent America that he had enjoyed in Chicago during his late teens: blackjack, dice, and the horses. He enjoyed it because he was good at it—or lucky. And now he had more money in his belt than he ever dared dream about back then.

He decided to go downstairs to the desk and ask Ziggy if there was any action.

SALLY Parkins stepped down from her coach car on the Seaboard Air Line train from Miami and quickly entered the station.

"Jeepers, it's cold here," she said to no one in particular. "Isn't St. Augustine supposed to be in Florida?" Three people on the station benches looked up but said nothing.

A Negro porter appeared in front of her. "You lookin' for a porter, ma'am?" he asked.

"Yes, I am," she said smartly. "I have two suitcases and a trunk"—she handed him the check stubs—"and get me a cab with a driver who knows the better hotels."

"Yes'm."

While the porter went about his business, Sally studied her pale reflection in a station window. Removing her hat, she patted her ginger hair into place, reflecting as she did so on what an unjust world this was, what with her skills as a hoofer and being one of the nicer-looking Jills around in every respect. But the Miami clubs were hiring nobody but blond tap dancers. Well, she was damned if she was going to dye her hair for thirty dollars a week. She hadn't left Manhattan to do that, especially when there was bigger money to be had.

When a Daddy Warbucks likes a doll, he will show it in diamonds, and she had collected her share, which she had sold to get cash, because once the daddies started getting romantic with rocks, they tended to neglect the bankroll, as though cash were beneath the dignity of their relationship. That's when you had to start rifling daddies' wallets while they slept.

Which had caused all kinds of problems recently, what with one guy planting a roscoe in her ribs to get his C-notes back and another waving a six-piece and threatening to call the police. Two heaters in a row, plus mention of the police, and she figured her contribution to the Miami scene this season was over.

And so here she was in this pony burg St. Augustine, which people said was also a winter resort but without the tap dancers and the horses. There were plenty of daddies about, but most had their wives in tow. Still, there had to be pigeons here somewhere.

"Got yer bags, ma'am," the porter said. "Taxi's waitin' at the curb."

Sally handed him fifty cents and carefully replaced her hat. Getting into her cab, she directed the driver to head toward the center of town. "And fill me in on the best hotels," she added.

"That would be the Ponce de Leon, ma'am," he answered, "followed by the Monson, the Buckingham, and the Castle Warden."

"What's the tab at the Ponce?" she asked.

"Ten dollars a day, American plan."

"Well, is there another hotel you'd recommend?"

"There's a room or two at the Alhambra, opposite the Ponce."

"Is it a decent place? I'm a respectable lady, as you can see."

"Oh, yes, ma'am. Just stay away from the bar when the servicemen are in town, and you'll get along just fine."

The driver pulled up to the Alhambra. As Sally got out, she looked resentfully at the huge twin-towered Ponce, across the street, and pledged that somehow she would dance in its ballroom, if it had one, before the week was out. Her cabbie fetched a gray-jacketed bellhop. After paying the fare and straightening her hat, she glided into the lobby with as stately a step as she could manage.

"Good evening, ma'am," the desk clerk said. "May I help you?"

"I'm told that you may have a vacant room."

"One left, ma'am, I'm pleased to say." The clerk—a short, wiry, balding man—reached for a registration form. "On the second floor. Two fifty a night. I'm sure you'll like it."

As she filled out the form, Sally heard a group of men approach the stairs behind her talking loudly about large sums of money. "See you guys in twenty-six after food," said one.

Sally asked the clerk, "And what is twenty-six, may I ask?"

"Oh, that's a room on your floor, ma'am, but far enough away that you won't be disturbed."

Sally leaned forward. "I'm very interested in people. What happens in room twenty-six?"

"The fellas have a high-stakes dice game in there, ma'am. Not anything a lady like you would be interested in."

"As I said," Sally confided, "I'm *very* interested in people."

IT WAS not hard to find room 26 after supper, as Sally simply followed the sound of brassy voices and the mixed fragrance of whiskey and tobacco. She was in her tightest, if not her best, dress. A confident knock, and the door opened to a very smoky space crowded with bodies.

"Yeah?" said a guy packing a Betsy in a shoulder holster.

"Hi, big boy," Sally said.

The door guard smiled, said, "Come on in, doll," and followed her movements with a low whistle of approval.

Quickly, with a practiced eye, she checked the table: real money in high denominations, no chips, and serious rolling. These shooters were pros. The men ranged in age, she figured, from the early thirties to the late sixties. Each held a fistful of banknotes in one hand and a drink or a broad in the other.

She made her first move alongside a thickset old crutch, who held the biggest wad at the table. "Bring me some luck, cutie," he said, and slipped his right hand around her waist. "I've got plenty on the table that says Blinker George won't make his six."

Blinker George went belly-up on a seven, which gave her the right to say, "If I had a daddy who'd stake me to a couple of C's, I could have fun, too."

Which the old crutch did right away, knowing it was a small price to pay where someone this gorgeous was concerned. "Are you for rent, pancake?" he asked.

"No, I'm not, Daddy. Only long-term lease." She moved quickly away to take a position alongside a very handsome thirty-odd the rest were calling Lucky Krug, admiring his gentleman's face and tall, muscular frame. And, of course, she studied the green-and-gray contents of his left hand. After a moment he turned to acknowledge her with a thin smile. "Good evening, miss."

"The name's Sally. How come they call you Lucky?"

He laughed. "Oh, I just hit nine straight. Real name's Peter."

"I like Peter better," she cooed. "What's your dodge?"

"Dodge?"

"Yeah. Whaddaya do for a livin'?"

"I'm an artist."

"You paint pictures? Well, slap the mooch! I didn't know artists gambled. Do you dance, too? You know, ballroom dance?"

"So-so. It's been a while."

"There's nothing I want more in all this world than to go dancing on Saturday night at the Ponce de Leon Hotel across the street. Before dinner I asked the desk clerk if there was a band there, and he said yes—in the Venido Room. I would just love to go dancin'."

"Well, why don't you?" Krug asked.

"I need an escort," she said, and lowered her eyes in mock shame. "You must think me forward for saying that."

Krug paused for a moment, then said, "I have to stay here through Saturday anyway. I'll take you."

Sally seized his right forearm. "Oh, Peter, we'll have a lotta fun! I'll go get us some drinks."

On her way, she swore that her hand had felt a shiv.

6

AT NAVAL Air Station Norfolk seadrome, Bo Burke nursed his newly assigned PBY-5 into position for takeoff. This was his crew's first operational scouting-and-search mission in the two and a half days they had been here on detached duty from Jax. They had learned how to load and fire guns. Then how to arm and drop depth bombs. Here at Fifth Naval District everyone seemed to know there was a war on.

Bo looked out with satisfaction to port and starboard at the four 325-pound depth bombs that hung from racks on the wing. The crew had .50-caliber guns in waist blisters, a .30-caliber in the bow, and another in the tunnel. Bo's Bombers were loaded for bear.

"Norfolk tower, P-six ready for takeoff," he advised the sea-drome controllers.

"P-six, you are cleared for takeoff," was the reply.

Bo turned to First Pilot Ray Hope. "Ray, let's uncoil this spring."

Reaching overhead, he slowly pushed the throttles to the wall. P-6 got under way, and the nose came up as Bo held the elevator control back in his belly. Abruptly P-6 broke away and became airborne.

Bo pulled the mike closer to his lips. "Sam, give me a heading. The big, bad Atlantic is dead ahead."

"All right, Bo," Singer answered from the nav station. "Fly one five zero. That'll put us on the northwest edge of the search grid."

"Roger that. One five zero."

Bo nosed over into cruise altitude, trimmed, and reduced power to 2000 rpm. Then he stood on the right rudder pedal and turned the aileron control slightly to starboard. The lumbering Catalina agreed, finally, to bank onto course 150 degrees.

To date, no U.S. Navy aircraft had positively identified, much less attacked, a U-boat off the Carolina capes. Meanwhile, the U-boats—no one knew how many were grazing in the Carolina pastures—had sunk sixteen freighters and tankers in this immediate vicinity alone. If Bo and his crew failed tonight to attack a U-boat, they might at least perform a lifesaving service by making some German commander keep his head down and stay out of the hunt.

But, of course, Bo wanted more. He wanted a German commander's cap, with or without the head inside it. He remembered with searing humiliation the greeting he had received from the refueling U-boats off Florida. Getting shot at focused your hostilities. Apart from Belle's love, there was nothing he wanted more in life than a U-boat kill.

"Navigator to pilot. You're at the corner," Singer reported. "Take new course heading zero nine zero."

"Zero nine zero," Bo acknowledged as he wrestled the Cat to port and established the first leg seaward of their search sector. "Cranking in the autopilot," he told Ray. "Let's go to glasses." On the intercom he called, "Pilot to blister lookouts. Continuous sweep. Report any disturbance of the surface. Any crease in the sea may have a periscope sticking out of it. Look for a feather wake. Out."

Ahead, the Atlantic was choppy from the passage of a mild, fast-moving front. Sunset was fifteen minutes away, the time U-boats would start to appear on the surface. Contrary to popular belief, U-boats did most of their traveling and fighting at night and on the surface, where their high-speed diesel power enabled them to make textbook bow-position attacks. Underwater, their speed was too slow, and their battery power too limited, to make periscope attacks practical.

In these particular waters, large numbers of ships nightly plied the dangerous passage around the Outer Banks and their extended shoals—Wimble, Lookout, and Diamond. The preceding midnight a U-boat sank the American bulk iron ore carrier *Marore,* bound from Chile to Baltimore. Survivors reported that following the torpedoing, the U-boat used its deck gun to fire over a hundred artillery rounds at the abandoned hulk.

Twilight would last for an hour more. Bo darkened the instrument lights as far as it was safe to do so, then grabbed for his glasses. They were coming up on some low-flying scud—wispy clouds—so that the ocean surface could only be seen in patches.

The Cat droned on until, "Port blister to pilot."

"Pilot. Go ahead."

"Sir, I have a long black object appearing on the port quarter. It may be a sub surfacing. I think it is, sir."

"Good work. Keep it in sight. Plane is banking your side." Automatic pilot off. Hard aport. "Pilot to crew, battle stations."

Ray reached over and activated the bomb-release key on Bo's control wheel. "Firing key activated," he reported.

"Roger." Bo pushed the yoke forward to begin a power glide.

"Port blister to pilot. I still have him, sir. Not fully surfaced. Decks awash. Scud makes it hard to get a constant sighting."

"Pilot, roger. Ray, break out the recognition book."

"Two points more to port and you'll be right on him, Bo.

Looks like a seven-hundred-forty-tonner, according to the book."

"Okay. I don't see him yet," Bo responded. "Descending to two hundred. Okay, now I see him. Bow gunner, open fire."

The forward hull of the aircraft shook from the recoil of the .30-caliber fire in the nose. "Tunnel gunner," Bo ordered. "After bomb drop, sweep the deck with your fire."

"Aye, aye, sir."

Altitude descending to a hundred feet. Speed one fifty. Now Bo saw the U-boat's conning tower in sharp detail—a narrow black form passing through a gray mass of bubbles and foam. Wordlessly, in deep concentration, he selected the exact moment to press the firing key, and watched eagerly as the four depth bombs severed from their wires in perfect sequence. He pulled into a climbing turn and looked aft. The DBs detonated in train, sending white water skyward in four violent geysers. Bo climbed to five hundred feet and began circling the attack position slowly, looking for results on top of the tangled water.

IN THE control room Böhm stepped around the periscope housing and checked the clock on the port wall. "Chief," he said to engineering officer Heinz Brünner, "prepare to surface in ten minutes. I'll give the order after I inspect the forward torpedo room."

"*Jawohl, Herr Kaleu.*"

Once through to the forward torpedo compartment, which had four torpedo tubes to the aft compartment's two, Böhm was relieved to find the men alert, excited, even buoyant. The launch of one or two "eels" would allow them to place a reserve torpedo or two in the tubes and free up room to bring down the folding bunks. Because of the unexpended torpedoes, the men who were assigned to bunks here had been taking turns sleeping on the floor plates—"hard lying"—which was normally a form of at-sea punishment.

Böhm looked into the eyes of each crewman. "Men, I know that this has been a sour-pickle time. Five weeks delivering a passenger to Florida, then standing offshore for a full day and night, and we can't claim a single ship in the locker. I'll try my best tonight to bring down a bunk or two for you hard-liers."

The men smiled broadly at their commander. Böhm made his

way back to the control room, where technicians stood by valves, levers, and handwheels, poised for action.

"All right, Chief," Böhm said to Brünner, "keep the boat heavy just in case. Be prepared for hard adive. Periscope depth!"

The chief engineer yelled, "Blow negative!"

At once, the always startling sound of compressed air filled the control room, while experienced hands whirled rapidly in unison among the wheels and levers. As ballast water vented, the boat bounced once, then began a steady ascent from its shallow bed on the continental shelf.

"Bow up fifteen," Brünner observed. "Stern up ten."

Böhm pounded up the ladder into the conning tower, followed by the bridge watch. The bow planesman reported the depth until he sang out, "Tower hatch is free. Boat's on the surface."

Böhm and the watch clambered up the final ladder to the tower-hatch wheel, where Böhm disengaged the spindle and pushed the hatch cover open. Built-up pressure in the boat nearly propelled them onto the dripping bridge platform.

Quickly Böhm swept the horizon with his binoculars. Nothing. No destroyers. No patrol craft. No merchant ships, either. Low, scattered clouds obscured much of the evening sky. The lookouts took their stations and began scanning their assigned sectors.

Böhm looked fore and aft with his bare eyes. The hull, still three-quarters submerged, pitched and rolled in the Atlantic swells. It was safe to come fully to the surface. As he was about to give that order, his eyes, quite by accident, caught the dark, terrifying form of an aircraft diving out of the clouds.

"Flying boat!" he screamed down the voice pipe. *"Alaaarm!"* As Böhm and the bridge party poured through the hatch in a blur, Brünner banged the diving bell.

Böhm, his boots hitting the floor plates with a loud pop, ordered Brünner, "Rig for depth charge. Go to seventy meters." Böhm took a position by the navigator's table, and, like everyone else, held on.

"Fifteen meters," Brünner barely got out of his lips when—

Click-*clang!* The boat shuddered and teeth shook.

Click-*clang!* Deck plates rattled and the hull ribs moaned.

Click-*claang!* Instrument glass cracked, sparks sprayed, knees buckled.

Click-*claaang!* The pressure hull lurched, steel shrieked, glass flew from wall to wall, lights flickered. The boat listed at an angle of sixty degrees and began falling out of control.

Round-eyed men struggled to keep their footing.

The lights flickered twice more—and went out.

Bo's watch read 0140. He could see the fourteen-mile beam of the Hatteras lightship on the port bow as P-6 neared the finish of its last westward leg of the night. Both Ray Hope and Sam Singer had spelled him in the port pilot's seat, enabling him to stretch out for a while, though not to sleep. Who could sleep after the excitement and the frustration they had been through that night?

What he had expected to see on the ocean's twilight surface— caldrons of water and bubbles mixed with oil, floating debris, perhaps a commander's cap—he did not see. For forty-five minutes he had not sighted the least evidence of a sub's destruction.

It was a textbook attack—the sub just underwater, the swirl plainly visible, the DBs an imperfect straddle maybe, but a straddle. He had every right to claim a kill. But the German navy had not cooperated, blast them.

FIRST, there was the slender stalk of the sky periscope and the short, foaming V-wake that followed it as the U-boat commander trained the lens around the sky. Then, that periscope down, he elevated the attack periscope and surveyed the ocean surface.

Finally, the entire wide frame of U-*Böhm* broke the surface in a froth of bubbles, like a shark's head, ugly with menace. It rose to its full buoyancy as heads quickly appeared on its narrow bridge and glass lenses bristled, reflecting glints of moonlight.

In the belly of the steel tube, oil-black hands fired the diesels, and the U-boat sliced slowly through the dark surface, gray suds scalloping from the bow. The exhaust roar of explosions from eighteen diesel pistons filled the air. Astern, the bronze starboard propeller left a greenish trail of phosphorescence.

"WHADDAYA got there, Bo?" Ray asked as he came upon his patrol plane commander on a bench outside the operations office.

"It's a Little Orphan Annie decoder pin," Bo answered, looking

211

up with a squint in the late afternoon sun. "Writing a note to Belle. I have to encode it."

"You have to *encode* it?" Ray protested. "On a Little Orphan Annie pin?"

"Those were her terms for continuing a correspondence. Said it would keep our letters short, which means unromantic."

"Seems this gal really wants to hurt you," Sam said. "First the Dear John letter. Now this."

"Actually, I don't mind doing this," Bo insisted. "I count myself lucky to still be in the game. I just can't use any gushy words. For a while it's going to be strictly business."

As Bo got back to his encoding, Ray looked over the official notices posted on the board outside operations.

"Did you see this?" he said. "An oil tanker, S.S. *Hennapoil,* sunk at 0200 today off Wimble Shoals. Bo, that's in our district. In fact—"

Bo leaped up to look at the notice, then hurried inside operations to verify the position on the area of operations chart.

When Ray joined him, Bo said, "I made a terrible decision." He put his finger east of the Hatteras lightship. "If we had turned north-northwest to base here as we were supposed to do—"

"We would have gone just east of Wimble Shoals," Ray interjected. "We had no bombs, Bo."

"But we had guns, and our mere presence would have kept that sub commander down. I wonder if it was our sub that did it." Bo sat down hard. "Just wish I knew what happened to that damn sub."

In the midafternoon light the southbound British-flag nine-thousand-ton tramp steamer *Battersea* hugged the Carolina coast as far as its capes and shoals would allow, in order to avoid the northbound Gulf Stream. Passing far out to sea around Diamond Shoals had been more of an inconvenience than a danger, for she had been able to do so in daylight, when the U-boats reported to infest those latitudes were on their seabeds asleep. Even so, she had zigzagged and mounted double watches. Now a confident *Battersea* thrust her blunt bows southwest toward Cape Lookout.

Lacking in grace, like all deep-sea tramps in ballast, *Battersea* stood high in the water, her red underbody embarrassingly revealed, most of her hull painted wartime gray. Prominently mounted on the poop was a 4.7-caliber gun. In lumpy, confused water *Battersea* was making a respectable twelve knots.

Above, the sky was overcast, like a plain linen spread. Most of the men just off the afternoon watch went to their bunks to nap or read. Others, out on deck, gazed lazily toward the Carolina shore, anticipating the evening's first electric lights.

Battersea was known in the merchant fleet as a pusser ship—one commanded by a captain who went strictly by the book and demanded exacting compliance with naval etiquette. More, she was known as the public school ship, since her captain required his officers to study Latin and Greek as well as nautical history.

When the third officer took the bridge to begin his watch, Captain Dudley Schofield—thickly compact, graying, with a face like crinkled chart paper—stepped out to the open weather. On his visored cap he presented the anchor-and-crown insignia of the merchant navy.

"Excuse me, Captain," the third officer reported, "young Purvis is here to see you, as you ordered."

Schofield turned to see a jacketed, nervous lad, apparently underage, clutching his watch cap in both hands.

"Come out here, son," he said.

When the boy made only mincing steps forward, Schofield urged, "Come, come, lad. I'm not Abdul the Damned."

The youth before him now, Schofield inquired, "Your name on ship's articles makes me ask, are you perhaps Jack Purvis' son?"

"Yes, sir."

"He had you late in life."

"Yes, sir."

"A fine man, your father. We served together on the *Rockpool* in the last war. A braver officer I never met. No doubt the salt runs in your blood. So you lied about your age and found yourself sent to me as an apprentice."

"I'll be sixteen in August, sir."

"Where are you assigned now?"

"To the steward."

"Well, eventually you'll get to try all the other jobs on board, except mine, the officer of the deck's, and the engineers'."

"I really want to shoot the gun, sir."

"Ha! So you want to be a warrior, do you? Well, the gunners had to take a week's course onshore and another week in practice. When we come up from the sea, you can apply for that."

"It's just, sir, I don't think going to Florida for sling loads of grapefruit has much to do with the war."

"And after Florida, to Savannah for cotton and to Philadelphia for lumber. I hope you think that's all right." He paused. *"Primum vivere*—first you have to live. You have to be alive to do battle. And to live, you have to have food and vitamins, which in England means you need ships like *Battersea.*"

He went on to explain how since September 1939, he had transported citrus and smoked fish from Florida, soybeans from Wilmington, canned goods from Philadelphia, wheat from the Midwest—foods that became the lifeblood of Britain's people. Sever the vital arteries, as the U-boats were trying to do, and Britain's defeat would only be a matter of time.

"I see the point now, sir," Purvis said.

"Have you had Latin?"

"No, sir."

"I want you to start. And don't let your bunkmates give you a hard time about it. Latin won't make a seaman of you, but it will put you in touch with great minds of antiquity—with Cicero, Virgil, Caesar. I'll give you a beginner's book. Are you game?"

"I guess so, sir."

"After the war you may want to go to college. I'm thinking of what your father would say."

"Yes, sir."

THUMP-thump-thump. In the U-boat sound booth Puster Kurt Schneewind pricked up his ears at the hydrophone effect reaching their hull. Twenty-three sensors on either side of the grounded boat were feeding a distinct audible wavelength both into Schneewind's earphones and into an electric timer, which enabled him to take a rough fix on the source. *Thump-thump-thump.* It was not the sound of breathing whales or porpoises, nor a destroyer's characteristic swish. It was clearly the propeller of a coal-fired steamer.

"Herr Kaleu," Schneewind said across the passageway to Böhm, who was reading on his bunk, "I have a southbound steamer seaward of us, course two four zero, range four miles."

Böhm threw his legs around to the deck, bounded into the control room, and ordered Brünner, "Chief, periscope depth."

When the depth reached 13.5 meters, Böhm was on his saddle in the tower. "Up attack periscope," he ordered.

The high-magnification periscope, fitted with cross hairs, came hissing up from its well. Böhm got a good view of the oncoming steamer. "Good size," Böhm observed. "Hand me the *Gröner*," he said to Second Watch Officer Baumann, standing by the deflection calculator.

Flipping through the *Gröner* book of merchant-ship silhouettes, Böhm commented, "Thank goodness our bomb damage was not as bad as I feared when we went plunging toward the bottom the way we did. The chief did a first-class job in righting the boat. We lost nothing serious. A few bent valves and busted pipes, that's all."

"We—I—simply have to do better in anticipating those flying boats," Baumann said. "This was the same kind of aircraft that caught us off Florida."

Böhm came to the silhouette that fit best. "British steamship, nine to ten thousand tons. I like her. Sunset's three hours off. We could trail her and, after sunset, catch up and make a normal surface attack, which would use up a lot of fuel. Or we can make an underwater launch now, when she's coming right to us, like a duck toward the blind." He made a decision. "Set for multiple launch."

As the steamer loomed larger in the lens, Böhm called out the target range, bearing, course, speed, and bow angle. Baumann worked the calculator, feeding the data into the torpedoes' gyrocompass steering mechanism.

When the range closed to eight hundred meters and the steamer filled the lens, Böhm said, "Tube three, launch!"

Rummms!

"Tube four"—he waited eight seconds—"launch!"

Rumms!

The first hit sent up a towering column of smoke and debris from the steamer's forward hold, while the second punched a hole aft of the bridge, causing a flaming water cloud pitted with splinters.

"Scope down," Böhm ordered. He turned to Baumann. "I missed

the engine room, but she's mortally wounded. The forward torpedo crew can bring down their bunks. They'll be happy about that. We'll steer around the stern to her port quarter. Both engines ahead full."

JUST seconds before, *Battersea* had been proceeding cheerfully toward Cape Lookout, her bows shouldering the long, easy swell with a sober steadfastness.

Then, with fate loaded heavily against her, *Battersea* shuddered from two savage explosions. The wakeless electric torpedoes had shown no sign of their coming. Forward, the tramp's thin half-inch hull plates gave way like paper and surrendered in a terrible swift uprush of fragments, deck machinery, planking, flame, water, and smoke. Seconds later another torpedo exploded, destroying the master's cabin, the engineer's accommodation, and one of the starboard lifeboats.

On the bridge, Captain Schofield flew six feet in the air against the gyro repeater, breaking three fingers on his left hand. Standing upright, he grabbed the whistle lanyard with his right hand and gave six short blows to signal the gun crew to stations. He ordered his second officer to signal the engine room to stop.

"There's no response from the engine room, Captain."

"Very well. Get the chief engineer down there to cut off steam. Send the damage-control crew forward to start pumps. Have the wireless officer send an SOS and our position."

Schofield ran to the wind boxes to look for their U-boat assailant. He saw nothing. Then, with dismay, he looked forward and saw not only that the ship was listing to starboard but that the vessel was going down by the bows.

"The crew forward reports that there is little the pumps can do, Captain," the second officer reported. "Numbers three and four holds both are flooding. The bulkheads have buckled."

Schofield could hear rivets and seams shrieking as the bows continued to settle. He did not feel the pain in his hand. "By Harry, if we don't stop our steam," he said loudly, "*Battersea* is going to drive herself underwater like a submarine. Find that engineer! And I don't hear any gunfire."

There was no artillery action, because there was no target for the gunlayer to aim at. The nine-member crew stood resolutely at the loaded piece on the poop, but they saw no sign of their attacker. Finally the chief engineer emerged from *Battersea*'s vitals. "The torpedo blast ruptured a steam line, Captain. The crew were driven out by the steam. They couldn't approach the valves. I'm going to try to get down myself."

While the chief donned an overcoat, gloves, cap, scarf, and goggles, Schofield addressed the second officer. "Have all hands assemble on deck in life jackets to abandon ship, on my signal, by jumping from the starboard side. The water will be cold, so we'll need help soon. Detail lifeboat crews to release the three remaining boats. The wireless did get our position, did it not?"

"Aye, aye, sir," the officer confirmed.

Meanwhile, the chief went down the steep, greasy iron ladder into the engine room, which was filled with a blinding, scalding fog. No man could stay in it for long. He made his way as quickly as he could by feeling along the tilted catwalk and deck. The engines were still turning, but slowing somewhat, he noticed, as steam dissipated through the pipe fracture. At last, his feet deep in water, he found the main steam wheel and turned it off. Gradually the engines ceased their loud labor and the propeller shaft abandoned its spin.

From his canting perch on the bridge, a relieved Schofield used what little steam was left to signal abandon ship with the whistle. The two port lifeboats made it down the side but in much damaged condition. The lone remaining starboard boat hung up in the after fall.

One by one the crew jumped overside from the slowing vessel, some not pausing, others lingering at the rail to screw up courage. One ran back to his bunk to retrieve a picture of his wife; he was not seen again. Another stood at the rail with no life jacket. Schofield recognized him. It was young Purvis. Schofield grabbed his megaphone and called, "Purvis, where is your life jacket?"

The youth looked around, confused.

"Here," Schofield called, throwing down his own jacket. "Put that on. Get in the water and swim to the lifeboats. Now!"

Purvis donned the jacket and, looking back at Schofield, jumped into the Atlantic swell. He, too, would not be seen again.

Once satisfied that everyone was off, Schofield hauled a wooden stool to the rail, threw it overside, and jumped after it, his captain's hat flying off as he fell. When he bobbed to the surface, he swam until he found the floating stool and held on, his left hand beginning to hurt now.

Withdrawing from him was the saddest sight of all his years at sea—the grotesquely tilted, wounded frame of *Battersea* on her knees, crawling slowly underwater. Schofield could hear the boilers come apart from their seatings with a deep thunder, followed by a loud sizzling as steam met cold water. Then her funnel lay over, and she simply went.

Tears welled in Schofield's eyes.

WITH his high-magnification periscope Günther Böhm saw it all. He held back from his victim on her port quarter. At the end he figured that the last man jumping off was her captain. Taking the usual periscope sightings as a precaution, he surfaced.

Under diesel power, he passed the survivors, tossing them life jackets, and reached the position where he thought the last man to jump might be. The forward starboard lookout sighted him. Böhm came alongside at dead slow and called Baumann up to interpret.

"What ship are you?" Böhm asked through Baumann.

"*Battersea*. British," came the reply from the stool.

"Are you the captain?"

"Dudley Rodger Schofield, master, merchant navy."

"I'm going to throw you a line and invite you aboard."

"I should prefer not, sir, if it's all the same."

"It's not all the same. You are a captain, and I must insist. No captain of any flag is going to die in cold water if I can help it."

To Franz, Böhm said, "Number One, throw the captain a line." But Franz did not budge.

"Did you hear me?" Böhm shouted. "I gave you an order."

"I will not assist the enemy," Franz said stiffly.

Outraged, Böhm grabbed a life preserver on a weighted line, and in his anger threw it too quickly into the water—not noticing a coil of line around his right ankle, which carried him overside, too.

When he finally got the line unwound from his foot and emerged from beneath the water, he swam to the life preserver. With the ring held before him, he kicked his way out to Schofield.

"Here," he said in German. "Take this line, sir, and we'll pull ourselves to the boat."

Schofield, understanding the gesture more than the words, was reaching with his good hand to take the line when two loud shouts came from the U-boat's bridge. "Flying boat! *Alaarmm!*"

Without looking at Böhm in the water, Franz waved frantically for the two lookouts on deck to drop the line and climb the ladder back to the bridge. Franz followed them down the hatch. The diesel exhausts closed, and the hatch cover was locked. The boat moved forward and down.

Böhm had never observed a dive from this close—outside. He turned his attention north to the horizon, where yes, there was a flying boat of the same type that had caught them on the surface twice before. Franz had done the right thing in diving. Fifty men in a U-boat were worth more than one—or two—in the water.

Böhm looked Schofield in the eye. "*Sprechen Sie Deutsch?*"

"No," Schofield answered. "Do you speak English?"

"*Nein.*" Böhm thought for a second. "*Dicisne Latine?*"

"*Utique,*" Schofield answered, pleasantly surprised.

The two men smiled at each other briefly, acknowledging the rarity of the coincidence. Then Böhm continued in Latin, "I regret sinking your ship, for reasons that will soon become clear."

"If that's an apology, I accept it," Schofield replied. "For my part, I wish I could have given back as good as I got."

"Are you a Christian man?" Böhm asked.

"More or less."

"Then I advise you to say your prayers, sir. When the bombs fall in the water, their concussion will kill us."

"Will kill us?" With a cold wave upon his heart, Schofield looked over his shoulder at the aircraft, now almost on top of them.

Böhm reached across the wooden stool and took Schofield's right hand. "*Vale! Auf Wiedersehen!*" he said.

"*Vale!* Good-bye!" Schofield closed his eyes, reserving all further communications for the Almighty.

To Böhm and Schofield, it all seemed to happen in slow motion. The four vaned canisters came off the aircraft's bomb racks simultaneously and made a curving fifty-foot descent to the water, the port forward bomb entering some twenty yards from their position.

The high-explosive charges sought their prescribed depth, where detonators released their awful fury.

In milliseconds each charge converted into a gas bubble that expanded outward radially as a pressure wave, traveling through the water at the speed of sound. When the waves reached Böhm and Schofield, they shredded the tissue of their abdomen, thorax, and lungs. Each man's hands uncurled from his flotage, vital systems shut down, and the sea closed over him.

The attacking aircraft droned in circles overhead.

7

IN CASSOCK and biretta Tony made his way through the sacristy and into the darkened cathedral, blessing himself from the holy-water font and genuflecting toward the tabernacle. As he walked to the confessional, Tony saw an array of civilians and servicemen waiting for confession this Saturday, though he lowered his eyes and took care not to notice any faces as he neared his post. He opened the small wooden door, placed the purple stole around his neck, closed the door, sat down, and slid open the grille panels on either side.

Footsteps and a rustle of curtain to his right. He closed the sliding panel to his left and waited until he heard knees meet kneeler. A penitent, a woman who sounded middle-aged, began, "Bless me, Father, for I have sinned. It has been two weeks since my last confession. I was uncharitable in my speech two times. I had three bad thoughts, I neglected my evening prayers two times, and I denied my husband conjugal rights one time. That is all, Father."

Good heavens! Tony reflected. The woman is a saint.

"For your penance say one Our Father and one Hail Mary," he told her. "And spend a few minutes thanking our Saviour for his merciful love. Now pray a good act of contrition." Tony then recited the absolution, ending, as he always did, with, "Go in peace."

A young male voice coughed behind the grille to his left. A high schooler. Predictable confession, Tom thought. Disobeyed parents, entertained bad thoughts. He slid back the panel.

"Bless me, Father, for I have sinned. It has been two weeks since my last confession. During that time I have had a terrible experience, and I need to ask you a question, Father."

"Of course. Go ahead."

"Is it true, Father, that what you say in confession is a secret? I mean, always remains a secret?"

"Yes, son. It's called the seal of confession. The priest who hears your sins can never reveal them, or anything else you say, to anyone else—not even the pope. Secrecy about what takes place in the confessional is the gravest obligation of a priest. I would be excommunicated if I revealed anything you told me. Does that make you more comfortable?"

"Yes, Father. I just have this terrible thing, and I feel it's a sin—the worst kind of sin there is—and I can't sleep. It's driving me crazy."

"Just tell me what it is."

Tony recognized the voice. It was Paul Ohlenburg. Definitely.

"Well, I was involved in . . . getting a man killed, Father."

"I see. Go on."

"It's complicated, Father."

"I have plenty of time. Go on."

The youth described in riveting detail the espionage work of his father—here in St. Augustine!—the arrival by German U-boat of the agent Homer and his chance encounter with Joe Capona, the night watchman of Marine Studios; the killing of the watchman; and the burial.

"I helped to bury him, Father. I shoveled sand with my hands. All he was doing was fishing. My father says no, but I feel it was murder. I feel that I'm—I can't think of the word."

"An accomplice?"

"Yes, Father. I wake up at night, and I see that body and the fish on top of him. I see his eyes opening up and staring at me."

"What does your father say to you?" Tony asked.

"He says that every German is a soldier and every soldier must kill for the fatherland because we're at war."

"All right. And you've not said anything to the police?"

"No, Father. If I said anything to the police, the FBI would trace Homer right to my father. They'd hang my father. I love my father." The boy broke into a single loud sob, followed by sniffling and silence.

221

"That's all right," Tony said. "Do you agree with what your father is doing?"

"I don't know, Father. He makes it sound so right. I'm confused. Right now, I'm all mixed up."

Tony stalled for time. What should he say? "No wonder you are," he said finally. "If I were in your shoes, I'd be confused, too. You love your father, and you love your father's country. On the other hand, you love your adopted new country. You respect the orders of your father, yet on the other hand, you believe and honor God's commandment against the unjust taking of life. Furthermore, you're unclear if this is a case of justifiable killing, as in war, or of murder. Does that seem to sum it up?"

"Yes, Father."

"You are very right to be upset about the death of an innocent man. But I'm sure that God knows that you never *intended* for it to happen. Sin is in the *intention,* son, not in the actual deed. You see, if I set out in my car to murder someone but had a flat tire on the way and couldn't get there, I'd still be guilty of murder in the eyes of God. Similarly, if some evil occurs over which I had no free control, I am not guilty in God's eyes. Your participation in the burial was forced on you and was not in itself a sinful act, except to the extent of covering up a crime. And we may be able to do something about that. Are you beginning to feel a little relieved now that you've got this much off your chest?"

"Yes, Father. Thank you, Father."

It was a leap well beyond what needed to be asked in this confession, but Tony knew that he would later regret it if he didn't. "You don't have to answer this if you don't want to, but is Homer, as he calls himself, living with you at the beach?"

"No, Father. He moved to town, to the Alhambra."

"Do you know what his mission is?"

"No, Father."

"And he's registered under the name of Homer?"

"I don't know. He may be using his real name, Peter Krug."

Peter Krug. Tony fastened the name in his memory. Leaning close to the grille, he said, "Now, I think we can do something about the body on the beach. Let me ask you this, son: Do you remember *exactly* where the man was buried?"

222

"Yes, Father."

"All right. Will you come back to this same confessional on Monday afternoon at three thirty?"

"Yes, Father."

"Good. I'll have something worked out. In the meantime, I assure you, everything you have told me is under the seal of confession. Is there anything else you wish to confess?"

"No, Father."

"All right. I'll give you general absolution for all the sins of your past life. Now make a good act of contrition."

All through the formula of absolution, which Tony gave by mindless rote, he kept thinking, Jesus, Mary, and Joseph!

AT SUPPER Tony fiddled with his food while Tom and Larry discussed the upturn in collections. The bishop was in Orlando. Excusing himself before dessert, Tony mounted the stairs to his room and exchanged his cassock for his street garb of black suit, clerical collar, and black hat.

He walked out on Cathedral Place and made his way briskly to the Alhambra Hotel. He thought he would pay a courtesy visit to the owner, Mrs. Olga Mussallem—compliment her on the faithful service her sons were rendering the church as altar boys. All right, he knew that was not the real reason. But uncomfortable as it was, even scary, Tony thought he had a moral obligation to throw himself into the middle of this situation as far as church rules allowed. Human lives were at risk. Maybe even the course of the war. What a burden! As long as he didn't *say* anything to anyone, couldn't he keep his eyes and ears open? Surely that was within the rules.

He approached the hotel and opened the door. Never having been in the Alhambra, he was surprised by the luxuriant expanse of Oriental rugs, white wicker chairs, couches, and tables. A parlor with a fireplace was to his right. The front desk was to the left, just before a large stairway. His ears recoiled from a volley of loud music and high voices passing through a closed doorway also to his left.

A slight, balding man behind the front desk greeted him. "Good evening, Father. Can I help you?"

"Good evening. I'm Father D'Angelo from the cathedral. I was wondering if Mrs. Mussallem was in."

"No, she isn't. She's here in the daytime only." He put out his hand. "Miles Zeigler, Father. Everybody calls me Ziggy."

"Very glad to meet you, Ziggy," Tony said just as two soldiers burst drunkenly through the nearby door.

"Sorry, Father," Ziggy said. "On Saturday nights the bar's full of plastered soldiers. Life's a lot different outside the rectory. But let me emphasize, Mrs. Mussallem runs a good Christian hotel."

"I'm glad to hear that," Tony said. "And I'm not surprised, knowing Mrs. Mussallem's fine reputation and her two altar-boy sons."

"You got it right, Father. She is one fine lady. We got a real nice lady guest in the hotel right now, too. She's waiting for her escort in the parlor. We have lots of decent folk who come to the hotel, and I try to take care of them nice as I can."

"I'm sure you do, Ziggy," Tony said. "Please tell Mrs. Mussallem that I dropped by to pay my respects. I'll come by again in the daytime."

"That I will, Father. You take care of yourself."

Tony turned and walked toward the front door. He paused for a quick peek into the parlor. At the moment, it was nothing more than an act of idle curiosity, though later he would acknowledge that it was as fateful an idle action as he had ever taken in his life.

Seated on a sofa, facing the door, was an attractive woman—late twenties or early thirties, red hair, formally dressed—whose eyes caught his at once. "Oh, Father!" she called.

"Yes, ma'am," he said.

Sally Parkins stood and said, "I hope I'm not botherin' you. It's just that I haven't seen a priest before in this whole state. I was beginnin' to think they didn't have 'em down here. They're all over New York. Do you know Father McGowan in New York?"

"No, I'm afraid I don't. I'm from New York, as a matter of fact, but there are hundreds of priests in the city I've never met."

"Father McGowan baptized me. But I haven't been to church much recently. I guess you'd call me fallen away."

"Well, you can do something about that," Tony encouraged her. "Did you ever go to catechism classes?"

"Never did. I asked my mother once if I could go to Sunday school, but to tell the truth, Father—I gotta be honest with a priest—the real reason was I wanted to be with this dude I had a

224

crush on, who actually grew up to be a pretty good trumpet player and not bad with the horses, either."

"Uh, Miss—"

"Sally Parkins is my name, Father. Honored to meet ya." She extended her hand.

"I'm Father D'Angelo," Tony said, accepting her hand. "Could we sit down for a moment? I can explain what you could do to get your religious life back on track, okay?"

"Okay," she agreed, and plopped down on the sofa.

"You need to begin," Tony explained, "by taking a course of instructions. Once you finish the course and have convinced the priest that you truly believe in God and are prepared to lead a Christian life, you can be prepared for Holy Communion."

"Can I take instructions at any time?" she asked, stalling.

"At any time," Tony assured her.

"Well, I'm willin' to talk about it. But I may be traveling soon. Suppose I started and then had to hit the road?"

"You can continue the instructions elsewhere. Could you come by the rectory—say, tomorrow at one o'clock—to talk with me about it some more? Do you know where the cathedral is?"

"I can ask my gentleman friend where it is."

"And let me recommend that you go to Mass tomorrow morning. I'm saying the one at eight o'clock." Tony smiled. "Well, it's been a pleasure meeting you, Miss Parkins."

"And you, too, I'm sure, Father—oh!" She looked toward the door. "Here's my gentleman friend now."

Tony turned and saw a man about his own height—long face, wide mouth, blue eyes, light hair—dressed in a navy-blue suit.

"Peter!" Sally said excitedly. "This is a father I just met."

"Good evening," the man said smoothly. "Peter Krug." He reached for Tony's hand, from which blood drained all the way to his clerical black shoes.

Tony stuttered his name in return. Awkwardly he smiled and took a step. "Well," he found himself able to say, "I was just leaving. I hope you—you both have an enjoyable evening." And, turning to Sally, "See you tomorrow." He nodded to Krug. "Good night."

"Good night," Krug said evenly.

"Good night, Father," Sally said cheerily.

Tony managed to make his feet work—left, right, left, right—toward the hotel doorway. Once through it, he expelled two lungfuls of frightened air.

Jesus, Mary, and Joseph.

WHEN Tony reached the rectory, Mattie Mae emerged from the kitchen with a bucket of ice.

"The bishop said for you to take this ice to his rooms when you get back."

"Oh, sure, Mattie Mae. Thanks." The bishop liked to have a nightcap. Tony took the ice and bounded up the stairs. Garvey responded in Italian to his knock.

As Tony entered, Garvey laid his wire-rimmed spectacles on the lamp table beside his chair. "We have a first-class fool in the Miami paper," he said, tossing the *Herald* to the floor. Tony began mixing two Scotch and sodas on a side table beneath a large framed print of Rogier van der Weyden's *Saint George and the Dragon.*

"An authentic tin-plated fool," Garvey went on. "Says that Floridians need not fear the Germans. The enemy is too far away to present any real danger. Doesn't the fool know that U-boats are blowing up ships just off our shores—right now?"

Tony handed him a glass. The bishop stared at it for a moment wordlessly, then took a sip.

"Do you think we'll get involved here in St. Augustine?"

"We are involved," Garvey answered. "Everyone is involved. This is total war. We are all in the trenches. When the evil force approaches, each man must do his duty. War happens with such frequency, you simply must take it into account and, when necessary, wage it. Look at the warrior saints. Joan of Arc is an example. Saint Barbara, the patron of field artillery. For the sake of religion itself, there are times when good simply must contend physically with evil—Saint Michael against Lucifer, Saint George against the dragon."

"Eccellenza"—Tony used the Italian form of address, which the bishop enjoyed, since it recalled his years in Rome—"just as speculation, suppose in the course of hearing a confession, I learned of the murderous activity of a German agent here in Florida. What could I do about it?"

Garvey leaned forward. "You can never violate the seal."

"Of course not, Eccellenza. But without betraying the seal, could I try to stop such a person?"

"Make use of confessional knowledge, is what you're asking."

"Yes."

"Under certain well-defined circumstances . . . What you need to do is consult a moral theologian."

"If, because of the knowledge I held, I was the only one who could prevent that agent from doing harm to our country or to individual Americans, would I be justified in so acting?"

Garvey paused to savor his malted barley, looking abstractedly to the ceiling. He then recited from Psalm 17: *"But who is God except the Lord? Who trained my hands for war and my arms to bend a bow of brass? And you girded me with strength for war."* He lowered his eyes.

For whatever reason, Garvey was not giving a direct answer, and Tony respected him for that. He would consult an authority in the morning. And then he would make up his own mind.

He fixed his eyes on *Saint George and the Dragon.*

LATER that Saturday night the Ancient City and environs presented numerous tableaux of varying hues and intensities.

On Marine Street, Tommy Williams and Bubba Davis weighed the advantages of the dollars gained by theft of linen left on a front porch against the advantages of an airplane ride, and decided to fly.

In her apartment on Riberia Street, Belle Hart, with a glass of milk in hand, read an article in the latest *Civil Aeronautics Journal* urging private pilots to join the Civil Air Patrol.

In his oceanfront room on the beach, Paul Ohlenburg finished his homework while listening to *Saturday Night Serenade.*

At the rectory, Tony lay in bed staring, wide-eyed and unseeing, at the ceiling, listening to the clock in the campanile strike ten o'clock.

And at the Venido Room of the Ponce, flanked by tall Tiffany stained-glass windows, Miss Sally Parkins, in long-sleeved black velvet top with bouffant pastel blue satin skirt, glided gracefully in the arms of Peter Krug to the strains of "I Guess I'll Have to Dream the Rest." It was wonderful to be dancing again. And with such a man! She did not resist when Krug brushed her cheek with his lips. Hardly so. She giggled and kissed him back, on the lips.

Not missing any of those signals, Krug knew that their highway partnership was ready to be sealed.

8

THE cathedral parishioners at eight-o'clock Mass more than half filled the nave. With altar boy Eddie Mussallem in tow, Tony descended the altar steps to distribute Communion at the marble rail. Halfway down, he looked up and caught sight of Sally Parkins, kneeling in the second pew. In the brief moment that their eyes met, Sally winked and waved at him.

Unfortunate, he thought. For the remainder of Mass he was plainly off his stroke. It was not because of Sally's innocent gaffe. It was because her presence starkly reminded him of Krug, whom he had made a conscious effort to exclude from his early morning thoughts and prayers. But now he nearly forgot the ablution, and had to read the prayers that he had always recited from memory.

Tightening his concentration, he prayed aloud with particular fervor and purpose. But as he unvested in the sacristy after Mass, he realized that Krug continued to encompass his mind. At breakfast he tried to put the man aside, at least long enough to read the Sunday paper, but again he was not successful. There was nothing to do but call Eddie Hagerty, his fellow *ordinandus* from Dunwoodie, now at Catholic University, in Washington, D.C.

"HEY, Fast Eddie! This is Tony D'Angelo in Florida."

"Tony, what a surprise! Great to hear your voice. How is it down there? Great, I bet."

"Yeah, it's pretty nice."

"I hear a bunch of our Dunwoodies are down there tearing up the golf links. Hey, what gives?"

"I've got a moral theology question, Eddie, and since you're the only doctorate in the field I know—"

"Still working on the dissertation, buddy."

"That's close enough. Listen, what I need is anything up to date on the use of confessional knowledge."

"Under-the-seal stuff? Well, we went through that. I've got my notes. Hold on."

After a few minutes Eddie came back on the line. "Okay, here's what I've got. There's not a lot written on it, actually. The main sources are the Fourth Lateran Council in A.D. 1215 and a decree of the Holy Office in 1682. The basic rule is this: Confessional knowledge may never be used if there is any resulting harm to the penitent. Having said that, theologians have noted certain cases where confessional knowledge can be used. For example, if the penitent discloses something that is public information, an event of which the confessor was not previously aware, the confessor may certainly discuss it afterward in the external forum. There's another possibility: The penitent may give the confessor permission to use confessional knowledge to warn others of impending harm and—personally, I would carry it further to say—to prevent that harm. But the circumstances really must be extraordinary."

"Very interesting. Very helpful."

"Tony, if your case is anything like that, I would ask in the sacramental forum if the penitent would agree to give you that same permission in the external forum. Just to be sure."

"Yes, Eddie. Thank you very very much."

"And, Tony, remember, the penalty for violating the seal is confinement in a monastery for life. You don't want that, unless you like cheese."

"Got it. Thanks. Bye!"

PROMPTLY at one o'clock Sally Parkins rang the rectory doorbell. Tony welcomed her into the office, leaving the door slightly open as he always did when the visitor was a woman.

"So you say you're leaving town quite unexpectedly?" he asked in a surprised tone, acknowledging her first words to him after she was seated opposite his desk.

"Yeah—yes, Father. My gentleman friend, Mr. Krug, and I decided to drive south together. He's an artist, you know. He's lookin' for good places to paint pictures and invited me to go along. For some reason, this morning Peter thought we should leave at once. One of those spur-of-the-moment things, as they say." She smiled.

"I see," Tony said, seeing a great deal more than he could tell her.

"Well," she said, "you mentioned something about instructions."

"Of course," Tony said, smiling broadly and reaching into a desk drawer to pull out a paperbound book. "This is what we normally use for instructions. You can take it with you on your trip." He handed it across the desk.

While Sally paged idly through the text, Tony's mind raced. Krug leaving . . . Where to? Why is he taking this woman? Should I, could I, warn her away from him? Not possible. She would tell him. Krug would know I'm onto him. Krug would find out Paul Ohlenburg is Catholic. . . . Paul and his father dead, maybe me, too.

It took only seconds for the inspiration to form. Reaching into another drawer, Tony brought forth a large packet and spread its contents on the desk.

"That book is background reading," he told her. "But what I want you to study is this extension course. You can do it while you travel."

"That's really keen," she said approvingly.

"Yes. Now, you have to be serious about it. Each lesson is paired with a question-and-answer sheet. Each time you finish a lesson—I recommend you do one every day—write out your answers and send the form back to me by mail. Here's my address. Maybe I should give you some three-cent stamps—"

"Oh, no! I have lots. This is such a neat way to learn. I like it already. And all this time I didn't know how easy it was to get straight with the church. Thank you, Father. You are one nice guy."

Tony debated whether to say anything about the impropriety of an unmarried couple traveling together. But she would read the material on the Sixth Commandment for herself. He dared not risk fumbling the ball on this play.

"Thank you again, Father," she said as they stood up. "You'll hear from me real soon. And that's a fact."

As he walked her to the door, Tony remarked as casually as he could, "You know, religion is a very personal thing. If you have any questions about the lessons, you can address them to me. I don't think it's advisable to discuss what you're doing with anyone."

"Including Mr. Krug?" she asked.

"I would say so."

Though the scent of danger was strong in his nostrils, there seemed no way for him to warn her. With Krug such an apparent good friend, she would regard it outrageous to suggest that he meant her any harm. Obviously he was using her. But how could Tony prove that?

"Miss Parkins," he ventured, "it's none of my business, and I don't mean to be intrusive, but are you completely certain it will be safe for you to travel with a gentleman you have only just met?"

"You mean Peter? Oh, he's a *dear*. I know a gentleman when I meet one. Don't worry. I'm very experienced."

"Good-bye, then, and God bless you," he said. "And please be very careful on your trip."

KRUG's black Pontiac bumped over the coastal highway, State 140, south from St. Augustine, past the Ohlenburgs' beach cottage, across the toll bridge at Matanzas Inlet, and along the sand dunes that held the body of the meddlesome bass fisherman. Krug gave the last site only a glance. His mind was fixed on getting down to business.

The wait for his watercolor paper had been an inconvenience, but he had used the time well. He had three completed paintings. And he had picked up a considerable amount of intelligence from soldiers and sailors in the Alhambra bar. He knew now that the principal army airfields were Drew and MacDill, in Tampa, and Eglin, at the west end of the Florida panhandle. But first he had to make contact with Lorenz.

No one could track him now. No one could connect him to his license plate or car, which he had left parked some distance from the hotel. His hotel registrations henceforth would be in other names. Heydrich had been emphatic: "Never leave a trail."

He looked over at Sally and feigned a caring smile. She responded with a hand on his arm. "Isn't this swell, Peter?" she said, pointing to the shoreline.

He agreed that it was, looking at the scenery for the first time now that he had resolved his intentions. He even began to envisage how the ocean scenes might be translated onto paper. To their left, miles of curling gray-blue surf were framed by undulating sand dunes, palmettos, sea oats, and slow flights of pelicans.

"Well, you really swept me off my feet, didn't you?" Sally said.

231

"This must be what they call a whirlwind romance," she mused.

"I guess so." He laughed. "Hang on to your hat!"

"Speaking of hanging on," she said, running her hand along his right forearm, "how come you wear your money belt to bed?"

"Oh, it's just a habit. I guess I'm a creature of habit. Sorry."

"Well, why do you wear a knife on your right wrist?"

"To protect the money belt."

"Oh."

"And if I may ask a question," he said, "did you say anything to that priest about where we were going?"

"How could I when I don't know myself?"

"Okay."

They engaged in desultory conversation for a while more. Then Sally dozed for a quarter hour and, on awakening, started reading one of her several copies of *Modern Screen*.

About an hour after leaving St. Augustine, the Pontiac began entering the populated areas around Daytona Beach and Port Orange, where the going was a little slower. Krug determined to reach the Canaveral Peninsula by dinnertime.

The afternoon sky was a porcelain blue above white, mountainous clouds when they pulled into the dune-ridge resort of Cocoa Beach. Krug registered them as Mr. and Mrs. Winslow Homer. After inspecting their tiny cabin, the two of them drove a short distance down the road where the clerk said they could get a decent seafood dinner, which they found to be the case. They lingered long in conversation before returning to the cabin.

9

MONDAY was the cathedral rectory's biggest personal-problems day of the week. Usually Tony looked forward to Mondays. He liked grappling with the problems parishioners brought him. And follow-up sessions enabled him to acquire a measure of satisfaction that his advice actually brought about a positive good in somebody's life.

On Monday morning Tony had appointments at eight fifteen, nine o'clock, nine forty-five, and ten thirty. Then lunch at the rectory, where Bishop Garvey was full of that morning's news of

Japan's stranglehold on Java. Then prayer and back-and-forth pacing in his room, which lasted until three, when, with a leaden heart, he descended to the empty cathedral and entered the confessional. The anticipation of this moment had clouded his entire day—made his lunch indigestible, Garvey's lecturing insufferable, and his whole sense of priesthood a daunting mystery. Was he really capable of doing what he planned to do?

The question festered until three thirty-five, when, to his responding heartbeat, someone entered the right curtain and knelt behind the grille.

"Father?" a voice asked.

"Yes, I'm here," Tony answered. "Thank you for coming back, son. Are you doing all right? Are you feeling better?"

"Yes, Father, a little."

"All right. Now, you told me last time that you remembered the place where Mr. Capona was buried."

"Yes, Father. It was a quarter mile north of the studios. It was at the only part of those dunes where there were no sea oats."

"All right. Here's what I'd like for you to do. You see, Mr. Capona, being a Catholic, deserves a Christian burial, and Mrs. Capona deserves to see her husband laid properly to rest. After dark tonight I want you to place a stick with a white rag into the sand where the body is buried. Will you do that?"

"Yes, Father."

"All right. Now, there's one other thing, and then we're through with this whole tragic experience. I've prayed and studied a lot about this matter, and I've found that without revealing anything about your confession, I can do something perhaps to prevent other people from being hurt by this man Homer—if you would give me permission to do so. Would you give me that permission?"

"Yes, Father."

"Would you also give me that permission outside the confessional? In other words, if I go out and kneel in a pew, would you kneel behind me and say, 'Father, I give you permission to try to prevent others from being hurt by Homer'?"

"Would my confession still be secret?"

"Absolutely. Yes, absolutely."

"Okay."

Tony closed the grille and, leaving the confessional, stepped out and knelt in a pew. The youth knelt behind him.

"Father?" he said.

"Yes, son. You have something to tell me?"

"Yes. I give you permission to try to keep other people from being hurt."

"By—"

"By Homer."

"Thank you, son. Now go in peace. If I can help you further in any way, please come to see me."

AFTER an early morning start, Krug and Sally made good time down U.S. 1, which paralleled the coast and was flanked by salt lagoons and low-lying islands. Sally studied the landscape, so strikingly different from her native New York—a motionless blue heron looking at its reflection in the water, oxen standing in ditches chewing water hyacinths, cowmen on marsh ponies driving cattle with long whips.

At Fort Pierce, Krug found his way into the center of town, where he located a movie theater. The marquee read DOUBLE FEATURE— SONG OF THE ISLANDS; KEEP 'EM FLYING. He parked the car nearby, and the two of them went into a newsstand. Krug bought a day-old Miami *Herald*. He invited Sally to pick up all the magazines she wanted. Then they went into a coffee shop for breakfast.

"Now, today," he told her over pancakes, "I've got to scout sites for painting. It's the kind of thing I have to do by myself. It's long and it's boring. When I actually start painting, I'll make sure you're with me."

"That I want to see," she agreed. "But what do *I* do?"

"You have your magazines. You can stay here until the movie theater opens. Here's a ten-dollar bill."

"A ten-spot?" she said disgustedly. "I've got more than that in my change purse."

"I'm sure that's all you'll need today. Now be a sweetheart and enjoy yourself. I'll find you back here at the coffee shop later. Tonight we'll go out to the best restaurant in town."

"In this burg? What's that, the diner?"

"Don't be naughty. We'll order some champagne, too."

235

STATE 140 SOUTH HUGGED THE west bank of Indian River, past weathered fish houses, rickety piers, boat sheds, and signs: LIVE BAIT, DANCE & DINE, REPENT. Eden was so small it did not show on the road map, but Krug had been told by Abwehr that it was south of Fort Pierce. He drove the narrow road slowly, troubled that he saw no signs. On rising ground to the right, there were occasional clusters of houses. When he came upon a man walking with a cane fishing pole, he stopped to ask, "Can you tell me, sir, if Eden is up ahead?"

The man pointed forward. "Yeah, it's ahead up there."

"How will I know when I'm there?"

"You'll see mailboxes and a dirt road, maybe a mile."

When, after a mile, a clump of mailboxes came into view, Krug turned right up a heavily wooded incline. All he could see was an occasional frame house. There was no town as such. To his right, an elderly man in overalls led a mule across a small field. Krug parked on the shoulder of the road, got out, and walked briskly after him.

"I'm looking for a man named Emil Lorenz. Do you know where he lives?" Krug called out.

"Fellow with the boats?"

"I suppose so."

The man pointed. "See that yeller house, second down?"

"Yes. Thank you. Much obliged."

Krug walked along a path until he came to the small yellow house, where he knocked on the door.

A slight but well-proportioned man—about fifty, with blue eyes and wispy gray hair—answered the door. He wore a frayed white short-sleeved shirt, navy trousers, and tennis shoes.

"Yes? May I help you?" he asked in a thin, reedy voice.

"My name is Peter Krug."

"Emil Lorenz. Come in." Lorenz led Krug through a small, neatly kept living room to a screened-in porch facing the river, where he motioned his visitor to a bamboo chair.

"Do you care for coffee?" he asked before sitting.

"No, thank you."

Lorenz looked at him carefully. "You say your name is Krug. What can I do for you? Are you selling something?"

"I'm not selling anything," Krug answered, smiling.

"Perhaps, then, you can tell me your business, Mr. Krug."

236

Krug realized with a chill that this might not be Lorenz at all. Maybe Lorenz had been picked up by the FBI and this man was luring him into a trap.

Krug decided to play a card. "I'm going to tell you something, Mr. Lorenz. I once knew a man named Böhm."

"Is that a fact?" Lorenz said. "And?"

"Günther Böhm," Krug added. "He recently came to Florida by boat and made a visit to Marine Studios."

"Yes? I wonder if you're thinking of the man I know who once met up with a fellow named Heyse."

There! That did it. No FBI agent could possibly know the linkage of those two names. Krug relaxed.

"Have you had any luck?" Lorenz asked.

"So-so," Krug replied.

"I'm glad that you came here straightaway, because, to tell you the truth, I may be picked up before our scheduled rendezvous, and I've been worried what you'd do without my help."

"Picked up? By the FBI?"

"Yes. Not because they know of my activities, but for general purposes. I think all us registered German aliens living on the coast will be detained. The U-boats have the authorities very nervous— they think German nationals are providing shipping information."

Krug nodded.

Lorenz stood up. "Come with me," he said. He opened a screen door, and Krug followed him down a white sand path through heavy growth. Lorenz led Krug across State 140 and out a forty-yard pier to a driftwood-gray boathouse with a tin roof. He turned a key in the door and flicked a light switch. "There's a power line underground from the house. People know I have boats and that I work on them a lot. You couldn't find a more secluded spot for my kind of work."

Inside, Krug saw two midsized runabouts in the boathouse slips. "The open boat is a Gar Wood twenty-eight-footer," Lorenz said, "top speed in the forties. The canvas-top job is a twenty-five-foot Chris-Craft Express Cruiser, speed only in the thirties but a much better sea-keeper. But either one will get you out the St. Lucie Inlet, seven nautical miles south. Your U-boat will be three miles due east of the inlet. Do you know anything about boating?"

"A little. Enough, I think."

"Whatever you do, don't go when the tide's going out. I can handle the bar at the inlet when the tide's shifting, but you can't. Currents can run seven knots in that cut."

"I understand."

"Read the tide tables. I've got 'em posted right over the tackle box. Leave here an hour before high tide."

Lorenz pulled a rope on the ceiling that opened a door and lowered a ladder. "The FBI probably won't care about my boats," he said, climbing up. "They'll want to know what else I own."

Krug followed him. Reaching the top, he saw a chaotic storage scene: boxes, rugs, lamps, jalousie window frames, papers—the typical attic detritus of an American household.

"That pine floor's a false bottom," Lorenz said, lifting up a whole section on hinges. The junk on top of the section fell off. "I just brush it all back when I'm through."

Underneath the false bottom and an oilcloth cover were a forty-watt dual channel transmitter and a receiver. Lorenz pulled up a folding table. "Here is my Morse key, my bug. And here are the U-boat frequencies and the pad ciphers for each date. And a folding canvas chair to sit on."

"Where's the antenna?" Krug asked.

"In the wall framing. I'll show you." Lorenz pressed a spot on an upright wood slat. Immediately two portions of the wall spread open from floor to ceiling, revealing shelves filled with cameras, enlargers, film, paper, and chemicals, as well as a typewriter.

"This is where I do my cards and documents. And you asked about the antenna." He pointed to a handwheel in the wall. "Here I can crank it up from its hidden position. I only do so at night, of course."

Lorenz closed the doors, and they climbed back downstairs. After raising the ladder, he added, "One more thing. See the black coffee cup next to the tackle box? If you see it turned upside down, it means I've been picked up here in the boathouse. There's another cup just like it on the windowsill in the kitchen. If it's upside down, it means I was apprehended in the house."

With that, Lorenz closed and locked the door, then gave the key to Krug. "I have another," he said.

At the house, Krug said his good-byes, ending with a click of the heels, a stiff arm salute, and a "Heil Hitler!"

Seeming not to notice, Lorenz opened the back door and smiled thinly. "Heil Hitler," he said.

AFTER Tony parked the rectory car on the sand off State 140, he opened the trunk and removed the spade and the Coleman lantern he had found in the rectory toolroom. With nervous hands he withdrew a large kerchief and a bottle of alcohol from the trunk, doused the kerchief with alcohol, and placed it in his left pant pocket. Then, in flannel shirt and tan trousers, he traipsed through the palmettos and cordgrass down to the beach, got a glow going on the mantle of the lantern, and paced slowly north, half spooked by the drumroll of the nighttime surf, looking for a stick and a white rag.

No more than five minutes into his search, he saw it clearly in the full moon. He set the lantern firmly into the sand. Then, after satisfying himself that he was alone, with a nauseated gulp he vigorously began shoveling sand to his left side.

It would have been much easier just to tell the sheriff that his deputies would find a body underneath the white marker, and let *them* dig for it. But Tony did not trust the sheriff's department to search for a marker. They might take his message as a crank call and dismiss it. But if he reported that there was a body *on the beach*, he knew that the sheriff would act.

The point of his spade hit something. He gently worked the blade around the object and half lifted it. It was a large, sand-coated fish. Digging deeper, he hit another object, which came up length-wise: the end of a cane pole, as the lantern revealed. The German lad had mentioned the fish and the pole. This was the place all right. As he set the lantern aside so that he might resume digging, the plain form of a man's fingers appeared in the hole left by the pole, and a foul odor entered his nostrils. He fumbled for his alcohol-soaked kerchief and wrapped it around his face.

Tony shuddered. He knew that it would come to this—he would have to touch a dead body. He found that he could not reach down and grasp the hand. His emotions would not let him. There was something about a hand.

Instead, he continued digging, taking care to expose the whole body so that he could remove it all at once. Here the left arm and shoulder came into view; there the trunk and head emerged. A cold shiver came over his ribs when he saw that the two dead eyes were open and staring at him.

The body moved with his tug, though it was difficult in the soft sand to maintain footing, and he had to haul the rigid deadweight out in jerks. After struggling in this fashion, he finally got the body down the dune onto harder sand. He set the lantern on the beach and knelt beside the ungainly, bent, stiff corpse. Taking out a copy of the *Rituale Romanum,* he read the prayers aloud.

That completed, he stood to go. He made a sign of the cross over the remains of Joseph Capona—"May his soul and the souls of all the faithful departed, through the mercy of God, rest in peace. Amen"—and, with lantern and spade, walked over the dunes to the car.

Driving back, he sensed a general decompression. He had done the right thing. He experienced a certain exhilaration at discovering that he could undertake a physical task—a horrible, sickening one at that—and carry it off without hesitating, without blubbering.

It was three thirty when he parked the car at the rectory.

Inside the rectory office, he dialed the sheriff.

"I have an important message for the sheriff," Tony said, disguising his voice through the kerchief. "There is a dead body on the beach about a quarter of a mile north of Marine Studios. Please act on it right away. Thank you."

Up in his room, he took off his clothes and placed them, with the kerchief, in an old suitcase. He would dump it somewhere later today. Then he took a bath and got into his pajamas. Probably he would not be able to sleep. He knelt and prayed, *"And you girded me with strength for war. . . ."*

10

THE drive across the Florida peninsula to Tampa seemed longer than Krug had anticipated. The flat, open, sparsely settled countryside made one think the road would never end. The scenery was eye-glazing grassy prairies interrupted only by herds of cattle and thin stands of pine.

Reaching Lake Wales, with its citrus groves, palms, and subtropical flowers, Krug was glad to stop and give Sally, who was visibly more torpid than he, a chance to recharge her batteries. This was not the Florida she was accustomed to, as she had made plain several times, including last night when the dining establishment Krug had picked out proved to be well below her usual standards.

"I'm going to the ladies' room," she said now as they pulled into a service station. "See if there's something here worth seeing. If I don't see a building soon, I'll die."

From the pump jockey filling his gas tank, Krug learned that Mountain Lake Sanctuary, with its Singing Tower, was the principal local attraction.

"And I'll need a good camera store," Krug told the attendant.

"That'd be Buddy's Camera and Film, near the entrance to the sanctuary," the man said, handing Krug his change. "Can't miss it."

Sally seemed in better spirits when she reentered the car, especially after he told her they were going to see a building—a carillon tower. After driving up a low mountain slope, Krug stopped at the camera shop and bought a Kodak Brownie and ten rolls of film. Inside the sanctuary, camera in hand, Sally made for the tower as fast as she could, while Krug, carrying his art equipment, lingered among the shrubs and multihued azaleas to find a site for his easel. He would need more finished watercolors when he got to Drew and MacDill fields. These flowery scenes should provide him with two or three acceptable paintings. He worked rapidly, pausing only at twelve noon when the carillon began a plangent recital.

After another hour's painting, he felt a hand on his shoulder.

"I've been standing back here watching you." Sally laughed. "I saw the whole picture just pop up. It's real pretty."

"Thank you," Krug acknowledged. "Did you take some photos?"

"Shot the whole roll. And then I got mad 'cause I wanted a picture o' me in front of that bell tower."

"Give me the camera, and I'll change rolls. I'll take a few pictures of you here and then a bunch more in Tampa."

While he worked in the shade, Sally called to him, "That's one of the highest buildings I've seen in this whole state. It looks like the GE Building—you know, at Lexington and Fifty-first?"

"Lexington?" he asked, walking out from the shade.

"Yeah. Near a fancy all-night bar where my friend Harold takes me when he comes in big on a ten-to-one shot at Pimlico."

"Come on," Krug urged her, "show me the bell tower and strike a few poses in front of it. Then we better start driving again."

AFTER driving an hour and a half, Krug and Sally finally entered Tampa, where Krug secured accommodations at the Gasparilla Hotel. As they followed the bellhop with their luggage upstairs, Sally whispered, "Why did that desk clerk call you Mr. Pimlico?"

"Because I signed the register 'Mr. and Mrs. Harold Pimlico,' " Krug answered.

"Pimlico?" Sally asked incredulously. "The track?"

"Sweetheart, wait until we're in the room." After they were, and the bellhop was tipped and gone, Krug said in his most reassuring voice, "We're not married, but we're traveling as though we were. Someone could use our joint registration to embarrass us. Now why don't you relax here in the room for a while? I'm going to go out and scout some painting locations. At the same time, I'll look for places to take photos of you. Okay?"

"Okay."

After Krug left, Sally sat down heavily in the upholstered chair by the window. Well, there he goes, she thought—money belt, knife, and all. Would someone please tell her how to get inside that belt? How much more time did she have to invest in this guy?

Oh, well. She reached for her Catholic-instructions packet and started reading lesson two. She had dropped the form for lesson one in a mailbox near the coffee shop in Fort Pierce. Maybe she'd do another lesson this afternoon. She read the words slowly, thinking about what they meant and wondering if she believed them.

WHEN Krug returned two hours later, he found Sally dozing in the chair. "C'mon, sleepyhead," he roused her, "I've found a good place to take some photos of you."

Sally was groggy but managed to get up on her feet. "I'm not in a picture-taking mood," she complained.

"You'll feel better after a few minutes," he encouraged her. "Change into something nice."

When Sally was ready, Krug walked her downstairs and to his car.

They drove west into the suburbs and then along the fence of a military airfield that Sally saw identified at an entrance gate as Drew Field. Olive-drab airplanes were noisily taking off and landing. Abruptly Krug stopped the car alongside the roadway, commenting, "A good place for taking pictures."

Sally did not particularly see why, but she got out of the car. "You see?" Krug said. "There's good light here and some nice natural groupings of bushes and trees."

Sally looked up as loud, low-flying aircraft went overhead.

"Don't mind the airplanes," Krug urged her. "Concentrate on looking pretty." He positioned her near a line of bushes. "Just hold it right there while I adjust the framing."

Krug went down on one knee. He stalled for time until an aircraft came over the fence; then he pushed the shutter button.

"There! That's one," he said. "That's right."

When another aircraft came over the fence, Krug clicked again.

Sally stood hands on hips and declared, "I want some pictures of me straight ahead, not up my nose."

"Sure." Krug complied, taking six pictures of her at eye level. "That's all for now. Let's get something to eat."

Which they did, and enjoyed greatly, Sally getting giggly on New York State bubbly, which he encouraged because it made her less acutely disapproving when, at the hotel, he put her to bed and said he had to go out and would be back later.

"You're going out?" she slurred as he pulled a blanket up to her chin. "You're always going somewhere."

"I'll be back soon. Get some sleep." In fact, as he noticed, she passed from stupor to unconsciousness before he left the room.

In his car again, he drove out by Drew Field. Driving back and forth around it, questioning naïve soldiers outside the fence and in bars, he acquired a fairly good picture of the base. Drew was headquarters for the Army Air Corps's 3rd Interceptor Command. Its mission was to train pilots in the single-seat P-39 Airacobra. By ten thirty he knew the entrance-gate routine, the MP patrol schedule, and the location of the parking apron for the P-39s. What he needed now was a uniform—preferably a sergeant's.

At Chappie's Tavern, Krug had seen a handful of uniformed noncommissioned officers. He parked in back and ordered a bottle of Schlitz at the bar. He waited until he saw a sergeant about his own height and weight get up and go to the men's room. He followed him at a careless gait and, once inside, closed the door.

Krug's arm grabbed around the sergeant's throat. The fellow made no real effort at resistance and went lamely to his knees. Leaving some life in his victim, Krug changed clothes and shoes. The uniform was a good fit. Then he walked out calmly in the direction of the back door.

It would be too risky to go through the main gate of the airfield, so, in a remote west corner of the field, Krug clambered over the fence. Reminding himself to salute if he encountered an officer, he walked casually around the perimeter to the parking apron.

He counted thirty Airacobras in three neat rows. There were no lights, except for the moon, and, as far as he could see, no sentries. The P-39 had a distinctive look about it. The engine intake and exhausts were jarring. They were aft of the pilot.

When he reached the apron, he chose an aircraft in the center row, stepped up on the wing, and tried the cockpit door. It opened. He climbed inside, sat, and studied the panel. Nothing unusual. After groping about, he found the pilot's handbook. He leaned down and opened it up on the floor, where his penlight would not show outside, and copied the numbers. An Allison V-1710-35 engine rated at 1150 horsepower. Maximum speed 368 at 13,800 feet. But no turbo supercharger! And a gross weight of 8200 pounds. The engine was mounted in the rear so that a 37-mm cannon in the nose could fire through a hollow drive shaft. He noted the additional armament: two .50-caliber and four .30-caliber machine guns.

Well, Krug bet that the new Bf-109Gs coming out of the Messerschmitt factory would fly pirouettes around these planes. The thing was a flying machine gun, but it had to be hard to get to altitude, and it couldn't be too nimble once it got there. So the 109s and Focke-Wulf 190s had nothing to fear from this plane.

Next time he'd look at bombers.

BACK at the hotel room, Sally seemed fast asleep when Krug let himself in. He took his picture case, eyecup, and Pyramidon tablets into the bathroom, where he removed one of his Lake Wales paintings from the case. Next he brewed a solution of pill and water and, with a toothpick, began writing. Forty-five minutes later he shredded his notes and disposed of them in the toilet. Then, for a few winks, he slipped into bed. It did not take him long to fall into a fitful sleep.

Sally, who had not been asleep when he returned, watched him twisting and turning and listened to his loud breathing. What did he do in a bathroom for a full hour? Read? Was Peter an insomniac? Was this the way artists behaved? Maybe he wasn't reading. Maybe he was counting money. Maybe he had been burglarizing and was now counting his take.

She drifted off, and the two of them awoke about eight. Sally took a bath first; then Peter took one. They said very little to each other while dressing. Sally wondered if there was any point in continuing this relationship. Then abruptly she ventilated it all. "The next time you go out at night, Peter, I intend to go along with you and find out what the heck is going on. It is weird that you stayed out so late and then came back and spent an hour in the bathroom. What did you do in there?"

Krug—who prided himself on never being surprised—was surprised. So she hadn't been asleep after all.

"I'm sorry, sweetheart. I had some business to take care of. When I got back, I read a little to help myself sleep."

"I think I have a hangover," Sally said, stepping into her shoes.

"I'll find you some Alka-Seltzer when I go out this morning to scout painting locations. And this afternoon we're going boating. That should be fun."

After breakfast Krug gathered up his watercolor equipment—all but the carrying case—and left. Sally sat down and returned to lesson two. An hour later she had the form ready for mailing.

She got up and checked the dampness of her rose blouse, which she had washed that morning. It was ready for ironing. She walked downstairs and asked the desk clerk for an iron. She also asked for a board, but none were available. No matter—she could iron it easily on top of the writing table. Back in the room, she cast about for something to place underneath.

The Tampa *Tribune* would not do—the print might come off. The pillowcases were soiled by Peter's Vaseline hair tonic. The towels were too wet. Her eyes lit on Peter's flat artist's case, standing against the wall. Of course. She laid the case on the bed, undid the ribbon knot that held it closed, and pulled out his latest three paintings, which she held up to admire. They were the scenes at Lake Wales, with lots of flowers. Really nice. Peter might be strange, but he knew how to paint.

Then she laid the cardboard case on the tabletop, and the three watercolors, one on top of another, paint down, on the case. When the iron was warm, she spread the blouse on the paper. Perfect. She ran the iron back and forth on the front and both sleeves. She stood the iron on end while she turned the blouse over and, looking down as she did so, saw brown spots on the paper.

Oh, no! She had ruined Peter's painting! The paint was coming through. She placed her hands over her face in distress. Then her eyes slowly widened as the brown spots grew to what looked like words, except that she did not know any of them.

Secret ink? Sally sat down hard and studied the few words that resembled English: BOMBE . . . 75-GALLONEN . . . PILOTEN HIER IN TAMPA. Was this about airplanes and bombs?

She stood up and ran the iron over the remainder of that sheet, bringing out at its top: BELL P-39D AIRACOBRA DREW FIELD 04.3.42. HÖCHSTGESCHWINDIGKEIT 368 MPH.

Drew Field. That's near where they were yesterday. What were these numbers? What was the language?

Taking the watercolor paper with her, she walked downstairs, placed a nickel in the hallway pay phone, dialed information, and asked for the number of the public library. With the returned nickel she dialed that number.

"Library," a woman answered.

"Yeah. I'd like to speak to someone who knows languages. I've found some writing and don't know what language it's in."

"Perhaps Mr. Templeton can help. Hold for a moment, please."

"Arthur Templeton. Can I help you?"

"Yes. I'm at the Gasparilla Hotel. I've found some writing on a piece of paper, and I can't read it. If I spell some of it out, can you tell me what it means?"

"I'll certainly be glad to try, ma'am. Let me get a pad and pencil. . . . All right, go ahead."

"Well, one of the lines goes—I'll spell it—'T-r-o-t-z,' and a space, 's-c-h-w . . . ' " It took two and a half minutes to complete the sentence, after which there was a long pause at the other end.

Finally Mr. Templeton said, "The language is German. A rough translation would be, 'Despite poor climb performance, the P-39 is well armed—in the nose a 37-millimeter cannon plus two .50-caliber machine guns.' You say you found this somewhere?"

"Yeah. Here's another sentence: 'D-i-e,' space, 'l-a-g-e . . .' " which, when she finished, Templeton translated, " 'Engine position makes it vulnerable to a wide range of attacks.' You know, the P-39 is an Army Air Corps plane. They have them at Drew Field locally."

"Well, Drew Field is mentioned, too, and numbers that look like a date: 'Zero four, period, three, period, forty-two.' "

"Yes, that's today's date in European form. Ma'am, I must say I'm very troubled by this document that you've found—"

Click.

She returned to the room and sat down to think. The thoughts came clearly for the first time in days. Peter was not an artist. He was a spy! He got information on American planes at night and wrote it down in secret ink on the back of his paintings in the bathroom. Yesterday, at that camp, he was only pretending to photograph her. He was really photographing those loud airplanes.

She carried the painting down the hall to the maids' linen closet, where she inserted it between the sheets on the shelves. Then she took the form she was mailing to Father D'Angelo downstairs and asked the clerk if he took mail at the desk. He said no, that there was a postal box on the wall to his right. Sally added, "I'm Mrs.—uh—Pimlico in twenty-two. I'll be checking out today. Mr. Pimlico, I think, will be staying. I'd like to have my bags brought down. Would you send a bellhop up in forty-five minutes? I'll ask you to call me a cab when I'm ready to go."

"Yes, ma'am, of course. I hope you enjoyed your stay."

"Yeah. Very nice."

As she turned toward the postal box, she jumped to hear, "Sally!" Krug was approaching. "I needed my case after all. Is everything all right?" Looking down at the envelope in her hand, he read, " 'Father Anthony D'Angelo, Cathedral, St. Augustine . . .' "

"Yes," she responded nervously. "I have to mail a letter."

"I'll drop it for you," he said.

"I'll drop it," she said sternly, and walked over and did so.

"You seem on edge, sweetheart," he whispered, taking her arm and moving her toward the stairs. "Why are you writing to that priest?"

"I'm taking Catholic instructions and sending in my answers."

"Have you been mailing them elsewhere on this trip?"

"Mailed the first one from Fort Pierce."

"I see."

When they reached the stairway, the desk clerk called, "I'll have the bellhop to your room in forty-five minutes, Mrs. Pimlico."

Sally nodded.

"Bellhop?" Krug asked.

"I'm leaving, Peter," she said.

"Leaving?" he asked. "Why?"

"Come in the room and I'll tell you."

When Krug entered the room, he saw his case and two of his paintings spread out on the table. The iron was standing upright next to them.

"So what have we here?" he asked.

"You want to tell me, or should I tell you?" Sally said, her arms folded across her rose blouse.

He flipped through the paintings and examined the case. "One of my paintings is missing," he said evenly. "I'd like to know where it is." He unfastened the cuff button of his right sleeve.

"At the police station," she answered. "I had somebody translate the writing on the back. You think you're so smart. Well, I can tell you that a P-39 airplane has two .50-caliber machine guns. Whaddaya think about that?"

Damn her eyes, Krug thought. "Who translated?" he asked.

"Someone I called on the phone. And the police sent an officer, and I gave him the painting with a note about who you were but all rolled up in newspaper and tied shut. I told him it was important evidence and to hold it until two o'clock, when I would reclaim it. And all you have to do, you Nazi pig, is go with me to the station and I'll reclaim it and give it back to you."

"For a price, no doubt."

"Whaddaya take me for? I wasn't born Sunday. Three G's."

"Three G's," he repeated.

Then, in an instant, he had her hair in his hand and the point of his blade pricking just outside her right carotid artery.

"This is the biggest pile of garbage I've ever heard," he said menacingly, his mouth inches from her wide eyes. "Now you tell me where you really hid that painting."

"All right," she gasped. When Krug released her hair, she reached for her throat with both hands.

"Now!" Krug ordered coldly.

"In the linen closet," she said, shaking, and moved sideways toward the door.

"Then get it. And I will be within a knife thrust of you every step of the way."

She led him down to the closet and retrieved the painting. He directed her to return to the room. For the next ten minutes, while Sally stood trembling, her face forced against the wall, Krug grilled her about Father D'Angelo and her conversation with the librarian.

"I suppose you told him you were staying at the Gasparilla."

"I may have—" she began, which a touch of the knife in the side of her neck changed to, "Yes, yes, I did."

It was clear now that Krug had to get out of this hotel fast.

"It really is such a pity," he said, placing his left arm around her narrow neck. Sally could have proved a very useful person. But there would be no boat ride today.

Professionally, he would miss her.

11

O N Thursday, March 5, Joseph Capona was finally laid to rest. Because of the publicity attending his death, and at Tony's urging, the cathedral thought it appropriate to offer him and his family a Solemn High Requiem Mass. Tom Murphy was officiant, Tony deacon, and Larry subdeacon. At the conclusion of Mass the three clerics gathered around the casket in the center aisle while a crossbearer stood at the head of the coffin between two acolytes.

From where he stood, Tony could see the tear-streaked face of Joe Capona's widow, Maria. He wondered what must be passing through her mind. There was so much she would never know about the circumstances surrounding her husband's death.

After the graveside ceremony, when the three priests returned to the rectory, the mail had arrived. Tony took his small stack to the dining room and joined Tom for coffee. He smiled to see an envelope from Sally Parkins postmarked March 2 from Fort Pierce. He smiled again when he saw that she had filled in the answers correctly. Was she all right? He supposed so. But what was Krug—that murderous Nazi thug—up to? He closed his eyes and recited a brief prayer for Sally's continued safety.

While Tom read the sports pages of the Florida *Times-Union* from Jacksonville, Tony looked idly through the Florida State News of the Day on page 5, where there were a dozen or so stories. Tallahassee: Florida Farm Prices Go Up; Tampa: FBI Searches 59 Homes—Rounds Up Enemy Aliens. Tampa again: Woman Found Dead in Hotel Room. Tony skimmed this one. "A young woman guest was found dead in her room at the Hotel Gasparilla on Wednesday. . . . Identified by documents in her purse as Miss Sally Parkins. . . . Her age given as 31." Sally Parkins! "The body is in the custody of the coroner while a search is made for next of kin and local police complete their investigation."

Tony stood bolt upright, scraping his chair across the floor and startling Tom with his ashen expression. "Oh, no!" he exclaimed.

Tom was agape. "Tony, what's wrong?"

Tony said in a raspy whisper, "A woman I was giving instructions to by mail—dead in a Tampa hotel room."

Tom reached over, found the story, and began reading.

"Just today," Tony continued, "her first answer form arrived in the mail," but he clutched his throat to stop himself from saying what was increasingly obvious and damning: And it's my fault. He should never have let her go with Krug. He had a chance to save her, and he did nothing! The whole point of getting permission to use confessional knowledge was to prevent others from being hurt.

Use of confessional knowledge, indeed. What arrogance, what foolhardiness on his part. And now another life was gone, a life on the rebound maybe.

Looking at Tom, he said, "I'm sorry, Tom, if I seem shaken, but I am. I feel responsible to see that she gets a Catholic burial."

"You're the judge, Tony."

"Tom, I want to ask a big favor. I'd like to go to Tampa. Could you possibly cover for me? You'd have to double up on confessions."

"Oh, that's no problem," Tom assured him. "Glad to do it."

"You're a saint, Tom. I'll call you as soon as I know what the situation is. Many thanks."

Tony went to the office phone to call Motor Lines at the Alhambra. A bus was leaving in five minutes—Tampa via Orlando. He could never make that one. Next bus at three thirty. He mounted the stairs to his room, exchanged his cassock for street garb, and packed a small overnight bag, making sure he had his breviary.

The more he thought about it, the more he became convinced that he needed not just transportation but freedom of movement. He needed a car.

And he needed to talk to Belle.

BELLE taxied her plane up to the manager's office at the St. Augustine airport, shut down her engine, and bounded out to greet Father D'Angelo.

"Hello, Father. Did you decide to take that ride?"

"No, Miss Hart, not right now, thank you. I just wanted to talk with you a few minutes if you have the time."

"Of course. Please call me Belle."

"All right. Thank you—Belle."

"Look," she said, "could you stand by just a minute while I tie this bird down and fill in my log?"

"Sure, of course."

He watched her do that, admiring her practical skills.

"I hope you don't think it forward of me to ask you a few questions," he said. "I'm something of an empiricist. I gather as much good thought and advice as I can from various sources and then make my own decisions, or at least I think I do. You strike me as being the same kind of person, and—"

"Thank you. I'm flattered."

"And I wonder how you would handle a situation where you learned in an absolutely confidential setting about a person who intended great harm to our country and to innocent individuals. And no one but you could stop him."

"Well, Father, I assume that this is a hypothetical case. And you couldn't go to the police?"

"No. I don't see how."

"And it has something to do with the war?"

"Yes."

"If I was the one who could do something about it, without betraying the confidence you speak about, I'd be on my horse—or in a plane—this instant to stop him."

"You really would?" Tony asked.

"Yes. That's what I'm doing right now—searching out U-boats to prevent them from doing harm."

"Of course. Well, if it were a real case"—he chuckled—"I'd be at a disadvantage, since I don't have access to either a horse or a plane. In fact, I don't even have access to a car, and they don't have rental agencies down here. How would you handle that?"

"Hypothetically, I would ask someone like me, who has a car."

"But I would never ask for your car," Tony protested.

"I know," Belle continued. "We're only talking hypothetically. And, furthermore, my car, a black Ford, would be found parked outside your rectory in one hour, with my home telephone number on the dashboard in case the driver ran into any problems."

"But I didn't come here to—"

"Remember, Father, we're only talking hypothetically."

"Of course."

She smiled. "The word we use is roger."

EARLIER that day Peter Krug sat in the office of an Atlantic Richfield station across the Tampa Bay toll bridge in St. Petersburg scanning old and current copies of the Tampa and St. Pete papers while waiting for his Pontiac to be gassed and greased. The afternoon before, following the unfortunate business with Sally, he had registered in a new hotel, in St. Pete, then painted two beach scenes at Indian Rock. After five o'clock, when officers came from work at MacDill and Drew to stroll the beach, he had cased the uniform blouses left in their cars until he found a major's gold oak-leaf insignia and a full colonel's silver eagles.

A headline in the Tampa *Tribune* made him worry anew about Lorenz, across the state in Eden: FBI ROUNDS UP 124 AXIS ALIENS IN TAMPA RAIDS. He read quickly through the story. Germans, Italians, and Japanese in the Tampa area classed as "potentially dangerous" were taken into custody. Seized in the mass raid were two Swiss rifles, seven hundred rounds of ammunition, coastal maps and charts, shortwave receivers, and stacks of foreign-language propaganda.

He read with particularly acute interest the story on Sally Parkins. "Body found by a policeman. . . . Autopsy being conducted." A not very accurate description of Mr. Pimlico followed. Police assumed that he had a car, but they had not been able to obtain a license-plate number. Krug was relieved. Nothing to worry about. He had left no trail.

In another story an Air Corps sergeant who had been assaulted in the men's room of a local tavern was reported in improved condition at the Drew Field hospital.

"Your car's ready, sir," a smartly uniformed service attendant told Krug, who paid the $2.50 bill and drove back to MacDill Field, a bomber base that occupied a peninsula jutting out into Tampa Bay. He parked his car a block away from the main gate and marched up to the MPs at the gate, who gave his uniform, gold oak leaves, and Major Peter Krug ID card only the barest notice.

Once inside, he walked briskly, with eyes set straight ahead, and returned the salutes of junior officers and enlisted men in the U.S. Army style that he had practiced before his hotel mirror. He identified the principal buildings—one marked 29TH BOMBARDMENT GROUP, another marked B-17 OPERATIONAL TRAINING UNIT, and three hangars—studied the movements of the MP guards, identified the runways, and stood for a while on the flight line watching the olive-drab four-engine B-17s take off on training flights.

These must be the new B-17E Flying Fortresses. They were considerably changed from the B-17C type the British had used last year with less than impressive results. Herr Joseph Goebbels called the plane a flying coffin. This new model had a lengthened rear fuselage, an enlarged tail assembly, and increased armament. But Krug guessed that there were spots where its guns were blind, where a Fortress could be approached without fear. He would have to fly in one to find out.

Krug saw a sergeant line chief break away from his duties and attend to a C-47 transport that had landed and taxied up to the chocks. Krug backed off somewhat, but not out of listening range, when a full colonel alighted and said to the line chief, "Colonel

Howard from Southeast Training Command. Top off my tanks and tell the next Fort crew I'm going to ride with 'em."

"Yes, sir!" the line chief acknowledged.

"And get me a chute and some high-altitude gear. That fits."

"Yes, sir!"

Krug was impressed. Obviously a colonel could throw his weight around here. He reached into his pocket and took out his colonel's insignia. A rapid promotion, he thought, but well deserved.

THE next morning Tony talked with the Tampa chief of police in his office. When the chief entered the detectives' room with Tony in tow, Detective Jim Boney stood up from his worn wooden desk.

"Boney, Father D'Angelo from St. Augustine. He's come here about Sally Parkins. I told him we'd found her mother and got her permission for an autopsy. Father D'Angelo just called her and suggested that Sally might have wanted to be buried as a Catholic. Why don't you tell him what happened, Detective? Let's sit down."

Boney·sat, reached for his typed report, and summarized its contents in a clinical drawl. The man, Mr. Pimlico or whatever, gave the bellhop some baggage and told him Mrs. Pimlico would not be needing a cab after all. "Once outside," Boney went on, "Mr. Pimlico carried his baggage up the street, so neither the desk clerk nor the bellhop got a look at his car. Then one of our police cars pulled up at the hotel with Mr. Arthur Templeton, one of the city librarians, who had called here very concerned that a woman registered at the Gasparilla had found a paper all in German about one of our Air Corps planes at Drew Field. The policeman went up and found Mrs. Pimlico's—Miss Parkins'—body. We gave Mr. Templeton's notes to the FBI. Our reasoning at this point? Harold Pimlico is a German agent interested in warplanes. The FBI is having all the gate guards at Drew and MacDill fields keep a special lookout for anyone answering his description. The problem is, the description we have is so general, it's not much help."

The chief explained, "A death like that, with the man disappearing, is suspicious to start with, even with no visible wounds on the body. The man grabbed the woman round her throat from behind and choked her. The autopsy confirmed the death as homicidal."

There was not much that Tony could do, unless, of course, he provided the chief with Pimlico's real name, verified his physical description, stated that he represented himself as an artist, and revealed that he had earlier killed a man on St. Augustine Beach, where he had landed from a submarine. But Tony decided that the virtue of prudence still dictated caution and silence.

He said his good-byes to the chief and Detective Boney and looked at his watch. Ten a.m. already. Where was Krug now? he wondered as he walked to Belle's car. Even with a name and an accurate description, the authorities probably would not be able to locate him. Krug would be a step ahead of them, and even more deeply underground than before. Only a Jack Russell terrier like Tom Murphy's could run this varmint to ground.

Who would that be if not himself?

By TEN o'clock Colonel Krug was already back inside MacDill. This time he had driven through the main gate, where the guards examined his credentials a great deal more closely than they had yesterday. Probably they had his description. But he passed inspection nonetheless. No doubt being a colonel helped. From the gate he drove to the rear of hangar number three and parked. From that point he marched officiously around the hangar to the flight line, where pilots and crewmen were assembling around their Flying Fortresses. In one group he sighted the same line chief he had seen before.

"Sergeant," he called, "Colonel Krug from Southeast Training Command. Line me up with one of these crews. I'll need high-altitude equipment and a parachute. I'll want a pencil and a clipboard. And I'd like to talk with the engineering officer."

"Yes, sir!" the line chief acknowledged, and sent a corporal scurrying to fill Krug's order. "You can ride with Lieutenant Parry, sir. Tail number one nine zero two four."

Most of the ten-man crew entered the Fort through a door near the tail assembly. Following their lead, Krug tossed his heavy protective clothing and parachute through the hatch. Then, grabbing the hatch frame, he swung up with all his might. In the pilots' compartment he donned the fleece-lined pants, boots, jacket, and helmet. Lieutenant Parry and his copilot dropped the jump seat for him. A crewman stowed his chute.

AT TEN THOUSAND FEET KRUG activated his throat mike, copying the pilots. "Lieutenant Parry, level off. I'm going to do a walk-around."

"Yes, sir."

"Engineer, I want you to accompany me."

"Yes, sir."

During the climb Krug had studied the bombload and armament data included in the pilot's handbook. Estimated average bombload was six thousand pounds, more than the Heinkel 177 was scheduled to carry. Next he had studied the machine-gun data.

Now Krug disconnected his headset, stood up, and gestured for the engineer to lead the way.

"We'll look at the tail guns first," he yelled.

"Yes, sir," the engineer responded, and led Krug aft across a catwalk in the bomb bay past the two waist gunners, squatting by their lateral gun apertures, and back to the tail gunner's station, where the engineer called the gunner out so Krug could enter.

BACK on the ground, Krug dropped through the nose hatch into the company of Captain Ehrlich, the engineering officer.

"Did you have a good flight, sir?" he inquired solicitously.

"Yes, very good," Krug replied. "Good crew. The guns tested well."

As Krug divested himself of the high-altitude gear, Ehrlich looked up at the two-story tail. "Big bird, isn't she, sir?"

"Yes," Krug agreed, but a better name, he thought, reflecting on her bristling firepower, was four-engine fighter. Except that she was incredibly vulnerable to an attack closing from forward—a fatal flaw. The .30-caliber nose gun was inadequate, and there was no armor in the nose, no bulletproof glass. With luck, a 109 or 190 could destroy nose and cockpit, then rake along the fuselage.

"Guess we'll be sending these men overseas pretty soon, sir," Ehrlich ventured as they walked back toward the hangar.

"I'm not at liberty to say, Captain," Krug answered.

"Of course, sir. It's just that I heard the Forts were leaving and being replaced by B-26 Marauders. I dread it if it happens, sir. Those planes are highly intolerant of pilot error."

"I hope you're wrong, Captain. Now I want to see your map room."

"Yes, sir. It's in operations. I'll show you, sir."

AFTER SAYING A PRIVATE MASS for the Dead at the Jesuit Sacred Heart Church on Florida Avenue and getting the pastor to telephone an introduction to the Catholic chaplain at MacDill Field, Tony drove Belle's car to the airfield's main gate, where he was met by First Lieutenant Timothy Feehan, from the archdiocese of Boston. Feehan drove them in an olive-drab Ford sedan to a wood-frame building adjoining the field chapel. "The name's Tim," he said, showing Tony into his small office. "I hear you've got something confidential and urgent."

"Yes, I do," Tony said. "Confidential because it's under the seal of confession. Urgent because it relates to national security and the lives of innocent people. Tim, the key person in all this is possibly on your airfield. I know what he looks like. So I'd like your help in looking around the field to see if I can spot him."

"Of course," Feehan said. "I want to help."

Feehan went to the door and called to an enlisted man at a desk. "Corporal Wozniak, Father D'Angelo needs to take a look around the field. It may take a while. Use the sedan, okay?"

"Yes, Lieutenant."

While Wozniak headed for the car, Tony asked, "If I don't find what I'm searching for here, are there any other airfields where I might look? I already know about Drew."

"Then I guess you gotta go to Eglin out in the panhandle. I'll walk you out to the car and show you on the map."

At the car Feehan took a road map out of the glove compartment. "See Choctawhatchee National Forest here? It's been taken over by Eglin. And they're clearing auxiliary fields out in the swamps. You need boots to make your way around there."

Tony put out his hand. "Thanks for your help, Tim. I owe you one."

"Just solve the problem, Tony, and when you do—as me sainted mother in Ireland says, nail 'im."

IN THE ops map room at MacDill, Peter Krug found exactly what he wanted: a sectional air map of Eglin Field and a field advisory dated February 15, 1941. Eglin Field, it turned out, was a two-runway main field near Valparaiso. Eglin's mission was tactical testing of aircraft and armament. There were extensive bombing and gunnery ranges. Engineers had begun construction of seven auxiliary fields. Satellite Field 1, east of Highway 218 and below Mossy Head, was now complete, with two paved runways for special projects training. Krug made a rough trace of the graphics and copied down the pertinent numbers. Then, clipboard in hand, returning salutes all the way, he walked aggressively to his car.

As he made the turn onto the gate road, at ten-miles-per-hour posted speed, and approached the PX and commissary, he sighted in the distance two men, one in black, the other in khaki, stepping out of an Air Corps vehicle and walking in his direction. The man in black had a white square at his throat, indicating that he was a priest. Krug would have thought no more about it, except that when he drew closer, he saw that it was—it was that priest from St. Augustine! D'Angelo! What was he doing here?

Now, suddenly, the priest stopped walking and stared through Krug's windshield like two headlights on bright. He had left a trail after all. But how? Sally, of course. She must have been in the papers up there. And the priest knew his name.

Krug watched him step out to the edge of the road, apparently for a better look. Krug swerved sharply, accelerated, and aimed at D'Angelo's black legs. Just as the priest was about to be crushed, the man in khaki reached out and pulled him back. *Verdammt!*

AFTER watching his assailant drive out the main gate, Tony rushed back to Belle's car. He spent the rest of that day and all of the next looking around Tampa. Though he sighted many uniformed men who had Krug's stature and hair color, none turned out to be his quarry. On Sunday morning he helped with a late Mass at the local parish church, then struck out in the Ford for Eglin Field in the distant panhandle.

Passing north of Tampa into Pasco County, he realized that he was truly on his own now, feeling his way in the thinly settled backcountry, with only a few Catholic rectories should he need an inn or a port in a storm. He decided to skip the rectories. He had enough cash to stay at tourist cabins. And that would free him from intrusive questions. He also considered the fact that he had no Mass kit or portable altar stone, so the obligation of daily Mass would have to be dispensed with. No matter. He was making his own rules now.

The narrow, rough state roads took him through alternate

stretches of dense pines and hardwoods. Where the land was cleared, he could see dilapidated farmhouses and roving cattle followed by white herons, but very few humans. When he finally reached Tallahassee, he stayed overnight at a small tourist court on U.S. 90.

12

THE next morning Tony pressed westward on U.S. 90. The long drive to Eglin was uneventful except for his stop, between Bonifay and De Funiak Springs, at Strickland's Country Store: SALT PORK, CORN MEAL, HORSE COLLARS, CLOTHING FOR MEN AND WOMEN. Tony parked in front of the large, low building with a tin roof and wraparound porch filled with potted plants and flowers. Inside, three men in bib overalls discussed dogs around a black wood stove.

Tony acknowledged the storekeeper's "Howdy" and walked past wooden barrels of dill pickles and pole beans in bulk, hundred-pound cotton bags of scratch feed and cracked corn. Throughout there was the scent of peppermint, shoes, soap, coffee, and oilcloth. When he reached the clothing section, he decided it had exactly what he needed: corduroy trousers, cotton shirts, and a wool sweater. He tried on a couple of pairs of hunter's boots until he found the right fit.

Tony put his purchases on the counter. The storekeeper looked up and said, "I think you need a collar to go with that shirt you're wearin', mister."

"No, thanks," Tony said. "These will be fine."

The storekeeper totted up the cost and observed, "You're the second Yankee what's been in heah in the last two days. Normally I don't get two in three months."

Suddenly interested, Tony asked, "Do you remember what the other one looked like?"

"Sort o' long and muscle thick and talked kinda funny, like you."

"Do you remember what he bought from you?"

"Hunter's boots, waterproof, and field glasses," the storekeeper said, wrapping Tony's clothes in newspapers and string.

"Did he say where he was headed?"

"You Yankees are awful curious. Didn't say."

"Thanks." Tony paid his bill. "I like your store a lot."

"You're country welcome."

Unlike the smell of the store, Krug's scent fouled the nostrils.

BY MIDAFTERNOON Tony reached Mossy Head, where, as his map showed, State Route 218 descended south through the Eglin forest. He made the turn and plunged into a narrow paved defile between tall pines. At Valparaiso, on an arm of Choctawhatchee Bay, he found a room at the Bay View tourist court. In the early evening, after bathing and finishing his prayers, he dressed in his clericals and drove down to the Gulf of Mexico. Along the coastal highway he decided to try the seafood at a place called Bacon's by the Sea.

"Red snapper," he told the waitress. "With iced tea, please."

He looked around. There were only a few tables empty. Half were occupied by Army Air Corps officers with their wives or dates. In the background a jukebox played "I'll Get By."

"Excuse me, Father."

Tony looked up to see a young officer. "Yes? Good evening."

"I happened to see you here, Father. Can I buy you a beer?"

"That's very kind of you, sir, but no, thanks."

"Is your church around here, Father?"

"No. Actually, it's in St. Augustine, on the Atlantic coast."

"Do you happen to know Father Showalter in Omaha?"

Tony smiled. "No, I'm afraid I don't." He was about to utter a breakaway phrase that would let the officer get back to his table, when he said something very different—"Is that your home?"—in order to hold the officer in place and shield himself from the view of a male civilian who just entered the room and resembled—more than resembled—*was* Peter Krug.

"Yes, Father, it is."

His heart pounding, Tony managed to ask distractedly, "Do you live here now, uh, is it Lieutenant?"

"Yes, Father. I'm sorry, I can't talk about it—military regulations."

Krug was being led to a table in the center of the room.

"Of course. It was stupid of me to ask. Let me just say, whatever you do, I pray that you will be kept safe while doing it."

"Thank you, Father. Will you bless my rosary?"

"Of course." As he did so, Tony saw that Krug was seated

with his back to him, absorbed with a group of officers and ladies.

Saying good-bye to the officer, Tony struggled to make sense of the moment. He felt his chest fill with a new emotion he could not at first identify. He did his best to eat his snapper, while examining the back of Krug's head and his broad, evil shoulders. As he drained his iced tea, he decided what his emotion was. It was anger.

The taste in his mouth was not tea. It was spit and vinegar.

HAVING changed into his uniform and colonel's insignia at the Bay View tourist court in Valparaiso, Peter Krug and his Pontiac presented themselves at the Eglin Field main gate at ten fifteen that night. The guards here, he had found on penetration earlier in the day, were serious. They carefully compared his face to the photo on his card and asked his destination.

"Officers quarters," he answered this time, blandly.

The guards here might be more intimidating than the casual patrols in Tampa, but their weakness lay in their regularity. Tonight he would time the patrols on the main field, where twenty-four B-25B Mitchell bombers were parked in two rows. There was something very curious about these B-25s. They had been modified. They had no gun turrets on their undersides and instead sported twin guns in Plexiglas tail cones.

After parking at the officers quarters and walking to the flight line, Krug stood in the dark corner of a maintenance building and timed the patrols. There were few lights. The quarter moon was hidden by clouds. After concluding that one of four guards would pass each aircraft every five minutes, Krug selected the third aircraft in the first line.

After a guard passed at eleven forty-two, Krug waited ninety seconds and then made his move in a running crouch. When he reached the tail cone, he looked up to check the twin guns for caliber. Curious. Even in the darkness he could see that the barrels had no air-cooling apertures. He jumped to feel the barrels. Wood! These "guns" were nothing but black-painted broomsticks!

He had to get inside the fuselage quickly, and found to his relief that the rear door came down easily. Once inside, he looked about with his penlight. The broomsticks, of course, had no firing mechanisms. In the interior space that would have been occupied by the gun turret, he saw that a fuel tank had been installed. Why? Farther forward, he came upon a large, rolled-up, collapsible fuel cell with a hose line. How much more fuel did that provide? Why the extended range?

In the pilots' compartment, Krug looked around for the usual equipment. Something was missing from aluminum brackets. Radios, to judge from the disconnected wiring. Removed, he assumed, to reduce weight. He poked around for the pilot's handbook and checked performance specifications. He stepped down into the bombardier's compartment. No Norden bombsight in the nose. Instead, he found a curious, seemingly handmade, two-piece aluminum device like the sight of an air rifle. What was this all about?

He checked out the .30-caliber gun in the nose and then looked at his watch. A guard should be coming down the line now. He looked out the nose glaze and saw one coming. After the soldier passed, Krug waited ninety seconds and then let down the trapdoor. Within another minute he was back at the maintenance building.

What was going on here?

Perhaps he had to give more time to the plane in the air. He had noticed this morning that six planes flew off in the direction of Mossy Head. He had called the telephone operator in Mossy Head and asked her if she had heard a flight of bombers come over her town, and the answer was no. So the Mitchells were stopping somewhere short. And he bet it was at Satellite Field 1.

IT WAS on one of Eglin's forest highways that Tony found himself this morning, on the trail of Peter Krug's Pontiac. He had set up the trail immediately upon paying his check and exiting Bacon's by the Sea the night before. He tracked Krug to the Bay View, whose quarters they shared, ironically, and then, following again in his vehicle, watched Krug, in Air Corps officer's uniform, drive to the Eglin main gate. About midnight he saw Krug emerge and return to his quarters.

Krug did not leave his room until seven thirty a.m. Putting on his new clothes and boots, Tony watched through the curtain as Krug's car moved out the driveway and turned north. Tony got into his own car and followed, though not closely. The road was familiar. He looked at his road map. The next town was Mossy Head.

After about ten miles Krug's car pulled to a stop on the shoulder, and Tony saw him get out and look east to the sky. Without slowing, Tony looked, too, seeing, just over the trees, several olive-drab airplanes wheeling against the luminous blue. There was nothing to do but drive on past, blowing into his handkerchief as he came abreast. In the rearview mirror he saw Krug remove equipment of some kind from his trunk and walk into the scrub.

Tony stopped his car over the next rise and also walked east into the forest. It was not like any walk he had taken before. There were no forests in Manhattan. But he made his way steadily forward, keeping the morning orb of the sun and the sound of airplane engines in front of him.

KRUG was familiar enough with the carry of aircraft engine noise to know when he was drawing close to its source. After walking a mile and a half, he figured that he was about an eighth of a mile distant.

Near the tree line, movement in the scrub! Krug ducked behind a pine. Within a minute's time he saw two helmeted soldiers, with rifles, crossing in front of him.

Security at Eglin Field was tight, but this was incredible! What was there about a wilderness airstrip that required guards? He decided to wait before proceeding farther. Two men again, after exactly twelve minutes, a little closer to the tree line. And at fifteen minutes, somewhat deeper. Krug decided that he could rely on twelve minutes, less two minutes on each side, for forays.

He set up his easel, stool, and paints so that he would have an innocent position to retreat to if needed. Then, two minutes after the next patrol, he ran for the tree line. From behind a pine he fastened his eyes on the airstrip.

One Mitchell was just lifting off, wheels retracting. Two others were in the pattern overhead. A fourth was holding for takeoff. The airstrip had flags placed on both sides along its shoulders, beginning about thirty meters ahead of the holding aircraft, and ranging forward at sixty, ninety, a hundred and twenty, and a hundred and fifty meters, or—let's see—five hundred feet. They had to be indicators for landing practice, Krug concluded, since the normal takeoff distance for a Mitchell was fifteen hundred feet.

The B-25B in takeoff position now spooled up its rpm, but

higher, Krug thought, than was needed. It trembled behind its howling engines and frenzied props. Suddenly the plane came off its brakes and lunged forward in a takeoff roll. Abruptly, *before the last flag,* it yanked up in a near stall, brought its wheels up and its nose down, built up speed, and remained airborne! *Donnerwetter!* If he had not seen it, he would never have believed it.

He checked his watch and quickly retreated to his easel.

Krug observed twelve more practices. They were baffling. What was there about this amazingly abbreviated takeoff that was so important? He had had to practice short-field bomber takeoffs himself in Germany, but never anything like this. Here the bombers were getting off in the space of a postage stamp.

Perhaps he could find some answers from the air. He decided to rent a plane.

TONY had to walk perhaps a mile and a half—not as far as he feared. What he really had cause to fear was stumbling face to face on Krug or on the military sentries, whom he sighted just in time to avoid detection. He imagined that Krug was similarly stalled, so he turned south, hoping to catch a long-distance view of the agent. After ten minutes he sighted Krug at his easel.

Tony knew that Krug was not here to paint. He was here because of the planes. Sure enough, every fourteen or fifteen minutes Krug dashed in the direction of the tree line. He must have timed the sentry patrols, Tony figured. He hung back in the trees, but he could see, barely, Air Corps planes taking off and landing one after another. It had no meaning for him, but it must have for Krug. Tony watched Krug painting, leaving, returning, painting, leaving—

Until eleven forty-five, when, apparently, the planes all left—and Krug disassembled his easel. Tony took off for his car at his best speed. As before, he followed Krug at a safe distance. Krug turned west on U.S. 90 and stopped at a gas station at Crestview before driving east four miles to a flying field with a metal hangar. Three small planes were tied down on the edge of a grass field. Krug's car was parked near the hangar.

From the shoulder, a quarter mile off, Tony kept his eye on Krug's parked vehicle and, after about fifteen minutes, saw Krug reenter it and drive back toward Crestview. Tony followed and saw Krug driving south on State 54, which Tony knew was another route through the Eglin forest. When it seemed Krug was headed all the way to Valparaiso, Tony made a U-turn and drove to the airfield. There he found a man in overalls working on a bright red plane in the hangar.

"Excuse me," he said. "Have you seen a man here named Krug?"

"Yes, sir," the man answered. "A fella by that name was just here. Wanted ta rent a plane."

"Oh, were you able to take care of him all right?" Tony asked.

"Well, yes and no. I told 'im our only rental, a J-3 Cub, was bein' flown up in Alabama today by a couple of hunters, but it'd be back tomorrow afternoon. So he gave me a deposit to hold it."

"Good. I'm glad it worked out." Tony reached into his pocket for a ten-dollar bill and handed it to the mechanic. "I'd appreciate it if you wouldn't say I was asking about him."

The mechanic winked. "You got it."

BACK at the Bay View, Peter Krug considered his deadline, the dawn hours of March 13—three days hence—when he would rendezvous with U-*Böhm* off St. Lucie Inlet. The deadline was approaching too quickly; in order to have a time cushion, he should leave today. But an air view of the Mitchells' takeoff field was absolutely essential. And a call to other nearby airports had failed to turn up any rental earlier than the Cub at Crestview tomorrow.

"BELLE Hart speaking."

Tony deposited thirty cents.

"Belle, this is Father D'Angelo."

"Oh, yes. How are you *doing?*"

"Fine, thanks. I think I'm ready to take that airplane ride."

"Wonderful."

"And you said that you liked to go from point A to point B."

"Yes?"

"And what if point B is a good distance from point A?"

"Well, try me."

BELLE started out toward the panhandle in the only rental plane available that day, a yellow 1940 J-3 Piper Cub. She made a good seventy miles per hour ground speed tracking U.S. 90 and spent the night in Tallahassee with an old classmate. In the morning she pressed westward, remembering scenes from the Ruth Darrow Flying Stories she had read as a girl. What exactly was the adventure Father D'Angelo had in mind?

Tony met Belle's Cub when she landed at Fort Walton, on the Gulf, and drove her to a nearby restaurant for a bite of lunch. He expressed his deep gratitude that she had come so quickly and so far.

"I ordered my tank topped off," she said, opening her map. "How far do we have to go? The Cub doesn't have much range."

"To the north edge of the forest below Mossy Head," Tony said. "We'll have to fly east about twenty-five miles, north to U.S. 90, then west a short distance to Mossy Head."

Belle examined her aeronautical map as Tony continued. "Just below Mossy Head we're going to be looking at a small Army Air Corps landing field built on a clearing in the forest."

"And can you tell me why?"

"No, Belle. I'm terribly sorry. There's that matter of privileged information I told you about. I have to ask you to trust me."

"Oh, I do," she assured him. "You have my car after all. And I wouldn't have flown all the way out here for any other man I know—except one. But can you be just a little more specific about what I should be looking for?"

"No, I can't. I just want to know what *you* see. And I think as soon as we finish lunch, we should get going." Remembering that Krug was expecting his plane this afternoon, Tony wanted to make his flyby before Krug got in the air.

On returning to the airport, Belle showed Tony how to strap himself in the back seat of the small, fabric-covered aircraft.

"And here're some earphones to put on. They're connected by a hollow tube to my voice piece," she explained. "Through it I can talk to you over the engine noise. Unfortunately, you can't talk back. If you need to tell me anything, undo your seat belt, lean forward, and yell in my ear. Okay?"

"Okay." He had never yelled in a woman's ear before.

At one o'clock the yellow Cub lifted off and headed east along the Gulf of Mexico, then north along the eastern edge of the forest. When Belle turned west at the top of the forest and came abreast of Mossy Head, Tony could make out the narrow north-south cut of State 218 through the woods. With the help of Belle's binoculars, he soon was able to sight the airstrip. He handed the glasses to Belle and shouted, "Directly to your left—an airstrip, and olive-colored airplanes landing."

Belle eased the throttle back and peered through the lenses. "Is that what you wanted me to see?"

"Yes and no. I want you to see the planes. They take off and land again and again."

"Then I'll fly on past and come back on the same track."

Twenty minutes later she was back, due north of the strip. Now she could see one of the planes readying for takeoff.

"It's a B-25," she said. "Twin-engine medium bomber. There he goes—off the ground awfully fast, I'd say, and before reaching a double white line painted across the runway."

"What does it mean?" Tony yelled.

"I don't know," Belle answered. "It looks like short-field takeoff practice. I'll watch the next one."

She did. And the next one. And the next. "They're lifting off before that marker," she said. "And it's a very short distance—almost the takeoff distance of a Cub." She paused. "There's a white line down the center of the strip, and it ends at the double white stripe about an eighth of the way down the strip. It could be practice for short jungle-strip takeoffs, or . . . those lines may really be meant to mark off a carrier deck. No, it can't be!"

"So you think something important's going on?" Tony yelled.

"I can't be sure," Belle answered. "But if it's medium bombers training to take off from carriers, it's *damn* important—excuse my language."

Tony looked out the window to his left and—*Oh, no!*—could no longer see the ground on that side. His whole frame of view was filled by another yellow Piper Cub, only tens of feet away, its pilot, with field glasses, studying their faces.

PETER Krug had decided to drive out to Crestview immediately after lunch, just in case the hunters in that rental Cub got back early from Alabama. He was not disappointed.

"Shot their limit already," said the mechanic, who seemed also to be lineman and general factotum. "She's all topped off."

267

After a brief checkout flight with the mechanic, Krug took off, heading east to the point where State 218 entered the Eglin forest. At forty-five hundred feet he held the stick between his knees and sought the auxiliary airstrip through his binoculars. And there it was, with the last of a flight of six Mitchells landing on its paved surface and one of them poised for takeoff. It was not the aircraft, though, that froze his attention—it was the runway. Two white painted lines across the runway! And another line down the center that ended at the double line.

These bombers were flying off a simulated carrier deck!

Of course! That's it!

He slowed the aircraft, watching the first bomber take off in the space defined by that double white line. He watched the second bomber do the same. The Air Corps pilots were going to fly these Mitchells off a carrier to—where? Not Germany or the occupied countries, since they didn't need a carrier to get them there. No, it had to be a target in the Pacific. And what target did the Americans most want to hit right now?

Tokyo.

Remember Pearl Harbor.

He had to get word out right away. Only a U-boat's transmitters could reach Germany, which, in turn, could reach the Imperial Japanese Navy. He would call Lorenz as soon as he landed.

Tokyo was why the Mitchell pilots had installed fake guns—to discourage Zero attacks from astern—why they added extra fuel tanks, and why they installed the handmade bombsights—they were much better at low altitude.

He had begun a right turn and a slow descent to Crestview when his eye caught sight of another yellow Piper Cub ahead and above him by some hundred and fifty meters. *What the—* He added power and easily overtook the other craft, which was on slow cruise. Coming from behind, he knew he was out of sight. He pulled close alongside, the binoculars in his right hand.

There were two people on board the other Cub—a blondish young woman in front and a man. Krug adjusted the focus. It was that Father D'Angelo! How had he followed him here? What was he doing in the air? And now D'Angelo apparently recognized *him.* He shouted something at the woman, who suddenly accelerated forward and then made an evasive diving turn left, reversing course.

Krug followed, but found it hard to keep up with the other craft as it banked below him. With his rudder hard left and stick forward, he dived on the other craft, his thrashing propeller aimed at its tail.

As BELLE pulled out of her dive, she looked back out the port window to see the other plane following her. "What's going on with that guy?" she asked through the voice tube.

Tony, his stomach still moving in a different direction from the rest of him, leaned forward and yelled "He'd like to see me dead. If he's got a gun, he'll use it."

Belle whipped the plane into a sudden right bank, then level again, so that she could see her pursuer. The other Cub was diving on them. Was it going to chew them up with its prop?

Belle dived, too, with throttle wide open. "Be sure your belt is on tight," she warned Tony. Abruptly she pulled the stick back, and the plane shot up in a loop. The other Cub whipped by to the left, only inches away. Tony gasped as Belle's plane dropped inverted out of the top of the loop. Dirt fell off the floor into his face.

At the bottom of the loop Belle made a tight turn to the right, hoping to gain some separation. But the turn slowed them, and she looked back to see the other Cub coming on fast. She checked the altimeter: thirty-five hundred feet. A quick turn to the left; then she laid the stick all the way back again, and when the steeply climbing plane trembled into a stall, pushed hard on the right rudder. The maneuver caught their pursuer out of position. Breaking off the attack, he made a slow roll off to the left.

Belle's Cub went spiraling down toward earth, seemingly out of control, and thoroughly frightening Tony, who made an audible act of contrition. After a seven-hundred-foot drop Belle applied left rudder, pushed the stick forward, and pulled the Cub into level flight. Tony looked around for their foe. Krug was spiraling down right after them like a fallen angel.

"Did you say you went to an airfield in Crestview?" Belle asked.

"Yes," he yelled.

"Try to find it," she urged him, handing the glasses back while she concentrated on the other Cub, which, to her distress, she could not find. Where *was* it?

With all their maneuvering, Tony estimated that they were to the west of Mossy Head. Ahead was the other forest highway, State 54, that led to Crestview. He saw the town in his glasses.

"Straight ahead," he yelled just as their plane shuddered violently and whipped sharply to the right. They were hit!

Belle dived to escape, then leveled off. The rudder pedals flexed freely back and forth. The cables were shot. She would have to steer with the ailerons and elevators alone. Could she land?

"If he gets the rest of the tail," she shouted into the tube, "we're goners. Come on, Cub," she coaxed.

Her mind laced with hope against hope, Belle flew on toward Crestview, knowing that their only chance was to outrun their attacker. She jockeyed the plane forward, banking and yawing, but flying steadily in a shallow full-throttle descent. She dared not turn to look back, for a turn would bleed off miles per hour. So far, she had the speed advantage—why, she didn't know.

Now, with Tony gesturing forcefully to the right ahead, she saw a building with CRESTVIEW written across its roof and a grass field alongside. She pushed her nose down and headed for the grass. Five hundred feet . . . four hundred . . . She could see the wind sock. They could make a straight-in approach. Thank God!

Just before touchdown the plane yawed suddenly right, hitting the ground with the left tire and bouncing them into the air again. Belle held the ailerons hard over right, and the plane righted itself enough for both tires to hit together. Two more bounces and they were down, rolling to a crawl.

As soon as she could, Belle braked the Cub into a turn back to the hangar and taxied over the rough grass at her best speed. She saw with relief that the other Cub had not followed them. Searching the sky, she finally saw the yellow wings at a low altitude to the south. Her heart was pounding and her hands were shaking when they climbed out of the stricken plane. Tony leaned against the fuselage and tested his legs. Belle walked to the rear of the aircraft to study the tail. The entire fabric-on-aluminum rudder was gone. Cables dangled on either side.

"Well, I ain't seen nothin' like that b'fore," said the overalled mechanic, who came alongside. "Get yer tail caught by a buzzard?" he asked Tony.

Belle didn't know how far Tony wanted to carry this. "We had a small midair," she said. "With another yellow Cub."

"Musta been with my plane I rented," the mechanic ventured. "Wonder why he don't come in. He's a friend o'yourn, ain't he?" he asked, remembering Tony's visit and the ten-dollar bill.

"I'll make a report to the Civil Aeronautics Administration," Belle said. "And I'll want you to repair the tail if you have the parts."

While Belle and the mechanic talked repairs, Tony walked over to Krug's car. The keys were in the ignition. When he returned to the plane, he took a ten-dollar bill from his wallet and handed it to the mechanic. "Here. I'm going to call you from the road to find out where that other pilot goes after he lands. Okay?"

"Sure 'nough."

Tony took Belle by the arm and led her to Krug's car, saying over his shoulder, "Tell my friend that I've borrowed his car."

As Tony and Belle drove off in the Pontiac, he said to her, "We'll exchange this car for yours, pick up my things, and get you home."

"Thank you," she answered. "But whose car is this?"

"The man who tried to chop us up."

"And we're stealing his car?"

"Borrowing it. After what he did to us this afternoon, I think he deserves a little inconvenience, don't you?"

"I think I'm seeing a new side to you, Father."

"Yes, I suppose so. Perhaps it's about time."

"Why don't we press charges? You say he wants to kill you!"

"He'll disappear. I have a feeling things are moving too rapidly. I may be the only one who can nail him. The police would slow *me* down, not him."

"But I'd at least like to know why he tried to kill you—and me with you. Don't I have a right to know at least that?"

"Yes, Belle, you have a right. No, Belle, I can't tell you. It's a terrible position to put you in, and I'm extremely sorry. I'm trying awfully hard to keep a solemn secret. Maybe I'm being too scrupulous. Anyway, my main desire right now is to get you safely home. And also I'll take care of the costs to your plane."

"Well, it's all very mysterious to me, and I'll pursue it another time. I'm scheduled for an antisubmarine patrol tomorrow afternoon, and I'd like to be back in time for that."

"We'll drive. On the way I'll have to call the Crestview airport to find out, if I can, where our attacker is going next."

"You really are onto something, aren't you?"

"The most that I can say is yes."

FLYING back and forth aimlessly, Krug simply did not know what to do next. Should he land at Crestview, pay for damage to the prop, and drive off to Eden? No—the priest would probably have the police there. Should he land at another airport and abandon the plane? Perhaps—but he would have no transportation. Should he keep this plane and fly on to Fort Pierce with the nicked prop? No—the prop might not last, and the Cub was so short-legged he would have to land at airports all along the route for refueling, and the police could be on the lookout.

Finally he decided that he would land at Crestview, explain that he had had a midair accident that was his fault, and offer to pay for repairs to both planes.

Which is what he did. But just as he feared, a sheriff's deputy was waiting with the mechanic when he taxied up to the hangar and the Cub with the torn-up rudder. But no sign of D'Angelo and the woman.

"I'm afraid I had an accident with your plane," he said to the mechanic after getting out.

"Well, I 'spicion so." The mechanic fingered the dented brass leading edges and the splintered blades. "You're darn lucky this prop didn't fly apart on ya. It's junk now. And look what you did to the other plane," he said, pointing to Belle's Cub.

"Can you replace the prop and rent me the plane through tomorrow? I'll be glad to pay you whatever it costs. And I'll pay for the other plane, too. The pilot did a fine piece of flying to get it down. Is he around so I can apologize?"

"It was a she. No, she's gone. And I don't have a new prop. Have to order one."

"Can you rent me one of these other planes tied down here?"

"They're privately owned. No way I could. You said you'd pay. Have ya got cash? I reckon one hundred for the new tail and two hundred for the prop."

Krug peeled off three hundred dollars and handed it to him.

The deputy spoke up for the first time. "You got some identification, mister?"

Krug produced a pilot's license and his selective service card.

The deputy looked them over and handed them back. "I got a call from a hog farmer that said he saw two yeller planes hit each other. Well, no one was hurt, and you paid up, so I'm gonna git me some barbecue. Runnin' late on eatin' today, Virgil." He winked at the mechanic as he left.

"Do you have a phone?" Krug asked. The mechanic pointed to a corner of the hangar.

Krug called Lorenz person to person. No answer. He had to get Lorenz to send word out about the carrier bombers right away, so Japan could get ready. He would try again from the Bay View.

When he exited the hangar, he looked across to where his car had been parked. "Where's my car?" he asked the mechanic.

"Your friend took it what was in the plane with the woman."

"My *friend?* He's no friend! Where did he take it?"

"Don't know."

"Darn! And I have to get to Fort Pierce." Krug regretted the words as soon as they left his lips.

"There's a train leavin' tonight fer Jax," the mechanic offered. "I'll git you to the Crestview station in my pickup."

"Can you drive me to Valparaiso to pick up my suitcase?"

"In the pickup? Heck, it can't git *that* far."

WHEN Tony called Crestview airfield from a pay phone in De Funiak Springs, there was no answer. When he called an hour and a half later from Marianna, the mechanic picked up.

"I'm the man who gave you the ten-spots," Tony said. "What can you tell me about the fellow who rented your plane?"

"He said you ain't his friend," the mechanic replied.

"Yes. He's right. And I apologize for deceiving you—"

"And that you stole his car."

"Well, I didn't. Did he say what he was going to do?"

"Said he had to git to Fort Pierce. I took 'im down ta Crestview station. Leaves at seven on Louisville and Nashville number one. He was madder'n a wet hen. All he was carryin' was a flat cardboard thing. An' he forgot his field glasses. Where'd you put his car?"

"After the train leaves, call the sheriff and tell him to look at Fort Walton airport. I'm afraid I carried the keys away in my pocket."

"The ticket agent said he's got to change at River Junction to the Seaboard mail and express that gets into Jax at six fifteen tomorrow, then buy another ticket south. He's got a wad of money. Is he a gangster?"

"You could say that. Okay, six fifteen a.m. at Jax. I think I owe you another ten-spot. What's your name and address?"

"Virgil Bass, Rural Route 2, Crestview. God bless America."

"Amen to that."

13

THE Ford V-8 droned on eastward through the night into the early morning hours, the mile markers on U.S. 90 flipping by like page numbers in a book. Tony and Belle took turns driving. As people who are only acquaintances are wont to do on a long trip, they revealed much of their personal selves to each other.

"For most of my classmates," Belle said, "college was just a way station before marriage and children. But not for me."

"What was it for you?" Tony asked.

"It was a chance to grow up, to learn how the world works, to debate ideas, to test myself in sports and aviation."

"Is it too personal for me to ask—did you have gentlemen friends and go out on dates? You're a very attractive person."

"Thank you. Yes, I did. And I have a gentleman friend right now. But our relationship is on inactive status for the time being because he's in the military and I'm trying to get overseas, too. How about yourself? Do you have any lady friends?"

Tony smiled. "A fair question. No—it's not allowed."

"Do you have a problem, then, with just you and me alone, late at night, side by side? Does your church have rules about that?"

"*Numquam solus cum sola,*" he answered.

"That's Latin, I guess. And it means?"

"A priest should not be alone with a woman in a tight space."

"Like this?"

"Like this."

"Don't you feel guilty?"

"You certainly know the right terms, don't you? But, you see, our traveling together is something perfectly correct because it's something that must be done. Besides, I enjoy your company."

"Breaking the rule gives you a little exhilaration, doesn't it?"

"Yes, as a matter of fact, it does." He laughed.

"Well, I think if you can dodge death in the air the way we did yesterday, you can certainly resist my advances on the road."

Tony looked over to see Belle's mischievous smile, and laughed again. "Don't think I discount the power of your charms."

"Thank you for that. You know something? Calling you Father D'Angelo is too stiff and formal for what we've been through. I think I'll call you Solus if you don't mind."

"Okay, Sola," he said, surprised at the pleasure that filled him.

STILL nursing her wounds, U-*Franz* sighted the lights of Savannah to starboard on her scheduled cruise south to St. Lucie Inlet. The air attack ten days before had bent the starboard propeller shaft, set the motors on fire, and jammed the main oil-pressure pump.

Repairs had been made to all the equipment except the propeller shaft, which would have to await return to the yard at Lorient. Over all, it had proved easier to mend steel than mind and emotion. The boat's interior was thick with unassuaged grief and anger. The shock of losing Kapitänleutnant Böhm had afflicted every grade and rank, with the seeming exception of Oberleutnant zur See Wolf-Harald Franz, formerly first watch officer, now interim commander.

The damaged boat had surfaced in the general vicinity of the flying boat's attack, but there was no trace of Böhm or of the U-boat's life preserver. "Needle in a haystack," Franz had observed on the dripping bridge. "I doubt we'll ever find his body. No one could have survived the concussion of four bombs."

"Still, we have to keep searching," Baumann had insisted.

"No, we don't have to keep searching," Franz had answered coldly. "What we have to do is sink ships, complete our mission, and get home. I'm not going to waste precious fuel searching for a cadaver. One more hour at slow cruise and that's all."

But in the intervening ten nights Franz had not sunk any ships. Four times he lost his target, missed, or miscalculated. Word of his decision to give minimum time to hunting for Böhm had circulated among the crew; men of lower rank wondered how much time he would spend looking for *them*. And, in marked contrast to the leadership style of Günther Böhm, Franz had instituted severe punishments for minor infractions of the rule book—seven men committed to hard lying, an unprecedented number in U-boats.

Baumann argued with Franz that his iron discipline was self-defeating. "You're killing the fighting effectiveness of the crew," he attempted to persuade him.

"These men were coddled by our Latin scholar," Franz answered acidly. "With me they will have to meet higher standards."

"At least their Latin scholar, as you call him, sank ships."

"That impertinence will be duly noted in your fitness report."

BELLE dropped Tony off at Union Terminal on West Bay Street in Jacksonville. At four thirty a.m. she was an hour away from St. Augustine. When she got home, she assured Tony, she could get in a good sleep before flying her antisubmarine patrol.

"Oh!" Tony remembered as he reached into the back seat for his bag. "I forgot to tell you the Crestview mechanic said that the man who attacked us paid for the repairs to both planes. But I'll still pay for your trip back out there to pick up your plane."

"Please don't," she said. "I can afford it." She put out her hand. "Good-bye, Solus. I won't forget our adventure together."

"Good-bye, Sola. Neither will I. Maybe someday I can tell you about the service you've rendered. Thank you from a grateful heart, and God bless."

Tony was well ahead of time to meet the Seaboard mail and express when it pulled in at six fifteen. From a secluded position he watched Krug alight and walk into the cavernous waiting room. The German carried a flat case. For what? Tony wondered.

Krug walked to the ticket window and purchased a ticket. After checking the time on his watch, he walked across to a coffee shop and sat down to order.

Tony went immediately to the same ticket window and told the agent, "The gentleman who just purchased a ticket from you—I want to go to the same place. We're together."

"Walton?" the man asked.

"I thought we were going to Fort Pierce," Tony said hesitantly.

"Walton's a flag stop south of Fort Pierce," the agent said. "Actually, he's getting off at Eden, but you have to buy a Walton ticket."

"A ticket to Walton, then," Tony said.

"Eleven o'clock, track three." The agent handed him his ticket.

Tony paid the agent and walked to a corner of the waiting room where he could watch Krug without being seen. It was going to be a long wait, nearly four and a half hours before departure.

AT NORFOLK seadrome, Bo Burke and his crew, in another PBY-5 Catalina, lumbered into the early morning air, bound for Florida, except that neither Bo, Ray, nor Sam was piloting. They, their crew, and their gear were being flown down to NAS Jax, where their orders were to pick up their original Cat, now repaired, and fly it to the air station at Banana River. The U.S. Navy Gulf Sea Frontier command, headquartered at Key West, needed a long-ranger for patrol duty. So it was so long, Norfolk, hello, Banana, to join that station's six PBM Mariners and the OS2U Kingfishers. GSF wanted the Mariners to concentrate on transitional training, and the Kingfishers were too short-legged for extended seaward patrols, so Bo, much to his liking, would have the first choice on bombs.

From the navigator's compartment Bo and Ray looked out over the Atlantic—calm, flat, unmoving, gray-flannel. "I've been thinking, Ray," Bo said. "Luck probably plays a big role in all this, and one of these days—or nights—Bo's going to get lucky and a bomb from our boat is going to pop right inside the lethal range and Bo's going to win a Kewpie doll."

"I know you're right, Bo," Ray encouraged him. "It's gonna happen. All we need is a little bit of Lady Luck."

THE blue-and-white Taylorcraft crabbed left into the wind in order to maintain course parallel to the coast on Belle's first anti-submarine patrol leg, north to Jacksonville Beach. Westward the sky was darkening—a sign, she thought, of typical Florida afternoon cumulus buildup. The CAA had no special weather advisories for the p.m., so Belle concentrated on the calm ocean surface a thousand feet below.

At Jax Beach she made a slow 180-degree turn to the south and crabbed right on the return to St. Augustine. Ahead she noticed low-lying scud pushing off the land. The horizon was darkening there, too. She wondered if she should continue her intended patrol south to Flagler Beach. There probably was no need for concern. Enough gas was sloshing around in her tanks to make Flagler in case St. Augustine closed in. She kept her attention on the sea, looking for a U-boat's feather wake.

South of St. Augustine, she found the weather a bit more menacing, with embedded dark masses. Wind intensity picked up, and her little craft began to bump in the gathering turbulence. By the time she reached Flagler Beach and began her turnaround, she was surprised at how strong the westerly wind had become. It seemed that her Taylorcraft was standing still as it faced the shore, which now, she discovered as she continued the turn, was lost to view behind unbroken cloud. And she could no longer see the ocean.

Her heart beat palpably, and her hands became moist. Reducing power, she bounced her way below the seven-hundred-foot overcast only to find herself in light rain with about two miles visibility. She had never before experienced such a rapid deterioration of flight conditions. Could she push hard west through this stuff and regain sight of land?

She tried, but the turbulence was so severe, the head wind so strong, the rain so intense, she had to turn back out to sea, aided violently by the overpowering air currents. Don't panic, she told herself. Don't become disoriented. Stick to the panel.

She reached for the radio earphones and hand mike. "Taylorcraft NC two three six nine one to St. Augustine airport. Over." Only static crackled over her earphones. She repeated the call ten times. No answer. From anyone. Atmospheric conditions may have shot communications. The radio was only a one-watter. And maybe she was too distant. She checked her fuel—one eighth to empty. Would she have to ditch? Yes, yes, yes! Only seaward could her little craft continue airborne—and for how long? Grimly she tried flattening her course and found that she could stay ahead of the weather. But she was still going out to sea. To crash.

It was four fifty on her watch when, ominously, the four-cylinder engine coughed and lost power. Belle pushed the nose down to maintain airspeed. Altitude: five hundred feet. The last quarts of usable fuel fed from a new angle in the exhausted tank. Four more times Belle made her futile radio calls. Then, abruptly dry, the engine quit altogether, and, in the strangely peaceful silence that followed, the plane descended gently toward the ocean.

Belle cut the switches and cracked open the doors. She checked the pockets of her slacks to make sure she had her wallet and the Saint Christopher medal that Solus had given her during their drive from Fort Walton. The main thing was to stall the aircraft just before touching water. She tightened her seat belt, knowing that as soon as the wheels hit, the plane would flip over on its back. She had only to keep her head. Forget the sharks. Just keep her head.

FRANZ disengaged the hatch spindles and stepped out onto the frothy bridge platform, the lookouts right on his heels. He quickly checked the horizon and sky with binoculars, then called, "Starboard ahead one third."

As the first diesel exhaust fumes and noise came up from starboard, the bridge watch steadied into their rhythmic routine, lenses sweeping the four quadrants of a choppy sea and dark, messy sky, wind-force 6 or 7 westerly. Of a sudden, the port aft lookout shouted, "Herr Leutnant! An aircraft going down!"

Franz turned his glasses. Northeastward he could see the dark form of a single-engine aircraft ditching in distress. It had its wheels down, so it was fixed-gear and not likely to be military. But what was a civilian plane doing this far out?

"Both ahead full," he ordered. "Come left to zero five zero." Ordinarily a U-boat would dive at the sight of any plane, but this one was crashing and ought to be investigated. Franz went forward to the voice pipe. "Deck force, prepare to recover survivor."

Turning again to the stricken plane, he watched its final moments. Just before the wheels touched down, a large black object came out the starboard door. Then the wheels hit and the engine dug in with a white splash and the fuselage overturned forward. The pilot extricated himself and swam back toward the black object, which must be a life preserver.

Coming alongside the still floating aircraft, Franz saw that it was no more than a brightly painted sport plane. What was a plane like that doing in a war zone? There was an insignia of some kind on the fuselage. He would interrogate the pilot and, if there was nothing useful to be gained, throw him back like a too small fish.

Brought aboard, the pilot surprised all the deck force with his slim build and delicate features. The chief bosun, checking him for side arms, abruptly stopped and drew back. Then, stepping forward again, he undid the pilot's chin strap and pulled the helmet off.

Belle's damp blond hair fell to her shoulders.

Stunned, the bosun made an about-face and shouted to Franz on the bridge, "Herr Leutnant! It's a *woman!*"

WHEN the train pulled out of Fort Pierce, Tony asked on which side of the tracks the Eden station would appear.

"The left, sir," the black-clad conductor replied.

"Okay. Will you make sure the train stops there for me?"

"Sure. There's another man getting off."

"I'd like to get out on the right side, opposite the station."

"I can't do that, sir. It's against the rules."

"Just this once." Tony handed him a ten-dollar bill. "And I want to get off on a different car from the other fellow's."

"Just this once," the conductor said.

It was the fourth time Tony had offered a ten-spot. Were they bribes or payments for service received? If bribes, were they justified by the good result that was intended? He'd sort it out later.

If Krug had walked through the coach cars, Tony had not seen him, because he had slept four hours with his hat over his face. Then he had gone to the toilet, where he remained for the rest of the trip.

At five thirty-five p.m., when the train slowed down for what had to be Fort Pierce, he had emerged from the toilet to strike his deal with the conductor. Now the train slowed again as it passed Walton. The conductor came by to show Tony the between-cars steps where he could alight. When the Eden flag stop was reached, Tony grabbed his bag and jumped from the lowest step to the ground, flinging himself into a thick patch of palmettos by the tracks.

The train jerked away. When the last car cleared, Tony looked up carefully to see Krug standing with his case in front of the tiny station, turning slowly in a circle to observe everything around him. Apparently satisfied, he walked east down a dirt road.

Tony remained motionless. And it was a good thing he did. Five minutes later Krug reappeared at the tracks and made another searching observation. Then again he turned and walked east.

Tony left his bag in the scrub and dashed for the tree line alongside the road. As quietly as he could, he moved forward, pausing from time to time to listen for Krug's step, anxious that his quarry might reverse his course once more.

Suddenly, where the woods thinned ahead, Tony saw movement crossing from right to left. He stopped behind a tree. Krug was walking slowly, head down. Tony looked along his line of march and sighted a yellow house half hidden by bushes. Krug knocked on the door. When, after numerous knocks, no one came, he cupped his hand against the glass and peered through a window.

Abruptly he walked off in an easterly direction. Tony followed, keeping to the high cover. After about two hundred yards he broke into the clear and saw ahead a crossing roadway, a river, and a boathouse at the end of a long, weatherworn pier.

He watched Krug walk with his case along the pier to the boathouse, place a key in the lock, and enter. Tony was looking for a better position, where he could sit down to rest and watch, when he was surprised by a sudden grinding noise from the boathouse. A minute later there was a muffled roar. A covered boat sortied into the water, with Krug, barely visible, at the controls. The boat turned south and picked up speed, leaving a considerable wake, which lapped the shore.

Had he lost Krug after all this?

Tony quickly walked the length of the rickety pier and tried the boathouse door. It was open. Inside, he took a quick look around the brightly lit interior. There was a second boat in the water below, an open runabout of some kind. Along the three walls of the boathouse were catwalks and shelving.

Whose house, boats, and boathouse were these, anyway? he wondered. Another agent's, like Ohlenburg at St. Augustine Beach? If so, where was he? How did Krug know to come here? Where was he now with the boat?

Suddenly Tony's eyes opened wide at something leaning against the wall: Krug's case! He opened it and looked inside. Watercolors on paper. Eight or nine. Very good, professional work. Nothing else. But Krug would not have deliberately left his work behind, would he? It meant that Krug would be back. Enormously relieved,

Tony walked back along the pier, across the road, and into the trees, where he established a comfortable position from which he could keep watch. His empty stomach growled.

At eight twenty-five p.m. he heard an engine on the river to the south. Five minutes later he sighted the black form of a northbound boat. It slowed and turned into the illuminated boathouse.

BELLE sat stoically in seaman's clothing at the wardroom table. Across from her, Franz and Baumann sat examining the contents of her wallet, spread out in damp, neat rows.

Baumann translated each document for Franz. "This is a license to drive an automobile," he explained. "These two are licenses from the Civil Aeronautics Administration—"

"What's this?" Franz asked, picking up a card marked with the same insignia he had seen on the fuselage of the plane.

"'Civil Air Patrol,'" Baumann read.

"Ask her what that is," Franz directed.

When Baumann did so, Belle answered in a straightforward fashion, "It's an organization of private pilots who fly missions to help in emergency situations like forest fires and lost airplanes."

When this was translated, Franz exploded, "You're a liar, woman! There are no forest fires out here in the ocean! Do you take me for a fool? And if a plane was lost this far out to sea, your government would not send a tiny sport plane like yours to hunt for it." He slammed his fist against the table. "You were reporting on U-boats! You are a spy!" He turned to Baumann. "Translate."

Belle was startled by the commander's guttural outburst, and for the first time felt fear at the hands of her captors. When Baumann finished, Franz added, "Tell her I want detailed information on coastal air patrols off Florida, and if she does not supply it, I will throw her back in the sea."

As Franz glared threateningly at Belle, Baumann translated Franz's demands, interspersing, "Be advised this man is a cold-hearted warrior. . . . He will treat you badly. . . . If you do not know information, make it up."

Belle nodded obediently. Baumann translated into German as she spoke. "Several hundred patrol planes originally destined for shipment to the British have been reassigned to antisubmarine patrols off Florida. These include PBYs and PBMs, OS2U Kingfishers, and even a squadron of the new B-17Es. The intention is to give saturation coverage to every merchant lane in Florida waters, and to make it suicidal for U-boats to operate here."

"When will these forces be in place?" Franz directed Baumann to ask. "And where will they be stationed?"

"The end of this month," Belle answered. "At Jacksonville, Banana River, Key West, Tampa, and Pensacola."

"Give her some paper and a pen to draw silhouettes of these planes," Franz said. "And when she's finished, dump her in the forward torpedo room until I decide what to do with her. I will not have a spy defiling the officers quarters."

"Jawohl, Herr Leutnant."

When Belle began sketching, she found it easy to do. She knew all these planes cold—as did most schoolboys. If a spy wanted to know what a given warplane looked like, he need only open *Life* magazine. She was not giving anything away. And if the commander believed her story of massive antisubmarine patrols, she might be doing more to keep the U-boats away than the entire state CAP.

But what would happen to her when she finished her sketches? Would she be thrown back into the sea? Or be taken to Germany?

She reached into the pocket of her seaman's pants and fingered the Saint Christopher medal. Irrational though it seemed to her Protestant soul, she prayed, "C'mon, Chris. I need you."

When Belle finished her sketches, the chief bosun led her into the forward torpedo room and made Franz's order clear to every hand: The prisoner was sentenced to hard lying. At 0910 German war time—2:10 a.m. local time—Franz made one of his chilling inspection turns through the boat and seemed satisfied that Belle was where she was supposed to be—flat on the cold steel floor plates. After Franz returned aft, Puster Schneewind, who spoke English, came in from the radio room to report that Franz had doused the light in his cubicle for a few hours' bunk time. He said that he would make a click on the loudspeaker system if Franz woke up. Then he knelt beside Belle and invited her to get up off the plates and use a bunk. He gave her a hand to pull up on.

"Don't worry about us here, miss. We respect you as a lady. We want you to feel at home, as far as that's possible."

"Thank you," Belle said. She had reached her breaking point, and she covered her face with her hands while the tears flowed.

How her mother must be hurting at this moment. Would she ever see her again? Would she ever see Bo? Or her friend Solus?

Schneewind touched her elbow and said, "Why don't you lie down now on this bunk, miss? If the commander or the bosun comes, we'll have to remove you to the floor, you understand."

"I understand," Belle said sorrowfully, and laid her head on the pillow, where sleep soon practiced its consoling ministry.

Krug forced himself awake and looked at the phosphorescent dial on his watch. Four a.m. He stood up and turned on the boat-house light. The Chris-Craft cushions had made for a comfortable mattress, and he felt refreshed for the U-boat rendezvous.

Lorenz's tide tables scheduled high tide for 5:17. Dawn, he knew, would be about 7:15. He would have to get through the St. Lucie Inlet two hours before dawn in order to avoid the perils described by Lorenz. And, speaking of Lorenz, where, he wondered as he looked at the still upright coffee cup in the boathouse, had the FBI spirited him after his apprehension in the house? Fortunately, the Bureau had left everything intact and unexamined. Krug had found an old pair of binoculars upstairs.

The trial run to the inlet last evening took only sixteen or seventeen minutes to cover the seven-nautical-mile distance. Once through the inlet at high tide, he would still have to go three nautical miles seaward to reach the position where U-Böhm was supposed to be waiting. Had better be waiting.

He decided to go ahead and make his start now. He could stand in the river off the inlet and wait there for the tide.

Tony was awakened by the noise of the boat's engine. He raised himself up from his woodsy lair and watched as the boat went forward slowly and then, building speed, turned south. He ran to the boathouse, which was still unlocked, and switched on the light. Krug's case was gone.

Tony stepped into the open Gar Wood boat, with its sleek wood deck and front-and-back seating compartments. He studied its controls. They seemed simple enough if he could get it to go. He stepped back up to the catwalk and cut off the light. Then he untied the lines and sat down behind the wheel. Remembering what Belle had done in the Piper Cub, he cranked what looked like a throttle and pushed what might be a starter. The engine's loud response surprised him. Another lever with a round ball on top seemed to be a gearshift, and he pushed that forward. His neck whipped back as the boat shot from the boathouse.

He retarded the throttle, and when the boat slowed down, he turned south, close to the right shore in order to veil his pursuit. Scanning the river, after twenty minutes he caught his first dim glimpse of Krug's boat. He could just make out the off-white canvas top. The boat was proceeding slowly along the left shore; then it came to a stop. Had Krug thrown out an anchor? It certainly seemed so. Tony cut his engine.

On boarding the runabout, Tony had noticed that the rear seat compartment was filled with nautical and fishing gear. He wondered if an anchor might be included. While the boat drifted, he crawled back to see. Amid ropes, a life preserver, sinkers, lures, and—ouch!—gang hooks, he discovered a four-pronged anchor, connected by line to a cleat on the transom. He lowered it into the shallow river and shortened up the slack in the line. Then he donned the life preserver and waited—but not for long.

At five fifteen by his watch, he heard Krug's engine start up. Immediately Tony hauled up his anchor. Then he switched on his own engine and followed at what he hoped was a safe distance. Was Krug going to meet someone? Tony could not see any other boat.

Krug turned east and pressed steadily toward the Atlantic. After ten minutes the flat river gave way to waves and whitecaps. The bow of Tony's craft began to slap down hard against black currents. This was an inlet, he realized. They were going out into the ocean!

Fifteen scary minutes later Tony entered calmer water. He was actually out in the ocean itself now, he reasoned, rising and falling on more agreeable swells. And ahead of him, perplexingly, he could no longer see Krug's boat in the predawn light.

What to do now? With no reference points, which way should he head? The boat's compass read 80 next to an E, which he assumed meant east. Reducing power to a crawl, he maintained that heading as best he could. Had he lost Krug now for good?

14

Bo's crew were relieved when the big wing leaned right and P-10, out of Banana River, settled onto her homeward leg to St. Lucie Inlet. They had made no sightings along the two-hundred-mile arc they patrolled that night, and everyone was a mite bored.

Their aircraft, in fine repair, flew as sweetly as she ever did. While Ray, in the right seat, searched ahead with glasses, Bo fine-tuned the throttle quadrant and checked the gauges all around. Oil pressure on the money, still plenty of fuel. He looked out the windows. Visibility five to six miles, sea mirror calm. Ten minutes to sunrise.

Bo switched on the intercom mike. "Look alive, everybody. This is the time when subs submerge for the day. We might see a swirl. A periscope wake. Wipe your glasses and your eyeballs."

To his left the cloud bases were catching first light.

In U-*FRANZ* the deck force scrambled to their stations to make the pickup. As Baumann prepared to mount the ladder, he overheard Franz commanding the bosun, "I don't want that woman spy interfering. Take these handcuffs and shackle her to a stanchion."

"*Jawohl, Herr Leutnant.*"

After the bosun had gone forward, Baumann said to Franz, "Suppose we're attacked and have to abandon ship—"

"She'll be the last one I'll be concerned about."

"It's not honorable," Baumann protested.

Franz brushed past him and up the ladder. "The victors define what is honorable."

Baumann caught the bosun returning from his mission. "Good job, Bosun," he said. "You can give me the key."

"*Jawohl, Herr Baumann.*"

Baumann reached the forward gun deck. Looking in the direction of shore, he saw nothing but mist and broken cloud cover. Turning, he saw that the sun was throwing up its first faint suggestions to the east. Under him, the boat rocked gently on the warm Florida swells. Above, the bridge watch swept the horizon.

At seven thirty a.m. the starboard forward lookout broke the silence with a yell and pointed to the southeast. Franz stared intently through his binoculars in that direction.

"A small dot, Herr Leutnant," the lookout explained.

"That's interesting," Franz said. "I see two dots."

WHEN the first thin band of orange-gray light appeared on the horizon and the overnight sea mist began to lift, Tony sighted Krug's boat about three football fields distant. It was not moving fast but tossed casually on the swells, as though waiting—waiting for what? So far, the German seemed not to have noticed him.

Then, abruptly, about half a mile ahead, a strange dark form with a narrow superstructure materialized. Its silhouette became more defined, displaying guns, periscopes, and men on deck. At the same instant, Tony heard Krug's engine speed up.

Krug was meeting a U-boat!

Tony revved his own engine and headed toward Krug's craft. Krug mustn't reach the U-boat. He knew too much. He knew about the bombers. And the carrier—if Belle was right. Rashly throwing his throttle to full power, Tony aimed his prow directly at Krug, who was now staring back, binoculars raised. Tony was surprised how rapidly he was intercepting him. He certainly seemed to have the faster boat. Ten yards distant, Krug turned sharply to his right, but Tony's boat would not be eluded. At the last instant Tony threw seat cushions against the bulkhead and hurled himself behind them.

The banging, grinding collision knocked Tony about badly. He reached up to ease the throttle and take a look. His prow was smashed and splintered, and he figured that he was taking water. But Krug ran back and forth between the engine hatch and his controls, seemingly unable to get his boat to run.

Tony went back to the wheel, circled around, aimed his prow at Krug's forward hull, threw his throttle to full, and dived for the cushions before impact. This time the collision was fiercer. As his boat, gravely wounded, glanced off, Tony felt hurt over his entire body. He managed to reach up and reduce power. Lifting himself painfully, he saw with satisfaction a five-foot gash in Krug's hull down to the waterline. Krug climbed to the front deck, waving both arms frantically toward the U-boat.

Tony got his legs to move well enough to regain his seat. He brought his boat alongside, grabbed his anchor, and hurled it. It bit into the open rear part of the Chris-Craft. While Krug ran back to dislodge it, Tony took up the slack in the line, put his engine into gear, and slowly pulled the larger boat away from the U-boat.

Krug glowered at him across the twenty feet of line. "Damn you, priest! Why do you follow me?"

Tony shouted back from his wheel, "I'm not going to let you get to that sub, Krug!"

"You have no business—a damn priest!"

"I'm stopping you not as a priest but as an American."

"You're supposed to be a man of peace. I will kill you, priest!"

Krug dived into the sea and began swimming to Tony's boat. Alarmed, Tony leaped into the rear seat, grabbed a long fish knife and cut the anchor line. Then he jumped back to the throttle and pushed it all the way forward. The crumpled and waterlogged boat edged away just as Krug laid a hand on it.

Now, as Tony circled around Krug's boat, he saw Krug begin swimming back to it. Suppose he got it going again? He could yet make his rendezvous with the submarine. Tony wheeled his stricken craft about, and, ice in his heart and "Lord have mercy!" in his throat, he aimed the jagged prow at Krug. When he came close enough to be heard, he yelled, "Stop swimming! Halt, or I will run you down!" Which he prayed he would not have to do.

Krug swam directly at him, reducing the distance between them and making it harder for Tony, in his broken boat, to accelerate enough to do him mortal damage. Tony started to turn away. Krug grabbed a board on the prow and hauled his body up on deck.

Tony swung the wheel back and forth, trying to throw Krug off balance, but the German held on and sprang over the windshield at Tony and—unseen to Krug until, in midair, it was far too late to do anything about it—onto Tony's upraised knife.

Just as the blade drove home in Krug's chest, the boat was rocked violently by the wave action from two nearby explosions, and Krug was propelled into the sea.

THE sun lit up the sea below as P-10 droned closer to the terminus of its search sector. At exactly 0743, Ray, who was still on glasses, shouted, "Tallyho!"

Bo grabbed his own glasses and followed Ray's lead. "Bingo!" he exclaimed, and reached for the mike. "General quarters! General quarters! Sparks, transmit to base and all ships." Then he cut autopilot and pushed over into a power glide.

Ray activated the bomb-release key.

Sam Singer ran to the bow gun turret, where he loaded and charged the .30-caliber. Aft, the tunnel .30 cleared.

Sparks transmitted a broadcast directly afterward. "All ships, all planes, P-ten attacking sub immediately. Position follows."

"All right," Bo said. "We're going to release two DBs, then make a second run for a salvo of two. Understood and set?"

"Set," Ray confirmed.

With the submarine now in full view, Ray reported, "Two guns, manned—large number of men on deck, course parallel to shore. *There's* something odd—a couple of small boats just to the east."

"Might be fishing boats," Bo suggested.

"Would a U-boat surface in the presence of fishing boats?"

Bo knew that coming out of the cloud bases with the sun at 180 degrees relative, he had a very good chance at a class-A attack. But two miles off, it was clear that P-10 had been detected. Crewmen rushed down the hatch, and the sub began a forward submergence. "Okay, it's gonna be class B plus," he said to Ray.

Bo banked sharply to 160 degrees so as to come up the track of the sub and lay down a straddle. At half a mile Singer opened up with his gun. The sub's conning tower was still visible as P-10 came over its port quarter to starboard bow. Bo eyeballed the release, hit the firing key on his yoke, and made a sharp evasive turn to port.

Looking back, he saw two towering plumes of water rise, one forward, one abaft, of the conning tower, lifting the sub's hull back to the surface. As he climbed higher, he could see a silvery green iridescent oil slick form around the sub.

"She's wounded, Ray," Bo shouted exultantly.

Ray could see for himself. "Looks like she's still trying to dive."

"Yeah. Her stern's going down but not her bow. Let's complete this turn and come at her again with the salvo."

"Aye, aye."

When they were at 270 degrees on the return, Ray observed excitedly, "They're abandoning ship!"

"They sure are," Bo confirmed. "Pourin' outta that tower hatch like rats from a hole. Let's finish her off."

P-10 made a shallow bank into the second bomb run. At the optimum instant, two vaned canisters of high explosive splashed together in a perfect bracket—right out of the textbook.

FRANZ struggled to make sense of what he was watching. There were two different small boats, two different men, and they were colliding. Was one of them Krug? If so, which one? And how could U-*Franz* decide? He was about to order up diesel power and make a run in that direction when the port aft lookout cried, *"Flugboot!"*

Franz turned to see with horror that a flying boat was almost on top of them. He leaned to the voice pipe and shouted, *"Alarmmm!"*

Then he shouted the same to the gun and deck forces on the fore casing. He had to slam the hatch shut with two men still on top. Even so, before the conning tower could be fully submerged, two explosions convulsed the boat—Click-*claang!* Click-*claang!*

Mighty forces made the floor plates tremble and the steel ribs moan. In emergency lighting Chief Engineer Brünner tallied the reports: The boat had been blown to the surface. Starboard fuel bunker ruptured. Overhead compressed-air line severed. Salt water in the battery acid, and chlorine gas forming in the bilges.

Franz stood by in the control room. "We're on the surface, stern down. Dive the boat!"

"I don't think it's safe," Brünner replied.

"Dive it anyway!"

Brünner rang the bell and gave the order. The control-room crew hit the buttons and turned the handwheels. The electric motors produced way. No submergence.

"The forward diving planes are jammed in an up position," Brünner reported. "We can't override by hand."

"Then we'd better abandon the boat," Franz replied. "Damn it to hell!" He wheeled around to Baumann, standing by. "Tell the men to prepare to abandon ship. Remind Puster to take all secret materials. You take the confidential papers." Then back to Brünner: "As we leave, set the timer on the scuttling charge."

"What about the woman?" Baumann protested.

"The woman was dead the day we found her. Now act!"

When everything was set, Franz gave the final order on the loudspeaker mike: *"Alle Männer aus dem Boot!"* After Franz the rest of the life-vested crew went up the ladder, Brünner the last, after setting the charge.

The last except for Baumann, holding the soluble confidential papers, who lingered until Brünner was out. Then he donned one life vest and grabbed a spare. Just as he began to run toward the forward torpedo room, the boat suddenly plunged sharply on her stern, and Baumann had to pull himself laboriously up through the bulkhead hatches. Behind him he could hear seas crashing through cracks in the hull.

Finally he gained sight of a none too happy aviatrix hanging from her handcuffs in the torpedo room. Reaching Belle, Baumann pulled the cuff key from his pocket and unlocked her restraint. Belle fell awkwardly into his arms, and he helped her into a life vest.

"Oh, thank you, thank you!" she exclaimed.

Baumann wrestled a ladder against the forward torpedo access hatch. Climbing up, he disengaged the spindles and opened the hatch cover. But almost the moment he started down to get Belle— Click-*claang!* Click-*claang!*

Baumann was thrown against a torpedo-hoist I-beam, where his skull shattered in a profusion of blood.

"No!" Belle gasped. As she worked her way down to Baumann's side, she grimaced at the pain from being slammed about. Feeling his chest, she detected no sign of breathing. "Please, God," she prayed as she tried his pulse, but there was none.

So there was but one life to save now, and it was her own.

Excruciatingly, she clawed up to the foot of Baumann's ladder. By dint of will alone, she climbed rung by rung, hanging on to the ladder rails with a fierce, unyielding grip as the wounded U-boat rolled in its final throes.

Finally she was able to look out the hatch. The view was nearly horizontal to the sea, whose swells lapped just below the opening. With one ultimate effort she pushed herself out into the water, where she gently floated off and away.

The sun was bright orange. She blinked her eyes in its light. She looked behind her briefly when the U-boat, in her death ride, slipped beneath the surface with a frothy gulp. Then she looked around—

crewmen everywhere floated in their vests. She paddled to the nearest one. His head hung low, as though he were asleep. She tried to rouse him. When he showed no response, she felt his pulse.

Dead!

She went to another. It was Schneewind, who had befriended her. He, too, seemed unconscious. She felt his pulse. Dead.

She looked around at the rest and hollered, "Is there anyone alive?" But there was no response, only the soft sound of swells merging with one another, U-boat crewmen, faces down, bobbing on them in a macabre dance. And dead fish all around.

An underwater explosion from the U-boat ruffled the surface and made her legs tingle. In the distance she sighted what looked like two pieces of wreckage. Paddling in that direction through the briny mortuary, she saw the body of Franz, the only one for whom she had no pity. Why had everyone died? There were no marks on anyone.

As she drew closer to the wreckage, it began to look like two capsized boats. Where had they come from? What happened to them? Even closer, she saw that a man lay on one of the boat bottoms. He seemed to be alive.

"Over here," the man hollered, seeing her approach. He left his flotage and swam out toward her. "Grab ahold here."

When he was within ten feet of her, he stopped still in the water and stared into her eyes. "Miss—"

She stared back. "Solus?"

"Belle?"

He swam to her and placed his hand on her cheek. "Belle, is that you? What are you doing here? Are you all right?"

"Yes, I think so. Is this a dream? What are you doing here?"

"I can't tell you everything, but I'll tell you what I can. Come."

When they reached the wreckage, and had climbed onto it, Tony called Belle's attention to the navy plane that was circling over the site of the sinking. "We have to keep waving so it'll pick us up. So let's wave like we've never waved before."

While they did so, Belle explained how she had gotten picked up by the U-boat and saved by a German officer. In his turn, Tony explained as much as he could, including the fact that the man he had confronted at sea was the same man who had attacked them in the Piper Cub.

"What happened to him?" Belle asked.

"I don't know if he died of the knife wound or drowned. After the two bombs exploded, my boat capsized, and afterward when I looked around, I didn't see him anymore. All I saw was his picture case floating off on the swells."

"You still can't tell me who he was?"

"No."

"Well, I can tell you who you are. I never believed in guardian angels until now. And I've had two: a German officer and you."

Tony laughed. "Now keep waving!"

Their arms hurt more than either would let on.

MAKING their third low pass over the scene, Bo and Ray were struck by the fact that none of the U-boat survivors were swimming, or waving, or making any movement at all.

"I wonder if they're all dead, Ray," Bo said.

"Beats me, Bo. The rescue vessel you radioed for can probably tell us. But look over there to the right. Those two boats we saw earlier are sinking. And there's two people, I think, hanging on to them. And they *are* waving."

"Yeah. I see 'em," Bo acknowledged. "We better pick 'em up. Go back and break out the rubber raft."

Ray went aft to the tunnel and pulled the raft from its case. When Bo had the aircraft fifty feet above the surface, Ray pushed the raft through the hatch while holding on to the rip cord of a CO_2 bottle. As the bundle left the plane, the raft began to inflate.

Bo began a climbing turn to set up the sea landing. When ready, he established a final approach laterally between the swells. Just above the nap of the water, he put the Catalina into a full stall. The hull swished and settled in.

Back in his seat, Ray directed Bo toward the raft, which now had two occupants. One of them was paddling it in their direction.

"Ray, board them through the starboard blister hatch."

"Aye, aye."

After Ray and the waist gunners had assisted the survivors inside the aircraft, Ray went forward to report, "You won't believe this, Skipper. One of 'em is a woman. And the other is a priest."

"You're kidding."

"No, I'm not. The woman said she swam through the Germans, and they're all dead."

"I'll be darned. You get us back in the air, Ray, and I'll go aft to talk with her."

The survivors were wrapped in blankets and sitting on lower bunks when Bo reached them. The woman stood up slowly when she saw Bo's face and placed herself in his arms.

Bo's mind lurched. "Belle?" he asked incredulously.

"Bo," she replied in a thin voice.

He lifted her head gently from his shoulder and looked at her mottled face and red eyes. "Are you hurt, Belle?"

"I'm all right," she answered in a near whisper.

"Belle, what are you doing here?"

"Getting rescued, I hope." She glanced behind her. "This is my guardian angel, Father D'Angelo."

Bo looked at him blankly. "Father," he acknowledged.

"I have lots to tell you, Bo," Belle said, "but I'm so tired now."

"Don't talk anymore. Here"—he led her back to the bunk—"lie down and let me strap you in."

Which he did, kissing her lightly on her bruised cheek, while Tony, strapped in another bunk, stared at his hands and remembered, *And you girded me with strength for war.*

15

Sunday, April 19, 1942

WHEN he finished reading the St. Augustine *Record*, Bishop Garvey pushed it across the breakfast table to Tony and observed the young cleric closely as he read the full-page headline story:

JAPAN ADMITS KEY CITIES ARE BOMBED

U.S. AIRMEN ATTACK TOKYO AND OTHER CENTERS

(AP) Japan announced yesterday that her capital, her two greatest ports, and the center of her warplane production had been bombed by U.S. Air Force planes and that most of her home islands had spent hours under raid alarm. The raid appears to be the most daring of the war.

Garvey watched Tony lay the paper down, brace his shoulders, and gaze determinedly into space. There was no question that a change had come over him since his leave last month.

The bishop decided to make a guess.

"Tony," he said, "I think I'll call you George."

When Tony did not ask why right away, Garvey knew that he had made a pretty good guess.

SEVEN blocks away, a jubilant Belle Hart showed the telegram she had just received to her mother and her gentleman friend:

YOUR APPLICATION APPROVED RAF AIR TRANSPORT AUXILIARY. REPORT 27 APRIL 1000 HOURS TO HDQTRS ATA RAF FERRY COMMAND DORVAL AIR STATION MONTREAL. BRING ALL CREDENTIALS. MARY NICHOLSON FOR JACQUELINE COCHRAN.

Taking the telegram back, she kissed it and, arms outstretched like the wings of a plane, twirled around the living room.

Her mother smiled and left the two of them alone while she returned to the kitchen to snap beans.

Belle asked Bo if he still had his decoder pin.

"Of course," he said, reaching into his pocket.

"Give it to me."

When he did, she laughingly threw it into the wastebasket. Then she placed herself in Bo's arms, and they kissed for a long time—a very long time—long enough, Belle thought, for her mother to become concerned.

But then, she also thought, what the hell!

ABOUT
THE AUTHOR

Michael Gannon

On the night of April 10, 1942, in St. Augustine, Florida, teenager Michael Gannon and his friends heard on the radio that a ship was in flames off the coast—bombarded by the deck gun of a submarine. "Everyone in Jacksonville was watching. Riding our bikes to the tip of Anastasia Island, we could see the red glow." Thus began the author's lifelong fascination with U-boats and military history.

Much later, while doing research for his acclaimed nonfiction book *Operation Drumbeat*, Gannon was to discover that the incident represented the first attack by the Third Reich on the United States. Exactly how did he find out? By a surprising coincidence, Gannon interviewed the German commander of the U-boat responsible for the very attack he had witnessed as a teenager.

Gannon's contact with things military has by no means been confined to research. Kept out of the army during World War II by a bad eye, he signed up with the American Field Service to drive ambulances for the British. And a stint as a war correspondent in Vietnam left him disenchanted with war but more interested than ever in military matters. Today a history professor at the University of Florida, Gannon is engrossed in writing a suspenseful follow-up to *Secret Missions*. After all, he muses, "how can we know that Krug is really dead?"

PHOTO: © 1994 BY JERRY N. UELSMANN

Eyes of a Child

Richard North Patterson

The nightmares wouldn't go away.

Caught in a brutal tug-of-war between her parents, little Elena kept waking up terrified, certain that something awful was about to happen.

Or had it already happened and now she was only dreaming?

Just what dreadful thing had she seen through her child's eyes?

"Patterson's new thriller is a miracle of agonizingly focused suspense."

—*Kirkus Reviews*

THE NIGHTMARE

October 16

ONE

RICARDO Arias' face filled with fear and disbelief.

"If you're going to kill yourself," the intruder repeated softly, "you must leave a note."

Richie's eyes would not move from the gun. Pulled from damp and darkness, it had not been fired for years. The intruder wondered if it would fire now, but Richie Arias did not know this.

Sitting at his desk, Richie began groping for the pen.

His movements were sluggish, like those of a man struggling underwater. Fixated on the gun, he seemed blind to the darkened living room: the worn couch and armchair, the cheap coffee table, the computer on the desk, the answering machine he used to screen creditors. A chrome standing lamp cast a pall on his skin.

His face was thin, with black eyes that shifted from softness to anger as suited his needs. Blood trickled from one nostril.

"I never write." His head twitched toward the computer. "Everyone knows I use that."

"Suicide is different." The intruder's voice was strained now. "The handwriting must be yours."

Richie's face looked drawn. Slowly he picked up the pen.

"I am ending my life"—the intruder spoke for him—"because I have faced what I am."

An instant's pause, the instinct to resist. Then Richie's pen began to inch across the paper. The effort was awkward and hesitant.

"What I am," the voice instructed, "is selfish and pathetic."

301

Richie stopped writing. His eyes filled with resentment.

"*Do it,*" the intruder ordered.

Wiping the blood from his nose, Richie stared at the paper. It was a moment before his hand moved.

"My only business is extortion. I have used my wife and child, out of greed and shamelessness, because I myself am nothing."

Richie flushed with anger. He stopped, staring at the words he had already written. His hand would not move.

The intruder hesitated, irresolute, then saw, on the bookshelf next to Richie, a photograph. Gun aimed at Richie, the intruder retrieved the picture and placed it carefully on the desk. A dark-haired girl, her solemn brown eyes gazing at Richie Arias.

Richie's face showed that he understood the rest.

"You see," the intruder said softly, "I know who you are."

As if by instinct Richie stood. "Wait," he cried out. "You can just leave. I won't tell anyone. We can just let it go, okay?"

Slowly the intruder started toward him. Five feet, then four.

Richie's face was taut with fear and calculation. Backing toward the coffee table, he seemed to have forgotten it was there. His eyes flickered toward the bedroom hallway, searching for a way out. His throat worked. "Shoot me now, and it's murder."

The intruder stopped, raising the gun.

Richie's eyes changed. "I'll give her up," he whispered.

In silent answer the intruder's head moved from side to side.

Richie turned to run. The gun jerked up at his first panicky step. As he stretched forward, straining for the hallway, Richie's leg slammed into the coffee table. There was a scream of pain.

The next few seconds were like freeze-frames: Richie snapping at the waist, arms flailing; sprawling forward, head bobbing like a rag doll; temple hitting the corner of the table. And then Ricardo Arias rolled sideways, flopping onto the carpet, and was still.

Gun hand trembling, the intruder knelt beside him.

There was a red gash on his temple. Blood dribbled from his nose. The luminous wristwatch on his arm read 10:36.

Gently the intruder pushed open Richie's lips with the barrel of the gun. As the barrel slipped into his throat, Richie's mouth clamped down, the reflex of choking.

Eyes shut, the intruder took one breath and pulled the trigger.

A metallic snap. An instant later the intruder, forced to look at Richie's face, knew the ancient gun had not discharged.

Richie blinked, the first tremor of consciousness. Watching him taste the black metal, the intruder prayed that the gun would fire.

Richie's eyes widened in terrible comprehension. His head rose, twisting feebly. His mouth opened around the barrel to form a single word. *"Please."*

The child shuddered.

It was dark. She was damp from the struggle to escape. Her legs could not move, and her voice could not cry out. Knees drawn up tight against her stomach, she lay there waiting.

The banging on her door grew louder.

As the door burst open, the little girl awakened with a soundless scream, torn from her nightmare.

She did not know where she was. But in her dream she had imagined what would break down the door: a savage dog with bright teeth and black curly hair, eyes searching for her.

A shadow moved toward her.

The girl shivered, stifling her scream, hugging herself so tightly that her fingers dug into her skin. And then her grandmother spoke softly in Spanish, and Elena Arias stopped trembling.

"It was only your dream," her grandmother repeated, and swept Elena into her arms. "You're safe now."

Elena held her tight, tears of relief springing to the child's eyes.

As Grandma Rosa lowered her head onto the pillow, Elena shut her eyes. She felt Rosa's fingertips gently touch her forehead. In her mind she saw her grandmother's jet-black hair, the slender face still almost as pretty as that of Elena's own mother, Teresa, whose room this once had been. The sounds of Dolores Street came to her: Latin voices on the sidewalk, the squeal of cars at a stop sign.

"Where is Mommy?" Elena asked.

Rosa repeated the words like a favorite story. "Your mother is still at her house. Tomorrow she's flying to a place called Italy. But she'll be back in ten more days. And in the morning when you get up, we'll find Italy on the map."

Elena was silent for a moment. "But Daddy's not with her, is he? Mommy's going with Chris."

"Yes." Rosa's voice was quiet. "Mommy's going with Chris."

Elena opened her eyes. In the faint glow of the night-light her grandmother's gaze looked tired and sad.

"Will I see Daddy tomorrow?" Elena asked quietly. "After Chris and Mommy leave?"

"No, Elena. Not tomorrow."

Tomorrow was as far ahead as Elena wished to think. "Please, Grandma, sleep with me," she said. "I'm afraid of being alone."

In the dim light Rosa slid into the bed next to the child.

Nestled in her arms, Elena felt the rise and fall of Rosa's wakeful breathing as the caress of love and safety, until she fell asleep.

THE ESCAPE

October 19–October 24

TWO

THREE days later, seven months after they had first made love, Teresa Peralta found herself in Venice with Christopher Paget, astonished to be in Italy, fearful that their time together was coming to an end.

Chris stood on the balcony of their suite at the Danieli, dressed in shorts, the late afternoon sun on his skin. From the living room Terri watched him as she held the phone to her ear.

Halfway around the world, Richie's telephone rang again. It was her third call to his apartment in an hour.

Ten rings later Terri slowly put down the telephone.

She was fresh from the shower—a slim, dark-haired young woman who barely came to Chris's shoulder. She had olive skin and a sculpted face that he kept trying to persuade her was beautiful: a chiseled nose, too pronounced for her liking; high cheekbones; delicate chin; a quick smile that transformed her seriousness without ever quite changing her green-flecked brown eyes, watchful by habit. Pulling the towel around her, she studied Chris in silence.

Chris gazed out at the Grand Canal, hands in his pockets, head tilted slightly, taking something in. Terri walked toward him, making no sound, until she could see what he watched so intently.

At another time it would have enchanted her. A broad stone walk below, filled with people ambling among food and curio stands and the white-covered tables and umbrellas of outdoor restaurants, the edge of the walk lined with gaslights and parked gondolas. And beyond them the Grand Canal. There were no cars; save for the motorboats, there was little Terri saw through the iron-framed balcony that was not as it had been five hundred years before.

"It's timeless," Chris said. "I don't know why exactly, but I take comfort in that. As if we can survive Richie, after all."

Terri was quiet for a moment, and Chris turned to face her. He looked ten years younger than he was. His face was barely lined, his coppery hair had no hint of gray, and spartan self-discipline kept him trim and well muscled. The ridged nose, a certain angularity, lent his features strength.

"His machine is off," she said.

Chris's blue eyes narrowed. "Perhaps they're out."

"No way. It's eight in the morning, California time. Richie picked Elena up from my mother's last night for her week at school." Terri's voice quickened. "We've been gone two days, and now I can't reach her. It's part of the mind games Richie plays with her—'Your mommy doesn't love you like I do.'"

Chris studied her face. "It's hard," he said. "But somehow, at least for a few days, we have to leave him behind." He kissed her forehead. "After all, we're two people in love, alone in a beautiful place. Until we get to Portofino, I'd like to talk about Richie and our children as little as we can. It's quiet there, and we'll have time enough. Even to decide our future."

Silent, Terri took his hands in hers. His right hand, she saw, was still swollen and discolored, just as it had been two mornings ago when he picked her up to drive them to the airport.

"Terri?" Chris's voice was tentative, an inquiry.

Looking up at him, Terri met his searching gaze. Then slowly she led him to the bed and looked into his face. In the last instant before becoming lost in Chris entirely, Terri thought of the day eight months before when her life—and Elena's—had changed forever.

IT BEGAN quite unexpectedly at the end of the Carelli hearing, when Terri had taken her five-year-old daughter to the beach. As they walked along the sand, hands entwined, the sound of the waves was deep and lulling. Terri was only Chris's law associate then, not his lover; her sole thoughts were of Elena.

She and Elena had found a small cove carved into the cliffside. As Terri gazed out toward the Golden Gate Bridge, Elena played at her feet. With a child's solemn concentration she arranged toy people around pieces of plastic furniture. There seemed to be a mother, a father, and a little girl. Elena began talking to her plastic people. "You sit *here*," she insisted, "and Daddy sits there."

"Who are you talking to?" Terri asked.

"You. You're sitting next to Daddy."

"And where do you sit?"

"Right there." Elena placed the little girl between her parents.

A child, Terri thought sadly, ordering the world of adults. Terri had been certain that she had given Elena no sign of the marital problems she felt like a weight inside her—the fights over money and Richie's failure to get a job; the fantasy businesses he had used her money to finance; the subtle manipulations, always denied. But Elena must have some intuition.

"Do you like playing that?" Terri asked.

"Yes." Elena stopped. She gazed at her imagined family and then looked up at her mother. "Why are you so mean to Daddy?"

Terri was momentarily speechless. "How am I mean to Daddy?"

Elena did not answer. But her voice held deep conviction. "He cries, you know. When he's alone, after you hurt his feelings."

Terri felt herself stiffen. Calmly she asked, "How do you know?"

"Because he tells me." Elena's voice held a kind of pride. "When he tucks me in at night, we talk about our feelings."

Terri recognized the note in Elena's voice now: the false wisdom of a child flattered by the contrived confidences of a manipulative adult. When she spoke again, it was without thinking. "Daddy shouldn't say those things to you."

"He *should*. Daddy says I'm old enough to know things."

She had been foolish, Terri realized. This could not—should not—be resolved between Elena and herself. Terri forced herself to remember that she had come to play with her daughter. They did that until the breeze grew cold.

Later, as they drove home, Terri only half listened to Elena. Her mind felt as cold as the breeze had been.

Richie was in the kitchen. At the sight of Elena he flashed an incandescent smile, bending his dark-curled head to hers. "How's my sweetheart?" His voice was almost crooning.

Perhaps it was her mood, Terri thought, but something about it made her more edgy. "Can you put away your toys?" she asked Elena abruptly, and watched the little girl scamper down the hallway, unusually cooperative.

"How was *your* day?" Richie asked. "Court all right?"

"Fine." Terri's voice was cool. "And did you spend yours crying?"

Richie looked startled and then tried a puzzled half smile.

"The funny thing," she said, "is that you never cry. Sometimes I'd feel better if you did. But the deepest feeling you can dredge up is self-pity, and that's only to manipulate me or Elena."

"People express emotions in different ways," he said.

It was dusk now; facing Richie, Terri felt darkness closing around them. "What have you been telling Elena?" she asked.

"I'm just being a parent," Richie said coolly. "I want Lainie to know the difference between real love and infatuation."

"Oh, and what *is* real love? I'm not sure I'd recognize it."

Richie spoke with exaggerated patience. "Real love is when people make a commitment to family and carry it out even through the bad times. It's the opposite of this stage you're in with Christopher Paget, an infatuation with surface instead of substance."

"Chris has nothing to do with this and never has."

Richie shook his head. "You want me to parent Lainie, and then you complain when I do. I can never win."

"You always win, Richie. But this time I won't let you." Her throat felt dry. "I won't let the rest of Elena's life be about her father. I'm leaving you."

Richie stiffened. "You can't do that. Not without counseling."

It took Terri a moment to accept what she had said, another to tell him what she believed most of all. "You have an uncounselable problem, Richie. And so do I."

Richie looked wounded. "What's so wrong that we can't fix it?"

His voice was suddenly plaintive; for an instant it made Terri want to comfort him. But it was too late. "You can't see other people as separate from you," she told him quietly. "Elena most of all. I can't change it, and I won't fight it."

"You can help me, Ter. That's what marriage is about."

"No," she answered. "Only *you* can help you. It's too late for us, and I have Elena to think of."

"If you were thinking of Elena, you'd give her an intact family."

"It's all I ever wanted, Richie—a family. But there's a difference between intact and healthy. We're no good for Elena."

Richie moved closer. "It's not up to you to say what's good. It's up to a judge, and he'll listen to me."

"And what will you tell him?"

"That *I've* been the caretaking parent while you've worked long hours with a man who may be your lover. That I want Elena. That I can't provide care for her without sixty percent of your income."

"That's crazy."

His voice filled with triumph. "It's the law, Ter. I've checked it out. And even if you get custody, you think it's easy to find a man who wants to raise someone else's kid? You'll be all alone."

Terri tried to keep her voice steady. "If I have to be alone, I will. And if I have to fight you for Elena, I'll do that too."

"You'll lose." His next words were soft, insinuating. "But don't worry, Ter. Every other weekend I'll let you see my daughter."

It was near the surface now: her fear of Richie, which connected them more deeply than love. Richie would be smooth and plausible; how could Terri explain to a judge how things really were?

She forced herself to speak slowly and evenly. "I'm taking Elena and going to my mother's. We need to decide what to tell her."

He was standing over her now. "You're not going anywhere."

His voice trembled with an anger she had never heard in him before. When she tried to step past him, his hand jerked upward in the dim room. She flinched. *"Don't,"* she managed.

"Do you still want to leave, Ter? Or are you ready to talk?"

Terri was breathing hard. "Do it, Richie. Do it twice. That way the family court won't miss it."

Crimson spread across his face. But his hand did not move.

Terri looked into his eyes. "At least you weren't abusive, I used to tell myself. Not like my father with my mother." She stopped herself. "Whether you hit me or not, I'm leaving. And if you *do* hit me, I'll make sure it's the last time you'll ever hit anyone."

He stared at her. Then his hand dropped to his side.

Don't let him see your fear, Terri told herself. She knew that this was not over; with Richie, things were never over until he won.

"I'll think of something to tell Elena," she said. And then she walked past him, going to get their daughter, not looking back.

THREE

Two days after leaving Richie, sleepless and afraid for herself and for Elena, Terri found herself on Chris's doorstep.

He knew nothing about what she had done. For what she had said to Richie—that Chris had nothing to do with their marriage—was what Terri believed. Chris and she were too different for it to be otherwise; even his home, a sprawling three-story Edwardian in the Pacific Heights section of San Francisco, reminded her of all the ways in which their lives were not the same.

Chris had become famous sixteen years earlier, at age twenty-nine, for his part in exposing the Lasko scandal, the corruption of a President; Terri was barely twenty-nine now, and her career had hardly begun. Chris had been raised with wealth and a sense of entitlement. His only marriage had been to a well-known ballerina, graceful and elegant. Terri was from a family of Hispanic immigrants. She was a scholarship student who had worked her way through college and law school; the daughter of an auto mechanic who had drunk too much and abused her mother, Rosa—the one person, Terri sometimes felt, to whom she truly mattered.

Standing at Chris's door this morning, Terri wondered how it was that Chris and not Rosa had become the person she would turn to.

During the first six months she had worked for Chris, she would not have guessed this. Something at the core of him had seemed unknowable. Terri did not even know then that the center of Chris's life was his fifteen-year-old son, Carlo. And then the television journalist Mary Carelli, Carlo's mother and Chris's onetime lover, was charged with the murder of a celebrated writer.

Chris and Terri had defended her. For Terri the crucible of *People* v. *Carelli* made her see Chris as he was. As Chris came to trust her with the Carelli defense, then with parts of his life no one else knew, Terri saw that the man he showed to others—ironic and aloof—concealed such feeling that she sensed it frightened him.

But this discovery, Terri realized, made her feel safe with him. She told Chris things she had never told anyone, and he listened without judging, asking questions until the shape of her own feelings became clearer to her. In some deep way Teresa Peralta knew that Christopher Paget was helping her become truer to herself. For that, and for being who Chris was, Ricardo Arias hated him.

Standing straighter, she knocked on Chris's door.

When he opened it, Chris looked startled. He smiled then, as if to cover his surprise. "The Carelli case ended a couple of days ago," he said lightly. "You can go home now. Sleep, even."

Terri hesitated, abashed. "I'm a little at loose ends, I guess."

"Sometimes that happens after a trial." Chris looked at her more carefully. "I was just out on the deck. Care to join me?"

"Maybe for a while."

Chris led her to his deck. The morning sun was bright. A few sailboats flecked the bay. Terri went to the railing, leaning on it with her palms, gazing out at the water. A breeze rippled her hair.

"I've left Richie," she said softly.

Chris seemed unnaturally still. Terri wanted to ask what was wrong and then saw the realization in his face at the same moment that the sudden knowledge left her own face hot, her skin tingling. She had not come for his help, Terri realized, or his advice. She had come because she had fallen in love with him.

All at once Terri felt alone. "Is this all right? My being here?"

As if to himself, Chris shook his head. "I'm forty-five years old," he said, "with a teenage son. You're twenty-nine. You're newly separated. And you work for me. Any counselor in America would tell you I'm a bad idea and that you just need time to see that."

Humiliated, Terri gazed out at the bay, trying to collect herself.

"Tell me why you're leaving him," he said gently.

After a time, she began to talk, and then the dam of her emotions broke. She told him everything.

Chris leaned on the railing next to her, listening intently, careful not to touch her. But as Terri described the night she had left Richie, his hand grazed her cheek.

"Has he ever hit you?" he asked.

Terri shook her head. "Until the day before yesterday, not even close. He didn't need to. Somehow I was always afraid of him."

Chris studied her. "You're still afraid, aren't you."

It was hard to speak her fears aloud. "It's like he has this instinct for other people's weaknesses," she answered finally.

"Whatever else, Terri, I *am* your friend. I can represent you—or lend you money."

Terri turned to him, suddenly fearful. "That's not why I came here. I don't want you involved with him."

"Why? There's nothing Richie can do to me."

She shook her head. "I need to do this on my own."

Terri watched him study her and decide not to argue. She felt her tension ease. His smile was like a gift. She went to him, and he held her quietly. His closeness became a warmth inside her. It was somewhat the same, she thought, as when her mother had held her at night when she was small, offering and perhaps seeking comfort from the rages of Terri's father.

LEAVING Chris's house an hour later, Terri smiled to herself—an instant before she saw Richie's car parked across the street.

He leaned through the window on the driver's side, as if waiting to pick her up. His look was almost casual; his eyes had the strange blankness that she knew meant danger. "Hi, Ter. How're things?"

Terri walked toward the car. "What are you doing here?"

"Waiting for him to finish with you," he said amiably, and handed her a sheaf of papers.

A form petition for divorce. With an odd detachment Terri scanned the pleading for its essentials: the date of their marriage; Elena's name and birth date; a listing of Terri's sole asset—her pension plan—and Richie's request for half of it; a list of debts, incurred by Richie; dollar amounts for Terri's salary and Richie's projected expenses; his demand for alimony. The signature showed that Ricardo Arias, attorney-at-law, would serve as his own lawyer.

Terri turned to him. "You're representing yourself?"

"I can't afford a better lawyer." She caught the gleam of satisfaction. "Unless I ask the court to make you pay for one."

Terri stared at him. Then she asked, "What about Elena?"

A faint smile appeared at one corner of his mouth. "I can't support her without money," he said, and handed Terri another form.

A request for child support to be paid by respondent, Teresa

311

Peralta, collected by means of a wage assignment: a portion of her salary to be paid directly to Ricardo Arias.

How many hours, Terri wondered, had he spent planning this? Choosing the sequence of papers to give her, rehearsing.

"This little performance of yours needs work," she told him.

"It's no act, Terri. You forced me to do this." His voice hardened. "I'm just responding to the crisis in my daughter's life. You're so swept up in your affairs that you've got no time for her *or* me."

Terri's temple throbbed. "I've got the time, Richie. Right now."

"Then sit down and talk to me, Terri."

Slowly she walked to the passenger's side and got in. The inside of his beat-up car seemed hot and close.

He rested his hand on her knee. "It's all right, Ter. It's really not fair—someone like him picking on someone like you."

She removed his hand. "Leave Chris out of this," she said.

"As long as you see him, he has everything to do with the welfare of *my* child and your ability to devote suitable attention to her in the limited time your job and relationship allow."

Certain phrases sounded stolen from a primer on family law. Richie's mutability had always jarred Terri. If he needed to seem a compassionate parent, he would read six handbooks on what compassionate parents did, then weave what he had learned into his persona of the moment.

"Giving up your boyfriend," he went on calmly, "is what's best for our daughter. That should be obvious to anyone."

"What's obvious to me," Terri answered, "is that Elena is a five-year-old girl who needs her mother. Don't use her as a pawn."

"I'm not *using* her, Terri. I'm saving her." Richie reached into the back seat and gave her another document. "Read this. Any expert on child custody would tell you that this is what's best."

She stared down at the agreement. "What's in it?"

"Custody to me. Appropriate spousal support, and child support at forty percent of your income to keep me at home with Elena. And to make sure I can stay with her, you'll assume our community debts. So that I'm not forced to work outside the home."

"That's a real sacrifice, considering how much you like working." Terri fought to control her anger. "Just out of curiosity, when do I get to see her?"

"Every other weekend. And under certain conditions, a dinner with Elena one night a week." He rested his hand on her knee again. "If I have plans some night, I can drop Elena with you instead of getting a sitter." He looked content, almost happy. "I may even give you more time than that. But there's another condition. Outside of work you will never see Christopher Paget again."

The car felt stifling. As Terri cracked open the door, Richie grasped her arm. "We're required to meet with Family Court Services to see if we can work out custody. Our meeting's in ten days. Sign this, and we won't need to go through that." Richie's eyes were suddenly soft. "It's him or me, Ter. Please get rid of him, okay? Then maybe there's a chance for us."

Terri pulled away from him, pushed open the door. "The only chance for us," she answered slowly, "was for me to never see you as you are. In a way, I wish I never had."

WHEN Terri had returned to her mother's from Chris's house, still clutching Richie's divorce papers, Elena was waiting.

"Did you go to make up with Daddy?" she asked.

"I *saw* your daddy." Terri placed the papers on the mantel in Rosa's living room, then knelt to hug Elena.

"But were you nice to him?" Elena asked. "Are you guys going to be married again?"

Instinct caused Terri to look past Elena to the hallway and see her mother watching them both. Terri focused on the child's face. "I know you're sad, sweetheart. And I know you want your daddy and me to stay together. But we don't love each other anymore. And I don't want you *ever* to see us fight."

She felt Elena stiffen, and then the little girl began to cry. Terri drew her close. "I'll help you," Elena managed. "I'll talk to Daddy."

Terri glanced up at her mother. In the gaze that passed between them Terri saw Rosa remember, as vividly as she did, the night in this same living room when Terri had stepped between her father and her mother, begging him to stop.

"That's not your job," Terri told her daughter now. "Kids can't fix things for adults, and you shouldn't worry over us. It's your daddy's and my job to take care of *you*."

"But you can't," Elena said, a child's anger filling her voice.

313

"Daddy told me if you aren't still married, you can't live with us."

Terri was furious, but she kept her voice steady. "Your daddy and I haven't decided who you're going to live with. But you'll see both of us. Because we both love you very much."

Terri watched the thin veneer of the grown-up Elena vanish in the tears of a frightened five-year-old. "Then why can't you love Daddy?" Elena's look became pleading. "Daddy's nice. If you didn't work with Chris, you could be friends again."

Rosa appeared, touching Elena's shoulder. "I have a coloring book for you, precious. At the desk in your mommy's old room upstairs. If you color a picture for me, I'll put it on the refrigerator."

Elena hesitated. And then, choosing the world of a child, she went with Rosa to find her crayons.

Terri sat on the couch. Her thoughts tired and diffuse, she looked around the house where she had become who she was: a small square living room with a low ceiling; the smaller dining room, where Terri and her younger sisters used to sit, talking to their mother, watching their father from the corner of their eyes; the dark stairway to the bedrooms.

Her father had been dead for sixteen years now. Yet she could never sit in this room without the guilty fear that she had done something to displease him. Even the silence reminded her of the things she and her sisters could never speak of outside the house. Like the sound of his open palm as it struck their mother's face.

Rosa came down the stairs and crossed the living room to sit next to Terri. Somewhere between Terri's childhood and now, her mother had lost the habit of smiling. But she still had the arresting brown-green eyes, the even mouth and well-defined features that Terri knew to be her own. Today, as always, Rosa's jet-black hair was drawn back and her makeup applied carefully.

"I can't go back," Terri said to her mother.

"Is it really so bad?"

"Worse. He served papers this morning. He wants custody."

Rosa leaned back in the couch. "Where were you?"

Terri felt her gaze. "At Chris's. Richie was waiting."

"That is like him." Rosa's eyes were grave. Terri sensed that her mother was not surprised, and then remembered that this was like her father, Ramon Peralta. "Ricardo means to make you pay for

Chris," Rosa said with weary certainty. "The price will be Elena."

Terri shook her head. "It goes deeper than Chris. Or jealousy. Richie wants me alone, without anyone except him. He always has."

"Ricardo frightens me," Rosa said. "So I have to ask: Should you leave him without trying? At least for a time."

"I don't think I *can* try anymore. There's something damaged about him, and we're terrible for Elena."

"But this is not just about Richie, is it?" Her mother leaned forward. "You're my daughter, and I love you deeply. For many years it was you, before anyone, who gave my life its meaning. But you're also Elena's mother now. And mothers are not free."

"I know how important a family can be," Terri answered coolly. "That's why I left him."

"Then you must stay away from Christopher Paget."

Terri felt her stomach tighten. "I don't know if I can. Or even should. For Elena's sake as well as mine."

Rosa shook her head. "Elena has no interest in your love life. When you chose to have Elena, you chose to put her first. Her life was given to you to protect. That's how it must be now, however hurtful."

Terri paused for a moment. "I don't know what this will become. And you don't know Chris."

"I know enough. I have heard you speak of him. And I hoped, in spite of what I saw in your face, that you would never fall in love with him."

"Well," Terri answered softly, "I have."

"Chris will cost you Elena. After she's gone, you will see Elena every time you look at Chris's face."

"I'm not choosing Chris over Elena." Terri's voice rose. "He's a wonderful father, Mama. You should see Carlo. Chris may be my chance to be happy."

Rosa stared up at her. "And what is that," she said at last, "without Elena?"

THE next morning Terri returned to Chris's with Elena.

Carlo was eating cereal at the kitchen counter, a baseball cap shoved backward over his black curly hair, lean body arranged in a pose of languid cool. Elena walked directly up to him.

315

He looked down at her with a slightly bemused smile, as if a cartoon character had just walked into his kitchen. "Hi, squirt," he said casually. "Remember me?"

Terri knew the answer. Three weeks before, when Elena had met Carlo for the first time, he had contrived to let her beat him at a game. Winning was something Elena did not forget.

"You're *Carlo*," Elena responded. "I beat you at Blockhead. I'm the champion of this house."

Carlo looked askance at her. "Only as long as I let you be."

For the first time in days Elena's eyes danced. "I can beat you," she teased. "I can beat you all the time."

Carlo flashed his crooked smile. "Tell you what," he said, "let me finish my cereal, and I'll play you again. If you can get my dad to dig the game out."

Chris and Elena went to the library. Carlo resumed munching his cereal while he gave Terri an expectant look.

"I guess your dad said something," Terri ventured.

Carlo nodded at his cereal. "A little."

This was touchy, Terri thought. In their own way, children— even teenagers—were the most moral people in the world. "I have to say this," Terri told him. "Your dad had nothing to do with my leaving Richie. I'm not even sure it's fair to him. Or you."

Carlo gave a slight smile. "Don't worry about me. He was in such a great mood last night it was absolutely obnoxious." He angled his head toward the library. "Does Elena know?"

"Not really." Terri hesitated. "It's hard explaining divorce to a five-year-old who just wants things the same."

Carlo gave a philosophical shrug. "I'd better go amuse the munchkin," he said.

Chris was back shortly, glancing over his shoulder. "Talk about the Odd Couple. This is a side of Carlo I've seldom seen."

"He's a good kid, Chris. And he's had a good dad." Terri smiled. "Think we can go for a walk? I don't want Elena to hear this."

Chris nodded. Telling Elena they'd be back soon, they stepped outside. Terri found herself looking for Richie's car.

They walked to Alta Plaza, a gently rolling park that looked out toward the blue water of San Francisco Bay. They sat on a wooden bench, looking out at the bay.

316

"You must feel pretty isolated," Chris said at last.

A few simple words of understanding, Terri realized, could bring her close to tears. "I should never have come yesterday," she said simply. "Richie sees you as a threat."

"I'm sure that's how he wants you to feel." Chris's voice had a trace of suppressed anger. "If you really think seeing me means losing Elena, then you can't see me. At least outside the office."

Terri felt her throat constrict. "I don't need you to be rational. I just need you to hold me, all right?"

His face softened, and then he brought her close.

Terri rested against his chest. "I can't take the money you've offered," she said finally. "And you can't be my lawyer."

"Why not?"

"This morning Richie subpoenaed my bank records. You know what that's about. If you're giving me money, he'll claim that I can afford to pay him even more support. Plus he'll use it to imply that you enticed your impressionable young associate to leave her happy home. Which won't help me at all when it comes to Elena. He'll try to make any relationship we have seem bad for her. Trust me about this." Her voice rose. "We're lawyers, Chris. We know what lawsuits can be like."

"There must be *some* way for you to buy him off."

"Not in exchange for Elena. He needs her too much. He'll do anything to win her over—play the martyr, lie about me, treat her as a little wife—because he's in love with the man he sees in his daughter's eyes. And because she's his one excuse for not working."

Chris gave a grimace of disgust. "What's his problem?"

"I don't think he can work for anyone. Before he stopped working entirely, he lost three law jobs. Or quit them—I could never quite tell. It was always someone else's fault."

Chris's look was searching. "What will you do now?" he asked.

All at once Terri felt the pressure of facing Richie alone. "First we have to meet with the mediator. If that doesn't work, we're off to court to see who gets interim custody of Elena until there's a trial. Richie's going to make a good impression—he always does. Unless I show them the real Richie, he's got a chance of taking Elena. Once I start doing that, he's going to retaliate any way he can. You're already on the list."

Chris shrugged. "I'm only concerned that you won't let me represent you. Unless you mean to handle this yourself."

Terri shook her head. "I don't know family law, and I don't want you near this—for your sake *and* Elena's. I have to be careful, that's all. Just until this hearing's over."

FOUR

THE mediator's office was a bare rectangle in the Alameda County Administrative Building, in Oakland. Terri and Richie had sat against a wall, several feet from each other. The mediator, Alec Keene—fortyish, with a salt-and-pepper beard and horn-rimmed glasses—had turned his chair from his desk to face them.

Terri felt tense, concerned about Keene's first impression. In a gray suit and white blouse she looked like what she was—a lawyer who had come from work. But with his corduroy slacks, checkered shirt, and sweater with its sleeves pulled up, Richie resembled the benign head of a creative preschool.

"My purpose here," Keene said, "is to see whether we can resolve custody of Elena without the ordeal of the courtroom. We have thirteen days before the hearing on support and interim custody. If the two of you can't come to some agreement, this office will make a recommendation to the court regarding interim custody."

Terri leaned forward. "Doesn't that put too great an emphasis on this one meeting? As I understand it, interim custody orders tend to become permanent."

"Not always. But if the status quo seems to be working, the court may be reluctant to change it. Absent compelling reasons."

"What are those?" Richie interjected.

Keene touched his beard. "I'd say the real hot-button issues are child neglect, substance abuse, the mental instability of a parent, or evidence of physical or sexual abuse." His tone became cautionary. "Those kinds of allegations are becoming more and more common. In cases where parents start playing to win, it's sometimes hard to tell whether we're dealing with truth or tactics."

Richie shook his head, as if to signal his wonderment that people would exploit such problems. He was an actor, and Terri could only hope that Keene would see through him.

"Let me gather some data, just to get the mundane out of the way," Keene said. He turned to Terri. "In the past year, what have been your normal hours of work?"

"Nine to five thirty. Sometimes later."

"Weekends?" he asked sympathetically.

"Sometimes. Only when I was in trial, really."

"When you were later or in trial, who watched Elena?"

"Her preschool has her until six," she said. "As of twelve days ago, when Richie and I separated, I told the partner I work for that weekends are out and that I have to leave promptly at five thirty. So I'm ready to give Elena a predictable routine."

Keene raised an eyebrow. "And your boss understands?"

"He's a single father," Terri answered simply.

Keene turned to Richie. "I believe you work at home."

"I do." Richie's face became alight with pleasure. "On a new computer program called Lawsearch. I think it'll revolutionize legal research. It's been a good compromise between work and parenting." He leaned back, spreading his hands. "Terri and I tried having both of us work in offices for a while and decided it just wasn't right. So we agreed to put the emphasis on Terri's career and have me at home for Elena. It just makes sense—of the two of us, I'm the entrepreneurial one. It turns out I was also the lucky one. Watching Elena grow has been more rewarding than I ever dreamed." He paused, seemingly touched by the thought, and softly said to Terri, "No matter what, Ter, I'm really proud of what we've done."

"I'm proud too," she said to Richie. "Of some things. The problem is, none of the things *you* just described ever happened. When I got pregnant with Elena, I asked if I could just stay home with her. At least for a while. 'Of course,' you answered. And as soon as Elena was born, you quit your new job and decided to get an M.B.A."

Richie's eyes shone with resentment. "That's not how it—"

"That's *exactly* how it happened." Terri leaned toward him. "So I had to return to law school when Elena was six weeks old and then scrambled to find the first job I could, at the public defender's office, while you took out a loan for grad school. I'm still paying off the loan.

"In the first year after you got out of grad school, you quit or got fired from two more firms," Terry went on. "When your credit card charges got too high for me to carry, I left a job I'd gotten to like and took one with Chris's office. When I came home that night and told you what I'd be making, you said you were proud of me because now you could work at home." She turned to Keene. "Elena has one stable parent—me. I want custody."

With a look of deep sorrow Richie shook his head. "Why are you saying this, Terri? We made those decisions together." He spoke to Keene. "The simple fact is that for the last year and a half I've been home with Elena. In the structure of our family I'm the one she turns to. She's the center of my life."

"How many times," Terri asked, "have I left work to pick up Elena because you were too busy? Parenting is more than hanging around the house."

"All right," Keene said. "I think I've got the flavor of your disagreements. Have you discussed solutions?"

"I've tried," Richie put in quickly, and then made his tone more soothing. "Look, I know Terri. She's a good mom. I just think I should raise Elena." He turned to Terri. "At some other time, when your thing with Chris has calmed down a little, I'm sure we can work this out in Elena's best interests. Just give me a trial period."

Keene removed his glasses. "I missed something," he said to Richie. "This thing with Chris . . ."

"It's hard for me to face. Terri's having an affair with her boss. Since it started, it seems I can't do anything right."

"That," Terri answered, "is not true. Chris and I are friends, and I may be seeing him, but I wasn't during our marriage—"

"We *are* married," Richie broke in. "Two weeks ago we were living together. So don't tell me that Christopher Paget has nothing to do with the hell we're putting Elena through."

"All that Chris has to do with Elena," Terri shot back, "is that he's given me shorter hours so that I can raise her. Which is far more help than you've ever given me."

Richie flushed. In the silence Keene looked glumly at them both. "Our time is up," he said finally.

As SHE entered the bleak and dingy family court building with her lawyer—a pert red-haired divorce specialist named Janet Flaherty—Terri felt a rising dread.

A cheery voice spoke out behind her. *"Abandon all hope,"* it quoted, *"ye who enter here."*

Turning, Terri saw Richie's too bright smile. He extended his hand to Janet Flaherty. "Janet? I'm Richie Arias. We've spoken on the phone." Richie with his party manners, Terri thought grimly.

They took the elevator to the third floor and stood in the green tile hall outside the courtroom. Ignoring Terri, Richie fixed Flaherty with a serious gaze. "Can we talk for a moment, Janet? I was hoping you might help mediate between Terri and me."

Flaherty stayed unimpressed. "What's the proposition?"

"A package deal. Nonmodifiable spousal support of a thousand a month. Child support: fifteen hundred a month—"

"That's half my take-home," Terri put in.

"Let me finish. Please." He turned to Terri with limpid eyes. "For one year I get weeks and you get weekends. At the end of that year we sit down and see how it's working. If we can't agree, then we can come back to court for a permanent order."

"I'll up your spousal," Terri said. "But I want preponderant custody."

"You know this isn't a matter of money, Ter," he replied.

Frowning, Flaherty looked at her watch. "We're due inside," she put in. "Terri and I should talk."

They walked down the hallway, Terri glancing over her shoulder. "He's nervous about spousal," she murmured.

Flaherty nodded. "By making spousal support nonmodifiable, he avoids having to report to the court about looking for work and maybe getting cut if he's been sitting on his rear end."

"Did you follow the rest of his scam?" Terri asked.

Flaherty nodded. "Richie knows that child support is his meal ticket—he can live off that till Elena turns eighteen. Come the end of the year, he'll tell the court that it shouldn't disturb the status quo. The court will probably buy that. Once he has permanent custody, he can ratchet up child support every time you get a raise." Flaherty finished in astringent tones, "And he's got every weekend free. In short, the deadbeat's version of a perfect life."

"There's no way," Terri said, "that I can let him raise Elena."

"Then we've no choice but to go in there and fight him." Flaherty touched Terri's shoulder. "But I should warn you about how quirky

Judge Scatena can be. Twenty years as a family court judge has taught him to hate pretty much everyone—lawyers included."

They went inside.

The judge's chair was empty. The wall behind the bench was covered with gold paper; the American and California state flags stood to either side. In front of the bench were two wooden tables, each with a brass nameplate, marked PETITIONER and RESPONDENT. A low wood partition with a swinging door separated the litigants of the moment from those waiting their turn.

Gazing around, Terri spotted Alec Keene in the front row. Richie had taken a seat next to him and was chatting amiably.

"What's Richie doing?" Terri murmured to Flaherty.

"Don't worry—Alec's already met with the judge to make his recommendation. And Alec's a pro."

A door at the rear of the bench swung open, and Judge Scatena abruptly entered. "All rise," intoned the judge's deputy.

Judge Frank Scatena was an erect white-haired man in his sixties, with a seamed face, a hooked nose, and, it appeared, painfully arthritic hands. He surveyed the room with a jaded bureaucratic displeasure. "All right," he said. "What have we got first?"

The deputy glanced at his docket. "Case number 94-716. *Ricardo Arias* versus *Teresa Peralta*. Petitioner's motion for alimony, child support, and interim custody; respondent's cross motion for interim custody and that the petitioner seek employment."

Richie rose and walked through the low swinging door to sit at the table opposite Terri and Janet.

"I'll hear petitioner," Scatena said to Richie. "The first issue is spousal support and whether you'll get work."

Richie walked to the podium, head held high. "Good morning, Your Honor. Ricardo Arias, appearing in pro. per.—"

"Why haven't you got your own lawyer?" Scatena cut in.

"If I had any money, I wouldn't be standing here," Richie said.

"You can ask me to order your wife to pay for a lawyer."

Richie nodded. "That's true. But it's my position that any resources should be preserved for Elena's benefit."

Scatena assessed him. "Why don't you just get a job, Mr. Arias? You seem able-bodied enough to me."

"Well, the thing is, Terri and I agreed that I would raise Elena.

323

As a result, my law career has fallen way behind now. I can't earn half of what Terri makes." His voice was humble. "Terri has resources: a high-paying job and a wealthy boyfriend who happens to be her boss. Because I thought we would always be married, I have none. It's not fair—to Elena or me—to push me out of the house."

Terri gripped the table. The reference to Chris was deft.

"That depends, doesn't it," Scatena said, "on who gets custody."

"When I say fair to Elena, Your Honor, I mean to include economics," Richie said. "I intend to help support my daughter. I certainly haven't been sitting around. I've used my role in the family—the at-home parent—to start my own business."

Scatena sat forward. "So how much do you want?" he asked.

"Spousal only, fifteen hundred a month. But that's based on my wife's current salary, of course."

"All right," Scatena said. "Let's hear from Mrs. Arias."

Flaherty went to the podium. "Janet Flaherty, Your Honor, for respondent Teresa Peralta. Mr. Arias' position—on everything—stems from the assertion that Teresa Peralta implored him to stay home. The truth is that Ms. Peralta implored him to work, and he refused. The truth is that Mr. Arias has been on a self-declared sabbatical from his responsibilities—both to Teresa and to his daughter. Who supports Mr. Arias? Teresa does. Who supports Elena? Again, Teresa. Who watches Elena?" Here Flaherty paused. "*Not* Mr. Arias. A day-care center. Paid for by Teresa Peralta—"

"What about summers, Counselor?" Scatena put in.

Terri recalled the bitter argument she had with Richie when money was tight last summer and Elena had stayed home. "Last summer, Mr. Arias," Flaherty answered. "But that was an economic necessity—he had again declined to work. And Elena's summer was not satisfactory."

"But she did leave Elena with Mr. Arias, correct? I don't suppose she'd have done that if the child's life had been in danger."

"We don't think that's the standard, Your Honor—"

"According to Mr. Arias," Scatena interrupted in a hectoring tone, "he was also working."

"According to Mr. Arias," Flaherty replied. "But his so-called enterprise has yet to generate a dime. Where is his business plan? I wonder. Where are the buyers for his supposed breakthrough?"

324

"I have no clue, Counselor. Maybe Mr. Arias doesn't, either. But our business here is determining what he gets in the meantime."

For the first time, Flaherty looked disconcerted. "What Mr. Arias should 'get,' in our view, is a directive to find work."

"She makes over twice the national family average, Counselor."

The argument, Terri saw, was sliding downhill.

"In San Francisco," Flaherty rejoined. "The most expensive city in America. Look at our income and expense statement. Your Honor, my client's paycheck can't stretch any more."

Scatena folded his hands. "Well, it's going to have to. I'm awarding Mr. Arias interim support, and I'll decide how much after we address custody." He glanced at Richie. "If Mr. Arias were an unemployed wife, there'd be no question about spousal support."

Richie nodded, as if deeply impressed by the judge's fairness.

Watching Flaherty return to her seat, Terri could not repress her fear. "He's buying Richie's act," Terri whispered.

"It's okay," Flaherty murmured back. "Custody is a separate deal. A lot depends on Alec Keene."

"Next," Scatena snapped, "is custody. Mr. Arias?"

Richie walked slowly to the podium. "It's exactly as the court said. I'm at home with Elena, and Terri isn't. At least in the near term, that should decide custody." He gazed up at Scatena. "I love my daughter," he added softly.

"Don't let him get away with this," Terri whispered to Flaherty.

Flaherty rose. "As we know," she began, "being a parent is very complex. It certainly isn't as simple as who's home between nine and five—a time during which, for most of the day, Elena Arias will be in school. No, parenting is a number of things—love, understanding, stability, and financial support—which flow from a sense of responsibility."

She paused, turning to look at Terri. "Teresa Peralta is the responsible parent. The one who calls Elena's teachers. Who takes her to the doctor. Who puts her to bed at night, drives her to day care in the morning. And yes, who supports her. The reward for being the responsible parent should be the responsibility of parenting. That is what Elena has in Ms. Peralta."

Scatena held up a hand. "Frankly, Counsel, if Mr. Arias had hired you first, I'm sure you could make him sound as much like

325

Walt Disney as Ms. Peralta sounds like Snow White. Professional couples are the bane of this court, and lawyers are the worst. The child might as well be a football."

The courtroom was still.

"Here's my order," he snapped. "Interim custody to petitioner, Mr. Arias. Interim spousal support to Mr. Arias: one thousand two hundred fifty dollars. Interim child support to Mr. Arias: a thousand dollars." The judge looked back at Terri. "Visitation to Ms. Peralta: alternate weekends, Friday evening to Sunday evening." He cracked his gavel. "Next case."

Terri sat there. She felt numb.

"Come on," Flaherty said gently. "Let's go."

Terri did not see the courtroom as she left it. Outside, she felt a hand on her shoulder. She turned, ready to face Richie.

It was Alec Keene. "I shouldn't tell you this," he said, "but that wasn't what I recommended." His tone mingled weariness with disgust. "Half the time the man doesn't listen to us."

Terri stared at him. "The man," she said tersely, "doesn't know anything about my daughter."

THE look in Elena's eyes, frightened and inconsolable, made Terri fight back tears.

They stood in Rosa's living room. "I don't want to just live with Daddy," Elena said. "I want to live with *both* of you."

Terri hugged Elena. "It's just for a while," she told her.

"But why? Why don't you want to be with me?"

"I want to be with you," Terri said, and then spoke the lines she had rehearsed. "But Daddy's at home right now, and I have to work. So we decided he should take care of you. Just for now."

"But who's going to take care of Daddy?"

In her bitterness Terri wished she could take the child to Scatena, demand that he answer her himself. But the custody trial would not be for at least nine months, and after yesterday, Terri could not imagine winning. "I'll still help him," Terri said quietly. "Daddy will be fine, and some weekends you'll come live with me. Next weekend, if you want, we can go to the zoo."

It did not seem to reassure Elena.

There was a knock at the door.

"It's your daddy." Terri mustered a smile. "It's time now."

"How's my princess!" Richie exclaimed, picking up Elena. He turned to Terri. "I'll need my check. The whole amount."

Terri stared at him. "It's not the first of the month yet."

"Well, I need it." He kissed Elena on the cheek. "I promised Lainie we'd go to the movies, and there's not enough food."

Terri saw Elena's eyes, fearful and confused. In silence she went to her purse and wrote him a check. She hoped there was a special place in hell for men who made their daughters worry about them.

"Okay, Lainie," Richie said in a cheerful voice. "We're off."

He walked briskly away, Elena looking over his shoulder.

IN THE days and weeks that followed, Chris tried his best to give Terri a life she could cling to without Elena.

They found Terri a place she could afford, a bright five-room apartment in a sunny part of the city, Noe Valley. Terri enjoyed the outdoors; on a weekend without Elena they drove across the Golden Gate Bridge to Marin County to hike to the beach. They both enjoyed modern art, so they went to galleries, and Chris got them tickets to the ballet. Most of all, he gave her his time without demands or even plans beyond the moment.

Terri devoted her weekends with Elena to the child alone; they would visit Chris and Carlo only for a few hours, and only when Carlo was there. To Carlo's embarrassment the little girl worshipped him.

"Carlo," she would shriek, and run through the house to find him. The boy reacted with amusement and chagrin; his charm, he remarked to Terri, was sure to end with kindergarten.

Terri smiled. "I'm not so sure."

Once, Carlo and his red-haired girlfriend, Katie, had read Elena stories; Elena positioned herself in Carlo's lap.

"I'm marrying Carlo," she told Katie. "When I'm twelve."

Carlo checked his watch. "In exactly five hundred seven thousand, one hundred thirteen hours and eighteen minutes," he told Katie, "your time is up."

That was enough for Elena. And a few days later, on an afternoon when Carlo seemed particularly tolerant, he walked her to the park near Chris's house. Terri watched them go—a tall, handsome boy in a baseball cap with a raven-haired child who came to his waist but insisted on holding his hand. Unlike Terri, and perhaps Chris, Carlo seemed to make Elena forget how angry she was. Terri decided this was a blessing, for Elena—when she wasn't listless—was so angry that she seemed out of Terri's reach.

At first this anger seemed sporadic. The normally spirited little girl would become recalcitrant, throwing toys, telling Terri that she hated her apartment, or demanding to call her father so that he would not be lonely. Whether spoken or silent, the message was the same—the divorce was Terri's fault.

"You hug and kiss Chris now," Elena told her flatly one day.

They were tie-dyeing T-shirts at the kitchen sink; Terri had thought it a happy day. She searched her memory of the time since the separation for some slipup that had occurred in Elena's presence, and found none. "How do you know that?"

"Daddy told me." The child's voice was accusatory.

"Chris is my friend, Elena. He's nice to me." She paused and then asked, "Don't you think I deserve someone to be nice to me?"

Elena frowned. "*I'm* nice to Daddy," she said.

That night when Elena had gone, Terri waited until ten and then drove to Richie's.

Elena answered the door. Surprised, Terri bent to hug her. "It's past your bedtime, sweetheart."

The little girl pushed her away. "It's *not*. Daddy said there was no bedtime tonight."

Walking past Elena, Terri saw Richie in the living room, an empty bottle of wine in front of him, candles on the coffee table. Instinctively Terri looked for a second adult, then perceived from Richie's flush that he had drunk the bottle alone. For an instant he looked cornered, and then his eyes took on a strange glitter.

"We've stayed up playing games," he said. "Just like you, Terri. Coming here." The words had a sibilant hiss.

Without answering, Terri picked up Elena and tucked her in bed, read her stories until the little girl was asleep.

When Terri at last went to find Richie, the lights were off. That and the smell of wine gave Terri the trapped, eerie feeling of her childhood: a man sitting alone in the darkness, ready to explode.

"Miss me, Ter?" Richie's voice from the darkness was slurred and insinuating. "We're all alone now, and Christopher Paget's nowhere in sight. Just the way it should be."

"If you ever do this around Elena again," she told him softly, "I'll kill you." Then she turned and walked out. She did not know whether she had only imagined Richie laughing as the door shut.

FIVE

"H E DOESN'T usually drink," she told Chris the next day.

They sat in his office. "Maybe he's beginning to unravel," Chris said. "I'd start keeping a journal. Everything Richie does."

"Assuming anyone will believe me." She paused. "Elena's not right, Chris. I may go back to Alec Keene."

Chris nodded. "I think you should."

As Terri stood to leave, he raised a hand to stop her. "Have another minute? There's something I need to talk to you about."

His tone was somehow different. Slowly Terri sat again.

Chris folded his hands. "I've been asked to consider running for the Senate, Terri. In the Democratic primary, two years from now."

It startled her. "As in *United States* Senate?"

Chris nodded. "Amazing, isn't it? When Wally Mathews called, I thought he wanted money again. Instead he wanted me."

She was quiet for a time. "You might be good, Chris."

He shrugged. "Some people want a candidate who hasn't been handpicked by James Colt, Jr. Our inevitable next governor."

Once more Terri felt surprise and a little unease. James Colt was a prominent Democrat of about Chris's age. Most local politicians, including the ambitious district attorney McKinley Brooks, were allied with Colt. Chris had resources and name recognition, but it would not be easy for him to build support.

"What reason," Terri asked, "does Wally give for wanting someone independent of Colt?"

"A lot of party people feel that beneath his public charm James Colt is mean as a snake and utterly devoid of principle."

Why, Terri thought, did she feel a sense of apprehension? "And you're thinking about it," she ventured.

"To my surprise. When Wally called, I realized that there are things I'd like to say, and this may be a chance to say them in a way that matters. At my age you start to ask yourself what it's all meant."

"I worry about Richie. He's jealous of you, Chris."

"Richie? What can he do to me?" Chris changed the subject. "Whatever Richie does when he has Elena, don't save him, and don't cover for him. He may start screwing up Elena's life in a way that other people notice." His voice turned cool. "No matter how painful, let him. Because then Elena will be with you."

This, Terri knew, was the best advice Chris could give. But the mother in Terri found it hard to follow.

Perhaps Richie knew that she could not help but salvage him if Elena was at risk. When Richie suddenly "gave up" the old apartment because he had stopped paying rent, he let her know that he was looking in neighborhoods Terri knew to be unsafe; after a week of this, Terri found them another apartment in the city so that Elena would be closer. When the landlord balked at Richie's credit, Terri co-signed the lease. She hated herself for it, just as—in the twisted logic of a custody battle—she despised herself for finding Elena the best possible school once it was clear that Richie would not bother. Richie knew nothing about the school, but at Elena's first open house he cornered the teacher, Leslie Warner, a willowy dark-haired woman with wide-set eyes and a credulous demeanor. Terri could not stand to watch.

Elena, though still defensive of her father, no longer asked whether he and Terri might reconcile. Instead she would sit alone for long, listless periods, barely speaking. She would not sleep by herself, began demanding the night-light she had proudly discarded a year before. She complained of stomachaches. Yet Richie claimed to see nothing.

They were standing in Terri's kitchen after Richie had dropped off Elena. "She's always fine with me," he said. "That leaves you and your boyfriend. If you were a little more sensitive, Ter, you'd see that your relationship is a form of abuse, and give him up."

Terri controlled her temper. "She's been listless at school too. And she used to make friends so easily."

Richie grimaced. "I'll keep an eye out, okay? But I think *you're* the problem. In fact, I think that all you're proving is how right Judge Scatena had it. I don't know why you imagine you can change his mind—especially when you're still chasing Paget."

"This isn't a contest, Richie—"

"You're damn right it isn't." His voice turned low and angry. "I'm broke all the time now—no money for Lawsearch, no nothing." He gazed up at her. "Sometimes, without you, I just feel so lost."

From some buried instinct of their marriage Terri wanted to comfort him. But she knew that even Richie could not tell where his vulnerability became artifice. It was that knowledge that kept her from touching his shoulder.

"Please, Richie, just let me have Elena. I'll see you're taken care of. Please. I'm frightened for her."

"Elena needs me." Richie gave her a look of bitter knowledge. "You think you can take everything away from me, don't you? But you can never kill my daughter's love."

He turned and walked from the kitchen.

Terri stood there awhile. Then she heard him in the bedroom, talking to Elena. "It makes me sad too," he was saying quietly. "I'll come back for you just as soon as I can."

As he drove away, Elena watched him from the window. She did not want dinner.

That night Terri found the little girl sitting rigid in her bed, tears streaming down her face. "Was it a nightmare, sweetheart?" Terri asked gently. But Elena would not speak.

In the morning Elena's eyes were puffy with sleeplessness. When Terri asked about the dream, the child shook her head.

Back off, Terri told herself; try to leave her alone.

ALEC Keene's venetian blinds cut the afternoon sunlight into ribbons on his gray tile floor. "Terri's been pretty specific," he said to Richie. "Listlessness, insecurity. Repeated nightmares."

Richie looked at him with folded arms. "I haven't seen it, Alec." His voice was polite but cool. "I hate to say so, but these things seem to happen when Elena's with Terri. If they happen at all."

"Are you saying that Terri made all this up?" Keene asked.

At once Richie's tone became apologetic. "Okay, maybe that last remark wasn't fair. What Terri says surprises me, that's all. She's a good mother, but since her involvement with Christopher Paget she has a hard time thinking about Elena." He turned to Terri. "And you *are* involved with him, Terri."

"Yes." Terri kept her voice steady. "*Now* I am. But that has nothing to do with Elena."

Richie turned to Keene. "Alec, all that I'm asking is that Terri agree not to expose Elena to Paget."

Keene looked glum. "Would it be so difficult?" he asked Terri.

"Not difficult," she answered. "Pointless. Elena adores Carlo. And Chris and Carlo aren't giving her nightmares—"

"No?" Richie cut in. "Then you are."

"We're getting nowhere," Keene said. "There's a final custody hearing in a few months, and you two can't even agree on how your daughter is acting. I'm going to recommend a family evaluation."

Richie looked puzzled. "What's that?"

"It's an assessment of the parents and the child, conducted by a child psychiatrist or psychologist. The evaluator will interview you at length, as well as others who may be in contact with the child."

"Will it include Chris Paget?" Richie asked.

"If Terri intended to live with Mr. Paget, it probably would."

"Good." Richie shot Terri a quick glance. "I want him tested." He leaned back in his chair. "Look, if there's any way to work this out, I want to." It was, Terri knew, Richie at his most deceptive. "Tell you what, Ter. I'll give you Lainie every weekend, and we'll see how that works. If she's okay, maybe we could make it permanent. And if there has to be an evaluation, at least we'll know how Elena does with much more time with you."

Terri shook her head. "I want an evaluation now—"

"And in three months, if you still want one, we'll have one. With all of us *and* Christopher Paget." Richie spread his hands. "I'm offering you more time without even requiring you to keep Elena away from Paget. Although I think you should."

"You're stalling, Richie."

"Stalling? I'm giving you a lot more than I need to."

Feeling Keene's gaze, Terri saw that Richie had boxed her in. If she contested custody after turning down more time, and Judge Scatena ever learned of it, she would have no chance at all. Meanwhile, Richie's preponderant custody would be that much more the status quo, and his checks from Terri would continue.

Terri exhaled. "All right. We'll try it. Just for a few weeks."

Keene gave a hopeful smile, then shook hands with both of them.

Richie walked with Terri out Keene's door, chatting pleasantly until they reached the hallway and the two of them were alone.

He took her elbow, speaking quietly. "I told you to stay away from Paget. But you wouldn't listen. So now this is the best you'll ever get from me. You'll never beat me, Terri. Ever."

Turning on his heel, Richie left.

Watching him go, Terri tried to be grateful for her weekends with Elena, resolving to spend all her time this weekend with her.

And except for Chris's debut in politics, she would have.

Chris's speech was scheduled for Saturday. Terri had not expected to have Elena then. Rosa was in Los Angeles visiting Terri's sister, so Chris, who wanted Terri to come, offered to pay Carlo to watch the child.

Elena, of course, was delighted. When Terri dropped her at Chris's that morning, she ran through the door after Carlo, armed with a dollhouse and a basket full of plastic Fisher-Price people.

Terri watched her climb the stairs. "Poor Carlo," she said to Chris. "I bet he can hardly wait."

They walked into the bright morning sun, laughing.

But it was not, they found out on the way, a good morning for politics. It should have been. The venue was well chosen—the annual convention of the California Society of Newspaper Editors. Chris's speech—a call for reform of the justice system—played to his strengths. But then an unbalanced father, angered by a custody fight, took an AK-47, walked into a recreation center in Oakland, and slaughtered his two children and five others.

Chris and Terri heard the news while they were driving to Moscone Center. "Oh, my God," Terri murmured automatically.

Chris merely listened. "The right to keep and bear arms," he finally said. "Our most sacred freedom. No cost can be too great."

When they reached the center, the news had not yet filtered through the audience, a group of perhaps five hundred. Terri sat in the first row. When Chris was introduced, she did not know what he would do.

He gazed out from the stage for what seemed minutes. "This morning," he began, "while I was polishing my speech, a man walked into an Oakland play center with an assault rifle and killed seven children. Two of them were his own."

A groan went up.

"My speech," Chris went on, "was quite well written. It was a balanced review of the shortfalls of our criminal justice system. Had I given it, it might well have served the purpose of showing how qualified I am to be a United States Senator. And like most speeches on crime—even by liberals—it mentions gun control only in passing." His voice held the barest trace of irony.

"I don't own a gun," he said quietly. "Outside the army, I've never fired one. Perhaps that makes it easier for me to notice that the chief use of handguns in America is domestic violence and robbing the corner store." He paused; for the first time, his words had an undertone of passion. "Since when, I wonder, is an AK-47 a tool for sportsmen? Empty one into a deer, and there wouldn't be enough left to hang up on the wall. The truth is that other countries use assault weapons to fight wars; we use them to butcher people in our streets and stores and homes."

Terri could not take her eyes off Chris.

"I suppose this speech is impolitic," he continued, "but what passes for politics isn't serious anymore. It's not about serious things. If anyone requires proof of that, consider that seven children died today because our political system is too cowardly and indifferent to protect them."

He lowered his voice. "This is an easy speech to give," he said. "Anyone can be angry about dead children. But I'm going to try something more difficult: to talk about serious things and to propose serious answers. Otherwise there's no point to this." Chris stood straighter. "I hope people listen. But if they don't, at least I won't feel any worse than I do this morning. Thank you."

He sat abruptly. Only after a moment did Terri realize that people were standing, sending up waves of applause washing over Chris, one upon the other.

An hour later, as Terri drove them home, Chris said, "Know what I feel like doing? Something with our kids."

But when they got home, Chris's house was silent. Then from upstairs they faintly heard a child talking. Together they went upstairs, walked through Chris's bedroom, and found Elena splashing in Chris's oversized bathtub. Carlo was sitting against the bathroom wall, watching her and listening to a Giants game on his transistor radio. Elena was surrounded by the bobbing plastic heads of miniature people. "I'm taking a bath," she explained to Terri. "With Carlo and my friends."

With a comic expression Carlo pulled the baseball cap down on his head. "She wanted to," he said. "Wouldn't even go for ice cream."

"I'll take over from here," Terri told him with a smile.

Carlo stood, looking relieved. "I'm going to see Katie," he said to Chris. "If that's okay."

"Sure."

Chris and Carlo went downstairs, talking about Chris's speech, leaving Elena staring after them. For the rest of the afternoon the little girl was sullen.

Terri passed this off as the child's devotion to Carlo. And then on a Friday shortly after Elena entered school, Leslie Warner, Elena's teacher, called Terri at work. "I don't mean to disturb you," Warner said, "but something happened at school today, with Elena." Warner paused. "The playground supervisor found Elena with a little boy. She had pulled her panties down."

Terri sat back in her chair. "What did she say?"

"Nothing."

"What do you think I should do?"

"Nothing, really. There's a lot of acting out at this age. Plus there's a divorce going on, and these things overstimulate children. New relationships, whatever . . ." The phrase trailed off.

"Have you called Elena's father?" Terri already knew the answer.

"Yes. But he told me Elena would be with you tonight."

"She will be," Terri said politely. "Thank you for calling."

That evening when Terri asked Elena what had happened, the little girl turned away, arms clasped, as if holding herself together.

Terri said softly, "You can talk to me whenever you want to."

Elena shook her head, mute.

That night when Terri went to check Elena, the child was crying. Her nightmare had come again.

"You want an evaluation *now?*" Richie had demanded in irritation. "Two weeks after we agree to a new arrangement?"

Terri kept looking at Alec Keene. "Elena's still not right," she said quietly. "And now there's this thing at school."

335

Keene propped his chin on tented fingers, gazing at them. "I'm inclined to agree with Terri. It may be time for a psychologist."

"I can't agree to a process that's not objective," Richie said.

Keene spoke with exaggerated patience. "It's not a matter of the parents agreeing. If there's no settlement, a family evaluation report is mandatory. But what do you mean by objective?"

Richie leaned forward. "I'll object to any evaluation that doesn't include intensive scrutiny of Christopher Paget and his son."

Keene looked puzzled. "Perhaps some time with Mr. Paget might be helpful. But at this point his son seems peripheral."

"Peripheral?" Richie turned on Terri. "Let's take your extra weekend time with Elena. Tell me how much time Elena spent alone with Carlo Paget on the first weekend after our agreement."

"I don't know." Terri was edgy now. "Chris was giving a speech, and I didn't have a sitter. It wasn't long."

Richie nodded. "And what did they do? Play with dolls?"

Terri held her temper. "I wasn't there."

"But you *do* know, Terri, what they were doing when you and your boyfriend came home."

Terri felt her pulse quicken. "Elena was taking a bath."

Richie's voice was silken now. "Alone?"

"No." Terri paused again. "Carlo was watching her."

Richie raised his eyebrows. "And where is the bathroom?"

"Upstairs, off Chris's bedroom—"

"All right," Keene interrupted. "What's your point, Richie?"

"It's this," said Richie. "The last time we were together, Terri began ticking off symptoms: listlessness, lack of close peer relations, regression, bad dreams. Things our daughter had left behind at the age of four. What Terri said puzzled me, so I went to the library and took out some books. And as I read, I began to worry."

His eyes narrowed. "I didn't want to believe it, of course. No parent does. But then there was this incident at school—sexual acting out, they called it. And everything Terri had told us suddenly fell into place." He turned to her. "It's a symptom of sexual abuse, Terri. Of our daughter, by your lover's pervert son."

It startled Terri. "That's crazy. . . ."

"*Is it?*" Richie demanded. "Then how did I know about that bath?" His voice lowered. "Because Elena told me."

"Carlo was just watching her," Terri began. Her stomach felt hollow. "What did Elena tell you?"

"It was more what she didn't tell me. She was withdrawn, spacey. Just as you described. When I asked her what was wrong, she turned away. All she said was, 'I took a bath with Carlo.' "

Terri felt a visceral fear. "Why didn't you tell me?"

Richie opened his palms. "These kinds of charges are *very* serious. I wanted to think it over."

Keene faced Terri. "I don't know what's happened here," he finally said. "These behaviors don't necessarily mean child abuse. But once the charge is made, people don't back off. And it affects everyone for a long time."

"I don't believe that Carlo would abuse Elena," Terri said. "What I do believe is that Richie's been saving this as a bargaining chip—"

"Terri!" Richie exclaimed. "Are you still clinging to Paget?"

"I want Elena tested—"

"That's a cop-out. I want some guarantees from you."

"You've got one. Elena won't go near Carlo, all right? For *both* their sakes. But there *will* be an evaluation. Elena *will* get help. We *will* get to what's happening with her."

"All right. *Enough*," Keene interrupted. "I'll be in touch, with names of three prospective evaluators. Try to agree on one. Otherwise Judge Scatena will choose one for you."

WHEN Terri had called about Richie's charges—from a phone booth outside the administrative building—the softness in Chris's voice scared her more than anger would have. "For eight years the major purpose of my life has been to tell Carlo, less by words than by being there, that no one in the world was more important to me. The funny thing is, it worked. Terri, I love that boy more than Ricardo Arias will ever comprehend."

"I wish this had never happened, Chris."

"It never did." Paget's tone was hard now. "You were there. Carlo was giving her a bath because we asked him to watch her."

"I don't think anything happened, either," said Terri. "But Elena told Richie something. She's a mess, Chris. I can't pretend that Richie never raised this."

There was silence. "I'll talk to Carlo," Chris said in a flat voice.

337

Terri made one more telephone call, then drove to Elena's school. When Terri appeared, the little girl ran into her mother's arms. Terri held her close. "Come on, sweetheart," she murmured. "We're going to see Dr. Nash—it's time for your checkup."

Elena's pediatrician was a brisk, no-nonsense woman in her mid-thirties. Elena lay on the examining table with her eyes shut, stoic and silent. Afterward Dr. Nash took Terri aside. "I can pretty much rule out intercourse," she said bluntly. "Beyond that, it's always hard to tell. Unless the child says something."

Terri looked toward the examining room. Elena was engrossed with coloring books. "You can't tell me *anything?*"

The doctor frowned. "Nothing physical," she answered. "If something else comes up, please call me." She hurried off.

At least, Terri realized, it was Friday; she could take Elena home.

They sat together on the living-room rug with Elena's plastic people. But Elena seemed merely to play by rote. When Terri put away the toys, she did not protest.

Terri pulled her daughter close. "Do you remember," she began gently, "when we talked about good touching and bad touching?"

Elena glanced at her, eyes veiled and cautious. She gave an almost imperceptible nod.

"Tell me about bad touching, okay?"

Elena stood abruptly and walked to the corner of the room.

Terri went to her, kneeling. "Do you remember," she asked, "the day you took a bath at Chris's house? When Carlo was with you?"

Elena's eyes froze.

Terri forced herself to stay calm. "Did Carlo ever touch you?"

Elena turned sideways. Her profile was a line of tension—pursed lips, folded arms, stiff body. Terri slid in front of her. "Did you say something to Daddy about Carlo? Or a bath?"

The child's eyes flickered. Terri knew what it meant. Six-year-old children, when planning to lie, do not disguise it well. "No," Elena said, and turned away.

Frustrated, Terri clutched her shoulder. "You can talk to me, Elena. Just like with Daddy."

"I can't." Elena whirled angrily. "You want to take me away from Daddy. I can *never* talk to you." She ran to her bedroom, crying. She would not come out for dinner. Whoever first conceived of a broken heart, Terri thought to herself, must have loved a child.

An hour later Chris called. "Carlo wants to talk with you," he said. "We both do."

"I'll try to get my mother to stay with Elena."

It was nine when she got to Chris's. Carlo was in the library. For once, he did not wear the baseball cap. She sat across from him, with Chris standing to the side. Carlo was pale; the effort to look stoic made him seem younger than his age. But his eyes did not waver.

"I never touched her. Not that way. Not even close."

Terri fought her sympathy. "Richie claims she was upset."

"She wanted to take a bath, she told me." His words were shot with pain. "Terri, she's a *little kid*."

"Did you help her undress?" Terri asked. "Anything like that?"

"No way. She had her clothes off before I even started the water."

"How did taking a bath come up?"

"Kids *do* things, that's all." Carlo exhaled. "Maybe Richie believes this lie. Maybe he doesn't. Either way, he thinks he's going to put me through a lot of crap—social workers, shrinks, whatever." His voice turned raw. "Let him. I didn't do this stuff."

Abruptly Carlo left the room.

Chris watched him climb the stairs until he disappeared. "*This*," he murmured to Terri, his voice level, "is one of the worst nights of my life. I know Carlo better than I know anyone. He's not lying."

"Are you saying that Richie put her up to this?"

"Think about it, Terri. I know you're worried for Elena, and so am I. But the first time you sat down with Keene, Richie asked him to spell out the hot-button custody issues—including child molestation. The hardest thing to prove or disprove. When Elena came home that weekend and told him about the fun bath with Carlo, Richie must have salivated. All he had to do was tack on the disturbed behavior you'd described to him and take it to Keene."

"The behavior is real. And Elena won't talk."

Chris shrugged. "That's why you need an evaluation."

Terri held his gaze. "Even one that involves Carlo?"

"Especially then. He didn't do this, Terri. How would he feel if he ran away from it?"

Terri walked to the window. "Richie's desperate, Chris."

"Richie," Chris cut in, "doesn't know what desperate is."

Turning, Terri gave him a questioning look.

"I'm going to wait," he told her, anger in his eyes, "until you've got Elena. And then I'm going to destroy him."

ALTHOUGH Terri could not have known this, their deepest troubles began with a call from a reporter. It came at a moment of frustration. Terri had just put down her office phone after talking to the evaluator Alec Keene had recommended, a warm-sounding psychologist named Denise Harris, only to learn that Harris could not start with Elena for at least eight weeks. The phone rang, and Terri, distracted, picked it up again.

"Ms. Peralta? Jack Slocum. Have a moment?"

Slocum worked as a reporter for the morning paper, Terri recalled. "Concerning what?" she asked.

"The article in this week's *Inquisitor*. Do you have a comment?"

Terri could not fathom why she should care about a tabloid filled with celebrity gossip and citings of spaceships. "I missed that one," she said. "Did Elvis die?"

"They didn't call you? On page seven your husband claims that Christopher Paget broke up your marriage."

It was as if, Terri thought, she were dreaming. "Let me ask you something. The *Inquisitor* pays for slime like this, right?"

"Uh-huh," said Slocum. "Mr. Arias got ten thousand dollars."

"This isn't news," Terri said. "It's compost."

"Come on, Ms. Peralta. Christopher Paget may well run for the Senate. We're obliged to explore questions of character."

"Whose character?" Terri snapped, and hung up.

She found Chris at his desk. He did not look up. Slocum had called him, she realized. The *Inquisitor* lay in front of him.

At the center of page 7 was a news photo of Chris and Terri emerging from the Carelli hearing and, next to that, a color picture of Richie holding Elena. Elena looked bewildered. The photo caption read, "Ricardo Arias raises six-year-old Elena by himself. 'She's all I have now,' Richie says. 'We're barely making it.' "

The writing was florid but effective: the story of a stay-at-home father abandoned by his wife for her rich and powerful boss. "We had so much in common," the article quoted Richie as saying. "We were both Hispanic and poor, working together for a better life. Then Terri became caught up in another world. *His* world."

Terri felt a rush of shame. "Has anyone else run this drivel?"

"Not yet," Chris said in a flat voice.

Terri kept herself from apologizing for Richie. It was pointless and would sound too pitiful. "I could sue him," she said.

"Not as long as he's got Elena. It can't seem like you're seeking custody to spite him." When he looked up, his expression held sympathy. "If it weren't for my flirtation with politics, Richie would rate no interest at all."

"What are you going to do?"

"I've already done what I can. Our friend Slocum's publisher agrees with me that this isn't news—at least for now. If all this turns out to be is an *Inquisitor* story, it'll probably go away."

"But you don't think it will," Terri said.

"That may depend on what else Ricardo feeds them. Or what the media, or someone like James Colt, dig up on their own." His eyes were hard now. "It's time for me to have a talk with Richie."

Terri felt her nerves tingle. "You can't, Chris. Not yet. It will only make things worse."

"Carlo's my son, damn it." Suddenly Chris's anger burst into the open. "This little weasel thinks he's immune, Terri."

Terri forced herself to be calm. "Richie and I are contesting custody. I don't want Richie telling Scatena that you tried to prevent him from learning the 'truth' about Carlo and Elena."

Chris stared at her. "He has a genius, doesn't he? He's put us on opposite sides. Anything I do to protect Carlo may hurt Elena."

"I'm so sorry," Terri said. "But if he keeps on doing stuff like this, he's going to reveal who he really is. I'll try to tell him that."

Back in her office, Terri picked up the phone.

"Richie Arias," she heard him answer in a cheery voice.

"I've read the article," Terri said calmly. "It captured you perfectly." Her voice remained level. "In a way, I'm glad you did it. You're usually better at concealing what you are."

"Look, I'm out of money." His voice rose. "You think I wanted to embarrass myself? You and your boyfriend made me."

"No, we didn't. As I told you once, you're a self-made man."

There was a tense silence. "And now you've found the perfect lover, haven't you." Richie's voice grew quiet. "Tell me, Terri, what makes you think that he'll choose you over the Senate? You know, when things get *really* hard for him."

"What do you mean by that?" Terri snapped.

He laughed softly and hung up.

SIX

ROSA sat down on the couch. "You're going to Italy with Chris," she repeated to Terri. "Eight months after leaving Richie."

"The evaluation doesn't start for almost a month." Terri kept her voice calm. "Chris and I need this time, Mom. Somewhere away from the office and Richie's constant presence."

"For months," Rosa replied, "I've said nothing to you. The courts have taken away your daughter. The man who you claim loves you is a millstone. The child I love is a shell. And still I've said nothing. But your decisions have been wrong, Teresa. Every one of them. Beginning with Christopher Paget. And Elena has paid the price. Please, ask Chris to step aside."

Terri felt the guilt of all that had happened. "That's why we're going to Italy—to talk, to see if there's any future for us that is good for our children. Like the adults we happen to be." She heard the edge in her voice. "You'd be surprised how well that works—talking."

Her mother's face remained impassive. "Are you so certain, Teresa, that Carlo didn't molest your daughter?"

"I can't swear to it," Terri said, "but I don't believe he's capable of that. The evaluator will try to find out."

Rosa's face was still a mask; only her eyes showed her anguish. "To abuse a child is a terrible thing. Whatever else you blame me for, I never would have let that happen to you or your sisters."

For an instant, in what Rosa did not say, Terri felt the presence of her father, Ramon Peralta.

"I imagine," Rosa said, "that you've already told Ricardo."

"Yes." Richie had hardly reacted. He had simply taken down the dates of their trip. "If there's an emergency, Richie has to know where I am," Terri said. "I would never leave, Mama, if Elena were with me for more than weekends. But she isn't. If you take Elena on the weekend I'll be gone, it'll be good for both of you."

Rosa fell silent. Terri kissed her, the offering of peace, and left.

It was dark, just past ten. The inside stairs to her apartment were quiet. Climbing them, Terri promised herself a good night's sleep.

The door was ajar.

Terri gazed at it, stepping back for a moment. Then slowly she pushed it open and peered into her living room. She saw nothing. She stepped forward, head turning to each side. Softly, someone shut the door behind her. Terri turned, a scream caught in her throat. In front of her door stood Ricardo, grinning at her.

"What's wrong, Ter? You used to like a little excitement."

Her heart was pounding. "How did you get in here?"

"Remember when I borrowed the car, when mine was in the shop?" He flipped Terri a set of keys. "You shouldn't keep your extras in the glove compartment. Someone might steal them."

Terri looked down. Her keys lay on the floor: to her apartment, to her mother's home, to Chris's house.

"You scum," she said softly.

"That's not fair, Terri. Actually I came here to effect personal service of an important set of legal pleadings. Regarding Elena. You remember her, don't you? Our daughter?" Richie handed Terri a flat sealed envelope. "I'm not leaving until you've read this."

She opened it. Inside were a set of pleadings marked FILED UNDER SEAL. The caption read, "Petitioner's Motion for Preliminary Injunction." The relief requested was simple: that respondent Teresa Peralta cease all contact between her daughter, Elena, and her lover, Christopher Paget. And his son, Carlo. The petitioner, Ricardo Arias, wanted the court to restrain respondent from exposing their daughter "to the unstable and immoral sexual patterns that pervade the Paget household."

Terri looked up at Richie in disbelief. "So you're bringing Carlo into this," she said quietly. "You just can't help yourself, right?"

"I'm *protecting* Elena." Richie folded his arms. "I thought it was time that Judge Scatena knew the facts."

"You'd drag them both into a courtroom. Elena too."

"Only if you make me. Notice that I've been very responsible—everything filed under seal. So none of this becomes public unless you force me to a hearing." Richie draped an arm around her. "Just think what a truly vindictive person would do with this—someone in politics, for example."

Deliberately Terri took his arm off her shoulder. "The hearing date. You scheduled it for when we'd be in Italy."

"In Portofino, according to your itinerary."

"Tell me what you want. Tell me and then get out of here."

Richie's eyes glinted. "Call off the evaluation. I want permanent custody, the support I've asked for, *and* fifty thousand dollars. Now. If you don't, we go to a hearing." He nodded toward the papers in her hand. "And those become public documents."

Terri's telephone rang.

"That should be your boyfriend," Richie said cheerfully. "He must have read his courtesy copy."

"So Colt found Richie," Chris said when Terri answered the telephone. "I suppose it was only a matter of time."

"You found the papers," Terri said.

"Carlo did. I need to see you, Terri."

She glanced over at Richie. "Oh, I'm leaving," Richie told her. "I know you lovers need time to talk."

"All right," Terri said to Chris.

As she hung up, Richie kissed her on the forehead and left.

Terri locked the door behind him and sat down to wait. Soon there was a knock on the door. She went to open it. Chris was standing in the doorway. He looked completely miserable.

He stepped inside. "I couldn't be sorrier, Terri," he said. "Most couples have bad moments, but they don't have them in public, with their children at risk."

"Unless I give him Elena *and* money," she said wearily, "she'll go through a hearing. You and Carlo will be spread all across the papers. The Senate will be history."

Chris nodded. "One of James Colt's people read the *Inquisitor*, I'm quite sure, and got in touch with Richie. Just in case he needed more encouragement."

Terri found it hard to look at him. "That gives us only one way out, doesn't it?"

Chris had made his face impassive. "You agree not to see me. And just to be safe, I get out of the race."

Chris sat on the couch staring at the ceiling. Terri began picking up Richie's papers, a lawyer straightening her desk. "The hearing's not for three more weeks. We've got that long to decide."

"Three weeks to be together." For the first time, Chris seemed almost angry. "Just time enough to go to Italy."

Terri turned to him in surprise.

"We could cut four days off the trip," Chris said, his voice soft, "and still be back to prepare for court."

Terri sat next to him. "We can't, Chris—not now. I won't be able to stop thinking about Elena. It would be a nightmare."

"Perhaps. But we'd be far away from Richie." He paused. "Whatever I've faced in life, I've never let anyone just run me over. I won't start now for Ricardo Arias. And neither should you."

"It's all right," Rosa said. "I'll make sure Elena's safe."

They were standing in the doorway of Rosa's home on the night before Terri left for Italy. It was seven o'clock; Elena was in her nightgown. When Terri let the little girl go and looked into her mother's gaze, she felt unutterably sad. "I know you will," she said.

Back home, she snatched at clothes, unable to pack.

The telephone rang. It was Chris, she knew, calling to take her to dinner. After that, she would stay with him. Right now, Terri felt, only that would get her to Italy.

"Hi," he said. "Ready yet?"

"Getting there. What's for dinner?"

"Actually I think I'm coming down with something," he said. "Is it okay if I just pick you up in the morning?"

"Sure," Terri said automatically. "Are you all right?"

"A little queasy. I've got the twenty-four-hour whatever, I think. I don't want to give it to you or take it with us on vacation."

"That's fine," Terri said. But when she hung up, she found that she had far too much time to think and too much need to talk.

An hour later she had still not started packing. Terri sat on the edge of the bed, lost in the past. Remembering the night she had packed for her honeymoon, filled with hope and uncertainty. Looking into the face of her new husband, Ricardo Arias.

She picked up the telephone to call him.

IN THE stillness of night Terri knelt before the confessional. Behind the screen the priest was a shadow. The church was dark. Terri was afraid. Trembling, she confessed what she had done.

The church was hushed. The priest rose. Terri could feel his anger. The only sounds were his footsteps on the stone.

The priest appeared from behind the screen. Terri could not bear to see his face. She turned to run. He called out, "Teresa . . ."

Terri awoke. Voices drifted through the window from the walk below; a church bell, deep and sonorous, echoed across the water—the lulling rhythms of an ancient city where she lay in the evening next to her lover, unable to forget Ricardo Arias.

Venice, Terri realized. She was with Chris. Next to him. They had made love, slow and sweet, and then she had fallen asleep.

He reached out to touch her. "Are you all right?"

With Chris, she told herself again, for the last two days. Together with him in Italy and yet lost in the past.

Terri lay back on the pillow. "It's an old nightmare. One I haven't had for years." She found that she could not look at him. She spoke to the ceiling. "I'm in the chapel at Mission Dolores. It's as it was when I was a child. I'm alone, confessing my sins. I can't see the priest's face. He's a shadow on the other side of the screen. But I recognize the profile; it's Father Anaya, the parish priest.

"There's a last sin, one I've never confessed to anyone. I lean my face to the screen and whisper it. The shadow moves. I hear footsteps." Terri closed her eyes. "I want to run, but I just stand there waiting. A priest in monk's robes appears. At first I can't see his face, but I know that he's filled with hate. His arm rises to point at me, and then he steps into the light." Eyes opening, Terri turned to Chris. "It isn't Father Anaya, Chris. It's *my* father."

Terri felt the breeze through the window. Her forehead was damp. Smiling slightly, Chris touched her face. "This particular sin of yours," he said. "What have you done that's so terrible?"

"I've never known. The dream just ends."

"Do you have any idea what it means?"

"It's obvious enough. Somehow I feel guilty about my father, perhaps for how I felt when he died. I don't waste a lot of time on it. It's nothing. Except that I seem to have passed my talent for recurring nightmares on to Elena, like some family curse."

Chris reached for an ice bucket beside the bed, poured a glass of pinot grigio, and handed it to Terri. "I thought she wouldn't tell you what she sees," he said.

"She won't." Terri sipped the wine. "But she always calls it the dream. Sometimes, Chris, I wonder what I've done to her."

He reached out, cradling her face. "Try calling her again."

Terri kissed his palm. Dialing Richie's number, she watched Chris flick on a bedside lamp and refill his wineglass.

Richie's telephone rang. At twelve rings she hung up.

Enough, she told herself. Be with Chris while you can.

Chris replaced the wine bottle. The purple discoloration on his hand had faded a little, but he still winced when he used it. "You should have that x-rayed," she said. "It might be broken."

He shrugged. "I doubt it."

Terri looked at his hand again. "I've never been the victim of a falling trunk. I can't imagine how you did it."

"Your reflexes are faster. I only wish you'd helped me pack."

Terri gave him a wry look. "It's your trunk. And it was you who canceled dinner at the last minute and left me alone all night."

Chris turned to the window. "I'll make it up to you. It's a fine night, and I know just the place for black squid pasta."

"*That*," Terri answered, "was the real subject of my nightmare. The other stuff I just made up."

They caught a vaporetto near the Danieli and took the long, slow ride to the Rialto Bridge. The night was purple; the lights of the floating bus swept the black water of the canal. With the breeze in their faces Chris and Terri seemed far away from everything.

WHEN Terri dialed Richie's number the next morning, there was still no answer. Holding the telephone, Terri imagined that Elena must feel as if she had lost her mother. Watching Chris, she felt guilt and self-contempt. "I wish he were dead," she said bitterly.

"Nothing?" Chris asked.

"No. And Elena should be in bed by now. If I can't reach Richie by tonight, I'm calling the school."

They went to an outdoor café on the Piazza San Marco. They chose a table, ordered croissants and double espressos, and surveyed the immense piazza. It was, Terri realized, quite wonderful.

"I'm sorry," she said finally. "About everything. I wonder, sometimes, if you can ever forgive me for what he's done to you."

Chris stared at his espresso. "I think it's more a matter of whether

348

you forgive yourself for staying with him. Enough to stay with me."

"You think I need a shrink, in other words."

"Is that a sin too? Like the one in your dream? Or whatever feelings you've never faced about your parents?"

Terri turned away. "I don't like thinking of my father. When I do, it scares me. Anyway, a lot of it I hardly remember now. It's done, all right? He's dead."

Chris gazed at her. After a time he asked, "How did he die?"

As if by reflex Terri shut her eyes. The image was like the shock of a flashbulb. Her father's head at her feet in the first morning sun, a ribbon of dried blood running from his temple. She felt her mind flinch, close down; then there was nothing.

Terri did not answer. Softly Chris asked, "What is it, Terri? That you blame *yourself* somehow?"

She opened her eyes, but she did not look at Chris. "The house felt safer afterward," she said. "Maybe I blamed myself for liking that." Her voice grew tired. "Sometimes, Chris, I think that's why I was so determined to become a lawyer. Because there were *rules*. No one got hit, and everyone had their turn to speak. The law protected even children, I thought."

CHRIS and Terri spent the day visiting the Doges' Palace and strolling along the Grand Canal. That evening they walked back to the Danieli from dinner at Harry's Bar. Other lovers, more carefree, drifted arm in arm beneath the gaslights. Part of Terri wished to join them. But she would have no peace until she spoke to Elena.

When they reached the hotel, she hurried through the ornate lobby and up the staircase ahead of Chris. Opening the door, she switched on the lights and began jabbing at the buttons of the telephone. Once more Richie did not answer.

She put down the phone. From the doorway Chris watched her. Then he stepped inside, closing the door behind him. In the dim light Terri looked up at him, silent.

"I'm sorry," she said finally. "Maybe I was crazy to come here."

Chris looked stung. "Maybe," he answered tersely, "you should have left your husband at home."

"I'm not going to respond to that. Not now," said Terri. "Maybe he's achieving exactly what he wants—us sitting here quarreling over him, as if he were pulling strings from seven thousand miles away. But right now all that matters, Chris, is that I can't find my daughter. I'm calling the school in an hour."

"I think you should at least find out if Rosa's seen Elena."

Glancing at her watch, Terri placed the call, the phone pressed to her ear. Six rings, then seven.

"Hello?"

The connection was bad.

"Mom? Thank goodness you're home. I'm looking for Elena. I'm worried sick about her."

A pause. Then Rosa's hollow voice saying, "She's here, Terri."

"With *you*?"

"Yes. I just took her to school."

Terri's eyes shut. "Elena's with my mother," she murmured to Chris, and then, as if in delayed reaction, leaned back against him. "Where's Richie?"

"He never came."

Terri sat up. "Have you tried to reach him?"

"No." Rosa's voice sounded faintly surprised. "Should I?"

"I don't know. Is Elena upset?"

"She was at first. Actually she seems quite happy now."

Covering the telephone, Terri turned to Chris. "Richie never showed," she said. "What do you think I should do?"

Chris shrugged. "Nothing. Devoted fathers aren't supposed to blow off custody. Why remind him?"

Terri frowned. "I was thinking about Elena."

"So am I. Let him rot awhile."

After a moment Terri spoke to Rosa. "Leave him be. He'll show up whenever he decides to. Tell Elena I'll call her."

"I will. And don't worry, sweetheart. Everything is fine."

When Terri hung up, Chris turned away. "A dozen times I've told myself I should let you go. But I can't." The raw feeling in his voice startled her. But when he spoke again, it was gently. "I *was* wrong to bring you here. I'm sorry for that, and for talking you into it."

PORTOFINO, on the Italian Riviera, was surrounded by steep hills that tumbled to sparkling green water. The hills were covered with palms and tall, slender evergreens and bright flowers. Chris and

Terri sat at the glass table on the balcony of their hotel room. The view was sweeping and beautiful, Terri thought. It was also very painful. When she drifted to the bedroom to make her call, Chris stayed on the balcony.

Elena was drawing pictures with her grandmother. "Mommy!" she exclaimed. "Where are *you*?"

"In a place called Portofino, sweetheart." Terri described it. "I wish you could see it."

"I can *draw* it for you," Elena answered. "There are palm trees outside Grandma's house too. On Dolores Street."

Terri laughed a little. "I've missed you so much, Elena."

"I miss you too, Mommy. How many more days is it?"

Thinking of Chris, Terri felt sad again. "Only three," she said softly. "Then I'll be home."

Elena was quiet for a moment. In a different voice she asked, "Do you know where Daddy is?"

Terri hesitated. "He hasn't called you yet?"

In the silence, Terri imagined Elena shaking her head. "Do you think he had an accident, Mommy?"

"No, sweetheart. Your daddy's just gone somewhere."

There was a long pause. "Mommy, I think Daddy's dead."

Terri felt a chill. "No, Elena," she said calmly, "Daddy's not dead. Why do you think that?"

"Because he's lonely." Elena's voice was frightened now. "Daddy wouldn't leave me alone."

"I think he just took a trip," Terri said. "He told me he might. So don't worry too much, all right? Besides, you've got a picture to draw for me."

"Okay, Mommy, I will. Grandma wants to talk to you now."

Terri heard instructions to find crayons, and then Rosa said in a muted voice, "Do you want me to call the police, Teresa?"

"No," she answered. "At least not until Elena makes you."

Terri got off the telephone.

"How is she?" Chris asked.

Terri turned, watching his face. "She thinks Richie's dead."

Chris's eyes narrowed. "Does she say why?"

"Only that he never came for her. So he must be dead."

Chris seemed to reflect. "Elena's world is pretty small," he said at last. "In the eyes of a child, everything that happens is about herself."

Terri walked to the balcony, looked down into the blue harbor. "A long time ago," she said finally, "my mother lost her belief in happy endings. Perhaps Elena has too."

That night Terri did not fall asleep for hours. When she did, the nightmare broke her sleep. Until the final moment it was the same as before. But this time the priest was not her father; it was Richie.

IN THE morning Terri did not tell Chris of her nightmare.

"If we're trying to decide our future," she said, "let's at least get out. I don't want to sit around in our hotel room being depressed."

They took a stone path winding down through the hills to the harbor below. The water glistened with early sun. They bought cheese and fruit and mineral water, hired a motor launch and a gap-toothed fisherman to pilot it, and cruised along the coast until they reached a rocky beach. The pilot left them.

They sat facing each other on the sand, the food spread between them. Terri opened her hands in a gesture of helplessness. "Where do we start? Elena, Carlo, the Senate, the hearing? How could we live with all the wreckage? And why would you even want to?"

Chris looked into her face. "Because I love you, Terri. More than I've loved any woman."

For a moment she was too moved to answer. But this was a time for truths to be spoken. "Even if you believe it now, Chris, you won't later on. Not after your career in politics is finished and Richie has dragged Carlo through the mud."

"That's not for you to say, Terri. Unless saving me from myself is your excuse for backing out."

Terri shook her head. "I'm not a fool. You can have pretty much anyone you want without turning your life inside out."

"As if women are interchangeable," Chris cut in sharply. "Where do you suggest I go to find *you* again, after I've thrown us away? Someone who, when I talk to her, feels right. Someone who, when I touch her or even look at her, makes the world different."

Terri felt tears in her eyes. She could not trust herself to speak.

"I know that it's different for you," Chris continued. "I used to think that once you got custody of Elena, you could see more clearly the life I wanted for us. But you have to be able to do that now. Because if you're not sure you want to be with me, then what Richie does—or where he is—matters not at all to us."

Terri gripped his hands. "What do you think is making me so sad? Oh, Chris, if you just eliminate Richie, being with you is more perfect a life than I ever imagined. But if I'm to be with you, I need to be able to love you with a whole heart. Even if I lose Elena."

For once, Chris had no answer.

They ate together, quiet. But an hour later when they had cruised back to Portofino, Terri asked to be alone.

"I just need to think awhile," she said. She went to walk in the garden, thinking of Elena and Carlo and Rosa, Judge Scatena and Alec Keene, and how they would react should she decide to be with Chris.

A little after four she found Chris on the patio. As she approached, he tried to keep his face impassive, concealing his apprehension. She sat across from him and touched his hand. "You're precious to me, Chris. I believe in you. We have to solve this terrible problem with Carlo and Elena. And if we can, our life will be something no one can ever take from us. Not even Richie."

Chris's eyes shut; it was then that Terri saw, beyond anything he could say or do, how deeply Christopher Paget loved her. This was the man she would spend her life with, she was suddenly certain.

The elderly concierge approached their table. "I apologize," the man said. "But I have a message for Ms. Peralta."

It startled her. Terri thanked him and read the slip of paper he handed her. She looked up at Chris. "My mother." Her voice felt thin. "The message says it's urgent."

All at once Chris looked apprehensive.

She hurried to find a telephone.

SLOWLY Terri put down the phone.

It was a while before she stood. The mini-world of the hotel lobby went on around her unnoticed as she returned to their table.

Chris watched her with a look of unease. "What is it?" he asked.

She brushed the hair back from her face. "Richie's dead."

His eyes widened slightly; that was all.

Terri watched him, taut. "Say something, Chris. Please."

353

He stood, walking slowly to the iron railing at the edge of the patio. "Would you care for me to put it into words? All right. I'm glad he's dead, and I hope it was slow and painful. How *did* he die?"

Terri kept her voice steady. "He shot himself. Apparently. My mother called the police last night, and they found him." She paused. "That's not like him, Chris."

He expelled a deep breath, the first hint of emotion. "Is killing oneself 'like' anyone? You're in shock, Terri. But Richie can't hurt you or Carlo anymore. Most important, you have Elena now."

Terri clutched his arm. "Oh, Chris, it will be so hard to tell her."

Chris's arms came tight around her. They stayed like that for a time, quiet and close. Then he murmured, "At least no one can blame us for *this*."

Terri looked into his face. "Only because it's suicide. From what the police told my mother, Richie may have died the night before we left."

Terri saw the flicker of some new emotion in his eyes. "We'd better pack," Chris said. "We can catch a plane in Milan."

THE INQUIRY

October 27–November 30

SEVEN

Christopher Paget was not surprised when, three nights after Ricardo Arias was found, two homicide inspectors came to his home unannounced, armed with a tape machine. In itself this was not too worrisome. But one of the inspectors was Charles Monk, and Monk would not have forgotten the Carelli trial, where it had been Paget's role to ask the questions. Within an instant of opening the door, Paget found that he was thinking like a lawyer, alert beneath the surface.

"Come on in," he told Monk easily.

Monk said nothing. Ushering in Monk and his partner, a graying and taciturn Irishman named Dennis Lynch, Paget sensed Monk taking in the surroundings. His appearance was striking—a six-foot-four-inch black man with gold-rimmed glasses—and off the job he had a certain laconic charm. But Paget thought of him as a monotone, with eyes and a brain that forgot nothing; an hour with Monk and his machine had ensnared Mary Carelli—a frighteningly clever woman—in a trial for first-degree murder.

"Why don't we sit in the library," Paget said, and led them into a high-ceilinged room with a fireplace and two sofas.

Terri was sitting on one of them, drinking coffee. "You remember Terri Peralta," Paget said to Monk.

Monk did not shake hands. Terri was also a potential witness, and Monk would not want his witnesses to hear what each other said.

"You can talk to us both," Paget said pleasantly. "I'm sure that Terri is on your list."

Monk paused. Paget could follow his calculations: Neither Paget nor Terri was under arrest, and to insist that someone leave was beyond his power. "We were trying to find you," Monk told Terri.

She looked at him over her coffee cup. "I was out all day," she said. "Trying to distract my daughter any way I could. It's been hard." Elena, in fact, had moved from tears to numbness, burrowing deep within herself, as if she blamed herself for Richie's death.

"Where is she now?" Monk asked.

"With my mother."

Monk set the tape machine in front of her. "Can you answer a few questions?"

Terri nodded. Monk glanced at Paget. Monk wanted him to leave, Paget knew, as surely as Paget intended to stay. He took a chair.

Belatedly Dennis Lynch introduced himself to Terri. A pose of diffidence came easily to Lynch, Paget sensed, which cast him as the good cop in any partnership with Monk. Lynch eased his slender frame onto the couch next to Monk, facing Terri.

Monk pushed a button, then began speaking. "This is an initial investigation into the death of Ricardo Paul Arias. It is October twenty-seventh at seven thirty-five p.m. I am Inspector Charles Monk; with me is Inspector Dennis Lynch. The witness is Teresa Peralta, and we are at the home of Christopher Paget, who is also present." Monk turned to him. "Are you representing Ms. Peralta?"

It was a game, Paget knew. "No," he said evenly. "I was just here with Ms. Peralta when you happened to show up. This is, as you point out, where I live."

Monk turned to Terri. Within moments he had her age, her work and home addresses and telephone numbers, and enough information for him to subpoena her bank records and interview her neighbors. Then he turned to the subject of Richie.

"At the time of Mr. Arias' death, were you still living with him?"

"No. We were separated."

"And where did your daughter live?"

"Richie had preponderant custody. But you've already interviewed my mother, so you know all this."

"Was there some question about custody?" Monk asked.

"I had questions. I didn't think that Richie should raise her."

"Why not?"

"He had emotional problems. I don't think he was stable."

Monk caught Lynch's eye. In a sympathetic voice Lynch asked, "Did he ever go to a psychiatrist, anyone like that?"

"No." Terri gazed down. "Richie thought he was fine."

"Did your husband own a gun?" Monk asked.

"No."

"Did he have any interest in guns?" Here Monk paused. "Because the gun we found with him was quite unusual."

"How so?" Paget asked.

Monk kept looking at Terri. "It was a .32-caliber Smith and Wesson safety model. Five cylinders. The last one was made in 1909, Ms. Peralta. It's practically a collector's item."

Terri looked puzzled. "Richie wasn't a collector," she said.

"Do *you* own a gun?"

"No." Her voice was emphatic.

Softly Monk asked, "Do you think Richie killed himself?"

"I can't imagine *anyone* killing himself," Terri said. "But I'm not sure I understood Richie. Now I'm less sure than ever. Still, there was something wrong with him." She paused. "Toward the end he seemed angry and more desperate. His mood swings were wider."

"Do you know why?"

"He lost me," she said simply. "And he had very little money."

"Was he employed?"

"No. Richie didn't like working for people."

"Did he ever ask you for money?"

"I *gave* him money," Terri answered. "Nearly twenty-three hundred a month. Much of that was child support."

Monk adjusted his glasses. "Are you sorry he's dead?"

"Not for me," she said. "But for Elena, yes."

"When was the last time you spoke with your husband?"

"The night before I left for Italy. By telephone."

Paget was surprised; Terri had not told him this. "That reminds me," Chris said to Monk. "Did you check his answering machine? When Terri tried to call from Italy, it wasn't on."

"Someone turned it off," Monk said tersely. "Seems like the tape was erased. What time did you call him the night before you left?"

"I don't know," Terri said. "Maybe nine or so. It wasn't for long."

Paget felt himself tense.

"What did you talk about?" Monk asked.

Terri stared at the tape recorder. "I'd been packing. Somehow it made me think of my honeymoon, how much hope I'd had and how sad things were now. So I called to ask if I could see him."

Paget felt a surge of anger.

"Why did you want to see him?" Monk asked.

Terri looked at Paget. "To beg him," she said softly. "To ask him for Elena. To see if I could give him something in return."

"Such as?"

"Money." Why, Paget asked her silently, didn't you tell me?

"What did he say?" Monk asked.

"That he had an appointment that night."

Paget watched her, edgy. "Did he say who with?" Monk asked.

"No. But I thought it must be a woman—'appointment' had a sniggering sound." Terri shrugged. "Maybe there was no one. That would be like him—trying to impress me or to string me out."

"What," Monk asked, "did you do after you hung up?"

"Packed. Then I went to bed."

"Did anyone see you that evening?"

Terri glanced at Paget. "Only my mother and Elena, when I dropped her off. That was around seven."

"Did you talk to anyone else?"

Now Terri focused on Monk. "Just Chris. He called me about our arrangements. Before I called Richie. We decided Chris would pick me up the next morning."

"And that was all?"

Terri glanced at Paget's hand. He raised it slightly. The bruise

357

and the swelling had vanished. "That's all I remember," she said.

"Your flight," Monk said. "When did it leave?"

"Very early. Eight o'clock, I think."

"You didn't go to Mr. Paget's the night before?"

"No."

"Or to see Mr. Arias?"

Terri stared at him. "No," she answered.

Monk stood, stretching himself, taking in the art on the walls. "Did you ever visit Mr. Arias' apartment?"

Terri nodded. "Sometimes. When I dropped off Elena."

Monk began pacing—two or three steps, then back again. He stopped. "And what is your relationship with Mr. Paget?"

"Just that." Her voice was terse. "We have one."

"A romantic relationship?"

"Yes."

Monk turned to Paget and back to Terri. "And when did that part—the romantic part—begin?"

Paget stood at once. "That's enough—"

"*After* I left Richie," Terri interjected. "Is that what you wanted?"

Unruffled, Monk gazed at Paget and then turned to her. "Yes," he said with courtesy. "And only because it's my job. The man's dead, after all, and we have to ask questions to find out why."

The last thing Monk did before moving on to Paget was to take out an ink pad and help Terri put her prints on a white card with boxes for each finger. She sat there, silent.

Monk turned to Chris. "Mind answering a few questions?"

"If you don't mind my asking a few. Exactly how did Arias die?"

Monk shrugged. "Gunshot wound. The bullet lodged in the brain stem."

Paget's eyes narrowed. "What was the point of entry?"

In a flat voice Monk said, "It looked like he ate his gun."

Paget saw Terri wince. The laconic phrase was police argot for a not uncommon suicide.

"Did you find gunshot residue on the roof of his mouth?" Paget asked.

Monk nodded. "There was powder on his tongue and palate, a little on the back of his throat."

Terri stood and walked to the window.

"Did he leave some sort of note?" Paget asked.

"There was a note," Monk said tersely, and inclined his head toward the tape machine. "Mind sitting over there?"

Terri turned to watch them. Her face was pale. When Paget sat, she walked to the sofa and rested her hand near his shoulder.

"So," Monk said to him, "the night before you left for Italy, you didn't see Ms. Peralta. Is that right?"

"That's right," Chris said. "I spoke to her by phone."

"About what time was that?"

"Perhaps eight thirty or so." He leaned forward. "There was one thing Terri's forgotten. We had plans to go to dinner. The first part of our conversation was me calling to cancel because I felt sick. It was some twenty-four-hour thing. By morning I was fine."

"Did you see anyone that night?"

"Carlo. My son."

"Was Carlo home with you?"

Chris shook his head. "He had a date. He came home around midnight. I waited up for him."

Monk sat back and looked at Chris; for the first time, Monk seemed tired. "How," he asked Chris, "did you feel about Mr. Arias?"

"Based on my observations, he was an undesirable human being. Terri had more patience than I ever could have managed."

"What do you base that on?"

"Richie's undesirability or Terri's patience? I base them both on the divorce proceedings. Richie's devotion to using Elena as a meal ticket was matched only by Terri's determination to keep that fact from Elena. That much forbearance amazes me."

It was, Terri saw, a clever response. In one answer Chris had placed her in the most favorable light while avoiding his deepest reasons for despising Richie. And Carlo's reasons too.

Lynch leaned toward Paget. "Can you think of any reason why Mr. Arias would kill himself?"

"I'm no mind reader," Chris said, "but his life was in a downhill spiral: divorce, financial problems, difficulty holding a job."

"So you stayed home that night, correct?" Monk asked.

Chris nodded and then cocked his head. "Satisfy my curiosity. We've spent a fair amount of time talking about a single night, and yet you found Richie a week later. All that time at room temperature couldn't have helped him much." Chris gazed at Monk with an expression of pleasant inquiry. "The medical examiner couldn't have given you time of death if she'd had a Ouija board."

Monk removed his glasses and began to wipe the lenses. "Mr. Arias," he said slowly, "liked air-conditioning."

"At thirty degrees? When did Richie stop opening his mail? Not until Saturday, at least. That's what you must be going on."

Monk did not answer, but the look on his face told Terri that Chris was right. Chris did not have to make his larger point: that Richie might have died the next morning while Terri sat with Chris on an airplane to Milan.

"Anyhow," Chris said carelessly, "it's kind of an academic issue. The man did leave a note."

Monk appraised him for a moment, then spoke into his tape recorder. "We are terminating the interview at nine oh two." He switched it off and looked at Terri. "We may have more questions."

He did not say another word as Chris ushered them out.

When Chris returned, he crossed the room to take Terri in his arms. "Sorry," he murmured.

She said quietly, "They don't think he killed himself, do they?"

"You were divorcing him, Terri. Plus we're together. Monk's going to ask the questions." He frowned. "After all, if he doesn't, the press may get ahold of this and pillory him."

Terri shook her head. "You think it's more than that, Chris. You were pretty careful to cover for me."

He shrugged. "I wish there was more I could do, for you and Elena."

"The only thing you can do for either of us is to love me. Because Elena's going to need all the patience I can give her." Terri looked up at him. "I'm starting her with that psychologist, Dr. Harris. But what the doctor can find out— I just don't know."

They walked together to his door. Stepping onto the porch, Terri remembered that Richie was not spying on her and would never spy again. The night was cool and silent.

She turned back to Chris. He stood inside the doorway, watching her. "For what it's worth," he said quietly, "I didn't kill your husband. I could never work out the details."

She was speechless. Then Chris leaned forward and kissed her.

DENISE HARRIS HAD BEEN A surprise to Terri. On the telephone Harris was crisp, quick to ask questions. But in the flesh the fortyish black psychologist was a person of much softer edges: quieter, with a welcoming manner and luminous brown eyes. They sat in Harris' office in a brightly painted Victorian in Haight-Ashbury. Sunlight streamed through a large bay window.

"How was it with Elena?" Terri asked at once.

"About what I expected," Harris answered easily. "For fifty minutes we sat on the rug, not playing with toys, while Elena didn't talk to me. It may take a while. Six-year-olds don't generally articulate their inner traumas right away. How was she at Richie's funeral?"

"The same." As tearless as Terri and Rosa, filing past the closed casket in Mission Dolores beneath the piercing stare of Richie's mother, Sonia. Richie had been Sonia's prize. When Rosa, Terri, and Elena left Richie's graveside in a bleak drizzle, the three of them holding hands, Sonia had said to Terri in an accusatory voice, "Ricardo did not kill himself—he did not commit this sin." In the car on the way home Elena had curled up in a ball, hugging herself.

Harris spoke gently, her eyes conveying concern. "This child has undergone a great deal in the last half year or so: her parents' separation, possibly some form of sexual abuse, her father's death. Some of what she must feel is impossible for a child to verbalize."

"But how will you get her to talk?"

"Slowly. You'll need to be as patient as you can. Some of the behavior you've described—listlessness, regression, acting out, even the nightmares—could be consistent with abuse. But even if that happened, sexual abuse is no longer the worst thing in Elena's life. Her father's death dwarfs anything she's ever experienced."

Terri felt despair. "But what will you *do*?"

"I may spend weeks just getting her to play. Perhaps with doll figures. It may be easier for her to express herself through surrogates. Which, necessarily, requires me to interpret quite a bit. That may be something you can help with."

"How?"

"I want to understand Elena's life," Harris said. "You can tell me about her, of course, but I'd also like you to tell me something about the family she was born into. Something about you. Tell me, Terri, what do you remember about being Elena's age?"

361

The seeming change of subject took Terri by surprise. "About being six?" She hesitated. "Nothing, really."

"Well, what are your first memories? At any age." Harris' voice became quiet. "Lean back, close your eyes, and try to pretend that Elena's happiness depends on your coming up with something. Pretend, just for a time, that you're her."

Terri gave Harris a sardonic half smile to signal that this was foolish. But when she closed her eyes, blackness descended.

"Anything at all," she heard Harris say.

Blackness descending like a blanket pulled over her head. Her mother is crying. The crying comes with the night. Terri grips the blanket, pulling it tighter. Perhaps if she can stop the sound, her mother will stop hurting. The cries grow fainter.

Terri opened her eyes. "Nothing. I can't remember anything."

EIGHT

CARLO put down the sports page. "So what did the cops want?" They were sitting on the deck; the weather was unseasonably warm, and white sails dotted the bay. Carlo had been leafing through the *Chronicle,* Paget the Sunday *Times.*

Paget turned to his son. "They're trying to figure out why our late friend Ricardo killed himself. And in the process, to ensure that his resignation was voluntary."

Carlo shook his head in mock dismay. "You have a great way of putting things, Dad. Law do that to you?"

Paget smiled. "Nope. My warm human qualities are all my own. Although the subject of Richie's passing stretches them a bit."

Carlo pushed the baseball cap back on his head. "Do they think he *didn't* kill himself?"

Paget shrugged. "They're considering it. They have to, really. It's part of their job description."

Carlo's blue eyes were serious now. "You know, Dad, I wouldn't make jokes about Richie. Not where anyone can hear you."

Paget was oddly touched; for the first time he could remember, he was aware of Carlo looking out for him. "Don't worry. I only share my bad taste with you. And on her lucky days, Terri."

Carlo looked curious. "How's she dealing with all this?"

"Terri's all right. The problem, really, is Elena. Now that Richie's dead, Elena seems to feel she killed him. Metaphorically speaking."

"Why would she think that?" Carlo asked.

"Who knows? It's magical thinking—placing herself at the center of the world. Kids do it all the time."

The rasp of the doorbell was clearly audible. Carlo disentangled himself from his chair. A minute later he returned with Charles Monk. Behind them was Dennis Lynch.

Paget looked up. "Morning," he greeted Monk amiably. "If we'd known you were coming, I'd have invited you."

"We have more questions. I'd like to talk to each of you. Alone."

All at once Paget's thoughts felt sharp and focused. "No thanks," he said coolly. "You care to talk to my son, you do it with me here—right now, once. Afterward *we* can chat alone." Paget gestured toward two deep canvas folding chairs. "Have a seat."

Monk gazed at the chairs. They were rather like hammocks. Sinking into them, the two homicide inspectors looked a little foolish. Monk, suddenly all arms and knees, did not seem amused.

Carlo watched Monk balance a tape recorder in his lap.

"You'll have to speak up," Monk said to him, and began his litany: that the interviewee was Carlo Carelli Paget, that his father was present, and that it was ten forty-five on a Sunday morning.

"Ready?" Monk asked him.

Looking first at his father, Carlo gave a brief nod.

"Did you sexually molest Elena Arias?"

The question struck the elder Paget like a slap in the face.

Carlo straightened in his chair. "No," he said.

The answer had a simple dignity—no protest, no elaboration. What Paget himself would do. But it did not stop the rush of anger he felt. "Nicely done," he told Monk sarcastically.

Paget saw his son's faint smile. Shrugging, Monk turned back to Carlo. "Have you ever met Ricardo Arias?"

A quick shake of the head. "No."

"Or been to his apartment?"

"I don't even know where it is."

"Are you aware of the materials Mr. Arias filed in family court?"

Carlo tried to look stoic. "About me and Elena. It's garbage."

"Did you and your father discuss that?" Monk asked.

363

"Uh-huh. He said that Terri's husband was using this stuff to try to break her."

"Did you and he discuss what to do about it?"

"Only that we might have to go to court. To prove it was a lie."

"Were you willing to testify?"

Carlo nodded. "If I had to. I told Dad that."

"And what did he say?"

"My dad said he was sorry. And that he was proud of me."

"The night before your father went to Italy, where were you?"

Carlo shifted in his chair. "With friends," he answered slowly.

What was this? Paget wondered. Surely they did not suspect Carlo. But Monk's face showed nothing.

"Between when and when?" he asked.

Carlo shrugged. "I'm not sure exactly. But my dad makes me get in by twelve thirty. So maybe from around seven."

"When you left, was your father here?"

"Yes."

"What about when you returned?"

"Yes. He was here then too."

"And where," Monk asked Carlo, "were you in the meanwhile?"

"With friends. Like I said." Carlo looked reluctant to go on. "There were a bunch of us. My girlfriend, Katie Blessing. Danny Spellman, Darnell Sheets, Jenny Havilland, Joey Arroyo."

"Were you with them the whole time?"

A longer pause. "Mostly," Carlo answered.

Monk watched Paget's face. "Was there a period," he asked Carlo, "when you weren't with them?"

"Yes. Around eight thirty." Carlo had begun to fidget. When Monk did not fill the silence, Carlo added, "It wasn't very long."

"And what were the circumstances?"

"We were all at Darnell's house, and we decided to go to a movie." He shot his father a quick glance. "I'd forgotten my wallet."

Paget felt himself becoming very still.

"What did you do?" Monk asked.

"I tried to borrow money, but there wasn't enough to cover us. We decided that I'd meet the rest of them at the Empire Theater."

Monk watched Carlo intently now. "And between Darnell's house and the Empire, how long were you gone?"

Carlo's brow furrowed. "Forty-five minutes, maybe."

"And where did you go?"

Carlo said simply, "I came home. I went to my room and got my wallet. Then I left."

"While you were home," Monk asked, "did you see anyone?"

Carlo stared at Monk. He did not look at Paget—deliberately, it seemed. In his son's silence Paget implored Carlo not to lie.

"No. I was just looking for my wallet. I ran up to my room, got the wallet, and ran down again. It took less than two minutes."

"To get to the stairs," Monk asked, "you pass the library and living room, right?"

A slow nod. "Right."

"Where is your dad's room?"

Carlo seemed to blink. "Next to mine."

"And no one called out to you?"

"I didn't hear anyone call me."

"Did you hear noises in your father's bedroom?"

Carlo leaned back, folding his arms. To Paget he looked suddenly pale. "I can't remember," he said. That, Paget was certain, was true.

"Was there any sign your father was here?" Monk asked.

Paget's stomach felt tight. He saw Carlo straining to think. "All that I remember is thinking maybe I heard footsteps in the attic. That would make sense. The attic's where we keep extra suitcases."

"Did you hear *Carlo?*" Monk asked abruptly.

It was a moment before Paget realized that Monk had turned to him. "No," he answered.

Monk asked him, "Where were you, anyhow?"

"I'm not sure," Paget said evenly. "But Carlo's right. We keep our bags in the attic. So I spent some time there." Paget looked at Dennis Lynch and then back to Monk. "If we're through with Carlo and on to me, I believe that Carlo had some plans."

Monk paused. Then he nodded.

Carlo gave his father a look that mingled concern with apology. Monk stopped Carlo from standing, asked him to stay for a moment, and took a set of fingerprints. Then the boy left.

Paget turned to Monk. "All right. Let's get this done."

"Did you ever meet Ricardo Arias?" Monk asked quietly, and Paget felt everything change.

He was in a field of evidence not yet discovered: questions yet to be asked, facts not yet sifted, connections yet to be made. But the questions *would* be asked—of Terri, of Carlo, of people Paget had never met and perhaps did not know existed—and the connections drawn, like lines between dots.

"No," Paget answered.

"Did you ever see Arias?"

"Yes. In the *Inquisitor*. With a touching caption beneath him. Something like 'For ten thousand dollars you can feed this boy.' "

Monk sat back, staring at him. "Where were you that night?"

"Here."

"Did you ever visit his apartment?"

Paget's temples began to feel constricted, as if in a vise. "No."

"Do you believe your son sexually abused Elena Arias?"

"Absolutely not."

"Do you know why Mr. Arias made that charge?"

"Yes." Paget's voice was firm. "He was a worthless deadbeat who wanted to live off child support. The best way was to trash his wife and anyone who might help her."

"Mr. Arias," Monk said, "filed papers charging your son with child abuse and you with adultery. Are you aware of that?"

"Of course."

Monk pushed the gold-rimmed glasses up the bridge of his nose. "You're running for the Senate, aren't you?"

"I may," Paget said. "But the race is almost two years away."

"Why did Ricardo Arias file these papers under seal?"

"I can only speculate. Clearly he intended to put pressure on Terri to give him permanent custody. Through me, if necessary."

"Tell me," Monk said, "did Arias ever ask you for money?"

"No."

Watching the recorder, Paget saw that the tape appeared to be close to ending. "Care for some iced coffee?" he asked.

"No. Thank you." Monk's voice was very polite now. "Did you and Mr. Arias ever speak by telephone?"

The recorder clicked.

Monk fumbled for another tape. It gave Paget a moment to ponder whether Ricardo Arias might have recorded phone calls. And then he realized quite certainly that Richie could not have.

Monk inserted the new tape and handed the machine to Lynch. "The night before you left for Italy, did you speak to Ricardo Arias by phone?" Monk asked.

"No."

"Or see him?"

"No."

"Or visit his apartment?"

"No."

Monk's rapid-fire cadence made Paget feel cornered. "Did Richie ever call *your* home?" Monk asked.

Paget hesitated. "I wouldn't know."

"Who, besides you, answers the telephone?"

"Carlo, obviously. Sometimes Cecilia, the housekeeper."

Monk folded his hands. "Do you own a gun?"

"No."

"Have you ever had one in your possession?"

"Only in the army."

"Ever fire one?"

"Again, not since the army. I don't like them."

"How about Ms. Peralta?"

It took Paget by surprise. "Terri told you already. She hates guns. I can't imagine her owning one."

"Do you think that Ms. Peralta intended Mr. Arias any harm?"

Paget shook his head. "All the time we were in Italy, Terri worried that he hadn't shown up. For Elena's sake and in spite of everything. While we were there, we had long and agonized discussions about whether our relationship was possible in light of Richie's malice. You don't put yourself through that for a dead man."

Monk's gaze hardened into a stare. "Unless one of you is an actor. How did *you* feel about Arias? You weren't exactly forthcoming with us about your reasons for disliking him. Your son, for example."

"I didn't like him then, and I still don't." Paget folded his arms. "You weren't asking me about Carlo, but about a death. About which, as it happens, I know nothing."

"So you don't have any information on how he might have died?"

"None. Except from you."

"Not even a theory?"

Paget stared back at him for a while. "Theories are your job. Not

367

mine." He tilted his head. "Although suicide's not a bad one. If I were you, I might take Richie's note as a sign of his sincerity."

Monk simply watched. "A man will do a lot of things," he said, "if someone holds a gun to his head."

Monk had what he had come for: answers, impossible for Paget to run from, recorded on tape. Noting the hour and minutes, he clicked off the machine. "We appreciate your time," he said.

Shepherding Monk and Lynch to the door, Paget said little. From the window of his library he watched them leave. Then he went to the kitchen, took out an oversized green garbage bag, and climbed the stairs to his room.

His walk-in closet was filled with suits, about twenty-five of them.

He pulled out a gray suit with a speckled stain on the cuff of one sleeve. He took the suit off its hanger and stuffed it into the garbage bag. It was only when he was outside, standing over the garbage can, that he realized the police might search his trash.

Paget went to the library, gazing into the fireplace. But Carlo, he realized, might come home. He hurried upstairs to his room.

Randomly he pulled out three more suits. Then he put the gray suit back on its hanger, threw it on his bed with the others, and began looking for the shoes—simple black ones that were almost new. Putting them in the garbage bag, he felt a twinge of sadness and then, more deeply, felt furtive and alone.

He had no choice, Paget thought; he could not keep the suit and shoes. He walked outside into the bright sunlight and drove to the Goodwill outlet in the Mission District.

NINE

WHEN Terri arrived at the office on Wednesday morning, Charles Monk was sitting at her desk, her telephone propped under his chin. Monk listened intently, taking notes. Over his shoulder was Terri's picture of Elena.

The room was quiet. Monk's concentration seemed so total that Terri found herself closing the door with extra care so as not to break his thoughts. Then she noticed Dennis Lynch sitting calmly by her window with the tape machine and studying the progress of the Sixth Fleet as it moved across the bay.

Only when Monk put down the telephone did he look up at her. "Would you like your chair back?"

"Yes. Thanks."

Rising, Monk walked around the desk and sat down. "We have more questions," he said. Terri managed a smile.

Lynch pulled his chair next to Monk's and switched on the machine.

Monk gave his preface again, then asked abruptly, "Did you ever threaten to kill Ricardo Arias?"

It startled her. "Of course not. Does anyone say I did?"

Monk ignored that. "Did you ever quarrel over Elena?"

"Yes. That was what the custody suit was about."

"But you never threatened to kill him?"

"I can't remember saying that. Certainly not meaning it."

"Did Christopher Paget ever threaten Mr. Arias?"

"Not in my presence."

"Do you have any reason to believe that Mr. Paget is capable of violence?" Monk asked.

Terri folded her hands. "Chris," she said slowly, "is the most self-controlled man I've ever known."

"That's not what I'm asking."

Terri felt herself flush. "Chris is not a murderer," she said coldly.

Monk did not blink. "Are you?"

"Not even in my dreams."

Monk studied her. "Do you know where he was that night?"

"Yes. At home. I know that because he told me."

"And how did his health seem the next morning?"

Fine, Terri thought. And then, although Monk did not know to ask about it, she thought of his swollen hand. "All right," she answered. "He seemed a little tired. That's what flu will do to you."

Monk leaned back. "Whose idea was the trip to Italy?"

"Both of ours. We needed to get away."

Monk waited a moment. "Who scheduled it?"

"Chris did."

"Remind me of the first day you tried to call Ricardo Arias."

"Monday morning, San Francisco time."

"Did you mention that to Mr. Paget?"

"Yes, of course," Terri said.

"And what did he say?"

369

"To call him again. Which I did. Monday night and again on Tuesday morning and throughout the day."

"And when he didn't answer, you still didn't know that Elena was with your mother, correct?"

Not unless I killed Richie, Terri thought. "That's right," she answered. "I didn't know *where* she was."

"Did you think about calling the school?"

"I thought about it. Then I decided to call my mother first."

"And after you called your mother and found Elena there, you decided not to look for Mr. Arias."

"Yes."

"Did you discuss that with Mr. Paget?"

Let him rot, Chris had said. Terri hesitated. "I believe so."

"And what was the substance of that conversation?"

Suddenly Terri could see the scenario Monk was building in his mind. A trip to Italy, planned as cover. A night alone, hours before they left. And all the days after that, knowing he was dead, letting his body decompose until no one could tell when he had died.

"It was my decision," she told Monk, "not to call Richie. We were in a custody dispute, and I was willing to let him be neglectful. Because in my mind he was very much alive."

In the quiet, Terri watched the tape silently winding her answer around a plastic spindle. "Thank you," Monk said politely. "We hope this wasn't an inconvenience."

They packed up their tape machine and left.

Terri waited until she was certain they had caught the elevator; then she went to Chris's office. He was putting down the telephone. "That was the phone company," he told her. "The cops have a search warrant for my phone records. Bank records too."

"I know." Terri sat across from him. "I just had a visitor. Chris, I think they're serious about this."

"WHEN I agreed to marry Richie," Terri said to Denise Harris, "I told myself that he wasn't like my father at all. He wasn't abusive. He never lost his temper. I couldn't see any parallel between them."

The psychologist touched her chin. "Did your father beat you?"

Terri found herself staring at a print on Harris' wall—two fawns in a lush African landscape with multiple suns. In Terri's mind

Ramon Peralta's face was contorted with drunken fury. Her mother's mouth was swollen. He raised his hand. . . .

"What are you remembering?" Harris asked softly.

Terri closed her eyes.

It is night. Terri is fourteen now; she can no longer hide beneath the covers or inside the closet, as she has taught her younger sisters to do. Her mother's cries have drawn her from the bedroom. Terri creeps down the stairs. In the dim light of a single lamp she sees her mother's face. It is beautiful and ravaged, drained of hope. Her mouth has begun to swell.

Ramon Peralta steps into the light.

His hand is raised. Rosa backs to the wall. Her eyes glisten.

"Whore," Ramon says softly.

Helpless, Rosa shakes her head. Her shoulders graze the wall.

"I saw you look at him," Ramon prods. He comes closer.

Her father's hand flashes through the light.

Terri flinches. Hears the crack of his palm on Rosa's cheek, the short cry she seems to bite off, the heavy sound of his breathing. In the pit of her stomach Terri understands; her mother's cries draw him on for more. Rosa's lip is bleeding now.

"No," Terri cries out. Tears have sprung to her eyes; she is not sure she has spoken aloud. And then, slowly, Ramon Peralta turns.

Seeing her, his face fills with astonishment and rage.

But Terri cannot look away. "You *like* this," she tells her father. "You think it makes you strong. But we hate you—"

"Teresa, don't!" her mother says. "This is *our* business—"

"We live here too." Without thinking, Terri steps between her parents. "Don't ever hit her," she tells her father. "Ever again."

Ramon's face darkens. "You little—" His hand flies back.

"*No.*" Her mother has clutched Terri's shoulders, pulling her away from him. Her father reaches out and jerks Terri by the arm.

Blinding pain shoots through Terri's shoulder. She feels him twist her arm behind her back, push her face down on the sofa. Terri wills herself to make no sound at all.

"What," her father asks softly, "would you like me to do now?"

Terri cannot be certain whether he asks this of Rosa or of Terri herself. She can sense only that her mother has draped both arms around her father's neck.

371

"Let her go, Ramon." Rosa's voice is gentle now. She whispers, "I'll make it up to you. Please, let her go."

With a sharp jerk Ramon Peralta releases his daughter's arm.

Standing, Terri turns to her mother. Her legs are unsteady.

"Go," Rosa tells her. "Go to bed, Teresa. Please."

Terri turns, walking toward the stairs. Knowing that in some strange way her father has accepted Rosa as a substitute for Terri. Her face burns with shame. She does not know for whom.

Harris listened, impassive. "Did you ever talk about this with your mother?" she asked.

"No," Terri said. "A few nights later my father died. My mother and I never spoke of him again."

TERRI and Chris had resolved to set their worries aside and spend a day at the park. The fact that it was easier to do that by skipping work, when Elena was at school, only enhanced their pleasure.

They had played tennis and then spent two more hours talking, picnic lunch spread on the grass, the sun on their faces. It was easy to be with him, Terri thought, to feel the deep friendship she always felt when they had time together. Perhaps in months or even weeks she would know what had happened to Elena and to Richie, and then the pieces would fall into place.

Suddenly she remembered to glance at her watch. "I've got to go," she said. "Another mom is picking up Elena, but I can't be late."

The drive home went easily. Chris had a new Bonnie Raitt disc; they cruised in warm sunlight all the way to Noe Valley.

Terri was humming a Bonnie Raitt tune as she climbed the stairs to her apartment. When she arrived, her door was ajar.

Terri felt fear; it was a moment before she realized that she had thought of Richie. Another moment until she realized who must be on the other side of the door. But when she pushed it open, it was not Monk who looked up from her desk; it was Dennis Lynch.

He gave her an apologetic smile. "Sorry. We thought we should do this when your daughter wasn't here."

Terri stifled her anger. "I guess you have a warrant."

"Oh, yeah. Showed it to the manager already." Lynch pulled the warrant out of his coat pocket and gave it to Terri, waving her to a couch. "Make yourself at home. We'll only be ten, fifteen minutes."

Terri sat. From Elena's bedroom came the sounds of drawers opening and closing. "Find anything interesting?" she asked Lynch.

"Just the usual routine," Lynch said. He was watching a crime lab cop in a white jacket, on his knees in a corner of the living room, picking at the rug with tweezers.

"If you're looking for fibers from Richie's rug," Terri said, "they're probably all over. I've been in his apartment, and he's been in mine. In fact, this particular search is a serious waste of taxpayer money."

And then it occurred to her: Perhaps they were trying to frighten Chris, to see what he would do.

Another crime lab cop came from the hallway with Terri's gray suit. "We'll want to keep that for a while," Lynch told her calmly. "We'll give you a receipt, of course."

"I don't have that many suits, Inspector. And I don't have any with gunshot residue, blood spatters, or traces of cerebral cortex on the hemline. I'd like you to leave that here."

The crime lab guy turned to Lynch. When Lynch gave him a querying look, the man pointed to a spot on the suit's lapel.

"Ketchup," Terri said disgustedly. "From McDonald's. Elena spilled it when she was sitting in my lap."

Lynch shrugged. "Got to check it out, that's all."

Ignoring him, Terri began to read the warrant. It told her nothing at all. Nor did Lynch say anything much before he left, taking with him two crime lab cops, three evidence bags of rug fibers, a woman's gray suit, and the tape from her answering machine.

WHEN Paget arrived home from the park, there were two squad cars in the driveway and Carlo was waiting for him on the front porch. The boy's face was pale. The door was open behind him, and Paget heard voices from inside. Carlo held some papers.

"Monk?" Paget asked. When Carlo nodded, Paget took the warrant. It allowed a broad search. As always, it did not explain the basis on which the police asserted that there was "probable cause" to comb Paget's home for evidence in Ricardo Arias' death.

"I tried to keep them out," Carlo murmured, embarrassed.

Paget paused to touch his shoulder. "There was nothing you could do," he said, and stalked into his house in search of Monk.

A red-haired cop was standing in Paget's library, peering into his fireplace. Carlo's childhood games had been pulled out of their cabinet and turned upside down. Paget's rage at this violation of his life was so deep that for a moment he could not speak.

"Where's Monk?" he demanded.

The cop looked surprised. "You're not supposed to be in here."

"I *live* here," Paget snapped. "I asked where Monk was."

The cop's youthful face turned cold. "You'll have to sit on the porch, sir. Unless you want me to cuff you."

Paget tilted his head. "Are you aware that I'm a lawyer?"

The cop took the handcuffs off his belt and started toward him.

"Because," Paget said coolly, "your warrant is screwed up. So before you do something truly stupid, go find someone who's capable of understanding why."

The cop stopped halfway across the room, the first flicker of hesitation in his eyes.

"I'll give you a clue," Paget continued. "When you find Charles Monk, take him aside and whisper the words special master in his ear. He'll be impressed with your insight."

The cop flushed. "Wait here," he ordered, and went upstairs.

Suddenly Paget heard the voice of his housekeeper.

Walking to the living room, he saw the dark-haired Cecilia, a Nicaraguan woman with haunted eyes whose husband had been murdered by guerrillas. She was warily answering the questions of a plainclothes detective with a tape machine.

"I'm sorry," Paget said to Cecilia, "but this will be over soon." She looked up at him with fear and shame; in the depths of her soul she knew that authority had no limits. "Tell them whatever they want. Nothing you say can hurt me."

Paget felt a hand on his shoulder. Turning, he discovered Monk, with the young cop next to him.

"I told him not to move," the cop told Monk.

Please, the cop's tone said, bust this guy. Paget smiled at him.

"Are there any legal files in the library?" Monk asked Paget.

"No."

Monk addressed the young cop. "Finish the library, then. And check with me before you do anything else."

Monk peered at Paget. "You keep files here?"

Paget nodded. "So let's review where we are. To inspect legal files, you need a special master to screen them for privileged materials. You haven't got one, or the warrant would have said so."

"True," said Monk, his voice calm and professional.

Paget stared at him. "The D.A. screwed up."

Monk appraised him. "Just tell me where your files are, and we won't look at them. 'Cause I could care less about files."

But Paget was determined to eke out this small victory. "It won't work—they're mixed in with other stuff. Besides, I bring work home at night, and sometimes I forget where I put my papers. So wherever you go, *I* go. Where have you been so far?"

"Just your bedroom."

"Then let me speak to Carlo, and we can go back upstairs. But the deal is that we take it a room at a time, with me present."

Monk gazed past him at Cecilia and spoke to the plainclothesman. "You can pack up your stuff and leave. I'll do the rest." He permitted the young cop to stay.

Paget turned to Cecilia. "Go home," he said to her. "Tomorrow, if I need it, you can help me clean up."

He went to the porch. It was perhaps five o'clock; Carlo was on the steps. Paget sat down next to him. "Sorry," he said softly.

When Carlo turned to him, Paget was startled to see that his eyes were moist. "This scares me, Dad."

It was all Paget could do not to hug the boy. "Didn't you and Katie have plans?" he asked Carlo. "Something about a movie?" He took some money from his wallet. "Here," he said. "Take Katie to dinner. Don't let Monk ruin her night too."

Carlo shook his head. "I just want to stick around."

"Please, son," Paget said quietly.

Carlo scanned his face more closely; in that moment Paget saw him understand how much this pained his father. He stood, still looking at Paget, unsure of what to say.

"Call me," Paget said, "if you're going to be past ten or so."

It made Carlo smile a little. "Ten thirty," he said, and walked down the steps to the used car Chris had helped him buy.

AN HOUR after sunset Paget sat in the dining room drinking brandy. At his feet were broken pieces of his grandmother's china serving platter. The cop had knocked it off the cabinet and, when

375

Paget turned at the sound, blandly apologized for his clumsiness.

It was the last room they had reached. By then the house was a wreck: Paget's and Carlo's drawers overturned, clothes strewn on the carpet, books tossed about like refuse. Paget had expected this.

They had taken very little, mostly from Paget's bedroom. Three gray suits. Several pairs of shoes. A checkbook register that might reflect the purchase of a Smith & Wesson older than his grandmother's broken china. Only when Monk had demanded the keys to Paget's Jaguar convertible, explaining that the crime lab people would return it in a week or so, had Paget noticed that the last item on the warrant called for the impoundment of his car.

Looking around him at the mess, he took the last warm swallow of brandy. His run for the Senate was in serious trouble. Tomorrow he would think about that; it seemed a small thing now.

He went to the kitchen and picked up the telephone.

Outside, through his windows, the city dropped toward the bay, a smooth oval of blackness, and the lights of Marin County twinkled in the hills beyond. The telephone he had dialed rasped in his ear.

"Hello?" the woman answered.

"Caroline? This is Chris Paget."

"Christopher!" The woman's well-bred voice was nasal and faintly New England. "What a pleasant surprise."

"Not for me, I'm afraid. It seems I'm in need of a lawyer."

Briefly Paget heard the silence of her surprise. "Well," Caroline Masters replied, "at least you can afford me."

TEN

CAROLINE Masters smiled over her coffee. "It's good to see you again, Christopher. I'm just sorry it's because of the police."

Paget was disoriented at seeing her again. Caroline had been the judge in the Carelli hearing, the star of a televised morality play watched by millions of viewers. Offers had poured in, Paget knew—law, politics, even the media. In the end, she had accepted a partnership in San Francisco's largest firm, Kenyon and Walker. For Caroline it meant four hundred thousand dollars a year, a panoramic view of the city, and a new base of supporters for her ultimate ambition—a high federal judgeship.

She had greeted him with the brisk assurance of someone who graced the firm by being there. At five feet eight she carried herself so perfectly that the first impression she gave was of some electric combination of aristocrat and stage actress. She was an extraordinarily handsome woman, a year or two younger than Paget—aquiline features, glossy black hair, deep-set brown eyes beneath a high forehead. But for Paget, one fact was enough: Caroline Masters was a superb lawyer.

"Well," she said after a time, "there's no doubt you have motive. What do the police know about where you were that night?"

"What I told them is that I was home all night."

Her eyes narrowed. "And the police have that on tape?"

Paget turned to the window. The day was sunless, and the tops of buildings vanished in morning fog. "That's right."

"And now they've taken three gray suits. I don't need to tell you what that may mean, Christopher."

Paget felt an eerie helplessness. "A potential eyewitness."

Caroline nodded. "At least one."

Paget fell silent. He was already certain that Caroline would not ask if he had murdered Ricardo Arias. For a defense lawyer this restraint was common sense—the answer, if it was yes, would prevent her from preparing the best defense.

"A word of advice," Caroline said. "No more chats with Monk. As it is, we're going to have to live with what you've said already."

"Do you know why I talked to them?" he asked. "Because I didn't kill him. In fact, I assumed that the little creep shot himself."

"And what do you think now?"

"That the cops think someone killed him. But it wasn't me. If it had been, I'd have come to you before I said a word to Monk."

Caroline shrugged. "Which, in Monk's eyes, would have drawn suspicion like a magnet. What do you think they meant to accomplish by turning your house upside down?"

"Scare me into doing something funny, I suppose. Perhaps trying to destroy evidence."

"Possibly. But what evidence could they hope to find?"

"The obvious. Bullets. A receipt for the purchase of a gun. Some small memento of the late Ricardo—blood or hair or tissue. Fibers from his rug. Which may be why they wanted the car."

Caroline nodded. "Fibers might help them. But only if you'd never been to Richie's at any other time. What did you tell them?"

"That I never had been. At any time."

Caroline paused. "So what do you think they'll find?"

"Nothing. Except maybe fibers from Richie's rug. From Terri. She went to Richie's regularly to pick up or drop off Elena. And of course, she's often at my place."

Caroline smiled. "It seems that your relationship with Terri has complicated a number of things, Christopher. Including the evidence." She leaned back in her chair. "Are you sure it's not Terri that Monk's after? They searched her apartment, after all."

Paget shook his head. "Maybe, in the middle of the night, Monk imagines that we plotted Richie's death together. But I'm pretty sure it's me they want."

Paget watched Caroline consider this thought and then saw it lead to another. "Isn't there something curious about all of this?"

"You mean how nasty they've been?"

Caroline nodded. "It's not like Charles Monk, and normally, it's not like the district attorney—even if McKinley Brooks is still angry about losing the Carelli case."

"I don't think it's the Carelli case Mac's mad about," Paget responded. "Try the magic words James Colt."

Caroline's lips parted as comprehension dawned. "Junior," she said. "Of course. McKinley Brooks' new best friend, ever since Mac conceived ambitions to be something more than district attorney."

Paget nodded. "Junior not only wants to be governor, he wants to control the party in this state should his ambitions become even loftier. He does not, he's made quite plain, wish for me to be a Senator, and I'm equally sure Brooks knows that. I think I've just been warned."

"Knowing that could be useful to us. If it's true."

"At trial? When we suggest that they're on a witch-hunt?"

Caroline did not smile. "You don't want a trial, Christopher. But what I will do, soon, is go see Brooks to find out whether I can talk him out of this—or at least hear what's on his mind."

Paget stood. "I guess that's it, then," he said, and shook Caroline's hand. "Let me know if you have any other thoughts."

"Actually," Caroline said, "there is one other thing."

"What's that?"

"When they give you back the Jaguar, put it in the garage. And mothball the Armani suits. From now until you're off the hook, imagine yourself on-camera and the television audience as jurors. For a prospective defendant, you're just a bit too elegant."

TERRI sat on her living-room couch wearing a flannel nightgown and her reading glasses. Legal files were scattered around her, and the television news was on mute. The apartment itself was bare. Worn couch and borrowed chairs, a cheap wooden breakfast table highlighted the room's bleakness. It was just past eleven.

"We're a long way from Italy," she said to Paget.

"Not as long as I'd like."

It was the first time they'd been able to talk since the police had searched their homes. Wary of the telephone and tied up in trials at work, they'd been reduced to meeting at Terri's after Elena was asleep. "What do you think is wrong?" she asked.

Paget hesitated. "Politics, is my guess. I think James Colt wants me to back off running for the Senate. Colt is clever enough to know that the stench of a criminal inquiry would scare most politicians and prejudice most voters. Particularly when the subjects are murder, adultery, and child abuse." Pausing, Paget realized how trapped he felt. "Damn Richie's soul. Never in his wildest dreams would he have believed his obsession with us would outlive him."

Terri appraised him. "Not unless he killed himself," she said.

The words hit Paget like a shock. "What does that mean?"

Terri placed her hand gently on his wrist. "That there's something you're not telling me, Chris."

He withdrew his hand as if from a flame. "Would you care to give me an example?"

Terri stared at him. "What I'd like is for you to tell me."

Suddenly Paget felt cornered. "This isn't relationship counseling," he snapped. "It's a possible homicide, in which you and I are potential witnesses. And as long as we're not married, there's nothing I could say to you that Monk or McKinley Brooks or some hotshot assistant D.A. couldn't grill you about." Paget tried to speak more softly. "One of us might have to testify about anything we say. That's why I so seldom ask you where you found the gun."

Terri gave him a startled look. "You don't think that *I* killed him."

"No, as it happens. But if we're ever forced to testify, even asking you the question could do great damage."

"Not talking," Terri said, "makes me feel dead inside."

"I know. About that and several other things, I'm very sorry."

She searched his face. "Just tell me the truth, please."

Paget looked back into her eyes. "Only this, Terri." He emphasized each word. "I did not kill Ricardo Arias."

Terri stared at him. "And you have no idea who did."

"None. Unless it was Richie, just as you said."

Terri glanced down the hallway to the bedroom, as if Elena might hear them. Paget saw a tremor run through her. Terri turned to him again. "But you think there's going to be a trial, don't you?"

"I don't know," he said finally. "But I no longer assume there won't be. That's why I hired Caroline."

Terri sat back as if absorbing this new reality, and then something at the edge of Paget's vision became part of his consciousness.

Turning to the television, he saw the face of James Colt. Reaching for the remote, Terri switched on the sound.

"I'm running for governor," Colt was saying into a microphone, "on the basis of trust." His voice was light but pleasant; his suntan and his white-gold hair brought a touch of southern California to the blue-gray eyes and cleft chin. "Private character is the key to public leadership. I believe that any person seeking high office in the state of California should live a life that voters can respect."

"Maybe I'm paranoid," Paget murmured, "but did you just hear a message?"

"So ELENA had the nightmare again," Rosa said to Terri.

They sat on a bench in Dolores Park, where Terri once had played. It was a sunny morning. Swings and slides were some distance away. Elena had climbed a playground structure and was gazing at the park. She showed no interest in the children playing around her.

Terri watched her daughter. "For a moment, when I came to her room, she thought I was Richie. She called out, 'Daddy.' "

"Did she say anything else?" Rosa asked.

"Not really. She seemed to realize where she was, and then she put her arms around me."

Pensive, Rosa watched her granddaughter. Even sitting on a park bench, Rosa was impeccable—a turtleneck sweater and wool slacks, earrings and makeup, a gold bracelet on her wrist. "And you?" she asked. "Are you still having your dream?"

It was the closest Rosa came to speaking of Terri's father. All Terri had told her was that she was having her dream again. Terri did not have to tell Rosa whom the dream concerned.

"Every few nights now," Terri said. "I've been wondering if I should talk it over with Dr. Harris."

Rosa grazed her hair with her fingers. "Do you think that's wise, Teresa? To stir things up inside you?"

It was, Terri knew, the credo by which her mother had learned to live. It struck Terri that there was too much silence in her life. She asked, "Why did you never leave him, Mama?"

In profile, her mother's eyes widened; her body became rigid. Only when the silence continued did Terri realize that Rosa meant to act as if she had not heard the question.

"Mama," she said softly, "I don't judge you. I never will. You loved me, and you got me to where I am. But there's a part of you, a part of my life, that is lost to me. Sometimes I think, because of that, I've failed Elena without knowing why."

Rosa lowered her gaze. "All right, Teresa. We will do this once. And never again." She exhaled slowly. "The answer is, I stayed with him because a girl I barely remember now thought that all Ramon Peralta needed to escape his fears was her. By the time she knew better, her first daughter had been born."

Terri felt unspeakably sad. "What was he afraid of?"

"Himself." Rosa's voice was filled with irony. "His father used to beat him. Ramon was afraid of ending up like that."

"My God, Mama," Terri said.

"You must understand the Ramon I met," Rosa went on. "He was just out of the navy, handsome and eager for life. I thought it nice just to watch him. But then I saw how uncertain his smiles were, how much he wanted me to like him. My heart went out to him. This man, who could be so much, needed me to help him."

Her mother, Terri saw, spoke more honestly than she ever had before. Only the look in her eyes, remote yet touched with shame, betrayed how hard this was.

Rosa reached for the thermos at her feet. She filled a plastic cup with coffee and handed it to Terri, poured another for herself. "The night we were married," Rosa continued, "we slept together for the first time. I was happy. But after, as I waited in the dark for him to hold me, Ramon said that I was not a virgin. When I began to cry, he slapped me." Rosa's voice became hushed with memory. "A month after you were born, the drinking started."

Rosa paused; her eyes shut. "Drink changed him, Teresa— brought out all the demons of his nature. He imagined you were not his. He'd slap me, and I would cry out for him to stop. And then when *you* began crying, he wept and begged my forgiveness."

Terri's stomach felt tight.

"It just went on like that," Rosa said. "There were weeks Ramon would not drink at all. He would go to the garage where he worked, come home, eat without complaint the dinner I had cooked for him. And then something would go wrong—a cross word from his boss, an expense we did not plan on—and he would come home and beat me for what the world had done to him. Father Anaya told me that I must obey Ramon and try to make our home peaceful and happy. There was nothing to do but go on with the life I'd made. And by the time I was twenty-two, I had three daughters."

"Do my sisters know this?" Terri asked through her horror.

Rosa sipped coffee, eyes reflective. "No. And they never will."

Terri met her mother's gaze. "Couldn't you still have left him, Mama? Even then?"

"To where? A jobless woman with children?"

"But how did you live?" Terri asked.

Rosa turned to her daughter. "You remember, I'm sure, that there were periods of peace in our home, when Ramon did not drink. He would play with you, even take you places he wanted to go. Perhaps you wondered why and hoped it would last."

Slowly Terri nodded. Rosa smiled a little. "You see, there was one other thing that scared Ramon—being without me. Because deep down inside, just like Ricardo, he was weak. So every few months, when things got too bad, I would tell him I was going away. The tears would come, and the begging. 'Please,' he would say, 'I'll change.'" Rosa's voice became ironic. "If you think about these periods of peace, Teresa, they always began with roses. A gift from your repentant father, with a card promising to love me all his life."

Terri remembered a dinner. Ramon, smiling at Rosa, had placed roses on the table. Terri had thought him wonderful.

Rosa looked at her as if trying to fathom her feelings. "He never harmed you, did he?"

"No, Mama. Not with his hands."

"There are men who do worse. Ramon was jealous of me because he was so frightened. And he was right about one thing. When I married him, I was not a virgin. One drunken night when I was fourteen, and more terrified than I can ever tell you, your grandfather found me alone. We never spoke of it again." Her voice was quiet and bitter. "So you see, Teresa, Ramon Peralta was nothing special. My own father taught me that."

FROM her first few moments in the office of McKinley Brooks, Caroline Masters knew that there was something wrong.

It started with the district attorney himself. Brooks' smile was tight; and his manner—the easy bonhomie of the city's most successful black politician—for once could not obscure the constant workings of his mind. But what concerned Caroline more was that the assistant D.A. with him was Victor Salinas.

Physically Brooks and Salinas were opposites. Brooks was rounding amiably into his mid-forties. A decade younger, Salinas had the leanness and intensity of a man who played his daily squash games not for exercise but to win, and his carefully trimmed mustache and hand-painted tie lent him a touch of the dandy that Brooks was careful to avoid. But Salinas burned with an ambition as deep as Brooks' own, and less well concealed. That Brooks would give this case to Salinas told Caroline that it was something special.

Brooks passed her a cup of the coffee he brewed fresh in his office. "This really is a treat, Caroline. You look wonderful."

Caroline smiled. "I have a question," she said amiably. "Is there some sort of pent-up demand for Christopher Paget's scalp that I've managed to miss? Or has it become the style to badger defense attorneys, harass their girlfriends, fingerprint their children, and trash their homes? Oh, and make off with their sports cars?"

Brooks leaned back in his chair and folded his hands. "Are you suggesting, Caroline, that we intervene with the police to make sure that Chris Paget is treated *better* than the average citizen?"

Caroline rolled her eyes. "Oh, McKinley, come off it. Name me a multimillionaire from an old family—let alone a famous lawyer and a senatorial prospect from your own political party—who isn't treated at least a little better than a drug dealer."

Brooks shrugged. "I can't let people think I'm affected by who he is," he said blandly. "Or what he might become."

"Really? I would have thought by now that you'd have had a conversation or two about the very seat that Chris may run for. Perhaps with someone seeking your support for some candidate other than Chris." She paused. "James Colt, for example."

"I can hardly play politics," Brooks answered, "in a race where one of the prospective candidates is involved in an active case."

Caroline smiled. "I never suggested you were playing politics. Merely that someone might have an interest in Chris's downfall."

Brooks spread his hands in a show of wonder. "Seems like anything Charles Monk does, or doesn't do, must have some hidden meaning for this office. And all because the dead body in question comes with a widow whose boyfriend happens to enter politics."

The last observation struck Caroline as carefully planted. "Are you suggesting that Chris might be better off if he *left* politics?"

Brooks' eyes widened. "Who am I to say? The only thing I know is that *I'd* be better off."

It was time, Caroline knew, to shift the focus. "Chris is the least likely killer this side of James Colt," she said. "Paget has wealth, political promise, and a son he treasures. He'd never throw it all away on a piece of scrofula like Ricardo Arias."

"Scrofula?" Victor Salinas put in. "Here's a broke young guy in a custody dispute, with a little girl he's worried sick about, up against his lawyer wife, a boyfriend who's got money, and a kid who may be a child molester. And yet somehow Arias manages to fight for what he thinks is right. Talk about an underdog."

Caroline was momentarily startled. Salinas, she realized, identified with Ricardo Arias. But what bothered her was something more—he was already thinking about his opening statement.

"Nicely done," she said to Salinas in her driest voice. "If only the late Ricardo were worthy of your talents." Turning to Brooks, she added, "If you have something better, enlighten me. Then we'll talk."

384

"Your *client* has already talked," Salinas said. "To the police, on tape. Does he have anything to add? Or change?"

Brooks tapped his chin, looking from Caroline to Salinas. "Victor's right. What do you have to offer us that's new?"

The word offer, elliptical in itself, might suggest some sort of deal. But Caroline could not know. "Right now," she said, "your complaint against Chris is that he had reason to dislike Ricardo Arias. Frankly, *I* didn't like Ricardo Arias, and I only met him at cocktail parties. I suggest you consider him more carefully before you imagine the jury weeping."

Brooks suppressed a chuckle. "Caroline, you *are* entertaining."

Caroline stopped smiling. "Mac," she said in her most clipped tone, "you haven't told me a thing."

Brooks' face went cold. "What I've told you is that we have an investigation and that it's ongoing. Until *you* tell me something better than that Chris is too pleased with life to shoot someone—no matter how good his motive—that's all I have to say."

For the next fifteen minutes, riding in a cab to her office, Caroline pondered the meaning of all that was said.

At four thirty her telephone rang.

"Find out anything?" Chris Paget asked.

"Two things. First, you told Monk something that they don't believe. Maybe about where you were that night."

There was a pause. In a level voice Paget asked, "What do they think they have? A witness?"

"They won't tell me that." Caroline exhaled. "But the second thing, Christopher, is that whatever it is Mac's doing, James Colt's fingerprints are all over it."

ELEVEN

"WHAT do you remember," Denise Harris asked, "about your father's death?"

It was the question Terri had been dreading. "I try *not* to remember it," she answered. "It was very traumatic."

"Which perhaps is one reason for your dream—a sort of jailbreak for your subconscious."

Terri hesitated. She could think of that moment, she found, only by shutting her eyes. But when she did, all she saw was blackness.

"Take your time," Harris said calmly.

The first wisp of memory was a sound: the closing of a screen door. A shiver ran through Terri's body.

"What is it?" Harris asked.

"We had a screen door," Terri said slowly. "On the back porch, where I found him. When you closed it, the catch on the door made a kind of soft click. I can hear the sound."

"When you found your father," Harris asked, "did you close the door and go for help?"

An image. Rosa behind her. The cat rubbing against her leg.

"No," Terri said finally. "I think my mom was there."

There was silence. "What's the first thing that comes to you?" Harris said. "From before you found him."

Terri leaned back in the chair. With her eyes shut, the image was like the particles of night broken by the first light of sunrise. The chair felt as soft as the warm mattress that Terri sank into as a child.

Terri cannot sleep. The rectangle of her bedroom window frames the first gray sheen of morning. Something is wrong. There are goose bumps on her skin. As she stumbles from bed, uncertain of her purpose, the hardwood floor is cold beneath her feet.

Terri pauses at the door of her bedroom, feeling the silent house. She does not know what draws her down the stairs. As she takes them, walking softly, something tightens inside her. And then she hears the screen door shut.

She stops. Her heartbeat is light and quick. She tries talking to herself: Fourteen is far too old for a child's fears. She continues. She reaches the end of the darkened stairs. As she edges through the dining room, toward the kitchen, she hears a sound that she knows by heart. It is the cat clawing the screen door.

Entering the kitchen, Terri fishes beneath the sink for a bowl and cat food. Pouring the dry cat food, Terri glances up. The inner door is glass, and Terri sees the outline of the cat standing on her hind legs, with her front claws digging into the screen. Spotting Terri, the cat cries out to her.

Terri opens the glass door. She speaks softly to the cat just before unlocking the screen to find Ramon Peralta staring up at her. The cat's dish, falling from her hand, scatters food across his chest.

Ramon does not move. A ribbon of dried blood runs from his temple past his mouth and then onto the stone in a carmine pool. One hand, stretching backward, must have clawed at the screen.

Terri begins to shake; the handle of the screen door rattles in her fingers. She knows her father is dead.

"Teresa!"

Terri starts, heart thumping wildly as she turns.

Already dressed, Rosa stares past her at Ramon and then into Terri's face. Rosa sweeps Terri into her arms. In the back of Terri's mind she hears the screen door closing. She senses Rosa looking over her shoulder into the face of her dead husband.

"Oh, sweetheart," Rosa says with trembling voice. "Oh, sweetheart, that this should happen to you."

It is that which Terri remembers now. She cannot know, and will never ask, to whom it was that Rosa spoke.

She does not know how long they stayed there holding each other as her father lay on the porch.

After a while her mother leans back from her, hands clasping Terri's elbows. "You must listen to me now," she says, "I must call the police. But I do not wish your sisters to see your father or to know until I am ready to tell them. I am going upstairs to wake them now. Then I will serve them their breakfast in the dining room. After that, you will go with them to school as early as you can. Tell Sister Irene that there's a problem at home and that I will call to explain. But do not tell her what the problem is."

Looking into her mother's face, Terri nods. Her mother would take care of this. From now on, Rosa would take care of everything.

"What should *I* do?" Terri asks.

Her mother thinks. "Stay at school," she says quietly. "Just until I come for you. It won't be long."

"But I want to stay with you."

Rosa shakes her head. "I don't want the police to bother you, Teresa. You help me most by helping your sisters. It will be bad enough for them that your father, filled with drink, has died from a fall on his own back porch."

Harris expelled a breath. "You seem to remember quite a bit," she said after a time.

Terri slumped in her chair. "More than I thought," she said.

PAGET's telephone rang.

He had been enjoying a peaceful breakfast with Carlo, their first such in days. Paget answered the phone.

"Mr. Paget? Jack Slocum."

Paget knew the voice at once: the reporter who had found—or been led to—the *Inquisitor* article on Ricardo Arias.

"I'm over in Alameda County, at the family court," Slocum went on. "There are some files in *Arias* versus *Peralta* that the clerk won't let me have. Apparently they're sealed. I was hoping you could help me. See, from what I understand now, Mr. Arias is the one who wanted them sealed. And he's dead."

Paget fought to control his anger. "That makes him a little hard to reach, doesn't it."

Slocum sounded nettled. "I hear you might have copies."

At that moment, looking at Carlo, Paget despised the press. "Oh," he said quietly. "And where did you hear that?"

Slocum ignored the question. "Actually, I hear the files involve you, Mr. Paget. And some members of your family."

Turning from Carlo, Paget made his answer soft. "Does that excite you, Mr. Slocum?"

A pause, and then Slocum let his aggression show. "Look, your character is news, Mr. Paget. As is your family. Are you going to give me copies or not?"

"No. Perhaps you should go to the person who fed you this tidbit and get a copy from him. Or does he prefer anonymity—just in case there's a lawsuit?"

"Our paper," Slocum retorted angrily, "can go to court and get those papers unsealed. Most courts believe that the public interest outweighs personal privacy. Especially for people who think we should elect them to something."

"I'll remember that," Paget said, "if I ever find you crawling through my sock drawer. Anything else?"

Now Slocum tried sounding aggrieved. "Look, I'm giving you a chance here, out of fairness, to come down on the side of being open about your life. If you don't cooperate, I'll have to write that you refused me. And no one will keep me from printing that."

"Fine. But when you do, be sure to mention that you're *not* on the list of people I discuss my life with." Paget hung up.

Carlo had left his cereal behind and walked to the window. He was staring out at the bay. "That was a reporter, wasn't it?"

Paget rested both hands on his son's shoulders. "They're trying to dig up Richie's molester stuff. And dirt about Terri and me."

Carlo turned to face him, worry in his eyes. "Can they?"

"Probably. The way to stop them is to give up on the Senate."

Paget could read Carlo's face: He already imagined the shame of being labeled as a child molester—his name in the newspapers, the snickers of peers. "I don't want you to give up, Dad. It's not right."

"What wouldn't be right," Paget told Carlo, "is to sacrifice you to my ambitions." He spoke softly now. "I'll have to take care of this reporter right away. The best way I know how."

But Carlo's thoughts had moved past Slocum. "What about the police, Dad? What about Richie?"

Paget looked into his face. "All I can tell you, Carlo, is what I've said before. Because I didn't kill him, they can't prove that I did."

"I DON'T think this problem with Slocum came from Brooks," Caroline said to Paget. "At least it didn't start there."

Paget watched her. "Colt?" he asked.

Caroline nodded. "Colt's the one with the most to gain. Even if Slocum doesn't get the files, the little article he's planning to run does you real damage politicswise. And it gives Brooks no way out. If Richie's death and these files hit the media together, Brooks would have to pursue you even if you were his brother."

Paget felt depressed. "Throughout my life I've had the illusion that I could control things if only I tried. But I don't even know where all the pieces of this are or who holds them."

Caroline leaned back in her chair. "The first piece," she said slowly, "is politics, where 'who shot Richie' doesn't matter. What's at stake there is Carlo's privacy, and the immediate way to ensure that is shutting off the press. What someone—Colt, I'm certain—wants you to do, Chris, is drop the Senate. But have you considered what you lose by dropping out? Not on piece one, but piece two—the police investigation, where 'who shot Richie' matters a lot."

Paget stared at her. "A deal," he finally said. "Never stated, but understood: I drop out of the race, and perhaps Colt tells Brooks to let Richie stay a suicide. Have I caught the essence?"

Caroline appraised him. "More or less."

Paget turned to the window. The morning sunlight, glinting on the windows of high-rises, left them opaque. Quietly he said, "I'm getting out, Caroline. As early as tomorrow. Not because I'm afraid of what Brooks has against me, but because this is the only thing I can do to prevent Carlo from becoming a media plaything."

Caroline raised an eyebrow. "It must be extraordinary," she said finally, "to love a child."

"There are *two* people I love, Caroline. First, and always, there's Carlo. And now there's Terri. I don't want either of them hurt."

WHEN the telephone call came to her office, Terri hoped that the caller would be Chris. Her desk was strewn with work she could not do, and she had been pacing. But it was a woman, taut and upset.

"Mrs. Arias, this is Barbara Coffey, Elena's day-care supervisor."

Terri checked her watch. Elena would not be in day care for a good three hours yet. "Is something wrong?"

"Yes. I came in early to bring some posters while the room was empty for lunch." Her voice rose. "Elena was there with two men—one white and one black. They were asking questions."

Terri stood. "You mean the school just let—"

"Her teacher's *with* them, Mrs. Arias."

Terri left immediately and found them in the schoolroom. Four desks were arranged in a circle—Monk and Lynch sat on top of theirs; Leslie Warner sat next to Elena, holding her limp hand as Monk asked questions. Monk's tape machine sat on Elena's desk.

"Mommy," Elena said, getting up. Leslie Warner gripped her hand.

Terri gazed down at the teacher. "Let her go," she said softly. "Right now."

Warner opened her mouth to speak, then shut it again. Elena's hand slipped free.

"I'm sorry, Mommy," the little girl said as Terri picked her up.

Through her anger, Terri's nerves tingled; she did not ask what Elena meant. Terri told her, "Just wait outside a minute, okay?"

The little girl nodded against her shoulder. Terri carried her to the doorway, where Barbara Coffey waited. "I'll take Elena to the playground," the day-care supervisor said.

"Thanks," Terri said. "You're the only one who thought of her."

Coffey took Elena's hand. As they left, the little girl looked back at Terri. It was all Terri could do to wait until Elena disappeared.

She turned, walking back into the room. She stopped two feet in front of Monk. "You scum," she said. "Both of you."

Monk's returning gaze was not angry. Terri had the sudden intuition that this had not been his idea. He turned to Leslie Warner. "Thank you," he said politely, and he and Lynch left.

Terri faced Warner. The teacher's gray eyes were at once defensive and defiant. "How could you allow this?" Terri asked.

"I have an obligation. To Elena, not you."

In that moment Terri understood. "*You* called them. Why?"

"You threatened to kill Richie. Elena told me months ago."

Terri felt her body stiffen. Slowly it came to her: the night she had found Richie drunk. She had tucked Elena into bed and then, thinking her asleep, had told Richie that she would kill him if he again became drunk around their daughter. Then Terri remembered Monk asking if she had ever threatened to murder Richie.

"You shouldn't raise her," Warner continued angrily. "Not with what Elena knows. She's *lost* without her father."

Terri looked into Warner's eyes. And then quite deliberately she took one step forward and slapped Warner across the face.

There was a sharp crack. Warner reeled backward, eyes shocked.

"You fool," Terri said softly, and went to find Elena.

ELENA pointed at the sea lion leaping to catch a silvery fish tossed by a zookeeper. "Look, Mommy, he's having dinner."

It was one of the few things Elena had said in the hour since Terri had picked her up at school. On first seeing her mother, the little girl had worn a fearful, guilty look. Being questioned about a parent would turn a child's world inside out, Terri knew. When she asked Elena if she wanted to go to the zoo, the little girl's anxiety seemed to ease, but none of her formerly favorite things—the petting zoo, the orangutans, or the merry-go-round—drew any response. Finally Terri suggested a ride in a motorized train.

Now, moving past the seal pool, Elena settled back on her mother's lap. The train was not crowded, and Terri and Elena—sitting alone near the end—could talk as they chose.

"Were you scared?" Terri asked her daughter.

Elena nodded. "They asked all about Daddy. About when you guys were fighting."

Terri studied her. "Do you remember us fighting?"

A short nod. "You said you would kill Daddy."

The words, fearful yet certain, made Terri's skin feel cold. "Your father was drunk," she said. "Do you know what drunk means?"

Elena hesitated. "You act crazy?"

"Very crazy sometimes. I love you too much to have let your daddy be like that around you. I was just trying to tell him that."

Elena looked up at her. "Did you want to kill Daddy?"

"Of course not," she said. "Why do you ask that?"

Elena turned away. "Because of me," she said.

Terri pulled her daughter close. "I love you more than anything, sweetheart. But killing people is wrong."

Elena's arms tightened around Terri. "I didn't tell them, Mommy. Only Miss Warner, a long time ago."

"Tell them what?"

"What you said to Daddy." Elena's voice was soft and fearful. "I won't get you in trouble. I promise, okay?"

Terri felt her stomach wrench. "You don't need to promise, Elena. You don't need to be afraid for me."

Elena shook her head. "They'll take you away from me. If a mommy or daddy gets in trouble, that's what they do."

Terri pulled herself back, holding Elena to see her face. "Daddy told you that, didn't he?" Terri said softly.

Elena nodded. "He told me about *all* his feelings. All the things that scared him."

"Like what?"

Elena looked down. "Chris took you away from Daddy," she answered. "He was helping you take me away too. I had to stay with Daddy or he'd be all alone."

The simple words, repeated like a catechism, frightened Terri for Elena more than anything the child had said. Her hatred of Richie returned as fresh as when he was alive. "Your daddy was a selfish man," Terri said without thinking. "He didn't love me or you or anyone. All he wanted was you to feel sorry for him."

Elena's eyes filled with tears. "That's not true!" she exclaimed. "Chris was Daddy's enemy. I told them all about it."

"Who?"

"The policemen." Elena paused. "I wouldn't leave Daddy, and so Chris killed him with a gun. He's going to jail, Mommy, forever."

WHEN there was a knock on his office door, Paget turned, hoping for Terri. And then Lynch and Monk came through the door with a bearded medical technician.

They've come to arrest me, Paget thought at once. Steeling himself, he asked, "What do you want?"

"All we want is prints," Lynch said evenly. "And blood."

Monk and Lynch sat at Paget's desk. Lynch put fingerprint cards and an ink pad onto Paget's blotter while Monk handed him some papers. A warrant authorizing the holder to take fingerprints and sample blood from Paget's body.

Paget held out his right hand. Silent, the technician took it; he placed one finger at a time on the ink pad and then on the card, rolling it from side to side. Paget turned to Monk. "You would have done this a while ago, Charles, wouldn't you, instead of stringing things out? If it had been up to you instead of Brooks."

Monk looked him in the face, but he said nothing. To acknowledge the question would be to admit that he could not answer.

The telephone rang. It might be Terri, Paget thought. As it rang, the technician turned the tips of Paget's fingers into prints on a white card.

TWELVE

"DO YOU think this will end it?" Terri asked. "Quitting the race?"

Chris gazed at the bedroom ceiling. The look in his eyes was distant. "I turn this over in my mind again and again. What do they have? I ask myself. What do they *think* they have?"

Terri had never seen Christopher Paget so lost. She had gone to find him, driven by the instinct that he needed her. Now, as she lay in his bed in the light of late afternoon, the duality of the moment left her without words. The man she loved and wished to comfort was suspected of killing the father of her child.

"What do we do now?" she asked softly. "I can't see past this moment, Chris. You're going to have to help me."

He touched her face. "Feeling lonely?"

"Not lonely, Chris. Alone."

Slowly Chris nodded. "If, after this is over, I never again feel distant from you, I'll have what I most want in life." He kissed her. "I love you," he said.

He heard a knocking on the door then. Slow and insistent.

They looked at each other. The knocking kept on.

Gently Paget kissed her again and got up from the bed. Terri watched him as he dressed in sweater and jeans, taking his time.

By now they knew that the knocking would not stop.

And then quite suddenly there was a cracking sound, like wood snapping. Footsteps now. In the doorway Paget glanced back at Terri. "Lock this door," he said. "And call Caroline."

Slowly Paget walked down the winding stairs. The front door was broken open. Monk and Lynch were in the alcove, waiting with the young policeman who had searched Paget's home.

"Three of you?" Paget asked.

"You have been indicted by the grand jury," Monk said gravely. "We have a warrant for your arrest in the murder of Ricardo Arias."

Monk began reading Paget his rights.

Paget felt a moment's lightness, like an oxygen shortage. As if by reflex, he nodded when Monk was finished, and then Monk took his arm and guided him past the splintered entryway.

THE twenty or so inmates of the Hall of Justice's holding tank, blacks and Latinos and a few Asians, seemed to study him with the lassitude that comes from the shock of arrest. Paget had to keep his thoughts focused and clear. Once he got out, he could think about Carlo and Terri.

Monk opened the door and walked over to Paget. "I'm going to walk you through this," he said. "Express check-in."

Another series of images: Monk shoving through the crowd to the booking window. A Latin deputy booking Paget for the murder of Ricardo Arias—name and address, fingerprints and photo. More fingerprints in a room that smelled like a latrine. Another photograph in a wooden seat that looked like an electric chair.

"I'm checking with my lawyer," Paget told Monk.

Monk shrugged. Paget went to a telephone on the concrete

wall and tried to call Caroline. No answer; only a taped message.

When he turned, Monk was holding out an orange jumpsuit. Paget stared at him. "I want my own cell," he said.

Monk shoved the jumpsuit in Paget's hands. "Put these on."

"Look—" Paget began, and then the telephone rang.

"It's for you," a deputy said to Monk. Monk took it, listened for a moment, and said a few terse words.

Hanging up, he turned to Paget and repeated, "Put that on."

Paget did. A deputy put his clothes in a bag and took them away.

"All right," Monk said. "Let's go."

A few steps later Paget found himself standing in front of the barred door to the county jail, flanked by Monk and a thick-bodied sheriff's deputy. Through the bars was a two-hundred-foot-long corridor with cells on either side and sheriff's deputies spaced in front of them. The sound of inmates shouting at one another echoed off the walls. The light was a sickly yellow.

Someone pushed a buzzer, and the door opened. Paget felt frightened and alert at once. On both sides of him now were cells full of prisoners—blacks on his left, Hispanics and Asians on his right, separated so that they would not attack one another.

"Where am I going?" Paget asked.

Monk stopped moving. "Shopping. Your assignment is to pick out five guys who look like you. If you can find that many."

Paget turned to him in surprise. "A lineup?"

Monk nodded. "Of course, they have to be volunteers."

Slowly Paget and Monk made their way down the corridor, staring through the bars of the next group of cells. The inmates, hostile or bored, gazed back. About twenty prisoners stood around or lay on bunk beds; none of them were Caucasians.

They went to the next cell. Inside, a twentyish olive-skinned Latin with reddish hair leaned against a bed. He shrugged when Paget pointed at him; he was bored, the shrug said—why not?

Cell by cell Paget added prospects. At the last cell Paget stopped, gazing at a Caucasian prisoner.

The man was younger than he, perhaps thirty-five, and his hair was redder than Paget's copper-blond. But their height was similar, their skin tone the same, and the man's eyes were as blue as Paget's. The two men watched each other, the bars between them.

Silent, Paget beckoned. The man was still, gazing at Paget.

"I need you in a lineup," Paget said.

"Why should I?"

Paget angled his head toward the line of prospects. "Man," he said, "*you* are my only ticket out of here."

The man shrugged. "All right," he said, and stuck his hand through the bars. "My name's Ray."

"Chris," Paget answered, and shook his hand.

Monk and the deputy let Ray out of the cell.

Paget and the five prisoners filed back down the corridor, Monk to one side, the deputy behind them. The jail door swung open; two other deputies waited to escort them down one corridor, then another, and into a barred mantrap that faced a metal door.

"There had better be a lawyer," Paget said to Monk, "on the other side of the door."

The metal door opened, and Paget and the others stepped through. They were standing on the stage of an auditorium. The stage was lit from above, but the theater seats were shrouded

in darkness. Gazing out, Paget could see shadows, hear whispers.

"Christopher," a voice called from the shadows, "I'm over here."

Silent, Paget nodded. The fact that Caroline had spoken to him meant that the witness was not yet there.

"All right," Monk said. "Spread out."

The six men formed a line. Monk gave them each a numbered card: Ray was three, Paget five. A flashcube went off. Paget blinked. It was the photo of the lineup, to be used in court.

There was silence, then a reshuffling of the unseen bodies who watched them. Paget sensed that the witness had been brought in.

From the darkness a cop's bored voice began reading. "The person charged with the crime may not be here. You don't have to pick anyone. Don't pick anyone to please us. . . ."

Somewhere in the darkness the witness watched them.

"Number one," the cop's voice called out.

The man stepped forward. More silence, then whispers.

"That's fine," the cop called out. "Number two."

The same: silence, whispers, a dismissal.

"Number three."

Ray stepped forward. He squared his shoulders.

"Turn right," the cop's voice said.

Ray did so; Paget felt himself grip the card he held.

"Turn left."

Ray turned again. Paget started counting the seconds that passed. "Step back. Next is number four."

Number four passed quickly. Swallowing, Paget hardly listened.

"Number five," the voice called out.

Paget stepped forward. He gazed out at the darkness. In the silence he felt the unknown witness. The lack of sound was oppressive.

"Turn right," the cop called out. "Turn left."

Paget did that. His palms were sweating. It seemed too long before the cop told him to step back.

Number six went quickly.

Then a new voice asked, "Could I see number five again?"

A woman's voice, low and hoarse. Paget could not recognize it. He stepped forward, facing the darkness again.

"That's him." The voice was shaking now. "I'm sure of it."

THE JURY

February 1–February 2
The Following Year

THIRTEEN

CHRIS Paget watched the jury pool—eighty or so strangers—wondering which twelve of them would decide his future.

After his arrest in November, Paget had spent the night in a solitary cell and remained there until the next afternoon, when, after an angry session between Caroline and District Attorney McKinley Brooks, the amount of bail had finally been agreed to—a half-million dollars. Upon his release, Paget attempted to reassure Carlo and Terri as best he could. Both conversations had been painful: It became clear that the best thing Paget could do was to start building a defense as quickly as he could.

Now, two months later, Paget sat in Judge Jared Lerner's spacious courtroom. The walls were a cheap blond-wood paneling. The worn theater seats behind the low wooden divider, packed with potential jurors, gave it the look of an overcrowded classroom in an underfunded school. But the presence of a black-robed judge lent gravity. Reporters lined the walls; the lawyers fidgeted or stared into space; Lerner himself—a bald, sharp-featured man with a dark beard—looked edgy and alert.

Paget, sitting next to Caroline, could not enjoy an unconsidered moment. Minute to minute he was aware of each potential juror watching him. He sat very still, trying to look serious yet composed. Part of him could still not believe that Ricardo Arias had brought him to this.

Of course, it was some comfort to have the best defense that money could buy: Caroline Masters and, seated discreetly behind them, private detective Johnny Moore—hired by Caroline to discover, as she put it, "every slimy little thing Ricardo ever did," along with the names of anyone with a reason to dislike him. Neither Carlo nor Terri was in the courtroom. As potential witnesses, they had been barred.

The prosecutor, Victor Salinas, had swiveled on his chair, eyeing the jury pool. Paget knew Salinas was gauging the ethnic composition of the panel, honing his strategy for selecting the jury that was most likely to convict Paget of first-degree murder. They were about to begin the chess game where cases are won or lost—the strange mixture of intuition, sociology, pop psychology, and racism through which Caroline and Salinas would winnow eighty people down to twelve.

On the surface Judge Lerner's rules were simple enough: The bailiff would call out twelve names, and the candidates would shuffle forward to the jury box to be queried by Judge Lerner for competence or bias. If some disqualification was obvious, Lerner might dismiss a juror on his own accord, or Salinas or Caroline could ask him to do so for cause. But the real art lay in the lawyers' use of peremptory challenges: the precious occasions, twenty in number, on which each side could demand dismissal of a juror.

"All right," Lerner said, turning to the first twelve panelists. "This is the case of *People* versus *Christopher Paget*."

Caroline touched Paget's arm as if to reassure him. But Paget knew that Caroline Masters must do more than pick jurors who claimed to be unbiased. She must find twelve people who would acquit a man who would not testify in his own defense.

PAGET watched Jared Lerner question the first potential juror.

According to Johnny Moore's inquiries, the middle-aged red-head, Alice Mahan, was an Irish Catholic mother of four, a telephone operator for twenty years, and the wife of a parochial school teacher. Paget, Caroline, and Johnny Moore had placed Alice toward the bottom of the list on the theory that she might be rules oriented and inclined to trust authority.

"Some people," Lerner said, "feel that if a defendant doesn't testify, he or she may have something to hide. What do you think?"

Alice cocked her head. "I don't think I'd be satisfied. A man on trial for murder shouldn't want to leave us with any questions."

It was the very mind-set Caroline and Paget feared.

Lerner stroked his beard. "Do you think you could judge the case fairly if he decides not to testify?"

Alice hesitated. "I'm not sure. But I'd certainly try, Your Honor."

Tensing, Paget saw Victor Salinas turn to Lerner with a hopeful expression. "Strike her," Caroline said under her breath. "Please."

Lerner gave Alice a nod of approval. "I'm sure you'd try, Mrs. Mahan. But in fairness, I think I should excuse you."

Salinas turned away.

"Bingo," Caroline murmured.

"ONE of the nasty little racist secrets of picking San Francisco juries," Johnny Moore had said to Caroline, "is for defense lawyers to strike as many Asians as possible. Do you disagree?"

They were meeting in Caroline's office—the detective, Paget, and Caroline herself—to strategize on the selection of a jury. But where Paget and Caroline Masters looked as if they belonged there, Moore—with his white beard and the ruddy face of a reformed drinker, his wool sport coat and corduroy slacks—seemed more like a pro bono client who had been sent to Caroline by Legal Aid.

"It depends," Caroline answered. "If we're talking immigrants or the unassimilated, I suppose I agree: They tend to defer to authority. But give me a second- or third-generation Asian, especially a professional with an advanced education, and things start to look quite different." She leaned back in her chair. "Who's next?"

"Latins," Paget said. "For two reasons. One living, one dead."

Caroline nodded. "Salinas and Richie. Too much identification."

"I wouldn't take a Latin male. Period," Moore put in.

"I'd add lawyer haters," Paget said.

"Of course," Caroline said. "So who *do* we want?"

Paget thought for a moment. "As a gross generalization, the old civil rights coalition—Jews and blacks. Jews because of a humanist bent that goes with a certain sympathy for the accused, blacks because they know that cops are not always free from bias."

Caroline looked dubious. "Monk complicates that. They'll respect him. What I need is *anyone* who doesn't trust authority."

Moore frowned. "That's why education is so important in Chris's case, as long as it's combined with imagination. If we were lucky, we'd get a jury of white Yale-educated poets who vote the liberal line and come from East Coast cities."

Caroline shook her head. "Even if we could find them, Salinas would mow them down." The smile she gave Moore was somewhat grim. "You might want to comb the jury pool for women with an obsessive attraction to blond, silent males."

The comment, delivered in a tone of mock innocence, carried a pointed barb. It reminded Paget that his lawyer was headed for a trial in which, for reasons Paget refused to explain, he would say nothing.

VICTOR Salinas was questioning the twenty-third of the first twenty-four initial panelists, a process that had yielded three jurors: a white male public school teacher, a black bank officer, and a middle-aged Filipina stenographer. The current panelist was an attractive sixty-year-old Jewish woman named Marian Celler, whose husband was a cardiologist, whose daughters were academics, and who had helped administer several charities. When Johnny Moore had leaned forward to say that they should take her, both Caroline and Paget had agreed.

Standing near the jury box, Salinas smiled at Celler. "Your family has distinguished itself," he said pleasantly, "by not having sent a single member to law school. Is this an accident, or is it another reflection of good parenting?"

The prospective jurors laughed at the mild joke, but Paget knew it had been planned. Salinas was disassociating himself from his profession: He was not one of *those* lawyers, but one who protected his fellow citizens from lawyers' worst tricks.

Celler gave Salinas a smile. "It's an accident. Neither of our daughters wanted to be doctors, either. And *I* married one."

"Have you had experience with members of the legal profession?"

"Yes. I've had the same lawyer for twenty-five years."

"And have you been satisfied?"

Celler gave Salinas a vigorous nod. "Oh, very."

Salinas said, "That's all I have, Mrs. Celler," and sat down.

Caroline rose. "Good afternoon, Mrs. Celler. I'm sure you're aware that Mr. Paget is himself a lawyer."

"Oh, yes."

"Based on your experience, Mrs. Celler, what is your opinion of the integrity of the legal profession?"

"It's quite high. My lawyer, for one, is a man of great integrity."

"It's been nice to know you, however briefly," Caroline said dryly.

There was suppressed laughter from the press. As Caroline sat down, Salinas gave her a look of anger. With one subversive comment she had made it clear to the panelists that Salinas was trying to cash in on anti-lawyer bias. Now he had the choice of confirming it or letting on a juror that he plainly did not want.

"Mr. Salinas?" asked the judge, a certain amusement in his eyes.

Victor composed himself, standing straighter for the jury. A little too loudly he said, "The people pass Mrs. Celler."

"Oh, Victor," Caroline murmured, "that really wasn't very smart."

JUST after five thirty they adjourned.

Marian Celler had been Caroline's finest moment. She had used fourteen peremptory dismissals, with only six left. Among the eight jurors passed, Caroline had been forced to accept the first two Asians—a Chinese medical technician whose parents came from Hong Kong, and a twenty-year-old Vietnamese immigrant. Most of her peremptories had been used on Latins, but Caroline did not like the message this might send.

By afternoon of the next day both sides had agreed on three more jurors: Luisa Marin, a slender young Hispanic woman, Catholic and lightly educated; a Japanese accountant; and a recently naturalized Irishman. Neither Paget nor Caroline was sanguine about any of them. As time wore on, Paget felt the jury slipping away from them.

Now, with the next two panelists blue-collar Asians, Paget watched Caroline question Joseph Duarte, an upwardly mobile Hispanic businessman in his early thirties with the cocksure manner of a leader and a lack of deference—to Caroline, in particular. Even before the questioning, Paget had mentally stricken Duarte. If Caroline used her last peremptory on him, one of the two Asians following might become the twelfth juror.

"Mr. Duarte," Caroline said pleasantly, "you are aware, are you not, that Mr. Paget is quite wealthy."

A brisk nod. "Sure."

"What experiences, if any, have you had with people who you would consider more than usually affluent?"

Duarte smiled. "I used to caddy at the Olympic Club to make money toward college. There were plenty of rich people there."

Caroline tilted her head. "You mean there were plenty of rich *men* there, all of them white."

It was a shrewd probe. The Olympic Club had a long history of restricting minorities and barring women altogether.

Duarte's smile flashed again. "I remember that," he said.

Watching, Paget sensed that it was ethnic and class resentment, and not a dislike for women, that underlay Duarte's manner.

"How," Caroline asked, "would you characterize your experiences with the rich folks at the Olympic Club?"

"Some treated me all right," Duarte said. "Others, like dirt. It was hard to forget that you were only welcome as a caddy."

Caroline nodded. "Do you think that this unpleasant experience with wealthy people would affect your ability to judge this case?"

Duarte sat straighter, as if she had insulted him. "No," he said tersely. "I can take people as individuals. I came here to listen to the facts and make a judgment. Just like I do in my business."

"Thank you," Caroline said. She turned away from Duarte.

"Mr. Salinas?" Judge Lerner asked.

Salinas stood. "The people pass Mr. Duarte," he said.

When Caroline reached the defense table, Moore leaned for-

403

ward. "Take him," he whispered, "and you have the jury foreman."

"Ms. Masters?" Judge Lerner said from the bench.

She glanced his way. "Please, Your Honor, a moment."

"There's another thing," Paget murmured to Caroline. "At least to a point, this guy could be Ricardo Arias—the disadvantaged Latin struggling to make it."

Caroline looked at him intently. "But he *isn't* like Richie, and we can turn it around if he believes Richie was a bum. And the race thing works both ways, Chris. We've bumped every Latin male on the panel. This guy believes he's made a commitment to me, and he'll try to honor it as a point of pride."

"Ms. Masters?" Lerner asked again.

When she turned, facing Joseph Duarte, the look she gave him was one of triumph and complicity. "The defense," she said, "passes Mr. Duarte."

Watching, Paget saw Victor Salinas smile to himself.

"Then we have a jury," Judge Lerner said. "Thank you, counsel. The trial will commence tomorrow at nine, with opening statements."

"So," Carlo said to his father, "how's your jury?"

"All right." Saying this, Paget wished that it were so. "A lot depends on how they respond to the lawyers."

They were shooting hoops in the driveway, under the lights Paget had installed so they could play at night. They were playing Horse, alternating shots until a player sank one, and the other had to make the same shot or receive a letter. The first one to spell out "horse" lost the game.

Carlo took his father's place and gazed at the basket, gauging his shot. "How do you feel about that? I mean, Caroline's smart, but she doesn't seem all that warm." Without waiting for an answer, Carlo replicated Paget's last jump shot. It landed inside the rim, swirled once, and came out again.

"Trying to beat me at my own game?" Paget asked.

Carlo shrugged. "We'll see."

Paget retrieved the ball. "About Caroline— I picked what I'm comfortable with, and I'm happier with cool and smart than some folksy gunslinger who thinks he's Mr. Populist." He paused for a moment. "Jurors don't like arrogance. But they *do* admire style and intelligence. And Caroline can adapt her touch to the audience. She'll do fine with these people."

Paget hoped that was right. He arched another jump shot, which fell through the hoop. "The pressure's on," he said.

Carlo got the ball. "Is Caroline going to talk to me again? Before I testify?"

"Sure." Inside, Paget ached for Carlo. Not only would Salinas try to make him testify against his father, but he would drag the boy through Richie's charges that he molested Elena. Paget wished that he could help his son prepare, and blamed himself that Carlo had to face this at all. But it would not help to say this now.

"You couldn't be in better hands," Paget added calmly. "Caroline will prepare you not only for everything *she'll* ask you but for everything Victor Salinas will ask you. That way you'll be as comfortable as possible."

Carlo turned to him. "I really *am* feeling the pressure," he said quietly. "But not from your stupid jump shot. I just want you around to shoot it, okay?"

Paget smiled. "Okay."

Carlo shook his head. "I wish I could talk to you about what to say."

Paget gazed at him across the half-lit driveway. "I know, son, but we can't. There's nothing I can say to you that Salinas couldn't ask about in court."

"Dad," Carlo said slowly, "I really don't want to screw up."

"Then just tell the truth. That way you *can't* screw up."

But Carlo only looked at him. Oh, Lord, Paget thought, you're not really sure, are you? "Look," he went on, "I've never told a serious lie that I haven't paid some price for, and there are some I've had to live with for a long time. Don't try to do that for me, Carlo. I'll know you're doing it, and it will hurt me. And if Salinas catches you at it, that could hurt me quite badly."

Carlo rested the ball on his hip, looking at Paget as if to fathom his meaning. "All this evidence they say they have—"

"Will be explained. Just be patient for two more weeks." Paget tried to smile. "Meanwhile, shoot the ball, okay?"

Carlo hesitated. Then he turned to the basket, breathing in once, and sank the jump shot.

"Grace under pressure," Paget remarked.

THE TRIAL

February 3–February 16

FOURTEEN

A MURDER trial is like a cocoon, Paget thought. The world outside seems barely to exist.

He sat at the defense table with Caroline Masters, waiting for Salinas to begin his opening statement. He could imagine the routines of daily life only by attaching them to Carlo, who had no choice but to go to school, or to Terri, whom Paget had asked to mind his cases. But his sole concrete image was that of the satellite trucks of news services—set up outside the Hall of Justice to feed live reports from the trial.

During the next two weeks, though, no matter how many reporters and voyeurs packed the courtroom, the only people who would matter as much as Caroline were Judge Lerner and the jurors. Paget turned to scan them—among them Marian Celler, attentive and carefully dressed, with reading glasses on a silver chain around her neck; Luisa Marin, the young Hispanic woman, hands clasped; Joseph Duarte, holding a notepad, with a look of skeptical alertness.

Finally, there was Jared Lerner. The judge took a long survey of the courtroom, then nodded to Victor Salinas. The trial began.

Approaching the jury, Salinas said, "This is a case about secrets and about lies. More than that, it is about arrogance—the arrogance of a man who decided that *another man* was too inconvenient to live and too insignificant for anyone to question how he died."

The jurors looked rapt.

"Ricardo Arias was a man like you or me," Salinas went on, speaking to Duarte. "He had a daughter he loved, a life built on family, a future he believed in. Most of all, he had his wife, Teresa."

His voice became flat with muted outrage. "Ladies and gentlemen, Christopher Paget took Teresa from her husband and her home. But Ricardo Arias still had his daughter, Elena, the child he adored. And Teresa Peralta would not let go. In spite of his limited funds—because *he* had cared for Elena while Teresa 'worked' for

Christopher Paget—Richie Arias suddenly found himself in a custody fight he never wanted.

"And then," Salinas continued, "strange things began happening. Despite all Richie's efforts, Elena became depressed. A teacher called reporting sexual play involving Elena." Salinas turned to Marian Celler. "To his horror Ricardo Arias concluded that his daughter had been sexually molested by Chris Paget's teenage son."

An involuntary flicker of distaste crossed Celler's face. Salinas nodded as if satisfied. "Like any loving father, Ricardo Arias went into action. He demanded that Teresa keep Elena away from Carlo Paget. And when, in the face of all that had happened, Teresa still insisted on trying to get custody, Ricardo Arias went to court.

"He accused Christopher Paget of adultery and placed the evidence of child abuse before the court. He filed the papers under seal, to shelter Elena's tragedy from public view. Only if Teresa refused to keep Elena from the Paget home would a hearing ensue, in thirty days, and Richie's concerns become public."

Salinas paused. "It was an act of compassion. And it was a fatal mistake. For Christopher Paget was running for the Senate."

Turning to Luisa Marin, Salinas slowly shook his head. "Ricardo Arias' act of love for his daughter was a death warrant. If his charges became public, Carlo Paget could be exposed as a molester and his father as an adulterer. Not only would Mr. Paget's lover lose her child, but his own ambitions might well be destroyed."

Abruptly Salinas spun on Paget. "What, Mr. Paget must have wondered, would life be like without Ricardo Arias? His son would be off the hook. His affair would remain buried. His girlfriend would have her daughter—at whatever cost to the child. And most of all, Christopher Paget could become *your* Senator."

Salinas turned back to the jury. "The only problem," he told them quietly, "was that Mr. Arias would have to disappear within thirty days. Christopher Paget had planned a vacation to Italy with Teresa. And despite this critical hearing involving *both* their children, Mr. Paget wanted to go. Why? Because the night before they left for Italy was a perfect time for murder. For unless Mr. Arias was quickly found, Christopher Paget could suggest that Ricardo Arias died in San Francisco while Paget made love to Ricardo Arias' wife in Venice."

Flushed with anger, Paget spotted Duarte gazing at Salinas.

"And," Salinas added, "if people thought that Ricardo Arias had killed himself, no one would question Christopher Paget at all. How do we know he thought these things?" Salinas pointed an accusing finger toward Paget and answered, "Because Christopher Paget *lied* to the police.

"When the police found Ricardo Arias," Salinas said, "it looked like a possible suicide. He was shot in the mouth, a gun was found near his hand, and on his desk was the beginning of a suicide note. But there were bruises on his legs, damage to his nose, a gash on his head—and there was nothing, not blood or even gunpowder, on the hand that supposedly fired the gun.

"And so, on Mr. Paget's return from Italy, the police decided to question him. And what did Mr. Paget say? That he had never met Ricardo Arias or even spoken to him. That he had never been to Mr. Arias' apartment. And that he was at home on the last night of Ricardo Arias' life."

Caroline Masters watched intently as Salinas surveyed the jury. "We will show that each and every one of these statements was a lie. Most important, ladies and gentlemen, we will show that Christopher Paget went to Richie's apartment the night before he left for Italy and that Ricardo Arias was never seen alive again."

The jury was grim-faced now. Joseph Duarte was writing in his notepad. Covertly Marian Celler glanced at Paget.

Salinas' voice rose. "By the end of the trial you will know that Ricardo Arias was murdered." Turning, Salinas gazed at Paget. "You will know that Christopher Paget made Ricardo Arias write his own suicide note. And then, quite coldly, killed him."

FACING the jury in a well-tailored black suit and gold earrings, Caroline Masters looked calm, almost serene. "Let me tell you," she said, "what, when this trial is over, you will *not* know. You will not know if Ricardo Arias killed himself. Or if he died while Mr. Paget was somewhere else. Or if, even assuming that Mr. Arias was murdered and assuming further that Mr. Paget was in San Francisco, Mr. Paget had any part in—or knowledge of—that crime."

Caroline paused. "And that, members of the jury, means that you must find Christopher Paget innocent of murder."

The jury seemed alert; by inverting Salinas' opening, Caroline got them to listen. But Joseph Duarte's eyes were narrow with doubt.

"What Mr. Salinas just told you," she continued evenly, "is a list of what he needs you to believe. He needs you to believe that Christopher Paget met Ricardo Arias. That he went to Mr. Arias' apartment. That he was there in some proximity to his death. In fact, Mr. Salinas offered so many lists that it was easy to miss what was missing: proof that Christopher Paget killed Mr. Arias."

It was good, Paget thought. Caroline had put a subtly satiric spin on Salinas' style without ever raising her voice.

"Mr. Salinas cannot even prove beyond a reasonable doubt that Christopher Paget and Ricardo Arias were ever within two miles of each other, let alone that Mr. Paget killed Mr. Arias." Pausing, Caroline gazed at Joseph Duarte. "The truth is that Mr. Salinas cannot prove that anyone killed Mr. Arias *but* Mr. Arias.

"And so," she said softly, "Mr. Salinas asks you to share his prejudice. He does this by offering you a cartoon: Ricardo Arias is a simple and loving man, courageously fighting for his daughter's welfare, while Mr. Paget is the arrogant son of wealth who stole Ricardo's wife. In short, Mr. Salinas wants you to convict Mr. Paget because you like Mr. Arias better. Aside from the lack of evidence, there are two problems. And the first is the *real* Ricardo Arias."

Caroline, Paget saw, would not take her eyes off Duarte. "As to Mr. Arias, let me offer you a list of my own. This was a man of minimal honesty. A man unable to hold a job. A man who lived off his wife. A man who used his daughter for money. A man whose selfishness and callousness drove Teresa Peralta out of the house and *then*—because she was the only responsible parent Elena had—forced her to support him by posing as the loving custodial father."

Duarte's face was attentive now. "Ricardo Arias," Caroline said with scorn, "who for ten thousand dollars used his daughter as the centerpiece of a self-pitying article in a scandal sheet. Ricardo Arias, who charged an innocent teenage boy with child abuse so that he would not lose the monthly support check Teresa provided for their daughter."

Pausing, Caroline scanned the jury box. "Ricardo Arias," she repeated. "A man who was running out of excuses. A man who,

409

after years of hiding behind his wife, faced a rigorous examination of his own life by a psychologist appointed by the family court. A man about to be exposed for what he was—a con artist.

"No one deserves to die," Caroline continued softly. "But I believe that we can understand why a man like this, faced with the truth of his life, might well consider ending it."

She looked at Marian Celler. "What is far more difficult to fathom is why Christopher Paget would choose to kill him. And that is Mr. Salinas' second problem—Christopher Paget. Unlike Ricardo Arias, Chris Paget already possessed those things he valued most: a warm relationship with his son, Carlo; a healthy and loving involvement with Teresa Peralta, *after* she had freed herself from the misery of her marriage; a distinguished career; and a chance to serve his larger community as a candidate for public office. Yet Mr. Salinas asks you to believe that this man was driven to murder."

Paget sensed Marian Celler appraising him. Caroline approached the jury box. "Ricardo Arias *was* who he was: an unstable man, capable of self-destruction. And Christopher Paget *is* who he is: a peaceful man who loves his son far too much to kill Ricardo Arias."

One by one Caroline met each juror's eyes. "This prosecution," she finished simply, "makes no sense. In the end, if nothing else, you will know at least that much."

CHIEF medical examiner Elizabeth Shelton was a slender blonde in her late thirties, with a clear-eyed gaze and a composed air.

Putting Shelton on the stand, Victor Salinas quickly established her extensive credentials and took her through a summary of her physical findings. Then Salinas began to lay the groundwork for murder. "When Mr. Arias' body was found," he asked, "could you describe the condition it was in?"

"Mr. Arias was lying on the floor with a revolver near his hand," Shelton said. "I found what appeared to be a bullet entry wound through his mouth. He had obviously been dead for some time."

Salinas picked up a manila envelope and pulled out several photographs. "Dr. Shelton, I hand you what have been pre-marked as people's exhibits one through four. Can you tell me what they are?"

Shelton took out a pair of tortoiseshell glasses. "These are crime scene photographs of the head and hands of Ricardo Arias."

Salinas collected the photographs and tendered them to Caroline. She spread them on the table, and Christopher Paget looked into the face of Ricardo Arias.

Richie's eyes were frozen in shock and terror. He did not look like a man who had resolved to shoot himself and then pulled the trigger. His face was waxen and puffy. His nose seemed swollen.

Paget made himself study each picture. In the final picture Richie's hand was shriveled like a mummy's.

Paget had seen enough. He pushed the photographs back. Salinas handed them to the jury, his expression grave.

One by one they inspected the photographs.

"In the course of examining Mr. Arias," Salinas asked Shelton, "did you form an opinion as to the time of death?"

Shelton shook her head. "No. However, we were able to establish from extrinsic evidence a probable range of time within which Mr. Arias died. Mr. Arias had opened his mail for Friday, October sixteen, but there was a stack of unopened mail behind the mail slot of his apartment. The local mail bore postmarks of from October sixteen until the day before we found him. Based on which, we believe that Mr. Arias died sometime between the delivery of his mail on Friday, October sixteen, and the next day's delivery."

In her seat, Caroline looked pensive.

Shelton continued. "In the kitchen we found a full pot of coffee. We determined that Mr. Arias had preset his automatic coffee-maker for seven thirty a.m., suggesting that he died before the coffee was actually made. We also found the morning newspaper for October sixteen on the kitchen table. But the newspaper for the *seventeenth* was still outside the door."

It was neatly done, Paget thought. He doubted that anyone on the jury did not now assume that Ricardo Arias had died before Paget left for Italy.

Quietly Salinas asked, "And were your physical findings, Dr. Shelton, consistent with a self-inflicted gunshot wound?"

"They were not," she answered. "When I first arrived at the scene, I assumed this might well be suicide, but within moments I found things that made suicide seem unlikely. It seemed that this was a homicide dressed up to look like suicide."

Caroline took out a pen and began scribbling on a legal pad.

411

"On what basis," Salinas asked, "did you determine that?"

"The first thing I noticed was Mr. Arias' hands." Shelton turned to the jury. "The bullet that killed Mr. Arias did not exit his head. That causes something called blowback—blood and tissue spraying forward through the path left by the gunshot. Which is why the pictures of Mr. Arias show specks of blood and tissue on his face.

"Similarly, the gun that killed Mr. Arias was old," Shelton went on. "A gun like that leaves considerable gunshot residue—what we call GSR—a sootlike deposit of unburned gunpowder. There was a significant amount of GSR on the roof of his mouth and his face." She paused, surveying the jury. "My point is, if Mr. Arias had placed the gun in his mouth and pulled the trigger, I would expect to find at least as much blood spatter and GSR on his hands and arms as on his face. There was almost none."

The jury had a rapt look, Paget saw.

"Perhaps most troubling was the other violence done to Mr. Arias," Shelton said. "First, his skull showed an abrasion—a gash on the back of his head—which was not caused by the gunshot wound. We determined from traces of skin and hair that Mr. Arias' head had struck the corner of his coffee table. There were also contusions and swelling to Mr. Arias' nose. Our autopsy revealed another anomaly: a bruise on the front of Mr. Arias' right leg. Its position reflected the approximate height of the coffee table."

In an involuntary reflex Paget thought of the suit he had taken to Goodwill, and then of Terri glancing at his hand as she had concealed his injury from Monk. He was glad she wasn't here.

"Also, in my experience," Shelton continued, "people tend to shoot themselves in three positions: standing up, sitting in a chair, or lying in bed. Here, based on the pattern of blowback and the angle of the bullet, Mr. Arias would have had to shoot himself while lying on the floor and with his head slightly raised."

Shelton's testimony was becoming deadly, Paget knew. But Caroline could do nothing but listen and wait to cross-examine.

Victor Salinas walked to his table, producing a small black revolver with an exhibit tag. "Your Honor, this has been pre-marked as people's exhibit five. I will ask Dr. Shelton to identify it."

"May we see it?" Caroline asked.

Without a word Salinas placed the revolver on the table. Looking down, Paget saw a small and worn handgun with a checkered handgrip monogrammed S&W and a safety catch inside the grip.

"Odd," he murmured to Caroline, "that it's so old."

Salinas took the gun back, then handed it to Shelton. "Is this the murder weapon?"

"It certainly appears to be," Shelton answered.

Salinas removed the gun, then asked quietly, "Did you find anything peculiar about Mr. Arias' eyes?"

"I did," Shelton said with equal quiet. "Virtually all the people I've seen who shot themselves died with their eyes shut."

"So based on the medical evidence, Dr. Shelton, do you have a belief as to the sequence of events that led to Mr. Arias' death?"

"I do," she said firmly. "The medical evidence is consistent with my belief that Mr. Arias sustained a blow to the face and that he spun and fell over the coffee table, resulting in an injury to his head. Together, the blows to the face and head rendered Mr. Arias unconscious." Pausing, Shelton spoke more quietly. "The evidence further suggests that as he lay there on the floor, someone inserted the gun in his mouth and pulled the trigger twice. But as ballistics discovered, the bullets had been kept in a damp place, and the first shot did not discharge. Finally, the medical evidence suggests that before the gun was fired again, Mr. Arias awoke. So that in the last instant of his life he was aware of the gun in his mouth.

"I may be off about a detail or two," Shelton added, "but the medical evidence is not consistent with suicide. Of that I'm quite confident. This man was murdered."

Salinas was finished. Beneath the table Caroline's fingertips grazed Paget's knee, a fleeting gesture of reassurance, and then she was on her feet. "Was Mr. Arias' alarm set?" she asked Shelton abruptly.

Shelton looked surprised. "No. I believe not."

"Perhaps," Caroline said dryly, "he didn't plan on getting up."

"Objection," Salinas called out. "Calls for speculation."

"Precisely, Victor," Caroline asserted, still gazing at Shelton. "And it's at least as reasonable as Dr. Shelton's testimony about the coffeemaker. Let's stick to the evidence, then. For all you know, Mr. Arias was alive when the newspaper was delivered, correct?"

Shelton gave a disinterested shrug. "It's possible, yes."

413

"And indeed, it's possible he slept well into the morning?"

"In theory, yes."

"So that even accepting your hypothesis, if Mr. Paget was driving to the airport before seven and on an airplane by eight, it's quite possible Mr. Arias died thereafter."

Shelton nodded. "It's all possible, Ms. Masters."

"Then you have no opinion as to whether Christopher Paget shot Ricardo Arias. Or even could have."

"None whatsoever."

"We've seen the revolver," Caroline continued. "It's a rather weak caliber, which would cause less blowback, correct?"

"Yes."

Caroline smiled. "And as I recall, the autopsy report showed traces of blood and GSR on Mr. Arias' right hand."

"A *small* trace. But there was far more on the gun itself. From which I concluded that someone else held it, receiving blowback on his or her hand or sleeve, and then placed it in Mr. Arias' right hand, leaving only the small trace of blowback and GSR."

Caroline walked forward. "There was also blood, was there not, on Mr. Arias' hand near his wrist? Quite a bit, in fact."

"Yes," Shelton said. "But that was a *smear* of blood, completely inconsistent with the speckling caused by blowback."

"Oh? And what *did* cause it?"

Shelton folded her hands. "In my opinion the smear was caused when Mr. Arias wiped blood from beneath his nose."

Caroline raised her eyebrows. "How did you determine that?"

"It makes sense. There was also a smear beneath his nose."

"And you never considered that it was blowback, and that Mr. Arias' hand, falling after he shot himself, smeared the blood as it crossed his face or body or even the rug?"

"I wasn't there, Ms. Masters, but I found no reason to believe it happened like that." Shelton was looking annoyed. "As I testified before, it's possible that I'm wrong about a detail or two, but the essence of my opinion is this: The medical evidence is all inconsistent with suicide. Period." Shelton paused. "And there was one other thing: the look on Mr. Arias' face."

"Wouldn't you be frightened," Caroline asked, "if you were about to shoot yourself? Even if you wanted to?"

414

Shelton thought for a moment. "The circumstances are hard for me to imagine. But yes, I suppose I might."

Caroline nodded. "I suppose I might too," she said. "Thank you."

Shelton stepped from the stand, staring straight ahead. Paget could see in the faces of his jurors that Ricardo Arias had moved much closer to being a victim of murder.

FIFTEEN

THE next morning Victor Salinas set out to prove that Ricardo Arias had meant to live forever.

He began with Leslie Warner. Taking the stand, Elena's former teacher arranged her long floral skirt and fingered her bracelets.

"You were going to meet Mr. Arias, were you not?" Salinas began abruptly. "The day after anyone last saw him."

Warner looked somber. "Yes. To discuss Elena."

"Were you surprised that he didn't appear?"

"Very much. At our first open house, and in subsequent conversations, Richie—Mr. Arias—spoke to me about Elena for some time. He seemed a very warm, very concerned father."

Salinas nodded. "How often did you speak to him?"

"At first only once or twice." Warner looked down. "And then, after a particular incident, he would drop by or call at least once a week, or I would call him. I mean, he *was* the custodial parent."

"This incident you mentioned—can you describe it?"

Here it comes, Paget thought.

"I observed Elena behind a Dumpster, pulling down her panties and asking a boy to look at her," Warner said in a flat voice.

"Did the incident you observed raise particular concerns?"

"Sexual acting out is fairly common in children. As a teacher, I see it a lot. Sometimes it's simply experimentation, or it may suggest deeper problems. In this case, Elena's distress when I spoke to her was so extreme that I decided to notify Mr. Arias."

"When you say deeper problems, what do you have in mind?"

Paget braced himself for what would come.

"It can be a symptom of sexual abuse," said Warner.

"Did you mention possible sexual abuse to Mr. Arias?"

"Yes. He was quite disturbed."

415

"Did there come a time, Ms. Warner, when Mr. Arias reported to you his concern that Elena had been molested?"

Warner glanced at Paget. "Yes," she said in a tone of suppressed anger. "About two weeks before he died, Mr. Arias called me, sounding very upset. What he shared with me, in confidence, was his fear that Elena had been sexually molested by Mr. Paget's son."

From the side Paget saw several jurors glance at him surreptitiously. But he could not control his look of outrage.

"And what," Salinas asked, "did Mr. Arias tell you?"

"That his wife let Elena spend time with Mr. Paget's son, Carlo. It had bothered him, Richie said, but he hadn't wanted to say something that might damage a teenage boy. Then Elena told Richie that Carlo had given her a bath. And when he questioned her, Richie said, she went into a shell. It frightened him."

Paget saw Caroline begin to rise and then reconsider. She was right, he knew. Objecting would only aggravate the damage.

"Did Mr. Arias tell you what he intended to do?" Salinas asked.

"Yes." Warner's voice became firm. "He intended to tell his wife to keep Elena away from Carlo and Mr. Paget. And if she refused, he was going to court."

"And when he told you this, what was his demeanor?"

"Determined. Confident that he was doing the right thing."

"Did you ever see any signs of despair in Mr. Arias?"

"Never. Except for worrying about Elena, he was a very optimistic man, looking forward to getting on with his future."

Salinas assumed an almost mournful look. "And when, Ms. Warner, did you last see Mr. Arias?"

Warner twisted her bracelet. "The day before his wife left for Italy with Mr. Paget. By then Richie had filed his motion in court. He expressed disappointment that—with all that was at stake for Elena—Ms. Peralta had chosen to leave the country with her boyfriend. We talked for a while, and then he asked if I could meet him the next morning, Saturday, at the Coffee Bean in Noe Valley. To talk more about Elena. I agreed. I live close to there."

"When were you supposed to meet him?"

"Around eleven." Warner's voice became almost wispy. "But Richie never came. I waited for an hour and then left."

Quietly Salinas said, "I have no further questions."

416

CAREFUL, CAROLINE THOUGHT AS she approached Leslie Warner. Right now the jury likes her; too supercilious, and you'll lose them. "You seem quite troubled by Mr. Arias' death," Caroline began.

Warner regarded her with wounded gray eyes. "I am. It's tragic when someone dies so young. Especially someone so full of life."

Caroline tilted her head. "How well did you know Mr. Arias?"

Warner rearranged her flowing skirt. "Fairly well, I think. When you talk to someone at least twice a week for several weeks, you get a sense of who they are. Especially someone as open as Richie."

"Oh? What kind of parent was Ricardo Arias?"

"He was concerned, as I said. We talked about Elena quite a lot."

"Did you ever actually observe the two of them together?"

Warner looked bewildered. "I wasn't in a position to do that."

Caroline made herself look pensive. "Would you say another sign of concern would have been to have Elena evaluated by a psychologist? One who specializes in children."

"Yes. I believe I mentioned that to Mr. Arias."

"Did he happen to mention that Ms. Peralta had asked for that?"

Warner looked surprised. "I don't believe so."

"When you called Ms. Peralta about the playground incident, did you mention your concern that Elena might have suffered sexual abuse?"

"No," Warner said. "Ms. Peralta didn't seem receptive."

"Do you make it a practice to decide to raise child abuse only if a parent seems receptive?"

Warner flushed. "Of course not. But I'd already told the custodial parent. And when I suggested that Elena might be overstimulated by Ms. Peralta's new relationship, she sounded annoyed. So I decided to leave it there."

"And how did you know about Ms. Peralta's 'new relationship'?"

"Because Richie told me."

"And on that basis you made a moral judgment about Ms. Peralta as a mother."

"Elena's problems came from somewhere," Warner snapped.

"Indeed they did. Don't you think that if you'd told Ms. Peralta of your concerns, she might have helped identify where?"

Warner stared at her. "I didn't consider that."

"And yet you did have a series of meetings and conversations with one parent, all supposedly premised on the specter of abuse."

"Many of these contacts were initiated by Mr. Arias."

Caroline nodded. "The custodial parent," she said. "Who, for all *you* know, was the one who had molested Elena."

"Objection," Salinas called out. "That is outrageous, Your Honor. There is no basis for that kind of diversionary slander."

Caroline spun on him. "From the moment you entered this courtroom, Victor, you have been just delighted to slander a teen-age boy so that you can convict his father. But I suppose it's not slander if it's also a career move."

"I resent that—" Salinas began, and the judge's gavel crashed.

"Enough personalities, both of you." He addressed Caroline. "I agree that your question's germane—if rephrased. Press on."

Caroline turned back to Warner. "Did you ever consider that Mr. Arias might have molested his own daughter?"

The teacher gave her a hostile look. "No," she said firmly.

"Is it fair to say that you didn't know anything about Mr. Arias' life—except what he told you?"

"I suppose not."

"Nor do you have any background in psychology."

"I don't."

Caroline paused, skipping a beat. "Or suicide."

Warner looked startled. "No."

"And yet you're convinced that Mr. Arias didn't kill himself."

Warner's mouth set in a stubborn line. "Yes."

Caroline half turned, taking in the jury for the first time. They were surveying Warner with a newly skeptical air. Facing Warner, she said, "You don't like Teresa Peralta, do you?"

Warner blinked. Slowly she answered, "No."

"Is there a specific reason?"

"Yes." Warner's eyes hardened. "Teresa Peralta slapped me."

"What was the occasion?"

"I was at school, in my room." A slight hesitation. "I'd suggested to the police that they question Elena."

"Elena? As in Ms. Peralta's six-year-old daughter?"

"Yes." Warner's voice rose. "Maybe a month before Richie died, Elena told me that she had heard her parents having an argument and that Ms. Peralta had threatened to kill Richie."

"Do you know the context?"

"No. When I told Richie, he said his wife had a bad temper."

"Did you see fit to inform Ms. Peralta that you were setting two homicide inspectors loose on her kindergartner?"

"No."

"For that matter, did you consult the school principal?"

"No."

"Or a psychologist?"

"No."

"Did you consult anyone on how the violent death of a parent might have affected Elena? Or how being questioned about it by the police might affect her?"

"No," said Warner.

"And because you never talked to Ms. Peralta about anything, you were unaware that she'd engaged a psychologist to help Elena."

Warner sat rigid. "I did what I thought was right."

"You always do, don't you? Isn't it true that before she hit you, Ms. Peralta asked if you had any idea of the harm you were doing?"

"She may have said something like that."

"And didn't you say she shouldn't raise her own daughter?"

A slow nod. "I think I did."

"And then she slapped you." Caroline appraised her. "How long after that did you call the police and offer to testify that Mr. Arias wasn't suicidal?"

Warner shrugged. "Sometime thereafter. I'm not sure when."

"Try the next day, Ms. Warner." Caroline gave a sardonic smile. "One more thing. When Ms. Peralta slapped you, did she also call you a fool?"

The insult was so subtle that it took Warner a moment to flush, Salinas to object. There was a snicker from the press.

"That question," Salinas said angrily, "is sheer harassment."

Caroline turned to Salinas. "Please forgive me, Victor," she said in rueful tones. "I was just doing what I thought was right."

FROM the moment he first saw her, there was something about Sonia Arias that Paget found disturbing. It was more than the bright, birdlike look of malice she gave him as she took the stand. For Paget there were too many hints of some inner dislocation: the

419

over-plucked eyebrows; the brightly hennaed hair, at odds with both her age and her sallow skin color; the way she darted looks around the courtroom, an uneasy meld of paranoia and the narcissism of a fashion model striking poses for a camera.

Richie had been scheduled to call his mother on the Saturday after he last was seen. When Salinas asked his first key question, she paused until every eye was on her. "Ricardo," she said, "would never take his own life. He was taken from us. That's why he didn't call me."

Gently Salinas asked, "Why do you say that?"

She gave him a prideful look. "Ricardo was strongly Catholic—from his childhood, *I* saw to that. He knew that suicide was a sin."

"Aside from Richie's religious convictions, are there other aspects of his character that tell you he didn't shoot himself?"

"He never even touched a gun. He was always happy, an optimist, ready to make the best of things. And if he ever needed anything, he knew that I would give it to him."

Salinas, Paget saw, was regarding Sonia warily. "Would you describe Richie's relationship to your granddaughter, Elena?"

"Devoted. Totally in love with the girl, as I was with him."

"Did you and he discuss the effect of his divorce on her?"

"It wasn't *his* divorce," Sonia answered grimly. "I want to make that clear to everyone who's listening." Suddenly she turned and pointed at Paget. "*She* left my son to take up with *this* man. She was always too ambitious to give Richie the support he needed."

All at once Paget felt the anger run through him.

"Did there come a time," Salinas asked, "when Richie told you he believed Elena had been molested by Mr. Paget's son?"

Sonia Arias folded her arms. "Yes. Of course. I can't imagine *what* a parent would have to do to turn his own son into a pervert."

"I've had about enough of this," Paget said to Caroline.

"Easy," she told him quietly, and was on her feet. "Your Honor, I move to strike everything after 'yes.' And I ask this witness, if possible, to distinguish between fact and anger. Whoever may be its subject at the moment."

"Motion granted," Lerner said promptly. "Members of the jury, I am directing you to ignore Mrs. Arias' comments regarding Mr. Paget and his son as speculative and unwarranted."

Looking unhappy, Salinas asked, "What did Richie tell you about the alleged abuse by Carlo Paget?"

"He was disgusted. Worse, Elena's mother had left him no money to get a psychologist to help her own daughter." Sonia gave the jury a proud look. "So *I* sent Ricardo a thousand dollars."

Next to him Paget saw Caroline look puzzled, then make a note.

"To your knowledge," Salinas asked, "did he intend to fight for permanent custody of Elena?"

"To the bitter end—and I was going to help him. Nothing was going to keep Ricardo from having his daughter."

"When did you last speak to Ricardo?"

"That Friday. The last day anyone saw my son alive."

"And what did you talk about?"

"That Elena's mother was going to Italy with her boyfriend. Richie said it was the final proof that he needed to fight for Elena."

Abruptly the atmosphere in the room had changed. The jury leaned forward to listen. "Did you respond to that?" Salinas asked.

"Yes." Sonia looked down. "I told him I'd come from New York to help. But he said he could take care of Elena, and what would really help was if I could send him the money I would have spent on airfare. He had powerful friends now, Richie told me. Other people who could help."

The last two sentences, Paget saw, were unrehearsed. For a second Salinas looked unsettled.

"Colt's people," Caroline whispered to Paget.

Quickly Salinas asked, "Did you talk to Ricardo often?"

Looking directly at the jury, Sonia said, "Every Saturday and Wednesday. Ricardo always called *me*, and he never forgot."

Salinas gave her a melancholy look. "But he didn't call on Saturday, did he? Or ever again."

Sonia looked down again. "No."

WHAT Caroline needed to do, she knew, would not be easy. Rising, she regarded Sonia Arias with a look of puzzlement. "When you said that Teresa didn't support your son, what did you mean?"

Sonia gave her a knowing smile. "I meant emotionally. She never appreciated how special he was—how imaginative, how attractive."

"So you weren't referring to financial support?"

Sonia's face seemed to tighten. "No."

"And in fact, she supported him through five years of marriage."

"Only after he quit the law so he could start his business."

Caroline kept her face bland. "How many jobs did he 'quit'?"

"Three." Sonia looked angry.

"And Teresa also sent him to graduate school for an M.B.A.?"

"She did. Richie wanted to become an entrepreneur."

"And then she gave him money to start his business."

"She may have. But so did I."

"Do you know what happened to the money? Terri's or yours?"

"No." A slight pause. "Richie had some bad luck."

Caroline angled her head. "Before Teresa married him, who supported Richie?"

Sonia Arias hesitated. "We supported him. And let me set the record straight again. I helped them get through the law school years, when Teresa had the baby. By getting a job."

"Did *Richie* ever work?" Caroline asked.

Frowning, the witness said, "I can't remember what jobs he had."

"What about when he lived at home?" Caroline asked casually. "When he was seventeen, didn't Richie have a summer job clerking at a sporting goods store in the Bronx called Bernhard's?"

Salinas half rose to his feet.

"Yes," Sonia said coldly. "I remember that now."

"And didn't Mr. Bernhard call your husband and demand reimbursement because he'd caught Richie skimming cash from the register?"

"Your Honor," Salinas called out, "the prosecution requests a bench conference."

"Of course," Lerner said, and motioned Caroline to the bench.

She and Salinas stood face to face, Lerner peering down at them. "What is this?" Salinas demanded. "Whether Ricardo Arias stole the milk money in fifth grade is completely irrelevant."

Caroline spoke to Lerner directly. "What Victor has been trying to do, right from his opening statement, is to paint Ricardo Arias as the compendium of virtue." She turned on Salinas. "You've asked for this, Victor. *My* Ricardo Arias is a cheat, a liar, unable to hold an honest job, and, quite possibly, a textbook sociopath humbly disguised as a second-rate con man. Not only does that suggest

emotional instability, but people like *my* Richie make other people mad—lots of them." She faced Lerner again. "This is a murder trial, Your Honor, not a memorial service."

Lerner said, "Next time you nominate someone for altar boy, Victor, you may want to screen him first." He looked at Caroline. "I'm going to give you considerable latitude. See that you don't abuse it."

"Thank you, Your Honor."

Turning to face Sonia Arias, Caroline saw a brittle woman, tensely guarding her image of her own son. Quietly she said, "Do you remember the question?"

Sonia Arias sat straighter. "This man Bernhard never caught Richie stealing anything. We paid him five hundred dollars because he threatened to call the police."

"Wasn't there another reason you didn't want trouble? A problem at the Latin School three months earlier? A suspension because Ricardo was accused of stealing a math test from his teacher's desk?"

"So another student said. But *he* was the one who stole the test and then blamed it on Richie." Sonia Arias turned to the jury. "Ricardo was innocent. He was a beautiful, talented boy, and—"

"Did there come a time in college," Caroline cut in quietly, "when Richie moved out of the dorm?"

"Yes." Sonia gave her a wounded look and then frowned. "It was when he decided to live with Teresa."

"Did Richie tell you that the dorm committee had asked him to move out? Because he'd been stealing from people's rooms?"

"No." Sonia gripped her chair. "*She* must have said that."

Caroline went on. "You mentioned that after law school Richie worked for three firms. Did he ever tell you that he'd been fired from two of them? And that one of the firms fired him for misrepresenting his grades?"

"No." Sonia's arms were rigid now, and her eyes darted from place to place. "And it's not true, either. I know my son."

I doubt anyone did, Caroline thought—except perhaps his wife. "Did you know that your son was seeing a therapist?"

"Of course." Sonia smiled. "*She* didn't send him enough money, so *I* helped him pay for it."

Caroline shook her head. "But wasn't all you really knew about Ricardo, from age eighteen to thirty, whatever your son chose to tell you?"

All at once Sonia Arias stood in the witness-box. "Ricardo Arias had a passion for living," she said. "And I was there for him. This young man would never do a selfish thing like kill himself."

Caroline watched the jury, looking at Sonia Arias with a kind of dread and pity. "No further questions," Caroline said softly.

SIXTEEN

O N THE third morning of the trial Victor Salinas called Richie's therapist as a prosecution witness.

Diana Gates was a composed brunette in her early forties, with short, straight black hair and a pleasant snub-nosed face. Her wide-set brown eyes conveyed a certain professional reserve, but the jury could not know how hard Gates had fought against testifying.

From the outset the therapist had refused to speak to either Monk or—once he discovered her existence—Johnny Moore. Her position was clear: Under California law, conversations between therapist and patient are confidential. In Gates' mind the privilege survived Ricardo Arias. This morning, urged by Salinas, Judge Lerner had ruled otherwise. No one knew what Gates would say.

Clearly, Paget thought, Salinas was willing to chance a terrible surprise just to be able to disparage Caroline's suicide theory.

Gates sat with her hands folded as Salinas established her advanced degrees and extensive experience in family therapy. "How long," he then asked her, "did you treat Ricardo Arias?"

"Twice a week for about four months. Until his death."

"When Mr. Arias first came to you, Dr. Gates, did he explain why he wanted therapy?"

Gates paused. "In general, Mr. Arias' concerns related to his daughter, Elena. At first he wondered if I might perform the family evaluation if it came to that. But I was able to persuade him that I might be more helpful in an individual capacity."

There was something, Paget sensed, buried in the bland response. Salinas seemed to hear it as well; the prosecutor hesitated and then skipped to the heart of things. "In the course of seeing Mr. Arias, did you form an opinion as to whether he was prone to suicide?"

The courtroom was completely still. "Nothing I saw gave me reason to consider that Mr. Arias might take his own life."

"Did you have a sense as to whether Mr. Arias was depressed by the breakup of his marriage?"

Gates considered this. "Depressed is not the word I'd use. He was deeply offended that Ms. Peralta had chosen to leave him. He also expressed concern that his daughter had been molested."

"How did Richie react to this concern?"

"By trying to educate himself. Mr. Arias asked me about the signs of molestation. He also asked me to recommend reading on the subject, and when I did, he read everything and discussed it at length."

"He seemed to take the therapy process seriously, then, correct?"

Gates gave Salinas an inscrutable look. "I would say that Mr. Arias was very engaged in what he was trying to accomplish."

"Would you consider these behaviors consistent with suicide?"

"I would not."

"When did you last *see* Mr. Arias?" Salinas asked.

"I believe it was on the Thursday before he died. Our appointments were generally for Monday and Thursday, and before leaving, he confirmed that he'd see me on Monday. I was quite surprised when he didn't show up."

"On that last Thursday, did he seem in a state of despair?"

"Not in my observation. He seemed generally upbeat."

Salinas turned to an easel on which was placed a photographic blowup of a handwritten note. "I am ending my life," the note read, "because I have faced what I am. What I am is selfish and pathetic."

The handwriting itself, irregular and childlike, had a certain haunting quality. Staring at the note, Gates seemed for the first time to be deeply troubled.

"This is a note found near Mr. Arias' body," Salinas told her. "I take it that you don't recognize the handwriting?"

"No. I've never seen Mr. Arias' writing, except on checks."

"But do those words correspond with Mr. Arias' self-image as you perceived it? Or with how he would wish others to see him?"

"I simply can't believe," Gates said, "that the man I saw on Thursday would turn around and write this."

As she slowly rose, Caroline felt tense. Gates had just done Chris Paget grievous harm, but Caroline sensed that something lay beneath the surface of the doctor's answers.

"In meeting with Mr. Arias," Caroline began, "did you explore his family background?"

Gates met her gaze directly. "To some extent."

"For example, did Mr. Arias tell you that his father beat him?"

Gates hesitated. "He said that, yes. During childhood and adolescence. He was quite resentful. He mentioned several times that he himself had never touched Elena in anger."

"But isn't it plain that abusive fathers are quite likely to have been abused as sons?"

Gates nodded. "Yes."

Caroline tilted her head. "Is that also true of sexual abuse?"

This time Gates paused for a split second, locking eyes with Caroline. "Yes. But I heard nothing that suggests the possibility you mention. In fact, his sexual interests seemed exclusively adult."

"Even though Mr. Arias had been abused as a child?"

"*Physically,* not sexually. They're quite different."

Caroline studied her. "You perform family evaluations, do you not? Of the kind sought by Ms. Peralta?"

"Yes," Gates said.

"Was your experience a reason why Mr. Arias sought you out?"

"That's what he told me. He said I could help advise him 'how to make it come out right,' I believe was how he put it."

"Did Mr. Arias explain what he meant by that?"

"What he asked for, Ms. Masters, was a list of positive attributes he should present as a father. As well as what kind of negative factors might cause Ms. Peralta to lose permanent custody."

"Did you describe them to Mr. Arias?"

"Yes. The main ones, in any event. Substance abuse. Child neglect. Violence. And of course, sexual abuse."

"Did you also discuss the evaluation process?" Caroline asked.

"In detail. Particularly after Ms. Peralta began requesting an evaluation in her mediation sessions. Mr. Arias was concerned to understand the process. Including psychological testing."

"Could you describe the nature of the testing?"

Gates gave a short nod. "The principal test is the Princeton

427

Personality Indicator, or PPI. The test subjects answer over five hundred true-false questions designed to reveal specific personality factors in great detail. The PPI is particularly helpful in diagnosing personality disorders."

"Did Mr. Arias ask for advice with respect to the PPI?"

"Yes." Gates' tone was still level. "He wanted to know how to give the right answers. I told him there was no way to help him."

"Do you know why he was so concerned?"

"Mr. Arias said he wanted an edge. But he also mentioned that his wife had told him he wasn't normal. It seemed to upset him."

"Do you know why?"

"No, but he was quite angry with her. I particularly remember a statement he made early on. That he wanted Ms. Peralta to suffer."

Caroline raised her eyebrows. "Mr. Arias seems to have been quite comfortable telling you things."

"He was," Gates said in a dry voice. "Assured that our talks were confidential, he seemed to enjoy sharing the workings of his own mind. Including how he intended to break Terri down."

There was something here, Caroline thought, that she did not quite understand. "Did he discuss Ms. Peralta's personality?"

"Certain aspects of it. For example, Ms. Peralta's father was an abusive alcoholic, and Mr. Arias asked how a child of such a family might react to the pressure of a custody suit. His own observation was that Ms. Peralta was afraid of conflict close to home and that he had doubted she could stick out a custody fight."

"Had she surprised him?"

"To a point." For the first time, Gates glanced at Paget. "He tended to blame that on Mr. Paget. He thought that Mr. Paget had propped up Ms. Peralta, while Carlo, Mr. Paget's son, was trying to displace him with Elena."

A certain calm came over Caroline now. "Do you recall when Mr. Arias first mentioned the possibility of sexual abuse?"

"I believe there was a playground incident. Elena's teacher had called him. That was when he started asking me about it."

"Did he consider it an opportunity to pressure Ms. Peralta?"

"Clearly. And perhaps to get back at Mr. Paget and Carlo for their sins against him, real or perceived. But—and I emphasize this— Mr. Arias didn't invent this concern: *That* originated with Elena's teacher. Nor could he summon Elena's symptoms out of nowhere. So I am not saying that nothing happened to this little girl."

"Did you give Mr. Arias any advice?" Caroline asked.

"Yes. To be very careful with Elena. I thought she might need help. I also suggested that the family court mediator, Alec Keene, would help find an evaluator for her."

"Did Mr. Arias agree?"

"He agreed that Elena should see *someone.* But he was still worried about how he would come out in an evaluation."

In the jury box, Joseph Duarte, Caroline saw, was very still. "Had you," she asked slowly, "formed an opinion as to what the tests would show?"

"My sessions with Mr. Arias," Diane Gates said, "indicated intense self-absorption, a disrespect for social norms, a tendency to project his own faults on other people, a lack of interest in anyone else's feelings or beliefs, a high degree of dishonesty and manipulation, a distrust of other people's motives, and, paradoxically, a tendency to see others strictly in terms of his own needs."

Caroline gazed at her a moment. "That's an impressive cluster of symptoms, Dr. Gates. Does it happen to have a name?"

Gates paused. "Sociopath."

"And did you offer this analysis to Mr. Arias?"

"What I told him," she said softly, "is that psychological testing might damage his case."

Caroline raised an eyebrow. "And how did Mr. Arias react?"

"Predictably, on one level. He said that tests like that were garbage, and he became quite angry with me. He redoubled his efforts to keep the evaluation from ever happening."

"How did he do that, if you know?"

Gates frowned. "By putting his charges about Elena in a legal pleading and filing it in court. At one of our sessions he described how he had served the papers on Ms. Peralta by waiting inside her apartment at night. He also thought the charges against Carlo Paget might drive her and Mr. Paget apart. If Ms. Peralta was alone again, he seemed confident he could break her down."

"Did you respond to any of this?"

"Yes. I implored him not to do it, for Elena's sake, and to let the evaluation take its course. He absolutely refused, of course."

"I take it," Caroline asked gently, "that you reached some conclusions about Mr. Arias' fitness to raise a child?"

"It is very difficult, Ms. Masters, to imagine the circumstances in which I would give Ricardo Arias custody of a child."

As Caroline returned to the table, Paget was buffeted by emotions in conflict. He felt a deep relief for Terri. Her decision to leave Richie—and to fight for Elena—had been vindicated. But Caroline had come no nearer to clearing Carlo. Furthermore, the Ricardo Arias who emerged from Gates' depiction—resourceful and pathologically vindictive—was a man worth killing. Clearly he was also a man who'd harm another person before he'd ever harm himself.

PARKING in front of Rosa Peralta's, Christopher Paget got out, looking around him.

It was close to nine on Friday night, after the first week of his murder trial. Paget had arranged to meet Terri at Rosa's. Oddly, Rosa had requested this, and Paget wondered why she wished to see him now. After all that had happened, this was the first time he would meet Terri's mother or enter the home where Terri had been raised.

It was a modest two-story stucco, neatly maintained, with concrete steps climbing to a covered porch. When the door opened, Paget was speechless. The woman he saw startled him.

"I just found out," Paget said to her finally, "how Terri will look someday. In that, she's lucky."

Rosa gave a slight nod. "Please come in," she said, and Paget stepped into the dimly lit living room. They were alone. "Teresa is upstairs putting Elena to bed," Rosa explained, "and I wanted to see you. Please, sit down."

Paget took a chair across from the sofa, where Rosa sat.

"I'm sorry for what has happened to you," she told him. "That is much of what I wished to say." She gave him a considered look. "You love my daughter very much, I know. For a time I was not sure. And she needed to be away from Ricardo and to get Elena away. I understand that now."

"Was that so hard to understand before?" Paget asked simply.

"I was afraid of what Ricardo would do."

"What Terri did took courage," Paget said. "She broke away from

Richie against your advice and, whether or not you accept this, without my help. If nothing else, the trial has justified her."

Rosa raised her head. "Perhaps. But now she has you."

It was a probe, Paget sensed. "Perhaps. Perhaps not."

Rosa appeared to study his face. "Do you think," she asked, "they will accept that Ricardo killed himself?"

The question surprised him; it could be understood on different levels. "No. In the end, they'll decide whether or not I killed him."

Something in Rosa's face became remote and almost hard. "It shouldn't matter how Ricardo died," she said. "Only that he's dead." In her voice was the tone of absolute dismissal. "Long ago," she added in a quiet voice, "I stopped believing in God. But I still believe that, in some terrible way, there is a balance in life. I know Ricardo's death is part of that. Just as I know that in the end you will survive. And so will your son."

The mention of Carlo startled him. And then he heard Terri's footsteps on the stairs.

As she entered the living room, Paget tried to smile at her. "Your mother just told me I'll be acquitted."

Rosa shook her head. "No. I said you will be absolved."

Terri gave Paget a veiled look, then turned to her mother. "We'd better go, Mom."

She bent over the sofa, kissing her mother. In profile, Paget could see how alike they were and how they might yet become different. At forty-nine there might still be light in Terri's face.

Leaving with Terri, Paget was aware of Rosa Peralta watching until she gently shut the door behind them.

SEVENTEEN

"How did it come about," Salinas asked Charles Monk, "that you first went to Ricardo Arias' apartment?"

The inspector sat in the witness stand wearing his trademark gold glasses and a crisp gray pin-striped suit that looked tailored for a football player. He looked around the courtroom. "I was contacted by a uniformed policeman on the scene," he told Salinas. "Mr. Arias' mother-in-law had called in. He hadn't been seen for a week or so, and she asked if we'd perform a well-being check. When

431

no one answered, they broke in the door and found Mr. Arias."

"When you arrived, what did you observe?"

"The body, of course. Near Mr. Arias' hand was a Smith and Wesson .32 safety revolver. On inspection we found that one of the rounds had misfired and that the bullet that killed Mr. Arias was the second attempt at firing."

"Did you observe anything else?" Salinas asked.

"Yes. The dead man had been shot through the mouth, and there was a note on Mr. Arias' desk, next to a picture of a little girl who turned out to be his daughter." Monk looked briefly at Paget. "In addition, someone had turned off Mr. Arias' answering machine."

"After you made these observations, what did you do?"

"We searched the apartment. To start, there was no sign of forced entry. That could have meant suicide, but it could also mean that Mr. Arias had been killed by someone he let into the apartment. Then we started finding things that didn't add up." Monk paused. "Someone had set the automatic coffeemaker to brew some coffee that Mr. Arias never got to drink. And in his computer we found a calendar showing appointments for after anyone had seen him and, as we'd calculated from the pile of mail and newspapers, after he'd been shot. Then there was nothing tying Mr. Arias to the gun—no permit, no record of purchase, nothing. Of course, it could have been a robbery. But Mr. Arias still had his watch and his wallet, with cash and credit cards inside. Also, in a gym bag in the bedroom closet we found ten thousand dollars. Cash."

Caroline looked up from her notes. "Colt," Paget whispered. "They must have paid Richie off in cash." Caroline nodded.

"So Mr. Arias was not financially desperate," Salinas said.

"Sure didn't look like that," Monk said coolly. "We also found a bank passbook showing another ten thousand or so."

"And when did you first speak to Mr. Paget?"

The prosecutor, Paget realized, had quickly changed the subject. "Victor knows something," he said to Caroline under his breath.

"Three days later," Monk was answering. "At his home, after he and Teresa Peralta flew back from Italy. She was there too."

"And what did Mr. Paget tell you?" Salinas asked Monk.

"Then? Only a few things. I asked Mr. Paget whether he'd been home that Friday night. I understood him to say yes. But when I

432

replayed the tape, I realized he hadn't said a thing. Just nodded."

"What did you do about that?"

"Nothing at first. Just started going over the papers we found in Mr. Arias' apartment." Monk adjusted his glasses. "I found a clipping from a tabloid, the *Inquisitor,* where Mr. Arias accused Mr. Paget of breaking up his marriage. So I started in on the papers from Mr. Arias' divorce. The last papers filed in the case were marked confidential. It was a motion by Mr. Arias to keep his daughter, Elena, from seeing Mr. Paget or his son. Mr. Arias' own affidavit accused Carlo Paget of sexually molesting Elena Arias."

"Did you then go back to Mr. Paget?"

"Yes."

"After you spoke to him," Salinas asked, "what did you do next?"

Monk glanced at Paget again. "We interviewed a neighbor, Georgina Keller, who lived down the hall from Mr. Arias."

"And what did Mrs. Keller tell you?"

"That she thought she heard angry voices coming from Mr. Arias' apartment that Friday night. Two men, and then a thud. Like someone hitting the floor. She opened her door a crack and looked out."

Salinas nodded. "What did she report seeing?"

"A tall blond-haired man in a light gray suit leaving the apartment. He was about six feet, with blondish hair, a strong jaw, and a slight ridge on his nose."

Paget felt the jury turn to him, matching him to the description.

"And did you then show her a photograph?"

"Yes." Monk paused a moment. "Of Mr. Paget."

"What, if anything, did Mrs. Keller say?"

"That this was the man she had seen in the hallway."

"And what did you do next?" Salinas asked.

"Detective Lynch and I obtained a warrant to search Mr. Paget's house and impound his car. According to the crime lab, there were fibers from Mr. Arias' carpet on the Persian rug in Mr. Paget's entryway, the runner up his central stairs, and the Chinese carpet in his bedroom."

"What about in Mr. Paget's Jaguar convertible?"

"More fibers," Monk said. "On the driver's side."

Salinas looked eager. "Did you then take Mr. Paget's fingerprints and attempt to match them with prints you found?"

433

"Yes. Mr. Paget had left a full right-hand print on Mr. Arias' answering machine. The one someone had switched off."

There was utter silence. "Perhaps," Salinas said softly, "we should play the tape of your second interview with Mr. Paget."

Paget braced himself as Salinas produced a black tape player. For Paget the next few minutes were a kind of death.

As if in slow motion Monk switched on the tape machine.

Listening, Paget could remember his tautness as he answered Monk's questions. That he had never spoken to Ricardo Arias. That he had never even seen Ricardo Arias. That he had never been to Ricardo Arias' apartment. And that on the night before leaving for Italy, he had been at home alone.

The jury leaned forward, looking from the tape to Paget's face. To Paget, his answers—terse and measured—sounded like lies.

CROSS-EXAMINATION started after the lunch break, with Caroline's opening question. "You mentioned, Inspector Monk, that you'd tried to trace the Smith and Wesson revolver to Mr. Arias. Did you also try tracing it to Mr. Paget?"

Monk nodded and folded his hands. "We did. We found no evidence that Mr. Paget has ever owned a gun."

Caroline looked bemused. "Did you happen to check this murder weapon for Mr. Paget's fingerprints?"

"Yes, Counselor. We didn't find Mr. Paget's prints. *Or* Arias'."

"Then let's move on. When you searched Mr. Paget's home, isn't it true that you searched Mr. Paget's closet? For clothing with blood spatters or gunshot residue?"

"Among other things."

"Come up with anything—like rug fibers on Mr. Paget's shoes?"

Monk was quiet for a moment. "No."

Caroline put one finger to her lips, as if the truth were dawning. "So let's summarize your evidence against Mr. Paget. After all that effort it comes down to rug fibers in his house and car, an eyewitness who saw a tall blond man, and prints on Mr. Arias' machine."

Monk gave her a pointed stare. "He also had a powerful motive."

"To dislike Mr. Arias, surely. But so did Ms. Peralta. Did you consider Ms. Peralta as a potential suspect?"

"For a time, yes."

"And did you also search her home?"

"Yes."

"And found rug fibers there, the same as at Mr. Paget's?"

"Yes."

"So you didn't pick him over her because of rug fibers."

"No."

"And in fact, you removed a suit from Ms. Peralta's closet because it had stains on the front. What did the stains turn out to be?"

A small smile. "Ketchup."

"So at that point your case as to Mr. Paget was the same as against Ms. Peralta. Motive and fibers."

"One big difference, Counselor. Ms. Peralta admitted that she was at Mr. Arias' apartment a lot. Mr. Paget denied being there."

Paget could feel the damage even before he saw Joseph Duarte's silent nod. But Caroline looked quite calm. "And that was why Mr. Paget's prints on the answering machine so troubled you?"

The question startled Paget. Abruptly Caroline had moved to the most damaging piece of evidence—Paget's fingerprints.

Monk regarded her with an air of interest. "Yes," he answered.

"Could you identify any *other* prints on that machine?"

Monk nodded. "Mr. Arias' and Ms. Peralta's."

"Why didn't Ms. Peralta's prints disturb you?"

"Because she had reason to visit the apartment a lot."

Caroline smiled. "Do you happen to know the history of this answering machine? Had it always belonged to Mr. Arias?"

Monk shrugged. "It was in his apartment."

"Did you happen to find Mr. Paget's prints anywhere else?"

"No."

Caroline's voice became very soft. "Tell me, Inspector Monk, when did you first discuss this case with the district attorney? Not Mr. Salinas, but the D.A. himself. McKinley Brooks."

Salinas was on his feet. "Objection. Law enforcement is the D.A.'s *job*. What Mr. Brooks may have discussed with Inspector Monk or any law-enforcement officer is irrelevant."

"Hardly," Caroline said to Judge Lerner. "We think that Mr. Brooks has everything to do with the case against Mr. Paget and, perhaps, with why there is a case at all. Justice will be blind, Your Honor, the day that district attorneys stop being politicians."

Salinas assumed an indignant look. "That," he said, "is an unwarranted assault on the integrity of District Attorney Brooks."

Lerner gazed at the courtroom clock. "I'll permit this," he told Caroline. "But if all you end up doing is making accusations in the form of questions, I'll cut it off."

Caroline turned to Monk again. "When *was* the first time you spoke to McKinley Brooks?" she asked.

"Two days after we found Mr. Arias."

"And how did that conversation come about?"

"The D.A. called me."

"Please describe the substance of that discussion."

Monk gazed at the floor, choosing his words. "District Attorney Brooks wanted to let me know that the case should be handled carefully. He believed this case had political implications."

"Which were?" Caroline asked.

"That it involved Mr. Paget."

She looked surprised. "How could Mr. Brooks know that?"

"Somehow the D.A. was aware that Mr. Paget was involved with Mr. Arias' estranged wife."

"How did he know that Mr. Arias had died?"

"I don't know."

Caroline's expression became curious. "During Mr. Brooks' tenure in office, how many homicides have you investigated?"

"Around a hundred. Give or take a few."

"And on how many have you worked directly with Mr. Brooks?"

After a moment's thought Monk answered, "Two. The high-rise massacre a couple of years back, where a gunman killed six people." Monk paused. "The second was the Carelli case."

"That involved Mary Carelli, right? The TV journalist accused of murdering the novelist Mark Ransom?"

"That's the case."

"And what was the result?"

Monk gave Caroline a droll look. "The D.A. lost."

"And who defended Ms. Carelli?"

Monk folded his arms. "Mr. Paget. And Ms. Peralta."

Caroline smiled. "And just for the record, who was the judge?"

"You were."

Caroline nodded. "In this initial conversation with the district attorney, Inspector, did Mr. Brooks ever mention the Carelli case?"

Monk nodded in turn. "He did."

"And what," Caroline asked, "was the context?"

"That anything involving Mr. Paget was sensitive—that people might be watching us for bias. He wanted me to report to him directly, even though Mr. Salinas was assigned to the case."

"Was this unusual?"

Monk seemed to consider the word. "It wasn't *usual*."

"Was there any other reason that the case was sensitive?"

"Mr. Brooks mentioned that Mr. Paget might be running for the United States Senate."

"In that conversation did you discuss the specifics of the case?"

"I reviewed what we had found in Mr. Arias' apartment. Brooks was interested in the ten thousand dollars we found in a closet."

Now Paget saw where this was going; it was hard not to smile.

"What did you tell the D.A.?" Caroline asked.

"That I wanted to know where the money came from."

"And how did Mr. Brooks respond?"

"He told me to check Mr. Paget's and Ms. Peralta's bank records and then get back to him." Monk's voice was flat now. "We couldn't trace the cash to either one of them."

"Did you so inform District Attorney Brooks?" Caroline asked.

"Yes. He didn't think the cash was relevant."

"Did he give you any specific instructions?"

Monk's eyes met Caroline's. "To drop trying to trace the money."

"I see." Caroline donned an almost innocent expression. "Tell me, in your experience, Inspector, are large amounts of money in cash often associated with criminal activities?"

It was all Paget could do not to laugh. The money was surely Colt's, Salinas could say nothing, and Caroline was about to kill him with it. Salinas, Monk, Paget, and Caroline all knew that; only the jury was in the dark.

"Large amounts of cash are often associated with activities that people don't want anyone else to discover," Monk said solemnly.

"Is drug dealing among those activities?"

"That's maybe the most common."

The jury, Paget saw, seemed enthralled. At the prosecution table Salinas stared at the wall, as if willing himself to stay calm.

"And did you," Caroline asked, "happen to inquire into whether Mr. Arias was dealing drugs?"

"No," Monk said evenly.

"And in your experience is drug dealing frequently associated with violence and weapons?"

"Sometimes."

"Do these weapons tend to be registered?"

"No. People who ignore drug laws don't make a habit of obeying the gun laws. It might start a bad precedent."

Caroline paused. "Did you consider the possibility that Mr. Arias was killed in a drug-related incident?"

"I had no reason to suspect he was a drug dealer, Counselor."

"Other than the cash?"

Monk shifted in his chair. "I couldn't explain it, that's all."

"You didn't happen to show your eyewitness—Mrs. Keller—photos of any drug dealers, did you?" Caroline asked smoothly.

"No."

"Did you show her *any* pictures—other than Mr. Paget's?"

Monk fixed Caroline with a level gaze. "No."

"Is that your usual practice?"

"It is not."

"Then why, Inspector, this exception for Mr. Paget?"

"Mr. Brooks wanted an ID immediately. To see if we could rule Mr. Paget in or out. We also had a lineup."

"Indeed you did. And where, Inspector Monk, did you find the *other* five members of Mr. Paget's lineup?"

"Mr. Paget found them. In the county jail."

Caroline raised an eyebrow. "Besides Mr. Paget, how many members of the lineup were Caucasian?"

Monk scowled. "One."

Caroline put her hands on her hips. "And whose idea was it to have Mr. Paget choose among prisoners?"

Monk stared at her fixedly. "The district attorney's."

Caroline's slow nod seemed a gesture of respect. "Thank you, Inspector. I have no further questions. At least about *your* role."

She walked slowly back to the defense table.

And then Salinas was up. He quickly established that Brooks had never told Monk to go after Christopher Paget, and that the evidence against Paget was gathered by the police and the medical examiner without interference. But in the end, Paget thought, the jury would remember two conflicting strands: Paget's fingerprints on the answering machine, and the suspicion that, for reasons of politics and spite, McKinley Brooks had kept the inquiry focused on Paget.

EIGHTEEN

WHEN Terri took the witness stand, she turned to Chris Paget and smiled.

It was a good smile, filled with confidence in the man at whom she gazed. But the smile was for the jury. Like Caroline and Paget himself, Terri had become an actress. She had taken care with her appearance. Gone was the severe look of the young professional; today Terri wore gold earrings, and her black dress was simple and soft. The effect was to make her prettiness and youth more obvious, her poise less so. Paget was quite certain that she had discussed all this with Caroline. But only he, Paget was confident, knew that Terri's folded hands were a sign of nerves.

Salinas began. "How long, Ms. Peralta, did you know Mr. Arias?"

Terri's voice was quiet but clear. "Nine years."

"And during all those years did Mr. Arias ever discuss suicide?"

"No."

"Did you ever see or hear anything that, in your mind, raised the concern that Mr. Arias might take his own life?"

Terri seemed to consider this. "That's hard to say. I came to believe that my former husband was emotionally unstable. I'm not sure I wanted to think about everywhere that might lead."

"Did you speak to him the night before you left for Italy?"

"Yes."

"For what reason?"

"I wanted to see him. To beg him to let me raise Elena. I was scared for her."

"And how did he respond?"

"That he had an appointment and couldn't see me."

"Did he sound depressed or discouraged?"

"No," Terri said. "But as I understand you've developed in this trial,

Richie hid things—from everyone. He was emotionally disturbed."

"She's doing well," Paget whispered to Caroline.

"Did you believe," Salinas asked Terri, "that Mr. Arias was emotionally disturbed at the time you lived with him?"

Terri regarded him calmly. "Only at the end, when I knew I should try to get Elena away from him."

"You're familiar with the contents of the note that was found with the body," Salinas said abruptly. "Did you ever hear Richie describe himself as selfish and pathetic?"

Terri shook her head. "No."

"And he certainly didn't on the night you last spoke to him."

"That's correct."

"You also had plans to dine with Mr. Paget, true?"

"Yes. But Chris called to say that he was sick."

"How did Mr. Paget seem the next morning?" Salinas asked.

"Tired. But all right."

"And between seeing him that morning and his phone call the night before, you don't really know where Mr. Paget was, do you?"

Terri looked nettled. "I know what he told me."

"But you have no firsthand knowledge, do you?"

"No," Terri said.

"When you went to Italy, did you try to contact Richie?"

"Yes. For two or three days. No one answered. I thought he was avoiding me. It was the kind of thing he would do."

"Did you call the school?" Salinas asked.

"No. I called my mother and found out that Richie had never picked up Elena from her house on Sunday night."

"Did you also tell your mother not to call the police?"

"Yes." Terri's voice was level. "Elena was happy with my mother, and Richie and I were in a custody fight. I didn't want to make him seem more responsible than he was."

For the first time, Salinas looked openly disbelieving. "Had Mr. Arias ever failed to pick up Elena?"

"No."

The prosecutor's tone sharpened. "Didn't Mr. Paget ask you not to find Mr. Arias? Isn't that what happened?"

Yes, Paget answered silently.

"I don't remember that," Terri said. "It was my decision."

"Your decision," Salinas repeated. "Because you were afraid that your lover had murdered your husband."

Silence. "No," Terri said tightly. "I've never thought that."

Salinas changed subjects. "How long have you known Mr. Paget?"

"A year and a half," Terri said softly.

"And when did you become romantically involved with him?"

"A year ago, almost. After I left Richie."

"How long after? 'A year ago' is cutting it pretty close."

Terri gave him a cool look. "Three weeks after, I would say. I can date it from the day I lost interim custody."

"So within three weeks you left your husband, lost custody of your daughter, and commenced an affair with your boss."

Terri stared at him. "You have a knack, Mr. Salinas, for making the most painful things in my life sound cheap. The only thing you've got right is the chronology."

"How did that happen, then—your involvement with Mr. Paget? Did you just happen to fall into bed one night?"

"No. It wasn't like that."

"It also wasn't like he'd never touched you before."

"Do something," Paget whispered to Caroline.

"I can't," Caroline said. "I refuse to make this worse for you."

"No," Terri said to Salinas quietly. "Chris had touched me."

"And when did *that* first happen?"

Terri sat back. "A few days after I left Richie."

"Getting closer, aren't we? Isn't it a fact, Ms. Peralta, that you were sleeping with Mr. Paget *before* you left Ricardo Arias?"

"No," Terri answered firmly. "I thought the feeling I had for Chris was only *mine*, and I didn't even know *that* much until after I left Richie." She glanced at Paget. "Then I told Chris that I cared for him—and saw that it had happened to us both."

"Isn't it true that Mr. Arias accused you and Mr. Paget of having an affair?" Salinas asked.

"Yes," Terri answered simply. "Just as he accused Carlo Paget of molesting our daughter."

Salinas stopped for a moment. Paget could see the jury consider anew that Ricardo Arias might be a liar. And then Salinas was back again, holding a scrap of paper in the air. "In fact, Ms. Peralta, didn't Mr. Arias accuse you and Mr. Paget—in the *Inquisitor?*"

"Yes." Her voice filled with disgust. "For ten thousand dollars."

"And was it one of the reasons Mr. Paget changed his plans to run for Senator?"

"No. If you're trying to suggest that politics drove Chris to murder, you don't understand him at all."

Salinas looked annoyed but kept boring in. "What about the hearing on Richie's motion?" he snapped. "He'd filed papers under seal, charging Carlo Paget with molesting Elena. And Christopher Paget with taking you away."

"Yes."

"In fact, Mr. Arias told you that unless you gave up Elena, it was going to a hearing. At which time all these charges would become public."

Terri looked steadily back at Salinas. "They would, yes."

"Did you discuss with Mr. Paget the possibility that his career in politics would end?"

"Chris thought that it might. That wasn't as important to him as the people in his life."

"Speaking of the people in his life," Salinas said, "Mr. Paget was also aware that the court might order you to keep Elena from Mr. Paget and his son. Did that damage your relationship?"

Terri started to say something, then stopped. "It was hard."

"So hard that you talked about breaking up?"

Terri's shoulders drew in. "Yes."

"Who initiated that discussion?"

"I did." She turned to look at Paget. "I love Chris. I didn't want him to go through all that because of me. And now he is." Turning from him, Terri saw the faces of the jury looking back at her with doubt and sympathy. "It was Chris who changed my mind," she told them, "in Italy. He told me that he loved me and that our future together was worth whatever he'd go through—"

"This was in Portofino," Salinas interrupted. "Eight days after you last spoke to Mr. Arias. Eight days after, according to the medical examiner, someone had murdered Ricardo Arias."

"You don't understand. Chris believed Richie was alive."

"Wasn't the purpose of your trip to Italy to decide the fate of your relationship?"

"Possibly. Yes."

"And as of the night before you left, you and Mr. Paget didn't know whether you would stay together?"

With piercing sadness Terri remembered. "No, we didn't."

"And then, eight days later, Mr. Paget proposed marriage."

"Yes."

Salinas smiled a little. "To your knowledge, had anything happened to make life better for you?"

"Yes. Chris and I had talked things through."

"But then, later that same day, you found that your husband was dead. And suddenly you had custody of Elena, *and* you were free of Richie, *and* Mr. Paget's career was still viable, *and* Carlo Paget was off the hook, *and* Richie's charges were sealed away. All true?"

"Yes. But not the way we wanted."

"No? Tell me, Ms. Peralta, how did Mr. Paget react to the news of your husband's death?"

Terri could feel Chris watching her. In a calm voice she answered, "He was shocked and appalled."

Salinas smiled. "Has Mr. Paget discussed with you whether he went to Mr. Arias' apartment?"

He's setting up the fingerprints, Terri thought. "Yes."

"And what did he tell you?"

"That he had never been there."

"You intend to testify for the defense, do you not, that Mr. Paget is a truthful person?"

"Yes, I do."

Salinas looked almost pleased. "And if you were to learn that he *had* been to Richie's apartment and lied to you, would that affect your belief as to Mr. Paget's honesty?"

"That's hypothetical," she said. "Chris would never lie to me."

Salinas' smile became cynical. "Of course. He's far too honest." In a dismissive voice he said, "No further questions."

TERRI saw Caroline Masters smile as she rose.

Caroline stood by Chris as if to draw the jury's eyes to him. "Ms. Peralta, I take it that you've had occasions to see Chris as a father."

Terri nodded. "Many times. It was one of the first things that drew me to him. Chris is a great dad, patient and kind. Carlo is the center of his life—the person he loves most in all the world."

"And how did Chris react to Richie's charge against Carlo?"

"He was filled with contempt. But Chris's ultimate feeling was that a measure of Carlo's courage was how well he faced it."

Caroline nodded. "Did you have any sense that Richie's charges would drive Chris Paget to violence?"

"I can't imagine it. There's no way that Richie drove him to murder. He intended to use the legal process to vindicate his son."

For the first time, Caroline moved forward. "When you were in Italy and worried about your future together, did Chris seem like a man who knew Ricardo Arias was dead?"

"No." Terri looked straight at Joseph Duarte. "I know Chris, and he's not that good an actor. For Chris, Richie was still alive."

"And during those eight days in Italy, from the morning he picked you up until the afternoon you learned that Mr. Arias had died, did you observe *any* sign that Chris Paget had been in a struggle?"

"No," Terri said flatly.

"Did you ever know Chris Paget to own a gun?"

Terri shook her head. "Chris despised guns. That was a lot of why he was running for the Senate—to stop the flow of guns."

"And how do you feel about Chris Paget now?"

When Terri turned, there was a shadow on Chris's face. She looked directly at Caroline Masters. "I love him. But I'm testifying about the reasons that I love him, not testifying *because* I love him. There's a difference." She finished quietly, "Because I could never love a man I believed to be a murderer. That's what I regret most. That by loving Chris, I brought these troubles to his door."

"Including rug fibers?" Caroline asked softly.

"Yes. Including rug fibers."

At the prosecution table Victor Salinas had suddenly tensed.

"Is it your belief," Caroline was asking, "that you tracked fibers from Richie's carpet into Chris's bedroom?"

"Yes. That was where we stayed together."

Caroline moved still closer. "The police also found carpet fibers on the driver's side of Chris's car. Can you explain that?"

"Yes. I'd never driven a Jaguar before, so Chris let me drive his several times. Including after visiting Richie."

"And did Chris also visit your apartment?"

"Chris came to my apartment quite a lot," Terri answered.

As if to bewilder Salinas, Caroline switched subjects abruptly. "Did Mr. Arias have an answering machine?"

"Yes."

"To your knowledge, how long had Mr. Arias used it?"

"This particular machine? About two months."

"And where did Mr. Arias acquire this machine?"

"From me. I gave it to him when I got a new one."

Salinas, Terri saw with satisfaction, looked as if he had been shot.

Caroline spoke in the same quiet voice. "And do you know, Ms. Peralta, how Mr. Paget's fingerprints came to be on that machine?"

"Yes," Terri said. "I'm sure that Chris touched the machine while it was still in my apartment. As I said, he was there all the time."

Was that even possible? Paget wondered. It had stunned him.

Terri stared straight ahead as the prosecutor walked toward her.

"You *knew*," Paget whispered to Caroline.

She gave him a sideways look. "Is anything wrong?"

NINETEEN

THE next morning Carlo took the stand.

He wore a white shirt, a blue blazer, and one of his father's floral ties. Taking the oath, he smiled uncomfortably at Paget.

Salinas asked him abruptly, "Do you know Elena Arias?"

"She's Terri's daughter." Carlo paused and then added, "She used to bring her to our house."

It had started. Victor Salinas would try to legitimize Richie's "concerns," Paget knew, while making the possibility of molestation real enough to be Paget's motive. All that Paget could hope for was that Caroline had prepared Carlo well.

"And were you ever alone with Elena?"

"Hardly ever. My dad would be there, and Terri." His voice became stronger. "Sometimes my girlfriend too."

"But you *were* alone with her," Salinas prodded.

Carlo squared his shoulders. "Only a few times. Three or four."

"Did Elena ever kiss you?"

"Sure. Little kids do that stuff."

Quietly Salinas asked, "Did you ever see Elena naked?"

445

Carlo's eyelids dropped. To Paget his son looked like someone who had received a blow to the stomach. In the jury box, Joseph Duarte—the father of two girls—watched with taut vigilance. "Once," Carlo said. "She asked me to give her a bath."

"Did you touch her?" Salinas demanded.

"Only with a washcloth," Carlo said. "And maybe to help her into my dad's bathtub."

"Who undressed her?"

"*She* did."

"Did you watch?"

"*No,*" Carlo said angrily. "She undressed before I got there."

"Did you touch her private parts, Carlo?"

Paget had to keep himself from standing.

"No," Carlo answered. "You can ask me that a thousand times, and the answer will always be the same. I didn't touch that kid in any way that was bad."

"So if Elena told her father you did, she was lying?"

"Objection." Caroline sprang out of her chair, turning on Salinas with a look of disgust. "There is no evidence, *anywhere,* that Elena ever said that. Not even Mr. Arias made such a claim. Frankly, Mr. Salinas, the biggest perversion I've heard so far is your effort to smear a teenage boy so that you can convict his dad of murder."

"That's offensive—"

"Really. Then show it to me, Victor. Show me where there's any basis for the question you just asked."

Lerner's gavel cracked. "That's enough." The judge turned to Salinas. "What's the basis for your question, Counselor?"

Salinas hesitated. Then he said calmly, "None, Your Honor."

Caroline said, "I'd like an apology, Victor. To Carlo Paget."

Watching, Paget felt his own outrage ease; Caroline was making Salinas pay.

"I'll decide who I apologize to," Salinas told her, "and for what. It's certainly not clear *what* this witness did."

But Joseph Duarte, Paget saw, was frowning at Salinas.

"Let's move on," Lerner snapped. "Objection sustained. And underlined."

Salinas turned to Carlo. "Did there come a time when Mr. Arias filed papers charging you with molesting Elena?"

"Yes. He left a copy on my dad's doorstep."

"Did you discuss this with your father?"

"Yes. Dad said we should stand up to him."

Salinas gave a skeptical smile. "But how did you feel? Did you want to go to court?"

"No. I don't think you'd like being charged with molesting a six-year-old, either." Carlo turned to the jury, his expression wounded. "But I was ready to say then, just like I'm telling you now, that Richie was a liar. I didn't need anyone to say that for me, and I didn't need anyone to kill him, either. All I need is my father back."

"Move to strike as unresponsive," Salinas snapped.

Caroline said, "And I move to strike that motion as pathetic."

"Motion denied," Judge Lerner cut in. "Spare us the critiques, Ms. Masters. As for you, Mr. Salinas, perhaps you would have been better off apologizing."

With that, Paget thought, Salinas' punishment was complete.

The prosecutor shifted subjects. "Let's discuss the night before your father went to Italy. You went out around seven thirty. Did you tell your dad where you were going?"

Carlo nodded. "Out with friends."

"Does he make it a practice to tell you if *he's* going out?"

"Yes. Pretty much."

"And what did he say on that night?"

"I think he was going out with Terri."

"Did he seem ill?"

Paget felt himself tense. "I really don't remember," Carlo said.

Salinas seemed to give the boy a second look. "Did you tell your dad when you'd be home?"

"Twelve thirty." Carlo's tone turned flat. "I have a curfew."

"And did you return home at twelve thirty?"

"Yes."

"And was your father home then?"

"Yes. He waited up for me. He does that a lot."

"And did he seem sick?"

Carlo hesitated. "I couldn't tell. It was dark."

"Do you remember what he was wearing?"

"Jeans and a sweater, I think."

447

"What about when you left at seven thirty. Was he wearing a suit then?"

Paget tensed again. "I think so," Carlo said.

"Do you remember what color?"

"No."

"Between the hours of seven thirty and twelve thirty," Salinas asked abruptly, "did you return home unexpectedly?"

The jury, Paget realized, had leaned forward. But Carlo's voice was firm now. "Yes, I did. About eight thirty. A bunch of us were at a friend's house. We decided to go to a movie, and I realized I'd left my wallet at home. So I decided to go home and get it."

"Did you see your father?" Salinas asked.

"Physically see him? No."

"Where did you find your wallet?"

"In my bedroom."

"To get to your room, you walk up a central staircase, right?"

"That's right," Carlo said.

"And going to the staircase, you pass the living room and library."

"Yes."

"Was anyone there?"

Carlo folded his arms. "Not that I saw."

"Your father's bedroom is next to yours. Did you hear anything?"

"I don't think so. I was hurrying."

"So at the point you climbed the stairs to your bedroom, you thought no one was home."

Caroline was watching Carlo with new intensity, Paget realized.

"I guess that's what I thought then," Carlo answered finally.

He was tense, Paget saw, hoping to give a helpful answer. "Salinas is going to sandbag him," he whispered to Caroline.

"As far as you were concerned," Salinas said, "no one was home."

"That's not true." Carlo's voice rose in anger. "I told the police I thought I heard a sound. And now that I know my dad was home, I'm sure the sound was him."

Salinas gave a too agreeable nod. "You told Inspector Monk that you thought perhaps you'd heard footsteps, right?"

"I'm sure I did."

"You're sure now?"

"Yes."

"Tell me, Carlo, about how long after that night did you give your statement to the police?"

"I don't know. Maybe three weeks."

Salinas walked back to the prosecution table. "And now it's about four months after that night, correct?"

Next to Paget, Caroline seemed to have stopped breathing.

"I guess that's right," Carlo said, and leaned forward. "That's a long time to think about you accusing my dad of murder. It makes remembering things more important. So I've replayed that night in my mind over and over. I remember walking up the stairs, finding my wallet, and then hearing footsteps in the attic, where Dad and I keep our suitcases. I've thought about it, and now I'm sure."

Listening, Paget felt almost sick. And then, as if he could not help himself, Carlo looked to his father for approval.

"Did you ever tell that to the police?" Salinas was asking.

Carlo's eyes flickered, and then he turned to Salinas. "No," he said. "The police never came back."

"Did you tell anyone?"

Carlo met Salinas' stare. "No," Carlo said.

"Not even your dad?"

"He won't talk to me about the case. Because I'm a witness."

"In other words, you just decided to save it for the trial."

Carlo stared. "You asked me, and I just answered. It's the truth."

Paget felt cold inside.

"Then you must have considered calling the police," Salinas said.

Carlo looked puzzled. "I don't understand."

"You thought your father was with Ms. Peralta, right?"

Carlo blinked. "That's what I *thought.*"

"So weren't you concerned about a prowler?"

"I don't remember what I thought exactly. I was in a hurry."

"Did you happen to mention it to your dad," Salinas asked in a pleasant voice, "the next time you did see him?"

Carlo seemed confused now. "I don't think so."

"I don't think so, either. Because you made it up, didn't you?"

"No," Carlo said, "I'm not making it up."

"No? When you came home at twelve thirty, did your dad tell you he'd gotten sick and stayed home?"

"I don't remember."

"Or did he simply tell you to come to court and lie for him?"

"No," Carlo said angrily. "My dad would *never* ask me to lie."

Salinas shook his head in disbelief. "No further questions."

Quickly Caroline was on her feet, moving toward Carlo with an air of confidence. "What kind of father *is* your dad?"

Carlo took a deep breath, as if to relax himself. "A great dad."

"Why has Chris been a good father, Carlo?"

"He's always been there." Carlo's voice grew husky and a little raw. "I always knew how important I was to him."

Caroline looked at Carlo gravely. "Based on all you've been through together, can you imagine your dad doing *anything* to jeopardize that?"

Carlo stared straight at Caroline. "No," he said. "I can't imagine it."

WATCHING Elena Arias play with a cloth doll she had named "Teresa," Dr. Denise Harris pondered the black dog of Elena's nightmare.

Elena had never described her dream, but she had wakened screaming the night before, telling Terri for the first time of a black dog that always frightened her. Harris guessed that Elena's repeated nightmare, like Terri's own, was the key to some buried trauma.

Now Elena sat on the rug as the late afternoon sun filtered through the window. Her mother sat outside in the waiting area reading summaries of trial testimony.

"Teresa's tired," Elena said of her doll. "She wants to lie down."

She laid the doll on its back and then turned it over, face buried in the rug. Almost to herself she said, "The robbers are outside."

Leaning closer from her seat a few feet away, Harris said, "Maybe she'd like the alligator to sleep in her room."

Elena was silent; it had taken two sessions with Dr. Harris for her to accept the presence of a plastic alligator as a protective figure, and the concept still frightened her. Harris placed the alligator close to the doll. "Teresa will be safe now."

Elena's brow furrowed. She rolled the doll on its back again and smoothed its red cloth dress. Darting a glance at Harris, she said, "Teresa's sleeping." Slowly Elena lifted the skirt up above the doll's waist. She stroked the doll's cloth stomach with two fingers.

Harris asked softly, "What's happening?"

"The robber is tickling Teresa's tummy."

Elena's fingers moved slowly downward.

Harris watched. "How does Teresa feel?" she asked.

"It feels good." Elena's voice became harder. "Sometimes she likes it. But sometimes she doesn't."

"Is there something the robber does that Teresa doesn't like?"

Elena stiffened. With an awful fascination Harris watched her slide one finger between the cloth legs of the doll.

"How does Teresa feel?" Harris asked quietly.

Elena's eyes filled with tears.

Gently Harris placed the alligator beside the doll. "It's all right. The alligator can help her. All Teresa has to do is call."

Elena shook her head. "She *can't*." Her face was tensed; her eyes were shut. The tears began to run down one side of her face.

Harris moved next to her. "Did someone touch *you* like that, Elena?" she asked. "Was it Carlo?"

Elena flung herself on the rug and covered her ears.

"The California roll was good," Carlo said.

It was merely something to say, Paget knew; his son did not require an answer. They sat on the Persian rug in the library, with plates of sushi scattered across the marble coffee table. Returning from court, they had ordered in. Paget felt sad; the words of thanks he had given Carlo sounded hollow even to him.

There were times, he had learned, when it fell to a father to lie to his son, or for him. But he had never imagined the moment when Carlo would lie for *him*.

"I'm proud of you," Paget said.

Quietly Carlo asked, "Do you think they believed me?"

"Yes," Paget lied. "You faced up to this thing about Elena, Carlo. You said what happened and backed Salinas down."

"But what about you? I couldn't do much for you."

"You helped me, son. Piece by piece Caroline is chipping away at this case."

Carlo frowned. "Once *you* testify, it'll be fine."

Paget had no stomach for more evasions. "*If* I testify," he said casually. "It's strategy. If the prosecution hasn't proven its case, you don't give them a shot at making you look bad."

"How can you not testify, Dad? You need to *tell* people. This isn't just about Salinas. It's about everyone."

Most of all, Paget heard Carlo saying, it's about *me.* Because I want to believe you. Watching Carlo's eyes, he saw the boy's sense of his father slipping away.

Slowly Paget shook his head. "I have my own reasons." He touched Carlo's shoulder. "I didn't need you to testify to know you didn't molest Elena. I knew even before you told me so. Because I know you. Within this family," Paget added quietly, "there are certain things we know. We know you're not a child molester, and we know I'm not a murderer. And that's what counts."

Carlo turned away, but not before Paget saw the look of wounded doubt in his eyes.

TWENTY

JACK Slocum, the political reporter, was a slight sandy-haired man with sharp features and an assertive manner. There was something unhealthy about him: His skin was pallid, his beard spotty, and his posture slumped. Paget loathed him on sight.

Slocum had not come willingly. Through his newspaper's lawyer he had claimed that his testimony was not relevant and would jeopardize his sources. But Victor Salinas had asserted that Slocum was needed to show Paget's outrage at the damage Richie had done to him, political and personal. Caroline had not fought this.

"After Mr. Paget began exploring a Senate race," Salinas asked the reporter, "when did you first speak to him?"

"Late summer. I'd seen an article in the *Inquisitor.*" Slocum darted a look at the jury. "Mr. Arias accused Mr. Paget of stealing his wife. The article raised questions about Mr. Paget's character."

"And so you called Mr. Paget?"

"I did. I told him about the article and asked him to comment."

"And how did Mr. Paget respond?"

"He was quite angry. His tone of voice was threatening."

"How did you respond?" Salinas asked.

"I told Mr. Paget I intended to report that the charges existed and that they could pose a problem for his campaign."

"And did the item actually appear?"

"No. My editor didn't run it."

"All right," Salinas said to Slocum. "When was the next time you spoke to Mr. Paget?"

"After Mr. Arias' death. I became aware that in Mr. Arias' custody suit against Ms. Peralta, papers had been filed under seal, which apparently involved Mr. Paget and his son. So I called and asked Mr. Paget if he'd discuss the filings or give me a copy."

"And what was Mr. Paget's response?"

"He mentioned a possible libel suit."

Salinas nodded. "The defense has characterized Mr. Paget as a very peaceable man. Was that your experience?"

"Not at all. He has a way of talking that is very hostile, very angry." Caroline kept watching the reporter.

"Did Mr. Paget's anger deter you?" Salinas asked.

"No. Like before, I intended to run an article regarding Mr. Paget's fitness for office."

"And did you run *this* article?"

"No." Slocum smiled. "My publisher called and told me not to run it. Because Mr. Paget was withdrawing from the race."

"In your opinion, Mr. Slocum, could Mr. Paget's candidacy have survived exposure of his alleged adultery *and* the claim that his son had sexually molested Ms. Peralta's daughter?"

Caroline was up quickly. "Objection," she said. "That calls for not only speculation but fortune-telling."

"Overruled," Judge Lerner said. "You may answer, Mr. Slocum."

"The short answer," Slocum said, pleased with his own importance, "was supplied by Mr. Paget himself. By getting out before my story could even appear. He was smart to do that."

Rising, Caroline looked at Slocum with faint distaste. The courtroom was very still. "You're not exactly a supporter of Mr. Paget's, are you?" she asked.

"It's not the function of the press to support anyone."

"So you don't feel you treated Mr. Paget unfairly?"

"Not at all. If anything, this man got off light."

Caroline raised an eyebrow. "Am I correct in understanding that if Mr. Paget had supplied you with a copy of the papers filed under seal, you would have published Mr. Arias' charges?"

453

Slocum nodded. "Yes."

"Did you intend to verify whether the charges were true?"

"Well, if Mr. Paget had been willing to talk to me, I'd have asked him. Or his son, for that matter."

"In fact, you don't know whether it *is* true that Mr. Paget had an affair with Ms. Peralta. And you *also* don't know whether Carlo Paget, then age fifteen, molested a little girl."

Slocum's mouth became a stubborn line. "No."

"Was I correct in understanding that one of your reasons for calling Mr. Paget was to get a copy of Mr. Arias' papers?"

A moment's pause. "Yes."

"But didn't you already *have* a copy?"

Slocum shifted in the witness-box. "Yes," he said finally.

"So when you suggested to Mr. Paget that you needed a copy, you weren't exactly candid, Mr. Slocum, were you?"

"I was trying to protect my source."

"I take it that the person who provided you with the papers was *not* Ricardo Arias. Or you would have called Mr. Paget about their contents long before you did."

Slocum looked to Judge Lerner for assistance. "Your Honor, I believe these questions impinge on my right to protect my sources."

"At the time of your second call," Caroline rejoined, "Ricardo Arias was dead. If *he* gave you the papers, it really *is* news."

Salinas, Paget thought, was curiously inactive.

"You may answer," the judge told Slocum. "Did you receive these papers from Mr. Arias?"

Slocum shook his head. "No, Your Honor."

Caroline moved closer. "How did you get them, Mr. Slocum?"

"A third party gave them to me."

"And did this nameless someone tell you where he'd gotten them? Seeing how they weren't publicly available."

"No."

"You didn't think your source got them from Mr. Paget or Ms. Peralta, did you?"

"I guess not."

"That pretty much leaves Mr. Arias. Dead or alive."

"Objection," Salinas said reflexively. "Calls for speculation."

Caroline turned on him. "As to what, Victor? Whether Mr.

Slocum's nameless source received the papers from Mr. Arias in a living state or after Mr. Arias was deceased? In which case I would think that the district attorney would be even more enthralled with talking to this person than I am."

It was lovely, Paget thought. In one deft response Caroline had introduced the anonymous source as a party to shady dealings with Ricardo Arias and, at least possibly, to his murder.

Even Salinas looked nonplussed. "Let me suggest this compromise," he said to Judge Lerner. "That Mr. Slocum identify the source by occupation only, but testify fully about the content of their conversations."

This was shrewd, Paget saw. It preserved Salinas' options until he spoke to District Attorney Brooks, while permitting testimony that might make the unknown source seem a little less sinister.

"Very well," Caroline told Lerner. As she turned to the witness, Paget saw that the jury was on edge. "How," Caroline said, "did you come to know the source who gave you Mr. Arias' papers?"

Slocum considered his answer. "I knew him before. From previous campaigns. He's a political consultant."

"And how did he get these papers into your hands?"

"My source called and asked to meet me confidentially."

"Did he happen to mention what his interest was in seeing that this material got published?"

"No. He wouldn't say. I assumed that my source represented someone hostile to Mr. Paget's candidacy."

"Didn't it bother you, Mr. Slocum, that you were being used by a politician to help torpedo a candidate he disliked?"

Slocum tried to summon a superior smile. "In my business, you learn useful things from a lot of people whose motives may not be the best."

"And you decided to publish that information without knowing its credibility?"

"Yes. I decided the story had value as it was."

"So much for journalistic integrity," Caroline said. "Now let me call on your expertise in another area—political disaster. Would you say that it would be damaging to a politician who had your 'source' leak this information if the *politician's* identity was known?"

Slocum hesitated. "It might be damaging, I suppose."

455

Caroline paused. "Did Mr. Arias appreciate that fact?"

Slocum looked startled. "He was dead. Just like you point out."

"He wasn't dead, was he, when you first talked to him?"

Slocum glanced toward Salinas.

"Did you," Caroline snapped, "ever talk to Mr. Arias?"

Slowly Slocum turned back to Caroline. "Yes," he said.

"And when was that?"

"After I saw the article in the *Inquisitor*."

"And who pointed it out? Mr. Arias?"

Another glance at Salinas. "No. My source did."

Caroline nodded. "Your friend the 'consultant.' I rather thought so. And when you subsequently called Mr. Arias, he didn't happen to ask you for money, did he?"

"Not exactly. He did ask if we paid for interviews. I said I didn't think I could."

"And how did Mr. Arias respond to that?"

Slocum paused. "He wanted to know who else might be interested and whether I'd talked to anyone like that."

"And what did you tell him?" Caroline said.

Slocum looked away. "That I couldn't reveal my sources."

Caroline stared at him in silence. "But you did pass on Mr. Arias' interest to your source, correct?"

A long pause. "Yes."

"Well," Caroline said with disdain, "then it looks like you helped set up a blind date. And you've already agreed that anyone who knew about your source's role—or the politician he worked for— might be in a position to damage that politician seriously, correct?"

"I suppose, yes."

"Including Mr. Arias? A man with a proven gift for extortion?"

"Objection," Salinas said. "The question calls for speculation."

"I'll change subjects, Your Honor." To Slocum, Caroline said, "Tell me, do you have reason to believe Christopher Paget to be a violent man? I mean, given how scary he can be on the phone."

Slocum folded his arms. "I didn't say that. I said he was angry."

"Do you happen to know Mr. Paget's position on violence in our society? Including gun control?"

A pause. "Yes."

Caroline turned to Judge Lerner. "Your Honor, I would like to show the witness a short videotape of Mr. Paget's speech to the California Society of Newspaper Editors."

Salinas stood. "I object, Your Honor. This is a murder trial, not a political rally. Mr. Paget's speech has no probative value."

"Nonsense, Your Honor. The speech was given well before Mr. Arias' death. I believe that Mr. Paget's distaste for guns and violence is more than a little relevant to whether he shot Mr. Arias."

Lerner touched one finger to his lips. "It's been an unusual day," he said with an air of bemusement. "Roll 'em, Ms. Masters."

Within moments the courtroom was dark. Caroline sat next to Paget as the television screen flickered in black and white.

To his surprise Paget was fixated by his own image—a man speaking with passion the day children had died. "I don't own a gun," he heard himself say. "Outside the army, I've never fired one. . . ."

Paget turned to look at the jury. Suddenly he felt grateful to Caroline; she had found a way for them to hear from him other than as a voice on Charles Monk's tape. And he knew that, whatever else, this had become a bad day for the prosecution.

TWENTY-ONE

ON FRIDAY all the energies of the courtroom flowed toward Salinas' final witness. Even Jared Lerner could not take his eyes off her.

Georgina Keller was a widow in her seventies—a rail-thin former teacher with a mottled face, her thinning hair dyed black. Her voice, low and raspy, filled Paget with remembered alarm: It was that of the woman who had picked him from the lineup. Next to her, on an easel, was a black-and-white photograph of Paget.

The questioning began in earnest. "And where is your apartment," Salinas asked, "relative to Mr. Arias'?"

Keller pursed her lips. "I'm at the end of the hall. His was the apartment next to me. On the left-hand side, if you're facing out."

"Did there come a time when you became concerned about him?"

"There did. I heard a noise in Mr. Arias' apartment—the walls aren't very thick. I heard voices and then a thud. Like something or someone hitting the floor."

"Did the noise worry you?"

457

"Yes. Because of the voices, you see. It was two men speaking like they were angry. One of them sounded like Mr. Arias. What disturbed me was what happened after I heard the thud. Suddenly I couldn't hear any voices at all."

"And what did you do, if anything?"

"I went to the door," Keller said in a brittle tone, "and cracked it open. As far as the door chain would permit."

"And what did you see?"

"Nothing at first. A noise frightened me—a door opening in the hallway. I flinched so hard that the door chain rattled."

The courtroom was still. "And what did you see then?"

"A man. Coming out of Mr. Arias' apartment. He was tall, in his mid to late thirties. He wore a gray suit, double-breasted, and his hair was kind of blond. Copper almost." Keller held her head rigid, as if straining to look not at Paget but into her memory.

"Did this man do anything?" Salinas asked.

"He stopped—for a moment. I thought he saw me, but he hadn't. He was holding something like a notebook or a journal. Then he put the journal in his left hand and began staring at his other hand. The next thing he did was odd. He shook his hand, like it hurt. Then he touched the sleeve of his suit coat and turned it over, as if he were looking for stains."

"And during that time, Mrs. Keller, did you see the man's face?"

She stared straight ahead now. "Yes. It was a *strong* face. With a ridged nose and a cleft on his chin."

As if by reflex the jurors turned to Paget. He could feel them studying the features Georgina Keller had described.

"Had you ever seen this man before, Mrs. Keller?"

"No, never."

"After looking at his sleeve, what did the man do?"

"He turned away. Then he disappeared."

Salinas asked, "Did you call the police?"

"No. It was none of my business, I thought, and I was leaving the next morning to visit my daughter in Florida. Until I returned, I didn't know that Mr. Arias was dead."

"And did there come a time, after you returned three weeks later, when the police came to your apartment?"

"Inspector Monk did. And his partner, Inspector Lynch."

"And did you tell them about the man you saw?"

"Yes. They had me describe him over and over. Then they showed me a picture. From a newspaper, I thought. Right away I knew I'd seen the face before."

Salinas walked to the easel. "And is this the photograph?"

"Yes." Keller gazed at it. "It was the man in the hallway."

A grimness had begun settling over the courtroom. Paget had seen it before: a turning point, when a jury begins to accept a defendant's guilt.

"Did Inspector Monk take you to a lineup?" Salinas asked.

"Yes. At the auditorium in the police station. It was like a play— the stage was lit, but all the seats were dark. There were six men on the stage dressed in orange coveralls and holding numbers to their chests. Inspector Monk asked if I recognized any of them."

"And did you?"

"Yes." Keller still did not look at Paget. "The moment I saw him."

"And do you also see that man in the courtroom, Mrs. Keller?"

For the first time, Georgina Keller turned to Paget. She raised her arm to point. "Yes, I do. The defendant. Mr. Paget."

AT FIRST Caroline seemed muted. "This crack in the door," she asked pleasantly. "About how wide was it?"

Frowning, Keller held her hands in front of her face, peering between them. "Like so. About two to three inches. But the door opens on the right side, and Mr. Arias' apartment was to my left. So I was looking straight at his door."

"About how long," Caroline asked, "would you say that this man paused, looking at his hand and sleeve?"

Keller reflected for a moment. "A good ten seconds."

"You were frightened, Mrs. Keller. That can make time stand still. In fairness, could it have been less than ten seconds?"

"I suppose it could have."

"Perhaps even five?"

Keller shook her head. "It couldn't have been that short a time. He looked at his hand *and* his sleeve."

Caroline tilted her head. "Did *you* look at his hand?"

"Yes. I thought maybe it was injured. As I said, he shook it."

"And when he looked at his sleeve, did you look at it too?"

"Yes. He was right beneath the overhead light in the hallway. I thought I saw a stain—dark speckles on the sleeve."

Each answer, Paget knew, was that much worse; for the first time, Caroline seemed to be floundering. "About how long, Mrs. Keller, did you look at this man's hand and sleeve?"

Keller squinted. "A few seconds at least."

"And during the time you were looking at his hand and then his sleeve, you weren't looking at his face, correct?"

A slight pause. "I suppose not, no."

"So out of the ten seconds—or maybe less—that this man was in front of Mr. Arias' door, how long did you actually see his face?"

"I can't say."

"Less than five seconds?"

"Maybe."

"Less than three?"

"I don't know." Keller's raspy voice rose slightly. "All I can tell you is that I saw his face clearly."

"Clearly? It was in shadows, right?"

"What do you mean?"

"It would have to be. If the light was right above his head."

Caroline had captured the jury's attention now. Keller said to Caroline, "I can't remember shadows. I saw him, that's all."

To Paget's surprise Caroline nodded agreeably. "And how much time passed until Inspector Monk dropped by with the picture you identified, Mrs. Keller?"

"Perhaps a month."

"And how long after that did you identify Mr. Paget in a lineup?"

"Maybe another month."

"In other words, two months or so from the time that you saw the man leaving Mr. Arias' apartment."

"I guess so. But I knew that I'd seen him before."

"How do you know that you weren't identifying Mr. Paget in the lineup because you recognized him from his picture?"

Keller shook her head, impatient at Caroline's obtuseness. "Because I'd seen the man in the picture before that. Just as I told Inspector Monk."

Caroline smiled. "Perhaps you can look at some other pictures."

In moments, with the aid of Judge Lerner's courtroom deputy,

Keller was gazing at a pasteboard with six color pictures—Paget's conscripts from the county jail, wearing jumpsuits.

"These are police photographs of the men included in the lineup," Caroline said. "Can you pick out Mr. Paget?"

"Yes." Keller pointed. "The second from the end."

"So Mr. Paget stood out from the others?"

Keller squinted at the board. "Except for the third man."

"Didn't you, in fact, also ask Inspector Monk to have that man step forward for a second time?"

Keller hesitated. "I believe I did."

"For what purpose?"

"Because at first glance certain things about him generally resembled the man in the hallway. The height and build."

"And so the man you saw in the hallway was slender, about six feet tall, with hair on the blond side and fair skin. Correct?"

"Yes."

"And about thirty-five years old?" Caroline asked innocently.

"About that."

Caroline smiled. "As opposed to Mr. Paget's forty-six?"

Reluctantly Keller gazed at Paget again. "He looks younger."

Caroline gave Paget a once-over. "Not ten years younger, I would say. Although I'm sure Mr. Paget appreciates your charity."

There was mild laughter; it seemed a small point. "Are you," Caroline asked, "familiar with the case *People* versus *Carelli?*"

A short nod. "That was Mr. Paget's case."

"As you may recall, I was the judge," Caroline said dryly.

"I know. I thought I recognized you."

"Really? How?"

Again Keller looked at Caroline as if she were slightly dense. "From television," she said impatiently. "You were *on* every day."

Caroline raised an eyebrow. "You watched every day? The Carelli trial was about two weeks long."

"About that."

"So before Inspector Monk showed you the picture, you *had* seen Mr. Paget—every day for two weeks. On television."

"That's true. But I'd never seen him in person."

"I quite agree," Caroline said. "But at the time Monk showed you this picture, you knew you'd seen Mr. Paget before."

"That's right. I just didn't place him."

"And when they put on the lineup, you'd already seen Mr. Paget's picture. As well as seen him on television."

Keller had begun to look confused. "That's true."

"And once more, you *knew* that you'd seen him before."

"Yes."

"But when you saw the man in the *hallway,* you didn't recognize him as anyone you'd seen before, did you?"

In the witness-box Keller seemed to go blank. "No."

"And until you saw his picture, you didn't recognize Christopher Paget as anyone you'd seen before, either. True?"

"I guess not." Keller shook her head. "I'm confused now."

The jury, Paget saw, was transfixed. But Caroline still had points to make.

"Tell me," she said, "isn't it true that you recognized Mr. Paget's picture because you'd seen him during the Carelli hearing?"

"That might be *one* reason."

"So isn't it also true that when you identified him in the lineup, you recognized Mr. Paget from his picture *and* from television?"

"Anything's possible, I guess."

Caroline plucked a plastic bottle from the pocket of her suit. "Is this anything you recognize, Mrs. Keller?"

"It looks like the bottle for my sleeping pill prescription."

"In fact, it is. Just how long have you been taking them?"

"Almost a year."

"At about what time of day?"

"A half hour before I go to bed. Sometime between nine and ten. They help me sleep."

"By making you drowsy and perhaps a little less observant?"

"Maybe," Keller said. "I've got no way of telling."

"Tell me this, then," Caroline said. "The night you saw the man leaving Mr. Arias' apartment—for maybe five seconds, perhaps with his face in shadow—had you already taken your pill?"

"I don't remember. I'd have to say it's possible."

"So would I," Caroline said. "You wear glasses, do you not?"

"Yes. But only for reading. Not for any distance."

"Were you wearing them the night you saw this man?"

"No. As I said, I use them just for reading."

462

Caroline put her hand on her hip. "Do you think you could look at the lineup picture again and tell me Mr. Paget's number?"

Before Keller even turned, Paget knew that she would squint. He could feel the jury watch her. "Five," she said finally.

"It is indeed," Caroline said. "Let me return to your testimony that you heard voices and then a thud, like someone falling. After this thud and before seeing the man in the hallway, did you hear anything else?"

Keller looked puzzled. "I don't believe so."

Caroline paused a moment. "Not even a gunshot?"

Joseph Duarte's head jerked up from the notes he'd been taking. There was a long silence. "No," Keller answered slowly, "I did not."

Caroline smiled. "Thank you. I have no further questions."

As she sat, Paget whispered, "That was classic."

"A minor classic, at best." Watching Salinas rise, Caroline kept her voice low. "Once Keller's neighbor told Johnny Moore that all she could talk about for two weeks was the Carelli case, this poor lady was as dead as Humpty-Dumpty."

Salinas did his best on redirect. Yes, Keller affirmed, she believed the man in the hallway was Christopher Paget. But as the key prosecution witness, Georgina Keller was damaged goods.

When it was over and the jury excused, Caroline asked Judge Lerner for a meeting in chambers. Glum, Salinas seemed to know what was coming. They sat in front of Lerner's desk as the judge contemplated the prosecutor with a certain sympathy.

"It's Friday afternoon," Lerner said pleasantly, turning to Caroline. "You're not planning to make me work, are you?"

Caroline smiled. "Not until Monday morning, Your Honor. But I wanted to discuss our plans for the defense. We plan to present no witnesses. Before final argument, though, I would like to move to dismiss this case for lack of evidence."

The judge nodded as if he had expected this. "Eight o'clock Monday morning, then. But be prepared for final arguments." He looked at Salinas. "Anything else, Victor?"

Salinas shook his head. "Not at this time."

His expression was unfathomable; perhaps Caroline only imagined his disappointment. She was quietly pleased.

Christopher Paget was almost home.

TWENTY-TWO

PAGET spent the weekend quietly. Unlike Caroline, he seesawed back and forth between believing that Lerner would either throw out the case or let it go to a jury. The hours passed slowly.

It gave him time to think. But the summing up depressed him— that Carlo and Terri had lied for him was deeply painful in itself *and* because neither relationship could ever be the same.

He saw Terri only once. There had been a call from Elena's therapist; Terri seemed quite troubled, although she would say little. But for the first time, Terri appeared to be uncomfortable in his home. Encountering Carlo, she was distant and preoccupied. She wished Paget luck and left shortly after.

The one bright spot was Carlo. Paget knew Caroline's dismantling of Georgina Keller for what it was: the guile of a gifted lawyer who knew that eyewitness testimony, which seemed so damning to lay people, was often not hard to discredit. But Carlo seized on it as vindication, as if to fill the vacuum of his father's silence.

Caroline, Paget thought, had done an extraordinary job. There had been a real comfort in her presence. Sometimes Paget wished he could tell her the truth.

But perhaps the truth did not really matter. Caroline was a professional; he knew she would spend the weekend preparing and would make an excellent final argument. By Monday, Paget had half convinced himself that within hours he would be free again.

THE first sign that something was wrong was the look on Salinas' face. They were in court, waiting for Judge Lerner. The jury was not present; reporters already packed the courtroom. But Salinas did not appear edgy and combative as Paget would have expected. His bland expression suggested a half smile.

Paget turned to Caroline. "What's with Victor?"

"All rise," Lerner's courtroom deputy called out.

Lerner ascended the bench. He said crisply, "Our first business is the defendant's motion to dismiss all charges. Ms. Masters?"

Salinas stood. "Pardon me, Your Honor, but within the last forty-eight hours there has been a development that renders this motion

464

premature at best. The people ask leave of court to reopen the prosecution case to present another witness."

Paget was stunned. Caroline quickly stood. "Just how did you discover this witness, Mr. Salinas?"

"She recognized Mr. Paget from television. A news report."

All at once Paget knew what had happened. But Caroline, of course, did not. "Who is this?" she asked Salinas. "Surely not another keyhole peeper."

Salinas shook his head. "This person met Mr. Paget in an entirely different context. A charitable donation, in fact."

Caroline turned to Lerner. "A moment, Your Honor, if you please." She sat, turning to Paget with a look of worry and annoyance. "Do you know what this new evidence is?"

Paget felt sick. "Yes," he answered, "I do."

LERNER gave Caroline the morning to prepare. At two o'clock the witness, Anna Velez, took the stand.

She was as Paget remembered her—brown eyes, gold earrings, and vivid makeup, pleasantly plump. He had been a fool to hope that she would not remember *him.*

Salinas still seemed calm, almost matter-of-fact. "And where do you work, Ms. Velez?"

"At the Goodwill outlet on Mission Street."

"And in November of this past year," Salinas asked, "did you encounter the defendant, Christopher Paget?"

"I did," she said. "At the store."

Quietly Salinas asked, "And why did you choose, at this late date, to bring this to our attention?"

"I was watching television on Friday night. The newsman was talking about this case, and they showed a film of Mr. Paget. 'I know that man,' I said to my sister, and so I started paying attention." Furtively she glanced at Paget. "It was about this lady who thought she saw another man leaving this dead man's apartment, and he wore a double-breasted gray suit with maybe something on the sleeve. And suddenly it all made sense. The reason I knew Mr. Paget is that he came to my store with three suits and a new pair of shoes. One of the suits was gray and had a stain on its right sleeve."

The jury, very attentive now, seemed startled. "Was there a par-

465

ticular reason, Ms. Velez, that the defendant stuck in your mind?"

She nodded. "At first it was that he was good-looking and that the shoes and suits were so expensive." She paused. "After our store closed, I looked at the suits again. And I saw the stain."

"Could you describe it?"

"It was like spots. Or a spatter of something. The suit was so nice that I decided to take it home and try to clean it, but the stain wouldn't come out." Her eyes narrowed. "It was like ink, I remember thinking. Or blood."

Caroline glanced up but otherwise did not react; to move to strike the answer would only drive it home.

"You mentioned shoes," Salinas said. "Could you describe them?"

"They were black leather and soft to touch. Almost brand-new."

"Do you know where the shoes are now?" Salinas asked.

Velez shrugged, shaking her head. "I couldn't find them at the store. So I guess we sold them."

"What about the suit with the stains like ink? Or blood."

"No," Velez said. "It's gone too. We don't know where it is."

For a moment Paget closed his eyes.

"Did you have a receipt," Salinas asked, "from Mr. Paget's visit?"

"We have a copy."

Salinas held up a small square of paper. "Your Honor, I would like to introduce this as people's exhibit seventeen." He passed the scrap to Velez. "Is this your handwriting?" he asked.

Velez held it gingerly. "It is. It shows that on November fourteenth Mr. Paget gave us three suits and a pair of shoes."

Salinas took the slip to the jury box and handed it to Joseph Duarte—a piece of paper with "Padgett" scrawled at the top.

"No further questions," Salinas said then.

Rising, Caroline looked puzzled. She inclined her head toward the jury box. "How did you get Mr. Paget's name?"

"I asked him," Velez said.

"So he wasn't trying to hide who he was."

"I don't know. He gave me his name. I just didn't spell it right."

"When Mr. Paget was in the store, how did he seem to you?"

"Nice. I remember joking with him about something or other."

"Did he appear nervous?" Caroline asked.

"Nervous? No. I never thought that. I thought he was generous.

I mean, you don't usually get things that nice. Even the suit with the stain."

Caroline nodded. "About that stain—you have no idea what it was, correct? You couldn't even tell what color it was."

Velez shook her head. "That's right."

"So when you said the stain reminded you of ink or blood, it was because the stain wouldn't come out? Ink or blood were just examples of stains you think are hard to get out?"

"That's right."

"When you found out over the weekend that the man you met had been charged with murder, were you surprised?"

Velez looked troubled. "Yes, I was."

"Because he seemed so nice. And because his behavior didn't seem suspicious."

"That's right. I thought he was careless, in a way. About his things. But he *was* nice."

Caroline smiled. "Some millionaires are like that, I suppose— careless but nice. By the way, Ms. Velez, do you like red wine?"

For a moment Velez looked bemused. "Sometimes," she said.

"Ever spill any?"

Velez grimaced. "Yes. On a new cotton skirt."

"How was it to get out?"

"I couldn't," Velez said. "Wine—that's hard to get out too."

"I've always thought so," Caroline told her. "Thank you."

"It was all I could do," Caroline said at last.

They were in her car, driving Paget home. The atmosphere was close and tense. "I know that," Paget answered.

Caroline stopped in front of the house. The only light came from streetlamps. But there was a yellow glow inside the house; Carlo was already home.

Caroline shook her head. "I'm sorry, Chris. But you really messed this up. This changes everything."

"It can't. I still can't testify, Caroline."

She stared at him. "So you want me to stick to this—no defense. Even after today."

"Yes." Paget paused. "I have no choice."

Caroline turned away. "Then it's closing argument tomorrow."

467

"Yes." Paget's own anger had died. He touched her shoulder and then opened the car door and got out.

Carlo was in the library. The television was on, a clip of Anna Velez leaving the courtroom. When Carlo turned to his father, tears were in his eyes. But what Paget saw was worse; for the first time, his son believed him a murderer.

WHEN Salinas rose to give his closing argument, Terri and Carlo were together in the courtroom.

The idea was Terri's. It was important, she said, that the jury remember the people who loved Paget most. If the case was over, there was nothing to keep her or Carlo from the courtroom. Now they sat behind his father, her lover, where the jury could see them.

The symbolism was effective. Terri waited until the jury filed in; then she leaned forward and squeezed Chris's hand. But even when she smiled, a part of her seemed elsewhere.

"Mr. Salinas," Jared Lerner said gravely, "you may begin."

Gazing at the jury, Salinas looked solemn. "This," he began, "was a murder. And from the moment that he killed Ricardo Arias to the final and devastating moments of this trial, Christopher Paget has been trying to get away with it." He paused, letting that sink in. The jury watched with open faces.

"The mantra Ms. Masters will repeat to you, I am sure, is that you must believe that we have proven Christopher Paget guilty of murder beyond a reasonable doubt, or you must find him innocent. So let us talk—right now—about what we're *not* required to show.

"We don't need a witness who saw Mr. Paget shoot Ricardo Arias. Nor does every witness have to be sure about every scrap of testimony. No, our job here is to present sufficient proof—in the form of circumstantial evidence—to satisfy men and women of common sense that Mr. Paget is guilty beyond a reasonable doubt.

"Is there a reasonable doubt that Ricardo Arias was murdered? There is not. The medical examiner spelled out for us the medical evidence. Mr. Arias did not beat himself up. Nor did he pirouette around the living room taking pratfall after pratfall and then shoot himself in the mouth. He did not make a coffee date to tell Elena's teacher that he had decided not to kill himself. No, ladies and gentlemen—this was a man who expected to live.

468

"Which brings us," Salinas went on, "to the defendant. As Judge Lerner will instruct you, motive is not an element of the crime. But does anyone doubt that Christopher Paget had several motives? The only 'reasonable doubt' is which one was the strongest—fear of political ruin, the loss of his relationship to his lover, or public knowledge that his son, Carlo, was charged with molesting Ms. Peralta's daughter.

"As became so abundantly clear to us all, here is a man who cannot account for several critical hours on the last night that anyone saw Ricardo Arias. Because, for those same hours, no one at all saw Christopher Paget. Not Ms. Peralta and not his son—however hard he tried to *hear* things. In truth, there was no one home for Carlo Paget to see *or* hear. Because someone else did see his father—leaving Ricardo Arias' apartment.

"This is a touchy point for the defense," Salinas continued, "because if Mr. Paget was at Mr. Arias' apartment that night, he not only had every chance to kill Ricardo Arias but he lied to Inspector Monk about it—a telling admission of guilt. So it was doubly important that Ms. Masters discredit Georgina Keller. And she tried.

"Here I can only sympathize," Salinas said with irony. "For little did Ms. Masters know that her very best work, transmitted through television, would summon Anna Velez into our midst. The woman to whom, shortly after the police began their inquiry, Mr. Paget made a gift of a gray wool suit coat with a stained sleeve."

Salinas' voice turned hard. "With that, there is no doubt anymore that Georgina Keller saw exactly what she said she saw—Christopher Paget leaving Ricardo Arias' apartment, examining his injured hand and the stained sleeve of his gray suit coat.

"Common sense, ladies and gentlemen. It really is all you need. Mr. Paget killed Ricardo Arias. And for that he must pay the price. I implore you to return a verdict of guilty. Guilty of *murder* in the first degree." Victor Salinas was finished.

When Caroline rose, she walked to the jury box and stood gazing from one juror to the next. "Did you notice," she began, "how Mr. Arias disappeared from Mr. Salinas' closing argument? Yet when his case opened, Mr. Arias was the purehearted underdog, battling the rich and arrogant Chris Paget—wife stealer, protector of child molesters, and, of course, killer of the less fortunate."

469

Caroline paused, letting her startling first words make their own impression. "The banishment of Mr. Arias is the key to this case, for the one thing that Mr. Salinas has proven beyond doubt—and these were *his* witnesses, remember—is that the one decent man in this case is the one he asks you to convict of murder."

She looked directly at Joseph Duarte now. "But let us consider why Mr. Salinas has banished Mr. Arias. The real Ricardo Arias—a man who was twice accused of stealing. Who exploited his own wife. Who used his six-year-old daughter to collect ten thousand dollars from a tabloid. Who engineered his custody fight as the paid hireling of Mr. Paget's political opponents, to torpedo Chris's candidacy for the Senate.

"In sum," Caroline said, "Ricardo Arias was a man who hid his motives and his fears from everyone he ever met. And Ricardo Arias had so very much to fear. A life at the margins, unemployed and unemployable. A future of financial desperation. Exposure as a sociopath. And, almost certainly, the loss of his daughter.

"Mr. Salinas is so certain that Ricardo Arias did not kill himself. I say, who can know? When someone is as troubled as Ricardo Arias, I defy anyone to say anything else beyond a reasonable doubt.

"The medical examiner," Caroline went on, "cites the lack of blood spatter and gunshot residue on Mr. Arias' hands. But there *were* traces of blood and GSR on his hands. And there were also smears that suggest he wiped his nose—which, if true, shatters the notion that someone knocked Mr. Arias to the ground, shoved a revolver in his mouth, and pulled the trigger.

"I don't know how Mr. Arias got the abrasion on his leg and the gash on his head." Caroline paused for emphasis. "And neither does the medical examiner. But let us assume for the moment that someone murdered Ricardo Arias. If so, why Christopher Paget? The prosecution's case is founded on the notion that what Mr. Arias did was so ugly that Chris Paget abandoned the training of a lifetime and shot him with an ancient gun and a rusty bullet. Why on earth should you believe this? The two people who know Chris Paget better than anyone—Teresa Peralta and Carlo Paget—say that he's not a killer. They know him to be a kind and decent man."

Carlo raised his head to face the jury.

"Let us stop for a moment," Caroline said softly, "and consider

Carlo Paget. There is not a shred of evidence to suggest that he molested anyone, but that has never stopped Mr. Salinas from smearing this boy in order to convict his father. Because this is not a prosecution, ladies and gentlemen; it is a vendetta.

"Christopher Paget is a gentle and nonviolent man. And for that matter a skilled trial lawyer who knew what Ricardo Arias knew: that Ricardo wouldn't hold up under a cross-examination in the fight for custody of Elena. And then the supposed affair, and the alleged abuse, would turn back on Ricardo Arias—a pathological liar whose character was, at last, about to catch up with him. So when you look at motive, ladies and gentlemen, consider that Ricardo Arias had a better motive to kill himself than Chris Paget ever had to kill him.

"That," Caroline snapped, "leaves us with the 'evidence.' A fingerprint. But no one disputes that Chris Paget touched the answering machine while it was still in Terri's apartment.

"Carpet fibers. But no one disputes that Teresa Peralta left them in Mr. Paget's house and car.

"An eyewitness," she said evenly, "who heard everything but a gunshot. In truth, we don't know if this unknown man leaving Ricardo Arias' apartment—whoever he was—had come with a gun. And the only time Mrs. Keller *failed* to recognize Chris Paget as a man she'd seen before—on television—was when she saw this stranger leaving Mr. Arias' apartment carrying, she tells us, some sort of journal. And yet—once we eliminate the answering machine—without leaving a single print that was Paget's. Nor, you will recall, did the police ever find a journal in Paget's possession or ever explain what it was."

Caroline's voice had become softer yet. "Most damning of all, Mr. Salinas suggests, is that Chris Paget gave some clothes to charity. And then, just to conceal his evil intentions, he also gave them his name so they could record it." Her voice filled with irony. "Oh, yes, and one of the suits had stains on it—a pretty good reason, if you're financially comfortable, to give a suit away.

"There are stains, and there are stains. After all, the high point of the police interest in Ms. Peralta was the day they found a suit in her closet with stains on it. Ketchup stains.

"While Mr. Salinas touts all of this evidence, there is one piece of

471

evidence he treats like a dead mouse on the kitchen floor. And that's the ten thousand dollars in cash about which his superior, McKinley Brooks, has shown such a driving lack of curiosity."

Salinas stared straight ahead.

"Ricardo Arias lived a funny life," Caroline told the jury. "How many of you, I wonder, keep ten thousand dollars in cash sitting around your house? But drug dealers do, and people with secrets do. Perhaps drugs, or secrets, got Ricardo Arias killed. Perhaps he was killed for this mysterious journal. But you'll never know.

"You'll never know whether Mr. Arias was dealing in drugs or politics, or both. You'll never know because the district attorney, McKinley Brooks, didn't want you to know. And because of the district attorney you will never know who pulled the trigger. Even if this *was* murder."

Caroline stood straight, her gaze sweeping the jury. "From the beginning of this case Christopher Paget has been McKinley Brooks' only target. Now you are Christopher Paget's only hope of justice. That is your job now. If you cannot condemn Christopher Paget to a life in prison, confident that you are doing justice, then you must let him go free. Thank you."

THE EYES OF A CHILD

February 17–February 19

TWENTY-THREE

BY THE next morning the jury had begun its deliberations.

For Paget, the knowledge that what mattered now was out of his control, and would happen out of sight, hit hard.

By five o'clock, when the jury ceased deliberations for the day, they had not reached a verdict.

Paget picked up Carlo after basketball practice; as much as possible, he had insisted that they follow a normal routine. But when they arrived home, there was a cluster of reporters and TV cameras on the sidewalk, looking for a quote.

"I hate them," Carlo said.

"You're not alone."

They parked in the garage and entered the back of the house

without acknowledging the media. Two cameramen scurried up the driveway to film them as they disappeared. The murderer, Paget thought bitterly, and the child molester.

At ten forty the next morning Caroline called Paget at home. "You'd better meet me down at the courthouse. The foreman just sent Lerner a note—the jury wants to see him."

"They're hung," Paget said. His nerve ends tingled.

"Maybe they just want more instruction," Caroline answered.

By the time he arrived, pushing through a crowd of reporters, the word had spread. The courtroom was filled with media people, and Victor Salinas was there. Almost as soon as Paget arrived, the courtroom deputy led the jury back to the box.

Judge Lerner took the bench. He looked at the jury. "I have a note indicating that you have been unable to reach a verdict. Is that correct, Mr. Foreman?"

Joseph Duarte stood. "Yes, Your Honor. We're evenly divided."

Paget tensed. "Good," he heard Caroline murmur.

"How many ballots have you taken?" Lerner asked.

"Three," Duarte said.

"Without indicating whether the votes were guilty or not guilty, what was the division after the first ballot?"

Duarte paused a moment. "Seven to five, Your Honor."

"Is it your impression that you cannot reach a verdict?"

"It is," Duarte answered.

Lerner folded his hands. "Members of the jury, this trial took over two weeks. However difficult your discussions may have been, your deliberations have lasted less than two days."

"*No*," Caroline whispered.

At the prosecution table Victor Salinas sat up, alert with hope.

"I would like you to return to the jury room," Lerner continued, "deliberate with mutual courtesy and respect, and see whether you can reach a verdict."

At eleven fifteen the following day Caroline called Paget at his office. "They're in," she said.

Paget felt his chest constrict. "I'll be right down."

Carlo was in school. Paget had promised to call the principal's office after the verdict. He pushed open his office door—it seemed like an act of will—and hurried to Terri's office. It was empty.

Her secretary, May, sat outside. "I thought Terri was here," he said tersely.

May glanced at the calendar on her desk. "She will be. She has a doctor's appointment."

Paget felt suddenly alone. "With Dr. Harris?"

May nodded. "Shall I tell her to come find you?"

"No," Paget answered. "I won't be here."

WHEN Terri entered Harris' office, the psychologist looked like someone who could no longer hide bad news. "What is it?" Terri demanded. "You were so strange on the telephone."

"Sit down, Terri. Please."

When Terri took a chair, Harris continued. "I've been keeping this for over a week. Because of Chris's trial. I'm sorry, but in good conscience I can't wait anymore. I now believe that Elena has been sexually molested. And that it may be at the heart of her problem."

Tears came to Terri's eyes. "How do you know?"

"Play therapy, in part. Do you know the motif of the abandoned girl? Last week when I asked Elena what her doll was afraid of, she pulled up its dress and began tickling the doll's stomach. And then Elena turned her face from me and stroked the doll between her legs." Harris paused for a moment. "The things she said about it were very real. As if she knew exactly how that was."

Terri felt a faint nausea. "Has she told you how it happened?"

Harris shook her head. "Elena has never *told* me anything. But I'm morally certain she's been abused. *And* that it's probably why she seemed to feel at fault for Richie's death. She thinks she's a bad person. Once children feel that, they make themselves responsible for every bad thing that happens."

In the eyes of a child, Terri remembered Chris saying, everything that happens is about herself. "How can I help her?" Terri asked.

"By being patient. Whoever did this, I think, told Elena that awful things would happen if she ever told·anyone. Secrecy and shame are terrible burdens for a child to carry."

Terri found that she felt both anger and despair. "She's my daughter, damn it. Isn't there *something* I can do?"

Harris gave her a look of deep compassion. "Spend whatever time you can with her. Next week, or next year, she may talk. That's all I can tell you."

"ALL rise," the courtroom deputy called out, and for the last time in *People* v. *Paget,* Jared Lerner ascended the bench.

His face was grim. He took in the scene before him—the reporters quiet and waiting; Victor Salinas standing, seeming to fidget without moving.

Next to Paget, Caroline drew a breath and held it.

Paget's stomach felt hollow. They've found me guilty, he thought.

Joseph Duarte stood stiffly and appeared pale. "I understand," Lerner said to him, "that you've reached a verdict."

"We have, Your Honor."

Silent, Duarte handed the bailiff four slips of paper: verdict forms, signed by the foreman, for each of the four counts against Paget—first- or second-degree murder, voluntary or involuntary manslaughter. The bailiff handed them to Lerner.

One after another Lerner read the four slips of paper. When he was finished reading, he handed the forms to the courtroom clerk.

Lerner faced the jury again. "Members of the jury," he said calmly, "my clerk will read each verdict aloud. Thereafter I will ask each one of you whether this is your true verdict."

The clerk began reading. "In the Superior Court for the City and County of San Francisco, case number 93-5701, on the charge of murder in the first degree, we the jury find the defendant, Christopher Paget, not guilty."

A stunned murmur. Numb, Paget braced himself for the next count.

"On the charge of murder in the second degree, we the jury find the defendant not guilty.

"On the charge of manslaughter in the first degree . . . not guilty. On the charge of manslaughter in the second degree . . . not guilty."

The courtroom exploded in sound.

Caroline grinned in triumph. Clasping her shoulders, Paget said in a shaky voice, "You're wonderful."

Lerner banged for silence. "Members of the jury," he intoned, "I will now poll you individually." Silence fell.

The next few moments were only impressions as each juror answered yes in a firm voice.

As the polling ended, Victor Salinas stared down at the floor.

"Mr. Paget, you are free to go," Lerner said.

In the noise of the gallery Salinas walked across the courtroom. "Congratulations," he said to Caroline, and held out his hand. Silent, they shook hands. Then, to Paget's surprise, Salinas turned to him, hand extended. After a moment Paget took it.

Salinas faced Caroline again. "You out-lawyered me," he said.

Caroline shrugged. Paget was now rid of the specter that had haunted him since he first lied to Charles Monk; thanks to Caroline Masters and his own resolve, he had got away with it.

"Ready for the press?" Caroline asked him.

Paget was quiet. Another thought had struck him. No one would ever answer for the death of Ricardo Arias.

"First I need to call Carlo," he said softly. "And Terri."

SEEING her mother at the classroom door, Elena gave her a look that combined surprise, apprehension, and pleasure in such rapid sequence that Terri wanted to pick her up.

Instead she walked over to the teacher. "I'm sorry," she said. "But Elena has a doctor's appointment. I forgot to call."

"Oh, of course." Turning, the young woman beckoned to Elena.

The little girl took a few tentative steps from her desk. Then Terri smiled. "I'm here for you, sweetheart."

Elena looked at the teacher for permission. The woman nodded. "Your mother's taking you to the doctor, Elena."

The little girl turned to Terri again. "Dr. Harris, Mommy?"

"No." Terri smiled. "Dr. Mom."

The teacher gave Terri a puzzled look, but Elena went to her mother, touching her skirt. Terri took her hand, and they left.

Outside, Elena blinked at the sunlight. "Where are we going?"

"For ice cream. I was hungry."

Elena turned to her, delighted by the surprise, and then frowned at another thought. "You didn't tell the truth, Mommy."

"That wasn't good, was it? People don't always tell the truth. Next time I will. I'll just tell Mrs. Johnson that I missed you."

They went to Rory's on Fillmore Street and bought two cones.

Then, each licking her ice cream, they drove to Terri's apartment.

"We'd better wash our hands, Elena," Terri said as they entered.

The little girl looked up at her. "How come you never call me Lainie? Like Daddy did."

What, Terri wondered, was this about? "Because Elena's a beautiful name. I picked it myself—Elena Rosa, so you could have Grandma's name too."

Elena looked down, and then she went to the kitchen to wash her sticky hands. Terri followed her. They stood at the sink together.

"You're not going to leave me, are you, Mommy?" Elena asked. Her voice was filled with apprehension.

"What do you mean, Elena?"

"You know. Leave me at Grandma's tonight."

Terri picked Elena up. "Not if you don't want me to."

"I don't, Mommy. Please."

The telephone rang. Suddenly remembering Chris, Terri carried Elena across the kitchen and grabbed it.

"Terri," Chris said, "I've been looking for you." He sounded strange.

"Where are you?" she asked.

"In the car with Carlo, playing hooky. They acquitted me."

She felt herself trembling with emotion and sheer relief. "Oh, Chris"—her voice was choked—"that's *so* great."

"What is it, Mommy?" Elena asked.

"It's wonderful," Chris was saying. "Listen, can you get a sitter for Elena tonight? Carlo and I want to take you out to dinner."

Terri felt suddenly numb. "Dinner with you and Carlo?" she repeated in a shaky voice, and then saw the look on Elena's face. For a moment Terri could not find words. "I can't. I just promised Elena—" She tried again. "I have to be elliptical, but I'll buy you dinner tomorrow night. That way we can really talk."

"It's okay," Chris answered with attempted casualness. "Carlo and I will have a boys' night out. You can tell me later."

He sounded all right. But when he hung up, Terri realized that she had not told Christopher Paget that she loved him.

STARS was a sprawling, brightly lit three-level restaurant with high ceilings and splashy Parisian posters on the walls. It was jammed with people, the mirrored bar lined two-deep. Paget's choice of Stars was deliberate. If a lot of people noticed him, both they and he might as well get used to that. But one look at Carlo, and Paget realized that—for tonight—Stars was the wrong choice.

They were sitting along the wall at a table where they could talk alone. But Carlo seemed painfully aware whenever someone stared at him. "It's like we're zoo animals," he murmured.

Paget sipped a martini. "Forget them."

Carlo gave him a look both steady and opaque. "How are you going to live with this? People still think you *killed* someone."

"I'll be okay. Caroline once said I wouldn't make a politician. She was right. There aren't many people whose opinion I care about." He hesitated. "A long time ago I learned the painful truth that you have to have your own standards, both for how you act and for whom you should answer to."

Carlo looked at him. "Are you ever going to answer to *me?*"

Paget felt his eyes narrow. "I already have, Carlo. I told you that I didn't kill Richie. The things I haven't told you may involve someone else. If telling you everything I might know or guess would change this business with Elena, I'd do it in a heartbeat. But it won't, so you're just going to have to trust me."

"This may be selfish, Dad, and I'm glad you got acquitted. But no one is ever going to find *me* innocent." His voice rose slightly. "Admit it—not even Terri is sure I didn't do it."

Paget flinched inside. "Terri's been through a lot," he said softly. "Give her time. I know you didn't do it, and so do your friends."

A shadow crossed Carlo's face. "Maybe you can deal with it," he said, "but this thing with Terri is something *I* can't live with. I mean it. I'm not going to be around someone every day who thinks I molested a six-year-old girl. I don't have to live with Terri, and I won't." There were sudden tears in Carlo's eyes.

For a moment Paget felt his own pain. Then he reached across the table, touching his son's sleeve. "Carlo, I understand."

Terri pulled the comforter beneath Elena's chin, placed the book they had read on the child's bedside table. Turning out the light, she kissed Elena's cheek. At that moment Terri could not imagine loving another person as much as this child.

"Can you stay with me, Mommy? Just for a while, okay?"

Terri smiled. "Okay," she said, and lay down on the comforter.

"Get inside the covers with me, Mommy. Please."

Terri slid beneath the covers and turned on her side, putting her arms around Elena. "I love you," Terri said.

Elena burrowed closer. "I love you too, Mommy."

Gently Terri stroked Elena's hair until the child's breathing became deep and even, the pulse of sleep.

ELENA Arias awoke in a pitch-black room.

She was alone. She sat up, fearful. She was in her grandmother's house. Her mother was gone and could not help her.

There was banging on the door.

It was the black dog. Elena was certain of this. The dog had never come through the door, but tonight, Elena knew, he would.

The knocking grew louder. Elena began to tremble. She knew what the dog wanted. She tried to scream, but she could not breathe.

The door burst open.

Shivering, Elena could hear the dog, but still she could not see him. Then his shadow rose above the bed.

It was more human than dog. For an instant Elena prayed that it was Grandma Rosa, and then his face came into the light. Standing over the bed, Ricardo Arias smiled down at her.

Elena woke up screaming.

IN THE soft glow of the night-light Terri saw her daughter's eyes as black holes of terror. "Sweetheart," she cried out, and held Elena close. "It's okay," she urged. "I'm here."

Elena's trembling arms held Terri like a vise.

"It was just a nightmare," Terri said. "Only a nightmare."

Elena could not seem to speak. Softly Terri stroked the little girl's hair again, and then Elena began to cry.

After a time Elena was still. Gently Terri pulled away a little. "Tell me what it was," Terri said, "and maybe you won't feel alone."

The little girl watched her face. "Daddy was here. I saw him."

"It was a dream, Elena. Daddy's dead now. He died in an accident."

Elena shook her head, and the tears began again, ragged and shuddering. "I was scared, Mommy. He was going to hurt the little girl."

Terri felt her skin go cold. In a calm voice she asked, "How?"

Elena's voice was small. "He was going to take her panties off."

Terri felt herself swallow. "What else was Daddy going to do?"

"Touch her." Elena's face twisted. "It was their secret."

Terri stared at her. "Why is it a secret?"

"Daddy feels lonely. Sometimes he needs a girl." Elena looked into her mother's face. "To feel better. Because he's all alone now."

Terri's sudden rage was almost blinding. She pulled her daughter close. She did not know how long she held Elena, but it was some time before Terri realized that she too was crying—silently.

"Elena," Terri murmured. "How I wish you could have told me."

In a thin voice Elena said, "I did tell."

Terri looked at her in confusion. "Who? Dr. Harris?"

Elena shook her head. "No, Mommy. I told Grandma."

It was a moment before Terri spoke again. "When, Elena?"

"A long time ago. Before Chris murdered Daddy."

CHRISTOPHER Paget stared at the bedside clock.

The illuminated dial read 10:45. He could not sleep: Relief warred with confusion, pain over Carlo with sadness about Terri. Impulsively he picked up the telephone and dialed Terri's number.

"Hello?" A woman's voice, but wrong.

Paget asked, "Is this the Peralta residence?"

"It is. This is Terri's neighbor, Nancy. Terri's not in right now."

Paget hesitated, surprised. "This is Chris Paget. I was expecting to hear from her tonight."

A moment's silence. "I'm sorry," the woman said, "but Terri had some emergency. She was too distracted to say what. As soon as Elena was asleep, she rushed out the door. She's at her mother's."

TWENTY-FOUR

T ERRI banged on the door.

Her mother's porch was shadowed, and the house was dark. The only sounds were Terri's fist slamming the door. Light came from inside, the sudden glow of someone switching on a lamp.

The door opened. "Teresa," her mother said softly.

She was in a robe and nightgown, her hair down as Terri had not seen it for years. Without makeup her face looked older and

480

harsher, the face of an Aztec statue, her black eyes beyond surprise.

Rosa stared into her daughter's face. "Elena," she said simply.

Silent, Terri nodded. She stepped inside.

"So you know." Rosa's voice was quiet and clear.

Terri felt a calm, cold clarity. "When did she tell you, Mom?"

"The night before you left for Italy."

Before Terri could find words to answer, Rosa walked across the living room to an end table, opening a drawer. When she turned, she tossed a small burlap bag to Terri.

It clicked in Terri's hand like a bag of marbles, but Terri knew better. With trembling fingers she emptied the bag into the palm of her hand. One of the bullets fell to the wooden floor.

"For years," Rosa told her, "I hid these in the basement, with the gun. So that if Ramon ever harmed you or your sisters, I would have a way. With Ramon, it never came to that."

Terri felt a chill. "Why did Elena tell *you*?"

"Elena asked why you were leaving her. And then she asked when her father was coming for her. When I told her Sunday, she started crying. It took perhaps an hour to find out why. Her father had said that if she told anyone, the courts would take her away from him and he would go to jail." Rosa's face hardened. "I gave Elena a sleeping pill and held her close. By the time she fell asleep, I knew that I would never let him come for her."

Terri felt herself wince. "You should have told *me*. I could have made him stop."

Her mother stood straighter. "No. *I* made him stop. Now Elena is safe from him and from the courts. As well as from her own shame."

There was an eerie certainty to her mother's words. Softly Terri asked, "How did you do it, Mom?"

Rosa coldly smiled. "Sit with me, Teresa, instead of staring at me like a stranger." Turning, she walked to the couch and sat in one corner. Terri followed and sat at the opposite corner of the couch.

"It began simply enough. I went to the basement and took out the bullets and gun. For fifteen years I hadn't touched or even looked at them. I had trouble loading it—I kept dropping bullets.

"When I went back to see Elena, I felt drugged. I would think of Ricardo—and then Ramon." Rosa seemed to stare into her memory. "Elena was asleep. I picked up the telephone and called

Ricardo's number. When he answered, I knew he would be there.

"I hung up. And then I got my black raincoat, put the revolver in a pocket, and drove to Ricardo's. When I pushed the buzzer, I felt calm. The sound of his voice over the intercom made me want to smile. Because I knew that Elena would never hear that voice again."

Terri looked into Rosa's eyes with dread and awe. "When Ricardo heard it was me, he buzzed me in," her mother went on. "After all, what harm could I be? I went to the door and knocked. When Ricardo peered from behind the door chain, his nose was bleeding.

" 'You're too late,' he told me. At first I didn't know what he meant; then I realized he must be talking about Elena." Rosa's face turned to stone. "When he opened the door, it was like the beginning of a dream. I closed the door behind me and took out the gun."

Simply and sparingly Rosa described the next few minutes. As if in a silent movie Terri matched words with images—Richie backing fearfully from his door to the desk, picking up a pen, putting it down. Saw her mother, with lethal irony, placing Elena's picture by his note. Compared her mother's story to the medical examiner's flawed imaginings: the nosebleed when Dr. Shelton believed Christopher Paget had struck Richie in the face; the bruise on the leg and gash on the head when Richie had fallen backward. Except that Richie had been running from the gun in Rosa's hand.

"While he lay there," Rosa said with terrible calm, "I put the revolver in his mouth. I wanted him to die knowing how Elena felt. The last thing he said was, 'Please.' "

Rosa closed her eyes. In memory she pulled the trigger.

RICHIE's eyes froze in shock.

A fine red mist rose from his mouth. The bullet had ended his life; it had not, Rosa guessed, gone through his head. He looked innocent, even frail, surprised that life had not been fair to him.

The telephone rang. Rosa started. The phone rang twice more, then stopped. Gazing at the dead man, Rosa heard his voice.

"Hi there. I'm not in at the moment, but I want to talk to you. . . ."

"IT WAS you, Teresa," Rosa said. "Begging him to see you that Friday night. I listened to you plead for custody of Elena, while I looked into Ricardo's face. And then I placed the gun in his hand, wiped my fingers on the raincoat, and went to the phone machine.

"When you finished the message, I turned off the machine and erased the tape. I didn't want them thinking you might have come there, you see. They might have suspected you.

"It was the last clear thought I had. It took all my strength to walk to the car and drive home."

TERRI stood staring out the window at Dolores Street. Behind her Rosa sat on the couch, silent and still.

"You let Chris go to trial. You let Carlo believe his father a murderer. You let *me* believe him a murderer."

"Never did I suspect what would happen to Chris," Rosa said.

Terri turned from the window. "And when it happened?"

"I had Elena to think of."

Terri walked toward her mother in silent fury. "And Carlo?"

"Carlo," she answered, "is not my grandchild."

Terri jerked Rosa upright, grasping the front of her robe. "Carlo," she spat out, "is not a child molester. And you could have sent Chris to prison."

Rosa did not struggle. "No. I would never have permitted that. But now he is acquitted, and Elena need never know."

"What about *me?*"

"I would have told you, Teresa. In time."

"But you didn't." Terri's voice grew soft again. "You did what you thought was right. And so can I."

Rosa gave her a weary look. "Will you tell the police? Send me to prison and traumatize Elena? For what—Ricardo Arias?"

Terri shook her head. "For Carlo, and especially for Chris. For the rest of his life, people will think him a murderer."

"Ask him, then," Rosa said. "Let Christopher Paget do justice."

Slowly Terri released her mother.

Gazing calmly into her face, Rosa said, "You called Ricardo *twice,* didn't you? That was why, in Italy, you were so worried when you could not find Ricardo, why you concealed from the police that you'd called him again. Because you were certain that Ricardo died between those two calls." Rosa paused. "You thought *Chris* had erased your message. That was what you could never speak of."

Terri did not respond.

483

CHRIS ANSWERED HIS door. It was two o'clock.

"I have something to tell you," Terri said.

"It's okay. I was waiting up for you."

They walked through to the library. Chris flicked on a small lamp and sat on the couch looking up at her in the half-light.

Terri did not sit. "Chris, it was my mother."

He nodded. "Yes, I know."

"You knew?"

"I suspected. Tell me how she did it. I already know the why."

It startled her. "You knew about Elena?"

"I know that Carlo didn't abuse her."

Terri felt shame overtake her. "No," she said softly. "*Richie* did."

"Richie?" For the first time, Chris looked surprised.

"Yes."

He stood abruptly. "And your mother let Carlo hang there."

Terri did not flinch. "She let *you* hang there."

"I'm not sixteen. You'd better tell me everything."

She told him all she knew, without emphasis or inflection. His expression never changed. His body was unnaturally still. When she finished, Terri felt exhausted.

"Does your mother understand what she did?" he asked.

"No." Terri's voice fell. "I want you to clear yourself, Chris."

A first ironic smile. "I thought I had."

"You know better." Terri paused and then made herself finish. "I was afraid that you'd killed him."

He looked into her face. "What about Carlo?"

"I wasn't sure. That's why you should do it, Chris. For Carlo."

"You're right. But you're leaving out Elena. The only thing your mother got right is that if this came out, it would devastate Elena. That's not a decision I'm prepared to make by myself." He paused, finishing quietly, "Nor, in the end, is it my decision. Or yours."

Terri stared at him. "You'd involve Carlo? You can't do that."

"Your mother did."

"I can't permit that. Even if there weren't also *you*."

He gave a short laugh. "Me? I deserve whatever I get. If only for my own stupidity."

"For what? Loving me?"

"No," Paget answered. "For being at Richie's that night."

484

RICARDO ARIAS OPENED the door. Paget looked at him.

"Come on in." Richie's voice was oddly pleasant. "I've been looking forward to this."

Silent, Paget stepped into the living room, then turned to face him. Paget had worn a suit; this, at best, was business.

"You told me what you had," Paget said. "I want to see it."

Richie walked to the coffee table. "I have copies," he said, "so don't even think about doing anything crazy."

On the table was a red-bound journal. Richie picked it up and gave it to Paget. "Read the last entry. It's all you'll need to know."

Paget opened the journal to the first page. There was the faint smell of mildew. The writing was feminine, careful and precise, recording the events in the order they occurred. That the language was flat, without emotion, made the entries worse. Paget reached the final entry, finished it, then read the words again.

"Well?" Richie said.

In that moment Paget wondered if it was possible to hate another man this much. "How did you get this?"

"I copied a set of Terri's keys." Richie's voice held no apology. His eyes glinted. "It's not too good for *her*, do you think? Makes you wonder what kind of mother she'd make."

Paget handed the diary back. Softly he said, "She was fourteen."

"A hundred thousand dollars," Richie said. "Cash."

Paget did not trust himself to speak.

Richie seemed to misread this. "If she's not worth it to you, maybe we can negotiate some sort of global arrangement. Covering all our outstanding issues. Your choice," he said. "Maybe we—"

With all the force he had, Paget swung. His fist crashed into Richie's face. The shock ran through Paget's arm. Richie clasped both hands to his face, moaning, and fell, half sitting, onto the rug.

Gazing at him, Paget felt his right hand throbbing. The diary lay at his feet. He kicked it toward Richie. "Hand that up to me."

Richie looked dazed. His nose was swollen and bloody. He crawled mutely to the diary, then thrust it toward Paget.

As he took the diary, Paget sent the back of his hand cracking across Richie's face. With a short cry Richie fell sideways, one arm upraised to protect himself. Paget flinched at the pain in his hand. Blood from Richie's nose speckled the arm of his suit coat.

"I should stop," Paget said. "I'm getting you all over me."

Paget turned from him and walked toward the door. Then, facing Richie again, he rested his damaged hand on the answering machine on top of Richie's desk.

"If I let you do this," Paget told him, "you'd be in our lives forever. So you may wonder what I'll do to you if you ever try to use this diary or to ruin my son's life or Terri's. The truth is, I have no idea. Because it will be something I've never done to anyone."

Turning, he opened the door and left.

TERRI studied his face.

"Why were you there?" she finally asked. "No more lies, Chris. You thought you knew why my mother killed Richie. But you didn't know about Elena. I want to hear *everything*. Just like you did."

Chris's voice was flat. "He tried to sell me information."

Terri nodded. "From some sort of journal—the one Georgina Keller saw."

"Yes."

"What did you do with it?"

Chris turned from her and walked to the mantel. "It's here."

"Where? The police turned the house inside out."

"Not quite." Chris knelt, pushing the brick backing of the fireplace. A line of bricks turned sideways, exposing a square compartment. "The man who built this place was paranoid, and the cop who searched it very young. I managed to distract him." Reaching in, Paget withdrew a journal. He gave it to Terri.

She walked to the sofa and sat beneath the light. She opened the journal. The handwriting was her mother's. The first entry was dated shortly after Terri's birth.

"Last night," Rosa had written, "Ramon beat me until my cries woke Teresa." Tears stung Terri's eyes. She turned the page. Day by day, for fourteen years, her mother recorded what Ramon Peralta had done to her. The words were flat, emotionless. Some of the entries stirred Terri's memory. Most did not. When Terri reached that night in the living room—Ramon beating her mother—she set the book aside.

How could she have lived? Terri wondered bleakly. But part of her knew the answer: She lived for us. She lived for me.

Before Terri reached it, she knew the date of the final entry. "I cannot be certain," her mother had written, "that the shadow was Teresa. Or if it was, what she chooses to remember."

THERE was someone in the house. Half asleep, Terri could hear this, a whisper in the silence. Perhaps it was Ramon Peralta returning, filled with whiskey. Perhaps it was a dream. But the crawl of fear across her skin drew her into the hallway to seek her mother.

Her parents' door was ajar. Her mother was not there.

Terri was frightened now.

She would not abandon her mother. Slowly Terri crept down the stairs. The living room was empty. Terri stood there listening.

A creak, somehow familiar. It was the back door to the kitchen. That would be the creak—the door opening to admit light.

Terri crept through the dining room until, heart racing, she reached the alcove and gazed into the kitchen.

A crack of light. A shadow standing in the doorway. The shadow faced the porch. But Terri knew it, slim and still. And then her mother turned a fraction, and the porch light caught her face.

She was staring down through the doorway. Terri followed her gaze and saw that Ramon Peralta stared up at her. There was a trickle of blood on his face; his eyes were stunned, beseeching, like an animal's. "Please," she saw him whisper.

Silent, Rosa gazed down at him. Terri saw the blood beneath his head now, black in the half-light.

Rosa seemed to consider him. Then she straightened, closing the screen door. The latch clicked shut. In the light Terri saw her father's hand clawing at the door. And then quite calmly Rosa switched off the light.

Terri felt herself gasp.

The shadow spun. With blackness between them Terri and her mother faced each other. Terri could not be sure if Rosa saw her.

There had been something in her mother's hand.

Terri was still. *"Go,"* she imagined her mother saying. "I'm giving you time. Go back to your room and dream."

It was a dream, Terri told herself. A dream.

She turned without speaking and tiptoed across the dining room. As if walking in her sleep, Terri climbed the stairs. A dream.

"I'm sorry," Chris murmured. "I'm so sorry."

As he reached for her, Terri crumpled. She sobbed against him uncontrollably, her body shuddering.

"It's all right," Chris said. "In time, everything will be better."

Terri felt unspeakably tired. In her lap, where it had fallen, was her mother's diary. "What shall I do with this?" she murmured.

"Take it to your mother. Tell her it's a gift from me."

"Carlo needs to know. About Richie—and about Elena."

Chris nodded. "I meant to tell him."

Terri sat straighter. "We both should. If that's all right."

He did not answer, but when he climbed the stairs to Carlo's room, Terri was at his side.

THE FAMILY

April, The Following Year

TWENTY-FIVE

IT WAS over a year before Chris and Terri returned to Italy, and when they did, it was not to Venice but to Montalcino, in Tuscany.

The town itself was quaint yet lively. Church bells sounded; children kicked a soccer ball in the square, surrounded by benches and people talking. Smiling, Terri took Chris's arm as they meandered through the town. At the end of the street they found themselves gazing down at the tree-covered grounds of a white stone church. The grounds ended at a precipice and a startling panorama of hills and fields and valleys receding into the distance.

Chris and Terri sat on a bench beneath a white flowering tree beside the church. Before them were fields of tiny wildflowers. The spring morning was fresh and still. Terri felt at peace.

Chris turned to her. "We've earned this, don't you think?"

Terri smiled. "If we haven't, I don't want to know."

This made him laugh. But so much did now. It was something she was still learning about him. Terri gazed at the church.

"Shall we go inside?" she asked.

"As Carlo would say, I generally don't do churches."

She took his hand. "Come on. I'll show you. It'll be all right."

THAT NIGHT A YEAR BEFORE, when they told Carlo all that had happened, Terri had thought that nothing could be all right. Carlo sat up in his bed, back against the wall; Chris sat at the foot of the bed with Terri. Carlo was silent for a long time.

"I'm sorry," he said to his father. "But you should have told me."

Chris could have justified himself or at least tried, but he seemed to know that he should not. Terri felt overwhelmed.

"What are you going to do about Terri's mother?" Carlo asked.

"For myself?" Chris said. "Nothing."

Carlo studied him. "So if I say we should let the truth out, *I'm* the one who's sent Elena's grandmother to prison."

"No," Terri interjected. "We're not putting this off on you. I won't let you or Chris pay the price for Richie and my mother."

Carlo regarded her intently. "Thanks anyhow," he said at last. "I'll just have to deal with it." His voice grew hard. "Just don't expect me to pretend this didn't happen. Either of you."

IT WAS five o'clock in the morning when Terri got home. Elena was asleep; Terri's neighbor Nancy slept on the couch.

After showering, Terri apologized to Nancy and had a quiet breakfast with Elena. Softly Terri asked her, "Do you remember what we talked about last night? About your daddy?"

Elena nodded at her bowl of cereal.

"I'm so glad you told me, Elena. I know how hard it was."

Slowly Elena looked up. "Was it wrong, Mommy?"

"Very wrong, of your daddy," Terri finally answered. "That's not how parents treat their children."

That morning after she dropped Elena at school, Terri returned to her mother's. When Rosa answered the door, she was carefully dressed and made up. She saw the journal that Terri held. Silent, she opened the door.

When Terri was inside, Rosa extended an arm toward the couch. They sat at opposite ends, as they had the night before. Terri handed Rosa the journal.

Her mother seemed to flinch. "You have read it," Rosa said.

"Yes. Chris says that you should consider it a gift."

Rosa folded her hands. "Then Ricardo had it."

"Yes. He duplicated my keys and then prowled through your

house—perhaps to see if I kept papers here. Instead he found *this*."

Rosa gazed at the journal. "I never knew it was gone until after that night. I thought that you had taken it, but I could not ask."

All that silence, Terri thought. "Did you think I'd say nothing?"

Rosa looked into her face. "What do you remember?"

"Everything. What were you holding?"

"A wrench. *His* wrench. To use if I needed it."

Terri felt a wave of sickness. "We killed him, Mama."

"*I* killed him, Teresa. You simply protected me and then tried to protect yourself. As best a child could." Rosa's voice was soft. "So you see, Ricardo was not new to me. Long ago I learned that I was capable of murder. Because when Ramon lay on the porch reaching up to me, I knew that he must die if we were ever to be free."

But they had never been free, Terri thought, and were not free now. She squared her shoulders. "Chris will say nothing, Mama. Neither will Carlo. But I'm sure that Chris will never want to see you."

Rosa studied her. "Because of the boy."

"Yes. Even if Chris could forgive you for himself."

Her mother turned away. "What about you, Teresa?"

Softly Terri answered, "You're my mother."

Her mother's eyes closed. "And Elena?"

"I'll bring her to see you. As much as is possible, we'll act as we did before. Elena loves you. I don't think she can take another loss."

ONE more person deserved to know the truth. A few days later, with Terri's consent, the telling fell to Paget.

Caroline Masters leaned back in her chair. "*Rosa*," she murmured. An astonishing range of expressions crossed her face. And then, to her plain surprise, Caroline began to laugh. "Chris, I just love assisting justice by accident. It expands my sense of the possible." After a moment she turned serious. "Will you please tell me just what you thought you were doing?"

Paget shrugged. "I thought I was protecting myself. I'd already lied to Terri about being at Richie's; I wasn't prepared to confront her with what I'd learned about her father's death. Then suddenly there was Monk questioning Terri. All at once I sounded like a man who'd lied to her to build an alibi—"

"But lying to Monk . . ."

490

"Stupid, I know. You can also see now why I wouldn't take the stand. I refused to lie to the jury—to say I wasn't there—and admitting that I *was* there would be to admit lying to Monk. Which, with Brooks and Colt after me and no other suspect except Terri, might well have been fatal."

"Not to mention that you would have had to tell the jury about Rosa—and Terri. So you decided to take the chance that your gifted lawyer could walk you on reasonable doubt."

"Just so."

"And is that why you kept the diary? Because you thought it was Rosa's motive?"

"I wasn't at all sure that Rosa had killed Richie. But if I'd been convicted, she and I were going to have a little chat."

"And Terri?" Caroline asked.

"To me, an implausible murderer. But it had to be Rosa or Terri. I never believed that stuff you dreamed up about drug dealers and homicidal politicians, and I assume you didn't, either."

"Of course not," Caroline said. "To the extent I considered it, I thought it was either you or Terri or both of you, with Terri providing extremely clever testimony you'd auditioned in advance."

Even now the remark hit Paget hard. "Whew," he said.

Caroline gave him a look of compassion. "So perhaps you can forgive Teresa for suspecting what *I* suspected frequently. That I was representing a murderer I liked rather more than I should."

Paget did not smile. "You're forgiven, Caroline. Terri I'm still working out." He stood. "Somehow I don't think I've quite managed to thank you adequately."

"Oh, I should thank *you*." Caroline took him by the arm, steering him to the door. And when he turned to say good-bye, she kissed him on the cheek. "That," she said, "was for being innocent."

IT WAS several months before Paget encountered Victor Salinas, and then Salinas came to his office unannounced.

"Who did I murder now?" Paget asked.

Salinas gave him an edgy, delayed smile. "McKinley Brooks?"

Paget stared at him. "Sit down."

Sitting, Salinas looked around for a moment, taking in Paget's paintings and the small sculpture on his desk. To Paget he seemed

491

muted. "I would like to run for district attorney," Salinas said calmly.

Paget nodded. "Let me see if I follow you, Victor. After what Caroline did at my trial, McKinley's anonymous friend became too gun-shy to find Mac some higher office. On the other hand, Mac is insufficiently wounded not to run for D.A. again. Which leaves him in your way." Paget paused. "So you're wondering whether I want to get back at Mac so badly that I'd help you become D.A.—say by digging up more dirt on how Mac tampered with the Ricardo Arias inquiry. I could for example ask Johnny Moore to see what he could find—like the nameless 'source' who contacted Brooks after the cops found Richie dead. Is that about it?"

"You're in the ballpark," Salinas said.

Paget smiled. "That kind of information would ruin Mac politically. He might even get indicted. All you'd need is to feed the source to the U.S. Attorney, and a grand jury would have a field day."

"All right," Salinas said. "It's what I need. So will you help me?"

Slowly Paget drew a manila file from a drawer and placed it on the desk. "It's all here in Johnny's report to me. The 'source' who called Brooks is the same man who funneled the information to Jack Slocum and, no doubt, the ten thousand dollars to our late friend Ricardo. The file is yours. In the public interest, of course."

Salinas stared at it. "What do *you* want?" he asked.

"James Colt."

Salinas sat back. "This source has ties to Colt?"

"Yes. To a certainty, Colt is McKinley's secret friend. The one who tampered with your case. So if you accept this information, you're committing yourself to Colt's political demise."

Salinas eyed the file. Then he reached across and took it.

PAGET lined up the cue ball, carefully aiming at the black eight ball. With a smooth stroke he propelled the cue ball; there was a soft crack, and the eight ball glided into the corner pocket.

"There," Paget said with satisfaction.

Carlo stared at the spot where, a moment before, the last ball had resided. "Another game," he announced. It was not a request.

They racked up the balls again. In the last nine years they had shot countless games of pool in Paget's basement; over time, Carlo had become Paget's competitor and then his equal.

"Look," Paget said abruptly, "I know I screwed things up."

Lining up the cue ball, Carlo did not look at him. His cue flashed; the white ball sped into the pack, sending balls rolling at all angles. Two disappeared into pockets. Carlo then scanned the table. "You screwed up, all right." He lined up his next shot. "What made it worse is that since I was a kid, I expected you to be perfect. When you weren't, I was scared—and mad." Carlo made the shot.

Paget looked at him. He did not know what to say.

Turning, Carlo eyed another shot. "Guess being a parent's a rough deal, huh?" The ball disappeared.

"Only sometimes," Paget said. "Other times it's not so bad."

Carlo smiled and made a bank shot. "So what's happening with you and Terri?" He sank his fifth shot in a row.

Paget raised his eyebrows. "I didn't know you cared."

"I've decided to declare amnesty," Carlo said.

Slowly Paget shook his head. That Carlo had protected Elena made him sad and proud at once; from what Terri said, it might yet be the saving of her. "You'd get a lot of points for Elena," Paget said seriously. "Even if I didn't love you so much. You've shown more character than Terri or I had any right to ask."

Carlo shrugged. "Elena I'm learning to live with. I've sort of figured out that if you show up somewhere and *you* know you're okay, people will accept that." He paused, then made his sixth shot running. "Terri's a nice person—a lot better than her life."

Paget hesitated. "What made *that* occur to you?"

"Two things." Carlo sank another two balls and then smiled up at his father. "First, she can honestly talk about how she feels, sometimes in complete sentences. Second, she doesn't talk to me like a parent. But then she's closer to *my* age than yours." The grin widened. "That was eight, by the way. You lose."

Two months before the November election McKinley Brooks was indicted by a federal grand jury.

On the day of the indictment Paget met Johnny Moore downtown to watch the evening news. The two friends sat at a mirrored bar beneath a television, drinks in hand.

When the news came on, the lead story was Brooks' indictment. "San Francisco district attorney McKinley Brooks was indicted today," said the blond anchorwoman, "on five counts alleging obstruction of the Senate race and subsequent murder trial of prominent San Francisco lawyer Christopher Paget."

The picture changed. A grim McKinley Brooks appeared hurrying from the federal building, flanked by lawyers.

"The case against Brooks centers on the testimony of political operative George Norton, who allegedly spoke to Brooks on behalf of gubernatorial aspirant James Colt. According to sources close to the grand jury, Norton claims he funneled campaign moneys to Ricardo Arias, the estranged husband of Mr. Paget's associate, Teresa Peralta, to make sensational charges against Mr. Paget and his son in Arias' divorce case. After Arias' mysterious death by gunshot, Mr. Norton—supposedly at the insistence of an aide to James Colt—again contacted the D.A. to ensure that the police did not discover the ties between Ricardo Arias and the Colt campaign. At his home in Bel Air, James Colt denied all charges."

On the screen, Colt appeared, standing beneath a palm tree, tense but composed. He was surrounded by cameras.

"However," the anchorwoman narrated, "there were late reports that McKinley Brooks is negotiating for reduced charges in exchange for testimony regarding his conversations with James Colt. The damage to Colt's candidacy may be immediate and severe."

"Colt is toast," Moore said.

The anchorwoman reappeared. "Today's indictment seemingly assures the election of insurgent candidate Victor Salinas as district attorney. Asked for comment, Salinas said, 'The Ricardo Arias matter was a travesty. This indictment reaffirms the principle that justice should not be sold, no matter how rich and powerful the bidder.'

"As for Mr. Paget, who has been silent throughout, his only comment was, quote, 'I'm sure they'll treat Mr. Colt more fairly than he treated my teenage son. Of course, he'll need that.' "

Moore looked sharply over at Paget. "Nasty," he said.

Paget raised his glass. "It had a certain elegance, I thought."

Moore touched Paget's glass with his. "You've also redeemed Carlo's reputation. And your own." He gave Paget a sideways look. "So," he said, "who *did* kill Ricardo Arias?"

Paget smiled. "Colt, of course. Didn't he do everything?"

Teresa Peralta lay beside Chris in the quiet of his bedroom. It was just past Christmas. Elena, happy with her toys, was spending the night with Rosa. Fourteen months after Richie's death Elena showed no sign of knowing the truth; for Elena, the security of Rosa's love and of her life with Terri seemed more and more to define her world. Sensing this, Terri was content. The subject of Richie, so potentially explosive, might be dormant for a time.

Terri turned to Chris. He slept lightly, his face calm and dreamless. Earlier, lost in his arms, she had not been sure where they were going. "Are we the same?" she had asked him.

"We'll never be the same. We've been through too much."

The elliptical phrase made Terri sad. "I can stand all that. What I can't stand is the idea of losing you."

"You haven't lost me, Terri."

"I haven't *got* you, either. There's a part of you that's out of reach. I can't quite seem to touch it."

"Then keep trying." He kissed her forehead. "Because if you ever stopped, I don't think I could stand it."

There it was, Terri thought, after months of wondering. She could not understand the tears in her eyes.

Christopher Paget held her close. "So are you going to marry me," he said, "or do I have to ask you?"

Terri found that she was smiling against his shoulder. "No," she managed. "I'll marry you. But what about Carlo?"

"Carlo? Oh, I did ask *him,* a few days ago. It's okay by him."

Now, as Chris slept, Terri knew she would love him more than he had ever been loved. And so, in time, would Elena.

Paget entered the church in Montalcino. Carlo and Elena stood at the altar. Somehow Terri had persuaded a priest to marry her to Paget, a non-Catholic.

They approached the altar and stood in front of the priest, a stocky man with a peasant's face and warm brown eyes. Their children were beside them. The vows began.

The priest spoke in broken English. When the moment came that they were married, Paget smiled to himself and felt the pressure of Terri's hand. He kissed her then.

Carlo was the second to kiss Terri. "Nice going," he told her.

Terri smiled. Beside them Elena began tugging on Terri's yellow silk dress. "Can we go outside now?" she asked.

The priest smiled down at her. "Go ahead," he told Chris and Terri. "I'll give the papers to your son."

Outside on a bench was a bottle of cold champagne. But before they could retrieve it, Elena asked, "Mommy, can we go get some ice cream? Yesterday I saw a place in the town."

"Elena, we just got married. We have toasts to drink."

Elena turned to Carlo as he emerged from the church. "Maybe you can take me, Carlo. You're my stepbrother now."

Carlo gave her a wry look. "Does that mean I have to take you places, Munchkin?"

The old nickname made Elena's eyes crinkle. "Yes," she announced firmly. "You have to now."

Carlo smiled at her. "Oh, all right," he said. "But *after* I drink some champagne."

Quietly Terri took Paget's hand and walked toward the bench. "Now that we're married, I have something to tell you," she said.

As soon as he looked at her face, smiling yet watchful, he knew what it was. "A baby?" he asked.

Terri grinned at him. "Uh-huh. What do you think?"

Paget sat down, taking this in as he looked out at the lush green hills of Tuscany, then at his family. He was forty-seven. He would not be a Senator or do all that he might have wished to do. But he would be this woman's partner, their time together still ahead, filled with joys and sorrows and surprises and, most of all, people he cared for, their lives interwoven with the fabric of his own.

Taking Terri's hand, he leaned back on the bench, feeling the sunlight on his face, at peace for perhaps the first time in his life.

"A baby," he said again. "Seems like enough."

ABOUT
THE AUTHOR

Richard North Patterson

Richard North Patterson had to look no further than his own law career for the vivid courtroom details that give *Eyes of a Child* its ring of authenticity. Before his success as a best-selling author enabled him to write full time, Patterson worked as a trial attorney for nearly twenty years, serving at times as a prosecutor, other times as a defense attorney. Which did he prefer? "They both have their good points," he says. "As a prosecutor, you feel a certain moral righteousness about what you're doing. But I also enjoy the chess-game aspects of defending a case."

As for the book's setting, Patterson had only to step out his door to find authentic San Francisco details. A Bay Area native, he lives and works in the city's Pacific Heights section, in a large Victorian house that he shares with his wife, Laurie, and their six children. Before marrying Laurie, the author, like his lead character Chris Paget, was for many years a single father of a teenage son, and this experience, too, has found its way into his book. Paget has now appeared in three of Patterson's novels—including his first novel, *The Lasko Tangent,* which won an Edgar Award in 1979 for best mystery of the year. Is Paget likely to turn up in future novels? "No," says the author. "After what he and Terri have been through, I think they deserve to live happily ever after."

PHOTO: *PEOPLE WEEKLY* © ACEY HARPER

More Than Meets the Eye

The true story of one woman's
triumph over darkness

JOAN BROCK AND DEREK L. GILL

"All our tests have shown us that the deterioration in your eyesight is irreversible. . . ."

When a doctor spoke these fateful words to Joan Brock, she was thirty-two years old. She was terrified that she would never see her daughter's small face again. Or the rich colors of the beach at sunrise. Or so many other things she loved. Then disease struck again. This time the victim was her husband. And as she battled against still greater darkness, she learned to find beauty in her life once more— the beauty that can be seen only through the heart.

1
Winter's Twilight

EVEN had it not been the day before my thirty-second birthday, I could never forget the date. On awakening that morning, I was quite unaware that the compass of my life had begun to swing radically.

I had a slight headache and a mild sense of lassitude. Oh, gosh! I thought; hope I'm not in for a cold—not in this weather.

After showering, I used the sleeve of my gown to wipe steam from the bathroom window. This enabled me to read the outside thermometer. It showed twenty degrees below zero. I shivered and indulged in covetous thoughts about California, where I had grown up. I enjoyed recollected images of palm trees and golden beaches. My husband, Joe, was already downstairs and doubtless hungry for breakfast.

I peeked through the door of Joy's room. Our three-year-old was still asleep, her golden hair spread across the pillow and her eyeless teddy bear limply clasped above the covers.

Once I had gotten Joe out of the house, there would be time enough to stir and dress our daughter.

Life for Joe and me was more than satisfying. Both of us loved our work at the Iowa Braille and Sight Saving School. Joe was the director of leisure and recreational training, and I was liaison between dorm parents and classroom teachers. I was also involved with the school's public relations. Joy was always close at hand because her preschool classroom was on the Braille School's cam-

501

pus. I cannot recall contemplating the smallest shadow of worry about the future.

The reason for Joe's early departure from home that morning was a basketball game with his friends before work. He would be back to pick up Joy and me shortly after nine o'clock. Joy and I had an unhurried breakfast; then it was time to get her dressed.

Our daughter was showing early signs of independence. She bounced around her bedroom gathering a blouse here, pants there, a padded snowsuit, a thick scarf from behind the door. As usual, the business of getting all these garments on her in the right order was all squirms and squeaks. The task completed, she looked like a brown-eyed stuffed doll who could still move, but only barely. All she needed to cope with the outside temperature were boots and a cap with earflaps, both down the hall, and socks—ah, yes, socks.

I pulled out the second dresser drawer and pursed my lips.

"Pumpkin, what's happened to your pink socks?" I asked.

Joy waddled across to the dresser, where she stood on her toes. This allowed her to tip her nose over the top of the opened drawer. Then she pointed. "There they are, Mommy, in the corner."

I followed the direction of her finger. "But those are white."

An impatient sigh from Joy. "Oh, Mommy, they're pink, pink, pink, like my pants."

Joy went back to the bed, her feet in the air waiting for me to put on the selected socks. I went to the Winnie-the-Pooh lamp and slowly turned them over in my hand. They were white.

"What are you waiting for?" the stuffed doll squeaked.

"I—er—are you sure these are pink?"

Another deep sigh from Joy. "Oh, Mommy, don't be silly. You're going to make me late for school."

I closed my eyes and rubbed them, then looked again. The color hadn't changed. Gnats of worry buzzed across my mind. This was absurd. Maybe the incipient cold or my sinuses were playing tricks on me. Anyway, I heard the car in the driveway, so there was no time to argue further. By the time I had Joy fully dressed, Joe was stomping the snow off his boots at the kitchen door.

In moments we were on our way to the campus. Joe was aglow from his exercise and murmured something about having dropped nearly ten pounds in three weeks. He was built like a refrigerator, and he was in a permanent state of war with the bathroom scales.

"Didn't you hear me?" he asked. "Nearly ten pounds!"

"Great," I responded without adequate enthusiasm.

"Something on your mind?" asked Joe.

The car was slowing for a stop sign. "Yes," I said. "What color are Joy's socks?"

"For Pete's sake!" he exclaimed.

The car had stopped. "I'm serious," I said. "Just check the color, please."

He glanced at me, his brow furrowed. Then he swiveled around and asked Joy, in the back seat, to lift her pant cuffs. With mock gravity he said, "The news this morning is that the President is expected to make an important new statement about the Panama Canal. There was an airplane hijacking in Greece." A pause. "And our daughter is wearing a pair of pink socks." He guffawed.

I didn't even smile as I felt another small stab of concern.

The journey through the little town of Vinton was a short one. The current joke was that the birth of triplets to the Mifflin family had pushed the population over the five thousand mark. Boastfully, it was the county seat, and at Christmastime folks drove in from miles away to see the treelined streets and the public buildings sparkling with lights. It was a community full of friends. Everyone was on first-name terms with the mailman and the grocery clerks. It was a town where church pews were filled on Sunday and where people gave generously of their time and treasure to worthwhile causes. Vinton was just the right place for a school for blind kids.

Joe stopped the car near Joy's preschool. He leaned over and gave each of us a peck. Joy and I gripped gloved hands to walk across the street. A wintry sun was shining directly at us, and the snow was so bright that I made my eyes into slits. Suddenly I tripped over a curbside mound of snow.

"Oh, Mommy!" exclaimed Joy in alarm. "Didn't you see it?"

"No, I guess I didn't," I said breathlessly.

I looked back. With the sunlight now behind me I could clearly see why I had tripped. The mounds of snow threw shadows onto the road. Yet the moment I turned to move toward the sunlight, the landscape flattened out. It was quite puzzling.

Before Joy and I parted at the preschool door, she more than

503

compensated for my clumsiness and concern. She looked up at me and said solemnly, "Mommy, you look so pretty today." I gave her a hug.

When I reached my office, I bypassed my desk and made straight for the rest room. Looking back at me from the mirror was a face that looked pale. Figuring that a little more blush would correct the problem, I pulled out my compact. My hand froze. The blush looked like talcum powder.

I took the compact to the window, but the natural light did not change the white color to a roseate hue. I took several deep breaths. There had to be an explanation. It was eerie. Was it, I pondered, a sort of temporary snow blindness?

Heading for my office, I passed the staff secretary, Ione, who gave me her usual greeting. "Hi, Joan, how are you today?"

I stopped and turned to her. "Well, truthfully, not so hot," I said. "Think I'm getting a cold. Do I look okay to you?"

Ione gave me a second glance. "Fine, except—well . . ."

"Well what?" I asked sharply.

She laughed with embarrassment. "You're wearing enough makeup to play the clown at a children's party." She whipped a tissue from her purse. "May I try to improve things?"

I forced a smile. "Please go ahead. I was in a hurry this morning."

She tossed away the stained Kleenex. "There," she said, smiling, "now you look lovely."

The rest of my day went well. I took a couple of classes with the kids—to whom it mattered not whether I looked like a ghost or a clown—attended an administrative meeting, and met with a women's church group, who gave me a warm welcome. I managed to sign up a half-dozen volunteers to help kids on a one-to-one basis.

By the time I collected Joy, the wintry sun was setting. In the fading light my eyesight improved. I could definitely mark the undulations in the snow. On the way home I stopped in at a pharmacy to buy over-the-counter medication for my cold. As I was leaving, I noticed a rack of sunglasses. I tried on a pair. Everything looked much clearer. I bought the glasses too.

Joe was amused by the glasses, flashed a big grin, and asked if I had any Hollywood pretensions. "Don't those female film stars wear sunglasses even in bed?"

"How would you know?" I parried. Joe's grin widened. Then I tried to explain that the dark glasses helped a lot, but by this time his attention was on a sports program on TV.

The next day all the trillion cold bugs made a full-scale attack. I felt awful. I phoned the Braille School to tell them I wouldn't be in. When I had outlined my symptoms to Brenda Armstrong, a colleague and close friend, and related how pink socks looked white, she immediately advised me to see my doctor.

"Oh, it's not that bad," I protested.

Brenda said, "Perhaps not, but I don't like what you're telling me. Get to a doctor as soon as possible. Today if you can."

The urgency in Brenda's voice got to me. She was an authority on educating people with low or no vision.

"Okay," I told Brenda, trying to keep my voice casual.

"Good girl. By the way," she added, "isn't it your birthday?"

"That's the problem," I sniffed. "We've got Joe's brother and his wife coming. They're taking us out to dinner."

The doctor's appointments ledger was overloaded; however, his assistant squeezed me in for early the following morning.

That evening, when we went out to Vinton's plushest steak house with Joe's kinfolk, I assuredly wasn't an Emily Post. But I got through the evening and also half a box of tissues.

The following morning I was Dr. Tony Anthony's first patient. He greeted me warmly. Not only was he the official physician for the Braille School, he was also a good friend.

His first question was why on earth I was wearing dark glasses on a January morning. I explained how the glasses helped me to see better outside in the snow and under the bright lights of his office. Then I laughingly told him the story of Joy's socks.

He reached out and removed my glasses. "Okay, Joan," he demanded, "what color is this room?"

I squinted at the walls. "The same color as the ceiling," I said.

"Which is?"

"White, of course."

"Not quite," said the doctor.

I looked at the walls again. "Well," I conceded, "I suppose they could be a little off-white."

Dr. Anthony chewed his lip.

505

I asked, "They're not by any chance—"

"Yes, they are—a deep shade of pink."

I was aware of a missed heartbeat. The doctor went to the door and told his assistant to do routine tests, including eye pressure.

He must have observed my look of concern. He came back, patted both shoulders, and said, "We're going to find out what the trouble is. It may well be sinusitis."

My ears and throat were examined, my blood pressure taken, my eyes numbed by drops of anesthetic for the eye pressure test. I recalled how the kids at school regularly took similar tests. I'd often accompanied them, held their hands, comforted them. Now it was me in the chair. I needed someone to hold my hand.

As I sat alone waiting for the return of Dr. Anthony, the mild anxieties of the past forty-eight hours began to coalesce into a clot of fear. But no, I told myself, there can't possibly be anything seriously wrong. I had twenty-twenty vision. Anyway, no one's eyesight just deteriorated overnight—not insofar as I knew. But no matter how hard I tried to soar on thermals of optimism, the fear began to spiral into panic.

"Dear Lord," I prayed in a whisper, "You know what's wrong—if there's anything wrong—but please take away my fear."

Almost instantly my mind quieted. A moment later the door opened, and in came Dr. Anthony and his assistant.

"Joan, the eye pressure checks out just fine, but this visual loss of color is—er—confusing. So I want you to see an ophthalmologist."

"But isn't my cold causing the problem?" I suggested.

"May well be," he replied. "But it could be more serious."

"Wouldn't a couple of days in bed—"

Dr. Anthony cut in. "I've been on the phone. You've got an appointment to see a good man in Waterloo this afternoon."

Ten minutes later I was back home. Joe and Joy were dressed and ready to take off for the preschool and his office.

Joy asked, "Mommy, did they give you a shot?"

I gave her a smile. "No shot, but I'm afraid we're going to have to reorganize the day. I've got to be in Waterloo by two o'clock to see an eye doctor."

"Whoopee! No school!" exclaimed Joy.

Joe said crisply, "I'll phone the office."

While we were driving, Joy asked me to read to her. Because my eyes were watery, I suggested we recite nursery rhymes. We sing-songed "Jack and Jill" and "Little Jack Horner." But her favorite was "The Snowflake Song." After the second encore Joe joined in. For the next few miles "The Snowflake Song" and our laughter helped me to forget completely the need for the journey.

In now recalling that drive down the road between Vinton and Waterloo, I can re-create the scene with extraordinary vividness. I see whirling snowflakes. I hear squeaking windshield wipers. My nostrils even pick up the pungent smell of damp woolen scarfs and mittens.

I know now, of course, why the picture is so clear, why the sounds and scents are so deeply grooved upon my mind. What I did not comprehend at the time was that soon, so very soon, the harmony of all my senses would not experience the like again.

2
"That's My Wife!"

THE Waterloo ophthalmologist dilated my eyes and spent a long time peering through a sophisticated apparatus. Eventually he swiveled his chair around to a wall desk. His pen scratched on a notepad. My patience had rarely been more hard-tested. My mind was screaming, Tell me I'm going to be okay! Tell me something!

The scratching of the pen ceased. The doctor stood up. Disappointingly, he said, "Let's go to my office."

I remember the deep pile of the office carpet, the backs of silver photograph frames on the desk. Somewhere behind me a clock faintly ticked. Through misting eyes I could make out that the doctor was turning pages of a large volume. *Ticktock* went the clock as seconds mounted into minutes. I felt I knew what it was like to be in the dock of a courtroom when the jury had just returned with a verdict.

"Guilty or innocent?" I heard myself asking.

I could make out the doctor lifting his face from the volume and removing his spectacles. "What was that?" he asked.

My voice again, like a mendicant pleading for alms: "Please, Doctor, give me something. Give me the verdict."

The heavy volume was closed with a plop. His answer was about as anticlimactic as it could be. "I don't know," he said.

"You don't know!" I exclaimed. "But there must be something."

"Yes, Mrs. Beringer, there is obviously something. But without more tests, for which I don't have the facilities, I cannot tell you what the problem is."

Then he gave me a short lecture on "the astonishing miracle" of eyesight. He spoke as if he were talking to a child. He told me that the retina of each eye holds a hundred and seven million cells. Of these, seven million are cones. The cones provide color awareness.

"The cones are the cells which, when healthy, should have told you that your daughter's socks were pink, not white."

I interjected, "And the rods distinguish between black and white."

"Quite right," he said enthusiastically, as if he were a teacher congratulating a bright student. The doctor continued his mini-lecture, but now he upgraded my intelligence and threw in a few polysyllabic words. "There's obviously some neurological interference to your visual capacity—markedly, to the reception of the cones. Frankly, I do not know why, so I am referring you to a specialist at the University of Iowa Hospital."

It was two weeks before I could get an appointment at the hospital. When I awakened each morning, I hoped that my eyes would be better, but each day my vision was worse. I tried to convince myself that I could function adequately. I had been driving Joy the two and a half blocks to her preschool. When the windshield became more and more fogged up, I vainly tried to clean the glass. One morning I opened the window and stuck out my head, hoping that I'd be able to see better. The fog was still there. I drove over a deep gutter, causing the car to rock wildly and bump hard. Joy cried out in alarm. I acknowledged that I was endangering my daughter and others on the road. After delivering Joy to the preschool, I stumbled through the snow to Joe's office.

I blurted out to him, "I cannot drive again. I could have killed Joy this morning or maybe run down another child. I must not drive anymore. I'm so sorry, Joe. Forgive me."

He was gentle with me. "There is nothing to forgive," he told me. "They'll find the problem. They'll find the answer."

Colleagues at the school were no less sympathetic, no less helpful. My supervisor, Dan Wirth, gave me a magnifying device shaped like a golf ball but flattened at the top and bottom. When placed on a page, he told me, it would magnify letters fivefold.

One late afternoon I took the device to the deserted school library, which housed many braille and large-print books. The sun was setting, and the light in the empty library was low—a light that now best suited me. I took one of the large-print books to a corner desk, then placed the magnifying glass on a page. I couldn't make out a single letter. I turned the glass golf ball the other way around and tried again. All that was visible were faint blobs.

A brutal truth hit me with crushing impact. My central vision was all but gone. Many of the partially blind children could see better than I could now see. "Oh, God!" I cried. Tears welled up and fell upon the hand that held the golf ball magnifying glass.

As twilight moved to darkness, I remained at the desk, too numbed to move, until I remembered that Joe was to meet me in the lobby downstairs. My limbs jerked into action, for were Joe to see no lights, he would assume I'd made my own way home.

When we met in the lobby, I collapsed into Joe's arms. His rebuke stopped my slide into hysteria. "Snap out of it, Joan," he told me. "You've got to shape up and start to take a positive attitude. Isn't that what we teach them in this place?"

I sobbed, "But I couldn't read a single word."

He put an arm around my shoulders. "People don't go blind just like that. It doesn't happen that way, and you know it."

That's right, I told myself. It doesn't happen like that. I couldn't think of one child who had a medical history comparable to mine.

As we walked from the library to the car, I repeated Joe's words aloud. "You're right," I said. "It doesn't happen like that."

What was curious and initially encouraging, too, was that I still had some peripheral vision. When the light was low, I could, if I turned my head, make out objects, albeit colorless, and movement. There were moments, too, again when the light was dim or I was wearing dark glasses—which I now did most of the time—when I rediscovered a tiny window of central vision.

So I was not without hope when Joe and I set out for my first appointment at the University of Iowa Hospital in Iowa City. It is one of the biggest teaching hospitals in America, and it was only an

hour's drive from Vinton. The hospital's ophthalmology department was familiar to me, for I'd often taken Braille School children
there. It had not only the latest diagnostic equipment but several
specialists with national and even international reputations.

I was hardly less fortunate in being on the staff of Vinton's Braille
and Sight Saving School, where many of my co-workers were highly
trained and long experienced in helping the blind and partially
sighted cope with their totally dark or shadowed worlds.

As we turned onto the highway for Iowa City, I mentioned these
advantages to Joe. I said laughingly, "If there's one place I'd choose
to be blind, it's right here!"

I was shaken by his almost savage response. He thumped the
steering wheel with his fist and said, "For Pete's sake, Joan, it's not
funny. You're not going blind, damn it! You can't!"

In the ensuing silence I began to comprehend what a load I had
placed upon my husband. I felt sure he had already pictured himself with a blind wife, and because he was a perfectionist, the picture
would be grim, perhaps intolerable. I wanted to reach out and touch
his arm, but feelings of guilt and resentment held me back.

As we drove, I found myself reflecting upon the irony of my
situation. Here I was, a professional who each day had been giving
her physical, mental, and spiritual energy to helping children
scramble and claw their way up from their own dark pits into a
world of sighted people. Was I myself now going the other way?

When Joe opened the car door for me in the parking lot of the
huge hospital, he apologized and said, "Okay, Joan, let's get to these
guys who are going to fix you up." A grim laugh, then: "If they don't,
they're going to have to answer to me."

I now understood what really troubled Joe. This man at my
shoulder, who gave every outward impression that he was afraid of
nothing or anyone, was now, in fact, fearful. He was afraid for me,
afraid for Joy, and, I was sure, afraid for himself.

When we reached the appropriate waiting room, my fuzzy vision
indicated that at least three dozen people had arrived ahead of us.
It was nearly two hours after my scheduled appointment when my
name was called. Joe had left the room to find a water fountain. I
stood up and saw what appeared to be an immensely tall man beckon-
ing me. I followed his white coat until we reached another room,

where other white-coated individuals were grouped together. I was taken to a chair that could have been a prop for a *Star Wars* movie. There seemed to be a Viking-like helmet above my head.

When Joe arrived, one of the white coats asked if he was lost. What was he doing in this area?

"That's my wife," said Joe, "and I'm staying with her." He spoke with the authority of a marine colonel. I could see him move to an empty seat. I gave him a grateful smile.

The very tall doctor squatted on a stool beside me and said, "Now, Mrs. Beringer, will you please read the third line down on the chart on the wall in front of you."

"What chart?" I asked. My question created a sudden silence. I felt every white coat in the room staring at me.

ON THAT first visit to the University of Iowa Hospital, between fifteen and twenty physicians and medical students took turns studying my eyes. It was awful. The white coats, as I called them, seemed to regard me with very special interest. What irritated me was that they often talked about my case as if I weren't within earshot. And whenever I asked questions, I was patronized. "We'll let you know in good time," said one white coat. "We're still working on it," said another. "Just be patient," said a third.

The name of one doctor kept cropping up, and it was spoken with reverence: Dr. James Corbett, the chief of neuroophthalmology. I was given to understand that all the reports on my eye exams were being referred to him. The order came through from Dr. Corbett that I was to have an immediate CAT scan. It was not until very late in the afternoon and after the scan that I first met Dr. Corbett. Joe was at my side when we were taken to his office.

"So this is the famous Joan Beringer," he said as he shook my hand.

"Famous," I responded with surprise. "Oh, no, not me."

Dr. Corbett chuckled, and several white coats standing nearby chuckled along with him. "Young lady," he said, "you've been keeping much of my staff busy today, and you're a real puzzlement."

One of the white coats interjected, "Indeed, we're all very intrigued. Not come across anything quite like it. We're like astronomers picking up strange signals, and we're going to train our most powerful—er—telescopes on the—er—object."

I could sense Joe beginning to seethe. He had protested several times during this long day that I was being treated like an object.

"Ah, but we haven't given you the good news, Mrs. Beringer," said Dr. Corbett.

Good news! A surge of relief began to sweep over me.

From Joe's next remark it was obvious that he, too, now felt that the worst was over and that my loss of sight was temporary. He said, "Well, thank heavens. Can we go home now?"

"Afraid you've misunderstood me," said Dr. Corbett. "I was speaking about the CAT scan. The images show no brain tumor."

Joe snorted. "So that's what you call good news, Doctor!"

Dr. Corbett responded coolly, "It is good news. There seemed to be indications—the speed of the onset of the loss of vision, for instance—which suggested possibilities of a tumor. Yes, we're much relieved, but we want to continue with other tests at once. Your wife's to be admitted to the hospital immediately."

My knees felt rubbery. I leaned heavily on Joe's arm. "Oh, no," I said. "I can't possibly. We have a small daughter at home."

Dr. Corbett said quietly, "I think you don't understand how concerned we are and how determined we are to find the cause of the problem. I've given instructions for a spinal tap at eight tomorrow morning."

Protectively Joe moved half a pace in front of me. With that ring to his voice that could bring a sassy student to heel, he said, "Five minutes from now my wife and I are going to be on our way to our home in Vinton. She's had one heck of a day here, and she's going to have a restful night in her bed—in our bed. If you insist, I'll get here by seven o'clock tomorrow morning."

A pause, then: "Fair enough," said Dr. Corbett.

I asked the doctor, "Do I need to bring anything with me—a toothbrush, whatever?"

A laugh from everyone. Dr. Corbett said, "A toothbrush, certainly, and enough toothpaste to last you at least two weeks."

"Two weeks!" I exclaimed.

Dr. Corbett put his hand on my shoulder. He said, "Yes, I'm afraid at least two weeks. We're planning a lot of tests."

When we reached home, one of my first duties was to call our folks. Mom and Dad lived in Wisconsin, where Dad had his present ministry. Dad was a pastor of the Reformed Church in the United States, one of the smaller Calvinist denominations. Joe's parents, Ken and JoAnne, lived in South Dakota. Both couples were about six driving hours away. To all four of them we gave just the basic facts. My parents and Joe's insisted on being with us as soon as possible. They would be on the road before dawn.

Joy was not yet four, and I felt, as did Joe, that it was not the right moment to explain my vision loss. As I tucked her into bed, I told her simply that I would not be at home for a while, because I had to go to the hospital.

Joy mulled over this information for a few moments, then asked, "Can we ask God to help you, Mommy?"

Joy's prayer, spoken as we knelt at her bed, was surely as simple and as pertinent as any He has heard. And I felt God would have smiled when my daughter, hugging her favorite toy, added, "And Winnie-the-Pooh wants You to help my Mommy too."

Joe kept his word to Dr. Corbett. At seven the next morning I found myself in a small ward on the second floor of the neurology inpatient wing at the University of Iowa Hospital.

For the spinal tap I was obliged to wear one of those cotton hospital gowns with ties at the back. Joe was tying the last one when a team of doctors and medical students walked in.

Joe left, and I was instructed to lie in the fetal position, my back to the white-coated company. A female medical student, who blithely confessed that she had never undertaken the procedure before, was given the needle. I couldn't see what was going on, but from the ribbing by other students I gained a good picture of the scene behind me. The nervous young woman jabbed my back three times before finding needle entry to the spinal column. The drawoff of spinal fluid wasn't painful enough to evoke more than an ouch from me, but I didn't appreciate the students' banter.

After the procedure was completed, the physician in charge gave me careful instructions to lie on my back for the next six hours. He didn't want me even to wiggle a foot. So naturally I was puzzled when, a couple of hours later, a wheelchair was pushed into the ward and I was told that I was to be taken off for X rays.

To the radiologist who x-rayed me in contortionist positions I made some mild reference to the instructions given earlier about my need to remain absolutely still. However, I don't think he listened to me as he clattered fresh film into the table slot.

While I was being wheeled back to my room, an excruciating headache hit me, causing me to cry out and to cradle my head against the slightest jar. Nurses and physicians were alerted. They injected a strong painkiller. Then Dr. Corbett was in the room throwing out angry questions. It was obvious that whoever it was—nurse, physician, or technician—who had permitted me to be taken to the X-ray lab was soon going to be facing his anger.

The headache, caused by my being moved too soon after a spinal tap, continued for forty-eight hours, but the pain was made bearable by strong painkillers—and by the arrival of my parents and Joe's.

While I was in the hospital, I went through the whole gamut of emotions. I was given rich and loving support by family and friends, and I thanked God for the shoulders that absorbed the tears. However, there were moments of laughter too. I was alone when one of the funniest incidents occurred.

Above my bed there was a placard about six inches tall that read BLIND PATIENT. I'd had my supper, when a hospital volunteer bustled into my ward wheeling a cart.

"Art cart, art cart," she cried, explaining that she came around once a week to change the pictures on the walls. "I see you've got the Van Gogh irises. You like the French Impressionists? Got a Monet here, or would you like a pretty English country scene?" Lowering her voice conspiratorially, she continued, "Some of those naughty men often ask me for a nude!" Her laughter rattled the cart. "I tell them no nudes. Does the wrong thing for their blood pressure." The cart was again jiggled by giggles. "Of course, you can hang on to the Van Gogh if you want to, and I'll . . ."

I guessed at what had caused her bright chatter to trail into an embarrassed silence. She'd seen the sign above my bed.

The wheels of the art cart squeaked. From the door the volunteer murmured, "So sorry. Didn't realize. Tactless of me . . ."

She left me giggling. It was my first genuine laughter in far too long. It felt so good.

There was another unexpected visitor that evening. In the softest of Irish lilts, Mrs. O'Leary introduced herself. She was, she told me, the cleaning lady who worked the evening shift. "How are you, darlin', if you'll not mind me askin'?" She was speaking from the door and waiting, I assumed, to be invited in. I did so.

"I'd like to," she said, "but tonight I'm runnin' a tad late. There's a lad t'other side of the nurses station needin' some hand-holdin'. But I will be seein' you. That I promise."

Shortly after this visit I was given the evening's third bonus—an unanticipated phone call.

"That you, Mom?" asked a childish voice. "It's me, Jay."

My stepson had never called me Mom. His special name for me was Joannie. His mother lived quite close to Vinton.

"I'm so happy to hear you! Did your daddy tell you about me?"

"Yes. He told me your eyes are not seeing very well." Jay's words were uttered so loudly that I was obliged to hold the phone three inches from my head. He provided an explanation for his shouting when he asked, "Do your ears work?"

"Oh, yes, they're fine," I reassured him.

With words now softly spoken, Jay urged me to get well quickly. I promised I'd do my best.

"Okay. Bye, Mom," said my seven-year-old stepson.

I held on to the receiver for quite a while as I reflected on how pleasing it was to hear a young boy calling me Mom. Jay already had a special place in my heart. He spent every second weekend in our home, where he was hero-worshipped by Joy.

There were not many such happy moments, but they seemed to be given to me when I most needed them.

I ran through a gauntlet of tests—magnetic resonance imaging, more X rays, and at least a dozen more visits to cubicles where my eyes were examined through ophthalmoscopes. In one of my early physical examinations a swollen lymph node was found in my right armpit. I knew enough about medicine to understand that a swollen lymph node in this area of the body was not infrequently a sign of cancer. I was told that a biopsy would be taken on the Wednesday of the following week.

"Why the delay?" I asked weakly.

The physician who found the node said that pathology was "all backed up." I had six days to ponder the possibility of cancer.

I had to be ready by seven o'clock Wednesday morning to go to the oncology department. An hour after dawn I was washed and

515

dressed. Seven o'clock came and went. So did eight, nine, ten. My anger came slowly to a boil, then steamed. Then I blew my lid.

A nurse got the full blast of my fury. Within five minutes I was on a gurney being wheeled to oncology. There, of course, I was smothered with apologies, but my anger evaporated only when the surgeon who examined my armpit said, "You may have had a swollen lymph node when you arrived at the hospital, Mrs. Beringer, but there's absolutely no sign of one now."

Mom was with me on the most critical day of my stay in the hospital. Dr. Corbett came into my room and tweaked my toe. He had done that before. I presumed he saw this gesture as affectionate, tactile communication. "And how is our Joan today?" he asked.

I was out of humorous or courteous responses. When I failed to reply, he said, "You've been putting up with a lot, haven't you? We still don't have the answers. But it's time to tell you one thing."

"Yes?"

"All our tests have shown us that the deterioration in your eyesight is irreversible."

In the silence that followed, the word irreversible seemed to take on a life of its own. It became a serpentine thing—twisting, humping, stretching, and finally coiling around my heart.

The next thing I recall is Mom squeezing my hand. Then she rose from her chair and took a step toward the doctor. She said slowly, precisely, "Doctor, should you ever have to give another report like this to my daughter, I want you to be very sure that there is someone with her—someone who is close to her."

Her words struck a chord. There was genuine humility in the famous doctor's voice when he spoke again. "Thank you. I promise to be sure of that." A pause and then: "It is not easy to be the bearer of bad news. I do believe that it is best to be frank—at least with patients like your daughter who has"—he felt for the phrase he wanted, and I liked it when he spoke it—"an inner strength."

Mom asked, "May my daughter go home now?"

Dr. Corbett said, "A hospital is not a prison, so Joan has every right to go home. I hope she won't. Before she goes, I'd like to taper down the heavy doses of steroids that we're now giving her. Her pleurisy and arthritis are responding. But my main reason for asking her to stay on in the hospital for some days is that our continu-

516

ing research of her case may well prove helpful, perhaps sight saving, to others stricken down as she's been stricken."

Mom asked guardedly, "What do you mean by research, Doctor? My daughter is not a laboratory animal."

Dr. Corbett said, "I fear I've not made it clear how unique and important your daughter's case study is. The foe that hit Joan's eyes was fast, furious, and, speaking for the enemy, effective. It was like an attack from kamikaze pilots." He said to me, "We know you have macular degeneration—normally a malady of aging—but we don't know what caused it. If we can identify the foe, we may be able to set up a defense system that could save the sight of others."

Mom grasped my hand once more. "What do you say, Joan?"

I licked dry lips. I was already wondering how Joe was going to cope with a blind wife—could I cook for him, clean house, do the laundry, do the shopping? And what about my three-year-old?

I became aware of the long silence. Oh, yes, they had asked me if I would stay in the hospital—not for my sake alone. For the very first time, I was given the thought that I could be helpful to others. It was a good thought. I nodded. "Yes, I'll stay."

"Thank you, Joan," said Dr. Corbett. "You're a brave young woman."

I'm not brave at all, I thought. I'm scared, so terribly scared.

When the doctor had left the room, Mom pressed her cheek to mine. In her comforting me, I felt that I was myself a child again. I sobbed, "I'm blind. Mom, I'm blind. I'll always be blind!"

I remember one phrase in my mother's efforts to soften my sorrow. She said, "But you're the most beautiful blind girl in the world." She spoke the Lord's Prayer, too, and when my throat permitted, I joined her in some phrases. *"Thy will be done . . . Deliver us from evil."*

I was so grateful that my mother was there to see me through the first shock of understanding that I would not see again—not my daughter's sweet face, not daffodils or tulips, not an avenue of trees in springtime, not even a work of art.

After my sobbing had stopped, I asked Mom to phone the Braille School and ask Joe to come as soon as possible. "He must bring Joy too. I need to see them both. I want to tell them in my own way."

Mom promised, and said she would phone from the lobby. I was alone for perhaps half an hour before my favorite nurse, Katy, looked in on me.

"Just checking you out," she said from the door of my room. "I know the bad news. Dr. Corbett told us. I am so sorry."

"Please, Katy," I pleaded, "don't say any more at the moment. I want to look okay for my husband, who'll be here soon."

"Understood," said Katy. "But if your guy's on his way, I'd better give your hair a brush."

"Is it that bad?"

"Not if he likes haystacks," she said, and we laughed and hugged.

Thanks in part to Katy, I was ready for Joe when he arrived. I guessed he had wheedled something out of Mom, because after kissing me, he said, "News not so good, huh?"

"Right," I said, and then I went on to tell him Dr. Corbett's prognosis. He was sitting on the bed, and when I used the word irreversible, he jumped to his feet.

"I'm not going to believe that," he said. "Nor must you. Never did like that Dr. Corbett. What right has he to say that you're permanently blind?"

I helped him along. "Joe, we've got to come to terms with the facts. What hurts me most is that I'm going to be a burden to you."

I tried to picture his expression. Was it anger, fear, frustration, or horror? In a moment I had the answer. He pushed me to one side of the bed so that he could lie on the other. Then he cradled my head. Although he did not make a sound, I could tell from his breathing that he was trying to keep his crying under control.

It was strange, but I now found myself doing the comforting. I stroked his face and thanked him for his courage and care.

When I suggested that it was time for me to see Joy, he agreed, but told me that he was going to spend the night with me. "It's okay," he said. "I'm going to sleep right here on the floor."

Minutes later Joy arrived and came to my open arms. Joe left us alone. It was harder now to keep my resolve to hold back the tears. Joy's breath was soft against my neck when I told her, "Honey, I wanted you here with me—just the two of us—so that I could tell you something important. I think you knew that I wasn't seeing well, but now my eyes are not working at all."

I'd planned to give her a long silence so that she could digest what I'd told her, but Joy responded at once. She asked, "Mommy, can I kiss your eyes better?"

I gave her a hug, and tears were under my lids. "Whenever you kiss me, I always feel better," I assured her.

Joy planted butterfly kisses on my eyelids. A moment, then: "Mommy, why do your eyes taste salty?"

From my throat came an uncontrollable cry of pain. Alarmed, Joy pulled away. "Oh, Mommy, did I hurt your broken eyes?"

After a moment or two of holding her to my breast, I was able to say, "Honey, sometimes people cry not because they've been hurt, but because their hearts are overflowing with love."

She pondered this, then asked, "Mommy, do hearts make tears?"

"The most beautiful ones of all," I assured her.

And after another thoughtful pause: "Mommy, I'm glad your broken eyes can still make beautiful tears."

I touched my lips to her forehead and wept quite unashamedly into the silk of my daughter's hair.

JOE did, in fact, sleep on the floor in my room that night. I suspect that the nursing staff had been advised—possibly by Dr. Corbett—to pretend they had not seen or heard the snoring figure in the corner. But one midnight visitor, Mrs. O'Leary the cleaning lady, was so amused to find Joe with me that she had difficulty stifling her laughter. From an empty room she brought a pillow and blanket, and so gentle was she in covering him and placing the pillow under his head that Joe's snoring was not interrupted.

When he was awakened by the sound of the breakfast cart, Joe expressed guilt that he had slept so well. I did not tell him that on that night—and through almost all my nights in the hospital—I slept for less than two hours.

Most hospital patients discover that at night the swing of a clock's pendulum slows down and there are many more than sixty minutes to the hour. I began to dread the nighttime, when to the sleepless, the imps of anxiety become brooding ogres.

The solution to the problem of my restless, unprofitable hours came from an unexpected quarter. I was listening to a radio program when a talk-show host interviewed a former Vietnam prisoner of war who had survived four years of solitary confinement. Asked how he had managed to avoid going crazy under such conditions, the veteran replied that he had compiled an autobiography. "I had neither pen nor paper," he related. "But in my head I recalled the events of my life in minutest detail."

I was fascinated by the former POW's self-designed therapy. I was listening to this radio program shortly after I had had a second spinal tap. This time I was taking very seriously the instructions to lie still. Since I did not want to be carted off to the hospital's psychiatric wing, I was careful not to voice my story aloud. But a sensitive microphone might well have picked up my whisper when, with some excitement, I began my story.

"Once upon a time," I started in the tradition of every good story of early childhood, "in California, at seven in the evening of January 22, 1952, a baby girl was born to Vivian, the wife of the Reverend Robert Stuebbe. They christened her Joan. . . ."

3
A Serpentless Eden

I HAD little if any recollection of the first years of my life, but insofar as I could recall, my childhood was lived out in a serpentless Eden. I had—and still gratefully have—two brothers. Bob is seven years my senior, and Jon is five years older than I. Today Bob works in the higher echelons of national defense, and Jon is a California judge.

Indisputably, my early childhood's closest friend was four-legged and fictional. Stabled within my mind was Princess, a golden palomino mare that could gallop me along white-surfed beaches to distant continents. I was never more content, even into my eleventh year, than when riding that surefooted imaginary mare. Princess imbued me with a passion for riding that I have not relinquished. Watch the expression of a sightless person mounted on a horse, and you can sense his or her liberation.

As I lay wide awake at three o'clock one morning, I relived another fabulous ride. This time my mount was as real as rain, and I was a nineteen-year-old college student. The horse, a high-spirited gelding named Midnight, was owned by one of my father's parishioners. Dad's ministry then was in the little town of Menno, not far from the University of South Dakota.

On this particular ride I headed Midnight into what I've heard South Dakotans refer to as Nowhere Land—stretches of country-side where no habitation can be seen. I cannot recall what it was that day that created such a close harmony of nature—the trees (not many in this countryside), the gentle fold of fields, the sky with its blues shifting from soft hues where they touched the earth to deep azure in the dome above. The tympanic beat of Midnight's hooves added rhythm to the music and the poetry of the hour. The solitude was no less than spiritual.

So deeply engraved was this memory that, even lying in a hospital bed with almost totally sightless eyes, I could re-create it in all dimensions; in so doing, what would have been a restless, troubled hour was shortened and wonderfully sweetened.

While I lay there trying to relive my earlier years, I shifted from tears to laughter and back again to tears with what, in less traumatic circumstances, might have been regarded as unstable frequency. Favorite Nurse Katy came in to check on me and asked how the "autobiography" was going.

"It'll need a lot of editing," I told her.

Katy urged me to "keep at it—because the therapy is obviously doing you a power of good."

Perhaps this was true. On the following night I found myself thinking of my senior year in high school. It was a good year, and one reason for declaring it so was because at last I was filling out my sweater. At the age of fifteen I had reached my full height of five feet nine inches, yet I weighed only ninety-five pounds. My closest childhood friend, Louise, had charitably called me willowy, but more than a couple of guys had nicknamed me Twiggy.

I had had no intention of becoming a professional model—though the idea had been suggested—but I did entertain the notion of becoming a dancer. I was not thinking so much of the second line of the chorus at Las Vegas as I was of being a dance teacher. I particularly enjoyed modern dance, but I was constantly pulled toward a career that would be less self-serving, and the idea of work-ing with people who had special needs became more sharply focused.

My father's decision to accept a ministry in South Dakota was to prove critical to my own life. My parents had lived in California since before I was born. I had not thought of myself as a typical

Californian, but this was how I was regarded when, with long blond hair, a golden tan, and stereotypically long legs, I entered the University of South Dakota in Vermillion.

For me South Dakota was a foreign land, but a land that I quickly learned to love. Certainly I was shocked by the winter weather. I, who had spent about eleven months of the year in shorts and T-shirts, now had to invest in long johns, padded snowsuits, thick mittens, and earmuffs. I had never seen snow falling. An unforgettable memory is of my first crunching walk over virgin snow that streetlights had turned into a pathway of diamonds. It was not only the beauty of winter that I loved but the indescribable wonder of the spring and fall, and the people were so welcoming, so hospitable.

All too quickly, it seemed to me, I graduated from the University of South Dakota with the credentials to practice as a recreational therapist. My first job was at the Yankton mental institution and women's correctional facility—a euphemism for a grim gray stone jail—both sited on the same well-guarded grounds.

I was instructed to program and plan leisure activities. Several of my clients—as they were always designated—had been incarcerated for homicide. On my first day on the job I was introduced to a dozen clients, the majority of them weighing at least two hundred pounds and the heaviest having axe-murdered her unfaithful spouse. A colleague told me later that on my first day of work I had reminded him of a prairie dog caught in the headlights of a truck—rigid from alarm, paws defensively raised, and eyes like Frisbees.

There were new and often alarming experiences every day. In the gym one day I was naïve enough to toss a twenty-pound medicine ball to a woman who could have been a professional wrestler. The first time she tossed it back, the ball hit my chest with a sound like a bass drum. The woman's second throw bounced me into the wall of the gymnasium, which then echoed with maniacal laughter. I persuaded her to change the game to Ping-Pong.

A much more serious incident occurred on the institution bus in which we took quieter clients for trips into the country. I was the driver on the day that Dolly, a psychotic, was given her first outing in months. We had just gotten under way when she seized a fistful of my hair and started to drag me backward over the driver's seat. My hands were unable to reach the steering wheel, my feet unable to touch the pedals, and my neck seemed to be within an inch of fracture. Two assistants rushed to my rescue. The bus, which had left the road, stopped only one yard from a huge oak tree.

At the end of each workday my colleagues and I felt we had earned not only our modest salaries but also our right to relax and enjoy ourselves.

"What about your love life?" asked Nurse Katy, who when time permitted, had been catching up on the autobiography.

I raised my eyebrows. "Love life?"

"Don't play innocent with me," said Katy. "When a tanned California blonde drops out of the sky onto a South Dakota campus, the guys must have thought they'd joined Alice in Wonderland."

"Oh, sure," I told her. "There were two or three guys whose company I enjoyed a lot."

Katy clicked a skeptical tongue, then asked about Joe.

"Oh, he was much later," I said. "I'd first known him in college, when he'd been married to his high school sweetheart. Like me, he graduated as a recreational therapist. Eventually he found the job he wanted at the Braille School in Vinton."

I went on to tell Katy how, after Joe's divorce, I had met up with him again. At first I had admired Joe's dedication to his work. Then we had had a few dates and watched football and baseball games together. Then we realized we had fallen in love.

In the summer of 1978 Dad married us in Manitowoc, Wisconsin, where he had taken up a new—and his last—ministry. In the course of Dad's message to us he said, "I wish I could promise you a stormless voyage as you set out together. But that I cannot do, because only God knows what lies ahead for us. What I can promise is that if you seek God's navigation for your lives, you'll be able to face whatever storms you might encounter."

Now, as I recall the words Dad spoke on that carefree day when I married Joe, I find myself wondering whether we would have been too daunted to make our solemn vows had we but glimpsed the perils and pain that lay ahead for both of us.

ONE afternoon Dr. Corbett greeted me with his usual toe tweaking. He said, "Good news for you, Joan." I held my smile because the only good news I was ready to accept was that his prognosis had been horribly wrong and that my eyes would soon be on the mend.

He didn't tell me this, of course. I was now only too well aware that the prognosis was grimly correct. I knew that my sight was limited to the smallest aperture of peripheral vision, which in certain conditions allowed me to distinguish light from dark and to see the vaguest of shapes and movements. What Dr. Corbett did say almost jovially was, "Tomorrow you're going home."

In the word home, there was music. Yet all too quickly the music became a screech of alarm. I realized that this small room in this huge hospital had protected me from the real world, a world created for people with vision—a mobile world of automobiles, trains, planes, elevators, even supermarket carts. In theory I'd known about this world that I must now face. For five years I'd helped a hundred and more children cope with the most basic demands of living, like the simple task of laying toothpaste along the bristles of a brush. But from tomorrow it would be I who would be blindly feeling my way beyond the walls and safety of this room.

Dr. Corbett must have observed the sudden change in my expression. His voice was kind, almost sorrowful, as he said, "How we wish we could have done more for you, Joan. Perhaps one day we may learn how to replace dead optical nerves with receptors that will respond to light and transmit signals to the brain."

After a brief examination Dr. Corbett addressed me again. "My colleagues and I believe you've been the victim of a lupuslike ailment." He went on to explain that for reasons not yet understood, women in their third decade were the most vulnerable to lupus. He emphasized that they were not labeling my malady lupus, but that "kinship to lupus had been observed."

Before he left, Dr. Corbett pleaded with me to make regular outpatient visits to the hospital to help in the continuing study of my case. He assured me once again that I had been "a most cooperative and courageous patient." In an avuncular tone he added, "And the prettiest patient I've seen for a very long time."

Then I began to think about going home.

In some ways the last day of my hospital stay was my worst. For one reason or another I had no visitors on that last afternoon or in the evening, either. Perhaps this was one reason why my thoughts focused on chilling questions.

At the Braille School I'd become skilled in teaching sightless others the daily living skills. How many had I shown how to use the sensitive skin on the back of the hand to pour salt from a shaker into a bowl of soup or stew? How many had I shown how to use a cane to move around furniture, to find one's way across a campus? But could the teacher now teach herself?

It must have been around ten o'clock when I heard Mrs. O'Leary's soft Irish voice at my bedside. "So it's been your toughest day, I'm guessin'," she said, "and that's because tomorrow you're goin' home." She sat on the bed and grasped my hands.

"Did they tell you?" I asked.

"No. I don't need to be told," she said. "I've seen a lot of patients who've suddenly lost their sight—auto accidents, young uns playin' around with guns, you name it. I've seen the bravest come apart at the seams on the day they're told they're goin' home. What's scarin' you, darlin', is how to make it on the outside. Am I right?"

"Oh, yes, yes," I whispered as I leaned forward into Mrs. O'Leary's ample bosom and soaked the lapels of her cleaning-lady uniform with tears. She stroked my hair, patted my back, and cooed soothingly into my ear.

"There, there. You're goin' to be just fine, and the good Lord will still be wantin' to use your love and all your learnin'."

With my crying under some control, I told her, "You're wonderful, Mrs. O'Leary. You could be giving lessons to the psychologists and some of the chaplains too."

She snorted, "Get along with you, darlin'. I was but fourteen when I leave school. Had to help me mother run the farm in County Kerry—that were after me dad died. Not much time for book learnin'. But I'd like to tell these chaplains somethin'. I'd tell them to come a-visitin' at three in the mornin', not at three in the afternoon. That be the hour they're most needed."

She heaved herself off the bed. "Best be goin'," she said.

I was so reluctant to let her go that I felt for her hand, but I realized that she was at the door. From there she said, "I'll be lookin' in on you later, darlin', to see how you're farin'." A new thought struck her. She asked, "How's that story of yours goin'?"

On one of her earlier visits to my room I had told her of how I spent wakeful hours trying to recapture the events of my life. Now

I told her that I had not made much headway lately, because I was weighed down by the challenges of going home.

"Ah, no, darlin'," she said. "You need somethin' to be thinkin' about this night—somethin' good. Now tell me what be the happiest day of your life? Your weddin' day? Ah, you're already smilin' as you think about a happy day. What is it you're thinkin'?"

"I'm thinking about the day my daughter, Joy, was born," I said.

"There you are!" said Mrs. O'Leary triumphantly. "Tonight you be givin' yourself a treat. You be thinkin' about that little lass of yours, and she'll be leadin' you to dreamland."

I took Mrs. O'Leary's advice. I thought about my daughter.

Joe and I were two years into our marriage when Joy was born. Although I remained healthy, I could not free myself of a deep concern that my baby would be born with some physical defect—a pregnancy worry not uncommon among women who work with the physically and mentally disabled. There was no moment in my life of greater relief and exaltation than when the doctor who delivered my daughter told me that she was normal in every respect—"not just ten toes and brown eyes, but absolutely perfect!"

Mrs. O'Leary's soporific worked marvelously. On my last night in the hospital I enjoyed the most restful sleep I had had since being admitted as an inpatient.

I was packed and ready well before Joe arrived the next morning. When he phoned from the lobby to say he was signing the discharge papers, I felt so good that I told the senior nurse I wanted to make my own way to the entrance to meet my husband.

"Certainly not," said the nurse. "You'll find you're much weaker than you imagine. Besides, it's a hospital rule that patients must be wheeled out in chairs." There was an unintended sting when she added, "Your husband's got to get used to waiting on you."

When Joe reached my room, a couple of other nurses came to say good-bye. An orderly had my suitcase. Everyone, including Joe, was awkwardly hearty. "Sure you've got everything?" Joe asked.

"Can't help you there," I replied.

"There's a card or something on the nightstand. You want it?"

"I've no idea what it is," I told him. "Probably just a tissue."

Joe picked up what he described as a penciled note. He asked me if I wanted him to read it, and I told him to go ahead. He read,

"Good-bye, darling lass. Glad to see you sleeping like a babe. To have a vision you don't need no eyes. Your heart will tell you what to do. I'll be praying for you. The Lord has good sweetness and blessings for you. I be sure of this."

An embarrassed silence followed. I put out my hand to Joe for the note and pushed it into my pocket. And Mrs. O'Leary's prophecy—for that's what it seemed like to me—was so etched into my mind that I was to recall it again and again as my future unfolded into a time of anguish beyond my reckoning, and a time of sublime contentment beyond my imagining.

4
But Why Not Me?

As we drove home on that crisp March morning in 1984, I could sense that something was troubling Joe. His chatter about inconsequential things and the pitch of his voice convinced me he was evading some issue that he needed to talk about.

My first guess was wrong. I asked, "Are you as concerned as I am, Joe, that I'm going to be a burden to you?"

He shouted, "For Pete's sake, Joan, how can someone I love be a burden?"

I leaned across the seat and put my cheek against his arm. "Thank you, honey. That's wonderful to hear." And then I pressed the question. "But there is something on your mind, Joe, isn't there?"

"Yup. Okay. I've been asking myself, Why the heck you?"

"Me what?"

"You know what I mean," he said, his voice rising. "Why the heck should you be—be—"

"Blind. Say the word, Joe. I've gotten used to saying it."

His lighter mood was now gone. Almost harshly he replied, "I can say the word blind and all the euphemisms—sightless, vision loss—you name it. No. What I want to know is, Why *you?* There are more than two hundred and fifty million people wandering about this country, and most of them have never given a damn about helping blind kids, about helping anybody. Why should you be singled out to lose your sight? That's what I don't understand. It's

527

pretty hard to talk about a loving God when this happens. You know, I was raised Catholic, but I never heard any priest or nun explain why the best people get slapped down the hardest. You asked me what's worrying me. It's not just worrying me. It's been tearing at my guts. Why you, Joan? Why you?"

He was breathing heavily. I wasn't sure what to say—not immediately. My mind was jumbled, confused, scared. One thought came to mind like a quick benediction. Softly I said, "Joe, the only answer I have is, Why not me?"

When he didn't respond, I continued. "I suppose almost everyone who is, as you put it, slapped down hard is strongly tempted to ask, Why me? I'm thinking of Mr. and Mrs. Holman, who lost their only child to leukemia last year. You remember them? They'd waited twenty years for that child. Then it was taken. And you know what Mrs. Holman did when her little boy died? She's now got half a dozen little boys. She's one of our most loyal volunteers at the Braille School."

We were silent for a while. Then I said, "I'm hoping that my loss of sight can be used for the good of others. Obviously, there'll be things I'll have to do differently, like getting Joy to school. But I believe the Braille School kids might feel they've got a staff member who better understands their challenges and difficulties."

Joe asked, "You really want to go back to the school?"

"Absolutely," I said. "I shall beg and plead and smile."

Joe reached out with his right hand and touched my knee. "The smile alone should do it," he said. I was glad that his anger had waned—perhaps some of his worry too.

In a non sequitur he now told me that some of the trees were already in bud. I had a spasm of pain as I reflected that for the first time, I wouldn't see the April greening of the town or the tulips in the park or . . . I jerked my mind away from these negative thoughts. At the hospital I had solemnly promised myself that I would not allow myself to be sucked into self-pity.

I opened the car window and allowed the prairie air to play on my face. I surprised Joe when I told him I knew where we were.

A short laugh. "Have you been kidding us all along?" he asked.

"I'm learning to make use of my other senses," I told him. "A couple of minutes back we hit that big pothole that should have been filled in a year ago. I've just picked up the smell of coffee from what has to be Hank's Diner. That means that hideous wrecked-car dump must be out on the left. Correct?"

"Almost," said Joe admiringly. "We've just passed the dump."

"Well, that's one thing I'm glad I won't have to see again."

A couple of minutes later Joe swung the car left, and the sound of gravel under the tires told me I was home at last. Then Joy was in my arms. And as we entered the house, I picked up the perfume of spring flowers, perhaps hothouse grown, and the smell of Irish stew, doubtless the gift of a colleague or friend.

Joy pushed a vase of daffodils under my nose. I breathed in the scent. "Beautiful," I told her.

"There are more flowers in the dining room and upstairs," said Joy. Joe read the names and messages from the cards.

It was all too much too soon. I felt overwhelmed by love—indeed, I would have fallen had I not grasped the banister.

"I need to rest for a while," I said. "They warned me at the hospital that my legs would feel wobbly for a time. It's great to be home." I pulled myself up the stairs and, quite drained, flopped on the big bed. Joe left for the school. Joy went to play with a friend.

In the now quiet house I recalled that summer six years earlier when I had arrived in Vinton as Joe's bride. Joe had been working at the Braille School for a couple of years and already seemed to have made friends with half the community.

I recalled, too, the first day of my being employed at the Braille School. I was appointed housemother of a dorm of ten legally blind boys whose ages ranged from six to eleven. Two older, experienced aides who were to work under me were understandably nettled over having to take orders from a naïve twenty-six-year-old who had little experience of caring for sighted children and no understanding at all of how to help blind children. Fortunately, I had enough sense to recognize that I would fail miserably at my job unless I could win the aides' confidence.

The job of looking after ten small boys for eight hours a day had sounded simple enough. I was to find out differently. In the dorm to which I had been assigned housemother, five of the boys were not only legally blind but were handicapped in other ways too. One was autistic, another mildly retarded; a third was obliged to wear leg braces, a fourth had to use a wheelchair, and another had the use of only one hand.

I had immediately turned to the two motherly aides, confessed my ignorance and pleaded for help. The training I needed is not found in textbooks. The effective caring for blind children is a skill born of the heart and consolidated only by hands-on experience.

Indeed, my first lesson was as simple as teaching a sightless child how to make his bed. An aide demonstrated hand-over-hand instruction on tucking in a sheet, smoothing a blanket, placing a pillow. By watching his mother, a sighted child can learn to make a bed in two or three sessions. A blind child might take six months. The same patience is needed in showing how to tie a shoelace, how to sort clothes, how to eat in a mannerly fashion—using, for example, a hunk of bread as a "pusher" to the fork.

Although my early official responsibilities were limited to domestic care and social skills, it seemed very important to me to learn all I could about the classroom teaching and other activities of the children. Joe taught me much, of course.

He was very firm with any child who did not measure up to what he believed was the child's full capability. I was pained to see one child in tears after Joe scolded him. When I protested Joe's severity, he pointed out that he may have saved the child from death or injury because the boy had crossed a street without listening for traffic. He always gave a big hug to a child he had reprimanded.

At one of my early activities at the school, Joe gave me a lesson that I would not forget. His recreation department was holding the annual Saint Valentine's dance, at which the sweetheart king and queen were to be crowned. The students themselves voted for what was the equivalent of homecoming king and queen.

I had by now gotten to know a good many of the one hundred and twenty students on campus, but there were still a few I had not befriended. Among these was Joyce, a girl with rounded shoulders, buckteeth, and mouse-colored hair so thin that her scalp was visible.

The election count and crowning ceremony were being held at the gymnasium, and Joe was emceeing the occasion. Excitement mounted as Joe came to the mike to declare that the vote had finally been tallied. The name of the king was no surprise. He was a tall and handsome youth who had done well in wrestling and academics. Then as the gym rocked with cheers, Joe announced the name of the queen. Joyce, who was just about the plainest girl on campus, had been chosen by her peers to reign over the festivities.

When, later, I mentioned my surprise to Joe, he retorted, "Honey, you haven't learned yet that beauty is in the eye of the beholder, and on this campus the kids look more than skin-deep."

The classroom teachers were more amazed than amused when I started to turn up in their classrooms. I felt it important to understand what and how the kids were being taught if I was to help them with homework or other projects. I also felt it was important to learn braille, which I did in my spare time. It is not all that easy to translate the dots that make up the braille alphabet into letters, phrases, and pages, but in due course I became a certified braillist.

I loved my work—initially as a dorm parent, later in a classroom setting, and then as a staff liaison between the dorms and the classrooms. The blind children unwittingly gave me lessons that were to prove priceless in my own unforeseeable years ahead— lessons in patience, perseverance, and humor.

One of my dorm boys was a mischievous but lovable ten-year-old named Blake. One day I took Blake to be fitted with new prosthetic eyes. As a child grows, so do his eye sockets—hence the need to replace prostheses from time to time.

Appointments were running well behind schedule. As Blake and I waited in a room filled with perhaps forty people, the boy became restless. He asked me how everyone else was killing time. I mentioned that they were reading magazines. Blake discovered a magazine rack next to his seat. A few moments later I was aware of a heavy silence in the waiting room. Glancing over the top of my journal, I saw that all eyes were fixed on Blake. He had removed one of his glass eyes, and he was now holding it delicately between thumb and forefinger as he pressed it against a magazine page.

"Blake," I exclaimed, "put it back now!"

Before popping the glass eye back into its socket, Blake gave the room his best urchin's grin and said, "Too bad. I can see so much better that way!" He seemed genuinely disappointed that nobody laughed. But Blake and I giggled all the way home.

By the fall of 1983 life was great. I had been appointed to the liaison position and was doing the work I most enjoyed—work that kept me in close touch with the children, their parents, the dorm staff, and the teaching staff. I was often invited to give presentations on the work of the school to service clubs, church groups, women's associations, and the like.

As for the Joy of my heart, as I always thought of our blond, effervescent daughter, she was well out of babyhood and becoming her own engaging personality. Each day when I counted my blessings, I ran out of fingers, and each Sunday when I gave thanks for them at church, I almost ran out of amens.

Christmas of 1983 came in with the merry sound of carols and sleigh bells. Joe and I welcomed in the new year with a kiss and champagne and in the company of wonderful friends.

Then came that bitter morning in January, the day when I was dressing my daughter for preschool and I received that first sign that my life's trail was dipping rapidly from sunlight into twilight.

A FEW days before Joy's pink socks had seemingly been drained of their color, I had made a promise to the Braille School's peewee wrestling team that I would be at their annual match against their number one rival. Nothing could have stopped me from keeping this promise. I'd been home from the hospital only three days when the date for the big match came up. By phone I arranged with the bus driver to swing around to our home after he had collected the team.

As soon as I heard the crunching of gravel under the bus tires, I went outside the front door. The bus driver jumped out to give me a guiding elbow, but before he did so, I was aware of a little figure alongside him. Then a small sticky hand gripped my own, and a very familiar lisping voice said, "It'th me, Mith Beringer." I recognized the boy as Terry, an eight-year-old from the Braille School. He continued, "I juth wanted to tell you how very thorry I am about your eyes. I gueth all we can do, Mith Beringer, ith to hope."

I felt so absolutely overwhelmed by the little boy's sympathy that I choked up. Terry had lost his sight in an accident when he was an infant. But here he was, grasping my hand, giving me his compassion.

I knelt down in a patch of melting snow and hugged him. "Oh, Terry, Terry," I cried, "how wonderful you are."

The other kids, who had remained in the bus, gave me a warm welcome too. "Welcome back, Mrs. B.!" "I hope the doctors were nice to you." "We missed you very much." "We love you, Mrs. B."

The natural humorist, Blake, wasn't joking when he said, "You're kind of like one of us now, Mrs. B."

Wrestling is one of the very few sports that the blind can participate in and enjoy. There have been some outstanding blind wrestlers. Here I would like to report that my peewee team won their match, but this time they lost—in spite of my cheering myself hoarse from the bleachers of the gymnasium.

In those first weeks at home, there were moments when I felt lost, beaten and depressed, but Terry's lisped encouragement— "All we can do ith to hope"—rang out in my head like an encouraging cry from the bleachers.

Understandably, Joy was initially very confused by my inability to help find things she had mislaid—her crayons, for example, or a picture book. But there were other activities, such as bathing her, that I could manage as well as I had before losing my sight.

Especially for our small daughter's sake, Joe and I made every effort to keep laughter in our home. One evening when I was bathing Joy, Joe came home from work. "Hi, girls," he said as he pushed open the bathroom door.

"Hi, honey." "Hi, Daddy," we responded.

As Joe approached, he pretended to trip on a throw rug. A moment later he was sitting fully clothed in the bath facing Joy, who was, of course, squealing with laughter.

When Mom and Dad came to visit, I think they were impressed on finding the house running so smoothly. I showed them how I arranged clothes in closets so that I could find them readily. I demonstrated the arrangement of food in the refrigerator and the kitchen cupboards. I could find a carton of milk or a box of rice as easily as I could have done had I been sighted—unless, as often happened, Joe or someone else put it back in the wrong place.

I was learning, too, how to use my white cane, and it was a victorious day for me when I first walked downtown to the pharmacy unaccompanied. I had, of course, walked the route from home to the shopping area very often in the past—one block east, one block north, then four blocks east. Now mobility skills would be fully tested. In a manner I had previously prescribed for others, I swung my cane from fence to gutter. Ah, yes, I told myself, here's the fire hydrant, and this is where the roots of that big tree are breaking through the pavement, and that barking has to come from the Restons' German shepherd. Here's the corner where I turn left. Okay. Now four blocks east. Remember to count them.

Fortunately, the sight of a blind person tapping his or her way down a Vinton street was not rare. When crossing a street, I listened carefully for traffic, then took the offered arm of a stranger. Otherwise I made the short walk unaided.

Was this the door to the pharmacy or the shoe repair shop? I pushed it open, and the friendly voice of the pharmacist greeted me. I did it by myself! Marathon winners or cross-Channel swimmers could not have experienced a warmer glow of victory.

Another thrill was to be told by the school that they wanted me to keep my job as liaison staff person. But since there were some duties that I would now be incapable of undertaking, I was given a few different responsibilities. Among these was to spend a couple of evenings a week in charge of the study period at the library.

It was in the library that students could find a quiet place for homework or make use of a wide selection of reference books—typically, talking encyclopedias. When asked, I would try to give students help with homework, but increasingly students came to the library simply to talk to a staff person who, as one of them put it, "really understands what being blind is all about."

One evening I was approached by Betty, an exceptionally intelligent sixteen-year-old who, since her arrival at the school, had been first in her class. But as she approached the corner table where I usually sat, she was obviously distressed. Eventually Betty blurted out, "An absolutely awful thing happened to me today in the lab."

"Tell me about it," I said softly.

With a shuddering sob she uttered the word birds.

"Birds?"

Three tissues later she whispered, "It was so humiliating; I'd always thought that birds were about the size of my thumb. But in the biology lab they've got a stuffed seagull and a stuffed crow. I couldn't believe what I was feeling. They were the size of my head!"

I still couldn't fathom the reason for Betty's tears, and I said so.

"But don't you see, Mrs. Beringer, I thought I was pretty smart, and today I realized how ignorant I am. I thought that because birds go cheep-cheep-cheep, they had to be tiny. I've been getting straight A's, and yet I didn't know that. Well, I felt I should be thrown back into kindergarten."

It was a new lesson for me on how little understanding those born blind have of dimensions unless the concept has been explained to them or they have been able to measure things themselves.

In the evenings that followed, Betty and I had fascinating discussions on the sizes of things. She proved to be a quick learner. Eventually she graduated cum laude from a university, and today is an outstanding teacher of blind children.

5
"I'm Going to Die"

WHILE I was embarrassingly deluged by people using synonyms for courage and stoicism—if only these well-meaning folks had known how frail I often felt—few gave a thought to how tough Joe's life had now become.

Here was a man so strong, vigorous, and masculine that he gave the impression of attacking life with a rapier; here was a man who possessed the compassion needed to be a good teacher of the severely handicapped; and here was a man whose time and activities were now restricted by unanticipated duties and concerns.

He rarely complained about having to do the grocery shopping, or driving me anywhere I needed to go, or doing so many other chores, but in one depressed moment he revealed what most weighed on his mind. He said, "I work all day with the blind, and I come back at night to a blind wife."

As I mentioned, Joe was a perfectionist, a trait that can be admirable in some vocations and circumstances—was not Michelangelo so described?—but one that often exacerbates difficulties. Yet his high standards encouraged me to strive to improve my capabilities.

The three of us—or four of us when Jay was with us—had many exhilarating times together, including memorable camping and beach vacations. With pride we watched our daughter during those enchanting middle years of the first decade. Often when I would inquire as to what was so engaging his attention that he was silent for a long period, Joe would respond that he was watching Joy at play. I recall his once saying, "Our daughter is so pretty, so graceful, so happy that I could spend the whole day simply watching her."

This observation was made when we were on a beach and Joy was building a sandcastle. On such occasions I most coveted my husband's eyes. I would enjoin him to tell me more. "Tell me what she's doing this very moment. Oh, tell me, tell me."

When Joy was six, I gave up my position at the Braille School. One reason was that I felt it important to be available to Joy at all times. Her school was close, and there were few moments of my day I more enjoyed than recess, when Joy would bring half a dozen friends to see me—or perhaps to sample my home-baked cookies.

There were other reasons for giving up my job. One was that Joe had just been promoted. But the most compelling excuse was that my energy level was near its lowest ebb. Arthritic pain had surged, and I was constantly aware again of pleurisy. Because of this, I was obliged to spend more time visiting specialists who were trying to balance my medications—notably, steroids.

Joe supported my decision. I loved being a full-time housewife and mother, and he was now freer to enjoy outlets for his seemingly inexhaustible energy. He had always been a sports fanatic, and in his off-duty hours, if he wasn't playing basketball or softball, there were TV sports programs on one channel or another.

In the spring of 1988 I noticed that Joe was losing some of his enthusiasm, not only for his work and sports but for social engagements too. He would find a thin excuse for not playing basketball with his friends or for not going to a Friday night barbecue. One afternoon when his favorite baseball team, the Los Angeles Dodgers, was on TV, I was amazed to find Joe asleep on the living-room couch.

There were other omens. He was uncharacteristically irritable. He snapped at me, Joy, and Jay too. I excused him because I knew his sinuses were acting up. Joe had suffered from allergies all his life, and they were much worse that spring.

What triggered my anxiety into real concern was a suppertime incident. Mom and Dad were visiting, and so was Jay. Between us, Mom and I had prepared one of Joe's favorite dishes—pork chops. I was expecting a compliment, when Joe said sharply, "Where's the applesauce?" His tone shocked the table into silence.

I attempted to smother the awkward moment by speaking up

536

lightly. "How silly of me," I acknowledged. "I forgot that the jar was empty, but there's another in the basement."

Eager to make amends, I hurried to the basement. The next thing I knew, I was flat on my back. The playroom door had been left half open. My forehead and right knee hit the edge of the door at the same moment. I was badly shaken and very sore.

Before I returned upstairs with the applesauce and while I took a moment to rub the bruises, my anger gathered. Back at the table, I told the company what had happened, and then angrily told Joy and Jay to try to remember to close all doors. A half-open door is one of the more common domestic perils of the sightless.

I was shocked when Joe said, "It's your fault, anyway. Didn't you spend years teaching blind kids to go slowly? Why don't you practice what you preached?"

The rest of the meal was eaten in silence.

Later, when my parents and I had a moment alone, I explained about the sinuses. "He's really not himself at the moment, and he's been having awful headaches."

When Mom asked why Joe didn't go to see a doctor, I told her, "Because he doesn't like doctors. He doesn't trust them."

When Joe and I were in bed that night, I raised once again the problem of his sinuses and headaches. I said, "Honey, they seem to be so much worse this year."

Joe grunted. "Nothing seems to help."

After a long pause I asked him if he would please see a doctor. "Just Dr. Anthony," I said. "Remember, he's your friend."

"No quack has ever done anything for me," he protested, but I could tell from his voice that his opposition was weakening. I gained his promise that if within one week his headaches were no better, he would see Tony Anthony.

Exactly one week later I heard him on the phone speaking to the school office. I heard him say that he wouldn't be going to work that day, as he had "a cold or something."

I moved to his side. "What's really the matter?" I asked.

"Another damn headache," he admitted.

"Then you have another call to make—to Tony Anthony. You promised."

"Oh, yeah, maybe later."

I lifted the phone off the cradle. "Right now," I insisted as I gave him the doctor's number—one of about fifty important phone numbers I now had registered in my head.

That afternoon Dr. Anthony gave Joe a prescription drug to help dry out his sinuses, but he also made an appointment for Joe to see an ear, nose, and throat specialist in Cedar Rapids.

Three days later the ENT man gave a quick diagnosis. The cartilage in Joe's right nostril had grown, and it had shut down the air passage. The minor problem would require simple surgery. The operation was scheduled for June 10.

It was Joe's idea to take the family to a Twins ball game in Minneapolis. What balm to my ears to hear him explaining the intricacies of the game to Joy and her half brother. I suspected that Joe had earlier swallowed a mouthful of painkillers.

On the drive home Jay asked his father why he was going so slowly. When Joe didn't reply, I asked him if he had a headache.

Joe turned to me and said blisteringly, "Okay, Joan, you drive!"

I gulped, and replied softly, "That doesn't sound like you."

He touched my face—his gesture of apology—then said quietly, "It's not a headache. It's just—well—for some reason I'm seeing double." He pulled in a deep breath and added, "Don't worry, I'll get us home. Damned sinuses. Surgery will fix 'em."

The day before the surgery Joe's parents joined us in Vinton. It was they who drove us to St. Luke's Hospital in Cedar Rapids.

The septoplasty procedure lasted only half an hour. The surgeon told us that everything had gone well. Joe's nose would be sore for a few days, and he would stay in the hospital overnight just in case there was some postoperative hemorrhaging. He asked Joe to report back to his office in a couple of weeks.

It was a long two weeks. The nose did not heal as promised, and Joe's headaches intensified. The double vision remained. On the tenth day Joe had a bad hemorrhage. He went to the bathroom to clean up.

When he came downstairs, he said, "Funny thing, but I could swear that my right eye looks much bigger than my left eye."

"Probably bruising caused by surgery," I suggested.

"Probably," he replied, "but you'd think— Oh, forget it."

But I couldn't forget it.

When the two-week checkup day arrived, Joe insisted on driving us to the surgeon's office, adjacent to St. Luke's Hospital.

"What about the double vision?" I asked anxiously.

"Oh, I'm fine when I keep my right eye closed," he assured me. He feigned a light mood and said, "We only need one good eye between the two of us."

Joe was with the surgeon a surprisingly short time. "What happened?" I asked as he pulled me from my chair.

"Got to take this vial to pathology," he said flatly. "Contains some tissue from my nose."

Tissue! Pathology! The words sounded alarmingly ominous.

The pathology department was in the hospital's basement, and it necessitated a long walk. Joe was very calm as he handed over the vial to a pathology department nurse.

Because the doctor had said there would be no report until midmorning on Monday, we returned home.

Joe returned to the Cedar Rapids hospital on Monday morning. I sat by the telephone. It was about eleven thirty when he phoned. His voice was firm, but his words froze me. He said, "I'm on my way to the University Hospital at Iowa City." He paused for an intake of breath. Then, "I have a malignancy."

"Oh, Joe!" It was all I could manage to exclaim. I swallowed the huge lump in my throat and asked, "Should I call your parents?"

"Do that," he said. "Just my folks—and your folks too. No one else." A pause, and another intake of breath. Then, "I love you."

I heard his phone click. A moment later Joy came running to ask me if she could go play with a neighbor's child. She spotted my tears. "Mom, what's the matter? Was that Daddy on the phone?"

I wiped my cheeks on my sleeve. "Yes," I said. "He told me that—that he loved me."

"Oh," said Joy. "Well, it's okay, then. I can go play with Peggy."

"Of course," I said.

I was compelled to wait about twenty minutes before I was sufficiently in control of my emotions to call Joe's parents. I managed to avoid breaking down as I told them only what Joe had told me. They were ready to drive to Vinton immediately. However, I suggested they wait until Joe called me and we knew more.

Then Joy reappeared. With the directness of a seven-year-old she said, "Mom, I want to be with you when you are sad. You are sad, aren't you, Mom?"

"Yes," I said.

She was eager to comfort me. When we sat down side by side on the couch, she asked, "Will it help you to tell me about it?"

I tried to smile as I said, "Darling, you're only seven years old."

She giggled. "You're feeling better, aren't you?"

I squeezed her. "How could anyone *not* feel better when they're with you?"

I thought of how, since the age of three, Joy had had to shoulder unusual responsibilities. She was three years old when she first led me to ladies' rooms at restaurants and airports. At six she was reading me menus. She was also a beautician's apprentice—at least that's what I called her as she checked my makeup each morning. And now my seven-year-old was asking me to share the reasons for my grief. However, I found myself quite unable to do so.

Although I'd been expecting the phone call, when it came in midafternoon, the ring was as alarming as a gunshot at midnight.

"It's me," Joe said. "I have cancer."

My heart was pounding.

"Cancer of the sinuses," he said flatly.

A five-second pause; ten seconds; fifteen seconds. What was happening? Was he still there? Yes, I could hear his breathing. Then, "They want to take out my right eye."

"Oh, no! No! No!"

Another long and dread-filled moment. Then: "I'm coming home. You haven't told Joy?"

"No."

"Good. I want to tell her."

"Yes. Do you want your parents here?"

"Yep."

"Drive carefully, very carefully."

"Yep. See you soon."

I called Joe's parents, who said they were on their way. Then I called mine. Because Dad had recently retired, he and Mom had moved back to California. My voice broke, but I managed to tell Dad the tragic news. He asked if I thought Joe would like him to call back that evening. I said Joe would be sure to value his call very much.

On hearing the car arrive, Joy and I rushed out to greet Joe. After a brief exchange of kisses Joe distanced himself from us. I guessed that while he was driving home, he had thought out the best way of handling his arrival. He was clearly determined to keep his emotions on a very tight rein. Once inside the house, he sat on his recliner, and in simple terms he explained what had happened at the hospital. He mentioned the name of the specialist who had examined him, a Dr. Douglas Dawson.

"I liked him," Joe said. "He used a model of a head to explain where this tumor thing is growing." He turned to Joy. "A tumor is like an enemy—a very nasty enemy. The doctors are going to attack it so that it won't be able to hurt me anymore."

The conversation continued at this simple level until Joy was satisfied that the doctors were going to help win the war against a bad enemy who was hurting her beloved daddy.

It was an extraordinary conversation and for me, a new revelation of Joe's courage. Here he had been talking about the greatest crisis in his life, in our lives, in the same tone and manner as he told bedtime stories to his daughter. Since he had not mentioned to Joy that he was going to lose an eye, it was little wonder that she was satisfied and went upstairs to bed.

Of course the dialogue was on a different level when Joe's parents arrived late that evening. While I made sandwiches, Joe explained in technical detail how the doctors would try to save his life. The atmosphere was heavy with shock, sadness, and disbelief.

Only when we reached the bedroom did he loosen the tight reins he had kept on his emotions. Wordless, we held each other for half an hour. I tried desperately to hold back my tears. Then Joe whispered, "When your father spoke to me on the phone tonight, he recited the Twenty-third Psalm." He paused so long that I wondered whether that was all he was going to say.

But then Joe continued. Still in a whisper he quoted a couple of the fabulous verses: *"He leadeth me beside the still waters. . . . Yea, though I walk through the valley of the shadow of death, I will fear no evil: for thou art with me."*

After another long silence Joe said quietly, "I need to believe those words to be true. You must help me to believe them, sweetheart, because—because I'm going to die."

541

JOE BATTLED FOR HIS LIFE FOR seven months. In returning now to the scenes of his battleground, I find myself thinking of a black-and-white movie I saw on TV when I was young. I cannot recall the name of the movie, but I do remember a knight in full armor leading his army against a foe. Although the knight was mortally wounded, he went on fighting until he could no longer lift his sword.

Yes, that was Joe. His courage blazed.

From that first grim diagnosis he knew the chances of his surviving were very small. Joe was given three options. The first was to do nothing except take drugs to subdue the pain. If this was his choice, his doctor told him, he might live for two, possibly three, months. The second option was to go for surgery alone. He would, as he already knew, lose an eye. The chances of the cancer returning within the year would be high. His third option was to undergo the surgery and follow up with chemotherapy and radiation. There would be a chance that he could go on living.

No promises were given that Joe would even survive the radical surgery. We were told that it would last at least twelve hours. The cancer had already moved into the frontal lobe of Joe's brain. A section of the brain would have to be removed.

Joe had selected his option immediately. I was beside him when he said, "Of course I choose the third option. For the sake of my family I want you to do all you can to prolong my life."

Early in the evening before the surgery Joe settled into his room at the University of Iowa Hospital. The adult members of his family held a prayer service at his bedside. Dad had flown in from California. Dave, our minister from Vinton, had joined us, as had Joe's parents and brothers. We all held hands as Dave prayed. For me four words, *"Thy will be done,"* remained poised in the air over Joe's bed.

Then the large family group left Joe and me alone. We held hands, and Joe said, "Sometimes I forget to tell you that I love you."

"I know," I said. "I should say those words more often too."

Joe reminded me, although I'd not forgotten, that the following day would be our tenth wedding anniversary. He said, "Next year, honey, we'll be in a better place than this—I promise you."

I was calm until Joe said, "I wish I was as strong as you."

"Oh, but you are," I said urgently. "You're stronger." I clasped him then and found that he was trembling.

542

The next dawn began my longest day—a day of what proved to be sixteen hours of surgery. Sometimes by phone from the operating theater to the waiting room, sometimes in person, Dr. Dawson gave us progress reports.

At one point, and at my request, the doctor had traced with his fingernail on my own skull just what area of Joe they were cutting. I was appalled when the doctor's nail moved in an arc across my head from one ear to the other, then around the socket of my right eye, then down my nose and cheek to my upper lip. The doctor explained further that Joe would lose half his palate and some teeth.

We were cautioned that because a section of the brain had been excised, Joe might be in a coma for days. But the following morning, when Dad and I were first permitted to visit Joe in the intensive care unit, he recognized us and even thanked us for coming.

Joe was in the hospital for two weeks. His doctors were surprised by the pace at which he regained strength. However, his last day at the hospital was a particularly traumatic one for him. A nurse asked his family to leave the room. She was going to show Joe how to clean his eye socket—a task, she cautioned, that had to be performed with a special solution and a Water Pik twice a day.

Now, for the first time, Joe was to see his face without an eye patch or bandages. He asked me to stay with him, and added wryly, "At least you, honey, won't keel over."

The nurse removed the eye patch and led him to a wall mirror. Then I heard Joe hiss with horror. A moment later he was beside me on the bed, breathing hard. He gasped, "If I'd seen a face like that on a man lying in the street, I would have said he was dead."

All I could do was squeeze his hand.

The nurse pulled Joe to his feet again. She said gently but with authority, "If this wound gets infected, you're in big trouble. If you don't want to be back in the hospital with a septic head wound, you must learn to cleanse your eye yourself. Let's try again."

Instruction on the use of the Water Pik took quite a while. When Joe was finally ready to leave the hospital, he was wearing an eye patch, and also a cap to cover his shaved head.

Back home that night when we shared a bed again, Joe said to me, "Honey, I want you to know that I'm going to leave you soon.

543

I'm just glad I've been given time to put things right, to put my insurance papers and my will in order."

I felt that Joe understood my silence.

"We've got to be strong for Joy and Jay," he continued.

"Yes," I said. I was crying, but so softly that he didn't seem to hear me.

The powerful sleeping pill he had swallowed half an hour earlier began to take effect. He began to slur his words. Over and over again he said, "Good to be home . . . good to be home."

When I knew he was asleep, I got up, went downstairs, and made up a bed on the living-room couch. I was concerned that in my turning over in our bed I would awaken Joe. When he slept, he was pain free. When he was awake, he was rarely, if ever, free of pain.

Before dawn I was awakened by a bellow from upstairs. As I stumbled into our bedroom, Joe demanded, "Aren't you still my wife?"

"Of course."

"Then why didn't you sleep with me?"

"Because I—"

"Because nothing. I want you beside me. I need you beside me."

"Okay."

"Then climb back in."

ONLY two weeks after he had returned home, and only four weeks after he had undergone sixteen hours of surgery, I found Joe dressed, with collar and tie, and rattling the car keys.

"What's happening?" I asked.

"I'm going to work," he replied chirpily.

"But Joe, you can't—"

"I can, and I'm going to. My eye patch is in place. My mustache has grown back, and although my hair looks a bit tufty, I intend to keep my cap on."

"But Joe, you're not yet—"

His hand was over my mouth, effectively smothering protest.

In those early weeks back from the hospital, Joe's main frustration was his difficulty in being understood. Part of the surgery had been the removal of half his palate, and the plate that had been fixed over the roof of his mouth to allow him to eat, as well as to speak, would become loose. If he removed the palate plate, which he did when his mouth became sore, only Joy could understand him.

He now spent much more time with Joy than he used to, and with Jay, now twelve years old. I'd often find him sitting on Joy's bed late at night while our eight-year-old was fast asleep. He explained, "I can't see enough of her. I want a thousand photographs of her in my mind. Soon those photos will be all I'll have." Of Jay he said, "I want to share ideas with him—thoughts that may help him when he's grown up."

Joe changed. He was different in so many ways. He was making every day count and, I suspected, counting every day left to him. He was more caring, more courteous, and even more humorous.

He claimed to be pleased when he started to lose weight. He was delighted when friends told him that he looked in better shape than he had for years—possibly true, because he had previously been badly overweight.

For a while, only I knew how exhausted he really was and how sick he became following the radiation treatment. Then suddenly after Thanksgiving—when we had made the six-hour journey to his parents' home in South Dakota—Joe became very frail. It was as if a storm had swept away the leaves from a stalwart oak.

Joe, in his mid-thirties, was entering the winter of his days. He gave up going to the Braille School. Often he failed to clean out his eye or could not be bothered to do so anymore. I had to struggle every day to persuade him to eat. All he wanted to do was sleep.

Our home now became strangely quiet. We rarely turned on the TV. Joy and I tiptoed around the house. How many times at night did I awaken and anxiously listen for the sound of his breath?

But the heroic knight was not beaten yet. In the middle of December a Braille School houseparent and friend, Elaine, phoned to say that "Joe's blind kids" had asked if they could come that afternoon and sing carols to their beloved Mr. B.

Except for when he crawled to the bathroom, Joe had not gotten out of his bed for ten days.

"They're coming in about three quarters of an hour," Elaine said. "They'll just sing outside his window."

I promised to give Joe the message.

Joe was in such a deep sleep that I was reluctant to awaken him.

He was never now without a headache, too often a savage one. It took three shakings of his shoulders to rouse him.

"The kids are coming here?" he asked, half dazed.

"In less than an hour," I told him, "but you don't have to worry. Joy and I will welcome them. We'll get some candy. It's okay. Just go back to sleep."

When Joe made no reply, I assumed he had gone back to a drugged sleep. A neighbor took Joy to buy candy canes. I was in the kitchen when I heard an unusual thumping noise. Joe was coming downstairs on his hands and knees. He had dressed himself in a sweat suit.

"Oh, Joe," I cried out, "you didn't have to."

He reached the bottom of the stairs at the moment Joy burst through the front door and announced that the carol singers were now only two blocks down our street. Joe instructed Joy to put on all the house lights. I mentioned that the kids wouldn't see the lights.

"But I will," he replied, "and Joy will, and the neighbors will."

As soon as the kids arrived and began to sing "O Come, All Ye Faithful," Joe opened the door and leaned against the doorframe. A horseshoe-shaped circle of kids stood out there in the bitter cold. Joy walked around the circle handing out the candy canes from a basket, and I, with tears streaming down my cheeks, walked behind her and gave each child a hug.

Between carols the kids called out, "Hi, Mr. B.!" "Merry Christmas, Mr. B.!" "Get well, Mr. B., 'cause we miss you."

Joe called back something that sounded vaguely like "Merry Christmas." I guessed that his palate plate had slipped again.

Finally, the blind children broke into "Silent Night." I'd never heard the words sung more sweetly. I surely never will again.

The carol singers did more than provide us with an unforgettable evening. Joe, who had seemed to be running on empty, now tapped into a reserve of energy. His family came for Christmas, and he carved the turkey. He even attended a New Year's Eve party.

In thinking back to that movie in which the gallant knight had gone on fighting though mortally wounded, the hardest part for me to watch as a child had been when the knight had to take two hands to lift his sword. Joe had reached the point in his own battle when he could, as it were, no longer lift his sword.

Following a night in which he suffered excruciating pain, we all knew—Dad and Mom were with us—that it was time for Joe to leave home and go to the local hospital.

There was a richness even about Joe's last days. He and Dad had become very close. I was with Dad at Joe's bedside when Joe said with surprising clarity, "I am not afraid to die, but how do I free myself from the pain and the guilt of knowing that I could have been a better father, son, and husband?"

Dad said quietly, "There isn't one of us who could not have done things better with our lives." He went on to remind Joe that he had been forgiven and he could and should now forgive himself.

On the last day Joe was coherent, his concern was about our future. He asked where Joy and I were going to live. I told him that I had given much thought to this question and had decided that we'd go to California. "It's best, I think, that we be near my family. So we'll be going to Bakersfield."

"Good," he whispered. "Very good."

He said something now that I didn't understand. I bent over the bed, and he whispered, "Jay. Keep in touch with Jay."

"We will," I promised. "We'll invite him down for vacations."

"They're both great kids," he whispered.

"Yes, they're great kids."

I was aware of his sudden spasm of pain. For a while we were silent, simply holding hands. Then he turned my hands over and said, "Your hands have worked so hard for me." They were not the last words he spoke to me, but the last words that I understood.

Joe died at four minutes after the midnight of his thirty-sixth birthday. They called me from the hospital. Dad accompanied me there, where we had a prayer together at Joe's bedside. I reached out and touched Joe's still warm hand.

I phoned Jay's mother, who agreed to give the news to Jay. I was dreading having to tell Joy. She barely stirred when, at dawn, I got into her bed and snuggled with her. When she eventually awakened, she calmly said, "Daddy's died, hasn't he?"

"Yes," I told her. "Very peacefully." I reached out to stroke her cheeks and, to my surprise, found them to be dry.

"It's okay, Mom," she said quietly. "I've cried all my tears."

Ten days or so later I awakened from an unforgettable dream.

Joy and I were holding hands and facing a darkly shadowed mountain. An illuminated pathway traversed the forested lowlands and then soared through the rocky upper slopes. The sun of the new dawning had not yet risen above the mountain's burnished crest.

Strangely, I was not daunted but was comforted, indeed exhilarated, by this dream, for it seemed to hold a promise of good things to come, so long as we held the faith and had the courage to strive and to climb on.

6
Westward Ho!

JUST as I had mourned the loss of my sight—which, in a way, is another kind of death—so I now mourned the loss of Joe. I experienced, too, pangs of guilt. Why had I, with my damaged body, survived and yet Joe, so healthy, so strong, succumbed?

I needed therapy. I found it, but not in the office of a psychologist. I started to write down all the experiences I had gone through in the past six years. This would be my catharsis. It was also to become the raw material for this book.

To write, I used a Visual Tek loaned to me by the Braille School. This instrument is a type of closed-circuit television designed especially for the partially sighted. The Visual Tek screen magnifies print forty times. This allowed me, through the tiny foggy window of my peripheral vision, to read printed letters—and thus words—one at a time. I was able, for instance, to read on the screen the figures on my phone and electricity bills. Then, by placing my checkbook on the plate below the screen, I could write the figures and my signature on the check. The whole process of paying a bill initially took as long as twenty minutes. But I could do it myself.

With this marvelous invention I first recorded the story of Joy's pink socks and my feelings when told by Dr. Corbett that I would be blind for the rest of my life.

Another reason I was able to move purposefully through very difficult times following Joe's death was because we had a new beacon in front of us. More accurately, it was a signpost, and it read CALIFORNIA. I began to chip away at all the decisions that needed to be made in order to get there.

Above: a Beringer family photo before the storm. Joe and Joan with Jay, five and a half, and Joy, one and a half.

Joan, after her vision loss, celebrating Joy's fourth birthday, in 1984. Left: Jay, now grown up, in his high school football uniform, fall 1993.

Wedding day, June 27, 1992.
Left: Joan with her father.
Below: Joan's parents.

A beautiful day to begin a
happy new life. Above: the
bride and groom flanked by
Jim's best man, Bob Peace;
the maid of honor, Louise
Erreca; and bridesmaid,
Joy. Right: newlyweds
Joan and Jim Brock.

Left: in the kitchen in Tucson, Thanksgiving 1993. Below: Jim, Joy, and Joan in their backyard in Arizona, fall 1992. On Joy's cheek is a "pet" giant swallowtail butterfly.

Mother and daughter, Christmas 1993. Joan and Joy both love to ride horses.

After I met with Braille School business officers, the insurance figures were given to me. Financially, I was going to be okay—if I was careful. Then came the toughest tasks. What to do with Joe's papers, clothes, tools, bicycle? What about our car, bought new only nine months earlier? I really loved this car. I'd often go out and just sit in it. Sometimes I'd start the engine, rev it up, and press the buttons to move the electric windows up and down. I agonized over getting rid of a vehicle I couldn't even drive.

I could have saved a lot of the energy I'd spent worrying about the car. Dad bought it. His own car, he told me on the phone, had reached retirement age. The Blue Book was consulted and the deal made in minutes. My parents would fly out to Iowa, give their return tickets to Joy and me, and then spend a leisurely four days driving back to California. It was a perfect solution, as I told Dad after he assured me that the car to which I was so attached would be the car that would be meeting us at Los Angeles Airport.

"And you'll drive us to our new home?" I asked.

"Our new home?" queried Joy, who'd been listening to the phone call. "You didn't tell me you'd bought a house."

"I haven't," I told her. "Not yet, but we will."

Joy slid down from the packing case upon which she'd been sitting and stood in front of me. She said, "Please, Mom, let me look at the house before you buy it."

I reassured her that I wouldn't consider purchasing a house without her first checking it out. "Your eyes are my eyes," I reminded her.

She leaned into me, her arms around my waist. "Oh, Mom," she said, "it's sometimes hard to be your eyes."

"I know," I told her, "but you're doing beautifully. You're a gift straight from heaven."

It was a few days short of three months after Joe's death that the movers came—on the same day my parents arrived to pick up the car. They set off almost immediately for the journey home. Joy and I stayed with my friend Cathy Hummel for the next week to give the moving van and my parents time to reach Bakersfield.

Then came the day of our departure. Joe's parents came down from South Dakota to see us off. They drove us to the Cedar Rapids airport. For me there was, of course, no opportunity for last looks at the treelined avenues, the familiar stores, or the handsome red-bricked civic buildings. My only recollection of this final drive through Vinton was the whistle of a train and the scent of lilacs.

Before we boarded the airplane, there was one more tearful farewell. Joe's father said, "If there's anything, anything at all we can do for you, please promise to get in touch with us."

I thankfully gave him my promise.

Ninety minutes after leaving Vinton, Joy and I were seated in an airplane thundering down a runway. As the wheels left the ground and the plane soared, a new and extraordinary feeling overwhelmed me. It was a sudden sense of lightness of spirit, as if I'd left behind a crushing burden. Enshrouded though my eyes were by a veil of darkness, I became deeply conscious of space—space for breathing deeply, for movement, for adventure.

"What do you see through the window?" I asked Joy.

"Just sky," she said.

"You can't see the ground?"

"No. There are clouds covering the ground." She paused and then added, "It's funny, isn't it? Only we can see the blue sky and the sunshine." She corrected herself. "I mean I can see it."

"Well, today I sort of see it too," I said.

I wasn't sure she understood. But she squeezed my hand and said, "I'm so excited, Mom."

"Me too," I said. "Me too."

7
Letters to Cathy

On July 4, 1989, I audiotaped the following letter to Cathy Hummel in Vinton:

I'm lying in my swimsuit on the enclosed patio of my very own home! Water's tinkling and splashing from a nearby fountain in a man-made lake across the street. Whir of wings from hummingbird feeder hanging from a beam above my head. Temperature in low nineties. Humidity zero. Have your eyes turned green?

My friend Louise found this condominium for us. It's in a new complex, typically Californian—treelined avenues, several swimming pools, tennis courts, shopping center only a block away. Kissin' cousins and friends moved us into the place in one day. The next morning Joy awakened me and confirmed the choice by declaring, "Mom, doesn't it just feel like home!" It did. It does.

In the first week in my new home I did almost nothing except allow the past to sort of drift away and embrace the future, whatever it is, wherever it takes me.

Thank God for the insurance money, which paid for our home. I've splurged on a few things. The most important is a Visual Tek closed-circuit TV, which cost $2500 and is worth every cent.

You ask about my health. Feeling pretty good. Not yet ready to run a marathon, but I am swimming in the pool with Joy, who is developing into a really good swimmer. I've so often bumped my head on the tiled sides of the pool that I'm ready to patent edge-side cushions like the ones on a pool table.

Love to you and Dennis. Blow kisses to everyone I know in that little town with a big heart.

Letters were so very important to me. I became quite frustrated when Joy was not around to collect the mail from our box—one of about thirty boxes placed some two hundred yards from my front door. It was Joy who decided that it was time for me to collect the mail myself. She marked out the route to the mailboxes by helping me to feel two fire hydrants with my cane, pacing out the sidewalk to an appropriate right turn, picking up the fuzzy shadows of some trees where I needed to cross a street, and so on.

I was getting quite cocky about my mobility, but that old caution about pride heralding a fall is no less applicable to someone carrying a white cane. What my cane did not tell me one morning was that a gardener had parked his truck within a stone's throw of the mailboxes and that the steel handle of his Weed Eater was sticking out over the sidewalk.

The blow across my forehead and the bridge of my nose threw me to the ground. I was so dazed and bewildered that I had no idea where I was. I didn't even know what had hit me. Indeed, my first thought was that I'd been mugged. Farther along the street I could hear gardeners mowing a lawn. I somehow managed to find my way home.

So you scold me for not "doing anything." But I am, and it's exciting. I've signed up for a class at the junior college here. I met a fabulous professor, Dr. Chuck Wall, who's blind but has four master's degrees and a doctorate. Anyway, Chuck asked me to help him with a class of blind people. My first reaction was negative. I felt I'd given enough years to teaching the blind. But I changed my mind when he told me that in this classroom was the latest model of a talking computer. This incredible machine actually talks back to you in a robot voice. It tells you what you've typed.

However, I wondered whether there was any purpose in my learning how to use this sophisticated machine, because I could never afford to buy one. But then a miracle!

It all began with a terrible tragedy about fifteen years ago. Three twenty-one-year-old girls were killed when a car plowed into them. One of the girls was Maria, the daughter of a Dutch family who were members of my dad's church. Maria was one of my closest friends. I was a student in South Dakota when Mom phoned me with the news of this tragedy. I remember so well how I walked across to the college chapel and prayed and wept alone for an hour.

Well, all this happened a long time ago. Then three Sundays back, after church here, Maria's parents, Leonard and Margaret Van Doorn, came up to me and said they had heard I was interested in a talking computer. Mr. Van Doorn, who still has a very strong Dutch accent, said, "Ve vould like much to give you a talking computer." Mrs. Van Doorn said, "Yes, ve like to do that."

I was just bowled over. I told them that they couldn't possibly know what these computers cost and I couldn't accept such an extravagant gift. We're talking about thousands of dollars.

Mr. Van Doorn took my arm and said, "Now, you lizzen good, Joan. God has blessed us. Ve can do no more for our Maria, zo you let us do thiz for you, yes?" He added that others would like to come in on this gift.

Hugs! Kisses! Tears! Wonderment! So now I have this incredible talking computer at my home. I'm taking lessons on how to operate it, and I hope to be able to help other blind students use it.

Am enjoying a speech class too. The other people in the class seem intrigued to have a blind woman learning about voice and diction. After about five sessions the professor asked us to talk about ourselves for three minutes. The others were to be allowed to read their speeches. I was going to have to remember mine. I typed out the speech on my talking computer, which played it back to me several times until it was memorized.

I could sense some tension among my classmates when it was my turn to speak. Most of them had tended to avoid me, perhaps assuming that since I'm blind, I'm also half-witted. I found the podium quite easily. Here is what I said:

"I'm going to talk about a recent experience at Pismo Beach when my nine-year-old daughter, Joy, and I walked the beach barefooted. It was quite cool that early morning, with eddies of fog coming in from the sea—so Joy told me. It is nice for me to walk in the surf, because I love the feel of sand between my toes and I can count on there being nothing to bump into.

"We sat on a splintery wooden bench and listened to the music of the waves. It was a gentle time for both of us. Joy felt close and comfortable enough to speak of something that was troubling her.

" 'Yes?' I said, encouraging her.

"Joy half buried her face in my Windbreaker, and said, 'Lots of kids tell me that they feel sorry for me—having a father who died and a blind mother. I hate it when they tell me that.'

"I bent my head until my cheek touched her fog-dampened hair and suggested that other kids really wanted to be kind. I told her I didn't like it, either, when people smothered me with sympathy. We got up and walked again, her arm still around my waist. I was happy that my small daughter could share these deep feelings with me. What she had told me made me more ~~re that she, too, was having to deal with difficulties related to my blindness.

"That morning on Pismo Beach will remain with me, for the passing of this hour of my life contained moments of shared beauty, shared sadness, and shared love."

Cathy, there was absolute silence in the room following this mini-speech. Then someone at the back of the classroom clapped; then they all applauded. I smiled, but I had to pretend to look at my shoes as I made my way back to my seat. I didn't want them to see my tears.

HERE'S A LETTER TO CATHY, audiotaped two years later on November 30, 1991:

Six weeks ago I went to my first dance. Actually, I was dragged to it by my friend Sandy, who's into country and western. I'd learned the basic steps when I was in high school. Well, we'd hardly gotten ourselves into the dance hall when this guy with a southern accent and cowboy boots came up and grabbed my hand. I was trying to tell him that I was here only to listen to the band, but Sandy blurted out that I was "a pro."

Not sure whether this guy thought I'd come from the red-light district—if Bakersfield has one—or whether I'd understudied Juliet Prowse. So Sandy pushed me onto the floor, and I pleaded with Mr. Cowboy Whoever not to let go of my hand.

"Trust me," he said. Well, I did some trusting as he whirled me around to a familiar beat. Memory clicked into the right groove, and I felt I was performing reasonably well. Then the music stopped, and guess what? This cowboy gentleman left me in the middle of the dance floor! I think he tossed a "Thank you, ma'am" over his left shoulder.

But now what do I do? I heard some mocking laughter and started walking toward it. Yes, it was Sandy.

The good thing I got out of all this was appreciating that Mr. Cowboy Whatever had obviously not realized I was blind. In fact he came back later and asked me to dance again.

Through Joe's struggle against his mortal disease, through my period of mourning, I'd unconsciously suppressed desires for male companionship. But now, in a crowded mall or while sitting in a bus or in a restaurant, I was aware of men again. I enjoyed the bracing scent of aftershave. If I was introduced to a man with a pleasant laugh or an attractive voice, I found myself holding on to a hand a second or two longer than was required by courtesy.

What I was having a hard time doing was persuading myself that I was still attractive. Surely my sightless eyes had lost their sparkle. Surely the experience of watching my robust husband fade and die had left some scars upon my face. Hadn't I read somewhere that a face presents a map of one's life experiences?

557

There are few people who can picture their own faces. Yet curiously I am able to recall my own mirror image of the time before I lost my sight. I like what I recall. I see blond hair lying across my shoulders. I see a nose of quite respectable proportions, a slightly cleft chin, high cheekbones, and a smile—ah, yes, a smile!

Since I liked to smile and since I was doing a lot of smiling again, why did I give heed to those negative whispers inside my head that hinted I was a close cousin of Cinderella's ugly stepsisters?

But then there was an incident that did wonders for me. I was taking a walk with an elderly neighbor. The sounds of saws and hammers indicated that we were passing a building under construction. The banging and buzzing of labor suddenly ceased, and I heard whistles—a whole chorus of wolf whistles.

"Just who are they whistling at?" I asked my friend.

"Who do you think, my dear?" she exclaimed. "Certainly not me!"

"You're telling me that . . ."

"Indeed I am," said my friend, drowning my astonishment with more laughter.

I giggled in disbelief and embarrassment. Those guys up on the scaffolding had no idea what a boost they had given my morale.

However, gains in my self-esteem these days came from more than wolf whistles. I was receiving a number of invitations to speak to different groups. I'd started with church groups; then I'd received invitations from schools. Now I was getting requests from service clubs and associations of various kinds. Naturally, I gave a very different talk to sixth-grade kids than to Rotarians. But the theme was the same. I saw how important it was not to belittle the difficulties I had faced, but I was anxious to promote my belief that whatever the challenges, whatever the hurts, life still goes on, grimly at times, but also triumphantly.

By the fall of 1991 word had gotten around Bakersfield that there was this woman—me!—in the area who had a very unusual personal story to tell and that she knew how to tell it.

But here I must backpedal and speak of my connection with the blind celebrity Tom Sullivan. When I was in college—and later, working at the Braille School—I'd read and reread Tom's bestselling autobiography, *If You Could See What I Hear,* and I'd seen him as a featured actor in half a dozen movies. I knew him to be a composer, performer, athlete. In recent years he'd become one of the most in-demand speakers on the lecture circuit. For me and many others who are disabled, Tom Sullivan's extraordinary achievements were a tremendous inspiration.

My lawyer brother, Jon, was in the audience when Tom spoke to a convention of businesspeople in Bakersfield. Jon is not given to using superlatives, but he pulled out all the stops when he spoke to me about Tom's speech. I was asked by another member of Jon's firm, a man who knew about my own modest lectures, if I'd be interested in getting in touch with Tom. A few mornings later I found myself speaking to Tom on the phone. This first call lasted ninety minutes. What amazed me about this man, who was to become such a dear and influential friend, was that he was so genuinely intrigued by my story. I told him about my hopes of writing a book and of my daring to hope that I too could become an inspirational speaker. He promised to help me with both aspirations.

He said, "Joan, there are tens of thousands who are waiting to be given a lift by the story that only you can tell."

"Only me?" I queried.

"Only you, because all of us are absolutely unique."

This phrase was branded into my mind.

"We're going to have to get you moving," Tom said, "and one good place to start under the big tents is at the Million Dollar Round Table. It's an annual convention of high-powered business executives. They're always on the hunt for new and effective speakers."

"Are you talking about me, Tom?"

"Is there anyone else on this line? Joan, you've got to learn to lift your eyes to the far horizons."

"But my eyes don't work, Tom. Did I forget to tell you?"

"I'm speaking about the vision of your potential and creative ambition, and your guts," said Tom.

Two speeches I gave during this period were to have a far-reaching impact on my life. The first was to a Bakersfield Rotary Club luncheon meeting. I still don't know what it is that triggers an audience's total attention, but I do know that on this occasion the Rotarians were listening—I mean really listening. Some of the members knew my parents. Some had been in school with me.

A few days after the luncheon I received a call from one of the

559

club's members, Mr. Richard Sullenger, who said he had been out of town and had missed my speech. "But I'm told that I missed the best speech the club's had in a very long while."

"Why, thank you," I responded with genuine surprise.

Then Mr. Sullenger astonished me by asking if I'd ever heard of the Million Dollar Round Table.

I told him about my recent conversation with Tom Sullivan.

Mr. Sullenger went on, "It happens that I'm not only a member of the Million Dollar Round Table but I'm also on the committee that picks the speakers for the annual conventions. Now, Joan, I have two questions for you, and if you give a yes to each of them, I'd like to try to get you on the platform for the 1993 Million Dollar Round Table in Boston. First, have you got an audio- or a videotape of one of your lectures? And second, do you think you could muster the courage to speak to an audience of five thousand?"

After a deep swallow I replied, "Yes and yes."

The summer of '93 was still a long way ahead, so after hanging up, I told myself in words close to those used by Scarlett O'Hara, "Fiddle-dee-dee. I'll think about that in about eighteen months."

Then I returned to my talking computer and continued to work on a forty-minute speech I'd been asked to give to a Bakersfield high school on the Thursday before the Christmas break.

When that date came around, I found myself in a gymnasium setting. The kids had listened attentively and had applauded warmly. It was now question time. A girl's voice came down to me from the bleachers. "Mrs. Beringer, it's hard to imagine what it's like to be blind. I'm wondering, though, what you miss the most."

The girl's question caught me off guard. Curiously, I'd never been asked what she now wanted to know. "What do I miss most?" I repeated the query, playing for a few seconds of time. "Obviously, there are a number of things I miss very much," I said. "I miss seeing my daughter's face as she begins to grow from childhood to young womanhood. I miss seeing blue skies and the fresh green of springtime. I miss driving a car. I miss—"

My long response to a simple question was drowned by the sound of the school bell. The school's principal approached, took the microphone, and said some kind words that evoked applause.

While I waited for a guiding arm, that question from the bleachers began to haunt me. It stayed with me all through the lunch with the faculty. It continued to prod and jab during the long drive home chauffeured by a PTA member. The question returned to haunt me when I went to bed. It held sleep at bay until the small hours. What did I really miss most?

I missed a man. I missed a male shoulder upon which to rest my head. I missed whispers in the dark, dialogue at the breakfast table. I missed a male voice telling me that I looked pretty. I missed cooking him a T-bone steak, knowing he liked it medium rare. I missed dancing with him cheek to cheek.

It was not, of course, the first time I had thought about how nice it would be to get married again. However, the question had put a match to a fuse, and the fuse was hissing away in my head.

The small hours of the morning are not the easiest of times to curb deep yearnings. But there it was—this fresh interest in finding a mate and in creating a two-parent family once again.

When I thumped my pillows for the fourteenth time, there was no recognizable man upon the stage of my mind. Would I have slept at all that night had I known that he was standing in the wings?

8

The Butterfly Man

THERE are a few unwritten rules for those who have lost their sight. One of them is that when taking a shower, you don't drop the soap. On a morning between Christmas and New Year's, I broke the soap-dropping rule. I was on my knees in the shower when the bedroom telephone rang. Realizing that the answering machine wasn't on, I uttered a naughty word. Then, after dripping water across the bedroom carpet, I picked up the phone. "Yup?" I said.

A male voice responded, "Sorry—must be the wrong number."

"Who do you want?" I demanded.

"Joan Beringer," said the voice.

"You've got her," I said, "but if you're selling—"

"Sure doesn't sound like you," said the voice.

"Caught me in a bad moment," I apologized. "Who's speaking?"

It was Scott Clare. He'd been in high school with me. He was phoning to invite me to his fortieth birthday party. His wife, Diane, was giving him a surprise party. He'd been instructed to invite his friends and then told to forget whom he'd invited. He continued, "There'll be a few people you'll know, but obedient to Diane's instructions, I've already forgotten their names."

"Scott, is your domestic life always so complicated?" Both of us chuckled. "Anyway, I do have one problem. For some reason the DMV won't give me a driving license."

"Problem solved," he said. "I'll pick you up myself. In any event, Diane wants me out of the house to give her time to blow up balloons and put little sausages on toothpicks. Real informal. Okay?"

"Okay," I said enthusiastically.

Joy gave me every encouragement to get out and about. She also liked to have some say in what would be suitable for me to wear.

For Scott's party I chose a pair of jeans and a peasant blouse. Joy approved but reached for the Q-Tips. "Too much mascara, Mom," she said, "and with that blouse you should be wearing Gypsy earrings." This from an eleven-year-old.

I humored my daughter. I usually did. She selected Gypsy earrings and danced with me around the carpet. The sitter had arrived, and we were all laughing when Scott rang the doorbell.

"Are you fifty or sixty today?" asked Joy.

Scott drawled, "How can such a beautiful woman produce a daughter who teases me like that?"

"Yes, Mom is beautiful, isn't she?" said Joy. "And I'm so glad that I look like her."

I turned away. Oh, Joy. Oh, my Joy, I thought. How dark and empty my life would be without you. I firmly resolved that were I ever to marry again, the man would have to love my daughter at least half as much as I loved her right now.

When we arrived at Scott's home, he was blasted with greetings and applause. He pretended to be taken by surprise. Diane, who noted my confusion—the glare of lights eliminated even peripheral vision—quickly came across to me and suggested I might be more comfortable in the less crowded den. From the doorway she introduced me to about eight guests whose names meant nothing to me. Then she spoke the name of Jim Brock.

Jim Brock! I spun back in memory to my high school days. I could see a shy, boyish face. I'd had such a crush on him.

I must have made some sound, because Diane paused in her introductions and said, "Oh, so you do remember Jim?"

"I'd be more than a little put out if she didn't," Jim said, and added, "Know where I last saw Joan? She was dancing on a table at the senior all-night party after our graduation."

"Nonsense, Jim," I shouted. "I never."

"Did you ever!" he responded.

Everyone in the den was enjoying this exchange.

The next moment Jim was beside me. Scott, who'd been his college roommate, must have told him about my loss of sight, because he maneuvered me around furniture. "Come sit on a cushion by the fire," he said. "We've a lot of catching up to do."

That was an understatement. We barely moved from the den's fireplace for the next four hours. For me it was a revealing interlude when Scott's two young daughters bounded into the den and made straight for "Uncle Jim." They obviously adored him.

After Diane had packed them off to bed, Jim said, "I'm not their uncle, of course, but I'm never happier than when playing the role. I just love kids."

Then we approached graver issues. I told Jim of my sadness on hearing of the death in an auto accident of his sister Lori.

"It was a long time ago, but I still miss her," Jim said. "I always will." He paused, then asked, "Is it the wrong time to talk about what happened to you? The amazing thing is, Joan, that you don't look as if you've had bad things happen to you. Truthfully, I was absolutely amazed when Diane brought you into this room."

I tried to brush away this unexpected compliment. "What did you expect—a depressed widow bumping into the furniture?"

His laugh held no more humor than mine when he said, "Perhaps someone like that."

Jim broke the moment by rising to his feet and taking my wineglass. He murmured something about recharging at the wet bar. When he returned, I asked, "Now, what about you? What do you do, and how many wives have you had?"

I could almost hear his grin as he said, "As an astronaut, I'm scheduled for next week's flight to Mars. And wives? Henry the Eighth ain't got nothing on me."

I dug my elbow into his ribs. "The truth," I demanded.

"I'm a lepidopterist," he said.

"That," I responded, "sounds like a word in a crossword puzzle or a spelling bee. You're either an authority on Bohemian art, or you extract perfume from exotic flowers."

"You're not that far off," he said. "A lepidopterist is a student of butterflies."

"So you spend your time catching butterflies!" I exclaimed. "I'm somehow getting the wrong picture. The one I'm getting is like a *New Yorker* cartoon. There's a guy with knobby knees waving a little green net on the end of a stick."

He chuckled. "Well, I don't have knobby knees, and I look for butterflies in places like Brazilian rain forests and the West Indies. Also in Arizona, where I live now." Jim went on to tell me that he had recently co-authored a book on butterflies at his home in Tucson. Then he spoke of the need to preserve nature's threatened treasures.

I was intrigued by his intensity when he suddenly stopped in mid-sentence. "Oh, heck!" he exclaimed. "I didn't mean to have tunnel vision when I got onto butterflies. I don't want to scare you off."

"Do I look scared?" I asked.

"You look—you look—well, much prettier than anything I've ever encountered in the forests of Brazil."

I gave Jim my most dazzling smile and told him that this was the most original compliment I'd ever been given. I added, "But I can't wait to hear about your love life."

"You're going to have to wait," he said, " 'cause we're all but the last people to go home. If we don't move out now, Scott and Diane will boot us out."

We'd walked out of the den and were now near the front door, where Diane embraced me, and Scott soon led me to his car. On the drive home I casually asked Scott if his friend had ever married.

"Surprisingly not," said Scott. "No, I think Jim's been totally wrapped up in his specialty. He must have told you about the butterflies. I gather he's quite a significant name in lepidopterology. He's done what so many wished they had done. He's followed his dream. He's a nice guy."

"Yes," I agreed, "he's a very nice guy."

When my friends Louise and Sandy dropped in for coffee the next morning, they quickly picked up on my enthusiasm.

"Not Jim Brock!" exclaimed Louise. "When I was in junior college, he was just about the number one catch."

I told Louise and Sandy as much as I'd learned about Jim but bewailed my low expectation of ever being likely to see him again. Both took me to task, Sandy saying, "Joan, this is the '90s. We gals are allowed to phone up guys and ask for dates."

"Oh, I just couldn't do it," I told them. Then an inspired thought hit me. I could ask Jim about publishing a book. That, after all, was what I was hoping to do myself sometime.

Over our coffee mugs the strategy was laid out. I managed to find the Brocks' unlisted number through Scott Clare. Jim was not at home when I called, but his father promised to deliver my message.

Thus it was on the last day of 1991 that Jim Brock took me to lunch at a Bakersfield restaurant called the Olive Garden. Later I was to reflect that the very first love story also began in a garden.

THIS is a letter that I audiotaped to Cathy on January 18, 1992:

There's a man in my life! Oh, Cathy, I'm trying to be cautious. I tell myself, Joan, just you remember who you are. You can't even see his face. You can't run into his arms without tripping over the doormat. You can't . . . you can't . . . you can't.

But I did see his face—twenty years ago. We were in high school together, same class. I can still see the boy smile but not the man. Yet I hear his words, and I feel his touch. His name's Jim—yes, another "J" in my life. He's a scientist—an authority on butterflies.

Cathy, I know you'll be happy for me but anxious too. Both Jim and I understand that not only is something wonderful happening but that both of us must weigh the obvious problems and difficulties. We're told that love is blind, but when one of the lovers is actually without sight, the warnings to go carefully are red-lettered.

Guess what? He's given me a very unusual birthday present, a round-trip plane ticket to Tucson, Arizona, where he's lived for the past fifteen years. Southern Arizona happens to be just about the best area in the country for the study of butterflies. This may be irrelevant trivia to you, but it's no longer trivia to me!

Since that lunch on New Year's Eve, and his return to Tucson, we've talked for about a hundred hours on the phone. I hope

565

you've got some stock in AT&T. You might also invest in Interflora, because long-stemmed roses are arriving by the dozens.

He and Joy took to each other from the moment they first met. After her second meeting with Jim she said, "Mom, he's real neat and he makes me laugh."

Much love from my song-filled heart.

At the end of January my heart was still song filled, but there was a timorous quaver to the top notes as the airplane nosed down to the runway in Tucson. Earlier in the flight I had asked a stewardess to check my makeup. She told me that I looked just fine.

"Meeting someone important?" she asked.

I nodded.

"Then I'll be meeting him too," she said, "because I'll be taking you off the plane."

The real reason I was edgy was not that I'd overdone the eye shadow, but that I'd be meeting Jim on his home ground. Oh, we'd spoken half a million words on the phone, but we'd not seen each other in several long weeks. He'd surely find out now how much I'd depend on him, not only to guide my steps but for descriptions of everything going on around me.

In our last phone conversation he'd mentioned that he'd gotten tickets for a basketball game. I'd enjoyed playing basketball myself at college, and I knew the rules and skills. But if I were to become involved in the game, he'd have to be a radio commentator. Would he weary of this and other tasks?

The wheels of the plane touched the runway, and soon the airplane came to a halt at the terminal. The stewardess came to me. She said brightly, "Well, here we are. Give me your hand. I'll take you off ahead of the other passengers. Excited?"

A minute later I heard a familiar and loved voice say, "You look beautiful, Joan. I'm so happy you're here." His arms were around me. His lips touched mine. I heard him thank the stewardess. Then he pressed a rose into my hands. It was sealed in a vial of water.

He said, "I felt pretty goofy holding this flower, but since you grasped it, the petals have started to open up." He laughed, and all my nervous feelings lifted like a sea mist touched by the sun.

As I allow my mind to savor again the memories of my first visit to

Tucson, Arizona, I'm getting goose bumps. I'm like a kid on her first trip to the beach—all delight and bewilderment and fascination.

Yes, we went to the university basketball game, where Jim proved to be an excellent commentator. We went to a marvelous restaurant in the foothills. We drove above the snow line of Mount Lemmon, where we pelted each other with snowballs. Everywhere we went, Jim recorded our activities on video. He explained, "I don't forget that I'm courting two blondes. These pictures are for Joy."

Back in Bakersfield, it wasn't the snowball fight that gave Joy her biggest laugh. What sent her into hysterics were shots taken by me. On Mount Lemmon, Jim had put the camera into my hands and instructed me to pan across the valley below. The outcome, Joy told me, was like flying in a small plane that was doing aerobatics.

Joy was enchanted by another shot—a close-up of a butterfly emerging from its chrysalis. Jim had been waiting for this for two years. He had kept the chrysalis in his small lab. The shot showed the butterfly on his hand as it unfolded and dried off its exquisite wings— I quote from his running commentary, given on the day of my arrival.

"Is the analogy too obvious?" Jim had asked.

Laughingly I told him that I'd set a limit on the number of times he could refer to me as "one of his bugs." I was discovering, though, that he was a poet at heart.

Within a few hours of the hatching of the butterfly, which was indigenous to southern Arizona, we drove eight miles into the desert to release it among the flora upon which it fed.

In the midmorning of the third day of my four-day visit, Jim told me to close my eyes. "I've ordered up the magic carpet. It will take us to a place of enchantment," he said.

Outside, the air was cool, but the desert sun was warm upon my face. There was a delicate aroma of what Jim informed me was a creosote bush. He led me to his four-wheel-drive truck.

Shortly we were rumbling along on our way, and within thirty minutes were obviously off the beaten track, for I was being tossed about like a cork in a boiling cauldron. When Jim pulled the truck to a stop and opened my door, I heard the sound of tumbling water. As he helped me out, he instructed me to use my imagination.

"It may sound like a waterfall to you," he said, "but what you hear are tiny violins being played by red-capped elves sitting cross-legged on toadstools." He left me for a moment as he pulled a blanket and a picnic basket from the back of the truck. He spread the blanket on what he told me was a carpet of pine needles. He ordered me to lie down and test it for comfort. We enjoyed a long moment, stretching our limbs, breathing deeply of the pine-scented air.

"Yes," he said eventually, "this is why I love this country. I come here often simply to enjoy a sense of freedom and space. Here you can whisper, or shout for joy, or speak of gracious things."

He stirred. Then, because of the sudden loss of sunlight, I was aware of his head above me. There hadn't been a moment since I'd lost my sight that I had more desired to see. His fingers combed my hair, and he kissed me very tenderly.

I had guessed that this time would come. I had played it out in my mind, and I had known that I would have to freeze the frame, to stop the movement of the scene until I'd spoken lines that might risk my losing Jim.

I pressed my hands into his shoulders and said, "Jim, I must talk. I need to talk about things that I don't want to tell you."

"Then don't tell me," he said. "Just listen to the elves on their violins. Are they playing allegro, animato, or dolce?"

"I'm not completely with you," I said.

"A concert pianist friend has been trying to educate me in music. Allegro means brisk, animato is lively, and dolce is—oh, you can guess that one—it means gentle or sweetly. What do you hear?"

"The music I hear now is in the words of a man I've grown to love."

He drew in a deep breath. "And I'm looking down on the loveliest face I've ever seen. I love that face."

He bent his head to kiss me again. But once more I put pressure on his shoulders. "Oh, Jim," I murmured, "I have to talk to you about something that's really important."

He picked up the gravity of my voice. He rolled away from me and lay on his back. This small separation hurt. Almost choking, I said, "There can be nothing more wonderful than to love and be loved. But I'm afraid, Jim, so afraid."

"Of me?"

"No, no, not of you. Not of a man who takes a butterfly eight miles for its supper."

"Then?"

I was silent, but trying hard to force words from my throat.

Jim said gently, "Would it help if I held your hand?"

"Yes, it would help," I managed to say. His hand held mine. I found that I was able to speak calmly, logically. "We're not really children at play," I said. "We're both grown-ups, Jim, and we must think and act like adults. Not far from this peaceful, beautiful place there are supermarkets where I am unable to select from a shelf one can of soup or one bottle of soy sauce. There are cars out there on the highway—millions of them. Have you thought that I cannot drive even one of them? When I'm in a home and someone leaves a closet door open, I can hurt myself. I live in a world of glare or twilight. I've lived in this world for eight years. Whatever more years are given to me are going to be lived out in this shadowed world. I'm not being self-pitying. I've accepted this unseeing world of mine. I'm no heroine, but I've not been unhappy in it."

I continued. "You asked me, Jim, what I'm afraid of. I'm afraid that you will tire of me—not now, not for a few days, not for a few months, but in a year, five years, ten years."

My voice trailed into silence. Suddenly Jim drew his hand away from mine and sat up. My heart turned over. The sky's glare was shadowed over once again, and I was aware that he was looking down at me. Was he adding up the cost of my speaking the truth?

A moment—a long moment during which my thoughts moved from agony to sublime elation—for his lips were upon mine once more. After the kiss I whispered, "Oh, Jim, I thought I'd lost you."

"Joan, you still don't know who I am," he said. His voice was light, touched by laughter. "Do you believe that I haven't given a lot of thought to what you've spoken about? Don't you understand my love for you? I don't claim all the virtues, Joan, but a man who chases butterflies has to have lots and lots of patience. You spoke about the years ahead. Didn't I tell you the butterfly that emerged from its chrysalis had kept me waiting for two years? When I'm in the rain forests of Brazil, I can spend a month looking for a metal-mark butterfly, a critter smaller than a dime."

He kissed me again before continuing. "I've been waiting years for a wife. I've been lonely for far too long. Every Christmas my mother has asked me what I want for a gift. Every year for the past decade I've told her I want a wife. It's a family joke. Patience?

Gosh, Joan, do I have patience. Then I met beautiful you." He paused for breath. "After our lunch on New Year's Eve, I went back to my mother and I told her that I'd found the woman I want to marry. I didn't tell her more than that, because I wasn't sure that the woman I'd found would want me—yes, me, Jim Brock, a forty-year-old bachelor who seeks rare butterflies. But on the off-chance that she might agree to marry me, I asked my mother for advice on buying an engagement ring. Mother went to her bedroom wall safe and came back not with a ring, but this."

Jim now uncurled the fingers of my left hand and placed within my palm what felt like a hard, thin little stick.

I asked, "What is it, Jim? What is this?"

"You're holding my great-aunt Sadie's diamond stickpin," Jim said. "I gather she wore it on her shoulder when she entertained President Theodore Roosevelt—someone like that."

"Oh, Jim," I cried, "you have to be kidding."

"No, it's true," he said. "The pin is eighty years old. Oh, and by the way, I'm asking you to marry me. If your answer is yes, we'll find a jeweler to put Aunt Sadie's diamond into an engagement ring."

"Oh, Jim, Jim."

"That's okay," he said, laughing. "You don't have to hurry with your answer. You can think about it over lunch."

While we ate, I told him I could indeed now hear his cross-legged elves playing their violins.

"Allegro, animato, or dolce?" he asked.

"All three," I replied, laughing. "And what perfect harmony."

9
Twilight Also Heralds Dawn

AN AUDIOTAPED letter from me to Cathy dated August 7, 1992:

Oh, my dear Cathy, how to begin to tell you what's happened since I was last in touch?

Jim and I were married on June 27 in the small Bakersfield church where I was baptized and confirmed. Dad married us. Louise was my maid of honor. The Joy of my own bones and my flesh was the only bridesmaid.

The congregation was small because we'd invited only Jim's family and my own to witness the plighting of our troth.

I had so many memorable moments. The first was coming down the aisle on Dad's arm. Dad's so frail these days. He's undergone major surgery on a heart that's spent nearly half a century giving its best to the spiritual and emotional needs of others.

While he was giving us his message, he choked up several times. Our wedding may be the last church rite Dad is likely to perform. I sense this, and I think he did too, as he asked his only daughter and the man at her side "to have and to hold from this day forward, for better, for worse, for richer, for poorer, in sickness and in health, until death us do part."

Jim and I said our I dos, he kissed me, and I'm now wearing his gold ring alongside Great-aunt Sadie's diamond.

Louise drove Jim and me down to the Los Angeles airport, where we boarded a plane for Hawaii. It's the first time I ever turned left when boarding a plane. Stewardesses served us lunch on white linen—champagne, shrimp, and broiled peacock tongues—just kidding. Thus to our deluxe condo right on a beach in Maui. How close to paradise! Going to sleep on the shoulder of a man I love with all my heart.

Then the big move to Tucson. Jim's big truck was loaded to the gunnels (whatever gunnels are). My precious talking computer and Visual Tek were padded by cushions. Guess we looked like one of the Dust Bowl families in a scene out of *Grapes of Wrath*.

We were on the outskirts of Tucson when there was a rainstorm. Although we'd roped a tarp over the things in the back of the truck, I was nervous about my computer getting wet. So Jim pulled the truck under a railroad bridge. After the brief storm was over and as we were emerging from the bridge, Jim and Joy holl_____.

"Stop screaming!" I shouted. "What's happening?"

"It's a rainbow!" yelled Joy.

"So what?" I said. "It's not the first rainbow you've seen."

"But, Mom, it's the brightest rainbow I've ever seen."

Then Jim added, "The apex of the rainbow is right over my house—our new home."

That night when Jim and I were in bed, he brought up the subject of the rainbow again. He whispered almost shyly, "I'm

571

remembering your first visit to Tucson, honey, and how that but-terfly chose the time of your arrival to emerge from its chrysalis. And today we're greeted by the mother and father of all rainbows. Nature's sure giving us a thumbs up."

This was my husband, the poet, speaking while his arms were around me. What went through my mind was the story of the first rainbow. I'm pretty sure it's in Genesis, chapter nine, where God said to Noah that he had set a rainbow in the sky as a covenant that the days of tribulation were over. So here I am, Cathy, lying in Jim's arms, and my heart is overflowing with thankfulness, hope, and love, and I'm thinking, I'm oh, so blessed.

Dear love to you, as always.

In 1993 there was another major event in my life. Richard Sul-lenger, who had spoken to me earlier about the Million Dollar Round Table, had kept in close touch. He had cautioned that the international organization received annually at least five hundred applications to speak at each convention—the next one to be held in Boston. I was still not putting much store in my chances when he, as chairman of the selection committee, insisted that I was a "seri-ous candidate."

In March, I was invited to travel to Chicago to try out for the Round Table's main platform, for which only fifteen speakers would be chosen for the five-day convention in midsummer.

Phone calls were coming in several times a week—some from people in a professional production company who helped me refine my talk, which had to be reduced to twenty minutes.

In the midst of these exciting days Dad died. In my last phone conversation with him he said, "Joan, I am so very proud of you, so very happy for you."

Jim helped me through my grieving. He reminded me again and again, lovingly but firmly, that life goes on. I pulled myself together and focused again on the great opportunity being given to me.

At the end of March, I flew alone to Chicago, where I was treated like royalty at the Hyatt Regency Hotel. Without blushing and committing the sin of pride, I cannot repeat what Richard Sul-lenger said to me after my presentation in a small theater within the hotel complex. Suffice it to say that I was selected to speak in June in Boston on the main platform before five thousand top business executives from five continents.

Jim and Joy accompanied me to Boston. The production company had worked out every detail of the presentation. The only piece of furniture on the stage would be a stool. To make sure I found my way to it they had, on Jim's suggestion, tacked down a strip of broad white tape stretching from the stage wing from which I would enter. My peripheral vision would allow me to follow the white tape to the stool.

I was behind the curtain, just offstage, as the emcee made his introduction. I started walking along the taped pathway. The blazing spotlights seemed to be brighter than the Arizona sun. I was unable to see even one of the thousands of men and women out there in front of me. They had not been told that I was blind, nor were they to learn this until I was five minutes into my speech.

In the course of the welcoming applause I asked myself what an ordinary woman, a preacher's daughter from Bakersfield, was doing in this distinguished company. Determinedly I put aside the alarming thought that ten thousand eyes were now focused on me and ten thousand ears were awaiting my first words.

I've since reviewed a film of my speech, and I've cringed at my occasional nervous giggles. I choked a couple of times when I spoke about the moment Dr. Corbett told me that the damage to my eyes was irreversible and when I spoke about Joe's valor. "And now," I said in concluding, "I'd like to introduce you to my new husband, Jim, and to my daughter, Joy."

A moment more, and they were there beside me—these two I loved above all others. A clatter of briefcases falling to the floor, a great wave of applause surging toward me that went on and on.

Jim shouted into my ear, "They're on their feet. Everyone in this huge auditorium is standing up."

I was crying now, and without shame. This can't be for me, I thought. Later I was told that it was the longest applause given to any speaker in the sixty-six years' existence of the Million Dollar Round Table convention.

Eventually the emcee was back at the microphone. He said very simply, "Joan, you've just made five thousand new friends from all around the world."

Later many of these new friends came to invite me to speak. I was given invitations to travel to and speak in cities across the United States and in Australia, Canada, South Africa, and Asia.

Even as I now prepare to parcel up the manuscript of this book to mail it to my publishers in New York, I am recovering from jet lag, for I've just returned from speaking engagements in Malaysia and Singapore. And my publishers tell me that before the year is out, they will be taking me to the major cities of the United States to speak to millions of men and women—children too, I hope.

What am I going to say? What I want to say is that while none can know how steep will be the path, how rough the terrain, how often we may fall and be hurt, we must not give up the striving.

In quiet moments I've recalled that mystical dream wherein I saw a steep mountain with its golden crest. In this dream the craggy sunlit summit sometimes seems to have the form of a citadel there for my taking—so long as I have the humility to ask the Guide for his footholds and the courage to trust Him.

When we think of twilight, we think first of the mellow or sometimes melancholy hour that heralds night. We tend to forget that twilight also heralds the dawn.

In our journeying, not one of us can avoid those darkening times when the color of our lives bleeds to gray—times when we are shadowed by pain, fear, grief, or a sense of helplessness. Yet as certain as the coming of every dawn, there's the hour when darkness breaks, when life itself is bright and colorful once more.

How often in my own dawn's brightenings has my heart cried out—sometimes, indeed, my throat and lips—"Ah, there, up there, I see my pathway once again!"

ABOUT
THE AUTHORS

Joan Brock with co-author, Derek L. Gill

A remarkable woman with a remarkable story to tell, Joan Brock was determined to find the best co-author she could to help her tell it. With the aid of her friend Tom Sullivan, the blind musician and entertainer, she met Derek L. Gill—Sullivan's own literary partner for the book *If You Could See What I Hear*. Gill turned out to be the perfect collaborator. Author and co-author of numerous inspirational biographies, he was so captivated by Joan Brock's story that he postponed his planned retirement to complete the project. And he says he is glad he did. Helping Brock write *More Than Meets the Eye* "has been the most exhilarating experience of my professional life," says Gill.

The collaboration has been a great success. Both authors are in high demand for interviews. Brock's public speaking career has soared. And a TV movie based on the book is scheduled to be aired on NBC in late 1995. Family life for Brock is also a success. Her husband, Jim, continues to study butterflies and is himself at work on a book. Her daughter, Joy, is in eighth grade now. Jay, her stepson, is a high school senior planning for college. And Brock admits that she is thrilled with her busy new world in Arizona. "In all my life," she says, "I've never been happier!"

PHOTO: COURTESY OF JOAN BROCK

ILLUSTRATORS

Mark Schuler: *Prizes*

Jim Dietz: *Secret Missions*

Robert Hunt: *Eyes of a Child*

Greg Harlin: *More Than Meets the Eye*, title spread

ACKNOWLEDGMENTS

Pages 549, 550, 551: courtesy of Joan Brock.

The original editions of the books in this volume are published and copyrighted as follows:
Prizes, published at $23.95 by Ballantine Books, a division of Random House, Inc.
© 1995 by Ploys, Inc.
Secret Missions, published at $22.00 by HarperCollins Publishers, Inc.
© 1994 by Michael Gannon
Eyes of a Child, published at $24.00 by Alfred A. Knopf, Inc.
© 1994 by Richard North Patterson
More Than Meets the Eye, published at $20.00 by HarperCollins Publishers, Inc.
© 1994 by Joan Brock and Derek L. Gill